P9-CSA-500

Rules
of
Ascension

TOR BOOKS BY DAVID B. COE

THE LONTOBYN CHRONICLE
Children of Amarid
The Outlanders
Eagle-Sage

WINDS OF THE FORELANDS
Rules of Ascension

A TOM DOHERTY ASSOCIATES BOOK
NEW YORK

Rules
of
Ascension

✦

DAVID B. COE

BOOK ONE

OF

Winds of the Forelands

This is a work of fiction. All the characters and events portrayed in this novel are either fictitious or are used fictitiously.

RULES OF ASCENSION

Copyright © 2002 by David B. Coe

All rights reserved, including the right to reproduce this book, or portions thereof, in any form.

This book is printed on acid-free paper.

Edited by James Frenkel
Design by Heidi Eriksen
Maps by Ellisa Mitchell

A Tor Book
Published by Tom Doherty Associates, LLC
175 Fifth Avenue
New York, NY 10010

www.tor.com

Tor® is a registered trademark of Tom Doherty Associates, LLC.

Library of Congress Cataloging-in-Publication Data

Coe, David B.
    Rules of ascension / David B. Coe.—1st ed.
        p. cm – (Book one of Winds of the Forelands)
    "A Tom Doherty Associates book."
    ISBN 0-312-87807-9
      I. Title.

  PS3553.O343 R85 2002
  813'.54—dc21

                            2001057485

First Edition: March 2002

Printed in the United States of America

0 9 8 7 6 5 4 3 2 1

Once again, for Nancy,
who is with me at the beginning of every new journey

Though writing a book may seem to be a solitary endeavor, it would be impossible for an author to survive this process alone. I am fortunate to be surrounded by extraordinary people who make it possible for me to live the dream of my youth.

Many thanks to my agent, Lucienne Diver; my publisher, Tom Doherty; the terrific people at Tor Books, in particular Jenifer Hunt and Peter Lutjen; Carol Russo and her staff; my marvelous editor and good friend, Jim Frenkel; and Jim's staff, in particular Tracy Berg and Jesse Vogel. I also want to thank my siblings, Bill, Liz, and Jim, who continue to offer their support and love, even as they wonder how someone who started out so normal could end up writing fantasy.

Finally, my deepest thanks go to my wife, Nancy Berner, and our daughters, Alex and Erin. Without their love and support, I would never accomplish anything, and without the music of their laughter floating up to my office in the afternoons, I'd never know when to stop working.

A number of years ago, Nancy told me that just once she'd like to read one of my books fresh, like any other reader would, without having read a draft or served as a sounding board for plot ideas. Here it is, Love. Enjoy.

—D.B.C.

North

Amon's
Ocean

Mistborne
Island

Cape of Bian

Falcon
Bay

GALDASTEN ✳ Gal-
dasten
Galdasten Tor Castle

Wantrae
Island

the Moorlands
of Eibithar

CURGH Curgh
Castle

Strait of Wantrae

E I B I T

Heneagh
Castle Sussyn

HENEAGH

Heneagh River

Tremain
Castle ☐

TREMAIN

Kentigern Wood

Whispering
Falls

Kentigern
Castle

KENTIGERN
Kentigern
Tor

Harrier Fen

Caerisson

Mertesse

MERTESSE
Castle ☐
Mertesse

Forest

Tarbin River

Panya's
Falls

Eibithar

Ellisa Mitchell 2002

Top of the
Forelands

Binthar's
Point

Thorald
Castle

THORALD

the
North

Wood

EARDLEY
Eardley
Castle

The Narrows

Enwyl
Island

...nthar's Wash

DOMNALL
Domnall
Castle

H A R

LABRUINN
Labruinn Castle

Gulf of
Kreanna

River

CITY OF
KINGS

Auduns
Castle

Raven
Falls

Silver
Falls

RENNACH
Rennach
Castle

...River

...USSYN
...ssyn
Castle

GLYNDWR
Glyndwr
Castle

Lake
Glyndwr

Blood Falls

Glyndwr   Highlands

Rules
of
Ascension

Chapter
One

✦

Galdasten, Eibithar, year 872, Morna's Moon waxing

A fter the bright glare of the dirty road and sunbaked fields, it took Pytor's eyes some time to adjust to the darkness of the tavern. He stood at the door waiting for the familiar shapes to come into relief: the bar with its dark stained wood and tall wooden stools, the rough tables and low chairs, the thick, unfinished pillars that seemed to groan beneath the weight of the sagging ceiling, and, of course, Levan, stout and bald, standing behind the bar. The air was heavy with the scents of musty ale and roasting meat, but Pytor also smelled Mart's pipe smoke. It seemed he wasn't the first.

"Starting a bit early today, aren't you, Pytor?" Levan asked, filling a tankard with ale and setting it on the bar by his usual place.

Pytor sat on his stool and took a long pull. "I'll do without the commentary, Levan," he said, tossing a silver piece onto the bar. "I'll just thank you to keep the ale coming."

The barkeep held up his hands and shrugged. "I didn't mean anything by it."

Pytor frowned before draining the tankard with a second swallow. He set it down on the bar sharply and pushed it toward Levan, gesturing for more with one hand and wiping the sweet foam from his mustache with the other.

"Got yourself a thirst today, do you, Pytor?" came a voice from behind him.

He turned and saw Mart sitting at a table in the back, pipe

smoke hanging like a storm cloud over his head and curling around his gaunt face.

"Since when is my taste for ale the whole world's concern?"

Pytor glanced back at Levan and shook his head. The barkeep grinned like a ghoul and handed Pytor his ale.

"Don't be sore, Pytor," Mart called. "I was just talking. Come back here and join me."

He took another drink and sat still for a moment. Mart wasn't a bad sort. Back when Kara was still alive, she and Pytor had spent a good deal of time with him and Triss. Mart and his wife had been good to them when they lost Steffan. Better than most, if truths be told. They'd looked after Pytor's crop and beasts while he cared for Kara, and even for some time after she finally died. And Mart had continued to be a reliable friend since, accepting of Pytor's quick temper and rough manner.

Still, Pytor wished that he had been the first to arrive that day. Since early morning he'd been restless and uneasy, the way he sometimes felt before a storm. *Perhaps it's only that.* Morna knew they needed the water. But he knew better. Something was coming, something dark.

Kara used to say that he had Qirsi blood in him, that he had the gleaning power, like the Qirsi sorcerers who traveled with Bohdan's Revel. They always laughed about it, Pytor reminding her that he was much too fat to be Qirsi. Still, they both knew that he was usually right about these things. He didn't doubt that he would be this time, too. He was in no mood to talk. But Mart was here, and it wouldn't have been right to just leave him back there alone.

"Come on, Pytor," Mart called again. "Don't be so stubborn."

Pytor tugged impatiently on his beard. There was nothing to be done. He pushed back from the bar, picked up his ale, and joined Mart at his table.

"That's it," Mart said, as Pytor sat. He tapped out his pipe on the table and refilled it. Then he lit a tinder in the candle flame and held it over the bowl of his pipe, drawing deeply. The leaf glowed and crackled, filling the air with sweet smoke. "What's new, Pytor?" Mart asked at last, his yellow teeth clenching the pipe stem.

Pytor shrugged, not looking him in the eye. "Not much," he mumbled. "Grain's growing, beasts are getting fat." He shrugged again and took another drink.

"You seem troubled."

He looked up at that. Mart was watching him closely, pale blue eyes peering out from beneath wisps of steel grey hair.

"Is something brewing?" Mart asked.

Pytor held up his tankard and forced a smile. "Only this," he said, trying to keep his tone light.

Mart just stared at him.

"Nothing I can name," Pytor finally admitted, looking away again. "Just a feeling."

The older man nodded calmly, but Pytor saw his jaw tighten.

"It's probably just my imagination," he said a moment later, drinking some more ale. "We've been almost a fortnight without rain and I'm starting to fear for my land. It's affecting my mood."

Mart nodded a second time and chewed thoughtfully on his pipe. "Yes," he agreed after some time. "That's probably it."

Pytor could see that Mart didn't believe this either, but the man seemed as eager as he to let the matter drop. Draining his tankard again, Pytor motioned for Levan to bring him another.

"Can I buy you one?" he asked Mart, noticing for the first time that his friend had no drink.

Mart hesitated, but only for a moment. "No, thanks," he answered with a shake of his head. "Triss will thrash me if she smells it on me. She's stingy enough with my time without having to worry that I'm spending all of our money on ale."

Pytor looked at the man with genuine concern. That wasn't Triss's way, and they both knew it. Anyone who spent even a few minutes chatting with her could have seen that.

"Things that bad then?" he asked.

This time it was Mart's turn to shrug. "They've been worse." He paused, then gave a wan smile. "Though not in some time."

Levan walked over to their table and placed another ale in front of him, but Pytor hardly noticed, so great was his surprise at what Mart was telling him. True, they needed rain, but things weren't that bad. Not yet. Another turn of it would be a different story, but the planting season had been generous, and the ground still had a good deal of moisture in it.

"What happened?" Pytor asked. "You're not having trouble with mouth rot in your herd again, are you?"

Mart shifted uncomfortably in his chair and stared at his hands. "Actually, we are," he said at last, his voice barely more than a whisper. "But not 'again,' as you put it. It's still the same problem."

Pytor narrowed his eyes. "I don't understand."

"I'm sorry, Pytor," Mart said, his eyes meeting Pytor's briefly before flicking away again. "I should have told you at the time how bad it was."

Pytor just stared at him. He knew what was coming. He should have been used to it by now, but it still stung. "So?" he finally managed. "How bad?"

"We've lost all but three of our beasts. Most of them died at the end of the planting, just as the grain was starting to sprout, but four more of them died during this past waning."

"Your crop's all right though, isn't it?" he asked dully. "You can get through the cold turns."

Mart nodded. "Barely, yes. The crop's fine, and Brice has just sold me a half dozen of his beasts at a low price. It's been a hard time, but we'll get through."

"Why didn't you tell me the truth?" Pytor demanded, struggling to keep the ire from his voice. He knew the answer, but he wanted to make the man say it. "Why didn't you come to me? I'm doing fine; I could have helped you."

Mart looked away, his face reddening.

"We would have, Pytor. Really. But after all you'd been through . . ." He trailed off, making a small helpless gesture with his hands.

It didn't matter. Pytor could finish the sentence for him. *We didn't want to trouble you.* He could hear the words in a dozen different voices. It had been a constant refrain in his life since Kara's death. His friends had been so considerate of his feelings that they'd made him an outcast.

"The others know?" he asked.

"By now, they do. They didn't right off. At first I only told Brice. But now . . ." He shrugged.

Pytor nodded and pressed his lips together. He wasn't certain why he felt so angry. Mart hadn't done anything wrong; certainly it was nothing the rest of them hadn't done as well. Besides, the man's herd was no business of his. He couldn't fault him for going to Brice, either. Brice was a decent man, despite his bluster. He and Pytor spent much of their time together baiting each other, but even Pytor knew that he could be counted on when times got rough. And it was no secret that he was the most prosperous of them all. Had Pytor been in

Mart's place he might have turned to Brice too, in spite of their past quarrels.

So why was he so offended?

"Well, I'm glad it's worked out for you," Pytor said at last, breaking an awkward silence.

"Thank you, Pytor." Mart smiled, looking relieved.

Pytor returned his smile, though he had a sour feeling in his stomach. He drank some ale and Mart puffed on his pipe, sending great billows of smoke up to the ceiling.

They sat that way for some time, saying nothing. Mart filled his pipe a second time, and Pytor drained yet another tankard of ale, which Levan dutifully replaced with a full one. He wanted to leave, but it was early yet. The others hadn't even arrived, and there was nothing back at his house except the beasts and his now-too-big bed. So instead the two of them just sat, keeping their silence and trying not to look at each other.

When Brice and the rest finally walked into Levan's tavern they both nearly jumped out of their chairs to greet them. The comfort Pytor took in their arrival was fleeting, though.

"It doesn't come at the best of times," Eddya was saying as she walked in. She stepped to the bar, gave Levan a silver, and took her ale. "But it's certainly not the worst either."

"There's never a good time for it," Jervis said sullenly, buying an ale of his own.

The others got their drinks as well and all of them walked back to the table. None of them looked happy, but Davor least of all: He was the youngest of the group, and the most prone to worry. Brice, too, was easily disturbed, despite his money. If they had been the only ones who were upset, Pytor wouldn't have been concerned. It was the others who had unnerved him. Eddya had been through four husbands, eleven childbirths, and more difficult times than he could count. Little bothered her anymore.

Jervis and Segel were even tempered as well, Jervis and Pytor had often been mistaken for brothers. They had the same coloring— red hair, fair skin, green eyes—and though Jervis was far taller than Pytor and a good bit leaner, they had similar features. They also reacted to things the same way. They were quick to anger, but kept their wits about them in hard times. No matter the trouble, they always managed to muddle through.

Segel was a stranger to Eibithar; no one who looked at him could have doubted that. He was small and wiry, with dark skin and darker eyes and hair. He even spoke with the hint of an accent, although not one that any of them could place. Some said that he was from Uulrann. Eddya was convinced that he came from the Southlands. Pytor had never asked him, though he'd often wondered. It had never really mattered. In the important ways he fit in just fine. He was quieter than the rest; he tended to listen more than he spoke, and he rarely worried unnecessarily.

So when Pytor saw the dark expression on his face, and on Eddya's and Jervis's as well, he knew something had to be wrong. He felt his stomach tightening like a fist.

"Looks like you shouldn't have bothered with those beasts after all," Brice said to Mart as he sat.

Mart glanced at Pytor uncomfortably before answering. "It wasn't a bother, Brice," he said awkwardly. "Your price was more than fair."

"Price doesn't matter anymore," Eddya told him, with a chuckle. She always seemed to be laughing when she spoke, even when she didn't mean it.

Pytor frowned. "What does that mean?"

"The timing couldn't be worse for Bett and me," Davor said to no one in particular. "What with having just put up the new shed and all."

"The timing of what?" Pytor demanded, his voice rising. "What's happened?"

Jervis looked at him for several moments, licking his lips. Then he shook his head.

"We just saw a posting at the meeting hall," Segel finally said in a low voice. "The duke has called for a Feast on the tenth night of the waxing."

Perhaps Pytor should have expected it. But the ale had begun to work on him, and he wasn't thinking clearly. Or maybe that was just an excuse. Maybe on some level he had expected it, but didn't want to admit it to himself. Here, after all, was confirmation of his premonitions. He could almost see Kara standing before him, nodding with that sad, knowing smile of hers. He had to clamp his teeth together against a wave of nausea.

Davor was saying something else about his new shed and how many days it had taken him to build it, but Pytor was hardly listening. There was a noise like a windstorm in his ears, and his head had begun to throb. He wished he hadn't drunk that last ale.

A Feast, and on the tenth day no less. The duke had given them only four days to prepare, not that they could do much. This was the last thing they needed. With the weather working itself into a drought, mouth rot killing their animals, and the duke taking more than his share of what they managed to make, it was amazing that they got by at all. But a Feast, that was too much. Pytor had been through seven of them in his lifetime, including one the year he was born, but there were just some things a person couldn't get used to.

"Has it really been six years already?" he heard Eddya ask.

"I believe so," Jervis answered. Pytor heard surrender in his words, and he hated him for it. In certain ways, he and Jervis were nothing alike.

"Hard to believe six years can go so fast," Mart said softly. He would go meekly as well.

"It's been five," Pytor said, his voice cutting through their chatter.

None of them argued with him. None of them dared. Steffan had died on the eve of the last Feast. Indeed, his death had prompted it.

"Five years rather than six," Segel said thoughtfully. "It may be that the duke's Qirsi has gleaned something."

"I remember back some years we had an early Feast," Eddya said, cackling. "Turned out there were people dead of the pestilence in Domnall."

Segel nodded. "That could be it as well."

"That doesn't excuse it," Pytor said, not bothering to mask his bitterness.

"Come now, Pytor," Brice said. "We all know how rough the last one was for you. But that doesn't mean that we should abandon the whole practice."

"The Feasts are a barbarism! They always have been, and I'd be saying that no matter what!"

Brice shook his head. "They're a necessity," he said. "And getting all riled up about it doesn't do you or the rest of us a bit of good. There's nothing that can be done."

"You have to admit," Davor added. "It has worked."

"Davor's right," Eddya agreed, grinning like a madwoman. "Galdasten hasn't had a full-blown outbreak of pestilence in my lifetime. And my father never saw an epidemic either. Say what you will, but it works."

" 'It works!' " Pytor mimicked angrily. "Of course it works! But at what price? They could kill us all with daggers beforehand and that would work too! 'No pestilence there,' they'd say. 'Killing them ahead of time works just fine!' "

"You're being foolish, Pytor," Brice said. "No one's been killed. The Feasts are a far cry better than that."

Pytor took a breath, fighting to control his temper, struggling against the old grief. "And what about those the Feasts don't save?" he asked in a lower voice. "What about them? The Feasts don't always work."

"No, they don't," Brice said. "But that's all the more reason for us to be thankful that the duke is being vigilant. Better we should do this a year early than wait and let someone else lose a child. The risks of doing nothing are just too great. And the Feasts aren't nearly as awful as the fever itself. You of all people know what the pestilence can do. You and Kara were lucky to escape with your lives last time. All of us were." He looked around the table and the others nodded their agreement. All, that is, except Segel.

"Yes," Pytor said, nodding reluctantly. "I know what the pestilence does." He shuddered in spite of himself. He wasn't stupid. The pestilence was no trifle. Murnia's Gift it was called, named for the dark goddess by someone with a twisted humor. It had wiped out entire villages in less than three days. One particularly severe outbreak two centuries ago had killed over half the people in the entire dukedom in a single waning. It had taken Steffan in less than a day.

But though it worked quickly, it was far from merciful. It began, innocently enough, with a bug bite. It didn't matter where—Steffan's had been on his ankle. If the bite just swelled and then subsided, there was no need to worry. But if a small oval red rash appeared around the bite a person was better off taking a dagger to his heart than waiting for what was to come. Within half a day of the rash's appearance fever set in, and with it delirium. The lucky ones lost consciousness during this stage and never awoke again. Such was the one grace in Steffan's case. But those who didn't pass out—those whom the goddess ordained should remain awake for the entire ordeal—could expect one of two things to happen: either the vomiting and diarrhea would leave them too weak to do anything but waste away, or they would spend the last hours of their lives coughing up blood and pieces of their lungs. In either case, they were as good as dead—and so was anyone who came near them within a day of the bug bite. Given their unwillingness to leave Steffan when he fell ill, Pytor still didn't know how he and Kara managed to survive.

"I'm no stranger to the pestilence either," Segel said softly, a haunted look in his dark eyes, "but I must say that I agree with Pytor: there ought to be another way."

"There!" Pytor said, pointing to the dark man. "At least one of you has some sense!"

"But what could they do?" Brice demanded. "The duke has healers and thinkers, not to mention his Qirsi. If there was another way, don't you think they would have thought of it by now?"

"Why would they bother?" Pytor asked, throwing the question at him like a blade. "Their solution doesn't cost them a thing. And as you pointed out yourself, the pestilence hasn't reached the city in ages. If a boy dies here or there, who cares? They're still safe as long as they get their Feast in soon enough. They have no need to look for another way."

Brice shook his head. "Other houses have to deal with it, too. They haven't come up with much that's better. Some of them just let the pestilence run its course. Is that what you want?"

"I'd prefer it, yes!"

Brice let out an exasperated sigh and turned away. "He's mad," he said to the rest of them, gesturing sharply in Pytor's direction.

"They've been doing it this way a long time," Jervis said, his eyes on Pytor, the words coming out as a plea. "Longer than any of us have been alive. I don't like it either, Pytor. But it has kept our people alive and healthy."

" '*Our people*'?" Pytor repeated, practically shouting it at him. Jervis flinched and Pytor realized that Brice was right: he was starting to sound crazed. But he could barely contain himself. Surely Jervis and the others knew the origins of the Feast.

Nearly two centuries ago, the pestilence struck the House of Galdasten, just as it had every few years for as long as anyone could recall. Kell XXIII, who later became the fourth Kell of Galdasten to claim Eibithar's throne, hid himself and his family within the thick stone walls of his castle, praying to the gods that the pestilence might pass over the ramparts of his home and remain only in the country-side. But while Galdasten Castle had repelled countless invasions and endured sieges that would have brought other houses to their knees, its moat and fabled golden walls were poor defenses against the pestilence. The duke and duchess were spared, but not their son, Kell XXIV.

In the wake of the boy's death, Kell ordered the razing of the entire countryside. It was, most had long since concluded, an act born of spite and rage and grief. But because the pestilence is carried by the mice living in the fields and houses of the countryside, and spread by the vermin that infest the rodents' fur, Kell's fire actually ended the outbreak. Realizing that he had found a way to control the spread of the pestilence, Kell made a tradition of it. For a time, he looked to his sorcerers to tell him when outbreaks were coming, but it soon became clear that the interval between outbreaks remained remarkably constant: six years almost every time. So that's when the burnings came. Every six years.

Kell's younger son, Ansen, continued the practice after his father's death, but the new duke added the Feast as an appeasement of sorts, a way of softening the blow. It too became a tradition. All in the dukedom were invited into Galdasten Castle to partake of a meal that was unequaled by any other. The duke had his cooks prepare breads and meats of the highest quality. He had greens and dried fruits brought in from Sanbira and Caerisse just for the occasion. And of course he opened barrel after barrel of wine. Not the usual swill, but the finest from Galdasten's cellars.

All the while, as the people ate and drank, dancing as the court's musicians played and fancying themselves nobles for just one night, the duke's Qirsi sorcerers, accompanied by a hundred of Galdasten's finest soldiers, marched across the countryside, burning every home, barn, and field to the ground. Nothing was spared, not even the beasts.

In the morning, when the people left the castle and shuffled back to their homes, sated and exhausted, still feeling the effects of the wine, they invariably found the land blackened and still smoldering. Pytor still remembered the last time with a vividness that brought tears to his eyes. Steffan had been dead only a day and a half. There hadn't even been time for Pytor and Kara to cleanse him for his journey to Bian and the Underrealm. But when they returned to their land they couldn't find the walls of their home, much less Steffan's body. Such was the force of the sorcerers' flame.

No, the pestilence hadn't swept through Galdasten in generations. Instead, they had their Feasts.

" 'Our people,' " Pytor said again, more calmly this time. "The duke doesn't do this for us. He couldn't care less about us. He does it to protect himself and his kin, just like old Kell did, and Ansen after him. If the Feast comes a day or two late to save the life of someone else's child, so what? That doesn't matter to him. This Kell, our Kell, is no different from any of the rest."

"Fine!" Brice said, the look in his grey eyes as keen as the duke's blade. "He does it for himself! And never mind for a minute what we all know: that the Feasts have spared us more suffering than you can even imagine! What do you suggest we do about it? You've seen what Qirsi fire does! You think we can stand against that? You think we can fight it?"

Pytor glared at him, not knowing what to say, feeling the color rise in his cheeks.

Brice grinned fiercely, though his face looked dangerously flushed beneath his thick silver hair. "I thought so," he said at last. "You're all bluster, Pytor. You always have been. I thought maybe now that you were finally alone in the world, you might have balls enough to back up all the dung you shovel our way every day. But I guess I should have known better."

"That's enough, Brice!" Mart said sharply.

The wealthy man looked away and said no more.

Mart turned to Pytor, concern furrowing his brow. "Brice didn't mean anything by it, Pytor. He just doesn't always think before he speaks." He cast a reproachful glance Brice's way before looking at Pytor again. "Steffan was a fine boy, Pytor. We all liked him. And we know that losing him still pains you. But," he went on cautiously, as if he expected Pytor to strike him at any moment, "Brice does have a point. I hate the Feasts as well. We all do. But what alternative do we have?"

Pytor didn't answer him at first. What did Mart know of his pain? What did any of them know? Instead, he kept glaring at Brice, watching him grow more uncomfortable by the moment. In spite of the tone he had used and all he had said, Brice was afraid of him. He had been for some time now. Not because Pytor was bigger or stronger than he. He was neither. Brice feared him because Pytor had lost everything, or at least everything that mattered. Brice still had his family and his farm and his wealth, so he was vulnerable.

He kept his gaze fixed on Brice for a few seconds more, allowing the man's discomfort to build. Then he looked at the others. They were all staring back at him. Davor looking frightened and confused, Eddya with her crazed grin, and Jervis just looking sad, like an old mule. Segel was watching him as well, but speculatively, the way a man might regard a piece of land that had been offered to him at a good price. He was appraising Pytor, considering what he might be capable of doing. Pytor grinned at him, but Segel's expression didn't change.

"There are always alternatives," Pytor said at last. "It's just a matter of having the will to find them."

Brice let out a high, disbelieving laugh. "And I suppose you have such will!"

Pytor heard the goad in his words, and he knew then what he would do, what he had to do. None of the others would act. They weren't capable of it. But he was. Realizing this, he felt more alive than he had since he'd lost Kara. He turned slowly to face Brice again, allowing himself a smile. "I guess we'll see, won't we?"

"I'll tell you what we'll see," Brice replied. He looked scared still, but it almost seemed that he was unable to stop himself. "We'll see you at Galdasten, lining up at the gates while the sun's still high so that you'll be assured of getting your fair share of wine and mutton. That's what we saw at every Feast before the last one. This one won't be any different."

Pytor bared his teeth like a feral dog, hoping Brice would take it for a grin. "And you'll be there right next to me, won't you, Brice?"

"Absolutely," he said, laughing nervously. "Absolutely. We'll sit together and have a good chuckle over this. And we'll fill our cups with the duke's wine and drink to our good health."

The others tried to laugh as well, but they were looking at Pytor, trying to gauge his reaction. When he joined their laughter, their relief was palpable. Pytor just laughed harder. He had made his decision.

He glanced over at Segel and saw that the dark man was still eyeing him closely, a strange expression on his lean features, as if he could read Pytor's thoughts. Pytor was surprised to find that this didn't bother him, that in fact he found it comforting. Segel, of all people, might understand.

The others had begun to talk among themselves, all of them in great humor now that the unpleasantness had passed. But Segel's expression remained grim as he moved his chair closer to Pytor's and signaled Levan for another ale.

"I'm concerned about you," he said in a voice that only Pytor could hear.

"Concerned?" Pytor replied lightly.

"I like you, my friend. I think I understand you. I'd hate to see you come to harm."

Levan arrived with Segel's ale and placed it on the table. The barkeep pointed at Pytor's empty tankard and raised an eyebrow. Pytor shook his head and watched the barkeep return to the bar before speaking again.

"I like you, too, Segel. I respect you." He turned to face the man. "I wouldn't want anything to happen to you or your family."

Segel's eyes widened slightly, but otherwise he offered no response. When he reached for his ale, Pytor saw that his hand remained steady. After another few moments, Segel turned his attention to what the others were saying.

Pytor left the tavern a short time later. He was tired, he told the others. He wanted to check on his beasts before nightfall. But all the way home he could only think about Segel and their brief exchange. He hoped that he had made the dark man understand.

The next several days dragged by, like days spent waiting for sown seeds to sprout. Pytor didn't change his mind about the decision he had made, though given time to think about it, he felt fear gnawing at his mind like mice in a grain bin. He tried to keep himself busy by tending to his beasts and his fields, but knowing what was coming, he couldn't help but wonder why he bothered. Occasionally he would pause in the fields and stare beyond the pasture and the low roof of his own house to the towers of Galdasten, which rose like a thundercloud above the farms and the low, gnarled trees.

He didn't return to Levan's tavern. After what he had decided, he couldn't bring himself to face the others again. He should have known that they wouldn't let him off so easy. The day before the Feast, Mart stopped by.

"I was concerned about you," the man said, sitting atop his wagon and chewing on his pipe, even though it wasn't lit. "We all have been."

"I'm fine," Pytor said. He was putting out grain for the animals, and he avoided Mart's gaze. "I've just been busy."

"You shouldn't listen to Brice, Pytor," Mart said, no doubt trying to be kind. "He's an old fool. I can say that even after all he's done for me. He had no business saying what he did."

Pytor glanced at him briefly, making himself smile. "Don't worry about me, Mart. I've already forgotten it. As I said, I've just been busy."

Mart nodded. "All right. I'll leave you. We'll see you at the Feast though, right? Triss has been asking after you."

"I'll be there," Pytor said. "Right along with you and the others."

Mart had picked up his reins and was preparing to leave, but he stopped now. "Not all of us," he said.

Pytor froze, his heart suddenly pounding like the hooves of a Sanbiri mount. "What do you mean?"

"Segel told us yesterday that he's heading south for a while. He says he's going to see his sister in Sussyn."

Pytor felt himself go pale, in spite of his relief. Apparently the dark man had understood well enough. "Well, the rest of you then," he said, fighting to keep his voice steady. "I'll see the rest of you tomorrow."

Mart smiled. "Good." He whistled at his ox and the animal started forward. "Good night, Pytor," he called as his cart rolled away, raising a thin haze of dust.

Pytor lifted his hand in farewell, but couldn't bring himself to say anything.

The day of the Feast dawned clear and warm. Pytor rose with the sun and started out into the fields without bothering to eat. Now that this day had finally come, his fear had vanished, to be replaced with a sense of grim satisfaction. At least he was doing something. At least he was proving Brice wrong. Indeed, he thought with an inward smile, Brice was to be wrong about a good many things.

Pytor didn't line up outside the castle gates with the rest of the horde. He spent nearly the entire day in his fields, and though his arms and hands were covered with bites from vermin by midday, it took him several more hours to find what he had been searching for.

As he approached Galdasten Castle, the prior's bells tolling in the city and the sun hanging low to the west, he had to keep himself from scratching his arms. He wasn't certain which had been the killing bite—there were rashes around several of them—but it didn't really matter. All he cared about now was getting past the guards before delirium set in. He had his sleeves rolled all the way down and his hands thrust in his pockets to hide the red welts on his skin. But the day had grown uncommonly hot, and with the fever coming on, he was sweating like an overworked horse by the time he reached the great golden walls of the castle. If it hadn't been for Pytor's girth, and the fact that the guards could see him hurrying up the path that led to the gates, they might have suspected something and not let him inside. As it was, he felt rather unsteady on his feet as he walked by them.

This at least he had anticipated. He had forced down some ale on the way to the castle, and now he endured the guards' snide comments about his drinking with a good-natured smile and a deferential bob of his head. It was a small price to pay. Once he was past them he had nothing to fear.

Pytor made his way slowly through the outer ward to the great hall. The illness was fully upon him now. He had hoped that the pestilence would attack his lungs—that was said to be the quicker death. But it was not to be. He had to close his throat hard against the bile rising from his gut, and he stumbled through the doorway into the hall, barely able to keep his balance.

This is what Steffan went through, he thought, bracing himself against the open door. And one last time he thanked the gods for allowing his boy to slip into unconsciousness before the illness was at its worst.

He shook his head violently, as if the motion itself could rid him of such thoughts. He needed to concentrate. He had come for a reason.

Still leaning on the door, Pytor surveyed the scene before him. It was early still, but already there was food on all the tables and empty wine flasks everywhere. Though his vision was beginning to blur, he could see that the duke and duchess had arrived and were dancing near the front of the room. That was all he needed to know. It would have been nice to see Brice's face as well, but he didn't have the strength to look for him. He could feel himself starting to fall. It was all he could do to reach into the small pouch that was strapped to his belt, pull out the three mice he had found in his fields, and throw them into the middle of the room.

He fell to the floor retching, his body racked by convulsions. But he heard the music stop. He heard the incredulous silence and he could imagine the look on all of their faces as they stared at the tiny creatures who had brought the pestilence to their Feast. And then, just before another wave of illness carried Pytor toward his own death, he heard the screaming begin.

Chapter
Two

✦

Thorald, Eibithar, year 877, Adriel's Moon waning

hey had been in the king's tower since midday, as far from the city marketplace as they could be. The lone window in the duke's private chamber looked out over Amon's Ocean and its rocky coastline, and Filib could hear breakers pounding endlessly at the base of the dark cliffs. Gulls called raucously as they wheeled above the ramparts of the castle, and the sea wind keened in the stone like Bian's spirits.

Yet, with all this, and with his uncle droning on yet again about the proper method for keeping account of the thanes' fee payments, Filib could still hear music coming from the city. He toyed absently with the gold signet ring on his right hand, wondering where Renelle was at that moment. In the city, no doubt, enjoying the Revel with everyone else.

"Filib!"

The young lord looked up. His uncle sat across from him at the broad oak table, anger in his grey eyes, his mouth set in a thin line.

"Yes, Uncle?"

"You could at least do me the courtesy of pretending to listen. This may not be as fascinating as whatever you're dreaming about, but I'm sure it's every bit as important."

Filib grinned. "Important, yes. But as I've told you, it's not necessary."

The duke frowned, gesturing at the scrolls before him. "This method—"

"Is not mine, Uncle," Filib broke in. "I know that you like it. I know that you feel my method isn't as orderly or as clear as yours. But it works for me. If you really intend to give me control of the fee accounting, you're going to have to let me do it my way."

"This isn't just my method, Filib," Tobbar said, his voice softening. "It was your father's as well. And the king's before him. Dukes of Thorald have been accounting this way since before the Queen's War. Do you really think it's your place to abandon the practice?"

Filib closed his eyes. His father. How was he supposed to argue with that?

"All right," he said, opening his eyes again and passing a hand through his hair in a gesture his mother would have recognized. "But can we do this later? Please? The Revel—"

"The Revel?" Tobbar repeated, sounding cross again. He gestured impatiently at the door, as if the musicians, sorcerers, tumblers, and peddlers who traveled with Bohdan's Revel stood outside the chamber. "You're nearly two years past your Fating, Filib. You should know by now that dukes and lords don't have time for the Revel. We've more important things to do. Besides, the Revel will be here for another five or six days. You'll have plenty of time for all that later, after we're done." He picked up one of the scrolls again and began to study it. "The Revel," he muttered once more, shaking his head. "Do you think your father would have been more interested in what's going on in the city than in the thanes' fees?"

Filib had been expecting this. "Actually, yes."

Tobbar looked up again. Filib could see that he was fighting to keep the grin from his face.

His uncle sighed, then smiled. "You're probably right."

"I'm not sure I see the point of giving me control of the accounting anyway," Filib said. "I'll be king before long. And then it will fall back to you. Why bother with all this?"

"Maybe I want a respite from it," the duke said. "As you say, this will be mine to do for the rest of my life. I'd like someone else to do it, even for just a short while. And I don't want that person ruining my scrolls with poor work. Besides," he went on after a brief pause, "as I've told you before, kings have accounting to do as well. Where do you think our tithe goes every fourth turn?"

"A king has ministers to do this. Certainly Grandfather does."

Tobbar shook his head. "Only recently. When he was younger he did it all himself."

Filib let out a long breath. "Fine, you win. I promise to learn your method. But not today. Not until the Revel leaves for Eardley. Please."

The duke put the scroll down and leaned back in his chair, a grin on his face, much as Filib's father might have done. "It is good this year, isn't it?"

"The best I can remember," Filib said, grinning as well. "It seems a shame to miss any of it." He sensed his uncle's hesitation and he pressed his advantage. "The fee accounting will still be here long after the Revel is gone."

"True," Tobbar said, the smile lingering. "I suppose that girl of yours is down there as well?"

Filib felt something tighten in his chest. He had no doubt that she was still angry with him about last night. It had been the Night of Two Moons in Adriel's Turn. Lovers' Night. They should have been together, she would tell him. Of all the nights of the year, this was theirs. That's what she would say, her dark eyes flashing, or worse, brimming with tears. As if he didn't know. As if he had any choice in the matter. She knew the limits of what they shared, he'd have to tell her. Again. She knew that certain things lay beyond his control, that this was one of them. But still, she'd be angry and hurt. Who could blame her?

"Yes," he said, trying to keep his tone light. "She's probably there."

"You've grown quite fond of her, haven't you?"

Filib shrugged, looked away. "I care about her. Shouldn't I?"

"Of course you should. As long as you remember who she is, and who you are."

Filib kept his eyes trained on the window, but he nodded.

"What you said earlier about becoming king soon is true, Filib. I expect your grandfather to abdicate within the year. It's time you started thinking about a wife and heirs. We've been lucky. The king's long life has ensured the continuation of Thorald control of the crown, despite your father's death. It's time now that you did your part."

"Has Mother put you up to this, Uncle?" Filib asked, meeting Tobbar's gaze.

His uncle gave a small smile. "Not directly, no. But she has mentioned her concerns to me. She fears you've grown too attached to the girl."

"Her name is Renelle."

Tobbar's expression hardened. "Comments like that concern me as well. Her name isn't important. In the larger scheme of things, neither is she. If you wish to keep her as a mistress, I'm sure that can be arranged. But I don't want you—"

He stopped suddenly, a stricken expression on his ruddy face. "Last night!" he breathed. "You didn't . . ."

Filib looked to the window again. "No," he said, his voice thick. "We didn't."

His uncle let out a sigh. "Good. That would have been a terrible mistake, Filib. You need to be building ties to the other houses right now. And what better way to do so than with a good match."

"I know all this, Uncle!" Filib said, his voice rising. "I don't need to hear it again from you!"

Tobbar fell silent. Filib looked away once more, but he could feel his uncle's eyes upon him.

"I'm not even sure the legend applies in this case," the young lord said after a lengthy silence. "It says only that a love consummated on the Night of Two Moons in Adriel's Turn will last forever. My . . ." He swallowed. "My affair with Renelle was consummated long ago. Last night probably wouldn't have mattered."

"Perhaps not," Tobbar said softly. "But you were right not to take the chance."

Filib nodded again. A lone gull glided past the window, its cries echoing off the castle walls. *Tonight,* he promised himself. *I'll be with her tonight. After I ride.*

The two of them sat without speaking for some time, Filib staring out the window, the duke, no doubt, watching him. His uncle deserved better than his tantrums. In the five years—five years!—since the death of Filib's father, Tobbar had done everything in his power to prepare Filib for the throne. Where a lesser man might have allowed jealousy and resentment to keep him from such duties, Tobbar had embraced them. In Aneira, Caerisse, and every other kingdom in the Forelands, Filib knew, a man in Tobbar's position would have been next in line for the throne, with his heirs inheriting the crown after him. Only in Eibithar, with its ancient Rules of Ascension, did the line of succession pass over the younger brother in favor of the eldest son of the deceased king. The rules had been established by the leaders of Eibithar's twelve houses after the death of King Ouray the Second, the last of the early Thorald kings. By creating a peaceful process for sharing royal power among Eibithar's five major houses, the dukes sought to give the land some stability, while preventing one house from establishing an absolute dynasty.

Under the Rules of Ascension, only the king's eldest son or eldest grandson, if he had come of age, could inherit the throne. If the king had no heir, power passed to the duke of the highest-ranking house not in power. Thorald had always ranked highest of all the houses, for it was the house of Binthar, Eibithar's first great leader. After Thorald came Galdasten, Curgh, Kentigern, and Glyndwr. Thus, if Filib's grandfather, Aylyn the Second, had died in the interim between the death of Filib's father and Filib's Fating, the duke of Galdasten would have taken the crown. Or rather, the duke of Curgh, Filib realized, remembering with a shudder the dreadful incident at Galdasten that killed the duke and his family several years before.

Because Thorald was the preeminent house in Eibithar, and because power always reverted to the highest-ranking house, Filib's house had held the throne for more years than any other. Filib's father would have been pleased to know that his death would not keep Filib from taking his place in Thorald's pantheon of kings.

A knock on the duke's door broke a lengthy silence. Tobbar and Filib exchanged a look; then the older man called for whoever had come to enter.

The door opened and Enid ja Kovar, the duke's first minister, stepped into the chamber.

"Sire," the Qirsi woman said as she entered. "I was just—" Seeing the younger man, she stopped. "Lord Filib, I didn't know you were here. Forgive me for interrupting."

"It's all right, Enid," Tobbar said. He glanced at his nephew. "I think we're done."

Filib stood. "Thank you, Uncle."

"I'm going to hold you to that promise, though. When the Revel leaves, you're going to learn the old method."

"You have my word," Filib said, grinning.

"You're off to the Revel, my lord?" the first minister asked, her yellow eyes reflecting the light from the window. Like all the men and women of the sorcerer race, she had white hair and skin so pale that it was almost translucent. Enid wore her hair pulled back from her face, making her appear even more frail than most Qirsi. Filib sometimes found it hard to remember that she wielded such powerful magic. Yet just two years before, when a late-night fire threatened to sweep through the center of the walled city below the castle, he had seen this wisp of a woman raise a dense mist that dampened the flames, and a stiff wind that blew against the prevailing natural gale to keep the fire from spreading. Without her magic the towns-folk might not have been able to put the fire out before it claimed the entire city.

"Yes," Filib told her. "I'm heading to the Revel now. Have you been?"

She gave an indulgent smile, as if he were still a child. "I find the Revel . . . tiresome. However, I will be at the banquet tonight. I trust I'll see you there?"

The banquet. He had forgotten. He had no choice really; he had to be there. He was hosting it, along with his mother and Tobbar. But how would he explain this to Renelle? She'd be there as well, though not at his table, of course, and she'd expect to be with him after. But he needed to ride. It was going to be a very late night.

His uncle was watching him closely, awaiting his reply to Enid's question.

He made himself smile. "Yes, of course I'll be there."

Tobbar continued to stare at him, as if expecting him to say more.

"I give you my word, Uncle," Filib told him. "I'll be there."

Still, his uncle did not look satisfied. "Then why are you behaving as though it's the last place you intended to be? Is this about that—?" He stopped himself. "Is this about Renelle again?"

"No, it's not." He exhaled heavily. "I had planned to ride tonight," he said at last. "That's all. It's not important. I'll just do it after the banquet."

Tobbar paled. "I'm sorry, Filib. My memory is not what it once was."

"I'm afraid I'm a bit lost," Enid said, looking from Filib to the duke.

"My father was killed during a hunt the night of Panya's full," Filib said. Just speaking the words made him shiver. He still remembered being awakened by the tolling of the guardhouse bells and hearing his mother wailing in the next chamber.

"Forgive me," the Qirsi woman said. "I hadn't come to Thorald yet. But it was my understanding that this happened in Kebb's Turn."

Filib nodded, playing with the ring again. "It did. But each turn, on this night, I honor my father by riding to the place of his death.

And on this night in Kebb's Turn, after leading the hunt as he once did, I remain there until dawn."

"It seems a fine way to remember him, my lord," Enid said.

"Thank you."

"I'll see to it that the final course is served early enough, Filib," his uncle said. "I should have remembered. Forgive me."

"There's nothing to forgive," Filib said with a shrug. "Mother says I'm foolish to do this more than once a year." He smiled. "Actually she called it unhealthful. But I'll have to stop anyway once I leave for Audun's Castle, so I feel that I should continue until then."

"Each of us honors your father in his or her own way," Tobbar told him. "Including your mother. I see nothing wrong with your rides, and I'll tell her as much the next time I speak with her."

"Thank you."

"Be watchful tonight, though," he went on. "For all that the Revel gives us, it also attracts more than its share of knaves and vagrants. I'd feel better if you'd take one of your liege men."

"I'll be fine, Uncle. I ride every turn, and I always do so alone."

"Very well," Tobbar said, shaking his head slightly.

Filib glanced toward the window. The sunlight on the castle walls had taken on the rich golden hue of late day. He barely had time to find Renelle before he'd be expected back at the castle for the banquet.

"Go on, Filib," the duke said. "We'll see you soon."

He was walking toward the door almost before Tobbar had finished speaking. He stopped himself long enough to bow to his uncle and nod once to the Qirsi woman. Then he hurried out of the chamber, down the winding stone steps of the tower, and out into the daylight. With any luck at all, he'd find Renelle in the markets. He could only hope that in her happiness at seeing him she'd forget her anger.

The singer beside him was nearing the end of the first movement, her voice climbing smoothly through the closing notes of "Panya's Devotion," finding subtleties in the piece that most singers missed. This was a difficult passage, although no part of *The Paean to the Moons* could be considered easy, and she was handling it quite well.

Cadel couldn't remember her name, though they had been practicing together since the second day of the Revel. It was not unusual for wandering singers in the Forelands to meet up with others of their craft, practice and perform with them for a short while, and then, after a most careful division of their wages, part ways to continue their travels. It was especially common in the cities hosting Eibithar's Revel. Cadel and Jedrek had been making their way through the Forelands in this manner for nearly fourteen years; they had sung with more people than Cadel could recall.

He had never been very good with names, a trait that actually was quite useful in his other, true profession. But in this case, he would have liked to remember, merely as a courtesy. She had not been shy about showing her interest in him, allowing her gaze to linger on his face, even after he caught her watching him, and standing closer to him than was necessary when they sang. He liked bold women. Had he and Jedrek not had other business to which to attend, he might have been interested as well. She was rather attractive, with short dark hair, pale green eyes, and a round, pretty face, and she was just a bit heavy, which he also liked. But most of all, she was a fine singer, her voice strong and supple. For that reason alone, he felt that he should have known her name. Her interpretation of "Panya's Devotion" had earned his respect.

Jedrek and the woman's sister, whose name Cadel had also forgotten, were backing her with a strong, even counterpoint, their voices twined like lovers. The two of them had spent the previous night together, Cadel knew, and it showed in their singing. Jedrek gave little credence to the moon legends, although he wasn't above using the promise of a lifetime of love to lure a woman into his bed. He had been doing it for several years. Nonetheless, it still angered Cadel to see him behaving so recklessly under these circumstances. He hadn't gotten the chance to talk to Jedrek about it this morning—Jedrek and the woman had arrived only a few moments before their performance began—but he would as soon as they ended their performance.

The first woman—*what was her name?*—had reached the end of "Panya's Devotion." The counterpoint was to complete its cycle once, and then it was Cadel's turn. He took a long, slow breath, readying himself. The opening of "Ilias's Lament" was by far the most difficult part of the *Paean*'s second movement. It began at the very top of Cadel's range and remained there for several verses before falling briefly during the middle passages. It rose again at its end, but by then his voice would be ready. The opening, that was the challenge.

The counterpoint completed its turn. Cadel opened his mouth, and keeping his throat as relaxed as possible, he reached for the opening note. And found it. Perfectly. His voice soared, like a falcon on a clear day, and he gave himself over to the music, allowing the bittersweet melody and the tragic tale imparted by the lyrics to carry him through the movement.

Those who knew him—or thought they did—solely through his profession would have been surprised to see what music did to him. At times, he was surprised by it himself. How many times had he finished a passage of surpassing emotion, only to find that his cheeks were damp with tears? Yes, there was a precision to the art that excited him, just the way the precision demanded by his other craft did. But there was more. Music had the power to soothe him, even as it exhilarated. It offered him both release and fulfillment. In many ways, it was not unlike the act of love.

With no piece was all of this truer than with the *Paean*. Normally it was sung only once a turn, on the Night of Two Moons. But their performance last night had been such that all those who missed it and heard others speak of what they had done demanded that they repeat it this day. Jedrek and the women had been more than happy to oblige, but Cadel hesitated. The previous night's performance had been wondrous. Singing the second movement, Cadel had felt for just a moment that Ilias himself had reached down from Morna's sky to add his voice to Cadel's own. The others had sung brilliantly as well, particularly the woman singing Panya's part.

But magic such as they had found the previous night was not to be taken for granted. They could not be certain that they would find it again. Besides, he and Jedrek had other things to do this day. It was only when one of the local innkeepers offered them twice the wage they had earned the previous night to sing the *Paean* again that Cadel realized he had no choice in the matter. Not that he or Jedrek needed the gold. But they were supposed to be wandering bards, and no bard could turn down such a wage without arousing suspicion.

So here he was, singing the lament again, and, much to his amazement, giving a better performance than he had the night before. All of them were. He had only to see the expressions on the faces of those listening to them to know it was true. Even sung poorly, the *Paean* was a powerful piece of music, capable of evoking tears from the most impassive audiences. But when sung by masters, it could overwhelm listeners with its splendor and arouse within them the same passion, longing, and heartache it described.

It told of the love shared by Panya, a Qirsi woman, and Ilias, an Eandi man. The two races were young then, and the gods who created them, Qirsar and Ean, had long hated each other and had thus decreed that the Qirsi and Eandi should remain apart. But what Panya and Ilias shared went deeper even than their fear of the great ones. Soon Panya was with child, and Qirsar's rage flared like the fire magic some of his people possessed. For it was well known that Qirsi women were too frail to bear the children begotten by Eandi men. When Panya's time came, she lived long enough to deliver her child, a beautiful daughter, but then she died. Ilias, bereft of his love and unable to find consolation in the birth of his daughter, took his own life, hoping to join his beloved in Bian's realm.

Qirsar, however, had something else in mind for them. He changed the lovers into moons, one white and one red, and placed them in the sky for all to see, as a warning to Qirsi and Eandi who dared to love one another. For all eternity, the great one declared, the lovers would pursue each other among the stars, but never would they be together or even see each other again. Whenever white Panya rose, red Ilias would set, and only when she disappeared below the horizon would he rise again.

But so great was their love that even in death they were able to defy the god. The first time Panya rose into the night sky, brilliant and full, she paused at the summit of her arc. And there she waited until Ilias could join her. Ever after, they traveled the sky together, their cycles nearly identical.

Cadel moved slowly through the second movement, carrying his audience with him through the range of Ilias's emotions: his passionate love for the Qirsi woman, his fear of the wrath of the gods and his joy at finding that Panya was with child, and finally, as the melody spiraled upward again toward the lament's heartrending conclusion, his anguish at losing Panya. Jedrek and the second woman stayed right with him throughout, easing the tempo of their counterpoint as he lingered on Ilias's passion, matching him as he quickened his pace to convey Ilias's fear, and, at the last, slowing once more, to wring heartache from their melody as he sang Ilias's grief.

The third and final movement, "The Lovers' Round," which described Panya and Ilias's final defiance of Qirsar, was sung as a canon. It began with the first woman singing the lyrical, intricate melody in a high register. As she moved to the second verse, Cadel joined in, beginning the melody again, though at a lower pitch. He was followed by the second woman, who was followed by Jedrek. Thus the melody, first sung high, then low, then high again, then low again, circled back on itself, each voice drawn along by the previous one. Just as Ilias followed Panya through the sky, turn after turn, so their voices followed, one after the other, thirteen times through this final theme, for the thirteen turns of the year.

They finished the piece and the audience erupted with cheers and clapping. But much more gratifying for Cadel was the single moment of utter silence just after their last notes had died away and just before the applause began. For that silence, that moment of awe and reverence, of yearning and joy, told him more about what their music had done to those listening than all the cheers the people could muster.

He glanced at the woman beside him and they shared a smile. *What is your name?*

"You sing very well," he whispered to her.

Her smile deepened, though she didn't blush as some women might have. "As do you."

Each one of them bowed in turn; then the four of them bowed in unison and they left the stage, the noise from the audience continuing even after they were gone. Four times they returned to bow and wave, and four times the people called them back, until finally the innkeeper came to them and asked if they would sing the *Paean* once more, for another five qinde apiece.

Once more, Jedrek and the other woman were willing, but this time Cadel and the dark-haired woman refused.

"But, Anesse!" the second woman said, turning toward her sister. "He's offering gold!"

Anesse! Of course. Anesse and Kalida.

Anesse shook her head. "I don't care if he's offering fifty qinde. Twice is enough." Her eyes strayed toward Cadel for just an instant. "We found magic twice with the *Paean*. We'd be fools to chance a third time."

The younger woman opened her mouth, but Anesse stopped her with a raised finger. "No, Kalida. That's my final word."

Cadel nodded his approval and faced the innkeeper. "I'm afraid we must refuse."

The man looked disappointed, but he managed a smile. "I figured as much." He turned away and started toward the bar. "I'll get your wage and you can be on your way," he said over his shoulder.

Cadel glanced at Jedrek, who gave a small nod. The time for singing was over. They had business.

"Will you be joining us at the banquet tonight, Corbin?"

It took him a moment. The alias he had chosen for the Revel.

"I'm afraid not," he said, meeting her gaze. It was a shame, really. He would have enjoyed passing a night or two in her arms. "Honok and I will be visiting with some old friends this evening."

She gave a small frown. "That's too bad. I had hoped to spend some time with you, away from all this." She gestured toward the stage, giving him the same knowing smile she had offered earlier as they finished singing.

"I'd like that as well. Honok and I will be in the marketplace tomorrow, singing some Caerissan folk songs. Perhaps after we've finished?"

Cadel knew what she'd say. He had overheard the two women discussing their plans a few days before. Still, he had no trouble acting disappointed when Anesse explained that they would be leaving for Sanbira the next morning.

"So we're not going to see you again at all?" Kalida said plaintively, looking from her sister to Jedrek.

"It seems not," Cadel answered. "At least not for some time." He smiled at Anesse. "But perhaps Adriel will bring us together again."

"She will if she has an ear for music," the dark-haired woman said, grinning.

Truly a shame.

They all turned at the sound of coins jingling. The innkeeper was approaching, digging into a small pouch as he walked.

"I believe we agreed upon four qinde each," he said as he stopped in front of them.

Cadel gave a small laugh, but when he spoke his voice carried just a hint of steel. "And I'm certain it was eight."

The man looked up. He was quite heavy, with white, wispy hair and yellowed teeth. He walked with an exaggerated limp. This was not a man who was looking for a fight.

He merely nodded. "Of course, I'd forgotten. Eight it is. And worth every qinde."

He handed them each their coins and then smiled, his breath smelling of ale and pipe smoke. "If you're back for next year's Revel, I hope you'll sing for us again. At the same wage, naturally."

"If we're back," Cadel said, "we'd be delighted."

The four singers left the inn by way of a rear door that let out into a grassy area near the west wall of Thorald City. Immediately, Jedrek and Kalida moved off a short distance to say their goodbyes, leaving Cadel alone with Anesse.

The woman stared after her sister for a moment before facing Cadel, a wry grin on her lips.

"Well," she said, "if there's any truth to the old legends, we'll probably see each other again at Kalida and Honok's joining."

Cadel hesitated and Anesse began to laugh.

"Don't worry," she told him with obvious amusement. "Kalida doesn't believe in the legends any more than your friend seems to." Her smile changed, deepened. "I do, however, and I should tell you that I still was tempted to seek out your chambers last night."

"I almost wish you had."

She arched an eyebrow. "Almost?"

"I take the moon legends seriously, too. Even if you had come, I'm not certain what would have happened."

"Fair enough," she said. "But what about now? I don't think Kalida and Honok would mind a few hours together before evening. And we have nothing to fear today from the legends."

He was tempted by her offer. Who wouldn't have been? But he had to meet someone before sundown, and on days such as these he did not allow himself any distractions. Except for music, of course, which actually served to sharpen his mind. Besides, he needed to speak with Jedrek.

"I wish I could. But Honok and I must rehearse for this evening. We're visiting friends, but like all our friends, they'll expect us to sing, and we have nothing prepared."

"If I didn't know better, Corbin, I'd say you were putting me off."

He felt himself growing tense and he tried not to let it show. "I'm sorry if it seems that way. I meant what I said before: I hope the goddess will bring us together again. But I'm afraid this isn't our time."

45

Anesse shrugged and smiled. "Very well. Until next time then." She glanced back toward where Jedrek and her sister had been and, seeing that they were gone, looked at Cadel again, a question in her green eyes. "Where did they go?"

"I think they went around to the side of the inn for some privacy," he said. No doubt Jedrek had her pressed up against the building wall by now.

Anesse frowned. "Kal?" she called.

For several moments there was no reply.

"Just a minute," her sister finally answered, her voice breathless and muffled.

The woman faced him again, looking uncomfortable, and they stood that way for a few more minutes, waiting for Jedrek and Kalida to return.

He's gone too far this time, Cadel thought, his anger at Jedrek building as they waited. He and Jedrek had been together for a long time, but in recent turns Jedrek had started acting strangely, taking risks where once he never would have thought of doing so. Perhaps it was the inevitable result of success, or a natural response to so many years of caution. Whatever the reason, it had to stop before one of them got killed.

When at last Jedrek and the woman returned to the grassy area behind the inn, their hair and clothes disheveled, Cadel was ready to throttle him. Kalida, her color high, refused to meet her sister's gaze, but Jedrek seemed far too pleased with himself. He grinned at Cadel sheepishly and gave a slight shrug, as if the gesture alone could excuse his behavior. At least he had the good sense to keep his mouth shut.

"Goodbye, Anesse," Cadel said, as he and Jedrek turned to leave. "Gods keep you safe."

He didn't look back, but he sensed that she was smiling.

"And you, Corbin," she said.

For some time as they walked, neither of them said a thing, and even when Cadel did begin to speak, he kept his tone low and casual, so as not to draw the attention of passersby.

"I've half a mind to kill you here in Thorald, and leave your body for the duke's men to find tomorrow morning."

Jedrek faltered in midstride for just an instant before resuming his normal gait. The smile had vanished from his lean face. He swallowed, then whispered, "Why?"

Cadel looked at him sidelong. "You have to ask why?" He shook his head. "Perhaps I should kill you," he muttered. They walked a few paces in silence. "You understand your job, right? You know what I expect of you?"

"I've been doing this for fourteen years," Jedrek said, sounding defensive. "I ought to know my role by now."

"Yes, you ought to!" Cadel said, his voice rising. He glanced around quickly. Two or three of the street vendors were eyeing him, but no one else seemed to have paid any attention. "You ought to," he repeated in a lower voice. "I need you to guard my back, Jed. I need you to keep anything unexpected from ruining my plans. You've saved my life more times than I care to count, and I need to know that you're capable of doing it again should the need arise. And here we are in Thorald, the heart of Eibithar, on the verge of completing the most lucrative job we've ever had, and you're acting like a rutting pig."

Jedrek didn't say anything for some time. When he finally did respond, he sounded contrite. "You're right. It won't happen again. I swear."

"It better not, or I will kill you. This is a young man's profession. We all get too old for it eventually. I'd hate to think that your time had come already."

Jedrek halted and grabbed Cadel by the arm so that they were facing each other. "I'm not too old!" he said, his dark eyes boring into Cadel's.

Cadel grinned. "I'm glad to hear it. And I'm glad to see that I can still get a rise out of you."

Jedrek glared at him for another moment before giving in to a smile and shaking his head.

"You bastard," he said, as they started walking again.

They reached the inn a short time later. Cadel had arranged to meet with their employer just after the ringing of the prior's bells, which would come within the hour. He had agreed to come alone—his employers often asked this of him—and he gave Jedrek leave to wander the city and enjoy the Revel for a time while he changed clothes and kept his appointment.

He climbed the stairs and walked down the narrow corridor to their room. But as he approached the door, he saw that it was slightly ajar.

Instantly his dagger was in his hand, its worn stone hilt feeling

47

cold and smooth against his fingers. He crept forward, each step as delicate as a kiss, and, laying his free hand gently on the door, prepared to fling it open and launch himself at the intruder.

"It's all right," a woman's voice called. "I'd have thought you'd be expecting me."

Exhaling, he straightened and pushed the door open.

He had never met the Qirsi woman he saw reclining casually on his bed, though he knew her name, and her title. Enid ja Kovar, first minister to the duke of Thorald. He also knew that she was right. He should have expected her.

Chapter
Three

e were to meet by the upper river gate," Cadel said, stepping into the room and shutting the door behind him. "Why the change?"

Still reclining on his bed, the woman smiled at the sight of his dagger. "Was that intended for me? I hope not. It wouldn't be prudent to kill the duke's minister."

He returned the blade to the sheath within his tunic. "Why did you change our plans?" he asked again.

She sat up and gave a small shrug. "You have a reputation as a dangerous man, Cadel. I prefer to meet with dangerous men on my own terms, at places and times of my own choosing."

"You hired me because of my reputation. It strikes me as strange that you'd suddenly find yourself afraid of me."

The smile sprung back to her lips, though her pale yellow eyes remained grim. "I never said I was afraid of you. If you deal with the Qirsi for any length of time, you'll find that we're not easily frightened."

He shuddered at the thought. He had no desire to deal with the Qirsi for any longer than was absolutely necessary. It was not just that he found their powers daunting, though certainly that was much of it. But more than that, he didn't even like to look at them. With their white hair and pallid skin they looked more like wraiths than people, as if they had been sent from the Underrealm by Bian himself to walk among the Eandi.

They had first come to the Forelands nearly nine hundred years before, crossing the Border Range from the Southlands intent upon conquering the northern tribes with their magic and their bright blades. Instead they were defeated, the survivors of their invasion scattered throughout the kingdoms. Yet somehow, no doubt owing to their powers, they quickly assumed positions of great importance in every court in the Forelands. To this day, they wielded tremendous influence in all the seven realms, advising kings and queens, dukes and thanes.

Enid laughed gently. "You don't relish the notion of doing business with the Qirsi for an extended time. You should. We have access to gold, we live in every realm in the Forelands, and we don't tend to live very long, a trait that should be especially attractive to a man of your talents."

"I work for gold," Cadel told her, keeping his tone neutral. "I don't work for one set of people to the exclusion of others."

"I realize that. I just hope that you'll consider working for us in the future, when we have need. Everyone knows that Cadel Nistaad of Caerisse is the best assassin money can buy."

Cadel stiffened at the sound of his surname. Even Jedrek didn't know it. He had done everything in his power to leave it behind when he left his home in southern Caerisse sixteen years ago, even going so far as to stage his own death and have his family informed that he had gone to the Underrealm. An assassin couldn't afford to have a past or a name, at least not one that could be traced. So he had thought to eliminate his. Up until now, he felt certain that he had succeeded, that nobody knew.

"How—?" He stopped himself, not wishing to let her see that she had unsettled him.

"How did I know your full name?" She opened her hands. "I know a great deal about you. Your father is a minor noble in southern Caerisse, a viscount I believe, who's more interested in his vineyards and horses than he is in politics. Your mother is the daughter of a northern marquess who had hoped she would marry better. Her first pregnancy—as it turned out, her only one—dashed all hopes of that and forced the marriage. You left your home at the age of sixteen, without ever having your Fating. The reason for your departure isn't clear, though there seems to have been a girl involved, as well as a rival for her affections who turned up dead."

He crossed to the room's lone window and stared down at the lane below. "How can you know all this?"

"I'm first minister to the duke of Thorald. And I'm Qirsi. I have resources at my disposal the likes of which you can't even imagine. Never forget that, Cadel."

As if to prove her point, she produced a leather pouch that jingled much as the innkeeper's had, and held it out to him. He took it reluctantly. It was heavy with coins. He stared at her briefly, then pulled it open and poured the contents into his hand. There must have been twenty gold pieces. Two hundred qinde.

"This is more than we agreed," he said quietly, returning the coins to the pouch.

"You see? Sometimes a change in plans can work to your advantage." She watched him, as if waiting for a reaction. When he gave none, she went on. "Consider the extra gold an incentive. As I was saying, we may wish to hire you again."

He looked down at the pouch, feeling the weight of the coins in his hand. But it was the threat implied by her chilling knowledge of his youth that occupied his mind. An incentive, she had said. And, in case that didn't work, she had shown him the cudgel as well.

"What about tonight?" he asked, his eyes still on the money bag.

"He rides tonight, after the banquet. He'll be in the North Wood."

"The wood?" Cadel said, meeting her gaze.

"He honors his father, who died there several years back. A hunting accident, I believe."

"Do you know where in the wood he'll be?"

She nodded. "His father died near the Sanctuary of Kebb, on the north edge of the wood just east of Thorald River. Do you know it?"

"Yes."

"I assume he'll be there."

"And that's where you want it done?"

She smiled at that, her small, sharp teeth as white as her hair. "It seems fitting, doesn't it? It was good enough for the father, it will do for the son."

Cadel offered no response, and after a moment she continued. "I want this to look like the work of thieves. The boy's uncle pointed out today that the Revel brings with it a collection of miscreants and lawbreakers. He'll readily believe that one of them is responsible."

"All right."

"That means you can't be seen leaving the city; you can't use any of the gates."

It was Cadel's turn to smile. "That's not a problem."

"You'll have to be careful getting back in, as well. You should be seen here tomorrow. It might arouse suspicion if you were to just disappear."

He held up the pouch of gold. "You've paid me a great deal, First Minister, because you know I'm the best. Let me worry about the fine points. I won't be seen leaving or entering the city, and I have no intention of disappearing. In fact, I expect to be singing 'The Dirge of Kings' at the young lord's funeral."

"I'll look forward to that, Cadel. I hear you sing quite beautifully."

He bowed his head slightly, acknowledging the compliment. "Is there anything more that we need to discuss, First Minister?"

"No," she said. "Leave me."

He hesitated. "But this is my room."

"Yes. But no one should see me leave. Not even you."

"I need to change my clothes."

"Please," she said with a raised eyebrow and a coy grin, "be my guest."

Again he shuddered, as though from a chill wind. But the first minister showed no sign of relenting. In the end, Cadel stood in the far corner of the room, his back to her, changing out of the tunic and trousers in which he had performed, and into simple, dark clothes far better suited to what he was to do that night. When he was finished, he walked to the door wordlessly and put his hand on the knob. Then he stopped himself and faced her again.

"Why do you want him dead?" he asked.

He had never asked this of an employer before, but neither had he ever been asked to kill a future king.

She regarded him for some time, as if trying to decide whether or not to answer. At last she gave a small shrug. "We sense an opportunity, a chance to gain control of events here in the Forelands. We don't want it to slip away."

"With so many Qirsi in the courts, I would have thought that you already control everything you need."

She smiled, as if indulging him. "We don't control everything. Sometimes events show us the way. The deaths in Galdasten, for instance. An accident of history, the act of a madman. The same is true of the incident that claimed the boy's father. Another accident, or perhaps an act of the gods. But these events created the opportunity I mentioned a moment ago. And with your help we're going to turn this opportunity to our advantage."

He nodded, profoundly relieved to learn that at least some of what happened in the Forelands lay beyond the reach of Qirsi magic. Still, he couldn't help feeling that by killing on their behalf, he made it easier for the white-hairs to turn subsequent events to their purposes.

He turned and pulled the door open, but before he could leave, the Qirsi woman called his name.

He looked at her once more and waited.

"What is it about the Qirsi that bothers you so much? Our magic? The way we look?"

"Yes, both of those," he said. "But mostly it's that you don't belong here. Your place is in the Southlands. The Forelands were meant to be ours."

She nodded. "I see."

"Is that all?"

"Yes, that's all. Do well tonight, Cadel, and in time the gold in that pouch will seem a pittance."

He felt his jaw tense, but he bowed his head once more, then left her and went in search of Jedrek. Gold is gold, he told himself as he walked. It doesn't matter from where it comes. Certainly that was what Jed would say.

Cadel found Jedrek in the city marketplace, haggling with a peddler over the price of a Sanbiri blade.

"Leave it, Honok," Cadel said as he approached the vendor's table. "You can't afford it anyway."

Jedrek glanced at him sourly, before facing the merchant again. "I could if this Wethy goat would be reasonable."

"Twelve qinde is as reasonable as I intend to be," the peddler said in a raspy voice.

"It may be worth twelve qinde in Wethyrn, old man, but it's worth half that anyplace else."

"We'll give you ten for it," Cadel said. "Final offer."

The merchant eyed him warily for a few moments. "Done," he finally said.

Careful to keep the money from the Qirsi woman hidden, Cadel pulled out two five-qinde pieces and handed them to the man. The merchant took the money and made a point of handing the dagger to Cadel rather than Jedrek.

"Thank you, good sir," he said to Cadel, a toothless grin on his wizened face. Then he cast a dark look at Jedrek. "It's always a pleasure to do business with a gentleman."

Cadel nodded once, before walking away. Jedrek hurried after him, holding his hand out for the blade. But for several moments Cadel held on to it, examining the bright steel and the polished wood handle. It was actually a fine piece of work. Sanbiri blades were the best in the Forelands, except perhaps for those made in Uulrann, which were exceedingly hard to find. At last he handed the dagger to Jedrek.

"Thanks," Jedrek said, taking time to look at it as well. "You can take the ten qinde out of my share."

"I will," Cadel said. "It's a good blade." He paused, before adding, "Better than a musician needs."

Jedrek shot him a look. "Then why did you buy it for me?"

"The damage had been done. Better we should get out of there quickly, without a fuss, than have you argue with the goat until sundown."

Jedrek shook his head, a sullen look on his lean face. "So now I'm not even allowed to buy a dagger? Is that what you're saying? Come on Ca—" He stopped himself. "Corbin, I mean. You're not being reasonable. We just gave a great performance, and we did nothing to hide the fact that we were paid very well for it. Can't I enjoy that?"

He had a point.

"You told me earlier that I was growing careless," Jedrek went on, obviously struggling to keep his voice low. "I think it's just as possible that you're trying to be too careful. You're the one who's acting like an old man, not me."

Cadel had to resist an urge to strike him. But he also had to admit that Jedrek was right. It was one thing to be prudent; it was something else entirely to act out of fear. In many ways that was as dangerous as taking no precautions at all. Wasn't it possible that by trying too hard not to stand out, they could draw attention to themselves? Yes, the dagger was an extravagance. But wandering musicians needed to protect themselves from thieves, and fresh from their performances, Jedrek could be expected to celebrate a bit.

Cadel's meeting with the first minister had left him shaken, but he had no right to take that out on Jedrek.

"You're right," Cadel said. "Enjoy it. It's a fine dagger. Nicer than mine, to be honest."

Jedrek stared at him for several moments, as if not quite sure whether to believe what Cadel was saying. Finally he grinned. "I know it's nicer. That's why I wanted it." He slipped the blade into his tunic. "So where's your meeting?" he asked a moment later, as they continued to walk.

"I've already had it."

"What?"

"Our employer was waiting for me in our room."

"How did he know where we were staying? How did he get past the barkeep?"

Cadel saw no reason to correct him. "I'm not sure."

Jedrek dropped his voice to a whisper. "So are we doing it tonight?"

"Yes. In the wood. He'll be on horseback."

"That shouldn't be a problem."

Cadel nodded. "I agree. We also have to avoid the city gates."

"That shouldn't be a problem either. Did he pay you already?"

"Yes. More than twice what we were promised." Cadel grinned at the expression on Jedrek's face. "Wish you had held out for a bigger blade?"

"I should have gotten two."

They circled once through the city, then returned to the inn at which they were staying.

"Go upstairs and change out of your performance clothes," Cadel said. "Then join me down here. We'll eat supper and go back to the markets. From there, when, it's time, we'll make our way to the wall."

Jedrek nodded and climbed the stairs to their room, while Cadel claimed a table in the back of the inn and ordered two plates of fowl and greens.

The two men lingered over the meal, which, though not particularly good, was not as bad as some of the meals Cadel had endured in inns like this one over the years. They left the inn just as the sunset bells were ringing. The sky had darkened to a shade of deepest blue, except in the west where the last rays of crimson and yellow still blazed. To the east, Panya, the white moon—the Qirsi moon—hung just above the city wall. A handful of stars could be seen overhead, pale as Qirsi skin. The air was still, which would make it harder to slip by the guards, but easier to hear the approach of their prey.

Cadel and Jedrek walked slowly back through the marketplace. Many of the merchants' tables had been cleared away to make room for the Revel's street performers. Tumblers soared through the air, twisting and rolling like swallows on a warm day. Bright flames leaped from the mouths of fire-eaters, and jugglers tossed gold and silver balls into the warm, sweet air. A company of Qirsi sorcerers conjured flames of every imaginable hue that danced and whirled as though they were alive. Musicians played at intervals along the street, the music from one group mingling with that of the next.

In the center of Thorald City, outside a great tent, young men and women of Determining and Fating ages stood in a long, winding line, waiting to have their futures foretold by the Qirsi gleaner inside. For all the spectacles of Bohdan's Revel, the dancers spinning and gliding in the streets, the falconers displaying the talents of their birds, the tournaments of strength and speed and sword skill waged by men of fighting age, the gleaning remained its most important element, just as it lay at the core of the traveling festivals found in the other kingdoms of the Forelands. For children in their twelfth and sixteenth years, it was all they could think of during the turns leading up to the Revel's arrival in their city.

The gleaning was yet another custom of the Southlands, brought to the northern kingdoms by the Qirsi invaders. A Qirsi man or woman possessing the gleaning power, the ability to divine the future, would offer a glimpse of each child's fate with the aid of the Qiran, a great crystal said to be imbued with magic of its own.

Having traveled for several years with Eibithar's Revel, Sanbira's Festival, and smaller fairs in Aneira, Wethyrn, Caerisse, and Braedon, Cadel had learned a good deal about the gleanings and how they worked. He knew, for instance, that the Qiran itself was little more than a pretty rock. It served mostly as a medium through which the Qirsi sorcerers could convey what they saw to the awed children. The Determining, done at the younger age, also was not what it seemed, at least not anymore. Once, perhaps, there had been some magic in it. Over the years, however, it had become little more than a means for steering children into apprenticeships at the appropriate age. Still, for the children gazing into the Qiran as the Qirsi before them summoned forth an image of their future lives, it was a wondrous event. Cadel still carried vivid memories of his own

Determining, though he shouldn't have been surprised by what he saw: himself as an adult, presiding over Nistaad Manor, tending to the vineyards and stables, and collecting tribute from the surrounding villages. At the time he thought it prophecy. Later, long after he fled southern Caerisse, he realized that it had merely been an informed guess.

The Fating, however, was a different matter. Done in the sixteenth year, it relied entirely on Qirsi magic. Fatings foretold good marriages or failed love affairs, great wealth or grave misfortune, long life or untimely death. Those awaiting their moment with the Qiran might be giddy with anticipation or debilitated with fear, but no one took it lightly. Even Jedrek, who scoffed at the legends and paid little heed to custom, had once admitted to Cadel that his Fating, which offered glimpses of the life they were leading now, had left him troubled for many turns after.

Cadel had often wondered what his Fating would have revealed. He left his home early in his sixteenth year, before the festival arrived at the village closest to Nistaad Manor. Tall and strong for his age, with a dark mustache and beard already beginning to appear on his face, he was able to pass for an older man almost immediately. To have sought out his Fating in another village would only have served to call attention to himself.

At this point, he had little doubt about what the Qiran would have shown him. He was living the life he was meant to live. He didn't need a Qirsi sorcerer to reassure him of that. Yet, even now, seeing the children of Thorald waiting to take their turn in the Qirsi's tent, he could not help but feel the call of the stone.

"Corbin! Honok!"

Wincing inwardly, Cadel turned at the sound of Anesse's voice. He and Jedrek could ill afford to be trapped in a long conversation, or, worse, caught in a lie. It was nearly time for them to make their way to the city wall.

"I thought you had plans for tonight," Anesse said. She was wearing a long, blue dress that was almost a perfect match for the color of the sky. It had a tantalizingly low neckline.

He summoned a smile. "We do. We're on our way there now."

"You're certain we can't lure you to the banquet?"

"Sadly, yes. You're certain we can't convince you to remain in Thorald for another day or two?"

She nodded. "Sadly."

Cadel glanced for an instant at Kalida, who was steadfastly avoiding his gaze and Jedrek's, her face as red as her dress.

"Well," Anesse said awkwardly. "We should be on our way."

"So should we."

"Goodbye again, Corbin. Honok."

"I hope to have the pleasure of singing with you again," he said.

The two women turned and started up the road toward Thorald Castle. After watching them walk away, Cadel and Jedrek turned as well, and cut back across the market to the south end of the city. Cadel would have preferred to go over the city wall somewhere between the south and east gates. But all the land between the gates belonged to the Sanctuary of Amon, and Cadel wished to avoid any encounters with the clerics. Instead, they made their way to the southwestern wall, between the south gate and the lower river gate. There were a few small houses in this part of the city, scattered along a narrow lane. But most of the residents were at the banquet or enjoying the Revel. The houses were dark and the street empty.

At least six guards were stationed at each of the gates, and two more walked atop each of the three wall segments between the river gate and the south gate. A small watchtower separated one segment from the next, and each tower held two bright torches. Obviously, their best chance was to climb the wall near the center of the middle segment, as far from the torches and the well-manned gates as possible.

Cadel was most concerned about the timing of their climb, which, in turn, depended upon how the guards on that middle segment had decided to keep watch. If they were walking the wall together, they could be avoided with relative ease. If not, he and Jedrek faced a far more difficult task.

Walking as quietly as they could through the tall grass that grew behind the houses, the two men soon reached the wall. It was made of rough stone, and it stood at least twelve fourspans high. Doing his best to remain in the shadows, Cadel looked up at the torchlit tower, trying to spot the guards. He heard them before he saw them. They were talking loudly, laughing about something, walking northward atop the wall. Cadel and Jedrek waited until the guards had gone past; then they began to climb.

Over the course of their travels throughout the Forelands, Cadel and Jedrek had climbed rock faces in the Glyndwr Highlands, the

Grey Hills of Wethyrn, and the Sanbiri Hills that would have appeared impossibly sheer to most people. Once, several years before, they had climbed a peak in the Basak Range of southern Aneira to arrange the death of an Aneiran noble who enjoyed hunting bear in the mountains. This wall, rough as it was, offered ample handholds and footholds. They climbed quickly, like lizards on a rock, and were soon within a few fourspans of the top of the wall.

Hearing the guards again, Cadel raised a hand, indicating to Jedrek that they should stop.

". . . Three bloody nights in a row," one of them was saying, as they drew closer to where Cadel and Jedrek clung to the stones. "During the Revel, no less. There's no justice in that."

"Captain doesn't care much for justice. If he thought you'd give him your wage, he'd probably let you off. Me, I've been on the wall for two in a row. And it looks like I'll be up here again tomorrow night."

"It's the banquet that does it. That's where the captain is. Him and his favorites. They're filling their bellies with wine and mutton while . . ."

Their voices were fading, as was the clicking of their boots on the stone path atop the wall. Cadel nodded once, and he Jedrek resumed their climb. As he reached for his next handhold, however, Cadel felt the stone beneath his right foot begin to give way. Grabbing desperately for anything that would hold him, he dug his fingers into the first stone he could find. Only to have it come away in his hand. The foothold under his right foot gave way, and as it did, his left foot slipped, leaving him hanging by his left hand. Small pieces of rock clattered down the face of the wall and into the grass below. Flailing with his feet, he quickly found new toeholds, but the damage had been done. The guards had stopped talking and were heading back in Cadel and Jedrek's direction.

Cadel looked at Jedrek, who was glaring at him as if had just shouted Jedrek's name at the top of his voice. The guards had almost reached them. With Panya, the white moon, full and climbing into the sky behind them, they would be easy to spot against the dark stone. So Cadel did the only thing he could. He still clutched the stone in his right hand, and now, with the guards approaching, he heaved it with all his might, up into the night sky and over the wall to the other side. After several seconds he heard it land on the ground outside the city.

The guards did, too. They stopped just above Jedrek and Cadel, but on the far side of the city wall.

"What do you see?" one of them asked.

"Not a bloody thing. With Panya as low as she is, it's black as pitch down there."

"I'm sure I heard something."

"So did I. But I promise you, whatever we heard wasn't human. No person I know could see in that kind of dark."

"You think it was wolves?"

The other guard laughed. "Wolves? More likely it was rats from the river, or a fox from the wood." He laughed again. "Wolves," he repeated, as the guards began to walk away again.

"Shouldn't we tell the watch?"

"Sure, we can tell the watch. We'll tell them the city's under siege from a pack of hedgehogs."

Cadel took a long breath and looked over at Jedrek again. His friend was grinning, his dark eyes shining in the moonlight. Cadel had to grin as well.

When they could no longer hear the guards' voices, they finished their climb, peering cautiously over the edge of the wall before swinging themselves onto the walkway, hurrying across, and beginning their descent on the other side. Without any further mishaps to slow them, they were on the ground again before Panya had risen high enough to illuminate the outside of the wall.

"Where to now?" Jedrek whispered.

"The Sanctuary of Kebb, by the river."

His friend smiled, and Cadel knew why. Kebb. God of beasts, god of the hunt.

"How appropriate," was all Jedrek said.

The great hall of Thorald Castle shimmered with torch fire and candlelight. The smells of roasting meat, baking bread, and sweet wine filled the air. Dozens of long wooden tables, each piled with mutton and fowl, rich stews and dark breads, steamed greens and fresh fruits, and large flasks of light wine from the Thorald cellars, lined the walls of the enormous room. All of them were crowded with men, women, and children, whose voices and laughter blended into an incomprehensible din.

The floor in the center of the chamber had been left open for the dancing that would follow the banquet, and just in front of the main table, which had been placed on a great dais, a group of musicians played.

It was a scene that Filib had always loved. For as long as he could remember, the Revel banquet had been, along with his own naming day, and the Night of Two Moons in Bohdan's Turn, one of the high points of each year.

Somehow, though, this year was different. Perhaps it was the knowledge that he would soon be leaving Thorald. Maybe it was simply that he was growing up. Whatever the reason, it felt to Filib that this year's feast had been going on for hours, though townspeople were still trickling into the hall to start their meal.

It didn't help that Renelle was here, sitting on the far side of the room, wearing the black dress he had given her, her fiery hair down around her shoulders the way he liked it. Occasionally their eyes would meet, and she'd give him that small, inscrutable smile that usually made his heart dance so.

Your mother fears you've grown too attached to the girl. Filib wasn't even sure what that meant. Too attached. How was that possible?

She had been angry with him about the night before, just as he had feared. But she could never remain that way for long. After finding each other in the marketplace, they had stolen out of the city by way of thieves' gate, circled around the outside of the castle and its famed double moat, and taken their hidden path to the riverbank. There, as they had so many times over the past year, they made love in the shade of the willows.

Just before sundown, with the shadows deepening and the air turning cold, he left her there. But before he did, he promised her that they would be together tonight and, rashly, every night to follow. It was a foolish oath. Both of them knew it. But he would gladly have traded the entire kingdom for the smile it brought to her lips.

He could still taste her skin, he could still feel her hands splayed against his back. Yet sitting at the front of the great hall, flanked by his mother and his uncle, he felt as though the distance between them had never been greater.

I'll be with her tonight, after I ride, he told himself.

As if in answer, another voice—might it have been his father's?—echoed in his mind. *You'll be king within the year.*

I can take her with me to the City of Kings.

To what end? The two of you can never marry. The children she bears you will be bastards. And what of your wife? Are you ready to doom your marriage before you even meet the woman who will be your queen?

All he wanted was to ride. To get out of this hall, this castle, this city.

"Are you well, my lord?"

He turned in his chair and saw the first minister, seated to his mother's left, gazing at him, concern in her pale yellow eyes.

"Yes, thank you, Enid."

"Are you still planning to ride tonight, Filib?" his uncle asked.

Filib felt his mother stiffen beside him.

"Yes. As soon as the banquet ends."

"I think it's a fine way to honor the duke's memory. Don't you agree, Nerine?" Tobbar winked at Filib, who responded with a grin.

"I think the two of you have been plotting behind my back," she replied, her expression severe. After a moment her face softened, and she allowed herself a smile. "I suppose there's no harm in it."

"The rides are actually quite pleasant," Filib said. "Perhaps you should come with me, and you can see for yourself."

His mother gave him a doubtful look. "I'll enjoy the comfort of my chambers, thank you. I have no desire to go riding into the wood with nothing to light my way but the moons and the stars."

"A wise choice, my lady," Enid said.

A short while later, his uncle rose and offered the ritual tribute. As was custom, he honored each of the gods by name, citing the blessings they had brought in each of their turns during the previous year, and ending, of course, with Bohdan, god of laughter and patron of the Revel, for whom the year's final turn was named. He then thanked Aurea Crenish and Yegor jal Sennah, the Eandi woman and Qirsi man who ran the Revel, and who were seated at the table of honor with Filib and the others.

Once, when they first assumed leadership of the Revel, Aurea and Yegor's marriage had been the topic of much discussion. To some, it had been an affront. Unions of Eandi men and Qirsi women were forbidden by law, because of the danger posed by childbirth to Qirsi women bearing Eandi offspring. The sin of the moons it was called, because Panya died giving birth to Ilias's child. Unions between Eandi women and Qirsi men, on the other hand, were legal. But to those who believed that the races should remain separate—and there were many, not only in Eibithar, but throughout the Forelands—they were still offensive. Many of Eibithar's dukes refused to allow Yegor and Aurea to attend the Revel banquets. To his credit, Filib's father had not been one of them, and to their credit, Yegor and Aurea continued to take the Revel to each of Eibithar's walled cities, regardless of how they themselves were treated. With time, their marriage came to be accepted, and the other dukes relented. Even now, however, Filib saw that many of the people attending the banquet here in Thorald craned their necks to get a better look at the couple. Many of them wore expressions of distaste.

Finally, Tobbar ended his remarks by thanking all of their guests for coming to the banquet and sharing the celebration with the Thorald family.

"Very well done, sire," Enid said, as the duke lowered himself into his chair.

"Thank you, Enid." He glanced at Filib, a kind smile on his face. "If you've had your fill, you can go."

"So early?" Enid asked quickly.

"I agree with the first minister," Filib's mother said, before Tobbar could say anything. "It's too early yet. You needn't stay to the very end, Filib, but I think it would be rude of you to leave now."

Tobbar shrugged, as if to say, *Sorry, I tried.*

"Of course, Mother," Filib said. "I was going to stay anyway. I'd like to have a dance or two with Renelle before I go."

His mother paled. "You're not serious."

"Oh, but I am. Have you seen how lovely she looks tonight?"

She glared at him, her mouth set in a thin line. Tobbar snickered.

"Just a short while longer," she finally said, surrender in her voice. "Then you may leave."

Filib smiled. "Thank you, Mother."

Out of courtesy to his mother, Filib actually stayed a good bit longer, until most of their guests had finished eating and a few had begun to dance.

Despite what he had said to the duchess, Filib never had any intention of dancing with Renelle. While many knew that they were lovers, such a public acknowledgment of their affair would have been deemed improper. Both of them knew it. As he left the hall, however, he did catch her eye, and they shared a smile.

Stepping out of the hall into the central ward of the castle, Filib took a deep breath. He hadn't realized just how warm it was inside until he felt the cool air on his skin. He could smell the brine of Amon's Ocean and hear the music drifting up to the castle from the city.

Though anxious to be on his mount, he walked slowly across the west ward to the stables, enjoying the quiet and the soft breeze. Panya shone down on him, stretching his shadow across the stone path and the grass beside it.

Galdis, his grey, had already been saddled and was waiting for him just inside the stable.

"He's all ready, my lord," the stableboy said, as Filib stepped inside and stroked the beast's snout.

Filib nodded. "Many thanks, Doran," he said, tossing the lad a silver half.

He led the horse outside and through the west gate of the castle before climbing into the saddle. On most nights he would have ridden through the city to the south gate, but with the streets choked with performers and peddlers, he chose instead to leave the city by way of the upper river gate. Once outside the walls, he rode south along the river before cutting east to the wood. It was the longer way, but with Panya's glow shimmering on the river, it also proved to be the more pleasant. Before long he was in the North Wood, riding toward the sanctuary where his father had died.

He had started his rides nearly five years before, on the night of Panya's full in Bian's Turn, just a turn after his father's death. He had been in his thirteenth year then, awkward and unsure of himself. He had worshiped his father, and in the wake of the accident that claimed the duke's life, he had felt as though the entire world were falling away beneath his feet. As the duke's only child—Simm, his younger brother, had been taken by the pestilence as an infant— he was entitled to all of his father's possessions. His sword and armor, his dagger and hunting bow, his saddle, and the lynx-fur wrap he had been wearing when he fell. Filib's mother assured him that she would keep all of it for him, until he was old enough to use the weapons and wear the clothes. But Filib could not wait. Every item was like treasure to him, a small piece of his father's life. On some level he believed that if he surrounded himself with enough of them, the pain of his loss would vanish, the wound on his heart would heal. Long before his father's gold signet ring fit on his finger, Filib wore it on a chain around his neck. Every night for that first year, he would lie awake in his bed, staring at the seal on the ring as it glittered in the candlelight. The Golden Stallion, the Thorald crest. And he would talk to it as if it were his father, telling of the day's events and how his mother was doing.

Eventually, the pain did begin to recede, just as his mother and his uncle and everyone else had said it would. But the comfort he drew from his father's belongings never diminished. Training with his father's sword, he felt as though the duke were teaching him to fight. Hunting with his father's bow, he felt as though the elder Filib were tracking boar and elk beside him. Sitting in his father's saddle, he felt as though they were riding through the wood together.

He rode slowly among the trees, moving in and out of the shadows cast by Panya's white glow and the branches overhead. Night thrushes called to each other, their songs sifting through the limbs with the scent of fire blossom and the low gurgle of the river. An owl called in the distance and the breeze coaxed a gentle rustling from the leaves.

Just as Filib first glimpsed the sanctuary fires through the trees, another sound reached him, one that was utterly unexpected. Somewhere in the forest, not far, a man was singing.

He wondered briefly if he was hearing a cleric at the sanctuary, but he soon realized that the sound was growing louder too quickly. The singer was traveling the wood, just as Filib was, and he was heading in Filib's direction.

After several moments, he recognized the tune. It was an old Caerissan folk song that one of his nurses had taught him when he was a child. Filib shouldn't have been surprised. Eibithar's Revel attracted performers, including singers, from all parts of the Forelands. With relations between Eibithar and her southern neighbor as cordial as they had ever been, many of those traveling with the Revel this year were from Caerisse.

An instant later, the singer came into view. He was on foot, and illuminated as he was only by Panya's silver light falling irregularly through the canopy of the wood, he was, at first, hard to see. He was tall and thin, with long limbs and broad shoulders. His dark hair fell to his shoulders, framing a pleasant bearded face. As he drew closer, Filib could see that his eyes were pale, although in the moonlight he could not tell if they were blue or grey.

Mostly, though, Filib noticed the man's voice, which was sweet and strong, like the golden wine served this night at the Revel banquet. It was higher than he would have expected for such a large man, though not so high as to sound unnatural. His notes floated through the wood as those of the thrushes had a short while before, as if they belonged there, as if they were as much a part of the forest as the river and the whispering wind. There was something almost haunting in the sound, and Filib shivered even as he and the man shared a smile and passed each other by.

He rode on, still not hurrying, listening as the singer's voice receded like an ocean wave. The sanctuary fires appeared brighter now, though the stone walls, bathed in moonlight, were still a good distance off. The owl hooted again, closer this time.

Abruptly, Filib realized that the singing had stopped. He glanced behind him, but could see nothing for the trees and the darkness.

Facing forward again, he saw a man standing in the forest path before him. He was slightly smaller than the singer, though not by much. His hair was shorter, dark and unruly. And his eyes appeared black in the forest shadows.

Filib's heart was pounding like a smith's hammer. He reached into his wrap for his father's dagger, cursing himself for not bringing the sword.

"It's late for a prince to be about," the man said. The accent was subtle, but Filib recognized it. Aneiran. He felt his stomach tightening.

Filib kicked at Galdis's flanks, hoping to ride past the man to the sanctuary. But just as he did, he felt strong hands grab his leg and arm from the side. An instant later he landed hard on the ground, the air rushing from his lungs and his dagger flying from his hand.

His shoulder and chest ached from the fall, but he struggled to stand. Someone held him down, then roughly turned him over. The singer. He held the point of a blade to Filib's throat.

"I have gold!" Filib managed, his voice little more than a whisper. "It's yours! All of it!"

"My apologies, my lord," the singer said, although there was little remorse in those pale eyes. "But someone wants you dead."

Filib flailed at the man and screamed for help, but the singer and his friend held him fast. After a moment, the taller man covered his mouth with a callused hand.

The singer looked Filib in the eye for another moment. Then, with a motion so swift that his blade was but a glittering blur in the moonlight, he slashed at Filib's throat.

It seemed to the prior that he had just drifted off to sleep when the screams awakened him. Out here in the wood, living among Kebb's beasts, one heard many strange things at night. In the final moment of its life, as the talons of a great owl closed around its throat, even a simple hare could cry out like a wraith from the Underrealm. He had grown accustomed to such sounds over the years. He rarely noticed them anymore.

These screams were different. They had come from a man.

He lit a candle, dressed, and stepped out of his chambers. One of the novices was sleeping in the antechamber. Apparently he hadn't heard the cries. The novice looked terribly young in Panya's glow. The prior hated to wake him. But if there was someone in the wood in need of aid, it would be best if he was not alone.

He shook the boy gently.

After a moment, the boy rubbed his eyes and sat up.

"Yes, Father Prior," the boy said sleepily. "How may I serve?"

"I heard something in the wood, boy. Fetch two torches and meet me by the gate."

The boy nodded, although for some time he didn't move. Finally he stood and shuffled toward the door.

"That's a good lad," the prior called after him.

He returned to his chambers for his healing bag, a small leather pouch that smelled of betony and common wort. He knew how to dress wounds and set broken bones, but in that moment he would have given anything for a Qirsi companion. He feared what he would find among the trees.

He hurried to the sanctuary entrance, where the boy was waiting for him, shivering slightly but looking a bit more awake. He took one of the torches and opened the gate.

"What's your name, boy?" the prior asked, gesturing for the lad to follow him down the path.

"Arvid, Father Prior."

"You're new in the sanctuary, aren't you?"

"Yes, Father Prior. I arrived here during Osya's Turn."

Osya's Turn! the prior thought. *That's three turns he's been with us. I need to give more attention to the novices.*

"Where is your family, Arvid?" he asked, though he could tell from the boy's accent that he came from Eibithar's eastern coast.

"We live on a farm, Father Prior, just outside of Eardley."

The prior nodded, scanning the forest as he did. He was walking quickly. Occasionally the boy had to run a few steps in order to keep up with him. The prior knew that he had been foolish to leave the sanctuary. Even with the white moon up, it would be nearly impossible to find someone in the darkness. He was about to say as much when he spotted a grey stallion standing just off the path a short distance ahead.

Seeing them approach, the horse nickered and stamped a hoof, but it didn't move from where it was standing.

The prior felt himself growing cold. Even from a distance he could tell that this was no farm horse. It was well groomed and well bred, and it wore a fine saddle on its back.

Had he seen the body lying next to the stallion soon enough, the prior would have warned Arvid to stay back. But by the time he spotted the man it was too late. Arvid let out a small cry and then emptied his stomach on the forest path.

The prior hurried forward and knelt beside the body. The poor man's neck had been slashed, blood pooling around his head on the fallen leaves and glistening in the moonlight. There was a stab wound in his chest as well, and another in his stomach. And the ring finger was missing from his right hand. This had been sloppily done.

The prior glanced down at the healing bag he still carried in his hand. He would have liked to throw it into the shadows. Instead he placed it in a pocket within his robe. Then he leaned forward to look at the man's face and let out a cry of his own.

Filib. The duke's son, the king to be.

He shook his head, feeling hot tears on his cheeks. First the father, and now the son.

"Thieves be damned!" he said, his voice quavering. He knew that Arvid could hear, but just then he didn't care. "Bian take them all!"

Chapter
Four

✦

Curgh, Eibithar, year 879, Amon's Moon waxing

tand ready, Tavis!" Xaver's father called, his voice as crisp as a harvest morning. "Keep your balance. Ready your sword."

The young lord gave a quick nod and lowered himself into a crouch, battle-ready and perfectly centered, the wooden sword held before him.

"Commence!" the swordmaster said.

Immediately, the other three swordsmen advanced. They were older than Tavis and Xaver by a few years, and it showed in their height and brawn. But they were commoners, probationers for the castle guard recruited from the baronies near Curgh. They had little experience with swords and formal battle, and it showed in the way they held their training weapons. Tavis, on the other hand, was the duke's son. He'd been fighting with swords of one sort or another almost since he could walk.

Their attack was clumsy and transparent. They rushed him as one, their swords held high, their bodies open to his counter. Tavis stepped forward, quickly closing the distance between himself and the largest of his opponents. The probationer leveled a chopping blow at Tavis's head that the lord easily parried. The crack of their swords still echoing off the castle walls, Tavis stepped to the side, and, with a motion so fluid that Xaver had to smile, delivered a blow to the man's ribs that drove him to the ground.

By then, the other two were upon him, but Tavis had used the motion from his last strike to put himself in the perfect position to meet their attack. Of course. His wooden sword a blur in the morning air, he blocked their blows in quick succession, stepped between them, and, pivoting like a Revel dancer, swung his sword first at one of the men, lashing him across his back, and then at the other. With this last blow, however, Tavis's back foot slipped. Rather than hitting the third man's body, his sword arced lower, catching the attacker just below the back of his knee. The man dropped to his knees with a howl of pain.

"Well done, Tav—"

Before Xaver's father could finish, Tavis pounced on the third man again, hammering his sword down on the back of the man's neck. The probationer toppled forward face-first into the grass and lay there unmoving.

"Demons and fire, boy!" Xaver's father said, rushing forward to check on the man. "What's wrong with you?"

"With me, Hagan?" Tavis asked with disbelief. He was standing over the man, his sword held by his side. He was breathing hard, and there was a slight sheen of sweat on his face, but he was unmarked. The fight had been a mismatch from the start. "You told us to fight as if in battle. In battle, that man would still have been a threat. I only struck his leg. I had to finish him."

"He was down, Tavis!" Hagan flung the words at him, an accusation, although he didn't even look up. "Had these been real swords you would have taken off his leg! He wasn't a threat anymore!" He turned the man over and bent his ear close to the man's face to check his breathing.

"He still had a sword, and two good arms to use it," the young lord said airily. He examined his sword for a moment, as if looking for cracks in the wood. "We Curghs don't leave anything to chance when it comes to battle."

Before Hagan could respond the man let out a low groan.

Tavis pointed at the man with his sword. "There, you see? He's fine."

"He's only fine because you're still too weak to give a killing blow!"

The lord's face colored, and Xaver noticed that the hand holding his sword had begun to tremble. But he managed somehow to keep his voice under control when he said, "I take it we're done for the morn?"

"You're done when I say so, whelp!"

The other two probationers exchanged a look, and Xaver stared at the ground rather than look at either his friend or his father. No one else in the castle save the duke and duchess would have dared speak to Tavis in such a way. Indeed, in his capacity as captain of the guard, Hagan never would have either. But here, in the city ward of Curgh Castle, in the shadow of the armory tower, Xaver's father was swordmaster, and Tavis his apprentice. Hagan could say anything to him, call him any name, no matter how insulting. He could take the young lord over his knee if he deemed it appropriate. Once, when Tavis and Xaver were nine, Hagan had done just that. As good as Tavis was with a blade, he was still just a student. Hagan MarCullet, on the other hand, was the best swordsman in the dukedom. Everyone knew it.

"Run the towers, boy," Hagan said. "Then you'll be done."

Xaver cringed.

"The towers?" Tavis complained. "But all I did—"

A withering look from the swordmaster silenced him.

"The towers," Xaver's father said again.

"Yes, sir."

Tavis returned his training sword to the stand by the armory and started up the stairs of the tower.

Hagan looked over at Xaver. "You'd better go with him."

Xaver nodded, returning his father's smile. Then he turned and ran to catch up with the duke's son.

Running the towers was perhaps the most onerous of all his father's exercises, which was saying a lot. One started with the nearest tower, ran up the stairs to its topmost turrets, then returned to ground level before running to the next tower and doing it again and again, until every tower had been climbed. Curgh Castle had eighteen towers in all. Some of them, the gate towers of the east and west barbicans for instance, were rather small. But most were quite high, at least fifty fourspans. The spire towers, which guarded the south gate, each had two hundred and sixteen steps. Xaver and Tavis had counted them more times than Xaver cared to remember.

Xaver caught up with his friend on the forty-second step of the armory tower. Without breaking stride, Tavis glanced at him briefly and grinned.

"You, too, eh?"

Xaver shrugged, and they continued up the winding stairs.

"I don't know what got Hagan so bothered today," the lord went on after a short while. "All I did was follow his instructions."

"You nearly killed that man, Tavis," Xaver said quietly, keeping his gaze fixed on the stairs. "You'd won already. You didn't have to hit him."

"In any real fight, that man would still have been a threat," Tavis said, his voice echoing loudly off the round stone walls.

Xaver said nothing, and for several moments the tower was silent save for the rhythmic beat of their feet on the worn steps.

"Is he all right?" Tavis asked at last.

At least he asked. "He will be." Xaver looked sidelong at the lord and smiled. "I don't imagine he'll be asking to help the duke's son with his training any time soon."

"Probably not, though they didn't fare much better against you."

"Do you know when the Revel will be arriving?" Xaver asked, eager to change the topic. Even when Tavis was offering compliments, it was usually best to avoid discussions of their swordsmanship. Like Tavis, Xaver had been raised with a sword in his hand. Both of them were acutely aware that swordplay was the one endeavor in which Xaver was, and always had been, the lord's equal.

Tavis regarded him for several moments, a mischievous grin on his face, as if he knew exactly what Xaver was trying to do. In the end, however, he relented.

"Father expects them to be here by the midday bells."

They reached the top of the tower, emerging from the shadows of the stairwell into the bright sunlight. They paused there for just an instant to catch their breath and to stare out at Amon's Ocean, calm today, and sapphire blue.

As usual, there were two guards atop the tower, and they looked at Xaver and Tavis with amusement. "Captain's got you running the towers, eh?" one of them said.

Tavis glared at the man as if he had called the duke a coward. He turned, and began to run back down. Xaver smiled weakly at the men, then followed.

"The city children are probably lining up for their gleanings already," Tavis said, as Xaver fell in step with him again. "Most of them probably haven't slept since the start of this turn."

"Have you?" Xaver asked.

"Of course. I know just what my Fating will show. I'm going to be king after my father. If old Aylyn would just step down and be done with it."

It had been over sixty years since the death of Skeris the Fourth, the last Curgh king. Under the Rules of Ascension, the dukes of Curgh did not get many opportunities to wear Audun's crown, but with all that had happened over the past few years in Thorald and Galdasten, Javan of Curgh stood next in line for the throne, and Tavis after him.

"What about you, Stinger? You worried about your Fating?"

Xaver smiled at his old nickname. A stinger was what the guards called a child's training weapon, and since his father had long been called the Sword, it was only natural that they should call Xaver Stinger. Few people used it anymore—his father, Tavis, a few of the older guards—but he was still fond of it.

"Sure," he admitted. "A little bit. What happens if you leave me here when you go to the City of Kings and I have to start earning an honest wage?"

Tavis laughed. "I think you're just afraid to find out that you're to marry a farm hag."

This time Xaver laughed, just as they emerged from the tower into the ward and turned toward the next tower.

"It sounds like the two of you are enjoying this too much," Xaver's father called. "Do I need to double your run?"

"No, sir," Xaver answered, turning to face his father so that he ran backward for several strides.

"Good. Less chatter then. Stop your dawdling."

"Yes, sir," both of them called at once.

Xaver faced forward again and they hurried to the next tower.

By the time they finished their run, the sun was high overhead and the midday bells had long since been rung. Xaver's father was nowhere to be found—no doubt he was off enjoying a fine meal with the duke.

Xaver and Tavis returned to the prison tower and used the sally port in back to reach the small yard between the moat and the outside wall of the castle. There, they stripped off their sweaty clothes and dove into the cold water. In another few turns, when the rains slackened and the moat waters grew stagnant and rank, they wouldn't dream of doing such a thing. But for now the moat was reasonably clean, especially here, behind the one section of the castle that had no privy shafts, and this was quicker than having servants draw bathwater from the well.

When they finished swimming, they climbed out of the moat and lay on their backs in the yard, letting the sun and the soft wind dry them.

"Do you remember your Determining?" Tavis asked suddenly.

Xaver, who had his eyes closed, smiled at the memory. "Of course. I was terrified."

"What did yours show?"

"Just what you'd expect. I saw myself as captain of the guard and swordmaster, just like my father."

"Mine showed me as duke."

"Of course. What—?"

"Duke, Xaver. Not king."

Xaver opened his eyes, shielding them from the sun with a hand, and looked over at the young lord. Tavis was sitting up, staring at the moat.

"I've wondered about it since Filib was killed. What it might mean."

"Why didn't you say anything?"

Tavis shrugged. "I don't know."

But Xaver did, almost as soon as he asked the question. Such a realization would have been terrifying for anyone, implying as it did any of a number of tragic fates—early death, disgrace for himself or his family, renunciation by his father. For Tavis, however, such a possibility would have been particularly devastating. He was a Curgh, Javan's son. That such extraordinary circumstances had combined to make it near certain that he would be king had been acknowledged only briefly. Since Filib's death, Tavis and his father had behaved as though their impending ascension to the crown had long been a given. Others in Curgh had looked upon their good fortune similarly, including Xaver's father. For centuries, the people of Curgh had been famous throughout Eibithar for their pride. Not just the Curgh family, but all the people of the dukedom. Never mind that their house ranked below Thorald and Galdasten in royal ascendancy or that nearly half of Curgh's eleven kings had died within five years of taking the throne. That was the past. None of that mattered now.

What did matter was that Curgh Castle was the most glorious fortress in Eibithar save for Audun's Castle in the City of Kings. Curgh's soldiers were the best trained and the most feared in battle. "Those who awaken the bear," it was said, referring to the great brown bear that adorned Curgh's crest, "will perish under its claw." Even Curgh's pale wine was said by the men and women of the dukedom to be the kingdom's finest.

Curgh pride. Small wonder Tavis had said nothing of his concerns, even to Xaver.

"Our fates can change," Xaver said at last, searching for any words that might comfort his friend. "When we were twelve, Filib was still alive. Ean himself couldn't have known that he'd be murdered. Your Fating will be different, Tavis. I'm sure of it."

The young lord nodded, his dark blue eyes still fixed on the narrow strip of water before them. "I know." A moment later he looked at Xaver, an unconvincing smile on his lips. "Of course it will."

Tavis stood and began to dress. Xaver did the same. Their breeches were dry now, warm from the sun and stiff with sweat. So were their hose and shirts, but these they carried rather than put on. They would have to change clothes anyway before going to explore the Revel.

They made their way back into the castle and started toward the personal quarters of the duke's ward at the northern end of the stronghold. As they crossed through the inner gatehouse, however, one of the guards stopped them.

"The duke's waiting for you, my lord," he told Tavis. "In his chambers."

"Tell him I'll be there shortly," Tavis said, turning to walk away.

"Begging your pardon, my lord, but from what I was told, he wants you sooner rather than later."

The young lord stopped and regarded the man coldly. "What did you say?"

"I was just saying that I was given to understand that the duke wanted you as soon as you could get there."

Tavis walked back to where the guard was standing. "Do you know who I am?"

The guard shifted his feet uncomfortably. "Of course, my lord."

"I'm Tavis of Curgh. I'm not some stablehand who you can order about like a child. I'm the duke's son. I'm to be king someday."

One of the other guards standing by the gate whispered something to the man next to him and they both snickered.

"I know that, my lord," the first guard said evenly. "I was just conveying a message."

"Well the next time—"

"Let it go, Tavis," Xaver said in a low voice.

Tavis spun toward him, his mouth open to berate Xaver as well. But after a moment he appeared to think better of it.

"You're right," he said, stalking away once more. "He's not worth the effort."

Xaver glanced at the guard, feeling the corner of his mouth twitch. The man's name was Olin, though Tavis wouldn't have known that. Nor would he have known that Olin lost a wife and daughter in the last outbreak of pestilence in the surrounding baronies. Xaver's father was captain of the guard. That was why Xaver knew. But somehow, he thought, the duke's son should know such things as well.

"Thank you, young master," Olin said.

Xaver shook his head and started after his friend. "It was nothing," he said over his shoulder.

"I wonder what Father wants," Tavis said as Xaver caught up with him once more.

"Why do you do that?" Xaver demanded.

The lord stared at him blankly. "Do what?"

"Treat the guards that way. These are to be your men someday, Tavis. Sooner rather than later, if the rumors about the king are true."

"I know that, Xaver. That's why I speak to them as I do. I have to teach them to respect me, as they do my father. I can't have them talking to me like I'm a child, telling me where to go and how fast to get there. They'll never learn to respect me that way."

"There must be a way to earn their respect without humiliating them."

Tavis laughed. "It's a good thing you're not going to be king, Stinger. You'd coddle your soldiers so, they wouldn't even be able to hold off the Wethy army."

Xaver thought about saying more, but there was nothing to be gained from it. If he pushed Tavis hard enough, the lord would turn on him, too, and he didn't want to ruin the first day of the Revel by fighting with his friend.

"Well, the duke will want to speak with you in private," Xaver said instead. "I think I'll go get dressed. I'll find you later at the Revel."

"No," Tavis said, a bit too quickly. "Come with me. Whatever it is my father wants won't take too long. Then we can get dressed at the same time and go to the Revel together."

He had witnessed more than his share of these meetings between the duke and his son. He had no desire to become entangled in yet another one. "I got the feeling that your father wants to see you alone."

"Nonsense. It's probably nothing at all."

Xaver gestured at himself—the dirty breeches, his bare chest and feet. "I shouldn't go before the duke like this. It may be all right for you, but I'm not his son."

"He knows we've been training. He's probably spoken to your father, so he also knows we were running the towers."

And he knows why. Tavis didn't have to say it. Xaver knew that was why the lord wanted him there, just as he knew that Tavis wouldn't give up until he agreed.

He stood there looking at his friend. Tavis was built like his father, with a lean, muscular frame, and he had his father's eyes as well. Even with a youthful face, he already had the air of a leader about him. When Javan left for Audun's Castle and Tavis became duke, he would at least look the part. But at that moment, dressed like a farm child, with his fine wheat colored hair matted and stuck to his brow, and the expression in his eyes an odd mix of mischief and fear, he looked far too young for his Fating.

"All right," Xaver said at last, sighing like a smith's bellows. He gestured toward Javan's chambers. "Lead the way."

Tavis grinned. "You'll see, Stinger. This will only take a moment. Then we can go down to the city and watch them set up the Revel."

He said nothing; he refused to give Tavis the satisfaction. After a moment, the young lord fell silent as well, and they walked slowly to the duke's chambers. Xaver couldn't have said which of them was dreading the encounter more.

Stepping into the cool shadows of the castle from the warmth of the ward, Xaver shivered, feeling bumps on his skin. Their feet slapping on the stone floor, the two of them made their way through the torchlit corridor and soon came to the dark oak door of the duke's chambers.

Tavis tried to smile. Then he knocked.

"Enter," came a voice from inside.

The young lord pushed open the door and stepped into the room, with Xaver following close behind.

Javan was seated by one of the chamber's large windows before a broad wooden table covered with parchment scrolls. He held one, reading by the sunlight streaming into the chamber. He was dressed simply in a cream-colored shirt and a black doublet emblazoned with the brown and gold crest of Curgh. The sun shining on his head seemed to make the grey in his hair stand out more, but his face was still youthful, despite his dark beard with its flecks of silver.

Off to the side, also by one of the windows, stood Fotir jal Salene, the duke's Qirsi advisor. He wore a simple white shirt and light breeches so that, with his pale skin and long white hair, the only color on him came from his bright yellow eyes, and the yellow gold ring on his left hand.

"Good day, Lord Tavis, Master MarCullet," the Qirsi said, nodding to each of them in turn.

"First Minister," Tavis said, directing a small bow at the sorcerer. "Please excuse our appearance. We've just come from training."

The duke glanced at his son with a dour expression. But he said nothing and quickly returned to his reading.

"Yes, we had heard as much," Fotir said. "Perhaps Master Mar-Cullet and I should retire to another room so that you and the duke can speak."

Xaver was about to agree, but Tavis was too fast for him.

"You're free to remain or leave as you choose, Fotir, but Xaver is staying. He and I have plans for what's left of the day."

Javan threw the scroll onto his table and shook his head.

"That's sheer cowardice, Tavis," he said. "I had hoped to teach you better than that."

Tavis paled, but managed a smile. "I don't know what you mean, Father."

The duke looked at Xaver. "You may go if you wish, Xaver. Or you can stay. It's your choice, not Tavis's."

More than anything, he wanted to leave. But he had told Tavis that he would remain.

"I'll stay, my lord."

"Very well." The duke nodded once to Fotir, who bowed in response and then left the chamber, closing the door behind him.

The duke rose and stepped around the table to stand directly in front of his son. He was not much taller than Tavis anymore—no more than half a span—but at that moment, the young lord looked like a babe beside him.

"Hagan tells me that you nearly killed a man today," Javan said, "for no reason at all."

"Hagan is mistaken."

"Are you calling him a liar?"

Tavis's eyes flicked toward Xaver for just an instant. "Of course not, Father. But to say that I nearly killed him is an exaggeration. And as to whether I had cause . . ." He shrugged. "Well, that's a matter of opinion."

"Hagan has been swordmaster here since you were still sucking at your mother's breast. Why should I trust your opinion over his?"

"Because I was the one doing the fighting. But you don't have to trust me. Just ask Xaver."

The duke regarded Xaver for several moments before shaking his head again. "I'll spare him that, if you don't mind."

"So you're just going to take Hagan's word over mine?"

"The man has a lump on the back of his neck the size of an apple, Tavis. Hagan says he was on his knees when you hit him. How much of a threat could he be?"

"In a real battle—"

"In a real battle you would have been justified. Hagan said so himself. But this was a probationer, holding a wooden sword, who you'd already knocked to the ground."

"He's going to be all right though?" It came out as a question, and Tavis cast a furtive look in Xaver's direction once more. The duke didn't seem to notice, however.

"That's not the point. The healers were able to help him, but even their magic couldn't heal his injury entirely. It will be at least a half turn before this man is ready to resume his training."

"He wasn't much of a fighter, Father. If you ask me, the new men recruited from the baronies seem even more inept—"

"That's enough!" Javan said.

Tavis appeared to flinch at what he saw in his father's eyes.

"When you're duke you can oversee the training of the probationers yourself! But until then, these are my men! You will treat them with respect! Abusing one of them is no different from abusing my sword or my mount, and I'll have none of it! Do you understand?"

Tavis swallowed, but he continued to meet his father's gaze. "Yes, sire. I understand."

The duke nodded. "Good." He stepped back around the table once more and lowered himself into his chair. "The Revel arrived a short while ago," he said. The harsh tone he had used a moment before was gone. "I was assured by Yegor and Aurea that the gleaning tent would be up and ready by the prior's bells." He offered a thin smile to his son and then to Xaver. "I imagine you're both eager for your Fatings."

That was their cue to leave. Xaver recognized it instantly. It seemed Tavis did as well.

"Yes, Father, thank you," he said. "Will you be coming to the city at all?"

"I'm sure your mother and I will get there at some point. She's busy with preparations for the banquet right now. But once that's finished, I expect we'll spend an evening or two in the streets. Aurea tells me that they have some marvelous singers this year." He smiled again, as if to remind Tavis and Xaver that their conversation was over.

"Is that all, Father?" Tavis asked, putting on a smile of his own. In some ways they were so much alike.

"Yes. Go put on some clothes."

The two of them turned and walked to the door.

"I look forward to hearing about your Fating, Tavis," the duke said, just as the young lord pulled the door open.

Tavis didn't turn, but he did pause on the threshold. "Of course, sire."

Fotir was standing in the corridor just outside the door, the torchlight making his eyes shine like those of a great owl. Tavis nodded to him, but said nothing as they walked past.

"May the stone glow with the glory of your fates, young masters," the Qirsi said.

Xaver glanced back at him. "Thank you."

They were back outside a moment later, crossing the inner ward to their quarters. Tavis muttered to himself as he walked, his eyes fixed on the ground in front of him. Xaver knew how angry his friend was, how humiliated, but he couldn't keep his own anger in check.

"You really would have asked me to lie for you, wouldn't you?" he asked, stopping in the middle of the ward.

Tavis stopped as well, but at first he didn't reply. When he finally did he looked puzzled. "What?"

"In there, with the duke. You tried to pull me into your fight, even though it meant pitting me against my father."

The young lord sagged. "Not you, too."

"I'm sorry, Tavis. But you can't treat people this way, at least not your friends."

"I wasn't asking you to lie," he said. "But you saw what happened. The man wasn't down yet, and he was still armed."

Xaver shook his head. "Stop it. This isn't about the probationer or our training, and you know it."

Tavis looked away, staring over Xaver's shoulder back toward his father's chamber. "What is it about then, Xaver? You and me? Me and my father? You and your father? I can't tell anymore."

"It's mostly about you." *It always is.* "It's about what kind of duke you're going to be. What kind of king."

"I suppose we'll find that out soon enough," he said. "The Qirsi gleaner can put all your fears to rest. And my father's."

So that's what it is, Xaver thought. *His Fating.* "It's going to be fine, Tavis," he said, trying without success to smile.

"Of course."

For several moments they stood there saying nothing, Xaver watching the young lord, Tavis's eyes still fixed on the windows of his father's chamber.

"I suppose we should get dressed then."

"Yes," Tavis said, starting once more toward his quarters. "Let's get this over with."

It was hot under the tent, despite the open flaps at either end and the steady ocean breeze that blew through the city of Curgh. Most of the performers in the Revel preferred the growing turns. They enjoyed singing or dancing or juggling in the streets on warm nights when flame flies lit the air and the infrequent rains brought immediate relief from the heat. Certainly they all preferred traveling when it was warm and the skies were clear.

But for Grinsa and the other Qirsi gleaners, the growing season meant not warm nights and cool breezes, but rather stifling days spent in the still air of the gleaning tent. Determinings and Fatings were intensely private matters—there could be no denying the necessity of the tent. There were even some gleaners who felt that the discomfort actually added to the mystery and gravity of the event, although Grinsa was not one of them. But all of them complained about it, usually to each other, occasionally to Aurea and Yegor.

The boy seated on a simple wooden chair across the table from him had yet to say a word. His name was Malvin Thanpole. He lived here in Curgh City with his mother, a seamstress in the castle, and his father, a wheelwright. He had come for his Determining, of course, but like so many of the younger ones, he had lost his nerve upon entering the tent. By custom, until the boy made his request with the ritual words, Grinsa could not begin. It didn't matter that Malvin had nothing to fear from the vision he would see in the Qiran, and even if such reassurances would have helped, they were not Grinsa's to give. The Determining was supposed to be an act of magic. Had Malvin seen the list of names and future occupations that Grinsa kept hidden beneath his own chair, he would have been shocked and, probably, deeply disappointed. Cities and towns had needs. If every boy and girl in the land realized their dreams of fighting in the king's army or dancing in the Revel, who would shoe the horses and plow the fields and fix wheels for peddlers' carts? There was magic enough in the Fatings. But apprenticeships had to start in the twelfth year and sometimes children needed to be steered toward their talents and their fates.

"If we sit here too long," Grinsa said gently, "your naming day will come again, and you'll be too old to look in the stone."

Malvin still refused to look him in the eye, but at least he smiled.

"Do you remember what you're supposed to say?" In the fear and excitement of the moment, some of them actually forgot, despite practicing day after day in the turns leading up to the Revel's arrival.

But Malvin nodded. "I remember," he said, the words coming out as little more than a whisper.

"Good. Why don't you give it a try. I don't think you have any reason to be scared, a strong, intelligent boy like you."

He smiled again, glancing up for just an instant before staring down at his hands once more. He swallowed. And then in that same low voice, he began at last.

"In this, the year of my Determining, I beseech you, Qirsar, lay your hands upon this stone. Let my life unfold before my eyes. Let these mysteries be revealed in the light of the Qiran. Show me my fate."

It was supposed to be "Let the mysteries of time be revealed," but Grinsa wasn't about to make him say it again.

"Very good, Malvin," he said. "Now look into the stone."

The boy leaned forward, his eyes wide as he stared at the Qiran. The stone was glowing as it always did, and now Grinsa melded his own magic with that of the Qiran.

Qirsi power was double-edged, like an Uulranni blade. Every act of magic—every conjured flame, every image coaxed from the stone—shortened a sorcerer's life just a little bit. Gleaning was a simple magic; the power it required was nothing compared with the effort necessary to summon mists and winds, or shatter a sword. But unlike other Qirsi, who might use their magic only occasionally, a gleaner laid his or her hands on the stone dozens of times each day. "Gleaning," it was said among the Revel Qirsi, "is like bleeding one's life away from a thousand tiny wounds." And perhaps this was true. Grinsa's people already lived far shorter lives than the Eandi, and Revel gleaners tended to die younger than most.

Still, Grinsa enjoyed gleaning. How could any Qirsi not? His people were creatures of magic. The same power that shortened their lives allowed them to do things of which the Eandi could only dream. If a musician's harp stole years from her life, wouldn't she still play? Did the risk of death keep warriors from going to battle? It seemed to Grinsa that the Qirsi were no different. Their magic was their craft. When Grinsa felt his power coursing through his limbs, cool and swift, like water flowing off the Caerissan Steppe early in the planting, he was reminded of how much joy was to be found in even the simplest act of magic.

Using that magic now, he summoned from the Qiran's depths an image of a tall man with corded muscles and sweat on his brow. He had straight brown hair and grey eyes, just like Malvin, and he was planing the rim of a large wagon wheel. The man moved gracefully, efficiently, like someone who had been doing this all his life. He could easily have been a master swordsman or a skilled rider atop his mount, such was the power and ease of every motion.

Grinsa had learned long ago that with the Determinings, it wasn't enough just to show the children their futures. He also had to make even the simplest profession appear heroic. Though Malvin

was seeing himself as a wheelwright, and not a soldier, he was also seeing himself as a grown man, muscular, handsome, and skilled in his
work. He would take that away from this tent as well, and perhaps
it would ease any disappointment he might feel at learning that he
would not be joining the King's Guard. Would Malvin really look
like the man in the stone? Possibly. But Grinsa thought it likely that
he would see himself that way for the rest of his life. Where was the
harm in that?

The gleaner held the image in the stone for a few moments
more, smiling at what he saw on the boy's face. Then he allowed the
vision to fade slowly. Even as the image vanished, disappearing in
the soft grey light of the Qiran, like a ship sailing into a morning
mist, Malvin did not look away. Only when it was completely gone
did he blink once, then look up at Grinsa.

"Was that really me?" he asked breathlessly.

The Qirsi smiled. "What do you think?"

"It must have been." The boy stood abruptly, almost toppling his
chair. "I should go tell my mother and father."

"Of course. Goodbye, Malvin. Gods keep you safe."

"Thank you, sir," he said, already spinning away from the table
and running out of the tent. "I wish you the same," he shouted over
his shoulder.

Smiling briefly, Grinsa leaned back in his chair and closed his
eyes. Malvin was his eighth Determining of the day, and he had done
two Fatings as well. That took a lot of magic, even for him. His back
and legs had grown stiff, and there was a dull ache in his temples.

"Morna have pity, it's hot in here!" came a voice from in front
of him.

He opened his eyes again and saw Cresenne, one of the other
gleaners, stepping into the tent.

"I hadn't noticed," he said.

"Liar."

He grinned. She was younger than he was and new to the Revel.
She was also exceedingly pretty, with long, fine white hair, pale eyes
the color of candlelight, and a soft smile.

"You look tired," she said. "Do you want me to take over for a
time?"

"How long is that line?"

She glanced over her shoulder, as if she could gauge the line's length from inside the tent. "There must be fifty children out there. Most of them are here for their Determinings."

Naturally. The younger ones were always the most eager. Those of Fating age tried to pretend they didn't care by waiting until two or three days into the Revel to approach the tent. But as far as Grinsa could tell, they were no less nervous than the twelve-year-olds once they got inside.

"On the other hand," Cresenne added, "the duke's son and his liege man just arrived. They're both of Fating age, I believe."

Tavis and Xaver, the two he'd been expecting. Grinsa tried to keep his expression neutral.

"Why don't I take the two of them and a few more of the Determinings," he said lightly. "I should be ready for a rest by the time I'm finished with all that."

"You're sure?" she asked. "As I said, you look like you could use a rest right now."

He smiled. The pain in his temples had disappeared at the mention of the duke's son. "Actually, I'm feeling fine. Give me a moment or two. Then send in Lord Tavis."

"As you wish."

She turned and stepped out of the tent, leaving Grinsa alone with the heat and the soft light of the Qiran.

Chapter
Five

avis could feel their eyes upon him and he knew what lay behind their stares. They envied him; for some that envy might even have spilled over into resentment. He understood, really. How could they help themselves? Here they were, waiting on line for a glimpse of their dismal futures or a chance to learn what lowly profession they would devote the next six years of their lives to mastering. Meanwhile, his future was as plain as the red moon rising into the deep blue of Morna's sky.

He was to be king, and duke before that. He would marry well and his wife would bear as many children as it took to give him an heir to continue Curgh's hold on the throne. He alone among those standing outside the gleaning tent in the marketplace of Curgh City had nothing to fear from the Qiran. His fate had been decided long ago.

Even Xaver could not say that. No doubt his friend would fare well with the gleaner. He came from a noble family, though he had little claim to the family seat. His father was the second son of a thane, which was akin to being the second to last man standing in a battle tournament. Everyone knew that Hagan's older brother was a wastrel who had none of Hagan's intelligence or fighting skill. But he was the eldest, and the thaneship belonged to him. Had Tavis's father not brought Hagan to Curgh to be swordmaster and captain of the guard, Hagan would have remained an obscure earl in the Curgh countryside, a fate he would have passed to Xaver as well. In a sense, then, the brilliance of Tavis's future would shine on his friend's as well. So long as Xaver remained by Tavis's side, his Fating could not show much that would give him cause to grieve. But still, Xaver's future could not be as certain as his own. No one's could.

Or so Tavis told himself again and again.

My Determining showed me as duke. Not as king.

It was such a small thing. A trifle. Yet it seemed to Tavis that it threatened the very foundations of his life. *Why not king? What could it mean?*

"We really ought to wait on line with the rest," Xaver said quietly. "They've been here since before midmorning bells."

Tavis dismissed the suggestion with a wave of his hand, as if it were a bothersome fly. "Don't be a fool. The duke's son and his liege man don't wait on line with the children of commoners. They wouldn't want that any more than we would."

"I'm not certain of that. Don't you see the way they're looking at us?"

Tavis turned to stare at him, unable to believe that his friend could be so dense. "You think that's why—?"

Before he could finish, a Qirsi woman emerged from the tent.

"Lord Tavis?" she said. "The gleaner is ready."

Tavis nodded, looked at Xaver again.

"May the stone be kind," his friend said.

Tavis forced a smile, then followed the woman into the tent.

He noticed the stone first, glowing on the table in the center of the space as if Panya herself had laid her shining hands upon it. It was as large as a building stone and jagged like a mountain peak, save for one side, the side facing him now, which had been cut and polished so that it offered a window into the depths of the crystal. It was just as he remembered from last time. His Determining, when he had seen himself as duke of Curgh. *But not as king.*

Behind the stone, seated at the table, a Qirsi man watched him. His eyes were medium yellow—not as pale as those of the woman standing next to Tavis, but not as bright as Fotir's. He wore his white hair loose and long, but while this often had the effect of making the Qirsi look even more wan and frail than they were, it did the opposite for this man. He looked formidable, as if the magic he possessed was bolstered by a physical strength that most Qirsi lacked.

"This is Lord Tavis of Curgh," the woman said. "He has come for his Fating."

The man looked appraisingly at Tavis, his expression revealing little. After a moment he nodded to the woman. "Thank you, Cresenne."

She smiled, her eyes flicking briefly toward Tavis, and withdrew.

The man stood and indicated the chair opposite his own with a slender hand.

"Won't you sit, my lord?"

"Thank you," Tavis said, lowering himself into the chair. He realized that his hands were trembling, and he tried to hide them from the Qirsi.

"My name is Grinsa jal Arriet," the gleaner said sitting as well. "We'll get to your Fating in a short while. I just have some questions for you first."

"I don't remember that from last time."

The man smiled. "You've had a Fating before?"

"No, you fool," Tavis said impatiently. "From my last gleaning. My Determining."

"Fatings are quite different from Determinings. I'm afraid your previous experience in this tent is poor preparation for this one."

"I've never heard of a Qirsi asking questions at any gleaning at all."

The man regarded him for some time. "We all glean in our own way, my lord. If you wish I can find another gleaner for your Fating, but he or she may need some time to prepare. You could have quite a wait."

Tavis twisted his mouth sourly. "No," he said, pressing his fingers together. "I don't want to wait. Just get on with it."

"Of course, my lord." But rather than asking him anything, the Qirsi merely gazed at him, until Tavis began to feel as if he would scream if the man didn't ask him something in the next moment.

"Well?" he demanded.

"You're concerned about your Fating, my lord." The gleaner offered it as a statement, but it seemed to Tavis that he appeared troubled.

"Why should I be?" the young lord asked, looking briefly at the glowing stone.

"I'm not certain. I was about to ask the same of you."

"I have no reason to be afraid. I'm the duke's son. I'm to be king someday."

"Then why are you so concerned?"

I don't know, he wanted to say. *Why didn't I see myself as king four years ago? Can a Determining be wrong?* Instead he looked away again. "I never said I was."

"There was an incident at the castle today," the Qirsi said. "You assaulted a man. Why?"

Tavis stared at him. "How did you hear of this? Who told you?"

"Why did you do it?"

Tavis stood abruptly, nearly upsetting the table and the Qiran. "Answer me! How do you know about this?"

"A man hears things," the Qirsi said, his expression infuriatingly calm. "People talk."

"Who?"

"Please sit, my lord."

"Tell me who told you!"

"No."

"I'll have you arrested!" Tavis said, whirling away from the man and stepping toward the entrance to the tent. "I'll call the castle guard right now!"

"If you leave this tent," the man said in an even voice, "you will never be allowed back in. You will never see your Fating."

Tavis stopped in midstride.

"Please, my lord," he said again. "Sit."

The young lord turned again. His heart was hammering in his chest and his hands were shaking again, though this time with rage rather than fear.

"Did you feel that the man you assaulted today was a threat to you?"

Something in the way the Qirsi asked the question caught his attention. His tone carried no hint of accusation. On the contrary. It almost seemed to Tavis that he was looking for a reason to forgive Tavis's actions.

"What's your name again?" the duke's son asked quietly.

"Grinsa, my lord."

Tavis took a uncertain step forward.

"Did you think he was going to hurt you? Is that why you struck him?"

"No," Tavis admitted, slowly walking back to his chair and sitting. "I'm not sure why I did it. I was training, I was acting on instinct. I didn't think about it at all. I just hit him."

Grinsa nodded. "I see. Do you think you were wrong to do it?"

Tavis narrowed his eyes, wondering if he had been mistaken a few moments before. "What does any of this have to do with my Fating?"

The man hesitated. "A gleaner needs to know something of those who seek their fates."

"I'm Tavis of Curgh, son of Javan, duke of Curgh. What more do you need to know?"

Grinsa smiled enigmatically. "Perhaps you're right. Do you have any questions for the stone, my lord? Anything you wish to know?"

Tavis almost said something then about his Determining, about how the Qiran had failed to show him a vital part of his future. But instead he shook his head and took a long, steadying breath.

"The words, my lord," Grinsa said, his tone almost gentle. "When you're ready."

He opened his mouth to make the ritual entreaty to Qirsar and the stone, but what came out surprised even him.

"Are Determinings always right?"

As soon as he asked the question, he regretted it. He felt his face redden.

"Determinings and Fatings offer us glimpses of our futures," Grinsa said, seeming to choose his words with care. "Nothing more. Are they accurate? Yes. Do they tell us everything about what our lives will bring?" The Qirsi smiled and shook his head. "Of course not."

Tavis hadn't realized how frightened he had been of a different answer until Grinsa spoke. He actually managed a smile.

"When you're ready, my lord," the Qirsi said again.

"In this, the year of my Fating," Tavis began, "I beseech you, Qirsar, lay your hands upon this stone. Let my life unfold before my eyes. Let the mysteries of time be revealed in the light of the Qiran. Show me my fate."

The soft glow of the stone began to give way to a brighter, harder light. Tavis sat forward to gaze into the stone, even as he felt his blood racing in his veins, like the waters of the Heneagh in flood. Slowly, the image in the stone grew sharper. And as it did, Tavis felt his whole world shift, as if Elined herself had torn it apart and put it together again in some grotesque parody of what it was supposed to be.

He had hoped for a vision of glory, of himself in Audun's Castle, sitting on the throne, leading Eibithar to victory against the armies of Aneira, or perhaps even Braedon. He had thought to see himself married to a woman of surpassing beauty and strength. He was to be king, and he had dreamed again and again of seeing himself as such.

True, he had feared that he might see something else: his own death at the hands of assassins or thieves, or worse, his body twisting with convulsions as he succumbed to the pestilence.

But neither his brightest hopes nor his darkest fears could have prepared him for the vision presented to him in the glimmering depths of the Qiran.

He was in a dungeon he had never seen before, his wrists and ankles manacled to the wall. His clothes were befouled and in tatters, his hair matted. His face was covered with bruises, his lips were cracked and stained with dried blood. Yet even through the injuries and the filth, Tavis could see that he was looking at himself as a young man, barely older than he was now. This was no image of his distant future. Whatever would bring him to this condition would happen soon. He gagged, fearing that he might vomit. He could almost smell the fetor of the prison.

But he couldn't bring himself to look away. This vision of his misery held him as firmly as those blackened iron chains bolted into the prison wall. Had he been captured in battle during some coming war? Had enemies of the House of Curgh abducted him in an attempt to gain the throne?

Even as these questions formed in his head, however, the Tavis within the stone, the wretched prisoner, turned his head to look directly at the Tavis in the gleaning tent. And this second Tavis, the boy enduring a Fating that exceeded his worst fears, cried out at what he saw in those dark blue eyes. Whatever circumstances had led to his incarceration had not resulted from battlefield heroism, nor had they been contrived by Curgh's enemies. The man in the stone did not believe in his own innocence.

A few moments later, mercifully, the image began to fade, like a castle obscured by the smoke of siege fires. Tavis closed his eyes and slumped in his chair, but he hadn't the strength even to wipe the tears from his cheeks.

"How is any of that possible?" he whispered.

"The Qiran seldom explains what it shows," Grinsa said softly. "As I said before, it merely offers a glimpse of the future."

"But that . . ." He gestured vaguely at the stone and swallowed hard, feeling the bile rising in his throat again. "That had to be a mistake." He looked up abruptly, staring hard at the Qirsi. "Or a trick."

"I assure you, my lord," Grinsa said, "it was no trick. And though it saddens me to say it, the Qiran rarely makes mistakes."

Tavis wanted to rail at the man, to accuse him of deception and have his white head impaled on a pike before sundown. But he knew better. There had been something too real about the image, about that look he saw in his own eyes. There could be no denying the truth of it.

"What do I do now?" the young lord asked, his voice falling to a whisper once more.

"You live your life, my lord."

"How can I? You saw what's waiting for me. How am I supposed to go back to living my life knowing where it all leads?"

Grinsa regarded him placidly. "That is the test of the Fating. You may not believe me now, but this is the easy part. The challenge of the Fating is living with the knowledge it brings."

"You're right," Tavis said, not bothering to keep the bitterness from his voice. "I don't believe you."

"You will in time, my lord."

Tavis stood. "No, I don't think so. Not after this. If that's the challenge that awaits me—learning to accept that I'll spend the rest of my life rotting in some dungeon—then I'd just as soon have Bian take me now."

At that Grinsa's expression changed, the maddening air of calm giving way to a look of shock and fear.

"My lord," the Qirsi said, starting to stand.

But Tavis cut him off with a violent shake of his head. "Leave me alone." He turned and hurried out of the tent, nearly crashing into Xaver as he did.

"Tavis!" his friend said. "How did—?" He stopped abruptly, seeing the look on Tavis's face. "What happened?"

Tavis just gazed at him for a moment before striding away. He could hear Xaver calling his name, but he didn't stop. The prior's bells were ringing at the sanctuary. There were only a few hours of light left in the day. He briefly considered having his mount saddled. But that would mean going back to the castle, where, no doubt, his father had sent word that he was to be directed to the duke's chambers once more.

I look forward to hearing about your Fating, Javan had said, and though there was little warmth in their relationship, there were expectations. Tavis was certain that the duke had meant what he said. He would be impatient for Tavis's report.

He felt tears starting to course down his face again.

"How do I tell him this?" he breathed. "How do I tell Mother?"

"All things considered," Javan said, with that half smile Shonah had come to know so well over the years, "it was a most agreeable message. I find it hard to believe that Aindreas penned it himself."

Shonah laughed, as did Hagan and their other guests.

"So they've agreed to the match?" she asked, when their laughter ebbed.

The duke nodded. "It seems so. There are conditions, of course. They want to wait another few years, 'until any uncertainties in our respective houses' futures can be resolved,' as Aindreas puts it."

"What in Bian's name does that mean?" Hagan asked.

"It means," Shonah said, before Javan could respond, "that they want to be absolutely certain that Tavis will be king before they make any final commitments." Once more the others laughed. Shonah looked at her husband. "And I promise you, my lord, that was Ioanna's idea, not the duke's. She's an eminently practical woman."

Javan smiled, glancing around the table at their guests. "That from a woman who would know."

She inclined her head slightly. "My lord is too kind."

Shonah picked up her goblet and took a sip of wine. Notwithstanding the banter with her husband, she was pleased. Lady Brienne of Kentigern would be a fine match for her son, one that would make both Tavis and the duke happy. She was a daughter of a major house, the only one even close to Tavis's age. With Javan expecting to take the throne within the year, the strengthening of ties between Curgh and Kentigern couldn't come at a better time.

Two years ago this union had seemed unlikely. There was talk that Aindreas wanted Filib of Thorald for his daughter's mate, and it seemed that Javan would have to choose a daughter from one of the minor houses for their son. Even then, he had already received overtures from the dukes of Eardley, Labruinn, and Rennach. But with Filib's untimely death and Curgh's impending ascension to the crown, Tavis suddenly became the most sought-after young man in Eibithar. Almost immediately, the duke of Kentigern sent a message to Curgh Castle stating his interest in a match. Javan, of course, had been delighted.

Shonah understood. As a woman who prided herself on knowing far more of court politics than most of Eibithar's other duchesses, she recognized Javan's need to improve Curgh's relations with Aindreas and the lesser nobles of Kentigern. But she was also a mother, and she was as pleased with this match for Tavis's sake as she was for her husband's. She hadn't seen Brienne in years, but by all accounts, the young lady of Kentigern was an uncommonly attractive and intelligent young woman, who was blessed with her mother's looks and her father's mind. Fortunate for the girl, Shonah thought with an inward grin. No daughter should look like her father, when her father looked like Aindreas.

Brienne would make a good wife, and, more to the point, a fine queen when the time came. Perhaps as well, the prospect of marriage, distant as the event itself remained, would instill some discipline in her son and force him to take his duties and his training to heart.

"I'd like to share these tidings with my son," Javan said, seeming to read her thoughts. "Has anyone seen him?"

Tavis should have been in the duke's hall at the start of their meal, when the sunset bells were rung outside the castle. That had been some time ago, and though Shonah was not usually one to worry, she was starting to grow concerned.

"I saw him just after his Fating," Xaver MarCullet said from the far side of the table.

That he was here and Tavis was not only served to deepen Shonah's apprehension.

"He seemed troubled when he came out of the gleaner's tent," the MarCullet boy went on.

The duke looked at him keenly. "In what way?"

"He didn't stop to talk to me, not even briefly. I called after him, but he just walked away."

Shonah and Javan shared a look. A bad Fating? Impossible. Yet the duchess felt as if cold fingers were squeezing her heart, like the hand of Bian reaching for her from the Underrealm.

"Different people react to their Fatings in different ways," Yegor jal Sennah said from his place between Xaver and the earl of Brintesh. "Disappointment comes in many forms. It may be that he has his eye on a girl and his Fating showed him with Brienne instead. Or perhaps he imagined himself taller or brawnier as a man than the stone showed. Chances are his dismay will be short-lived."

Shonah favored the Qirsi man with a smile. He and his Eandi wife had been seated at the table as far from Javan as possible, just as they were every year, just as they would be again a few days hence, when Shonah and Javan hosted the Revel banquet. For all his fine qualities, Javan was not without his faults, and chief among them was his prejudice. Prejudice against anyone or anything from one of the Foreland's other kingdoms, against anyone or anything from one of Eibithar's other houses, and most of all, against the Qirsi. He tolerated them. He might even have developed some fondness and respect for Fotir over the years. But the notion of unions between Qirsi and Eandi still disturbed him. Shonah had grown quite fond of Yegor and Aurea, and a few years before she had finally prevailed upon Javan to invite them to the banquet and other events at the castle during the Revel's stay in Curgh. But that was as much as she could do.

"The reason for his disappointment is of little importance," Javan said with asperity. "He should have been here long ago."

But Shonah was watching Xaver. He knew her son better than any of them, and he appeared unmoved by Yegor's reassurances. What if it really had been a bad Fating? What if Tavis had seen Javan's death or his own? She shuddered. First the incident in Galdasten, then Filib's death, and now, perhaps, this. It almost seemed that Bian was angry with them, that he had marked Eibithar for misfortune.

Not that she truly believed in such things. She had long since placed her faith in the cloisters rather than the sanctuaries. She worshiped Ean, as did her husband and son, though Javan still visited the sanctuary at the far end of Curgh City as well. He claimed that he was obligated to do so, that as duke he had to understand the lives and faith of all his people, whether they lived in the court or in the country. Shonah suspected that there was more to it than that. But when she lost her second child only a turn before the babe was due to be born, Javan joined her in the cloister. And she, in the privacy of her chambers, alone with her grief, cursed Bian's name. Faith could be a difficult matter, and the old beliefs lingered, even, she had to admit, in her own mind and heart.

"Are you well, my lady?"

Shonah started, then turned and looked at Fotir, who had spoken.

"Forgive me, my lady, but you look pale." He smiled. "If I can be so bold as to judge such a thing."

She smiled in return, though she felt cold and her stomach had balled itself into a fist. "I'm . . . concerned," she admitted. "About Tavis."

He nodded. "So is the duke."

Few people other than she could see so clearly through Javan's moodiness. Her husband was fortunate to be served by such a man.

"Do you think we have reason?"

The Qirsi seemed to consider this. "Perhaps," he said at last. "I wouldn't have thought so, but for what Master MarCullet said."

She was about to respond when a door opened at the near end of the hall and her son stumbled in. She was relieved to see him, but the feeling was fleeting. His hair was disheveled, his eyes red, and his face puffy, as if he had just awakened. He was wearing a simple shirt and breeches, not at all the attire that a duke's son ought to wear to dine with guests of the castle. He carried an open wine flask in one hand.

Leaning against the door, he lifted the flask to his lips and took a long pull. Then he took an unsteady step forward and bowed to his father, almost falling over as he did.

"My apologies, sire," he said, barely getting the words out. "It seems I'm a bit late for dinner."

"Just take your seat, Tavis," Javan said stiffly.

"Of course, Father."

Tavis made his way to the table, smiling at their guests as he did. Fortunately, this was a relatively informal occasion. All those in the hall were friendly to the House of Curgh and could be counted upon to be discreet. Had this been the Revel banquet . . . Shonah closed her eyes briefly, not even wanting to think about it.

"Hello, Mother," Tavis said as he stepped past her chair. His breath stank of wine. She said nothing.

Tavis sat at the duke's right hand and began to pile food on his plate. No one else made a sound, although most of them had the grace to stare at their own meals rather than at him.

After taking several mouthfuls, her son finally looked up from his plate and scanned the hall.

"Why isn't anyone saying anything?"

"Just eat, Tavis," the duke said. "Don't talk."

He shook his head. "No. Why won't the rest of you speak? Is it me? Is it because I've come late?" A smile spread across his face and he lifted the wine. "Is it this?"

Javan grabbed the flask from him. "There! Now eat, and be silent!"

"What's the matter, Father? Am I shaming you? Am I sullying the Curgh name?"

The duke opened his mouth to respond, but then appeared to think better of it. Instead he smiled, though Shonah could see that it was forced. "Your mother and I were just telling our guests of a message I received today from the duke of Kentigern. He and I have agreed on a match between you and his daughter, the Lady Brienne."

"Brienne," Tavis repeated, his mouth full of fowl. "I met her several years ago, didn't I?"

Javan's face brightened. "Yes, that's right. When you were ten, I believe."

"She was fat, and her voice squeaked like a rusted gate."

The duke closed his eyes for a moment, but recovered quickly, the same brittle smile returning to his lips. "We're to travel to Kentigern just after Pitch Night to celebrate the betrothal. I expect the duke will make quite a spectacle of it. Tournaments, feasts, musicians. It will be like a second Revel."

"It sounds like a damned waste of time, if you ask me," Tavis said, biting into another piece of meat.

"What is the matter with you?" Shonah heard herself say. "Is this about your Fating?"

Tavis closed his eyes and laughed weakly. "Ah, my Fating. Go ahead, Mother. Ask me about my Fating. Ask me to give you a full accounting of everything I saw in the stone."

Yegor cleared his throat. "I was just telling your mother and father, my lord, that Fatings often seem disappointing at first, but with time . . ."

The Qirsi trailed off as Tavis began to laugh again, quietly at first, but building quickly until peals of laughter echoed off the ceiling of the hall.

"Pardon me," the young lord said at last, shaking his head and fighting for breath. "I don't mean to be rude. Truly. But you have no idea of what you're saying."

"Tavis!" Javan cut in. "That's enough!"

"But by all means," the boy went on, as if he hadn't heard the duke at all, "let's talk about my Fating."

Fotir stood and walked to where Tavis was sitting. "Perhaps we should be going, my lord," he said, laying a hand lightly on the boy's shoulder.

Tavis twisted away from him. "Don't touch me, you Qirsi bastard! I've had enough of your kind today!"

He eyed the rest of them. "You want to know about my Fating?"

No one answered.

"*Do you?*"

"Only if you want to tell us, Tavis," Xaver said, his voice as gentle as a morning mist.

Tavis stared at him for what seemed to Shonah an eternity. Finally, he looked down at his plate and shook his head. "I don't," he whispered.

He stood abruptly and, glaring at Fotir, balled his hands into fists. The first minister took a step back, holding up his hands. Still watching the Qirsi, Tavis picked up his wine. But instead of taking another drink, he merely tossed the flask away so that it shattered on the floor, leaving a dark red stain. And without another word, he left the hall.

Servants scrambled to clean up the wine and sharp pieces of clay, and for some time the sound of their movements was the only noise in the grand chamber.

"My apologies, friends," Javan said at last, his voice utterly flat. "My son . . . is not himself today."

The guests murmured their understanding, and slowly, as the servants brought more platters of food, conversations resumed. People began to eat again.

Except Shonah, who just stared at her hands, struggling to keep from crying. After a while, she felt someone's eyes upon her, and looking up, she saw that the MarCullet boy was watching her, an expectant look on his youthful face.

If anyone could reach him it was Xaver. She took a breath, then nodded once.

An instant later, the boy was out of his chair, striding toward the same door Tavis had used.

Xaver knew just where to look for him. There were certain places Tavis went to escape the castle and his parents when he fell into his dark moods. One was the crowded city marketplace, where the singers, dancers, tumblers, and conjurers of the Revel were entertaining the people of Curgh. But the gleaning tent was there, and on this night, Xaver guessed that the duke's son would stay as far from it as possible. The second was the section of the moat where the two of them had gone after running the towers that morning. Xaver didn't expect that his friend would return there so soon.

Which left the third place: the high wall at the northern end of the castle, between the cloister tower and ocean tower. The wall overlooked the cliffs and the rocky shore of the Strait of Wantrae. There were guards in both towers—usually a pair walked the wall day and night—but whenever Xaver and Tavis went up there, the guards left them alone. No one had ever attacked Curgh Castle by climbing the cliffs from the strait. As high as they were, and as sheer, no one ever would.

Reaching the wall level of the ocean tower, Xaver was confronted by two guards, both of them looking tall and burly in the torchlight. He knew their faces, though not their names, but they, of course, knew him.

"You looking for the duke's boy, young master?" one of them asked.

"Yes. Is he here?"

"On the wall, as usual."

"He's in a foul mood, young master," the second one added. "Worst I've seen. He pulled his dagger on us both, when all we'd done was offer a 'good evening.' "

Xaver took a long breath. *What had Tavis seen in the Qiran?*

"Thanks for the warning," he said.

He stepped onto the wall and scanned the ramparts for his friend. At first he saw nothing, save the brown-and-gold banners of Curgh flying atop the cloister tower, illuminated by the rose light of the moons and snapping in the briny wind. He briefly wondered if Tavis had crossed the wall and descended the steps of the next tower without the guards seeing. Then, his mind turning in a darker direction for just an instant, he feared that the young lord might have jumped to the rocks below. But as his eyes adjusted, he finally spotted Tavis sitting on the stone walkway, his back pressed against the wall, his knees drawn up to his chest.

"Tavis?"

The lord turned his head to look at him before facing forward again. "Leave me. I don't feel like talking."

Xaver walked forward slowly. "We don't have to talk. I'll just sit with you for a while."

"I told you to leave me, Xaver. I just want to be alone."

"You always say that," Xaver said, still closing the distance between them. "I stopped believing you a long time ago."

"Stop!" Tavis said, scrambling to his feet. Moonlight glinted off the blade of his dagger, which he held out before him with a trembling hand.

Xaver nodded, stopping just a few strides from where the young lord stood. "All right," he said, leaning against the wall and looking out toward the water.

"You should go."

"I will, soon." He pointed at a dim yellow light bobbing up and down in the distance, just in front of the dark mass of Wantrae Island. "There's a ship out there. Remember when we used to sit up on the wall and count how many we could see in a single night?"

Tavis didn't answer. He just stood there, utterly still in the soft light of the lovers.

"What happened, Tavis? What did you see in the stone?"

His friend turned and slumped against the wall. "It's not important."

Xaver nearly laughed aloud. "Not important? You're drunk, you've humiliated your mother and father, you just pulled a dagger on two of the castle guards, and you want me to believe that it's not important?"

"I don't care what you believe," the lord said, bitterness creeping into his voice. "I've told you I want to be alone. Don't make me say it again."

"Tell me what you saw."

"No."

"Is something going to happen to your father, or to you? Is that what it is? Did you see your own death?"

Tavis laughed, a lonely, chilling sound. "Death would be a blessing compared to this."

"Is that why you came up here? To die?"

Tavis looked at him, his eyes glimmering with moonglow and the light of the far-off torches. "I thought of it," he admitted. "I had hoped that with enough wine in me I'd have nerve enough to throw myself into the strait." He gave a harsh smile. "But even drunk, I'm too much of a coward."

"You're no coward, Tavis."

"Aren't I?" He shook his head. "I fear death, even more than I fear shame, even more than I fear my family's downfall."

Xaver shrugged. "Who among us doesn't. We're young still, Tavis. Too young to die. So you're afraid of the Underrealm. Where's the crime in that?"

"Where indeed?" Tavis said, looking down at his dagger.

"Come down with me to your chambers," Xaver coaxed, starting toward him slowly. "We'll get you to sleep."

Tavis backed away. "Stay away from me, Xaver. I'm not going to my chambers. I'm not going anywhere."

"You'll feel better in the morning." He reached for him. "Just take my hand and—"

It happened so quickly that, at first, Xaver felt nothing. He saw the young lord's blade as a dim blur arcing through the darkness, saw a dark spot appear on the stone walkway, and then another. A moment later he realized that it was blood, his blood. Pulling his hand back, not quite believing it all, he saw that his sleeve was cut and that there was a long gash on his forearm.

"You cut me," he said, staring at the wound.

Tavis dropped the blade. "Demons and fire!" he breathed.

Xaver looked up at him.

"I'm sorry, Xaver. Truly I am."

Xaver didn't say anything. Instead he turned and walked back toward the ocean tower and the guards. He sensed Tavis watching him, but the young lord didn't call for him to stop, nor did he follow.

One of the guards saw him returning and held up a hand in greeting.

"I guess there's no reasoning with him when—" He stopped, his eyes widening. "Gods! Did he do that?"

"It's nothing," Xaver said, though the cut had begun to throb painfully. "But I should probably find the surgeon just the same."

"What about Lord Tavis?" the guard asked.

Xaver glanced back over his shoulder. He could barely make out Tavis's form, standing just as Xaver had left him.

"Leave him out there," he said, unable to keep the hurt from his voice. "That's what I should have done."

Chapter
Six

✦

T hey didn't finish the day's gleanings until well after the ringing of the bells signaling the locking of the city gates. It was this way on the first night everywhere they went. Often the children were exhausted, not only from their lengthy wait, but also because they were hours past their normal bedtime. But having stood outside the tent for so long, they were reluctant to abandon their place in line and start over again the next day. And more often than not, those who might have been willing to do so were accompanied by parents who were not.

After the gleanings of Tavis and Xaver, Grinsa rested, allowing Cresenne and then Trin, the eldest of the gleaners and the man in charge of the gleaning tent, to do their share, before he finished the final few. By the end of the evening, the three Qirsi gleaners were almost as tired as the last of the children filing through the tent for their Determinings.

Even at this late hour, the city was still alive with music and laughter when they left the tent. Dancers spun in the streets to the beating of tuned drums, and, in the distance, Grinsa could hear singers performing bawdy verses for an appreciative audience.

"I'd like a meal and some ale before I sleep," Trin said, glancing up at the Qirsi moon. "Either of you care to join me?"

Normally Grinsa would have declined. He longed for a comfortable bed. But he had taken a liking to Cresenne, and he glanced at her, gauging her response.

She was already looking his way, an inviting smile on her lips. "I'd like that," she said.

Trin nodded. "Good. I know of a place near here. The Silver Gull, I believe it's called. A Qirsi establishment that happens to serve the finest spiced stew in Curgh."

Grinsa had to laugh. Trin knew more about the inns of every city in Eibithar than anyone in the Revel. Not that Grinsa was surprised. In addition to being a discerning judge of fine food, Altrin jal Casson was also the only fat Qirsi he had ever met. His people tended to be quite thin, sometimes to the point of frailty. But Trin was as round as a suckling pig, with a fleshy chin and full cheeks. In other ways, however, he was as weak as any Qirsi, perhaps more so. The least bit of physical activity left him flushed, sweaty, and breathless. Grinsa often wondered how he managed to survive the rigors of life in the Revel, not to mention the heat of the gleaning tent.

They walked through the city, leaving the marketplace and taking a wide street west toward the Sanctuary of Elined. Just before the sanctuary gate, they came to the inn Trin had described. With its worn oaken door, its grey stone façade, and the dirty windows that shone faintly with candlelight, it looked like any of the other establishments found closer to the castle and center of the city. Only the sign hanging above the doorway set it apart. It showed a pale, almost wraithlike gull with golden eyes and outstretched wings. Every city in Eibithar, indeed, almost every city in all the Forelands, had at least one inn like this. The White Owl in Tremain, the Silver Nag in Thorald, the White Dragon in Jistingham on the Wethy coast, the Grey Falcon in Trescarri in southern Sanbira. Eandi patrons were welcome in all of them. Gold was gold, no matter the pocket from which it came. But these inns were run by Qirsi men and women, and most of their customers were Qirsi as well.

Inside, the inn once again resembled most of the other inns in Eibithar, with a single exception: nearly every person Grinsa saw had white hair and yellow eyes. The air was quite warm and smelled of sweet ale and a pungent spice that made Grinsa's mouth water.

"Trin, you fat drel!" a tall man called, stepping around from behind the bar, his arms open.

"Hello, cousin," Trin said, accepting the man's embrace. "You're looking well."

The man stepped back. "I wish I could say the same for you."

Trin raised an eyebrow. "How kind of you, cousin."

They weren't cousins, of course, at least not as far as Grinsa knew. Qirsi often addressed each other this way. It was an old, dark joke, dating from the years following the end of the Qirsi Wars, that had managed to survive the intervening centuries. There had been so few Qirsi warriors left after their failed invasion of the Forelands that it was assumed all the Qirsi born in the ensuing years had to be related. Some said only two thousand men and women of the Southlands made it through the war; others swore that it could have been no more than fifteen hundred. The Qirsi population had grown slowly in the nearly nine hundred years since—Qirsi women did not bear many children. Even now, after all that time, and with a steady stream of Qirsi wanderers coming to the Forelands over the Border Range, for every Qirsi man, woman, and child in the Forelands there were at least fifteen or twenty Eandi.

"Who are your friends?" the man asked, eyeing Grinsa briefly before smiling broadly at Cresenne.

"The poor child you're leering at like a drel in heat is Cresenne ja Terba. She's new to the Revel this year." Trin indicated Grinsa with a thick hand. "And this is Grinsa jal Arriet, another of our gleaners." Trin looked at Grinsa and then Cresenne. "May I present Ziven jal Agasha. The Silver Gull is his."

"Jal Agasha?" Grinsa repeated. "Your mother was Agasha ja Perton, of Riverway in Wethyrn?"

Ziven's eyes widened. "Yes. You knew her?"

"My own mother met her once, many years ago. She was said to be the finest cook north of the steppe."

"So she was," he said, grinning.

"I was sorry to hear of her passing. I hope Bian has been kind to her."

"My thanks." Ziven turned to Trin. "I was going to make you wait, Trin. See if I couldn't make you sweat away some of that fat. But since your friend here knows something of decent food, I'll give you a table now."

"Splendid, cousin. Something near the back, if you don't mind. I don't want any outraged parents interrupting our meal. You know the saying. 'The Qiran brings the vision, but the Qirsi bears the blame.' "

"Of course," Ziven said, smiling. He beckoned for one of the serving girls. "Ysanne will show you the way."

The girl who hurried to stand before him was slender and small,

107

with pale eyes and white skin. But unlike the other Qirsi, her hair was raven black. She couldn't have been more than a year or two past her Determining.

"You're hiring mongrels now, Ziven? I never thought I'd see the day."

Grinsa winced inwardly. Such prejudice was common among his people, and he had heard similar comments from Trin before, but they still rankled. Though his blood was all Qirsi, he had once been married to an Eandi woman. Had she not died of the pestilence so soon after their joining, they surely would have had children, and all of them would have been half-bloods.

"Careful, Trin," Ziven said, a steel edge to his voice. "This is my brother's girl, come to work for me from Wethyrn."

Trin's face reddened. "My apologies." He glanced at the girl. "To you both."

"Take them to the back room, Ysanne," Ziven said. "And pay no attention to anything the fat one says."

The girl looked down, suppressing a smile. "Yes, Uncle."

She led them on a winding course through the crowded inn, her head bobbing almost constantly in response to the stream of requests for more food and drink that followed her. The room in which she seated them was empty save for three unoccupied tables and several chairs. Candles burned on each table and several sconces were mounted on the walls. Moonlight filtered through the solitary window across from the door.

"This will do nicely," Trin said, smiling at the girl. "Thank you."

She nodded, but refused to meet his gaze. "I'll be back with your food shortly."

Trin stared after her as she returned to the bar. "I am a fool and a lout," he said. "I should never have said what I did in front of the girl."

"She's a half-blood," Cresenne said, before Grinsa could respond. "I'm sure she's heard worse."

The heavy man tipped his head, as if conceding the point. "Still, it's one thing to insult the innkeeper. It's quite another to insult the server." He smiled. "We'll be lucky to survive the meal."

Cresenne laughed, and after a moment Grinsa did as well, although he had to force himself. They claimed one of the tables, sitting just as Ysanne returned with three tankards of sweet ale.

"To a long day," Trin said after she was gone, raising his stoup and nodding first to Cresenne and then to Grinsa. "The first of many here in Curgh."

They drank the toast. It was fine ale, though Grinsa preferred the bitter, lighter brews of Wethyrn and eastern Eibithar.

"Will every day be like this one?" Cresenne asked. "Are the lines always that long?"

"Not always, no," Trin said. "The first day or two are the worst. That's when all the young ones come for their Determinings. There'll be a lull in the middle, and then a rush of Fatings at the end, as the older ones are forced by our impending departure to master their fears." He took another pull of ale. "Wouldn't you agree, Grinsa?"

"That sounds about right. Though even during the lulls, we'll each do ten or more every day. That's when most of the children come from the outlying baronies, earldoms, and thaneships."

"And we do this in every city?"

Grinsa smiled at her. "The major houses are the worst. And this stretch is particularly difficult. You missed most of our stay in Kentigern, but from here we go to Galdasten and then to Thorald. Once we're done with Thorald, though, we'll be in smaller cities for three turns before Glyndwr, which is the easiest of the major ones. This is really the worst of it right now."

"Well that's some consolation," she said, reaching for her ale.

"I actually prefer the majors," Trin said. "Grinsa tends to do most of the work, and I find that the food and the soldiers are much more to my liking."

Cresenne looked at him for a moment, a puzzled expression on her face. Then she seemed to understand, her cheeks coloring as she lowered her gaze.

"Ah, you didn't know that my tastes ran in that direction. My apologies, my dear. I thought it was common knowledge."

Grinsa sipped his ale, unwilling to look at either one of them just then. Cresenne's discomfort was palpable, and Trin's apology smacked of insincerity. He enjoyed setting people on edge. That was common knowledge as well.

"It's all right," she said, an awkward smiling flitting across her features. "It's none of my concern really."

"Actually, it should come as a great relief to you. Imagine how much worse it would be to find that I was attracted to you just as my friend Grinsa is." He glanced Grinsa's way for just an instant, his eyes dancing like candle flames. "Even I know that pretty young women don't like to be pursued by fat old men."

"That's enough, Trin," Grinsa said.

"I must apologize again, my dear. Apparently Grinsa wasn't ready for you to know how he felt about you." He turned in his seat to face Grinsa. "It is true though, isn't it?"

Grinsa could not keep himself from smiling. Looking at Cresenne, he saw that she was grinning as well, though her color was still high. "Perhaps," he said at last.

"Perhaps?" the man asked, arching an eyebrow.

"Fine, Trin," Grinsa said, laughing now and shaking his head. "You win. Yes, I've enjoyed the time Cresenne and I have spent together."

"Enjoyed the time," Trin repeated. He looked at Cresenne and gave an exaggerated sigh. "He wouldn't admit to being warm if his shirt was on fire." He reached across the table and took the woman's slender hand in his own. "And what about you, my dear? Are you similarly impressed with our companion?"

"Trin!"

"Quiet, Grinsa! You'll thank me for this later. Both of you will."

"I doubt that."

"You'd rather dance around each other for another six turns wondering who's going to be the first to say something? Don't be an ass. We're Qirsi. We don't live long enough to put up with such foolishness. Just because I prefer men, that doesn't mean that I know nothing of romance." He returned his gaze to Cresenne and smiled. "Now, answer my question, cousin. Are you taken with Grinsa as he is with you?"

She opened her mouth to answer, then grinned, her eyes on the doorway. "Here's our food," she said lightly.

Trin closed his eyes briefly. "Very well." He released her hand and sat back, allowing Ysanne to place three large bowls of stew on the table. "I'll leave this to you, Grinsa, although I've little confidence in your ability to win her heart for yourself. You would have been much better off with me speaking on your behalf."

Grinsa laughed, and he and Cresenne shared a look that left him wondering if Trin had already done enough.

"You were right, Trin," Cresenne said after a brief silence. "This stew is excellent."

"I'm glad you think so. Ziven's prices are too high, but he does find the most wonderful cooks." He paused to chew a mouthful of food. "So tell us about yourself, Cresenne. The Revel doesn't bring us new gleaners very often."

She shrugged, looking uncomfortable once more. "What do you want to know?"

"Where are you from?"

"I was born in Braedon, though I've lived most of my life in Wethyrn."

Trin stopped chewing for just an instant. "Braedon?"

"My father was captain on a trade ship. He met my mother there. After I was born, they left the empire and settled on the Wethy Crown. I haven't been in Braedon since I was a babe."

"Still," Trin said, his mouth full again, "I wouldn't mention your ancestry to any of our Eibitharian hosts. You're not likely to get a warm welcome."

"What were you doing before you joined the Revel?" Grinsa asked.

"I was a healer in our home village, just as my mother was. But when Wethyrn's north fair came the year of my Fating, I found that I possessed the gleaning magic as well. I'd always wanted to travel the Forelands, and becoming a gleaner offered the perfect opportunity."

"Why the Revel?"

She shrugged again, a wisp of white hair falling attractively over her brow. "It was either that or Sanbira's Festival—none of the other fairs can compare. Eibithar is closer to my home, so it seemed a good choice for now. Perhaps someday I'll travel with the Festival as well."

For several moments they fell silent, each of them enjoying the fine food and strong ale. Then Cresenne asked a question about one of the older Qirsi sorcerers, and for a long time Trin and Grinsa entertained her with stories of the Revel, most of them benefiting from Trin's singular knowledge of the smallest details of every romance, betrayal, and feud in question.

They filled themselves with stew—Grinsa ate three helpings and he lost count of how many Trin had. They also drank a good deal of ale. Tired and slightly drunk, Grinsa was gathering himself to say goodnight to his friends when someone knocked on the half-closed door to their small room.

Grinsa and Trin exchanged a look.

"Who is it?" the heavy man called.

In response, the door swung open, and there, framed by the doorway, stood a tall Qirsi man with long white hair, a thin white beard and mustache, and eyes as bright and yellow as an owl's. Grinsa knew that he had seen the man before, but until Trin spoke, he couldn't remember where.

"Cousin," his friend said without enthusiasm, a weak smile on his lips as he looked toward the door. "Are you here as the duke's man or as a Qirsi?"

The first minister. Of course.

"I wasn't aware that I had to choose, cousin," Fotir answered, his tone no warmer than Trin's had been. "But I'm not here at the duke's request, if that's what you mean."

"It's not. What is it that you want?"

The first minister stepped into the room, shutting the door behind him. "I'd like to know which of you was present at Lord Tavis's Fating today."

Before Grinsa could speak Trin raised a meaty hand, silencing him and Cresenne. "Why do you want to know?"

"The boy was quite distraught afterward. The duke and duchess were concerned."

"That's a common reaction, cousin. If I had five qinde for every boy or girl who went crying home to mother and father after a gleaning . . ." He shrugged. "Well, let's just say I'd be even fatter than I am."

"Is it common as well for a duke's son to arrive late and drunk at a formal dinner, to attack his liege man with a blade, and then disappear into the night?"

"Gods have mercy!" Grinsa whispered.

Fotir looked at him, narrowing his eyes. "It was you?"

"Yes. How's the MarCullet boy?"

"He'll be all right. He has a deep cut on his forearm, but it's nothing too serious."

Grinsa almost offered to return to the castle with him to help with the healing, but no doubt the duke had his own healers. Besides, he could not afford to reveal so much.

"Well, now you know it was Grinsa," Trin said. "If there's nothing else, you can be on your way."

Fotir took a chair from the nearest table, placed it next to Grinsa's, and sat, as if he hadn't heard Trin's comment. "What can you tell me about Lord Tavis's Fating?" he asked, his eyes fixed on Grinsa's.

"Nothing at all," Trin said pointedly. "You know that, Fotir. Gleanings are a private matter. We're not to share them with anyone."

"I also know," the first minister said, glaring at the heavy man, "that gleanings are not always what they seem. You have as much to do with what those children see as the Qiran does. Perhaps more."

"That's only true of the Determinings," Trin said, sounding defensive. "The Fatings come from the stone."

"Only because you let them. There's nothing to stop you from controlling the Fatings in the same way. Isn't that so?"

"What do you want to know about Tavis's Fating?" Grinsa asked, drawing Fotir's gaze.

"I'd like to know what he saw."

Grinsa shook his head. "That I can't tell you. As Trin said, it's a private matter. You'll have to ask Tavis."

Fotir clenched his jaw. "That could be difficult, given that no one knows where he is. His mother is afraid that he threw himself off the north wall of the castle. The captain of the guard is planning a search of the rocks below at dawn if he isn't found tonight."

"I'm sorry. But I don't see how knowing what he saw in the Qiran will help you find him. Isn't it enough that he's troubled?"

"I suppose," the first minister muttered, looking down at the worn floor. An instant later he met Grinsa's gaze again. "Can you at least tell me if what he saw was real?"

"It was real," Grinsa said. He considered saying more, but quickly thought better of it. He had spoken the truth. That would have to be enough for now.

"You know what he saw. Are you surprised that he'd behave this way in response to what the stone showed him?"

Grinsa looked away, exhaling through his teeth. "No."

Fotir nodded. "I see. I can't say that I'm surprised."

"I spoke with him briefly before his Fating," Grinsa said. "It wasn't an easy conversation."

"I don't imagine. What's your point?"

"I'm not trying to make a point. I'm wondering about the source of your concern for the boy. When I spoke with him he was arrogant and hostile, and he seemed to have little use for me or my magic. He didn't strike me as the type to inspire much loyalty, particularly from a Qirsi minister."

"Have you met his father, cousin?"

"No," Grinsa said, "though I know that he hasn't been very accepting of Yegor and Aurea's marriage."

"You're quick to judge. Too quick, it seems to me." Fotir glanced at Trin for just an instant. "It shouldn't surprise me, given the company you keep. But it's time the Qirsi understood that there's more to measuring the worth of an Eandi than just knowing his or her feelings toward our people. The duke is a thoughtful, intelligent man, certainly far more so than many Qirsi I know. He has his faults, as all men do, but he'll be a fine king. Regardless of what his son may or may not be, Javan does inspire loyalty."

"Spoken like the pet of an Eandi lord," Trin said.

The first minister stood abruptly. "I should have known better than to come here. You're fools in a circus, nothing more. You think we're so different. Where would you be without the Eandi? Do you really think your Revel could survive without them? There are Qirsi settlements throughout Eibithar. Yes, they're small, but they exist nevertheless. Yet, I never hear of the Revel stopping in any of them. It's always the cities, the courts of Eandi lords. You're just like me, all of you. Except that I'm the duke's minister, and you're his entertainment."

He turned smartly and stepped out of the room, not bothering to look at any of them again.

Grinsa and his companions sat in silence for a few moments. Then Trin began to laugh quietly.

"There goes the fool," he said. "His hair and his eyes are the right color, but his blood runs Eandi."

It was an old barb, dating back to the wars and the betrayal of the Qirsi army by Carthach, a Qirsi officer who, in exchange for gold and a promise of asylum for himself and his warriors, taught the Forelanders the secrets of defeating Qirsi magic. That his people still used it, that it could still be said with such venom, seemed to Grinsa terribly sad.

"I'm not concerned with his blood," Grinsa said, standing and starting toward the door. "I'm concerned with Tavis's."

He made his way quickly through the main room of the inn, which was still quite crowded, and hurried out into the lane. Fotir was a short distance off, his back to Grinsa as he strode toward the castle, his white hair illuminated by the moons.

"First Minister, wait!" Grinsa called.

The man stopped and turned.

"What is it you want?" he asked, as Grinsa stopped in front of him.

"Simply to apologize. Trin doesn't speak for me. If you say that the duke is worthy of your friendship, I believe you, without judgment."

Fotir eyed him suspiciously, but after a few seconds he nodded. "Is that all?"

"I'd like to help, if I can."

"What makes you think that you can be of any help to us?"

Grinsa shrugged. "I'm a gleaner. My power runs deeper than just reading the stone. Perhaps I can help you that way."

"Do you have any other powers, cousin?"

Desperate as he was to make amends for what his gleaning had wrought, Grinsa could not keep the lie from springing to his lips. He had been hiding the truth for far too long. "No."

"Well," Fotir said, "as it happens, I'm a gleaner as well. I'm also a summoner of mists and winds and a shaper. The castle has several healers and one woman who speaks the language of beasts." He smiled thinly. "The last thing we need is another Qirsi helping us with our search, especially one of such limited talents."

For the second time that night, the first minister turned and walked away from him, and this time Grinsa did not follow.

"His kind doesn't look for help from the likes of us," came a voice from behind him.

Grinsa turned and saw Trin and Cresenne standing a short distance away. He hadn't even heard them approach.

"We are his kind," Grinsa said with more fervor than he had intended.

Trin gave a gentle smile. "No, my friend, we're not. I'd have thought you would understand that by now."

Grinsa tried to smile in return, but knew that he failed. "I guess I'm just slow to learn."

"Perhaps. Or maybe you're slow to abandon hope. There's no shame in that."

"Thank you, Trin," Grinsa said, caught off guard by the fat man's kindness.

"I'm heading back to my room now," Trin said. "I have a skin of wine there that I'd be happy to share." He looked from one of them to the other, an eyebrow raised.

Grinsa followed his gaze to Cresenne and found that she was already watching him, a coy smile on her lips.

"Ah," Trin said knowingly. "I thought not. Very well, I'll leave the two of you. Do try to get some sleep. We've a busy day ahead."

Grinsa and Cresenne stood together in the moonlight for some time, watching Trin walk away. Then they faced each other.

"Let's walk," she said, the smile still on her face. "This is my first time in Curgh."

They started east, away from the sanctuary and the castle, back toward the marketplace. There was still music coming from the center of the city, and Grinsa had little doubt that it would continue until dawn. This was the Revel's first night in Curgh. Few people would get any sleep tonight.

"You're concerned about the duke's son." She offered it as a statement, but she was regarding him closely.

"I am. What I said before was true: he was difficult to talk to and he seemed to have a temper. But to take a blade to his liege man . . ." He trailed off, shaking his head.

"That must have been quite a Fating."

He nodded. "It was. I'm not certain that I would have taken it much better."

"Really?" she said, sounding surprised. "What was it he saw?"

He looked over at her. "You know I can't tell you that."

She met his gaze for an instant, then looked down. "Of course," she said. "I'm sorry. I wasn't thinking."

"It's all right."

She appeared so young just then, her smooth skin almost seeming to glow with moonlight and the glimmer of the street torches. A light breeze stirred her hair and she brushed a few strands away from her brow. Grinsa thought about stopping her there on the street and taking her in his arms to kiss her. Instead he faced forward again and continued to walk.

"You were very quiet at the inn," he said. "Were Trin and I talking too much?"

She let out a small laugh. "Not at all. I was listening, enjoying your stories about the Revel. Then that man came in."

"Fotir?"

"Yes. I didn't think it wise to get in the middle of all that."

Grinsa nodded. "You were right. It seems sometimes that the rifts among the Qirsi are even more difficult to bridge than those among the kingdoms of the Forelands."

She nodded. "It was that way in Wethyrn as well."

"It makes no sense," he said, shaking his head. "We've too much in common to be at war with ourselves this way."

"Maybe. But the Qirsi feud is as old as the kingdoms and Carthach's treachery."

"The Qirsi feud?"

She colored and looked away again. "That's what they call it on the Wethy Crown."

"I suppose it's apt. And do they also still refer to Carthach's choice as treachery?"

"Some do."

"You just did."

She smiled, though there was a brittleness to it. "That's what my father always called it. I do it by habit more than anything else."

He wasn't certain that he believed her, but it was not a subject worth pursuing. Discussing Carthach's betrayal with a Qirsi was as risky as asking an Eandi whether he or she followed the Old Faith or the Path of Ean. Most of the Qirsi in the Forelands viewed Carthach as a traitor, a man who abandoned their people in the time of their greatest need, for a few bars of gold. But some, Grinsa among them, saw Carthach as something else.

The Qirsi Wars were going to end badly for the invaders, regardless of what Carthach did. That much was clear by the time he struck his deal with the leaders of the Eandi army. The Qirsi advance across the Forelands had been stopped, and the two armies had fallen into a brutal war of slow attrition, one that the Forelands' defenders, who vastly outnumbered the invaders, were bound to win. By crossing over to the Eandi side, and showing them how to defeat the Qirsi magic and end the war swiftly, Carthach might have saved tens of thousands of lives.

There was an old Qirsi saying: "The traitor walks a lonely path." As one might expect, Carthach was reviled by the Qirsi. But he was never truly embraced by the Forelanders. They gave him gold and asylum, just as they promised, but he lived the rest of his life truly an exile, friendless, loveless, and scorned.

Even after his death, even after the Qirsi had lived for centuries in peace among the Eandi of the Forelands, Carthach remained the most hated man in Qirsi lore. Among the Eandi he was largely forgotten. Most Qirsi avoided discussing him at all, especially in the company of the Eandi. But his betrayal lay at the root of nearly every conflict that had divided his people since. Certainly it was the source of Trin's hostility toward Fotir. Those who hated Carthach the most believed that the Qirsi who served in the courts of the Forelands' kingdoms repeated his betrayal every day.

This was not to say that Fotir, or others in similar positions throughout the Forelands, had forgiven Carthach. On the contrary, some of them were nearly as vehement in their loathing for the man as Trin. But they saw their own influence as a way to improve the standing of the Qirsi in the northlands, to help their people become something more than merely a vanquished race.

Grinsa, while acknowledging that there was wisdom, perhaps even a sort of honor, in Carthach's actions, could not in good conscience align himself fully with either side. There were real dangers in the rage still carried by men and women who felt as Trin did, dangers that were beginning to manifest themselves in frightening ways in the Forelands. Yet there was also something offensive in the righteousness of men like Fotir. Nearly nine centuries after the end of the Qirsi Wars, Grinsa's people had done little to ease the pain of their defeat.

He and Cresenne walked for some distance without speaking. He sensed her unease and was very much aware of his own, but he could think of nothing to say.

"It seems we're on opposite sides of this," she finally said, her voice subdued.

"Yes, it does."

She halted, reaching out for his arm to stop him as well and make him face her.

"Does that mean that we can't . . . ?" She stopped. Even in the pale light of Panya and Ilias he could see that she was blushing.

"No," he said. "It doesn't mean that at all."

Their eyes met. After a moment Cresenne stepped forward and, lacing her fingers through his white hair, pulled his lips to hers, kissing him deeply.

"I'm glad," she whispered, resting her head against his chest.

Grinsa smiled. "So am I." He gave a small laugh. "Trin was right. This is better than waiting six turns."

She smiled up at him and they kissed a second time. While they were kissing, though, Cresenne suddenly yawned.

"I'm sorry," she said, starting to laugh. "I'm very tired."

Grinsa frowned. "Yawning during a kiss, especially a first kiss—"

"It was our second," she broke in, still giggling.

"Still," he said, smiling now himself. "That's a terrible thing to do to a man's pride."

"You're right," she said, trying with little success to stop laughing. "I'm terribly sorry."

He held out a hand to her. "Come on. I'll walk you to your room."

With that, her laughter did stop. "But our walk."

"We'll be in Curgh for another half turn," he said, gently brushing the hair back from her brow. It was as soft as Sanbiri silk. "And if you'd like, I'll walk with you every night."

She took his hand. "I'd like that," she said, although before she could finish, she had to suppress another yawn.

They both laughed, turning once more to walk back to the inn and their rooms.

Cadel had ended his singing performance some time ago, making his apologies as he left the other performers, claiming to be weary from the journey to Curgh. Jedrek had made a point of remaining to sing on. No sense drawing any more attention to themselves than was necessary. Cadel would have liked to stay as well. They sounded good tonight, and there were some fine musicians here for the Revel. But he had an appointment to keep. He had made his way, silent and watchful, over the city wall and around the base of the castle to the rocky promontory overlooking the Strait of Wantrae. There he had waited. And waited. Until his patience began to wear as thin as parchment.

Yes, they were paying him handsomely, but that did not give them the right to treat him like this. He almost wished that he hadn't taken so much gold from them in Thorald two years before. Ever since then, they had acted as though he was theirs to do with what they pleased, as if he were a servant, or a mount. No amount of gold was worth this.

As Panya reached her zenith and began her long slow arc downward to the western horizon, he resolved to leave.

"Let them find me tomorrow," he said aloud, his voice sounding small amid the pounding of the waves below and the rush of the water wind.

But even as he turned to start back to the castle, he saw a figure approaching over the rocks, white skin and whiter hair illuminated by Panya's glow. As the figure drew nearer, Cadel caught a glimpse of the pale eyes as well, and he shuddered. If it weren't for the gold . . .

The Qirsi stopped a few strides from where he stood, slightly out of breath, ghostly hair twisting in the wind.

"You're late," Cadel said, allowing his voice to convey the full force of his anger. "I've been here for better than an hour."

"It was necessary. Circumstances have changed."

He hesitated. "What do you mean?"

"The duke's son is missing. He had his Fating today, and apparently it left him . . . unnerved."

"Do you know what he saw?"

"Not yet," the white-hair said sourly. "That may take some time."

"Is it possible that he knows what we have planned for him? Might he have fled?"

"I don't think so. He got drunk, and he took a blade to his liege man. Hardly the actions of someone intent on flight. I think it more likely that he merely drank himself into a stupor. It's possible, however, that he's taken his own life."

"In which case my work here would be done."

"Hardly," the Qirsi said. "Such a death would complicate matters more than you could know. Regardless, though, we need to wait before we act. I need to know what Tavis saw in the stone and who he talks to about it."

"Can't you ask one of your Qirsi friends about the Fating?"

"It's not that easy. Gleaners aren't supposed to discuss the Determinings or Fatings they see, and Tavis's gleaner doesn't sympathize with our cause."

Neither do I. "So what do you want me to do?" He hated even asking the question. They had no right to order him about. Yet, it was their money.

"Meet me here again, two nights after the Night of Two Moons. By then we should know more. But prepare yourself for this: I don't want anything done while the Revel is here in Curgh. It was fine for Filib, but if we do it twice, we invite suspicion."

He had to admit that the Qirsi was right. "All right. When? Where?"

"I should know that the next time we meet." The Qirsi smiled, though the expression in those ghostly eyes didn't change. "Until then you should sing and enjoy the Revel."

I don't need your permission. "And what will you be doing?"

The white-hair was already turning away to return to the city. "Planning a murder, finding out what Lord Tavis saw in the stone. You're not the only one trying to earn some gold."

Chapter Seven

✦

T hey found him the next morning, shivering in his sleep in a corner of the wine cellar. The guards who discovered him there roused him and led him to the duke's chambers, stopping twice along the way so that the duke's son, the future king of Eibithar, could vomit in the gardens of the duke's ward. The men in question did not hear what the duke said to Tavis within chambers—they were told to leave the inner ward and return to their posts. But they said later that the duke's voice carried all the way to the south barbican on the far side of Curgh Castle.

Xaver heard all of this in bits and pieces over the following few days from servants, nurses, and guards. He had no part in the search. Even if the castle surgeon would have allowed it, he wouldn't have helped. Instead he kept to his chamber day and night. He was resting, he told his father, recovering from his wound. But his father knew him too well to be fooled. It was clear to both of them why he had shut himself away, like a novice seeking his first vision from the gods. He was hiding from his closest friend at a time when he should have been rejoicing.

His gleaning had been everything he had hoped, and more. He had seen himself in the court of the king in Audun's Castle, a captain in the King's Guard, serving under his father. He had seen his wife as well. He didn't know her name yet, or whence she had come. But she was beautiful, with long, shimmering black hair and a pretty oval face. And they were in love. That much had been clear.

It was a Fating straight out of his dreams, and his father's. He

123

should have been celebrating. He should have been enjoying the Revel.

Finally, three days after the incident on the castle wall, Xaver's father ordered him out of his chamber to the castle training grounds. He still couldn't practice, of course—his arm was wrapped in a heavy bandage. But his father had made it clear that he was to watch the soldiers hone their sword skills. "If you can't practice," his father had said, "at least you can learn a bit this way. It's better than sitting there in your chamber all day." Mostly, however, Xaver just scanned the ward for Tavis, dreading the moment when he would finally see the duke's son.

Had he attacked Tavis as the lord had attacked him, he would have been executed within a day. But Tavis would suffer no such fate. Xaver remained the young lord's liege man, of course, despite the blood that had flowed from his wound four nights before and the dull ache that he felt there still, beneath the surgeon's dressing. He had sworn fealty to the duke's son years ago, before their Determinings, in a ceremony that neither of them had understood fully. Certainly he had not. They had been children, best friends. And since one of them happened to be the son of a duke, and the other the son of the duke's liege man and captain of the guard, it had seemed the natural thing to do. Both fathers had urged them to wait, at least until after their Determinings. But Tavis, headstrong even then, had insisted, and Xaver, not knowing any better, had gone along.

He still remembered the words. They were emblazoned on his mind like the seal of Curgh on a castle banner.

"I, Xaver MarCullet, son of Hagan and Daria, free and noble born to the thaneship of MarCullet, swear fealty and service to you, Tavis of Curgh, sole heir to the House of Curgh, its lands and privileges. For as long as we both live, or until you release me from this pledge by your word, I am your liege man, sworn to protect you, honor you, and stand by you. My sword is yours, my shield is yours, my life is yours."

He had kissed Tavis's hand—both of them had thought this quite amusing—and Tavis had then laid his palms on Xaver's head and sworn an oath of his own. Those words Xaver had long since forgotten, though he knew that the duke's son had pledged to preserve the honor of both their houses and to receive Xaver's service in good faith. It had all been over in a matter of moments. Afterward they had run out of the room, through the stone corridors, and into the bright sunshine of the ward to resume their swordplay. It might as well have been another game, another imaginary adventure.

Except that as they grew older, and Xaver's memory of their other games faded, this one did not. Instead, that moment in the duke's chambers, under the watchful eyes of their fathers, had taken on greater importance with each year that passed, until it sometimes seemed to be all that remained of their childhood friendship. Tavis would never release him from the oath he had taken, and Xaver would never ask him to. They were bound to each other, like brothers. But there had been times, more numerous than he cared to acknowledge, when Xaver found himself wondering if he would have taken the oath at all if they had heeded their fathers' advice and waited.

He wouldn't have on this day. That was certain.

"They say he threw his first flask at the duke," one of the guards whispered to another, as they stood in the hot sun watching Xaver's father run a unit through their training exercises. "That's why he went down to the cellars in the first place."

"Actually that's not true," Xaver heard himself say. He kept his voice low, so that his father wouldn't hear.

"You're sure?" the guard asked.

"I was there. He just threw it at the floor. It wasn't aimed at the duke."

One of them nodded, but the other just stared at him.

"Why do you defend him?" he asked.

"I'm not defending him, really. I'm just trying to keep any more stories from spreading."

"If it was me, after what he'd done, I'd be starting a few stories myself. Truth be damned, and him with it."

Xaver had been leaning against the castle wall. But now he stood straight, and drawing his dagger with his good arm, he pointed the tip of it at the man's heart.

"Take back those words or defend yourself!" he said as forcefully as he could.

"But young master, I was just—"

"Your words are an affront to Lord Tavis, and so an affront to me, his liege man! I'm sworn to protect his name as well as his life, and unless you unsay what you have said, I'll cut you down where you stand!"

The guard glanced at his friend, before facing Xaver again, a puzzled look on his face. After a moment he shrugged. "I take it back, my lord."

Xaver stood there a few seconds longer, breathing hard, the hand holding his blade trembling slightly. Finally, he lowered his dagger. "Very well," he said quietly. Looking beyond the guard, he saw that his father was watching him, as were the rest of the men.

His father took a step toward him, a question in his gaze, but Xaver shook his head, stopping him.

He returned his dagger to its sheath and faced the two guards again. "Perhaps I should return to my quarters. Tell my father I was . . . not feeling well."

"Of course, my lord," the first guard said. "My apologies if we gave offense."

Xaver shook his head. "It's all right."

He started to turn away, but as he did the two men bowed to him. Unsure of what to do, he murmured a quick thank-you and hurried back toward the north end of the castle.

He couldn't explain what he had just done. The guard had been right. Tavis didn't deserve to be protected, not by him, certainly not with such ferocity. Yet he had drawn his blade on the man, for a comment that hardly deserved notice.

His arm throbbed as he walked across the city ward, his eyes trained on the ground. The guards at the inner gatehouse said nothing to him, and he entered the duke's ward in silence, almost afraid of what he might say if he spoke. Despite all the time he had spent alone in his room, he had slept poorly the past few nights. Perhaps rest was all he needed. That, and some time away from Tavis.

When he saw the duke's son standing in the corridor outside the door to his quarters, Xaver realized that he wasn't likely to get either any time soon.

"I've been waiting for you," Tavis said, looking uneasy.

Xaver stopped a short distance from him. "So I see." He kept his voice utterly flat. He'd offer no hope of forgiveness, at least not yet.

Tavis licked his lips, his dark eyes wandering around the narrow hallway like a fly searching for something on which to alight. Finally they came to rest on Xaver's bandage. "How's your arm?"

"It hurts."

"I'm sorry, Xaver," he said, his expression so pained that Xaver wondered if he was going to cry. "I didn't . . . I was drunk. I don't know . . ." He shook his head. "I'm sorry."

"What is it you want, Tavis?" Xaver asked.

The duke's son closed his eyes briefly. "Can we do this in your chamber? Please? It won't take long."

He wanted to refuse, to send Tavis away. But Tavis was the lord, and Xaver his liege man. Without a word he pushed his door open and gestured for Tavis to enter the room. Stepping inside himself, he closed the door and faced his friend.

"Now, what do you want?"

Tavis began to walk around the small chamber, pausing briefly at the lone window to gaze out at the ward before wandering again. He looked pale, as though he still felt the effects of his drinking. He had bathed recently, and he smelled faintly of perfumed soaps. Still, it seemed to Xaver that the stench of vomit and stale wine clung to him, as the smell of a horse stays with the rider after a long journey.

"I'm not very good at this," Tavis said.

"You've already apologized. You don't need to do it again."

The lord halted and for the first time that day he looked Xaver directly in the eye. "Yes, I do. I don't think I can ever apologize enough." He resumed his pacing. "But that's not why I'm here."

He took a long breath, stopping just in front of Xaver. This time, however, he didn't allow their eyes to meet. "I want to release you from your oath," he said, a slight flutter in his voice. "Actually, I don't want to, but I feel that I should offer after . . ."

He swallowed, not bothering to finish the thought.

Xaver couldn't believe what he was hearing. He had expected apologies, pleas for forgiveness, perhaps even excuses. But not this.

"You're releasing me?" he said, knowing how dull-witted he must have sounded.

"Yes. If it's what you want, I'll do so formally tonight, before both of our fathers and the rest of the court."

A voice in Xaver's mind screamed for him to accept the release, to unburden himself of this boorish young lord before his entire life was ruined. He knew, however, that he could not. He had taken the oath as a child, and there had been days when he had regretted his foolishness for doing so. But his friendship with Tavis was older than memory, and he had pledged himself to serve the lord for a lifetime. More than that, though, he had been sustained through the worst days of their friendship by the promise that he sometimes glimpsed within his friend. Beneath the spoiled child, beyond the selfish, hot-tempered youth, there was a man who carried both his father's strength and his mother's wisdom. At times, Xaver went for turn after turn without seeing this man, and he grew discouraged and fearful for the kingdom. But then he would appear again, just as Xaver began to lose hope. Just as he had now, in Xaver's chamber, with an offer bespeaking the humility and generosity of someone worthy of Audun's throne.

Tavis's offer hung before him, glittering like a jewel. He was drawn to it. He had longed for such freedom often enough, and none would blame him for accepting. Not his father, nor the duke. The duchess might. But none of that was to the point. He would blame himself. It was a jewel he saw before him. And the price—his honor—was too steep.

"I don't want to be released, my lord. I am your liege man, and I will be until one of us is called by Bian to the Underrealm."

In spite of everything, Xaver was moved by the look of relief that flashed across the lord's face.

"Thank you," Tavis whispered. "I didn't—"

Xaver stopped him with a raised finger. "I'll continue as your liege man," he said. "But . . ." He hesitated. "But I don't want to see you for a few days."

The color that had returned to the lord's face drained away again. "How many days?"

"I don't know. Not very many. Maybe just until the end of Amon's Moon."

"But . . . But that's more than half a turn." He sounded like a child learning that he was to be denied a favorite toy.

"All right," Xaver said reluctantly. "Then until the Revel leaves Curgh."

Tavis opened his mouth, no doubt to complain again. But he appeared to think better of it. After a moment he pressed his lips together and gave a single nod.

Once more they lapsed into silence, although they continued to stand facing each other, as if preparing to duel. Xaver would have liked to tell Tavis to leave, but he gave up that right when he refused Tavis's offer of release. So he just stood, staring off to the side, wishing the lord would say his goodbyes.

"It seems I'm to marry," Tavis said at last, a false, brittle brightness to his tone.

"Yes, I know."

The duke's son gave him a puzzled look.

"We were discussing your betrothal the other night at dinner. You don't remember?"

His face shaded toward crimson. "No, not a thing," he said, his gaze dropping to Xaver's bandage again. "If the guards and my father hadn't told me what I had done to you, I wouldn't even have remembered that."

Another silence, but Xaver didn't allow this one to last very long.

"So you're going to marry Brienne," he said.

"Yes. Not for some time yet, Father says. Apparently Kentigern wants to be certain that he'll be marrying his daughter to a king." He smiled weakly. "I can't really blame them."

"I'm happy for you, my lord. From all I hear of her, it seems that Brienne will make a fine queen."

"We're going to Kentigern with the start of the next turn," the young lord said, as if he hadn't heard. He hesitated. "You'll come, won't you?"

What choice did he have? "Of course, my lord."

"Stop calling me that."

"What would you have me call you?"

"Tavis, of course. What do you think?"

Xaver exhaled slowly and nodded. "All right," he said. "I'll address you that way the next time I see you, after the Revel is gone."

He intended the words as a farewell, and judging from the way Tavis's color rose again, it seemed that the lord took them as such.

Tavis stared at him for a moment before giving a nod of his own. "Very well." He crossed to the door and pulled it open. But he paused on the threshold and looked back at Xaver. "Thank you," he said. "I don't know what I would have done if you had left me."

He wasn't sure what to say. A thousand things leaped to mind. But in the end he just murmured, "You're welcome."

Tavis stepped into the corridor and closed the door behind him, leaving Xaver alone in his chamber.

"I had a chance," he whispered to himself, as the clicking of Tavis's footsteps receded down the hallway. "I had a chance and I chose to remain."

It was all he could have done. He knew it. He had made his decision years ago. Perhaps he had been too young, but he had made it nevertheless. Still, there was an aching in his chest, as if he had just lost something precious. And his arm throbbed with a pain that brought tears to his eyes.

The room was dark save for two candles burning beside the bed and the bright yellow flames dancing like tiny wraiths in the palm of Cresenne's hand.

"It's really not that hard," she said, her pale eyes fixed on the flames, a small smile tugging at the corners of her mouth. She had pulled on his shirt, but her legs were still bare, one of them stretched out to the side and the other tucked beneath her. Her hair, falling loose to her shoulders, seemed to glimmer in the firelight. "It's just a matter of using the healing magic at the same time you conjure the flame. As long as the two powers work together, you can't feel a thing." She turned her hand over slowly and the flames crept to the back of her hand, suddenly looking more like bright spiders than wraiths.

Grinsa, still naked beneath the light blanket, smiled. He had seen this done before—he had even tried it himself once or twice, although he could not tell her that—but never with such grace. Certainly never by anyone so beautiful.

"There was a man in my home village who used to do that," he said, watching her hand. Watching her. "He used to call it the fire glove."

Her smile broadened, though her eyes never strayed from her hand. "The fire glove," she repeated. "I like that. We always just called it balancing the flame." She turned her hand back so that the flames, which had turned purple and gold, like the seal of the king, could gather in a small circle in her palm. Cresenne stared at them for another moment before giving a small sigh. It almost appeared that her breath extinguished the fires, so suddenly did they vanish. Even with the candles, their disappearance seemed to plunge the room into darkness. It took Grinsa a few seconds to realize that Panya was up, her pale light seeping in through the thin white curtains.

"I wish I could teach that to you," Cresenne said, tipping her head to the side, her eyes shining like stars.

He smiled again. "So do I."

"Do you ever wish that you had access to other magics?"

Grinsa hesitated. He couldn't tell her the extent of his power. He knew that. But where was the harm in revealing just a little of himself? This was only their second night together, but already Grinsa felt that he could love this woman. It had been so many years since he had felt this way about anyone, more than he cared to count. For a long time after Pheba died he wondered if he would ever love again, and he had actually vowed never to love a Qirsi woman.

He had been away from their home in eastern Eibithar when the pestilence struck, on an errand he had long since forgotten. Had he stayed with her he might have been able to use his power to drive the illness from her body. Just as the village's Qirsi healers might have, had they gone to her when she summoned them. But like so many of his people—and Pheba's people as well, he had to admit—the healers did not approve of their marriage. It was an affront to Qirsar, they said. It was a betrayal, as loathsome as Carthach's had been. So they refused to go to her, leaving her to die when it would have been so easy to save her.

When he returned to their village a few days later, he found that their home had been burned to the ground, as were all homes that had been visited by the pestilence. Nothing of their life together was spared, save the golden ring he had given her on the day of their joining. And that he had to remove from her charred finger. Afterward, he vomited until his stomach was empty and all that came up was blood.

How was he ever to love again? How could he ever live among the Qirsi again? For some time he did neither. Even after he joined the Revel a year later, he avoided Trin and the other Qirsi, passing what little time he spent away from the gleaning tent and his room with Eandi singers and dancers. Gradually, however, his pain began to recede, and with it his hatred of his own people. He could never forget what the healers in his village had done, but neither could he deny who and what he was.

His willingness to love again was far slower to return. He had many affairs—it was easy, traveling with the Revel. There was no time to fall in love, which was just as well. Only recently had he begun to realize that his half-turn romances were not enough for him. And only when he met Cresenne did he understand that he was ready to love again.

It was not just that she was beautiful, though there could be no denying that she was. It was not just that she was a gleaner in the Revel, someone with whom he might have a future. What made him realize that he could love her was, ironically, the resentment she carried for Carthach. Such resentment had killed Pheba. That he could be drawn to her so powerfully in spite of this told him more clearly than anything else that he was healed. Pheba would always be a part of him. He had never stopped loving her, and he never would. But the pain of losing her had finally dimmed. At last, he was ready to give his heart to another.

Perhaps the way to begin was with a gesture of trust, even though she couldn't possibly understand the magnitude of what he was doing.

"Actually, I do have access to other magic," he said, abruptly making his decision.

He sat up, the blanket falling to his waist.

"What do you mean? I thought—"

"I'm a fine gleaner," he said, "but I have little skill with my other power. That's why I never speak of it." He grinned. "Still, I can do a few things that might amuse you."

Holding out his hand as she had done a few moments before, Grinsa summoned a small cloud of mist from the air. At first it was formless, like a lone white cloud on an otherwise clear day. But then it began to turn. Slowly at first, but building speed quickly until it looked, save for its size, like a whirlwind brought forth by Morna herself. It was an easy feat. Any Qirsi with the power of mists and winds could have done it. But it was all he dared reveal to her.

After allowing the tiny whirlwind to spin in his palm for several moments, he sent it up into the air, so that it hovered between them. It felt good to be using his power for something other than just gleanings, and he closed his eyes briefly, savoring the sensation of magic flowing through him. An Eandi friend of his had once asked him what it was like to wield such power, to tap into his magic.

"You might as well ask a soldier what it's like to use a sword," he had answered. "You might as well ask a musician what it's like to play his instrument."

His friend had not been satisfied by the reply, but Grinsa had been at a loss to explain it any better. In many respects the magic of his people was like the trades of the Eandi. They were taught to use it as children; just as the Eandi had their apprenticeships the Qirsi had theirs. And just as the trades of the Eandi soon become ingrained, so did the Qirsi magic, until the act of wielding the power was as natural and immediate as thought. The only real difference was that the magic he carried killed him just a little bit every time he used it. Few of the Eandi knew that. It was common knowledge that the Qirsi lived far shorter lives than did the Eandi, and that they tended to be weaker and more sickly. But few outside his own race knew that the use of magic further shortened their lives. Such knowledge might have caused those who depended upon Qirsi magic, as the duke of Curgh depended upon Fotir's, to hesitate when the use of power was called for. Or it might have given a weapon to those who hated the Qirsi. For whatever reason, this was not a fact that his people had seen fit to share with the Eandi.

On the other hand, the cost exacted by the use of their magic gave great meaning to the sharing of power by two Qirsi. Even Cresenne's fire glove and the tiny storm he was spinning for her now, though simple and small, were considered gifts of surpassing generosity, perhaps even a declaration of love.

"This is wonderful," Cresenne said, gazing at the whirlwind, a child's smile on her lips. She raised her hand tentatively toward the small cloud. "May I hold it?"

"Of course."

Her eyes met his for an instant before returning to the little storm. She placed her hand just under it and he made it touch down on her palm.

"It's cold!" she said, laughing. "It feels like snowflakes falling on my hand."

He said nothing. It was enough just to watch her watching the whirlwind. After some time, she lowered her hand again, leaving the spinning cloud hovering once more. He let it hang there for a few seconds more, before summoning a small wind that rushed through the cloud, leaving nothing but wisps of vapor that swirled in the air like smoke from a dying candle and then vanished.

"Thank you," she said after a brief silence. "That was lovely."

"You're welcome."

"I think you're being too modest, though. You're quite skillful with winds and mists."

Even feeling as he did for her, even as he sat on her bed, wondering if he might already be in love with her, Grinsa heard an alarm bell in his mind, as if some distant sanctuary were engulfed in flames.

"Not really," he said, keeping his voice light. "That's about the extent of what I can do. It's not as though I can summon a true whirlwind, one that could actually do any damage."

"Are you sure? I'd have thought that creating and controlling a small wind like that would be even harder than conjuring a big one."

She was right, of course. She was backing him into a corner, and he was helping her do it. Under any other circumstances, with almost anyone else in the Forelands, he would have felt as though he were under attack.

"I suppose you may be right," he said, pushing those thoughts from his mind. "One day I'll have to try conjuring some bigger winds. Perhaps you can help me."

"Gladly, though I doubt you'll need much help."

He grinned, but said nothing, hoping that the conversation would end there.

"You've heard that the duke and his son are traveling to Kentigern?" she asked after a moment.

It was the one other matter he would have liked to avoid discussing. But what could he do?

"Yes, I'd heard."

"It seems that Tavis has recovered from his Fating. The Lady Brienne will be a fine duchess and queen."

He nodded. "No doubt." But the mere mention of Tavis's impending journey to Kentigern was enough to darken his mood. Much of the image he had summoned from the Qiran during the young lord's gleaning remained a mystery to him, including the circumstances of Tavis's imprisonment. The Tavis who appeared in the stone had been young, so clearly they hadn't very long to wait before the events unfolded. But by the same token, Grinsa was certain that the duke's son would never be placed in a Curgh prison, and he had assumed from this that he still had some time to prepare. The announcement from the duke that he and Tavis would be traveling to Kentigern changed everything. Notwithstanding this arranged marriage, relations between the two houses had never been good; Grinsa had little trouble believing that the dungeon he had seen in the stone could be found in Kentigern Castle.

"You have doubts about the marriage?" Cresenne asked, furrowing her brow.

"No, not at all."

"Then what?"

Grinsa hesitated, trying to decide how much he could tell her.

"It's the Fating, isn't it?" she said, before he could answer. Her pale eyes widened. "Whatever you saw in Tavis's Fating is going to happen in Kentigern."

"I don't know that for certain." But there was an admission in his denial.

"You fear that it's so."

Grinsa took a long breath. "Yes."

"What are you going to do?"

He shrugged. "What can I do? It's his fate." Honesty had its limits, even where Cresenne was concerned.

She nodded. "I suppose you're right." She looked down at her hands, as if suddenly uncomfortable. "Is it terrible, this thing that's going to happen to him?"

"Cresenne—"

"I'm sorry," she said, quickly shaking her head. "Forget I asked. You've probably already told me more than you intended."

He smiled again and took her hand. "I'm afraid I have. But how could I help it?"

Her cheeks colored and she leaned forward to kiss him lightly on the lips. "You can't," she whispered. "You can't help it at all."

She sat back, staring at him, her face as luminous as Panya, and in a motion as graceful as the flames she had conjured a short time before, she pulled his shirt off over her head. She shook her head so that her white hair fell down about her shoulders, framing a smile that made Grinsa's heart pound within his chest. Her skin was so white it seemed to glow. His eyes wandered to her breasts, small and round and perfect, and slowly, as though of their own will, his hands reached for them. She leaned forward to kiss him once more, more deeply this time.

She was right, he knew. He couldn't help himself. And in that moment, he didn't really care.

Lying in bed, waiting for sleep and watching Panya's light move slowly across the walls of the room, the Qirsi couldn't help but smile.

A few days before, Tavis's Fating had seemed a dangerous complication, one that might serve as a warning to the young lord, one that would upset their plans. Not anymore. The boy had been seen in the city, wandering about, enjoying the Revel. Or at least trying to.

All who saw him thought he looked glum; some said he seemed always to be on the verge of tears. But at least he was out of the castle.

Tavis's Fating remained a mystery. With every day that passed, however, with every indication the young lord gave that he had recovered from the shock of that vision, the details of what he saw in the Qiran became less important. From what the Qirsi understood, no one knew what Tavis had seen except the gleaner and the boy himself. People in Curgh Castle and the city around it had heard only that the young lord had been deeply disturbed by his gleaning. And that, the Qirsi had also come to understand, might actually help deflect suspicion. Had his gleaning been of glory and long life, the fate that awaited Tavis in Kentigern might arouse memories of Filib of Thorald and his untimely death. As it was, this time next turn, people of Curgh would be talking of how Tavis had been marked for tragedy by the gods, and of how his Fating had already proven all too accurate. The substance of that Fating was no longer of any concern.

What mattered now was that the duke's plans to take his son to Kentigern were still in place. There had been some talk of delaying the journey, possibly even canceling it. Not anymore, though. The gods, it seemed, were with them. Kentigern offered the assassins they had hired the perfect opportunity to carry out their plans. It was far away from where the Revel would be, which, after Thorald, was absolutely necessary. But more than that, Kentigern was Curgh's rival, and Eibithar's first line of defense along the Tarbin. This was almost too perfect.

The only problem that remained was the gleaner himself, and in the end the Qirsi was fairly confident that even Grinsa wouldn't stand in their way. The man was bound by custom to tell no one what he had seen of Tavis's Fating. The only question was how long he would keep silent if the young lord's fate differed too greatly from what the stone had revealed.

In the end, the Qirsi decided, it wouldn't matter. Grinsa was a Revel gleaner, nothing more. Even if he tried to raise questions about the boy's fate, few would listen to him. Because in the days since Tavis's attack on Xaver, the Qirsi had formed a plan, a brilliant plan. It bore little resemblance to the murder of Filib in Thorald, but it promised to be no less effective in upsetting the Order of Ascension. In fact, the Qirsi had good reason to hope that it might do far more than that. If the assassin followed the instructions he had been given, nothing Grinsa did or said could save the boy.

Most importantly, the Qirsi knew that this plan would raise no suspicions. A simple murder might. Certainly another act of thievery gone wrong would. But not this. This would be utterly convincing. Tavis, by his recent actions, had made it so.

Chapter
Eight

✦

entigern Castle stood atop Kentigern Tor, forty leagues southwest of Curgh. A lone horseman pushing his mount, or even a small company taking advantage of the moons to ride past sunset, might have made the journey in four or five days. But the duke of Curgh had never been one to travel with a modest complement of servants, and leaving as they did with the first day of the new turn, they had no moonlight to speak of for the first several nights.

Before their departure from Curgh, Xaver's father had urged Javan to take a large contingent of guards.

"It's not just that I don't trust Kentigern," Hagan had said, "though I'll admit that I don't like you being under his roof without me there to keep an eye on things."

"I need you here," the duke told him. "I need to know that the duchess and my castle are safe."

"I know that. But you're going to be within sight of the Tarbin and a few thousand Aneiran soldiers. If I can't go, you should take one hundred men with you, eighty at the least."

Javan had laughed, laying a hand on Hagan's shoulder. "I can't show up at Kentigern with a force so large. Aindreas will think I've come for a siege rather than a betrothal. Besides, where would Aindreas put them all?"

Hagan tried to smile at the duke's humor, but his face colored in a way Xaver recognized. He was truly concerned about their journey to Kentigern. Probably it didn't help that Xaver was going as well. His arm had healed, but he had only begun to practice with a sword again a few days before they left.

"Sixty, then," Hagan said to the duke, as if haggling with a merchant in the city marketplace.

"I'll take forty, Hagan. Tavis and Xaver are quite skilled with their swords, as am I. And we'll have Fotir with us as well. You've nothing to worry about."

Stubborn as he was, Xaver's father knew when to back down in a discussion with the duke. "Yes, my lord."

Even with this relatively small number of guards, their company numbered close to seventy. As always, the duke and Tavis had a number of their servants with them, as well as several cooks and tasters from the Curgh kitchens, and a few of the castle's stablehands. As a result, the company had taken more than half the waxing to ride as far as they had, and still, on this, their eleventh day, they would be lucky to reach Kentigern before the ringing of the prior's bell.

It had not been an enjoyable journey for Xaver. They skirted the coast of the Strait of Wantrae, which afforded them some fine views of Wantrae Island and, far in the distance, the shores of Braedon. But there was little else to see, save the Heneagh River, and once they crossed that and entered Kentigern Wood, there was even less to look at.

Tavis was uncharacteristically quiet throughout their travels, although he insisted on riding with Xaver nearly the entire way. Fotir and the duke usually rode ahead of them, talking quietly about one thing or another and offering Xaver little relief from his boredom.

The nights were no better. After eating their evening meal, Tavis would sneak off with a wineskin, leaving Xaver alone with the duke and his minister. Perhaps the young lord thought that he was being discreet, or maybe he didn't care. But Xaver hadn't failed to notice the dark expression Javan always wore as he watched his son skulk off into the night. After the second night, Xaver considered saying something to Tavis. He soon thought better of it, however. Too often he had found himself trapped between the duke and his friend. He wouldn't put himself there again, not after all that had happened.

His anger at the duke's son had ebbed, but he could not say that it was gone entirely, nor could he be certain that it ever would be.

Every day since their conversation in his chamber, Xaver had railed at himself for refusing Tavis's offer of release from his oath. There was little else he could have done. He knew that. Yet, he punished himself anyway.

"What if I hate her?" Tavis asked suddenly.

They were riding side by side in the dense shadows of Kentigern Wood, their horses walking at a steady pace. The forest offered some relief from the heat of the day, but Tavis's face was damp with sweat, as was his own.

"Who?"

"Brienne, of course. What if I meet her and decide that I can't love her?"

"It's a good marriage, Tavis."

"That's not—"

Xaver stopped him with a shake of his head. "Loving her is beside the point." He couldn't help but smile. "You'd hardly be the first duke or king in Eibithar's history to take a mistress as compensation for a loveless marriage."

He spoke in a low voice, but apparently his words carried on the wooded path, for a moment later the duke glanced back at them from atop his mount, a wry grin on his bearded face.

"You've a wise friend there, Tavis," he said. "You'd do well to keep him by your side."

"Thank you, my lord," Xaver said, acknowledging the compliment with a nod.

Javan and Fotir slowed their mounts for a moment allowing Xaver and Tavis to pull abreast of them. The Qirsi nodded to the two boys, but said nothing.

"So you're worried about meeting Brienne?" the duke asked his son, as the four of them began to ride together.

"Not really worried—"

"It's all right," Javan said. "I was so afraid of meeting your mother that I couldn't keep down the food I ate at the feast. Her mother was so offended that she nearly called off the joining ceremony."

Tavis gave a wan smile. "I'm sure Brienne will make a fine wife, Father."

"I expect so, as long as she's not too much like her father. Or her mother for that matter." Javan and Fotir shared a grin. "The point is, Xaver's right. We need Kentigern right now. This marriage strengthens our house, and so strengthens the kingdom. Brienne will be a good queen. If you're lucky, she'll be a good wife as well. If not, you'll find someone else to warm your bed, just as others in your position have." Quite abruptly, the duke's face reddened. "That's not to say that I have. Your mother has been my love as well as my duchess."

Tavis suppressed a smile. "Of course, Father."

"It's the truth!"

"Best to move on, my lord," Fotir said, smirking and giving Xaver a quick wink.

Javan cleared his throat. "I quite agree." He looked over at Xaver. "Have you ever been to Kentigern, Master MarCullet?"

"No, my lord."

"Well then, you've got something to look forward to. No one is more fond of Curgh Castle than I, or more admiring of those who built it. Over the centuries the House of Curgh has withstood sieges that would have brought other houses to their knees. But that said, I've seen few castles as impressive as Kentigern and few cities as well fortified."

"My father has told me much the same thing, my lord."

"Don't expect it to be as spacious as Curgh, or as elegant. In many ways it's more a fortress than a castle. As close as it is to the Tarbin it has to be. But as Eibithar's first defense against the Aneirans for the last thousand years, it has rarely failed us."

A thousand years. The castle was older than the kingdom itself, as was the enmity between Eibithar and her neighbor to the south. Legend told that the wars over control of the Tarbin dated back to the days of Binthar and the ancient clan wars, when the only thing uniting the warring tribes of the north was their shared hatred of the southern clans.

"Has Kentigern ever fallen?" Tavis asked.

"Once, in Durril's War. The Aneirans managed to hold it for a time, and the castle's strength worked against Eibithar's army. But Grig, Kentigern's duke at the time, knew the fortress better than the Aneirans. One night, after Durril sent the bulk of his army northward to win Curgh and Heneagh as well, Grig managed to sneak a small force in through one of the sally ports. They took back the castle and Grig killed Durril." Javan frowned, looking at his son and then at Xaver. "You both should know all of this. I've paid your tutors enough silver and gold over the years to pave the streets of Curgh."

"We know of the war, Father. But the tutors leave the study of military matters to Hagan, and he's more concerned with teaching us sword craft. He says the other can wait until we're skilled enough to defend ourselves."

Javan glanced at Xaver, who shrugged.

"It's true," he said. "Father has never had much use for history, even when it pertains to waging war."

His frown deepening, the duke shook his head. "I'll have to discuss this with him when we return." He looked over at Fotir. "Make a note of it."

The Qirsi nodded, pulling from his riding cloak a small scroll and a writing quill.

"You were telling us of Durril's War, Father," Tavis prompted.

"There's little else to tell. After Durril's death, the Aneiran army was thrown into disarray. The king's forces had little trouble driving them back across the Tarbin."

"And that was the only time Kentigern fell?" Xaver asked.

"As far as I know. It withstood Aneiran sieges during the Bastard's War and the Harvest War, and it also fought off sieges by other Eibitharian houses during the First Civil War and the Thorald-Curgh Alliance."

Tavis's eyes widened. "Did we lay siege to Kentigern?"

"Skeris the Third did, yes, but that was more than three hundred years ago."

"And we couldn't take the castle?"

Javan shook his head. "No, we couldn't. To be honest, I wouldn't want to try it now either, even with Aindreas leading them." He glanced at Xaver. "Don't tell your father I said so."

All of them laughed. A moment later Tavis asked his father something else about one of the civil wars, and for a long time the four of them rode together, the duke giving Xaver and Tavis a lengthy lesson in Eibitharian history. For the first time since leaving Curgh, Xaver actually was glad to be traveling with the duke and his son, and much as he looked forward to arriving at Kentigern, he savored this last leg of their journey.

They emerged from Kentigern Wood just as the sun began to descend toward the the Strait of Wantrae. The air was hot and heavy and dark thunderclouds gathered to the east, above Harrier Fen. Before them, perched like a great eagle atop the craggy, white mass of Kentigern Tor, stood the castle.

It was simply designed. As Javan had said, there was little elegance here. Like most fortress castles, including Audun's Castle in the City of Kings, Kentigern consisted of an outer wall and a taller inner keep, both of them regular in shape and constructed of ponderous grey stone. Every wall of the fortress bristled with towers, some of them broader than others, but all of them lofty, no doubt affording the soldiers stationed on their ramparts clear views of the Tarbin, and the lands that lay beyond. Above the towers banners rose and fell lazily in the hot wind. Most bore the crest of Kentigern, a silver lynx standing upon a white mountain, framed by a bright blue background. But above the two towers that stood on either side of the nearest castle gate flew the purple and gold of the Kingdom of Eibithar and the brown and gold crest of Curgh.

Even at that moment, bathed as it was in the golden light of late day, Kentigern Castle could not be called beautiful, not as Galdasten was said to be, or Rennach. Rather, the castle looked as formidable and unassailable as the mountain on which it sat. It appeared as ancient as the stones that composed its walls, as though it had been there since Elined first laid her hand upon the Forelands. And it seemed to Xaver that the Goddess herself would never find the strength to topple it. Staring up at its towers and walls, he wondered how anyone could ever think to attack it. Which, perhaps, was what those who had built it had in mind.

On the slope of the tor and the broad plain stretching from its base, the small houses and markets of Kentigern City seemed to kneel before the castle, like the priests and priestesses of Ean offering obeisance in the cloisters. These smaller buildings were surrounded by an imposing wall that ran all the way up the tor to the castle. Towers rose from it at regular intervals, and Xaver could see at least two fortified gates from the edge of the wood. He could also see the spires of a sanctuary rising above the wall from the southeastern corner of the city. Xaver could not recall seeing any sanctuary with such tall towers, and he wondered which of the four gods the people of Kentigern honored.

"You're looking at the sanctuary?" Fotir asked him in a low voice.

Surprised, Xaver turned to face him. "Yes, actually I was. Do you know which of the gods they worship there?"

"Such grand spires," the Qirsi said, his yellow eyes still fixed on the sanctuary. "The people of Kentigern must love their god very much. Or perhaps fear him."

Xaver said nothing, waiting for Fotir to answer his question. But already he knew what the first minister would say.

"It's Bian's Sanctuary. They worship the Deceiver." He looked at Xaver and smiled in a way that made the young man shudder. "Don't look so aghast, Master MarCullet. The people of Kentigern live under constant threat of attack. While some of Eibithar's houses have gone centuries without fighting a battle, Kentigern has fought dozens of skirmishes with the Aneirans over the past five hundred years. Is it any wonder that they devote themselves to the god of the Underrealm?"

"We've still more than half a league to go," Javan called to them before Xaver could answer. "I'd like to make the nearest gate before the prior's bells."

The duke spurred his mount forward without waiting for a response and the rest of the company followed. But Xaver could not stop thinking about what Fotir had said. He was right, of course. It made perfect sense, though he could not imagine what it would be like to worship the god of death. He was called the Deceiver, because it was said that he seduced Elined, goddess of the earth, by taking the guise of Amon, her mate, and so begot the dark sisters: Orlagh, goddess of war, Zillah, goddess of famine, and Murnia, goddess of the pestilence. The mere sight of Bian's Sanctuary forced Xaver to consider once more the fears his father had expressed to Javan before their departure. The duke had dismissed them with a joke and a smile, and Xaver had forgotten them almost as soon as they rode out of Curgh. But he realized now that they were riding straight toward the Tarbin. If war broke out with Aneira, which was always a possibility regardless of the time of year, they would fight the first battle. Xaver did not slow his mount, but he found that he was suddenly aware of the dagger he wore on his belt and, almost without thinking, he reached back to make certain his sword, wrapped in its oilcloth, was still strapped to his saddle.

The road to the city and castle wound gently past open fields and scattered farms. At one point they passed a small boy standing by the road with a large herd of sheep. He stared openmouthed at the company as it rode past, before turning and running back to his small house, screaming to his mother that the castle was under attack.

When they had covered roughly half the distance remaining to the castle, Javan had them stop so that he could summon two of his guards to the front of the company. He positioned the two men on either side of him and had them unfurl the colors of Eibithar and a banner bearing the crest of Curgh.

"Tavis will ride with these men and me the rest of the way," the duke said, looking back at Fotir. "You and Xaver will ride behind us, followed by the rest of the guard and then the servants."

"Yes, my lord," the Qirsi said. "I'll see to it immediately." He wheeled his mount and started riding back through the company, shouting commands.

Javan turned to Tavis and then Xaver. "Say nothing unless you're addressed directly. Keep your bearing dignified, but remember to smile. We're guests here. Everything we do reflects upon the House of Curgh."

"Yes, Father."

"Of course, my lord."

They spoke at the same time, then glanced at each other and shared a grin. Xaver's pulse had quickened and he realized that he was far more excited about reaching Kentigern than he had imagined he would be. Given the expression on Tavis's face, it appeared that the young lord felt the same way.

Fotir rejoined them a short time later.

"All is ready, my lord," he said.

"Good. Let's ride."

Once more the company resumed its advance on the castle. Xaver could see the gate clearly now, as well as the guards standing on either side of it. As they drew nearer, two men joined these guards, both of them carrying golden horns that shone in the sun. Raising the horns to their lips, the men played "The Deeds of Binthar," Eibithar's war anthem, the notes ringing out across the open plain like the meeting of sword blades. Ending that, they moved right into "Roldan's Fleet," a ballad honoring Roldan the Second of the House of Curgh, who led Eibithar to a naval victory over Wethyrn in the early days of the kingdom. All the while as the men played, Xaver and the company of riders from Curgh continued their approach to the city gate. Just as they slowed their mounts, covering the last stretch of road to the city, the musicians ended this second piece and began another. Xaver did not know what this one was called, though he knew that it honored Grig, the hero from Kentigern of whom the duke had spoken earlier in the day. And as the first notes of this ballad soared into the warm air, the timing of it all so perfect that Xaver could not help but be moved, Aindreas, duke of Kentigern, rode out through the gate to meet his guests.

Xaver had never seen the duke before, though he had heard tales of him for years. The Tor Atop the Tor, they called him, and Xaver could see why. He was enormous, a mountain of a man, both tall and wide of girth. His hair and beard were the color of rusted iron, unmarked by grey or white, though he was said to be at least as old as Javan. His pale grey eyes were almost a perfect match for the color of Kentigern Castle, and his skin was ruddy, as if he had been standing for hours in a cold wind. He had an overlarge nose and his eyes were set a bit too close together, but his was a kind face nonetheless.

Behind him, riding as well, came an attractive woman who was as slight and delicate as Aindreas was large. Her hair was golden and long, her eyes deep brown. This had to be Ioanna, Kentigern's duchess. Xaver glanced quickly at Tavis, who was staring at the woman as well. If Brienne looked at all like her mother, the young lord was a lucky man indeed.

There was a Qirsi man with the duke, and a legion of soldiers resplendent in silver and blue. Kentigern and Curgh might have been rivals in the past, but it seemed to Xaver that Aindreas had spared no effort in honoring Javan and his company.

The duke of Kentigern sat motionless on his great black mount, regarding his guests coolly as the music played. When the horns fell silent, he raised a gloved hand in greeting.

"Be welcome to Kentigern, my Lord Curgh," he said. "We are most pleased to have you as our guest."

"My Lord Kentigern," Javan answered, "we thank you for this most splendid reception. You honor us with your deeds and kind words."

The two men swung themselves off their horses and, stepping forward, embraced each other like brothers as cheers went up from both companies.

Javan turned to face the riders from Curgh and made a small gesture that Xaver did not understand. An instant later, however,

Tavis and Fotir dismounted, and he realized that the duke expected him to do the same.

"Aindreas, duke of Kentigern," Javan said, "please allow me to introduce my son, Lord Tavis of Curgh."

Tavis took a step forward and bowed. "My Lord Kentigern," he said. "This is a great honor."

"It's good to see you, Lord Tavis. The last time we met you were but a boy. I hear you've some skill with a blade, now."

"A bit, my lord."

"Perhaps you'll show us what you've learned from old Hagan at our tournament two days hence."

Tavis grinned. "It would be my pleasure, my lord."

Javan nodded approvingly before indicating Fotir, with an open hand. "Perhaps you remember my first minister, Fotir jal Salene."

"Lord Kentigern," Fotir said, bowing in turn.

Aindreas offered a thin smile and a nod, but he said nothing.

"And this is Xaver MarCullet," Javan said, "liege man to my son."

"Hagan's boy!" the duke of Kentigern said, looking him over with a critical eye.

Xaver bowed, knowing as he did that he was not doing so with as much grace as Fotir, or even Tavis. "My Lord Kentigern."

"Are you a swordsman as well, boy? Is it in the blood?"

"My father has taught me well, my lord," he said. "I can't say if it's in my blood or not."

"It is, my lord," Tavis offered, surprising Xaver. "He's every bit the swordsman I am. Perhaps more."

Aindreas raised an eyebrow. "High praise indeed. It looks like we'll be making room for two more in the tournament."

Kentigern's duke placed a large arm around Javan's shoulders, something Xaver had never seen anyone do before, not even the duchess of Curgh. Together the two men walked back toward the city gate.

"Come, Javan," he said. "Ioanna's eager to welcome you. It's a shame Shonah couldn't make the journey as well, though I understand. The roads being what they are today, with thieves and knaves around every corner, I wouldn't take Ioanna or Brienne far from the tor unless I had to."

At Fotir's prompting, Tavis and Xaver followed the dukes so that they could go through another round of introductions. The duchess of Kentigern was somewhat reserved in her greetings, although she smiled kindly when Xaver bowed to her. Javan showed no more warmth in meeting Kentigern's Qirsi, a man named Shurik, than Aindreas had when presented with Fotir. Nor did the two white-haired men exchange more than a simple nod when they were introduced to each other.

After what seemed a long time and an endless exchange of greetings and names, the two dukes finally began to lead the rest of them through the city of Kentigern toward the castle. The city lanes were lined on both sides with hundreds of people, who cheered for the dukes and stared admiringly at the soldiers.

"They want to see the duke and Lord Tavis."

Xaver looked to the side and saw Fotir eyeing him closely, the hint of a smile on his lips.

"It's not often that kings come to Kentigern. Yet here are two men who will sit on Audun's throne. The people you see here will speak of this day for the rest of their lives." The Qirsi man spoke quietly, with a look in his pale eyes that made Xaver wonder if there was more to what he was saying than was immediately apparent.

"I hadn't thought of that," he said, not knowing quite how the first minister expected him to respond.

"I know. I think all of us forget at times. We must guard against that. They depend on us."

Xaver considered this for a moment before nodding slowly. Fotir smiled and faced forward again.

Ioanna was explaining that Brienne was in her chambers, preparing for the welcoming banquet that was to begin with the ringing of the twilight bells. There she would be presented formally to Javan and her betrothed.

"That's how I met Aindreas," she said. "It's a custom I thought worthy of being passed on to my daughter."

"I quite agree," Javan said. "Don't you, Tavis?"

"Of course, Father," the young lord said. "My Lady Ioanna is most wise."

Once more, Javan nodded his approval, and a moment later he and the duchess and duke of Kentigern returned to their conversation, leaving Xaver free to look around the city.

In many ways, Kentigern resembled Curgh. Both had large marketplaces that were filled with merchant shops, smithies, peddlers' carts, and inns. From what Xaver could see, Kentigern's outer lanes, like those in Curgh, served as avenues for shepherds and others bringing livestock to the markets from the surrounding country-side. The only important difference between this city and Curgh seemed to be the position of the castle. While Javan's castle was by far the greatest structure in Curgh, it was very much a part of the city. Shops and homes sat just beside it. Kentigern Castle, however, sitting atop its tor, towered above the walled city as if separate from it. The city ended at the base of the rise, giving way to large boulders, low grasses and stunted trees, jagged stone bluffs, and a single winding road that appeared to turn back on itself several times before finally reaching the castle gate. It was as if those who had built the castle sought protection not just from the Aneirans on the far side of the river, but also from their own townsfolk.

"Is it what you expected?" Fotir asked, drawing Xaver's gaze once more. The first minister had never before shown this much interest in him.

"I'm not sure that I was expecting anything in particular," he said, keeping his voice low. "It's a magnificent castle."

Fotir nodded and looked up at the castle. An instant later, though, he was facing Xaver again. "Lord Tavis seems to have recovered from whatever it was he saw in his Fating."

"I suppose," Xaver said, abruptly feeling uncomfortable.

"Do you know what he saw, Xaver?"

"No. And even if I did, I wouldn't tell you."

"Even after what he did to you, you still protect him. The duke is right: Lord Tavis is fortunate to have you."

Xaver kept silent, his eyes fixed on the road.

Fotir, though, had a knack for reading his thoughts. "Or perhaps that's not it at all. Perhaps you just don't trust me."

Xaver looked at him briefly, but still he said nothing.

"Good, Master MarCullet," the Qirsi said. "Very good. You're wrong about me. I'm a friend to both you and your lord. But there are far fewer of us than you may think. Trust no one. Better to mistake a friend for an enemy than an enemy for a friend."

Once more the first minister faced forward, leaving Xaver to ponder what he had just heard. There was a warning in Fotir's words, as well as an offer of friendship. If only Xaver knew which to believe.

Leaving the Revel had been no easy task. It helped that Jedrek stayed, though Cadel spent the better part of a day convincing his friend to do this. Had both of them left, it would have drawn the attention not only of the other singers, but quite possibly of Yegor and Aurea as well, and that was a risk he couldn't take. As it was, he went leagues out of his way to avoid raising suspicions about his departure or giving away his true destination.

The Revel left Curgh seven days before Pitch Night, traveling northeast through the Moorlands toward Galdasten. On the third night out, a full five leagues from Curgh, Cadel and Jedrek feigned a fight over a woman in a country tavern. It was a ruse they had used before. Indeed, several of the singers had been with them long enough that they were no longer surprised when the two of them came to blows. So when Cadel left the Revel, nursing a bloody nose and a cut on his cheek, it barely raised an eyebrow among the other performers.

He took a horse and headed toward Sussyn, turning in the direction of Kentigern only midway through the next day, when he was certain that no one who knew him could see. He stopped in a small village just outside the walls of Heneagh along the way, although only long enough to pay a visit to the village apothecary. From there, he rode as fast as his mount would allow to Kentigern Tor.

He knew that the duke of Curgh and his party would not be leaving the castle until the beginning of the next turn. Few chose to be abroad on Pitch Night, even during Amon's Turn, when the dark legends posed little immediate danger. So Cadel had several days to make up the distance he had traveled with the Revel. That, and the fact that he was riding alone, allowed him to reach Kentigern a full three days before Javan's arrival. Still, he did not enter the city until he saw the riders of Curgh emerge from Kentigern Wood, and then he did so through the north gate, on foot, in the company of several peddlers and a goatherd driving a flock from a coastal village.

As much as he relied on Jedrek, for companionship as well as his blade, Cadel was forced to admit that he enjoyed working alone. He had only himself to worry about. He could move at his own pace, make decisions without having to explain them. He felt free. He found himself taking greater risks and savoring the added danger. The Qirsi had offered to give him the names of some allies in Kentigern, just in case something went wrong, but Cadel refused. He explained that he had friends of his own scattered throughout Eibithar, which was true, though none of them were here. He said as well that he preferred to work alone, though at the time he hadn't realized how true this was. But he didn't reveal the real reason, that he wanted no more contact with white-hairs than was necessary. He certainly didn't want to be turning to them for help. It was bad enough that he would have to turn to them when the deed was done and he crossed the Tarbin into Aneira.

No, he didn't need the names of the Qirsi's friends. He had no intention of allowing anything to go wrong.

From the city gate, he made his way to the winding road leading up to the castle, where the people of Kentigern watched their duke escort his guests up the slope of the tor. When several of the city folk followed the dukes up the road to the castle gate, Cadel fell in with them. Most of them turned away before reaching the castle guards, but Cadel continued to the gate and started to walk through as if he belonged there.

"Hey, you!" one of the guards shouted, brandishing a gleaming pike. "You can't just walk into the castle. What do you think this is, Bohdan's Night?" He laughed, as did the other guards standing with him.

"No, sir," Cadel said, bowing his head and making himself stammer. "I'm one of the duke's men, sir. One of his servants."

"I never seen you before."

"Forgive me, sir. I meant the duke of Curgh."

The guard hesitated, then glanced at his friends. None of them had any idea what to do either.

There was never an easier time to slip into a castle, even one as well guarded as Kentigern, than when another noble was visiting. True, there were soldiers and servants everywhere, but none of them knew who belonged and who didn't, and all of them feared giving offense to the wrong person. These fools were no different.

"Better let him go," one of the other guards said, keeping his voice low. "Captain will have your head if Curgh makes a fuss and it's your fault."

The first guard stared at Cadel for a moment before nodding. "Go on then," he said. "Next time stay with the others."

"Yes, sir," Cadel said, bowing again, and hurrying through the gate. "Thank you, sir."

And just like that, he was in.

He had been in Kentigern Castle several times before, usually as a singer, and he knew just where to go. Stepping into the outer ward, he turned to the right and made his way to the north gate-house, which was just next to the kitchens. The guards there eyed him doubtfully, but let him pass, apparently assuming that since he had already satisfied the guards at the first gate, they needn't bother with him.

He caught the scents of roasting meat and fresh bread the moment he entered the inner ward, and he hurried toward the smells. As he often told Jedrek, there was no safer place for an assassin in a castle than the kitchens, and on this night Kentigern's kitchens were no exception. One of the duke of Kentigern's lesser ministers barked commands at servants, who ran in every direction, trying to prepare for the feast that was to begin within the hour. Cooks yelled for the pantrymen to bring more meats or flour, while the kitchenmaster shouted at the cooks to hurry the meal along. It was bedlam. Perfect.

A stout man emerged from the castle cellars struggling with three large containers of dark wine, and Cadel hurried to his side, taking two of them.

"Many thanks," he said with a grin. "I had a boy who was helping me fill these, but he disappeared when it came time to carry them."

"Glad to help," Cadel said. "Where are you taking them?"

The man gestured toward the steps leading up to the duke's hall. "There's a table inside the hall where we're to put all the wine. I'll be up and down these stairs a dozen times at least getting it there." He raised an eyebrow. "Unless I have help."

Why not. The busier he was, the less likely anyone would be to notice him. And having access to the wine would serve him well later. "Sure," he said. "I'll help."

"You must be from Curgh," the man said as they carried the wine up to the duke's hall. "I haven't seen you before."

"You're right, I am. My name is Crebin."

"Pleasure to meet you, Crebin."

They placed the containers of wine on a long oak table and the man held out a thick hand.

"I'm Vanyk, cellarmaster here in Kentigern."

Cadel smiled. "My father always told me that I had a talent for befriending the right people."

Vanyk laughed, as they started back down the stairs for the next load of wine. "Your father was right. Help me with these flasks and I promise you won't go thirsty while you're on the tor."

Even with two of them carrying the containers, it took Cadel and the cellarmaster nine trips to get all the wine into the hall. By the time they finished, the duke of Kentigern's guests had entered the dining chamber and started to seat themselves at the long tables arranged around its perimeter. Cadel scanned the hall for the dukes and Lord Tavis, but they hadn't arrived yet.

Both he and Vanyk were soaked with sweat and covered with dust from the cellar.

"I need to change my clothes," Vanyk said, wiping the front of his shirt. "The duke's cellarmaster can't come to a feast looking like this."

Cadel nodded. "I understand. Perhaps I'll see you later in the evening."

He started to walk back toward the kitchen, but Vanyk didn't let him get far.

"Those are your riding clothes, aren't they?" the man asked.

Cadel turned to face him. "Yes."

"Do you have any others with you?"

He made himself laugh. "My lord duke is generous, but not that generous. This is all I have."

Vanyk looked at him with a critical eye for a moment. "You're a tall one, aren't you?" he said. "Still, I think I might have something that will fit you."

Cadel narrowed his eyes. "What for?"

"I can't serve all that wine myself, and if that whelp who abandoned me before thinks he'll be pouring wine for the duke and his lady, he's in for a surprise."

The gods were smiling on him, though he didn't let Vanyk see how pleased he was.

"I'm not sure," he said. "I help in the kitchens back home, but I'm no server. I'd probably spill it all."

Vanyk smiled. "Nonsense. You'll be fine. And I can promise you five qinde for the night, plus a flask of my finest Aneiran gold wine."

It would have been a good offer even if he hadn't already made up his mind to accept.

"All right," he agreed. "But I prefer a Sanbiri dark."

"Done!" Vanyk said, nodding his approval.

They shared a quick smile before his new friend started back down into the castle cellars, gesturing for Cadel to come as well. He followed the cellarmaster down the stairs, and as he did his hand wandered briefly to the pocket of his breeches. The small vial he had gotten from the apothecary in Heneagh was still there.

Chapter
Nine

✦

The memory of his Fating haunted Tavis like one of Bian's wraiths, hovering at his shoulder during the day and darkening his dreams at night. At times he managed to forget about it, to immerse himself in whatever he was doing at that particular moment. But these instances were fleeting at best. Always the image of himself in the dungeon returned, flashing in his mind's eye like lightning on a warm day, and filling his heart with a dread that chilled him like sudden rain.

He had hoped the journey to Kentigern would bring some comfort, or at least a respite from his fears. Every time he looked at Xaver, however, and remembered what he had done to his friend, it all came back in a rush. Not the actual attack on his liege man; of that he could recall nothing. But he saw each day what it had done to their friendship, and he knew that it was all because of the vision offered to him by the Qiran. He slept poorly throughout their travels and had little appetite. His thirst for wine and ale, on the other hand, had never been greater, and though he had not drunk himself into a rage again, the way he did the night of his gleaning, he had been quietly drunk nearly every night since. If Xaver was aware of this, he had kept it to himself. His father, the duke, Tavis was sure, had noticed nothing.

Their arrival in Kentigern lifted his mood a bit. He was deeply impressed by the castle itself, and moved by the warm welcome they had received from Aindreas and Ioanna. At the same time, though, Kentigern presented Tavis with another problem: he was not at all

certain that he wanted to be married to Brienne. It had been years
since he had seen her, and his memories of their meeting had grown
dim and confused with time. He did not recall her being at all pretty.
She had been heavy, with thin yellow hair that hung limply to her
shoulders. Her disposition had been no better and they had spent
most of their days together teasing each other and fighting. When at
last he and his father started back toward Curgh, Tavis had been
glad to leave her and Kentigern behind.

Still, everyone assured him that she would make a good queen
and a fine wife. He wanted to believe them, and he had to admit that
his impression of Kentigern had changed markedly since his last
visit. He was grown now, nearly a man. Perhaps his impressions of
the Lady Brienne would reflect this as well. Certainly if she was anything like her mother, he would have to rethink his opinion of the
girl entirely.

"You'll be sitting with Brienne at the banquet," his father told
him, his voice low.

They were walking through a stone corridor in Kentigern Castle's inner keep. Following their arrival at the castle, Javan, Tavis,
and the rest of their company had been escorted to quarters on the
east side of the keep, where they were given ample time to shed
their riding clothes, bathe, and put on attire more appropriate for
the evening's celebration. Now four of Aindreas's guards, all of
them ornately dressed, led them to the duke's hall, where the banquet would take place. Fotir and Xaver were behind Tavis and his
father, as were two of Javan's servants, including, Tavis had noticed,
his taster. The display of warmth and friendship at the city gate
notwithstanding, his father was not yet ready to surrender all to
trust.

"I'll be just beside you with the duke and duchess." Javan was
looking straight ahead even as he spoke to Tavis, a smile fixed on
his lips.

"What about Xaver?"

"I don't know where he'll be. Close by, I'm sure. But your attention should be on Brienne. I want you to do your best to make a
favorable impression."

"I should think that she's the one who needs to worry about
favorable impressions. Curgh is about to take the throne, not
Kentigern."

At that, his father did look at him. "We need this match, Tavis," he said, his voice, though still quiet, carrying a hint of anger. "Don't do anything to muck it up."

Tavis almost protested. He was no stranger to court occasions. He had dined with dukes, thanes, earls, and barons. He once sat at the king's right hand for a feast in Audun's Castle. Hadn't he proven himself to his father over the past few years? Hadn't he acquitted himself well at the city gate that very day?

As if in answer, it all came back to him once again, sapping him of his certitude and resolve like an unseen blow in the middle of a sword fight. His Fating, what he had done to Xaver, his behavior at the banquet that same night, of which he remembered only scraps as well, though he had heard enough. His father had every reason to caution him in this way.

"Yes, sire," he said at last, his voice barely carrying above the echo of their footsteps. "I'll do my best."

Javan nodded once and faced forward again. "Very good."

They descended a narrow, spiral stairway, walked through another small corridor, and stopped in the wide doorway leading into the hall. With the exception of the enormous blue banner on the far side of the room, which bore an image of the silver lynx atop Kentigern Tor, the crest of Kentigern, there was little to separate this grand room from the duke's hall in Curgh Castle. It was long and wide enough to accommodate more than a dozen of the long wooden tables on which servants were piling roasts, stews, cheeses, steamed greens and roots, bowls of fruit, and large flasks of wine. It had a high ceiling, supported by great, soaring stone arches. Torches were mounted on the walls, and candles flickered on every table and on wall sconces.

Near the far wall, just below the Kentigern crest, another large table stood atop a dais. This, of course, was where the dukes and their families would sit, but for now the table remained empty. No doubt Aindreas was waiting to enter the hall until Javan and his company had taken their seats. Tavis knew that his father would have done just the same had the banquet been in Curgh, but still he saw that Javan's jaw tightened for just an instant.

"Come," the duke said, unable to mask the annoyance in his tone. "It seems we're to take our places before Aindreas makes his entrance."

"Javan, duke of Curgh!" a man announced as Javan stepped into the room. "Lord Tavis of Curgh! Fotir jal Salene, first minister to the duke of Curgh! Master Xaver MarCullet of Curgh!"

Those who had already arrayed themselves around the lesser tables looked up from their wine and food and began to applaud.

Javan forced a smile, as did Tavis, and they made their way to the dais, nodding and waving to Aindreas's other guests as they walked among the tables. Reaching the small stairway that led up to the main table, Javan hesitated.

"Do you know where we're to sit?" Tavis asked.

"No," his father said, looking annoyed again. "We'll sit where we see fit. Let Aindreas arrange his people around us when he arrives." He started up the stairs. "Just leave a place for Brienne beside you."

"All right," Tavis said, following him onto the dais.

Fotir and Xaver climbed the stairs as well, sitting to Tavis's right, farther from the center of the table. Several servants approached them bearing food and wine. Tavis had to keep himself from draining his goblet as soon as it was filled.

"Touch nothing yet," Javan said, looking at Tavis and then past him to Fotir and Xaver. "Seating ourselves is one thing. Eating or drinking without our host is quite another."

Fortunately, they hadn't long to wait. No doubt Aindreas had just been awaiting word of Javan's arrival in the hall to make his appearance. Only a few moments after he and his father took their seats, Tavis heard a flurry of whispers from the tables nearest the hall entrance. The man who had announced their arrival a few moments before now stepped to the middle of the room, commanding everyone's attention.

"Aindreas, duke of Kentigern!" he said. "Ioanna, duchess of Kentigern! Lady Brienne of Kentigern! Lady Affery of Kentigern! Lord Ennis of Kentigern!"

The duke entered the hall, followed by his wife, daughters, and son, all of whom looked tiny beside him. The other guests began to applaud.

"His Eminence Barret Crasthem, prelate of Kentigern, Disciple of Ean! Shurik jal Marcine, first minister to the duke of Kentigern!"

Tavis barely noticed the others. With the mention of Brienne's name, his pulse had started to race, until all he could hear was the surging of his own blood. Seeing her did nothing to calm him. She was as fair as her mother, perhaps more so. Like the duchess, she had long golden hair that fell to the small of her back in tiny ringlets. Her face was round, her cheeks and chin still slightly plump with youth. But already one could see in her features a hint of her mother's delicate beauty; the fine nose and full lips, the large, round eyes, though Brienne's were grey, like her father's. She wore a sapphire gown, cut low enough to reveal the flawless grace of her neck and the beginning of the soft swell of her breasts.

"Not quite as you remembered her, eh?"

It took Tavis a moment to realize that the comment had been directed at him. He tore his eyes from Brienne and found that Xaver was watching him, a smile on his boyish face.

The young lord shook his head. "Not even a little."

"Stand up!" Javan said in an urgent whisper. He and Fotir were already on their feet, and both of them were gesturing for Tavis and Xaver to rise as well.

They scrambled to their feet just as Aindreas ascended the steps to the dais.

"My Lord Curgh!" he said, his voice booming like a thunderclap. "We are most pleased to have you join us tonight." He held out a huge hand, indicating the others in his party, who were joining them on the raised floor. "Allow me to present to you my daughter, Lady Brienne."

Brienne curtsied deftly.

"A pleasure, my lady," Javan said. "I see that you are blessed with your mother's grace."

"Thank you, my Lord Duke," she said. "I am honored to see you again. Be welcome in our home."

Javan placed a hand on Tavis's shoulder. Tavis couldn't remember the last time his father had touched him.

"This is my son, Lord Tavis."

He and Brienne faced each other, and Tavis bowed, fearing as he did that he would topple over, or knock his head into her, or do some other fool thing to humiliate himself. For just an instant he wondered if a man could be thrown in a dungeon for offending a noblewoman. He thrust the thought away.

He straightened again. "My lady," he said, not trusting himself with anything more.

She curtsied once more, smiling coyly. "My Lord Tavis. The last time we met we teased each other and fought like wild dogs. I hope we manage to get along better this time."

The others laughed appreciatively, but Tavis merely smiled at her, searching for something clever to say in return.

"Our houses are on better terms now, my dear," Aindreas said, beating him to it. "If Javan and I can get along, I would hope the two of you can as well."

Once again the others laughed, and this time Tavis allowed himself to join in. But he and Brienne held each other's gaze for a moment longer, and Tavis wondered how that homely girl he remembered from his last visit to Kentigern could possibly have grown into this woman before him.

In the next instant, the duke of Kentigern introduced them to his younger daughter, Affery, forcing Tavis and Brienne to break eye contact. The younger girl was pretty as well, though she could not have been much past Determining age. Then he presented his son, Ennis, who, though no more than eight or nine years, was the image of the duke, with red hair and a solid build. Finally, Aindreas introduced the prelate of Kentigern's cloister, a tall, thin man named Barret who, like all of Ean's prelates, had shaved his head, giving his narrow, bony face a buzzard-like appearance. He smiled at Javan, Tavis, and Xaver as he greeted them in turn, but his eyes held little warmth. He did not even look at Fotir, nor, for that matter, did he pay any heed to Shurik, Aindreas's Qirsi minister. Nevyl, Curgh's prelate, was much the same way. Perhaps he was a bit friendlier toward Eandi strangers, but he had little use for men or women of the sorcerer race.

"Please sit," Ioanna said, pitching her voice so that all in the hall could hear her. "Our cooks have been days preparing for tonight's feast. Eat freely, all of you. And be welcome in our home."

Tavis almost sat, but remembered at the last moment to hold Brienne's seat for her first. Then he lowered himself into his chair, accidently brushing her arm with his as he did.

"Excuse me," he murmured, feeling his face color.

"You seem nervous, my lord," she said. "Would you rather I sat elsewhere?"

"No!" he said, a bit too quickly.

She giggled. "Very well."

Tavis gave a small smile. "Do you intend to keep mocking me for the rest of the evening?"

"Do I have to stop when the evening is done?" she asked innocently.

He couldn't help but laugh. "And what have I done to deserve such treatment?"

"You don't remember?"

His eyes widened. "Is this all about my last visit?"

"You were awful to me," she said, though the smile lingered on her lips. "I've never forgotten."

"I was ten years old," he said. "And you were no less awful to me."

"I was defending myself. I had to. You were merciless."

"Then I was a fool, my lady. I obviously knew nothing of beauty or grace or intelligence. For if I had, I would have showered you with gifts and praise, rather than with teasing and cruelty."

She blushed and her eyes lingered on his for an instant before looking away. They were the color of smoke from dying embers or of sea clouds carrying a storm.

"That was prettily said, my lord," she told him. "My mother taught me to be wary of men who spoke so sweetly."

He laughed. "Even the man who is to be your husband?"

"You mean the man who would be my husband."

He stared at her, opened his mouth to say something, then closed it again, not knowing how to respond.

After a few moments, Brienne began to laugh.

"You don't take kidding very well, do you, my lord?"

Tavis looked away. "No," he admitted. "I never have."

"You'll have to learn if you're to have me as your wife. I'm afraid I'm not always as staid as a court lady ought to be."

Once more, he wasn't certain how to respond. He was accustomed to the somber dignity of Curgh, where there was little room for mirth or gaiety. His mother and father were capable of engaging in lighthearted banter when their position in the court demanded it, but they rarely did so in the privacy of family conversation. He and Xaver joked with each other a good deal; Tavis thought of himself as having a sense of humor. But it was one thing to laugh with his friend, and quite another to trade jests with the beautiful woman sitting beside him. Yet, awkward as it seemed, Tavis liked the idea of it. It would be a complete departure from the way he had been raised, which perhaps explained why he found the notion so attractive.

"I think I can get used to that," he said.

For the first time that evening, she gave him a smile seemingly free of irony. "I'm glad."

163

Tavis reached for one of the flasks. It was filled with dark red wine, Sanbiri no doubt. As much pride as Eibithar's winemakers took in their vintages, most agreed that there was none finer in the Forelands. He reached for Brienne's goblet.

"May I pour for you?" he asked.

There could be no denying that they made an attractive pair. The young noblewoman, with her golden hair and her striking sapphire gown, and the boy who would be king, with his youthful good looks, his dark eyes, the color of which was almost a match for the lady's dress, and his festive silk shirt and doublet. They looked just the way young royalty ought to look: beautiful and spirited, shining like gems in sunlight. An entire country could fall in love with such a pair. No doubt the Qirsi men and women Cadel were working for understood that. No doubt that was why he was here.

They were on their second flask of wine, but Cadel had yet to add the sweetwort to their drink. For one thing, others at the table were also drinking from the flask and he could not risk having any of them affected by the herb as well. More important, sweetwort, when mixed with wine, worked quickly, and he had no desire to see his prey fall under its influence here in the duke's hall.

In large enough doses, sweetwort could kill, but Cadel wanted it for its narcotic qualities. A simple poisoning might work well under certain circumstances, but in this instance he needed something a bit more subtle. Sweetwort, the flavor of which could be masked by the wine, and the effects of which could be enhanced by the same, had the added benefits of being widely available and commonly used. Nearly every apothecary in Eibithar sold it, and none would think twice about doing so. Nor had he needed to buy much; the small vial he carried held more than enough for both Lord Tavis and Lady Brienne.

It was simply a matter of waiting for the right moment and slipping the extract into their wine without anyone noticing.

For an arranged betrothal, the two appeared to be getting along quite well. Before leaving his father's court in Caerisse, Cadel had witnessed more than his share of these feasts, and rarely had he seen them lead to any sort of romance, at least not so quickly. But Tavis and Brienne had spent much of the meal whispering to each other, laughing, and gazing into each other's eyes. The wine helped, of course. Up here, in the northern reaches of the Forelands, wine was known as the spirit of Bohdan, for the god of mirth and festival. But to the south, in Caerisse, Sanbira, and even Aneira, where the people truly knew something of making and drinking wine, it was called Adriel's nectar, for the goddess of love. Still, even without the wine, Cadel thought that the young couple might have found something in each other to love, if only they were given the chance.

The confections that concluded the feast had been served some time before, and now a number of guests at the lesser tables started to stand and stretch and make their way slowly out of the hall. The two dukes, taking little notice of the rest of their dinner companions, were in the midst of a sometimes heated discussion of the Aneiran threat and how best to cope with it. The duchess and Aindreas's first minister were deep in conversation as well, although their voices were pitched lower and Cadel could make out little of what they said. The duke of Kentigern's other children had long since been bundled off to bed.

Had he been taken with a young woman and eager to slip away with her, unnoticed by their parents, Cadel would have chosen that moment. Apparently, he and Tavis had this much in common. Or perhaps he and Brienne did; it was hard to say who was leading whom when they rose carefully from their places at the table and stepped off the dais, casting furtive looks back at the two dukes. For just an instant, Cadel feared that he had miscalculated. But as they reached the door leading out of the hall, the young lovers hesitated. A moment later, Tavis looked in Cadel's direction and raised a single finger.

Cadel smiled and nodded before turning to the table on which he and the cellarmaster had placed the wine. At the same time, he pulled the vial from his pocket, removed the small cork from its top with a quick motion of his thumb, and hid the open vial in the palm of his hand. With his back to Tavis, he glanced quickly to each side to see that he wasn't being watched. Then he pulled the stopper from a container of Sanbiri dark and in the same motion poured the sweetwort extract into the container. In all it took him just a few seconds, no more time than it should have to open a flask.

Lifting the flask, Cadel hurried to where Tavis and Brienne stood.

"Here you are, my lord," he said. "Would you like goblets as well?"

Tavis's eyes wandered once more to where his father sat. "No," he said, his voice low. "This is all we need."

He turned away, taking Brienne's hand again.

"Thank you," she said over her shoulder, as Tavis led her away.

Cadel made himself smile. "You're welcome, my lady."

It had been years since Cadel felt any regret for what he did to earn his gold. Yet in that single instant, when her eyes met his, he felt as though his heart froze in his chest and his own life stood balanced on the edge of a blade.

Then the moment was gone, and Cadel was left to consider what would come next. Tavis and Brienne would be going to the guest chambers on the southeast end of the castle, where Tavis was staying. Cadel was certain of it. He was noble-born and had spent much of his life studying the courts of the Forelands. He knew that Brienne's quarters were too near to those of her mother and father, and too closely attended by her servants. He knew as well that Tavis's quarters would offer ample privacy. Usually the son of a visiting duke would share his chambers with others in the duke's company. But Tavis was no ordinary lord; he was to be king after his father. To avoid offending either Javan or the boy, Kentigern would give each his own chamber. It would mean more cramped quarters for the rest of the visitors from Curgh, but that was of little consequence next to the comfort of the future kings.

Once again there was little Cadel could do but wait. The young ones needed time to make their way to Tavis's room and more time still to drink the wine. For now he returned to the wine table. Vanyk would expect him to help clean the empty flasks and return the unopened ones to the cellar. That was fine. Sweetwort worked quickly, but its effects lasted for hours. The later it got, the lower Panya would be in the night sky, and the harder it would be for the castle guards to see him climbing like a spider across the wall of the inner keep.

He was not a fool, nor was he blind, though his fool son seemed to think he was. Javan was just thankful that Aindreas hadn't seen

166

Tavis and Brienne sneaking off with that container of Sanbiri red. Their betrothal notwithstanding, the duke would have tried to take a sword to Tavis's neck had he known that they were alone together, with a full flask of wine no less. Fortunately, Aindreas had consumed a great deal of wine himself this night. He was too busy fulminating against the Aneirans and their allies in Braedor to notice how loud his voice had grown or how his continued pounding on the table was upsetting the plates and goblets. He certainly wasn't about to notice that his daughter had vanished with Javan's son.

As far as Javan could tell, neither the duchess nor Aindreas's Qirsi had seen them leave either. A small miracle. He could only guess how Ioanna would have felt about it. Had Shonah been here, she would have been furious.

For his part, Javan couldn't really blame his son. Brienne was a beautiful girl, and that dress . . . The duke shook his head. He and Shonah were not old by any means, but there were times when he wished they both were *that* young again.

At least Tavis hadn't done or said anything to offend Brienne. Given his recent behavior—his drunken appearance at the dinner in Curgh last turn, his attack on Xaver, his late-night drinking, which he tried so desperately to hide—that had been Javan's greatest fear. Considering what might have happened this evening, Tavis and Brienne running off together into the night was really not so bad. Just so long as Tavis didn't do anything stupid, like get the poor girl pregnant, everything would be fine.

The duke closed his eyes at the thought and took a long pull of wine. If that happened, Aindreas would kill Tavis, and probably Javan as well. He wondered briefly if Shonah had ever spoken to the boy of such things. Not likely. She probably saw that as a father's responsibility, and Javan couldn't really argue with her. His father had spoken to him about it, on a hunting expedition the two of them had taken when Javan was ten. He already knew most of what his father told him, having heard it all from guards, servants, and some of the older boys in the court, and their ride seemed to last twenty years. Even now, the memory of it made Javan squirm. Perhaps that was why he had avoided such a discussion with his own son. By now he had to assume that Tavis knew all that he needed to know. And more, no doubt.

"You will do tha', won' you, Javan?" Aindreas said, the words running together like paints on a wet canvas.

Javan stared at him blankly. The big man's face was even more flushed than normal and his pale eyes were red-rimmed and half closed.

"I'm sorry, Aindreas. My mind must have wandered. The wine, you know. What were you saying?"

"I said, I asked Aylyn t' sen' some of the King's Guard to the Tarbin an' he hasn' done a thin' 'bout it. But you will, won' you? I have jus' so many men, Javan. I can' protect the castle and the city and the river and continue to pay all of them. I'll be out of gold in no time." He leaned forward, his breath stinking of wine. "I don' need a lo' of men. Jus' a thousan' or so. Jus' enough to watch the river. You can do tha', right?"

He knew that this was what it would be like to be king. Aylyn himself had warned him, during his most recent visit to Audun's Castle a few turns back.

"Someone is always asking for something," the old king said at the time. "And more often than not, someone else is asking you to do the opposite. For all its glory, being king grows more burdensome with each year."

Javan just hadn't expected that it would start so soon.

"I'm not even on the throne yet, Aindreas," he said, sounding, he knew, like a parent putting off a demanding child. "I can't make any promises without knowing more about how the king's men are assigned currently."

Kentigern frowned. "If you need more men, you ca' recruit them. If you don' like the way they're assigned, you ca' reassign them."

"Forgive me, my Lord Kentigern, but I couldn't help overhearing your request."

Javan turned toward the voice and saw that Fotir and Xaver had moved closer, taking the seats that had been occupied by Tavis and Brienne. Fotir, who had spoken, was smiling now, though Javan could see that the smile was forced.

"What of it?" Aindreas demanded, eyeing the Qirsi with suspicion.

"Reasonable as your request is, my lord, I needn't explain to a man of your insight that my Lord Duke could not assign men to the Tarbin so soon after taking the throne. Such a move by a new king could easily be misinterpreted by the Aneirans as a prelude to attack."

Javan gave his first minister a grateful smile before facing Aindreas again.

"He's right, of course," the duke said. "Even if I were already king, there would be little I could do right now. I'll be happy to consider your request, Aindreas, but I think we should wait for a more appropriate time."

Kentigern shook his head and let out a sharp, loud laugh. "You're jus' like him, aren' you? Not even king yet, an' already acting like th' dithering old man you're t' replace. Hiding behind th' lies of your Qirsi, keeping your men t' yourself while th' rest of us guard your borders an' fight your battles." He drained his goblet and threw it on the floor. "I should ha' known better than t' trust a Curgh."

"Aindreas! That's enough!"

Ioanna was glaring at her husband, her cheeks as red as if she had been slapped. All other conversations in the hall had ceased and everyone who remained, even those at the lesser tables, was staring at the two dukes.

Kentigern, who had winced at the sound of his wife's voice, now turned toward the duchess.

"Look at yourself," she said. She glanced at the other tables and exhaled through her teeth. "Look at yourself," she repeated, her voice lower, but her tone no less severe. "Drunk as a soldier at the Revel, and insulting our guest. Insulting your future king!"

"We're jus' talking, my dear. Tha's all. Javan knows tha'."

"My deepest apologies, my Lord Duke," Ioanna said, looking past Aindreas to Javan. "At times my husband forgets that he can't drink the way he once did. The mind is always the first thing to age, but the last to mature."

Javan smiled at the adage, which was as old as the castle in which they sat.

"It's all right, my lady. As Aindreas said, we were just talking. I took no offense."

A lie, but a gracious one.

"You're too kind, my lord," she said, casting another withering look at her husband.

Kentigern did not seem to notice. His attention was elsewhere, although belatedly so.

"Where's Brienne?" He sat up straighter and shot a look at Javan. "Where did tha' boy of yours take her?"

Graciousness had its place, but enough was enough. He leveled a finger at Aindreas and opened his mouth, though he still wasn't sure what he was going to say. Mercifully, Fotir answered before he could speak.

"They left a short while ago, my lord, saying something about a walk through the ward and gardens."

Javan didn't believe a word of it. No one snuck off with a flask of wine simply to take a walk. But once more he was thankful for the minister's quick mind.

"A walk, eh?" Aindreas said, sounding doubtful as well.

"Let it be, Aindreas," Ioanna said. "We brought them together to build the foundation for a marriage. Let them have their romance."

"Romance? They're children!"

The duchess smiled. "She's six turns older than I was the first time we met. And you remember the walk we took, don't you?"

Aindreas's face turned the color of the wine. "If you're tryin' t' put my mind a' ease, you're doin' a damned poor job of it."

"When have I ever tried to ease your mind?" she asked, glancing mischievously at Javan.

The others at the table laughed, and after a moment Aindreas joined in. It clearly took an effort, however.

"You're lucky you've only th' one boy, Javan," he said, after the laughter had subsided. "A father can' help but worry about his girls."

"Don't you worry about Ennis?" Ioanna asked, raising an eyebrow.

Aindreas shook his head. "It's not th' same. My girls . . ." He stopped, shaking his head again. "Well, let me put i' this way: how much trouble can a boy get in? Right, Javan?"

Javan smiled weakly and made himself nod. Yet, even as he did, he found his gaze wandering to Xaver MarCullet. The sleeve of the boy's shirt hid the dark, angry scar that ran across his arm, but Javan could see it in his mind, an answer to Aindreas's question.

How much trouble, indeed.

Had Brienne not been leading the way, he would surely have gotten lost already. Perhaps it was all the wine he had drunk at dinner, but

Tavis was finding it difficult to follow the twists and turns of Kentigern Castle's passageways. He felt as though they had been walking for an eternity and still none of it looked familiar.

She was holding his hand, her skin smooth and warm, and now he halted, forcing her to stop as well. Her cheeks were flushed and she was just slightly out of breath, her chest rising and falling rapidly.

"Where are you taking me?" he asked, feeling a bit breathless himself.

She looked down for an instant, but then met his gaze again. "To your chamber."

He felt his heart begin to race. His hands were shaking. "But this isn't the way I came before dinner."

"No, it's not," she said, a conspiring smile on her lips. "That route would take us past too many of Father's guards."

Tavis grinned. "So are you just seeing to it that I find my way back to my bed, or did you have more in mind?"

Her color deepened, but still her eyes held his. They stood like that for a moment, staring at each other, utterly still. Then, as if performing a dance they had rehearsed a thousand times before, they each took a step forward, put their arms around each other, and kissed.

Her breath tasted of wine and her hair smelled of honey and wild flowers. Her body seemed to melt against his. Tavis could feel his heart hammering like a siege engine against his chest. His one free hand was pressed against her back, covered by silken threads of golden hair. He still held the wine in his other hand, and he almost threw it to the floor now so that he could unfasten the small, gold buttons that ran down the front of her dress.

Instead, he pulled away. "My quarters?" he whispered breathlessly, barely able to make himself heard.

"Yes," she said, kissing him again. An instant later, however, she pulled back from him. "But know this, my lord," she said, breathless as well. "Though I am yours, promised by my father, and bound now by my own heart, you will not bed me tonight. I'll share kisses with you." She hesitated, smiling shyly. "And perhaps somewhat more. But as to the rest . . ." She shook her head. "That will wait until the night of our wedding."

Perhaps he should have been angry. Perhaps in some small way he was. But he also understood. She was not a serving girl in a tavern or some such commoner. She was a noblewoman; she was to be his queen. He longed to lie with her. No doubt he would dream of it this night. If he wished to make this match work, though—and he did, more than anything he had ever wanted before—he knew now that he would have to accede to her wishes.

"Of course, my lady," he said. "If that's your desire, it's mine as well."

Brienne grinned. "Really?"

He had to laugh. "Well, maybe not," he admitted. "But I'll abide by your wishes. You have my word, your honor will be safe with me."

"Thank you," she whispered, favoring him with a dazzling smile.

They kissed again, and Tavis wondered if he had the strength to keep the promise he had just made.

"How much further to my quarters?" he asked, whispering the words into her hair.

"Not far. But first, some wine."

It was his turn to grin. "You make it difficult for a man, my lady."

"Yes, my lord," she said, taking the wine from his hand and drinking deeply.

She handed it back to him and he drank as well. Then she took his hand again and led him on through the corridors.

They hadn't far to go, but still they stopped several times more to kiss and drink and laugh, all the while urging each other to stay quiet so that they wouldn't be heard by Kentigern's guards. When finally they reached his chamber, they pushed open the door and stumbled forward onto the bed, nearly dropping the wine. There were no candles lit, but light from the moons spilled across the stone floor.

"The door," she said, lying on her back, her eyes closed. "Lock the door."

Tavis pushed himself up and made his way unsteadily back to the door. His head was spinning and abruptly he felt quite sleepy. He looked down at the flask, which was still half full. Maybe he had drunk more at dinner than he thought. Or maybe the day's journey and the night's festivities had finally caught up with him.

He locked the door and returned to the bed, putting the flask on the floor before lying down next to Brienne. Her eyes were still closed and her breathing had slowed.

"No fair falling asleep," he said, kissing her.

She returned the kiss, her eyes fluttering open for just an instant.

After a minute or two, Tavis moved his lips to the side of her neck, and then her throat, and then the top of her bodice. At the same time he began to unbutton her dress. Or at least he tried. He had to fumble with the buttons for several moments before he even succeeded in getting one of them undone. The buttons were small, and his fingers did not seem to be functioning as well as they had before his first glass of wine.

Brienne let out a soft sigh as he continued to kiss her, and she shifted slightly, making it easier for him to reach her dress. She certainly offered no objection to what his hands were doing, and so he didn't stop.

After what seemed an eternity, he finally managed to unfasten her dress all the way to her waist. He spread the dress open and gently kissed one of her breasts. Once more her eyes fluttered open for just an instant, but otherwise she offered no response. It took him a moment to realize that she had fallen asleep.

"Brienne," he whispered.

She didn't stir.

"Brienne." Louder this time.

Still nothing.

He kissed her on the lips, but she didn't kiss him back. He lifted his head and looked at her. Her golden hair flowing like a river over the pillow, her skin illuminated by Panya and Ilias, her breasts, full and soft, laid bare for him. He touched one of them, then the other. She was his, if he wanted her. Asleep, drunk, half naked.

He closed his eyes and lay down next to her. He would never have done such a thing. Besides, he was as tired as she, perhaps more so. He had spent much of the day riding. He needed to sleep. Just for a while. Just until dawn. Then he'd wake her and walk her back to her chamber. He had sworn that he would guard her honor, which not only meant controlling his own passion, but also keeping her reputation from harm. It was a promise he intended to keep. She was to be his queen; she deserved no less.

Later, after he slept.

Chapter
Ten

 n most nights, Fotir had no trouble getting the duke of Curgh back to his quarters at a reasonable hour. The duke had never been one to lose himself in conversation; social occasions were more a burden for him than a pleasure, just as they were for Fotir. Moreover, because Javan was a duke, few ever tried to prolong their discussions with him once he had made it clear that he wished to be done.

In this case, however, the evening had dragged on far beyond what Fotir felt was necessary. They had ridden much of the day, and had been journeying for the better part of the waxing. They needed rest. Judging from the frown that had been creeping onto the duke's face for the past hour or more it seemed clear to the Qirsi minister that Javan felt the same way.

But just as Curgh's duke was used to having people leave him alone when he grew tired of their company, the duke of Kentigern was accustomed to having people listen to him prattle on for as long as he wished. Add to that the fact that Aindreas was drunk, and there was little Fotir could do to end the evening. Ever since Javan and Aindreas's awkward exchange regarding the posting of the King's Guard on the Tarbin, the duchess of Kentigern and Shurik, Aindreas's first minister, had been trying to convince the duke to return to his quarters and sleep. Instead, Kentigern had called for more wine and taken their conversation in a new direction. He could barely speak anymore; Fotir doubted that Javan even knew what they were discussing. But that didn't seem to matter.

"Aindreas, we must let our guest sleep," the duchess said, trying once more.

"If you're tired, wife, go t' bed. I'll be along." He looked at Javan again. "'S jus' as well tha' Shonah didn' come with you, Javan. Two of them would be impossible."

"It's not me I'm worried about, you oaf!" The hall was empty now, save for a few servants and those sitting at the main table, and apparently Ioanna didn't care anymore if they heard her chastise her husband. "Javan and his company have come a long way. They need to sleep."

"Nonsense! Javan's fine! Jus' ask him."

"Actually, my friend," the duke said, taking this opportunity to stand and stretch his legs, "I could use some rest. It's been a long day. And we'll have plenty of time to speak further during the next few days."

Aindreas shook his head and laughed. "You're gettin' soft, Javan. Old and soft."

Javan clenched his jaw, his face shading toward crimson.

"Easy, my lord," Fotir said under his breath. "He doesn't know what he's saying. He hasn't for half the night."

Javan exhaled slowly and then nodded.

Two of Aindreas's servants helped the large duke to his feet and began to lead him off the dais and out of the hall.

Ioanna watched her husband leave before facing Javan. "My apologies, my lord," she said. She looked tired and pale, though she managed a rueful smile. "It's not easy for him seeing Brienne grown and ready for marriage, even with the wedding still a few years off. I believe he feels old."

Javan offered a smile that seemed sincere. "There's no need to apologize, my lady. Perhaps your husband is right. It may be more difficult with daughters than it is with sons. I won't presume to judge him."

"My lord is most kind," the duchess said, inclining her head slightly. "He will make a gracious king." Then she grinned. "Though only if he gets some sleep."

The duke laughed. "Quite true."

"This way, my lord," Ioanna said, starting toward the small set of stairs that led off the dais. "I'll have someone escort you and your company to your quarters."

"My pardon, my lady."

"Yes, Shurik," Ioanna said, as the rest of them stopped to look at the first minister as well.

The Qirsi gestured toward Fotir. "I was going to ask my colleague to join me for a journey into the city, but I wouldn't presume to do so without your leave and that of his duke."

"I have no objection," the duchess said. She looked at Javan. "My lord?"

The duke shook his head. "Nor do I."

Shurik smiled at Fotir. "What do you say, cousin?"

Fotir hesitated. He was weary as well, and he had matters to which to attend before he could retire for the night. But he didn't wish to be rude, nor did he feel that he could refuse an opportunity to speak with Kentigern's first minister.

"Very well," he said.

Shurik smiled. "Splendid."

Ioanna, Javan and the others started to leave.

"Master MarCullet!" Fotir called. "A word please."

This time, Ioanna did not stop, nor did Javan. Xaver did, however, and he regarded Fotir doubtfully as the minister approached him.

"Yes, First Minister?"

Fotir said nothing until he had stopped just in front of the boy. "I had hoped to speak with Lord Tavis before sleeping," he said, keeping his voice low. "Now it seems I may be another hour or two with Aindreas's Qirsi. Can I trust you to check on him for me?"

"I had planned to anyway," Xaver admitted.

Fotir offered a small smile. "So I guessed." Clearly the boy still didn't trust him, despite the assurances he had offered earlier that day, as they entered the city.

For several moments Xaver said nothing, his eyes fixed on Fotir's face, as if he could divine the Qirsi's thoughts if he but looked hard enough.

"I've told you, Master MarCullet, you have nothing to fear from me. But that's not to say you have nothing to fear. We're close to Aneira and now that the duke and your friend are in line for the throne, we can't be too careful. This is no time for you to be imagining enemies in your own court."

"You're contradicting yourself, First Minister, telling me in one breath to use caution and in the next to put my suspicions of you aside. Which would you have me do?"

The boy had a point, but Fotir didn't have time just then to argue the matter. "Both," the minister said, his voice hardening.

Xaver continued to stare at him for several moments more. Finally, he let out a sigh. "What do you want me to say to him?"

"Nothing at all. Just find out where he's been and make certain that he's safe." Again he hesitated, but only briefly. "And that he hasn't gotten himself into any trouble."

That, of all things, drew a wry smile from the boy. "All right," he said. "Good night, First Minister."

"Good night, Master MarCullet. Thank you."

The boy hurried out of the hall, leaving Fotir alone with Kentigern's minister, who still stood on the dais.

"Is everything all right?" the man asked.

"Yes, fine."

Shurik came down the small steps and gestured for Fotir to follow him through another doorway leading out of the hall. "I'm glad you agreed to join me," he said, as Fotir fell in stride beside him. "It seems our lords are determined to forge a stronger alliance between the two houses. We serve them best if we can work together as well."

Fotir nodded. "I agree."

Shurik glanced over at him. He was grinning again. "Good! I'd heard from some that you're not an easy man, Fotir. Many of my Qirsi friends tell me that you prefer the company of Eandi men and women to that of your own kind."

"I don't believe that's true. Some of my friends have yellow eyes; some don't. I have nothing against other Qirsi. But I've noticed that many of our people are resentful of me, because I refuse to hate Ean's children."

The other man nodded. "I understand. You'll find that here in Kentigern as well."

They fell silent for a short time, as Shurik led them out of the inner ward of the castle and toward the gate closest to the city. Fotir glanced at the man briefly, wondering if Shurik was waiting for him to speak, but the minister seemed content simply to walk. He was slight and tall, much like Fotir himself. He wore his white hair loose and long, which at first glance gave him a youthful appearance. His face, however, was narrow and long, with high prominent cheekbones and deep-set, pale eyes. The combination gave the minister an aspect of youthful ill-health that seemed to Fotir to be all too common among his people.

"Where are we going?" Fotir asked at last, breaking a lengthy silence.

"To a tavern in the city, a place called the Silver Bear." Shurik looked at Fotir once more and the two men shared a smile. "It seemed an appropriate place for the Qirsi minister of Curgh."

The Silver Bear was no different from any other Qirsi establishment Fotir had visited. It was filled with the sweet, musty smells of ale and burning pipeweed. Late as it was, the tavern was still crowded and loud, much the way Curgh's Silver Gull might be during the Revel. No doubt their visit had much to do with that. It wasn't every day that travelers from another of the major houses came to Kentigern, much less one of Javan's importance. Not surprisingly, most of the people in the tavern were Qirsi, although Fotir did see a few Eandi men and women scattered through the room.

The barkeep, a tall Qirsi man who was unusually brawny for one of Fotir's people, waved to Shurik as they walked in. He eyed Fotir briefly before offering a simple nod, which the minister returned.

"I've a table in one of the back rooms," Shurik said, raising his voice to be heard over the din. "We should have some privacy back there."

Fotir nodded and indicated with an open hand that Shurik should lead the way.

The two of them wove through the throng to a small chamber off the farthest corner of the main room. Closing the door against the noise, Shurik gestured to a chair at one of the room's two round tables.

"Please sit," he said. "Someone will be in shortly with ale and pipeweed."

"I don't smoke."

The Kentigern minister frowned. "A pity. This is a special blend. It comes from Uulrann."

Fotir raised an eyebrow. The growers of Uulrann were said to produce the finest smoking leaf in all the Forelands, but little of it ever found its way into any of the other kingdoms. Indeed, the same could be said of the blades forged by Uulrann's smiths, the mead made by its brewmasters, and the spices grown by its farmers. All were coveted by the merchants of the other kingdoms. Sometimes inferior products from other lands were falsely sold as exports from Uulrann. But just as the suzerain kept his court and his armies from

becoming entangled in the alliances and rivalries of the other kingdoms, so he kept his merchants from participating in the commerce
of the Forelands. It had been this way for centuries, though Fotir
had never heard a convincing explanation for why this was so. It was
true that Uulrann was surrounded by mountains and the ocean, and
bordered by its fiercest enemies, Braedon and Aneira. But among
the other kingdoms, trade thrived even between the most bitter
rivals. Eibithar traded with Aneira, as did Caerisse. All of them
traded with Braedon. "Kings must have their wars," an old saying
went, "and merchants must have their gold." But apparently, like
everything else, this saying stopped at the foothills of the Basak
Range.

"Uulranni leaf?" Fotir said. "How did they get it?"

Shurik smiled. "An enterprising merchant, no doubt. One who
was willing to pay a great deal of gold in anticipation of being able to
charge a good deal more. To be honest, I don't ask."

A moment later a serving girl walked in—Qirsi, of course—
bearing two tankards of dark ale and two pouches of pipeweed.

As she laid the pouches on the table, Shurik pulled a pipe from a
small pocket on the front of his doublet.

"You're sure?" he asked, eyeing Fotir.

He hesitated and the smile returned to Shurik's pale, narrow
face.

"Can you bring a pipe for my friend?" the minister asked the
girl. "Tell Tranda it's for First Minister Shurik."

"Yes, my lord," she said, bowing before she left.

"You won't be sorry," Shurik said. He filled his own pipe, lit a
tinder with the candle sitting on the table, and drew the flame into
the bowl. Smoke rose to the ceiling like steam from a kettle, the
scent of the leaf drifting to Fotir. He had to admit that it smelled
fabulous.

"I suppose I should apologize for Lord Kentigern's behavior,"
Shurik said abruptly.

"I believe the duchess saw to that quite gracefully. No further
apology is needed." Fotir thought the minister's comment curious.
Usually a minister wouldn't say such a thing unless expressly told to
do so. Aindreas had been in no condition to give such an order, but
perhaps the duchess had.

The serving girl returned with a pipe for Fotir. He quickly filled
it and lit the leaf, grateful for the distraction. It had been years since

he had smoked a pipe and in that moment he realized how much he had missed it. The pipeweed was as flavorful as it was fragrant. He closed his eyes briefly, savoring the sweet taste of the smoke.

"You must think the duke ill-mannered," Shurik went on, when they were alone again. "I would, were I in your position."

He did, of course, but he was unwilling to give voice to his feelings. Shurik had put him in an awkward position, and Fotir could not tell if that had been his intention.

"I think your duke is a passionate leader and a devoted father and husband," Fotir said, opening his eyes. "He'll be a valuable ally for my duke, and a trusted advisor when the duke becomes king."

Actually, from what Fotir had heard, the man was a fool and a drunkard. When he wasn't trying to mount some serving girl from the castle's kitchens, he was sending his soldiers on exercises that took them dangerously close to the Tarbin. There were those who said that he wanted to start a war with the Aneirans, to enhance his stature in the kingdom. Others said he took such risks out of sheer boredom.

Shurik grinned at Fotir's kind assessment of his duke. "And I have no doubt that Javan will lead our kingdom well. From what I hear he can be both strong-willed and compassionate, courageous and reasonable. Who can ask for more in a king?"

Fotir could tell that the minister had not given his true opinion of Javan, but after being more polite than honest himself, he could hardly say anything.

Seeing his expression, Shurik laughed. "We've fulfilled our duties quite well, wouldn't you say, cousin?"

"I'm not sure I know what you mean."

The minister gave a small frown. "Of course you do. Our dukes expect us to be tactful, to lay the groundwork for their better relations."

"Isn't that why we're here?"

"I suppose. I had hoped that we might move beyond that. Lord Tavis and Lady Brienne are to be married. The houses don't need our help to forge closer ties." He sipped his ale. "I saw this evening as an opportunity for us to start building a friendship of our own, Qirsi to Qirsi."

Fotir nodded, though he wasn't quite certain where all this was leading. "I'd like that as well, cousin. Such a friendship would further the interests of both our dukes."

181

"I suppose it would," Shurik said, a slight smile lingering on his lean face. "I hadn't thought of it that way. I was just looking for a friend. Do you have friends, Fotir?"

He laughed. "Of course I do."

"Qirsi friends?"

Fotir hesitated. "Some," he said. "There are other Qirsi ministers in Curgh Castle. I consider them my friends."

"I'm glad to hear that. As I said before, I'd been told that you were a difficult man." Shurik sat back, pulled the pipe from between his teeth, and drank some ale. "Tell me, Fotir, what powers do you possess?"

Once again, Fotir faltered. It was a question that Fotir would have asked only of a close friend.

"Forgive me," Shurik said, as if reading his thoughts. "The question makes you uneasy. Perhaps it would be best if I told you that in addition to being a gleaner, I also have the power of fire and speak the language of beasts."

It was useful information to have. While Kentigern's minister had several abilities, as many as Fotir, only the language of beasts was considered by the Qirsi to be among the deeper magics. Most men and women of the sorcerer race possessed only one magic or perhaps two. Those few who possessed three, like Fotir and Shurik, were among the most fortunate of their people, and among the most sought after by Eandi nobles throughout the Forelands. For centuries, the Qirsi had served the courts of the various kingdoms as ministers, offering not only counsel, but also gleanings of the future, and powers such as fire, shaping, or mists and winds that could benefit their lords in battle. Lesser nobles tended to have but one or two ministers, dukes as many as a half dozen. Kings often had ten or more, and some said that the emperor of Braedon was served by twenty Qirsi.

"And you?" Shurik prompted.

"Like you I'm a gleaner," Fotir said. "And a shaper, as well. And I have the power of mists and winds."

Shurik's eyebrows went up. "Very impressive. I can see why your duke values you so."

"Does he?" Fotir asked, curious again as to where Shurik was going with all this.

"Of course. Surely you must see it."

"I believe the duke respects me and is appreciative of my service."

"And that's important to you."

"Shouldn't it be?"

"I suppose," Shurik said, giving a small shrug and sipping his ale. "I think it's possible for the opinion of one's duke to become too important."

Fotir found himself thinking back to his unpleasant encounter with the Revel Qirsi in the Silver Gull. Trin had said something vaguely similar.

"Tell me, cousin," Fotir said. "Are you one of those Qirsi who find the Eandi tiresome and dull-witted?"

"Not at all. Do I give that impression?"

Fotir shook his head. "No. Forgive the question. Something you said reminded me of a man I know."

Shurik raised an eyebrow. "And he feels this way."

"Yes."

"A man in your position might think about taking more care in your choice of friends. Your duke would find it disturbing to know that you keep such company."

Fotir grinned and inhaled the sweet smoke of the Uulranni pipeweed. "He's hardly a friend. And I give my duke no reason to doubt my loyalty."

"That's very wise. I'm much the same way." The minister took a long breath. "I will admit, though: there are times I wish I could live in a Qirsi kingdom, serving a Qirsi lord." The minister smiled at Fotir's expression. "You find my candor unsettling, cousin?"

"I guess I should find it refreshing," Fotir said, smiling as well. "But after so many years in an Eibitharian court, I'm not certain how to respond to it."

Shurik laughed, though he quickly grew serious again. "I don't mean to sound ungrateful to my duke," he said. "It's true that he can be crude and foolish, sometimes even childish. But for all his faults, he can also be a wise and competent leader, particularly when he's sober. He commands his armies boldly and with imagination. He has, over the years, learned when to be firm with his people and when to be kind. At times he even surprises me with his graciousness and his wit." He made a sour face. "Obviously tonight was not one of those occasions. But still, as Eandi dukes go, he's not a bad one to serve. In all, I count myself quite fortunate."

Fotir nodded his head slowly. "I'm glad for you, cousin. And I appreciate your honesty."

"And yet, you offer none in return."

He felt his body stiffen. "What?"

"I've just been quite open with you about my feelings for the duke, but I've heard nothing from you beyond that drivel about the duke's respect and his appreciation for your service."

"It happens to be the truth."

Shurik sat back and rolled his pale eyes. "So Javan of Curgh is without faults, and Fotir jal Salene serves him with blind devotion."

"I never said the duke had no faults. He can be cold, at times humorless. He's stubborn and often ruthless, even in circumstances that demand flexibility."

The minister relit his pipe, sending swirling clouds of blue smoke up to the ceiling. "Now we're getting somewhere."

"There's very little more, cousin," Fotir said. "I'm sorry to disappoint you, but I admire the duke. I believe he'll be a fine king and I'm quite content serving him."

Shurik looked disappointed, although he recovered quickly. "Well, I'm happy for you, cousin. Who wouldn't be? Few of us are as lucky as you."

"I have been very fortunate," he agreed. Once again, though, he found himself thinking of his encounter with Trin in the Silver Gull. It disturbed him that Shurik had heard people speaking of how difficult he could be. The last thing a man in his position needed was a questionable reputation.

They sat without speaking for several minutes. At one point, the serving girl returned bearing two more tankards of ale. Fotir could still hear noise coming from the main chamber of the tavern when the door to their small room was open, but the crowd seemed to have grown smaller.

"Perhaps it's time we returned to the castle," Fotir said at last.

"What?" Shurik said looking up from his ale. "Oh, yes, soon."

"Is there something on your mind, cousin?"

The minister appeared to hesitate. "Actually there is. Perhaps you've heard talk of growing unrest among our people, fed by their resentment toward Eandi rule of the Forelands."

Fotir felt himself growing tense. Word of the Qirsi conspiracy had indeed reached Curgh. That people knew of it in Kentigern as well shouldn't have surprised him.

"Yes, I've heard of it," he answered. "From all I've been told, it seems the southern kingdoms—Sanbira, Caerisse, and Aneira—are especially at risk. But if the tales are true, none of us will be immune for long."

"I've heard much the same," the minister said. "I find it alarming to say the least."

"Of course," Fotir said. "All of us do. Have you seen any evidence of the conspiracy here?"

"Not yet. But like you, I worry that it won't be long." He paused again, as if he wished to say more, but was uncertain of whether to do so.

Fotir waited, and after a few moments, the minister went on.

"Living so close to the Tarbin, I'm used to contemplating all possible threats to Aindreas's rule. But these rumors disturb me in ways that similar ones in the past have not."

"Because the threat comes from our people?"

"Yes, there's that." He took a breath, swallowed. "But also because there's a part of me that's drawn to their cause." He looked embarrassed, and just a bit fearful, but he kept his eyes fixed on Fotir's face. "Don't you ever feel that way?"

Fotir wasn't certain how to respond. Shurik had made a most extraordinary admission, one few Qirsi, and fewer ministers, would have risked. Perhaps he hoped to cement their friendship with such a confidence, or perhaps he intended it as a snare, a way to determine if Fotir was party to the conspiracy. Whatever the reason, the minister had placed him once again in an awkward position. If he claimed that he had no sympathy for the conspiracy, he might sound overly righteous, or worse, he might make himself seem every bit the Eandi pet that Trin claimed he was. On the other hand, if he said that he shared Shurik's feelings on the matter, he might arouse the minister's suspicions.

"I know that many of our people feel as you do," he finally said, choosing his words carefully.

Shurik frowned. "But you don't."

Fotir shook his head. "I didn't say that. Our people's history in the Forelands has been . . . difficult. Time heals some wounds slower than others."

Shurik raised an eyebrow. "Am I to gather then that you think time will heal this one as well?"

"Don't you?"

"I hope it will," the minister said. "But hope is one thing. Believing it possible is another entirely."

They lapsed into another silence. Fotir eyed Shurik closely, try-ing to gauge the minister's response to what he had said, but the man's face revealed little.

"So what of the boy?" Shurik asked abruptly, catching him off guard.

"I'm sorry?"

"You admire the duke, but what about his son?"

"I'm quite fond of Tavis as well." He spoke the words forcefully enough, but he hadn't been able to keep himself from faltering for just an instant. He heard the lie as it passed his own lips; he knew that Shurik wouldn't miss it.

"I've heard it said that the young lord is a disappointment to his father," the minister said.

"The young lord is just that," Fotir answered. "Young. He'll grow out of his faults, just as he grows out of the clothes of his youth or the smaller mounts our stablemaster must still find for him."

Shurik's expression was grave. "Will he? Are you certain?"

"I have faith in his breeding, and in the guidance he'll get from his parents. He's mastered swordplay and horsemanship, just as his father did. I have no doubt that, with time, he'll master the finer crafts of running a dukedom and leading his people."

"But he hasn't yet." Shurik offered it as a statement.

"No," Fotir admitted. "He hasn't."

He probably should have stopped there, lest he appear to be betraying his duke's confidence. But Shurik had been open with him, and all the wine and ale had made him bold. "The boy has no discipline," he said. "He cares only for himself, and he's yet to realize that all he does reflects on his father and on their house. I speak of him growing beyond his faults, but he's actually getting worse as he grows older. Just last turn, he arrived at a banquet more than an hour late and as drunk as your lord was tonight. He stayed only for a short while, though long enough to humiliate his parents. And when his liege man followed him from the hall to see that no harm should come to him, Tavis attacked him with his blade. Master MarCullet still bears the scar on his arm."

"Demons and fire!" Shurik said, a look of disbelief on his face. "I had no idea things were so bad, or I never would have presumed to ask."

Fotir waved off the apology. "You couldn't have known. Even if you had heard such tales from another source, you probably wouldn't have believed them. I wouldn't have, had I not seen it all for myself."

"It's hard to accept that Javan's son could do such things."

"And no one is more disturbed than the duke by the boy's behavior, except perhaps the duchess."

"So they are disappointed in him."

Fotir nodded. "Very. I believe their hope is that Brienne will have a calming influence on him."

"She is an extraordinary young woman," Shurik said. "If anyone can help the boy, she can."

Shurik reached for his ale and Fotir chewed on his pipe for several moments, though the leaf had long since burned itself out. He had probably been wrong to say all that he had about Tavis—certainly Javan would be furious if he knew—but word of the boy's failings had already spread through the kingdom. And perhaps it was time he built more friendships among his own people.

"You must be tired, cousin," the minister said after a time. "Perhaps we should return to the castle."

"Probably. I'll be of no use to the duke if I don't sleep soon."

They both rose, made their way out of their small room, and crossed the main chamber of the tavern. Shurik tossed three silver coins onto the bar and bid Tranda goodnight. Fotir offered to pay as well, but the minister dismissed the idea with a wave of his hand.

"You're a guest in Kentigern Castle," he said as they stepped into the street. "The duke would insist, and so do I."

The night air was cool and still, and a light mist drifted through the city. Panya hung low in the western sky, her light angling sharply across the city wall and the low buildings, creating long, misshapen shadows. Ilias shone above her, giving a reddish cast to the hazy night sky.

They said little as they returned to the castle. Only now that he was on his way to bed did Fotir fully realize how tired he was. It was all he could do to climb the winding road to the castle gate. Shurik seemed tired as well, and by the time they had reached the castle, he was badly winded, the sweat on his brow shining in the moonlight.

"I never have gotten used to that climb," he said, struggling to catch his breath. "If it weren't for Tranda's Uulranni leaf, I'd never venture into the city at all."

They walked together to the base of the tower nearest the castle's guest quarters. There Shurik bade him goodnight and started back across the inner ward to his own chamber.

Climbing the spiral stairs to the guest quarters, Fotir wondered briefly if the MarCullet boy had found Tavis. Not that there seemed to be any cause for worry. The tower was quiet, and there were guards posted at the top of the stairs. Even the young lord couldn't have gotten himself into too much mischief.

The guards stopped him for a moment, asking his name before waving him on. No doubt Aindreas had taken every precaution. True, Kentigern's duke was next in line for the throne after Javan and Tavis, but for all his crude manners Aindreas was neither ruthless enough to try such a thing, nor foolish enough to do so while the men from Curgh were guests in his own castle.

Fotir had a little trouble finding the room he was sharing with Xaver—all the doors looked the same and he was loath to open Javan's door by accident. The first door he tried was locked. Probably Tavis's. Which meant the next one was his. Xaver had been kind enough to leave a candle burning by the small window. Fotir undressed quietly and slipped into bed without waking the boy. Lying in the darkness, he tried to think back over his conversation with Shurik. He believed the man wanted to be his friend, but he sensed as well that the minister had a second purpose. Had he not been so weary, and had he not had so much to drink, he might have been able to figure out what it was. But his thoughts were clouded and he soon fell asleep.

He couldn't be sure how long he slept. It felt like no time at all, though he awoke to find the first silver strands of dawn lighting the sky.

He thought he had heard something, though all was still when he opened his eyes. He glanced over at the other bed and saw that Xaver was awake as well, staring at him, his brow furrowed. Apparently he hadn't imagined it.

"Did you speak with lord Tavis?" the Qirsi asked.

Before Xaver could answer they heard the noise again. Someone was pounding on the door next to theirs. Tavis's door.

Xaver and the Qirsi were out of their beds in the next instant, throwing on their clothes as quickly as they could. Before they could dress, however, they heard something else, something that made Fotir's pulse race. A loud crash seemed to cause the stones of the castle to shudder, as if the earth itself were moving. Then there came a second, even louder than the first. They were breaking down Tavis's door.

A third jolt, and this time the Qirsi could tell that the door gave. Someone cried out, a woman screamed, and then the corridor outside their room echoed with shouts and footsteps and the ring of steel as swords were drawn.

Fotir leaped to the door, not caring any longer that he was only half dressed. Xaver was just behind him, and as Fotir pulled the door open he heard the boy utter a quick prayer to Ean, the god of the Eandi. Perhaps he should have joined the boy in his invocation. But the Qirsi had their own god, and Fotir thought little of the Ean worshipers and their new faith. And he was certain that what awaited them in the corridor lay beyond the reach of any god or any prayer.

Chapter
Eleven

✦

Claris had barely slept at all. How could she be expected to? With all due respect to the duke and duchess, Lady Brienne was her responsibility; she had been since the day the girl stopped suckling at her mother's breast. She dressed Brienne in the mornings when the girl was too young to choose her own clothes, and she sung her to sleep at night. She helped her with her lessons after the tutors were gone and played with her when the lessons got to be too much. As Brienne matured, Claris spoke to her of marriage and children and love, and she listened, holding the young lady's hand, as Brienne spoke in turn of her dreams and fears. It was Claris who was there when the girl's bleeding cycle began, to reassure her and quietly celebrate her first step into womanhood. And in recent years, when Brienne no longer needed a nurse, Claris continued to be the girl's friend. In almost every way, she was the one who had taught Brienne to be a lady.

No one knew the girl better than she. No one loved her as much, not even the duke and duchess, though she would never have said this to anyone. Actually, Ioanna seemed to understand the depth of her love for Brienne, for the duchess often consulted with her about decisions that would affect the girl: what course her lessons ought to take or who should be her travel companions when she ventured off the tor.

It was only this last decision, arguably the most important one in Brienne's life, in which Claris had been given no voice at all. She blamed the duke for that. This was a choice that had been guided by politics and ambition rather than by any concern for Brienne's happiness. How else could one explain Aindreas's willingness to marry his daughter to that spoiled boy from Curgh?

Claris didn't care that the boy's father was to be king, nor that the boy himself would be someday as well. She didn't like his looks or his reputation. And she certainly didn't like the way he gaped at her lady. He wasn't to be trusted. Anyone could see it. Except Brienne, of course. For all Claris had taught her, the girl remained an innocent. A cup or two of wine and some pretty words, and Brienne was ready to follow the boy out into the moonlight, where Adriel could work her dangerous magic.

Apparently that was just what had happened, because Brienne did not return to her quarters at all that night. Claris tried to sleep, to put her lady out of her mind and so find some peace, but she could not.

Brienne is a woman now, she tried to tell herself. *She is betrothed. She has no need of a nurse anymore. She knows her own mind and is free to love and be loved as she chooses.*

But though she knew all of this to be true, she couldn't keep herself from worrying. She lay in her bed, watching the candles burn down, listening for the girl's footsteps in the chamber next to hers, growing more and more concerned with each passing hour.

She must have dozed at last, for when she opened her eyes to the sound of the dawn bells ringing in the city, all but one of the candles had burned themselves out and the sky outside her window had started to lighten.

She decided then that she had waited long enough. Yes, they were betrothed, but they weren't husband and wife yet. She feared for the Lady Brienne's honor, but there was little she could do now to guard it. Brienne's reputation, however, she could still preserve.

Climbing out of bed and putting on her dressing gown, she hurried to the duke's chambers. She was met in the corridor by a pair of guards.

"I need to speak with the duchess," she said.

The two men shared a look.

"The duke and duchess are still asleep," one of them said. "You'll have to—"

"It's very important. It's about the Lady Brienne."

Again they looked at each other. After a moment, the one who had spoken nodded, and the other entered the chamber.

Several moments later, Ioanna appeared in the doorway, wrapped in a velvet robe, her face puffy with sleep and her hair tangled.

"Yes, Claris," she said in a flat voice. "What's wrong?"

Claris sketched a curtsy. "It's the Lady Brienne, my lady. She hasn't returned to her chambers. I haven't seen her since she left the banquet with Lord Tavis."

The duchess frowned. "Are you certain? Did you check her bed?"

"Yes, my lady." A small lie, but she was certain. She would have heard her lady's return.

The woman's frown deepened, so that a single crease appeared on her smooth brow, and she glanced over her shoulder back into the chamber. "I don't want to wake Aindreas," she said, as if thinking aloud. "Not so early, and certainly not with this." She looked at Claris again. "Take some guards to Lord Tavis's quarters and get her back to this side of the castle. Do it quietly, Claris. Try not to wake the duke of Curgh or any others in his company. Let's keep this to ourselves."

"Yes, my lady," Claris said, starting to turn away.

"And Claris," the duchess added, stopping her. "Be polite to Lord Tavis. You may not like him, but apparently Brienne does. Which is just as it should be. Do you understand?"

She nodded, but she made little effort to hide her displeasure. "Yes, my lady."

Accompanied by the two guards from the corridor, Claris hurried to the other side of the inner keep. There she found two more guards near the rooms of the duke of Curgh and his company.

"Which one is Lord Tavis's chamber?" she demanded.

"I'll show you," one of the men said, leading Claris and the other two guards down the hallway. He stopped in front of one of the large wooden doors and held out a hand. "This is it."

They all looked the same to her, and she almost asked the guard if he was certain. Instead she tried the door handle. It turned, but the door was locked. She knocked, but no one answered. She tried again, louder this time, but still got no response.

She looked at the guard who had shown her to the door. "Wake them!" she said.

"Them?"

"Him. Wake him."

The man stepped forward and pounded on the door with a gloved fist. Silence.

Claris's stomach felt like it had turned to stone.

He beat on the door again. Nothing.

"Something's wrong!" she said. "Open that door!"

The man stared at her. "But it's locked."

"So unlock it!"

"We haven't the keys, Dame Claris. Only the lockmaster has the keys."

"And where is he?"

The guard gave a shrug. "I doubt he's even awake, my lady."

She was losing her patience. Something had happened to Brienne, and these men were too stupid to find out what it was.

"Then you must break the door!"

The three guards exchanged glances.

"But Dame Claris," one of them finally said, trying to sound reasonable, "we can't just break into the room of a visiting lord. The duke—"

She had to fight to keep from shouting at them. "Your duke's daughter is in there!" Her hands were shaking and her voice sounded unsteady. "Now break down that door!"

Once more the men looked at each other, and once more the guard who had first spoken to her nodded.

"Very well," he said. "Stand back, my lady."

The knocking seemed to come to him from a great distance, as if sleep had carried him far out to sea. He knew that the sound was coming from the door to his room, that he ought to open his eyes and answer, but he couldn't. He was floating on gentle waters, his bed anchored leagues from shore. Sleep. All he wanted was to sleep. Again the knocking reached him, but slumber held him fast.

Leave me alone, he wanted to call. *Whatever you want can wait.*

But he couldn't even summon the words.

An instant later, though, when the knocking gave way to something louder, more insistent, Tavis fought to open his eyes. He had so far to travel—he was so far from that shore. His eyes fluttered open for just a moment, long enough for him to see where he was. Kentigern, the guest quarters. It was just dawn.

The pounding again, and then he remembered. Brienne. She was still there with him, asleep in his bed. Her father . . .

His eyes flew open.

"Brienne! You have to—"

It had to be a dream. Some horrible, twisted vision planted in his mind by Shyssir, or Bian, or perhaps both. But it couldn't be real.

Somehow he was on his knees on the stone floor, as if what he saw beside him had driven him off the bed. He heard a woman speaking outside the door, her voice spiraling upward toward a wail, and in the next moment something crashed heavily against the wood so that the lock creaked. Still Tavis couldn't look away. He felt his stomach heave and he vomited onto the blankets. But his eyes never strayed, not for an instant.

Her head still rested on his pillow, framed by her golden hair, just as he remembered from the night. The expression on her lovely face was so serene that he shuddered at the sight of it, and at the small spot of blood smudged on her smooth cheek. Her dress was still open at the waist. He remembered that as well, just as he did the taste of her lips and the softness of her breasts.

Again something crashed against the door. The wood of the frame had begun to splinter.

But that was his dagger buried hilt deep in her chest, and that was her blood caked on her chest and her stomach and running down her sides in dried black streams to the dark stains on the bed. There were several wounds on her chest and stomach. And blood. So much blood. Even on the stone handle of the blade.

The lock gave with the third crash. Or maybe it was the doorframe. Tavis never knew. Guards rushed in. And an older woman, who screamed like a wraith at what she saw and then collapsed to the floor.

"Look at his hands!" one of the men cried. "Her blood's on his hands!"

Tavis looked. The man was right. His hands were covered with so much dried blood that the skin felt tight when he flexed his fingers. Strange that he hadn't noticed before.

Two of the men grabbed him, pinning his arms to his sides. One of them brought his knee up into Tavis's stomach, doubling him over. A third man, the one attending to the woman, shouted for someone to rouse the duke and was answered by another voice, farther off. Sucking for air, his eyes now trained on the floor, Tavis could not make out what this person said.

"What is all this?" someone asked. "What—?"

Tavis looked up again. Fotir and Xaver were in the corridor just outside his chamber. The Qirsi minister was gaping at the bed, his yellow eyes wide, his face so pale he looked as dead as Brienne. Xaver stared as well, though he was flinching, as if he wanted to look away but couldn't.

"Why are you holding him?" the minister demanded, his voice suddenly raw and strained.

"He killed the lady," said one of the guards who was holding him.

"You don't know that." Fotir's words carried no conviction.

"Her blood's all over him, and the door was locked from the inside."

"Tavis?" Xavier whispered. He looked desperate, like a man so fearful of the truth that he would have gladly believed any lie at all.

"I don't think I killed her," Tavis said.

"You don't *think* . . . ?" Fotir repeated.

But Tavis's gaze was fixed on Xaver. If anyone could understand, it was his friend.

"We were drunk. Both of us. The wine from the banquet." It was so hard to keep his thoughts clear.

Xaver seemed to understand anyway. "You don't remember, do you?"

"I remember some of it. Not all." His eyes returned to Brienne, to her blood, his dagger. "I don't remember this."

"It had to be him," the guard said. "Look at his hands."

Before any of them could respond, Tavis's father appeared in the doorway. He paused, glancing at both Xaver and Fotir. Then he stepped past them and into the room. He looked at Brienne, absorbing what he saw like a man accustomed to battle and blood and death. Like a king. After a few moments he lifted his gaze to Tavis.

"What happened?"

"I don't know," Tavis told him. "I can't remember."

His father nodded, turning once more to the bed.

"I wouldn't have killed her, Father. I couldn't have. We . . . I liked her. I liked her very much."

Javan didn't look at him, but he nodded once more.

Tavis heard voices and footsteps echoing off the walls of the corridor. A good many people were approaching. Aindreas? The duchess? He felt like he was going to vomit again. He should have been crying, he realized. That's what people would expect from the man she was to marry. He wanted to cry, for her and for himself, but the tears wouldn't come.

Aindreas and Ioanna reached the room together and stopped on the threshold. Seeing her daughter's body, Ioanna fell to her knees, letting out a howl that chilled Tavis to his bones. Aindreas pushed past Fotir and Xaver, and stepped by Javan, glaring at him as he did. For several moments he stood beside the bed, staring down at Brienne, his expression hard and impenetrable, like the walls of his castle. Finally he reached down and pulled the dagger from her breast. Ioanna let out another sob. The duke raised his head and looked directly at Tavis. The guards tightened their grip on Tavis's arms.

"Is this yours?" Kentigern asked, his voice tight as a garrote.

Tavis swallowed. "It is, my lord."

With a single stride the duke was standing right in front of the boy, staring down at him with eyes that were red-rimmed and shockingly cold.

"Why did you do this? Did she spurn you? Is that it? You tried to force yourself on her and she fought you off?"

"I don't remember what happened, my lord," Tavis said, his voice quavering. "But I don't think I killed your daughter."

"This is your blade!" Aindreas said, his voice rising.

He held the dagger so close to Tavis's face that the boy flinched away. He grabbed Tavis by the wrist and held up his hand, wrenching Tavis's arm out of the guard's grip.

"This is her blood on your hands! And still you deny killing her?"

The duke released his arm, and almost immediately the guard took hold of it again.

"I wouldn't have killed her," Tavis said again. "I cared for her."

Aindreas raised his hand to strike him.

"Hold, Kentigern!"

The duke spun toward Tavis's father, his finger leveled like a sword at Javan's heart.

"You are not to speak!" he hissed. "Your son murdered my daughter, and now he lies about it like an Aneiran!"

"He claims to be innocent. And I believe him."

"Then you're a fool, or a liar as well!"

Javan's head snapped back as if he had been slapped. "How dare you!" he whispered. "I am to be your king! And you presume to speak to me in such a way?"

Aindreas took a step toward him, brandishing Tavis's blade.

Before he could take a second, however, there was a sound like breaking glass and the bloodstained steel of the dagger shattered into tiny pieces that fell to the floor like flakes of snow.

Aindreas halted in midstride, his eyes wide.

"My apologies, my lord," Fotir said, though he didn't sound sorry at all. "But let's not compound this tragedy with further violence." He glanced at Kentigern's Qirsi minister, as if seeking support, but the other man refused to look at him. "This is a time to mourn Lady Brienne's death," he went on, after a brief pause, "and to look for those who might be responsible."

"Fotir is right," said Javan. "We'll help you in any way we can with such a search, and with any investigation of—"

"We don't want your help," Aindreas said. He still held the hilt of Tavis's dagger, though he seemed to have forgotten it. "And we need search no farther than this room." He turned to the guards holding Tavis. "Put him in the dungeon. If any of our guests try to stop you—any of them at all," he added, glaring at Javan, "put them there as well."

He turned and started toward the door. But seeing his wife, who was still on her knees, her body shaking with her sobs, he stopped. Removing his cloak, he draped it over her shoulders, then bent to help her to her feet. There were tears on his face, though there had been none just a few seconds before. Ioanna climbed to her feet, clutching the duke's arm with both hands, and the two of them stepped into the corridor. She paused there, and though Aindreas kept his eyes on the floor, she looked back at Tavis. Her face was damp, her eyes swollen and red. She said nothing; her expression didn't even change. She just stared at him. Yet Tavis felt as though she were screaming at him, calling him a butcher, imploring Bian to torment him for the rest of time. When finally she looked away and walked out of sight, he sagged. Had the guards not been holding him, he would have fallen to the floor.

"Come on," one of the guards said, shaking Tavis roughly to get him to stand on his own again.

The two men started forward, compelling Tavis to do the same.

"Keep in mind that he's a lord," Javan warned as they walked past him. "He's soon to be duke, and one day king. Remember as well that he protests his innocence, and until he is proven otherwise he is not to be mistreated."

The guards barely slowed down.

As they led him out the door, Tavis glanced back at his father, who looked grim and pale, and, for the first time Tavis had ever seen, old as well.

"We'll find out who did this!" Xaver called to him. "You have my word."

The young lord nodded, but the last thing he saw as they took him to the dungeon was not his friend, but rather the bloodied corpse of his queen.

The room was silent save for the receding sound of the guards' heels on the stone floor as they led Tavis away. There were still plenty of the duke's guards there, along with Brienne's serving woman, Kentigern's first minister, Javan, Fotir, and Xaver. But none of them seemed to know what to do. Or perhaps they knew, but none of them wanted to be the first to touch her. Xaver didn't even want to look at her, though he was unable to stop himself.

At last, one of the guards went to the bed and covered Brienne with a blanket.

"No!" the serving woman cried out.

She tried to reach her lady, but was held back by the men attending to her.

"Your son will die for this!" she shouted at Javan. "The duke will see to it! And if he doesn't, I will! I swear it in Ean's name. He will die!" She was crying again, her entire body racked with spasms of grief.

"Take her to her chambers," Kentigern's Qirsi minister said quietly. "Have the healers sent to her."

One of the men nodded before helping her stand and guiding her out of the room.

"When can I see my son?" Javan demanded, planting himself right in front of the Qirsi.

The minister shrugged. "You'll have to ask the duke, my lord."

"Perhaps you can ask him for me."

"As you wish," the man said, bowing ever so slightly.

"Tell him as well that I wish to speak with him as soon as possible."

"I'll let him know, but I wouldn't expect him to grant you an audience anytime soon."

Javan's jaw tightened. "That's for your duke to say, not you."

"Yes, my lord," the Qirsi said with a shrug.

He turned to the guards and spoke to them in low tones, leaving Javan, Fotir, and Xaver to themselves.

"My lord—" Fotir began.

Javan silenced him with a gesture. "My chambers."

Fotir nodded, then glanced at Xaver. "I'd suggest that master MarCullet join us as well. I believe he knows Lord Tavis better than anyone."

Javan seemed to have forgotten that he was there, but after a moment's hesitation he nodded. "Yes, that probably makes sense."

They turned to leave, but two of Aindreas's guards stopped them. "First Minister?" one of the men said.

The Qirsi looked up from his conversation with the other guards.

"They're free to go," he said, "as long as they realize that they're not to go to Lord Tavis without leave from the duke."

"You've made that quite clear," Javan said.

The man actually smiled. "Good." It was all he said. An instant later he turned his back on them and returned to his discussion with the guards, as if the duke and Fotir were of no consequence at all.

Javan glared at the minister briefly before finally stalking out of the room.

Xaver and Fotir returned to their room to dress before joining Javan in his chamber.

"Do you think he did it?" Javan asked, after the first minister closed the door.

It was the same question Xaver had been asking himself almost from the moment he saw Brienne's body. He would have given anything to be able to answer with confidence, but his arm had barely healed and the wound on his heart was still raw. One turn ago he would have denied that his friend could ever murder anyone. He would have been equally vehement, however, in denying that Tavis could ever attack him. Too much had changed.

It seemed that the duke and his minister were thinking the same thing, for they were both looking in his direction.

"I honestly don't know, my lord," he said at last, meeting Javan's gaze. "Tavis has been acting . . . erratically."

The duke made a sour face and looked away. "I'm afraid you're being too kind, Master MarCullet. My son has been an ass. No one knows that better than you." He stepped to the window and stared out at the morning. "But being an ass is one thing," he went on, not bothering to face them. "Murdering the girl is quite another. I'd like to think that Tavis is incapable of doing . . . what we saw in there."

"He is, my lord," Xaver said. "When he's sober."

Javan turned at that. "Yes. That's right. Drink changes him, doesn't it?" There was a look in the duke's eyes that Xaver had never seen there before, as if he were desperate to believe what he had just said. It seemed to Xaver that the man was begging him to agree. For the first time he could remember, Javan was speaking to him not as his duke, but as Tavis's father.

"But even drunk," Fotir said, still looking Xaver's way, "do you really think he could commit so brutal a murder?"

He shrugged. What did the Qirsi want from him? He had done his best to be honest with Javan, at the risk of offending the duke and appearing disloyal to his liege. "He was drunk when he attacked me," Xaver answered. It was all he could think to say.

Fotir nodded. "I know." His voice sounded almost gentle, like morning waves lapping at a sandy shore. "What happened when he attacked you?"

"I've told you before. I don't think the duke needs to hear it again."

"I think he does. I think all of us do."

He considered this for several moments, his eyes fixed on the minister. "He was up on the castle wall," he began at last. "Sitting on the walkway. He warned me away, saying that he just wanted to be alone. I tried to talk to him, to get him to tell me about his Fating. But he wouldn't tell me anything. And when I tried to take his arm to bring him back down to his quarters, he swiped at me with his blade."

"Did he come at you a second time?"

Xaver shook his head. "No, he—" Suddenly, he understood. Whatever he thought of the first minister, he could not deny that the

201

man was clever. "No," he said again. The duke was watching him, but Xaver kept his eyes on Fotir. "As soon as he saw what he had done, he dropped the dagger. He tried to apologize to me, but I was too angry to listen to him."

"Understandably," the Qirsi said. "But those aren't the actions of a killer, even a drunk one." He turned to the duke. "Lady Brienne's killer showed no remorse, but instead struck at her again and again. Even at his worst I don't think Lord Tavis is capable of such savagery. To be completely honest, my lord, I don't believe he has the stomach for it."

Javan managed a smile, though it was fleeting. "I never thought I'd be so grateful to hear someone speak of my son's cowardice. Thank you, Fotir. And you as well, Master MarCullet. What I said yesterday I mean doubly this morning: my son is fortunate to have such a friend."

"Thank you, my lord."

The duke took a breath, and his body appeared to straighten as he did. "Well, the two of you have convinced me. But how do we convince Aindreas?"

Xaver said nothing. His own doubts remained, and he hated himself because of them.

"I'm not certain we can, my lord," Fotir said. "According to the guards, Lord Tavis's door was locked from the inside. It was his blade that killed her and you saw the blood on his hands. We, who wanted more than anything to believe in his innocence, found ourselves doubting him. The duke of Kentigern has no reason to believe us and, most likely, no desire to see Lord Tavis proven innocent."

"But at least for now, he has no knowledge of what Tavis did to Xaver. More than anything else, more than the blood and the dagger and the locked door, that's what made us doubt him. If we can just keep—"

"Qirsar, have mercy!" the minister breathed. His face had gone as white as it was when he first saw Brienne, and he appeared unsteady on his feet, as though he had been struck a blow to the head.

"What is it?" the duke demanded.

"Shurik knows, my lord."

"Shurik?"

"The duke of Kentigern's first minister."

Javan's eyes narrowed. "You told him?"

"Yes," Fotir said, nodding and lowering his eyes. "I knew nothing of Brienne's murder, of course. And we were speaking in confidence. But he knows, and I have no doubt that, under the circumstances, he will share this information with his duke."

"You told him," the duke repeated, offering it now as a statement, an accusation. "How could you do such a thing? You have condemned my son! Aindreas will never listen to us now! Tavis will be lucky to survive the day!"

Fotir started to respond, but Javan cut him off with a savage gesture. "Say nothing! This was not a matter for discussion, particularly not with the first minister of a rival house! What could you possibly have been thinking?" He waved a hand in Xaver's direction. "Even the boy knows enough to keep the scar hidden, and to say nothing of the incident! And you, you of all people, tell it to Aindreas's Qirsi?" He shook his head and muttered a curse under his breath. "Is that why you told him?" he asked a moment later. "Because he's Qirsi? Is that more important to you than the oath you took to serve me and my house?"

"No, my lord."

"Then why? Explain this to me!"

"Shurik and I were speaking as friends, sharing our experiences as ministers in court." Fotir swallowed. "In the course of our conversation, I expressed my concerns about Lord Tavis's recent behavior." He exhaled and shook his head, much as the duke had done a moment before. "As I said, my lord, I believed at the time that we were speaking in confidence. I had no idea how much damage I was doing." Once more, he hesitated. "If you wish to release me from my oath, I will understand, though I wish to continue in your service."

The duke dismissed the Qirsi's offer with another gesture and a quick frown. "And how would I replace you? With a Kentigern Qirsi? No, Fotir," he said, shaking his head. He took a long breath, which seemed to steady him. "No," he said again, his voice lower this time, calmer. "I do not release you from your oath. I shouldn't have said what I did. This isn't your fault. Even if Aindreas knew nothing of Tavis's attack on Xaver, he'd be eager for a quick execution. In truth, I would be too, if it was my daughter lying dead in that room."

"Forgive me for asking, First Minister," Xaver said, "but could a Qirsi have done this? Could that explain the locked door?"

The minister shook his head. "I don't see how. Only a few of our powers are physical in nature—mists and winds, fire, shaping—and of those, shaping comes closest. As it happens, I'm a shaper, which means that I can shatter a blade, as I did just now in Lord Tavis's chamber, and I can mend it as well. I can also alter its form, curve a blade that is straight, or straighten one that has been bent. I can do the same with wood or glass. But I can't throw the bolt of a lock without a key, and I certainly can't pass through wood."

"But you shattered Tavis's blade, and you say you can do the same with wood. Could another shaper have broken the door, entered the room, killed Brienne, then mended the door?"

"Not without waking everyone on this corridor. You heard the sound when I broke the blade?"

Xaver nodded.

"Breaking a door of such thickness and strength would have made a far greater noise. And mending it would take hours. We may be looking for a Qirsi, but we're looking for one with a key to the room."

"Or one who can climb," the duke said.

Xaver and Fotir looked at him.

"The window was open, wasn't it?"

"Yes, my lord," Fotir said. "But it was a warm night."

"I realize that. Nevertheless, if we're to assume that Tavis didn't kill her, then we have to consider every possible entry the real murderer might have used."

"But, my lord, the castle walls are at least ten fourspans high to these windows, and they're watched day and night."

"I've led soldiers who could climb walls that were far higher and more carefully guarded than these. For a single climber, it would be difficult, but far from impossible."

Despite the duke's surety, Xaver found it hard to imagine anyone climbing the walls of this castle. On the other hand, the duke was right about one thing: this was no time to be ruling out any possibilities.

"Even if we can figure out how," Fotir said, "that leaves us with who and why, both of which are likely to be far more difficult to answer."

Javan shook his head. "We're getting ahead of ourselves. We don't need to address those questions now. We merely need to find some evidence to suggest that Tavis didn't kill her. And we need to keep Aindreas from executing him before we do."

"What would you have us do, my lord?"

Javan rubbed his beard, his eyes fixed on the window again. He looked tired and pale, though even at that moment, he had the aspect of a king, dignified and strong.

"I'll go to Aindreas," he said after some time. "He probably won't speak with me, but I should at least try. I want you to go to your friend Shurik. See if he'll let you look around Tavis's chamber. Lie if you have to. Tell him that Tavis carried certain items of value to the house, and you want to make certain that they're safe." Xaver heard no rebuke in the duke's tone, but still the minister's face colored at the mention of Aindreas's Qirsi.

"What about me, my lord?" the boy asked.

Javan faced him, a sad smile on his lips. "Go to Tavis," he said quietly. "If the guards try to stop you, tell them the truth: you're his liege man. They should let you pass."

"But shouldn't you be the one to see him, my lord?"

"I will, later. After I've seen Aindreas. But chances are he'd rather see you than either of us."

Xaver nodded, though he had to wonder if Tavis really wanted to see any of them right now. Or, more to the point, if he wanted to be seen by them.

"We'll meet back here later," the duke went on a moment later. He was facing them again, his expression grim, his dark blue eyes catching the light in the room like the steel of a sword. "Watch yourselves, both of you. The two of you have convinced me that Tavis is innocent. But that means there's a murderer in the castle, one who's cruel enough to kill Brienne in this way, and clever enough to make it seem that Tavis did it. Neither house has been spared, which tells me that all of us are in danger."

Chapter
Twelve

✦

Usually Cadel would have left the castle immediately. Once his work was done, he had little to gain from lingering, and a great deal to lose.

But this time was different. The night before, just as Cadel was leaving the hall to make his way to Lord Tavis's chamber, the cellarmaster asked him to stay on as his assistant for the remainder of Javan's visit to Kentigern. It was a fine offer, a plum position for any castle servant. A refusal would have aroused Vanyk's suspicions. His acceptance, on the other hand, carried no cost at all. There would be no more banquets, though Vanyk didn't know this yet, and after Brienne's death and Tavis's imprisonment, no one in Kentigern Castle would care to have anything to do with those they thought were visitors from Curgh. All he had to do was show up this morning and let Vanyk tell him to leave. After that, he was free.

He passed the night hidden in the stable, and made his way to the cellars just after the ringing of the midmorning bells, carrying the flask, now empty, that the cellarmaster had given him the night before as part of his payment. Sanbiri dark. It had been a guess, really, though an educated one. The best wine in the Forelands came from the vineyards of Sanbira; every major house in Eibithar held it in their cellars. With the land's future king visiting it was only natural that Vanyk should serve it at the banquet. And with all that Cadel had heard from his Qirsi contacts about Tavis's thirst for wine, he could assume that the young lord would be drinking it.

Probably no one would notice the sweetwort in the flask that

Tavis and Brienne took back to the boy's chamber. Aindreas and his guards had their murderer; the existence of the container itself, its proximity to the bed, would answer most of the questions that remained. Moreover, Cadel's climb from the empty chamber on the east side of the castle to Tavis's window on the south wall would have been difficult enough without an empty flask tied to his belt. Most men in his position wouldn't have bothered.

But Cadel hadn't survived in his profession for so many years, building the reputation he had, by being careless or lazy. He did carry the flask to Tavis's room, and after killing Brienne, he switched the containers, taking the one with sweetwort when he left. He had emptied his; theirs still had a bit of wine in it. But Tavis wasn't likely to remember that, and given the depth of the sleep brought on by sweetwort, no one was likely to question an empty flask.

He found Vanyk in the cellar, arranging flasks on the shelves. His eyes were red, like those of many of the servants Cadel had seen this morning. Apparently Brienne was much loved by the people of the castle.

"Good morning," he said cheerily, approaching the man and holding out the empty flask.

Vanyk stared at him briefly before turning back to the wine containers again.

"Just put the flask on the shelf there," he said with a vague wave of his hand. "Then you can go."

"Go? Don't we have work to do?"

The cellarmaster faced him again, his eyes narrowing. "Do you think you're being funny? Can you really be so cruel?"

Cadel stared back at him blankly. "I don't understand. I thought—"

"Haven't you spoken with any of your Curgh friends today?"

He smiled. "No. I slept in the stable. You didn't think that I was going to share that Sanbiri dark with them, did you? Now if I had been able to find a woman, then I might—"

"So you don't know what's happened."

Cadel shook his head, still smiling. But as Vanyk just stood there, saying nothing, looking like he was about to cry, he allowed his smile to fade. "What is it, Vanyk? What's this about?"

The cellarmaster swallowed, and a moment later he was crying. "Lady Brienne is dead."

"Bian have mercy!" Cadel whispered. "How—?"

"Lord Tavis killed her. He's in the dungeon now."

He took a step back and shook his head again. "That's impossible!" he said, sounding angry, as any man of Curgh would. "It's a lie! Lord Tavis wouldn't do something like that!"

"The door was locked," Vanyk said, his voice hardening as well. "Her blood was on his hands and on his blade. It was him that did it. No doubt."

"I don't believe it for a minute! And I won't stay here listening to these lies! I don't care about your gold or your wine! Tavis is no murderer!"

Cadel turned on his heel and started up the stairs out of the cellar.

"Good!" the cellarmaster shouted after him. "Be gone then! I don't want to see you here again, you Curgh bastard! Bian take you all and let you rot in the Underrealm!"

When Cadel reached the top of the stairs, the kitchen servants eyed him darkly. No doubt they had heard his exchange with Vanyk. He stared back at them for a moment, as if daring any of them to speak. Then he stalked out of the kitchen tower and into the ward.

Two of the guards stopped him at the north gatehouse, brandishing swords and glaring at him much the way the servants in the kitchen had.

"Where you going, Curgh?" one of them asked.

"To the city. My duke needs herbs to calm his blood, and he doesn't trust the apothecary in your castle."

"Nor should he," the other man said. "If it was me, I'd give him a bit of hemlock. That'd calm him, all right."

Cadel felt himself growing tense. Even carrying just a pair of Sanbiri daggers, he knew that he could handle both of them. But that would only have made matters worse; servants weren't known for their skill with blades. No, if they chose to vent their hatred for the Curgh lord at him, he'd have no choice but to take it. Fortunately, their fear of angering Kentigern's duke overmastered their lust for vengeance.

"Go," the first one said at last, his voice cold. "May the apothecary have a heavy hand."

Cadel hurried through the outer ward to the east gate, retracing his steps from the day before. And just as the inner gate guards had let him through without a question on his way into the castle, now the outer gate guards let him pass with no more than a sneer.

Once he reached the road winding down the tor to the city, he knew he was safe. He would spend the balance of the day in Kentigern's marketplace before leaving the city with a group of merchants that evening, just to be certain. The guards were less likely to notice him that way. Even then, he wouldn't be finished. He still had to cross the Tarbin into Aneira and find his way south to the city of Noltierre. But compared with what he had done already, that was nothing. In all important respects, he had completed his job successfully. Again.

He should have been pleased. This had been a relatively difficult assignment, more complicated than most, and more dangerous as well. Certainly he was about to receive more gold than he had for any previous job.

Yet something bothered him. He couldn't say what it was. He had gone over everything in his mind several times, and he was certain that he hadn't forgotten anything, or made any mistakes. It all had gone just the way he planned. Even his luck had been good. How else could he explain his first encounter with Vanyk and the ease with which he had gotten the wine into the hands of Tavis and Brienne? Strange as it seemed, the gods had been with him.

But still the feeling stayed with him, mirroring his every move like a shadow. Notwithstanding his good fortune, and the fortune in gold that awaited him, he suddenly felt the hairs on his neck standing on edge, as if there were lightning in the air. He glanced back over his shoulder, half expecting to see Aindreas's entire guard bearing down on him. The road was empty. Cursing his own stupidity, he hurried on, fixing his eyes on the ground before him. He should have known better. He had often warned Jedrek not to look back like that under such circumstances. It only served to draw attention to oneself.

"Fool!" he muttered under his breath. "Calm yourself!"

The castle road leveled and merged into the avenues of Kentigern City, and Cadel quickened his pace, hoping that the bustle of the marketplace would divert his mind from this fear that had gripped him so abruptly. He knew better, however. Something was wrong.

Considering the way the memory of his gleaning had occupied his mind over the past turn, Tavis shouldn't have been so shocked by the familiarity of Kentigern Castle's dungeon. But in the confused horror of the morning, his Fating had been far from his thoughts. That is, until the guards dragged him to the prison tower and opened the door to the dungeon stairs.

The smells reached him first: excrement and urine, vomit and disease. He gagged, then retched, but he had already emptied his stomach onto the bed in his chamber. Then he heard the screams, not of pain, or even anguish. This was worse. These were screams of madness, of a man crazed by his imprisonment. Tavis recoiled at the sound and tried to flee. But Aindreas's guards held him fast, laughing as they practically carried him down the uneven stone steps into the darkness. Even before his eyes adjusted to the shadows, he understood that this was the prison he had seen in the gleaning tent. He recognized the small barred window high on one of the walls and knew from its position on which wall he would be shackled. He was even expecting the blow from the guard that would bruise his right cheek, though he could do nothing to prevent it.

"That's for Lady Brienne, you bastard!" the man said. The words seemed oddly familiar as well, though there had been no guard in the image offered at his Fating.

The man glared at him for another moment, as if considering whether to strike him again. Instead he walked away, leading the other guards up the stairs and out of the dungeon. The iron door slammed shut, the sound echoing through the prison like storm breakers hammering on a rocky shore.

The screams had ceased when Tavis and the guards descended the stairs, but now they started again, as if the mad prisoner had been waiting for the crash of the door. He couldn't see the prisoner; the sound seemed to come from another cell, farther from the stairs. Probably a forgetting chamber. Curgh's prison tower had such cells as well, places where prisoners were sent to waste away without food or water or even light. The young lord yelled for the man to be silent, but the prisoner wouldn't listen, or didn't care, or was beyond understanding. His screams filled the dungeon.

Closing his eyes, Tavis felt the entire prison pitch and roll, as if he were on a ship being tossed about by Amon's Ocean. His legs were weak, his stomach was sour and tight. He tried to sit, only to find that his chains were too short to allow him to do so comfortably. He could lower himself to the floor, his back against the wall, but he could not lower his hands past his shoulders, nor could he straighten his legs. Still, he was too exhausted to stand again, so he remained that way, crumpled on the filthy stone floor like a forgotten toy.

In the days after his Fating, as he struggled to throw off his despair at what he had seen in the stone, Tavis tried to convince himself that the gleanings were a farce, that they were empty prophecies conjured by the Qirsi. He knew better, of course. The tradition of the gleanings went back centuries. If there had been nothing to them, the custom would have been abandoned long ago. But he had nothing else, no other weapon with which to fight off his fear. So he clung to this hope, like a dying soldier clutching his sword.

But chained to that wall, folded awkwardly on the floor, Tavis knew that his hope had been in vain. Here was his future, stark, undeniable. If the Qiran was to be believed, his entire life had been leading to this place, to the hard rough stone pressing against his back and the cold iron cutting into his wrists and ankles, the foul stench burning his nostrils and the dim grey light teasing his eyes. This was all that was left for him. Imprisonment, disgrace, and soon, he knew, execution.

Once more, as he had in his chamber staring at Brienne's body, Tavis wished he could cry. But even in the dungeon, cramped and miserable, his mind buffeted by the other prisoner's shrieks, he couldn't summon a single tear.

He still smelled her perfume on his clothes, though the scent was mingled now with the smells of blood and vomit. Closing his eyes, he could see her face, her smile. Closing his mind to the screams, he could hear her laughter. He could almost taste her lips on his. He had been with her only a few hours, but somehow she had managed to touch his heart, as though Adriel herself had been guiding her hand.

"I'm sorry," he whispered, as if she might hear. "I don't know what happened, but I'm sorry."

She deserved his tears, if only he had some to give.

He sat for what seemed to him a very long while, though he had no sense of how much time was passing. At one point he thought he heard the bells ringing in the city. The sound was faint, and it was hard to be certain with the cries echoing off the walls, but he had heard them earlier in the day and he thought he recognized the cadence whispering like a soft wind. He couldn't begin to guess, though, which ringing he had heard. Midmorning? Midday? The prior's bell? How was it possible that within the span of a few hours, the passage of time could cease to have any meaning for him?

He must have fallen asleep—how he managed it with the screams and the manacles biting at his wrists and ankles he couldn't fathom—for he awoke with a start, jerking his arms painfully. It took him a minute to realize what had disturbed him.

The screams had stopped.

The door to the dungeon opened with a loud creak. He heard voices, one soft, the other louder and harsh. Then someone started down the stairs, slowly, as if unsure of each step.

"Tavis?" a voice called.

"Xaver?"

Tavis tried to stand, but his legs were stiff, and his chains were so short that he couldn't push himself up.

"Are you all right?" his friend asked. He was still on the stairs. Tavis could see him peering in his direction, looking young and afraid.

"I need help getting up. These shackles make it difficult."

"Of course," Xaver said, hurrying down the rest of the steps and crossing to where Tavis was sitting.

He took hold of Tavis's arms and hoisted him to his feet. Tavis gasped at the pain in his legs and shoulders, falling back against the wall and closing his eyes.

"I'm sorry," Xaver said. "I didn't mean to hurt you."

"It's all right. I just need to rest a moment. I don't know how long I was sitting there." He opened his eyes. "What time is it?"

"A few hours past midday. They should be ringing the prior's bells soon. I would have been here sooner, but the guards kept me waiting for a long time." He shrugged. "I still don't know why."

He must have heard the midday bells. Less time had passed than Tavis thought. He glanced up at the stairway, but it was empty. Xaver was alone.

"I guess my father couldn't bring himself to come."

"It's not like that," his friend said, shaking his head. "He went to speak with Aindreas, but he told me he'd be coming to see you later."

"He probably believes I killed her."

"He doesn't, Tavis. None of us do. You're no murderer."

Tavis let out a short, high laugh that sounded bitter and desperate to his own ears. "I wish I could be so sure."

Xaver's eyes widened. "Aren't you?"

"How can I be? Look at what I did to you." He lifted his hands

213

in front of his face, making the chains ring like coins in a pouch. "Look at my hands. Her blood is still on them."

"You said you liked her, that you cared for her."

"I did like her. I think I could have loved her. I don't think I killed her, Xaver. Truly, I don't. But I don't remember anything." He looked away. "And you know how I get when I'm drunk."

"We talked about that, your father, Fotir, and I. And we all agreed that there's a great distance between what you did to me and what was done to Brienne."

"My father really thinks that?" He was almost afraid to believe it.

"Yes. That's why he's with Aindreas: to convince him to begin a search for the real murderer."

He felt hope budding within his chest, like a seedling fed by a warm rain in Amon's Turn, and he moved with all the speed and ruthlessness he could muster to crush it before it took root. There was no room for hope in this dungeon. This was his fate. He had seen it.

"He shouldn't bother."

Xaver stared at him. "What?"

"He'll never convince Aindreas of anything. And I'll only leave this dungeon on the day of my hanging." He could barely get the words out without gagging on them.

"Don't talk that way, Tavis. Your father—"

"My father can't do anything for me. No one can."

"That's not true!"

He wanted to turn away, to end this conversation and go off by himself. But the chains held him. "You don't understand, Xaver," he said. "This is what I saw in my Fating."

His friend looked like he was going to be sick. "You saw Brienne's death?"

"No, not that. But this dungeon, these chains. This is where I'm supposed to be. This is what the gods have chosen for me."

For a long time, Xaver didn't respond. He just stood there, chewing on his lip, his eyes fixed on the stone wall. After some time, he began to shake his head, and he met Tavis's gaze again.

"I don't care," he said. "So what if the Qiran showed you this? There's no law that says you have to accept your Fating as the final word on your future. You didn't kill her. I'm sure of it. Which means that you don't belong in here, regardless of what the stone said."

Tavis wanted to believe him, but he didn't dare. Xaver seemed to sense his doubts.

"Just don't give up, Tavis," he said. "At least not yet."

Tavis nodded. "All right." He hesitated, but only for a moment. "Don't tell my father. Please."

"About your Fating?"

He nodded again.

"I won't say a word."

They fell into an uncomfortable silence. Tavis sensed that his friend wanted to leave—who could blame him?—but that he felt he should stay.

"Is there anything I can do for you?" Xaver asked, after some time.

"You mean aside from helping me escape?"

Xaver smiled, though it quickly changed to a grimace. "You know what I mean."

"I don't think there's anything. Although if you could get them to lengthen these chains just a bit, it would help."

Xaver's face brightened, as if he were eager to take on any task at all. "I'll do what I can."

"Thank you."

His friend cleared his throat and glanced up at the door at the top of the stairs.

"It's all right, Xaver," Tavis said, trying to smile. "I'll be fine."

"I'm in no hurry. I can stay as long as you want me to."

"I know that. But you can do more good out there, helping Fotir and my father find the person who did this."

"You're certain?"

No. I'm terrified of being alone in this place. "Yes."

"I'll come back tomorrow. I promise."

Tavis held up his hands, making the chains jangle again. "I'll still be here."

Xaver grinned. He gripped Tavis's shoulder and gave a squeeze, before turning and starting up the stairs.

Seeing him leave, Tavis was gripped by a cold panic that made him tremble.

"Xaver!" he called, before he knew what he had done.

His friend stopped, and even came back down a step or two. "Yes?"

"What did you see in your Fating?" he asked. It was the first thing that came to mind. "With all that happened, I never did ask you."

Xaver shrugged, looking uneasy. "There wasn't much to it."

"Please," Tavis said. "I want to know. Was it a good one?"

The boy hesitated. "Yes," he finally said, as if he was confessing a crime. "It was a good one."

"Tell me."

"Tavis—"

"Will you marry?"

"Yes."

"Is she very beautiful?"

"Yes."

"And what else?"

There was a long pause. Then, "I'm to be a captain in the King's Guard. If you believe the stone," he added, no doubt for Tavis's benefit.

Why couldn't I have had such a Fating? "That's wonderful, Xaver," he said, and he meant it. "I'm happy for you. At least one of us had a good Fating."

"You're going to get out of here, Tavis," Xaver said fiercely, like a man trying to convince himself. "We'll get you out."

He could think of no response, so he simply said, "Goodbye, Xaver. Come to see me again soon."

"I will."

Xaver climbed the rest of the stairs and pounded twice on the dungeon door. After a few moments, the door swung open and he left. It closed again, with a sickening crash, and Tavis heard the bolt thrown.

He closed his eyes, leaning his head back against the wall. And as he did, the screams began again.

The last time someone had kept him waiting for even close to this long, it had been Aylyn during Javan's visit to the City of Kings several years before. Patience had never been one of Javan's stronger attributes, but on that occasion he had managed to keep his temper in check. Aylyn was king and it was a king's prerogative to take as much or as little time with his audiences as he saw fit. That Aylyn was also a Thorald, possessing the arrogance for which all the Thorald kings were known, only made his willingness to inconvenience his guests that much less surprising. So Javan had waited, and, of course, when he was finally admitted to the king's hall, he addressed Aylyn with all the graciousness and humility demanded by the occasion. For regardless of what he thought of the king himself, he had been in Audun's Castle, standing before the Oaken Throne.

This day, however, was an entirely different matter. Javan was waiting for a Kentigern, not a king, and there was far more at stake than merely his pride and his time.

He had been pacing the anteroom to Aindreas's chambers for hours. He had heard the bells rung at midmorning and again at midday, and still the duke refused to see him. The two guards who first met him at the door and told him to wait had long since been replaced by a second pair, even taller and more muscular than the first. Soon it would be time for these men to be relieved, and still he waited.

Probably Aindreas had come and gone from his chambers a dozen times since Javan's wait began. There were no less than three ways to get to Javan's own chambers in Curgh Castle, for just this reason, though that didn't make the situation any less galling.

His daughter is dead, said a voice within his head. Shonah's voice. *Can you blame him for not wanting to see you?*

"And what of Tavis?" he mumbled, drawing dark looks from the guards. "Isn't he a victim here as well?"

Is he?

Javan faltered, halting for just an instant in midstride. There it was: his deepest fear, staring at him like one of Bian's demons from the dark recesses of his mind. What if the boy really did kill her? What if all the evidence—the locked door, his dagger in her chest, her blood on his hands— proved just what it appeared to prove? What if the boy's recent behavior, rather than being an aberration, was merely a prelude to this atrocity?

He had told Fotir and Hagan's boy that he believed Tavis to be innocent. Certainly he wanted to believe it. But in his heart, he was forced to admit, he still wondered. Which promised to make this meeting he sought with Aindreas that much harder.

As it was, facing the duke just hours after Brienne's death promised to be painful and awkward. There would be accusations, threats, talk of vengeance. But if he went into that chamber still doubting Tavis's word . . .

Javan shook his head, shuddering at the thought. Yet what could he do? His fear remained, undeniable, unmovable.

So when at last the door to Aindreas's chamber opened, and the massive guards stepped away, revealing the slight figure of Kentigern's first minister, Javan did the only thing he could. He pushed away all his doubts about Tavis, and thought only of Shonah. The boy's death would be the end of her. He knew it with a certainty that rendered moot the question of Tavis's guilt or innocence. He had to save the boy, despite his own doubts and no matter the evidence. For Shonah, and, if he was to be completely honest, for himself as well.

"The duke will see you now, Lord Curgh," Shurik said, his expression solemn and distant.

Javan started toward the door, but the Qirsi raised a hand, stopping him.

"You'll have to leave your sword out here."

At first Javan thought that he had heard the man wrong. An Eibitharian duke always wore his sword, particularly when meeting with another lord, be it a duke or one of the lesser lords. He had even worn his sword to meet with Aylyn.

"You're not serious," he said.

"Of course I am. We have already seen what Curgh violence has wrought. We won't chance the life of our duke as well."

"That's absurd!" Javan said, struggling to keep his temper in check. "My son is innocent and I am no murderer!"

The man shrugged. "I'm afraid I must insist."

"Insist all you like," Javan told him. "But I won't remove my sword. I am to be king of this land. I don't answer to the likes of you."

He took a step toward the door, but the two guards moved to block his way, drawing their swords as they did.

"You have no choice in the matter, my lord," the Qirsi said, his voice so calm that Javan wanted to strike him. "If you do not remove your sword, you won't see the duke."

It was an annoyance and little more, a defeat that signified nothing. But it was a defeat, and it stung. He sensed the Qirsi's amusement as he removed his belt and scabbard, and once more he wanted to hurt the man. Instead he handed him the sword and then followed him into Aindreas's chambers, like a prisoner.

The duke was standing at his window, his bulky frame keeping most of the light from the room.

"Leave us," he said, without turning.

The first minister bowed, then left, closing the door behind him.

Aindreas turned at the sound of the shutting door. His eyes were red, his face pale except for a bright red spot on each cheek. Javan had never seen him looking so poorly.

"You've been waiting to see me."

"Yes."

"Why?"

Javan opened his mouth, then closed it again, unsure of how to answer. Wasn't it clear? Didn't the morning's events demand a meeting?

"So we can discuss . . . what's happened," he said at last.

"Your son murdered my daughter. What more need we say?"

"I don't believe he did."

"Yes, I know. You told me the same thing this morning. I believe I called you a fool and a liar."

Perhaps the Qirsi had been wise to take his sword.

"This is a terrible tragedy, Aindreas," Javan said, fighting the impulse to respond in anger. "I'm deeply sorry for you and Ioanna. Brienne was a lovely girl. The Underrealm will shine like the sky with her light." It was the traditional epitaph, but it seemed truer than usual in this instance. For as long as he lived, Javan would remember the girl in the radiant dress she had worn to the banquet. As queen she would have been adored throughout the land.

"Do you know that's the first time you've expressed any sorrow at all at Brienne's death." His voice broke when he spoke the girl's name, but he recovered quickly. "Until now you've shown no regret at all. You've done nothing but defend your son."

He didn't doubt for a moment that this was true, and he felt ashamed.

"You're right, Aindreas. I should have said it earlier. My deepest apologies. No parent should ever have to see what you and Ioanna saw today."

"Nor should a father have to live with the knowledge that his son is a monster."

Javan closed his eyes briefly. He wanted to rail at the man, but he knew it would do more harm than good. "I honestly believe Tavis to be innocent of this crime," he said, as evenly as he could. "I understand that all you saw in that chamber has led you to believe him guilty. Were I in your position, I'd believe that as well. But you don't know the boy."

"I know that he attacked his liege man."

He should have been ready for this. Fotir had warned him. But still the words struck him like a fist to the gut.

Aindreas smiled thinly at what he saw on Javan's face, though the smile was fleeting and when it was gone, he looked even sadder than he had a moment before. "You're not to blame, Javan. Neither is Shonah. Sometimes fine breeding and wise guidance aren't enough to save a child. There's a darkness in your boy that even Morna couldn't light."

Javan understood that the man was trying to be kind, that under the circumstances it was an act of uncommon grace and charity. He knew as well that Aindreas was right, at least in part. There was something dark in Tavis, though he didn't know its source. Still, he wanted none of Aindreas's pity.

"You're wrong," he said. "No matter what you think you know about him, I assure you Tavis isn't capable of such butchery."

"Did he attack his liege man, as your Qirsi told mine?"

"Yes, but he was drunk at the time."

"There was an empty container of wine found beside the bed."

"That doesn't mean—"

"Enough!" Aindreas said, balling his fists until his knuckles turned white. "My daughter is dead, killed by your son's dagger, in a bed she shared with him! He is a murderer, and he shall be dealt with as such!"

"Aindreas, I am asking you duke to duke, as the man who will soon lead Eibithar, to allow me to look into this matter before you do anything that cannot be undone. Tavis is in your prison. He can't leave Kentigern, and he can't hurt anyone. Keep him there as long as necessary. But let's not compound this tragedy by executing the wrong man."

"You'll find, Javan, that justice in Kentigern is swift and absolute. No one in his right mind would need any further evidence to conclude that Tavis killed my daughter. You seek only to delay what you know is inevitable, and I will not allow it."

He had tried to keep his anger in check, but this was too much.

"And you will find, Lord Kentigern," he answered, "that Curgh's response to injustice is equally swift. I will consider any attempt to punish my son before all evidence has been brought to bear an act of war between our houses."

Aindreas took a step forward. "You dare to threaten me in my own castle?"

"If that's what it takes to get you to listen to reason. Think on it carefully, Aindreas. You don't want to start a fight with Eibithar's next king. You'll soon find yourself the loneliest man in the land."

"You'll not be king so long as I live! I don't care what the Rules of Ascension say! Yours is a house of butchers and liars! You're not worthy of the crown! Guards!" he shouted before Javan could say anything more.

Two men entered the chamber.

"Take the duke back to his room. He's not to be admitted to my chambers again."

"Yes, my lord."

Javan uttered a curse under his breath. "Let's not part like this, Aindreas," he said. "I'm certain we can reach an agreement that will satisfy us both."

"Leave me," Aindreas said, his tone severe. He had turned back to the window, his broad back as implacable as the walls of his castle.

Javan regarded him for another moment before turning and leading the two guards out of the chamber and into the shadows of the corridor.

He had threatened a war if Tavis was executed, and he had meant it. But somehow he didn't trust that it would be enough to save the boy's life.

Chapter
Thirteen

✦

Galdasten, Eibithar

He awoke with a start, opening his eyes to a small room that flickered with the lightning of a distant storm. It took Grinsa a moment to remember that they were in Galdasten now, the latest stop for the Revel. Cresenne stirred, saying something in a muffled voice that he didn't understand, before settling back into her slumber, her arm still resting on his chest.

He lay still for several moments, allowing his racing pulse to slow before gently moving her arm, rising quietly, and stepping to the window. As an afterthought he pulled on his breeches, which were resting on the chair beside him.

Often, after a dream of this sort, Grinsa needed time to sift through the images before he could divine the vision's meaning. In this instance, however, there could be no mistaking what he had seen or what it meant. It had never happened to him before; until tonight, he had never relived a gleaning in his sleep. Of course, this had been no ordinary gleaning. Perhaps he shouldn't have been surprised at all to see once more the disturbing image of Lord Tavis of Curgh chained to that dungeon wall. The boy was in Kentigern, just as Grinsa had feared. The vision itself hadn't revealed this, but the timing of it had. That was where Tavis and his father had gone, and Grinsa was certain that the recurrence of the image meant that the gleaning had already been realized. His powers went deep, and he had learned long ago to trust them in such matters.

"Why so soon?" he whispered, glancing back at the bed. "Why couldn't we have just a bit more time?"

As if in answer, a low rumble of thunder echoed through Galdasten City.

Already, the gleaning lay between them, undermining the trust they were trying to build like Amon's Ocean pounding at the base of sand cliffs on the Wethy Crown. Surely she knew that he could tell her nothing of what the Qiran had shown—she was a gleaner herself. Yet, perhaps because he had been so troubled by the Fating when their romance began, she continued to allude to it whenever his mood darkened.

He could not deny that she had reason. It had occupied his thoughts ever since Tavis's attack on his liege man. He had offered the vision as a warning, so that Tavis might be prepared for what the future held. What he had shown him was ugly, he knew, even shocking. But the image first offered by the stone would have raised more questions than it answered. Some of these might have led Tavis to make choices that would change the course of his own life and, thus, the course of events in the Forelands. Others would certainly have forced Grinsa to reveal things about himself that no one could know. At the time, he had been confident that he was doing what was best, not only for himself, but also for the boy and the land.

In the wake of all that had happened, that confidence had evaporated, leaving a residue of doubt that left him fearful and filled with remorse. Tavis might have been old enough for a Fating, but he was still just a few years past childhood. He couldn't have been ready for what he saw in his Fating, particularly in light of what he had probably been expecting. No doubt he had been shattered by it, too ashamed to confide in his friend or his parents, and too young and scared to face his future with courage. Better to have confused him than to have done this.

Regrets did him little good, however. He knew that he had to leave the Revel, that he had to get to Kentigern as quickly as possible. By offering this Fating to the boy instead of what the stone had intended for him, Grinsa had set himself on a path, one that tied him to Tavis's life.

And what of the life you wish to build with this woman?

That would be her question as well. He could tell himself that this was the price he paid for defying the Qiran, and the burden he bore for preserving his secret, but what would he tell Cresenne? Despite all they had shared, despite the passion that fired their nights and the love he felt building within his heart, he still had told her little about himself, aside from the fact that he could conjure mists and winds. He wanted to confide everything—he almost had on several occasions—but each time something held him back, until he began to question his capacity for trust and love. At such times he had to remind himself that they had only been together for a turn, that they had plenty of time.

Or so he had thought.

The curtains by the window stirred with a cool wind and another flash of lightning lit the room. A clap of thunder followed, louder and closer to the light than before.

"You can't sleep?"

He turned at the sound of Cresenne's voice. She was sitting up, her knees drawn to her chest.

"No, I guess not."

"The storm?"

He shook his head. "A dream."

It almost seemed that her ears pricked up, like those of a wolf when she catches the scent of prey. Her whole posture changed. "A dream, or a vision?"

He felt his defenses going up, no doubt because the dream had involved Tavis's Fating. Again it was coming between them. *It's just that she's a gleaner, too,* he told himself. *She understands the power of visions.*

"A vision actually."

"It was about Lord Tavis, wasn't it?"

"What makes you think that?" he asked. But he wasn't surprised. She already knew him so well.

"Was it?" she asked, ignoring his question.

Grinsa sighed, then nodded. "I think I'm linked to him in some way, maybe because I gleaned for him."

"That makes no sense. You've done thousands of Fatings. Why should you be tied to this one boy, but to none of the others?"

What choice did he have but to lie? "I don't know. Maybe because the stone showed us such a disturbing image. Maybe because he reacted to that image as he did." He shrugged. "I don't know," he said again. "But tonight I dreamed his Fating again. I think what he and I saw has already come to pass."

"So soon?" she asked, looking surprised. "Fatings usually look further ahead."

Once more, as he always did when the subject of Tavis's Fating arose, he felt that she was trying to make him reveal what he had seen. Perhaps some good would come of the young lord meeting his fate so quickly. At least this way, when he and Cresenne found a way to be together again, the matter would be behind them.

"Some do," he said. "Not this one."

"Well, if you're right," she said, smiling at him, "and it has come to pass, then it's over, isn't it? We can forget about Tavis and his Fating and just enjoy each other."

He turned back to the window. It had started to rain, and the wind was blowing large, heavy drops of water into the room and onto the white curtain. He should have pulled the shutters closed, but instead he just stood there, getting wet.

"It's not that easy. I have to help him, Cresenne. I have to go to Kentigern."

"What?"

He heard the bed creak and, facing her again, he saw that she had risen and was wrapping herself in a light robe.

"You're leaving the Revel? You're leaving me?"

Grinsa closed his eyes. "I don't want to, but—"

"Then don't!"

"I have to!" he said, his voice rising.

Someone in the next room pounded on the wall.

"I have to," he told her again, lowering his voice. "Somebody has to help him."

"His father is duke of Curgh! By this time next year he'll be king! If he can't help Tavis what makes you think that you can? You're a gleaner, Grinsa. We both are. We see the future, and we offer it to others to do with what they will. But once we've shown it to them, there's nothing more for us to do." She came forward and put her arms around him, resting her head against his chest. "I know that it's hard sometimes, but that's the nature of our power."

After a moment he put his arms around her as well. Qirsar knew, he didn't want to leave. He took a deep breath, smelling her hair, her skin. *Why so soon?*

She kissed his chest, and then, tilting her head upward, kissed him fully on the lips.

"Come back to bed," she whispered. "Let me convince you to stay with me."

They kissed again, but after a moment Grinsa stepped back.

"It wouldn't take much to convince me," he said, feeling a tightening in his chest. "That kiss almost did it. So I think I'd better gather my things instead."

Her expression changed so swiftly that one might have thought he had struck her.

"You're really going to do this." She offered it as a statement, a hard edge to her voice.

"I have to."

She threw up her hands. "Why?"

He couldn't possibly tell her all of it, but he felt that he owed her something, some small piece of the truth. "I told you before: I'm tied to him somehow. I think that his fate and mine are bound to each other."

That, of all things, caught her attention. She took a step back from him, narrowing her eyes. "How is that possible?"

"I don't know. As I said, it's probably tied to his Fating."

"That must have been an extraordinary gleaning," she said, sounding bitter.

"It was." As soon as the words left his lips, he regretted them, for he knew what would come next.

"What is it you saw, Grinsa? What is it that's dragging you away from me?"

He almost told her then, just to be done with it. But even with what he had done, this was not his fate to tell. It was Tavis's, and as a gleaner he was bound to silence.

"We've been through this. You know I can't tell you."

"Even now?" she demanded. "You're leaving me, running off to Kentigern to save a boy you barely know and don't particularly like. And still you can't tell me what you saw?"

"No, I can't. I'm sorry."

She turned her face away, but otherwise she didn't move. Neither did he. They just stood there in the darkness, saying nothing. He sensed her anger and he wondered if he should have been angry as well. But his sadness overwhelmed everything else.

Lightning blazed, illuminating the room like the sun for just an instant. Thunder followed almost immediately, rattling the walls and making the floor tremble like a frightened child.

"I'm not going forever, Cresenne," he said at last. "I'll do what I have to do to help Tavis, and then I'll return to the Revel, wherever it is."

She nodded, still looking away. "Of course," she said, but her tone carried no conviction.

He stepped closer to her and touched her cheek, making her meet his gaze. She offered a small smile, but it only lasted an instant.

"This is our last night together for some time," he said softly. "Let's not waste any more of it. Come to bed with me."

But she shook her head, and he thought he saw tears in her pale eyes. "I don't think I can," she whispered. "I'd better go."

She might as well have kicked him in the stomach.

"Go where?" he managed. "It's the middle of the night." He waved a hand vaguely at the window. "It's storming."

"Trin's down the hall," she said. "I can stay with him."

Trin. If he was going to drive her to another man's room, best it be his. How had this happened? He was reeling, like an army caught unawares by a more powerful foe.

He swallowed. "If that's what you want . . ."

She glared at him. "What I want? What I want is for you to tell me what this is all about! You wake up in the middle of the night from some dream that might have no meaning at all, and suddenly announce that you're leaving me to go to Kentigern to save a spoiled, arrogant boy who may not even need to be saved. And you have the gall to talk about what I want?"

"Cresenne—"

"No," she said, shaking her head. "You haven't been honest with me from the start. It's one thing to keep a gleaning to yourself because you're a gleaner and that's what you're supposed to do. But now you tell me that your fate and the fate of this boy are linked, and that changes everything. I thought we cared for each other; I thought maybe you were starting to love me."

"I am. I do already."

"I don't believe you. You can't love a person, and at the same time keep such secrets from them."

If you only knew, he wanted to say. Sometimes he wondered how one person could have so many secrets. But that hadn't kept him from falling in love with her. Once again he wanted to tell her all of it, to end all the lies right then. And once again, he found that he couldn't bring himself to do it. Perhaps he had been hiding the truth for too long and was no longer capable of sharing it with anyone. Or maybe he was just hurt at that moment and unwilling to confide in her. Whatever the reason, all he said was "Believe what you will. But I do love you."

She turned her back to him, pulling off her robe and reaching for her clothes. Another flicker of lightning lit the soft, pale skin of her back.

"There's no reason for you to leave," he said, his voice low. "I'll go. I just need to pack my things."

Thunder rolled over the city.

She pulled on her tunic, tossing her head to free her white hair. "No. I'll go. I need to get out of here."

Grinsa took a long, deep breath, but still he felt as though he were suffocating. It had happened so suddenly, and yet it seemed that he and Cresenne had been destined from the beginning to reach this point. "I will be back," he said again, but he knew that it wouldn't matter.

She paused, glancing over her shoulder at him. After a moment she nodded. She knew it as well.

Within a few minutes she was dressed. Grinsa had lit a candle and was absently gathering his things on the bed so that he could pack them into his satchel. Mostly, he was watching Cresenne. Her eyes were red, though he had not seen her shed any more tears, and her hair was disheveled. Still, he could not help but think that she was the most beautiful woman he had ever known. More beautiful even than Pheba. He had not loved this woman as he had loved his wife, at least not yet. But he had come to believe in the short time they were together that he could, given the chance. And now that chance was gone, stolen from him by a vision and the fate of Tavis of Curgh.

No, he thought, correcting himself. *This is not Tavis's fault. He didn't ask for the Fating you gave him, nor did he make you what you are. You stepped onto this path many years ago, long before you met Cresenne or Tavis.*

"What are you thinking?" Cresenne asked. She was watching him closely, looking sad and young and lovely.

"That I'm sorry. That I don't want to lose you."

"You don't have to. If you just explained this to me . . ."

Grinsa shook his head. "Please don't ask me again. Saying 'no' every time hurts too much. Maybe I can tell you when it's over. I want to. Truly I do."

She lowered her gaze and nodded. "I know you do." She looked around the room briefly as if checking to see that she hadn't forgotten something. Then she crossed to the door, stopping for just an instant to brush her lips lightly across his cheek.

Grinsa closed his eyes, breathing in her scent one last time.

Cresenne pulled the door open, but halted there. He sensed her looking back at him again, but he didn't turn to her.

"What should I tell Trin?" she asked.

Tell him to take care of you. Tell him to remind you every day of how much I love you. "I'll leave that to you. You can explain my decision to leave however you want. But don't tell anyone where I've gone or why. Please."

"I won't."

"And Cresenne."

"Yes."

He turned and their eyes met. "Make certain that Trin knows I'll be coming back." *Don't you forget that either.*

"All right."

She held his gaze for a moment longer, then turned away and pulled the door closed.

For some time he continued to stand there, staring at the door, hoping that it would open again. Lightning made the room glimmer, as if from a sputtering flame. Grinsa waited for the thunder, but it took longer than he expected. The storm was passing. But still the rain fell, gentle and cool, guided through the small window by the wind.

He shook himself, like a dog rousing itself from a long slumber, before shoving the last of his clothes and belongings into his satchel. Then he blew out the candle and lay down again, hoping that he might find a way to sleep a few hours more. It was a long ride to Kentigern—more than sixty leagues—and he would need to be rested if he was to get there in time to save Tavis.

She should have just gone to Trin's room as she had told Grinsa she would. This was a terrible risk. But though what she needed to do could wait until morning, she feared that sleep would rob her of her nerve. She had to do it now, while the pain of what had just happened was fresh and her mind set.

For almost all their time together, she had felt that Grinsa was hiding something from her, something more than just what Tavis's Fating had revealed. She thought she understood the night he revealed to her that he possessed a second magic, but even after that, the feeling lingered. Now she knew why. *I'm tied to him somehow.* Suddenly, Tavis's Fating mattered again. She would have given almost anything to know what Grinsa had seen, but she knew enough to see the danger. She had to do this, she told herself. No matter how she felt about the gleaner.

He shouldn't have been able to keep such a thing from her, not for this long. It bothered her that he had. He was just a gleaner. Or so she told herself. But there was something mysterious about him, something that would have drawn her to him even had she not needed to win his trust, something that made the nights she had spent with him more than just a lie.

There were some among her people who possessed mind-bending power, a potent magic that allowed them to touch the minds of others and convince them of nearly anything. Cresenne wasn't one of them. She had never needed such power. Men thought her beautiful and kind, particularly when she flattered them or made them believe she was attracted to them. She had learned long ago that she needed little more to make them believe her lies. That first night at the Silver Gull she had convinced Trin—even he was not immune—that she had feelings for Grinsa, and later, she had convinced the gleaner as well. The next night, when she and Grinsa had dinner alone, she continued his seduction.

Since that second night, however, something had changed. She knew that she had succeeded already in winning his trust and his affection. Indeed, she suspected that he was falling in love with her. But she sensed as well that what began as a seduction had become something far more dangerous. Only now, though, with the ache of leaving him twisting like a blade in her chest, did she know for certain. She loved him. Which was why she had to do this quickly, before she changed her mind, before she had the chance to gather her courage and go back to him.

So she walked silently down the corridor, passing Trin's room on her way to the stairs. Stepping out of the inn, she stopped at the edge of the lane, trying to get her bearings. It was raining steadily and the streets of Galdasten were dark. She knew that most of the Revel's Eandi performers were staying in two inns on the north side of the marketplace, just a short walk from where she stood, but it took her several moments to figure out which way was north. By the time she started walking her hair and clothes were already soaked. Usually she liked rains in the warmer turns, especially after a day as hot as this one had been. But tonight, the rain just felt cold. She crossed her arms over her chest and hurried across the marketplace.

She had made it a point to know where the man she needed to see was staying, which inn as well as which room. Cadel had given her the man's name before leaving the Revel, and it had been a small matter for her to inquire with the innkeeper. It was a precaution, one she had hoped would not be necessary. Certainly she had never imagined that she'd be sending this man after Grinsa.

"Damn him!" she muttered, as the rain ran down her face. "Bian take him to the darkest corners of the Underrealm."

It would have made all of this easier if she meant it. In the beginning, she had thought it a simple task. At first glance Grinsa had seemed rather ordinary. Kind, to be sure. Intelligent as well, and handsome in a plain sort of way. But a Revel gleaner and nothing more. All she had to do was seduce him, learn what she could of the gleaning, and leave him. What better way to demonstrate to the Weaver that the faith he placed in her had been justified than to assure that their plot against Curgh and his son succeeded?

But there was more to seduction, she soon learned, than merely luring a man to one's bed. And there was more to Grinsa than was apparent at first glance.

"Damn him!" she said again, quickening her stride.

She couldn't say when she first realized that she wanted to end Eandi rule of the Forelands. There had been no single moment, no sudden realization. Rather, it seemed to Cresenne that her entire life had been building to this. She still remembered the shame she had felt as a child, learning with other children, Qirsi and Eandi, of Carthach's betrayal and what it had cost her people. She would never forget how her father was treated, when, after his years on the sea, he became a lesser minister in the court of a Wethy duke. It was bad enough that the Eandi lord spoke to him with such disdain, dismissing his counsel with a wave of his hand and never even bothering to learn his name. But to see the higher-ranking Qirsi do the same filled her with rage.

Somehow her father accepted it all, but she couldn't. If the ministers could treat him this way while fawning over the Eandi, they were no different from Carthach. And if her father was willing to sacrifice his pride to remain in the court, then neither was he.

After her father died, the duke gave her mother and her twenty qinde and sent them out of his court.

"I cannot be expected to care for the families of every Qirsi who dies in my employ," he said at the time. "Your people just don't live long enough."

Cresenne was ten years old.

Her mother spoke of the incident only once before her own death five years later. It was just before she died. They had joined the Crown Fair, one of Wethyrn's traveling festivals, Cresenne as a fire player, her mother as a gleaner. They had finished a long day of travel and her mother had begun to show signs of the fever that would eventually kill her. It was dark in their room and Cresenne was certain that her mother had already fallen asleep.

"Your father was a good man," she said abruptly. "Strong, courageous, kind. I wish you had known him when he was still sailing, before Wethyrn."

Cresenne hadn't known what to say, so she had lain still in the darkness, hoping her mother would say more.

"The lords of the Forelands don't care about the Qirsi. They just collect them, the way they do war horses or swords. That's what the duke did. Your father wanted a good home for us, otherwise he never would have worked for such a man."

Those words stayed with Cresenne long after her mother's death. And though, with time, they had allowed her to forgive her father, even to love him again, they had only served to deepen her hatred of the Eandi and their Qirsi allies. She often wondered if that had been what her mother intended.

The first time the Weaver came to her, walking into her dreams like some white-haired god, Cresenne knew that she had been destined to join his cause. Perhaps he sensed this as well, for she quickly became one of his most trusted servants. It helped that she knew the festivals and was willing to travel the Forelands with them. The Weaver had recruited several ministers by then, but he also needed Qirsi who weren't tied to a particular court and could move freely about the land without drawing undue attention. There were others like her—chancellors, the Weaver called them—traveling with the Festival in Sanbira, the Emperor's Fair in Braedon, and one or two of the smaller carnivals in Aneira and Caerisse. But Cresenne was the youngest; the Weaver had told her so. Many of the older ministers seemed to resent taking orders from her, but she arranged their payments, and she spoke for the Weaver, so they never defied her.

The Weaver instructed her to eliminate Lord Tavis, but he left it to Cresenne to determine how this might best be done. She had no doubt that he would be pleased with her plan. She needed to make certain, though, that Grinsa didn't ruin everything. *I'm tied to him . . .* What could that mean?

Still making her way through the darkness and the rain, Cresenne reached the inn, hurried through the door, and started up the stairs that led from the tavern on the ground floor to the sleeping rooms above.

"Who's there?" a man's voice called from behind the bar. A moment later he lit a candle, spilling light across the open room of the tavern.

Cresenne pressed herself against the wall, hiding in the shadows.

"I—I was invited by one of your patrons to his room, sir," she said meekly.

The man stepped out from behind the bar and lifted his candle higher, but the light still did not reach her.

"Are you alone?" he asked.

"Yes, sir. He seemed a gentleman, sir."

"I'm sure he did," the man mumbled. "Bloody Revel." He turned and headed back to his room. "Go on then," he called, before shutting his door loudly.

She continued up the steps, walked carefully to his door, and knocked softly.

There was no answer for some time and she raised her hand to knock again. Just as she did, however, the door opened. It was dark in the corridor, and the man seemed to strain to see who had come. This was not a man she wanted to surprise, certainly not one she wanted to frighten. So Cresenne held out the palm of her hand and brought forth a small flame, summoning the magic as one would a memory.

He was taller than she expected, with dark eyes and dark unruly hair that gave him a wild look. He wore breeches but no shirt and Cresenne could see that he bore a small white scar on his shoulder, and another high on his chest.

"Who are you?" he asked, eyeing her suspiciously.

"You're Honok, aren't you?"

"Yes," he said. He glanced down the corridor, as if checking to see if she was alone.

"I'm a friend of Corbin."

His eyes flew back to her face, widening for just an instant. He stepped farther into the corridor and pulled the door closed.

"No," she said. "Not out here. In your room."

Jedrek frowned, but then opened the door once more and led her inside.

"Who is that?" a woman asked from the bed.

Cresenne brightened her flame, revealing a dark-haired woman sitting up in bed. She was naked and large-breasted, pretty for an Eandi woman.

"Who in Bian's name are you?" she demanded, looking Cresenne up and down.

"I'm his wife."

"His wife? But you're . . ." Hearing Jedrek's laughter, she stopped, glaring at one of them and then the other. "You bastard," she said to him. "You can both rot, as far as I'm concerned."

She rolled herself out of the bed, grabbed her clothes and walked to the door. Flinging it open, she started down the corridor, not bothering to shut it again. Jedrek walked to the door as well, watching her go before closing it.

"It took me three days to talk her into my bed," he said, facing Cresenne once more. "This had better be important."

She was in no mood to even pretend that she cared. "Get me a candle. I don't want to sustain this flame the rest of the night."

He brought her a large candle from the table by his bed. She held the wick to the flame in her hand before letting the conjured fire die out.

"What is it you want?" he asked, standing in front of her, his hands on his hips.

She sat on the bed, keeping her eyes on his face.

"You know where Cadel's gone?"

He nodded. "To Kentigern."

"And you know why?"

"I know enough. He doesn't always tell me everything. He says it's safer that way."

She considered this briefly. "He's probably right." She rubbed a hand across her mouth, then pushed her damp hair back from her brow. In spite of all that had happened that night, she didn't want to do this. She tried to tell herself that she had no choice, that everything was at risk if Grinsa wasn't stopped, but she wasn't certain it was true.

Can you risk letting him live? a voice asked within her.

"No."

"No, what?" he asked.

Cresenne hadn't even realized she had answered aloud.

"Nothing," she said. "I'm here because one of the Qirsi in the Revel, the man who was present at Lord Tavis's Fating, has decided to ride to Kentigern."

Jedrek looked puzzled. "Why?"

"He had a vision. He knows the boy is in trouble. He may even have seen what Cadel has in mind for the boy. It's possible that was what Tavis himself saw in his gleaning."

He whistled through his teeth. "Are you certain?"

She looked toward the window. The rain had slackened. "No. I'm not certain of anything. But I do know the gleaner is going to Kentigern. The rest is unimportant."

"All right. What do you want me to do?"

"Follow him. And when you've put some distance between yourself and the Revel, kill him."

He paled and lowered himself into a large chair near the window. "But he's . . . You said he's a gleaner. So that means he's . . . he's like you."

Cresenne couldn't help but smile. "He's Qirsi, if that's what you're trying to say." She leaned forward. "Is that a problem?"

"I've never killed a Qirsi," he said, averting his gaze. "Cadel usually handles them."

He wasn't making this any easier for her. "He's just a gleaner," she told him. "He shouldn't be any different from others you've killed."

Jedrek nodded, though he still looked disquieted.

"When were you to meet up with Cadel again?"

"Two turns from now, in southern Aneira."

She raised an eyebrow. "Two turns. It won't make much sense for you to rejoin the Revel when you're done."

"That's not a problem," he said.

"Perhaps not for you. But two of you leaving the Revel on the same day might attract unwanted attention." Cresenne chewed her lip for a moment. "Can you track him if he leaves a few days before you do?"

The man grinned, showing no trace of the doubts he had expressed a few moments before. "If he's in the Forelands, I can find him. All I need to know is his name and what he looks like."

Her heart was beating so hard she could hear it. She wondered if he could as well.

"His name is Grinsa jal Arriet." She almost didn't get it out for the trembling of her voice. "He's tall, broader in the shoulders than most Qirsi. He wears his hair long and untied. He has a wide mouth and high cheekbones." *And his hands are slender and more gentle than any I've ever known.*

"Is he a full-blood? White hair, yellow eyes?"

She nodded.

He frowned, but said nothing. Still, she knew what he was thinking. Like most Eandi he probably found it difficult to tell one Qirsi man from another.

"How many days do you want me to wait?"

She shrugged. "Can you afford to wait three or four?"

"It doesn't make any difference to me. Like I said, I'll find him."

"Four then. That should be enough. People will remark on the fact that you've both left, but they'll think it a coincidence, nothing more."

He nodded again. "Anything else?"

"I don't have any gold for you. All that I had for . . . for things of this sort, I gave to Cadel before he left."

"That's all right," Jedrek said. "Cadel handles the gold anyway. He'll make sure we get paid."

"Do you have enough gold to buy a horse? He'll be on horseback."

"Yes, I have enough."

Cresenne hesitated, then stood. There didn't seem to be much else to say, but she was reluctant to leave.

"I'll take care of this," he said, as if sensing her uncertainty. "He'll never make it to Kentigern."

Cresenne walked slowly to the door, but halted before she reached it, and faced him again.

"When the time comes," she said, "don't let him suffer. Do it quickly."

He took a breath, the worried look returning to his lean face. "Don't worry. I wouldn't do it any other way with a Qirsi. If I'm lucky, he won't even see me."

Chapter
Fourteen

✦

Kentigern, Eibithar, Elined's Moon waning

otir knew that he should have been grateful. On that dreadful morning, as Brienne's body lay covered with blood in Tavis's bed, he had wondered if any of them would survive the day. Certainly he'd expected that Tavis would be killed immediately. Late that day, when Javan returned to the guest quarters of the castle following his meeting with the duke of Kentigern, he too appeared to have lost all hope of saving his son's life.

"I've done all I can for him," he said at the time. "But I fear he'll be dead before sunset tomorrow."

The duke told Fotir little of his meeting with Aindreas, save that he had threatened war if Tavis was executed without fair consideration, and that Aindreas had vowed to block his ascension to the throne.

For his part, Fotir did little better with Shurik. The friendship they had started to build during their evening together at the Silver Bear crumbled under the weight of subsequent events. When he went to speak with the minister the morning after Brienne's murder, Shurik refused to see him. As much as Fotir wished to offer reassurances to his duke, he had none to give.

It seemed, however, that Javan's threats carried more weight with Aindreas than either Fotir or his duke had believed. Five days had passed since Brienne's death and Tavis's imprisonment, and still the young lord lived. He remained in prison, enduring conditions that Fotir could only describe as abominable. But at least he was alive.

The day before, four days after her death as custom dictated, Brienne was honored by the people of Kentigern. Despite his loyalty to the house of Curgh and his belief in Tavis's innocence, Fotir couldn't help but be moved by what he heard from the castle ward as the people of Kentigern filed into the castle cloister to view her body. Men and women alike wailed in their grief and screamed for Tavis's execution. At dusk, when Brienne's body was carried back to the ward and laid upon the pyre, the thousands who had lingered in the castle abruptly began to sing the lament from *The Paean to the Moons*. It was not at all the custom—they were supposed to remain silent as the fire was lit. But this only served to make their tribute more poignant. Recalling it now, though, as he walked with Javan and Xaver to the prison, Fotir realized that even this act of devotion and love had a darker side. It didn't matter if they proved Tavis innocent or not. Aindreas wanted the boy dead, and, it seemed, so did his people.

The Qirsi dreaded these visits to the dungeon, though he would never have dreamed of staying behind. Not only was the place foul and dismal, but the conversations between Javan and Tavis had grown painfully awkward. Yet each day the duke returned. Fotir would not have expected Javan to go to his son so often under such circumstances, but the duke surprised him. Perhaps he had not fully appreciated Javan's affection for the boy, or perhaps Javan himself had not realized until now how much he cared for his son. After the first day, Tavis seemed surprised to see his father as well, but he had the good sense to express only his gratitude at their return.

When they reached the dungeon on this morning, Tavis looked to be in worse condition than the day before. Javan had prevailed upon the jailers to lengthen the chains holding the boy's arms, but had been unable to do more for him. His legs were still bound, allowing him little movement. His meals remained meager and vile—mostly stale breads and half-rotten meat—and his allotment of water so small that his lips had grown dry and cracked. He was soiled and filthy, his hair matted with sweat and Qirsar knew what else. Overnight, the sores on his wrists and ankles where the manacles held him had grown darker and angrier. There were fresh bites on his arms and legs from the vermin in the prison. But more than that, Fotir saw nothing but despair and surrender in his eyes. The boy seemed to flinch at the merest sound, and he was shivering, though it was not particularly cold in the prison. It was as if the stench and the darkness, and the oppressive weight of the stone walls, had battered his spirit into submission. The duke and his men had yet to hang him, but their prison was killing him a bit at a time.

It took the young lord some time to realize that they had come, and even then, he did not appear to trust his senses.

"Father?" he said weakly, his chains ringing as he roused himself.

Javan regarded his son with a pained expression. "Yes, it's me. Fotir and Xaver are here as well."

"Good morning, my lord," Fotir said, trying to sound cheerful.

Xaver could not even bring himself to speak. He merely stared at his friend, looking like he wanted to cry, or perhaps kill.

"What day is it?"

"It's the first day of the waning," Javan answered. "Last night was the Night of Two Moons."

"In which turn?" Tavis grimaced. "Forgive me, but I can't remember."

"Elined's Turn."

The planting moon, Fotir thought. It hadn't even occurred to him until now. Throughout the land, farmers had sown their last crops the night before by the light of Panya and Ilias. Most of the planting took place earlier in the year, with the return of the rains and warm nights, but the last seeds were saved for the Night of Two Moons in Elined's Turn. Planting on this night, legend told, would bring a successful growing season. The same legends also warned that if these last seedlings were not up by Pitch Night, all the crops would fail. Had they been back in Curgh, the duke would have been riding last night, visiting as many of the towns around the castle as he could reach, sharing in the ritual plantings with the people of his realm. Instead, they were here, and the simple beauty of Curgh's farms seemed terribly far away.

"When am I to be executed?" Tavis asked.

Fotir shivered to hear the words spoken so plainly.

"They're not going to execute you," Xaver said. "We've told you before that we won't allow it."

The young lord closed his eyes and gave a small, sad smile. "There's no preventing it, Xaver. You haven't found anything yet, have you?"

For a moment none of them answered.

"No," the duke finally said. "They still haven't allowed us into the room. But one of the guards told us to return today, so perhaps Aindreas has had a change of heart."

"Have you told Mother yet?"

Javan's mouth twitched. "I sent a messenger the first day. I've heard nothing back yet."

"You should go to her, Father. You can do more for her than you can for me."

"Your mother is a strong woman. She'll be all right. And she'd never forgive me if I left you without doing all I could to win your freedom."

Tavis conceded the point with a nod.

"My lord," Fotir said, "have you remembered anything more from the night you spent with Lady Brienne? Is there something we should be looking for in the room?"

He shook his head, as he had each time Fotir asked him the question. "I was drunk. I remember very little. We were together, I remember that much. I remember kissing her and locking the door at her insistence. A few moments later she fell asleep; soon after I did as well. Too much wine." He shook his head a second time. "The next thing I knew the guards were pounding on the door and Brienne was dead." The young lord swallowed as if to keep himself from being sick. "I wish I could tell you more."

"It's all right," Xaver told him. "Maybe we'll find something in the room."

"You'll find nothing. It's been days. They've probably cleaned the room by now. Ean knows I would have."

"Did you see anyone in the corridors?" Fotir asked. "Do you think you were followed?"

"No. We followed a winding route back to my room. I barely knew where she was taking us. She wanted to be sure that we weren't seen by any of her father's guards. We were very much alone."

Javan let out a low sigh. "Well, someone must have known where you were going."

"Or perhaps I really did kill her."

His father looked at him, his dark blue eyes glinting like a dagger blade in the pale light let in by the dungeon's high window. "Is that truly what you think?"

Tavis hesitated, then shook his head. "No. I dream of her when I sleep and I think of her constantly when I'm awake. I honestly believe that I could have loved her. I just wish I could remember."

Listening to Tavis speak, Fotir found himself remembering how he had spoken of the boy to Shurik several nights before. At the time he had been truthful. He saw the boy as undisciplined and thoughtless. He resented the young lord's disregard for the standing of the House of Curgh and his father's reputation. But seeing Tavis now, listening to him struggle with his own doubts and fears, it was hard to hold onto such feelings. If the boy was innocent—and Fotir wanted to believe that he was—the gods had been terribly cruel to him. No one deserved such a fate.

"We should go," Javan said abruptly. He started to reach a hand out to his son, faltered, then grasped the boy's shoulder, causing the chains to rattle slightly. "Ean willing, we'll find something in your chamber."

"Thank you, Father."

The duke pulled away and started up the prison stairs. Fotir nodded once to Tavis before following. Xaver lingered, however, looking as if he wished to say more.

"We'll find something," he said at last. "I'm sure of it."

Tavis lowered his gaze, but managed a nod. The MarCullet boy frowned.

Xaver had offered similar assurances during earlier visits and they had started to sound forced. It was no longer clear if Xaver even believed them.

The MarCullet boy gripped Tavis's arm, then hurried to the stairs. A few moments later the guard at the door let them out and Fotir felt a cool breeze touch his face, like Morna's hand. Still, the stench of the dungeon seemed to cling to his clothes, and he longed to strip them off and bathe. Small wonder Tavis was losing hope.

They walked back to the guest quarters in silence, Javan setting such a quick pace that Fotir and Xaver struggled to keep up with him. The duke did not bother stopping at his own room, choosing instead to go straight to Tavis's chamber. The new door to the room had been put in place the day after Brienne's death, and had been locked ever since. On this morning, however, it stood slightly ajar. Javan glanced briefly at Fotir, a question in his eyes. Then he pushed the door open.

Shurik was standing in the middle of the chamber gazing at the empty space where Tavis's bed had been. There were three guards there as well, two by the door and one standing closer to the first minister.

The Qirsi turned at the sound of the creaking door hinges.

"My Lord Duke," he said, offering a halfhearted bow. His eyes flicked in Fotir's direction. "First Minister."

The duke stepped into the room. "One of your guards said that we would be allowed to examine Tavis's chamber today."

"I know," Shurik said. "I'm here to oversee your search."

Fotir entered the room as well, and as he did he felt what little hope he had left wither and die. Not only had the bed been removed, but so had all of Tavis's clothes and the flask of wine. The floor was spotless and smelled vaguely of soap. Tavis was right: there was nothing to be found here.

"Any evidence that was here has been washed away," he said, looking at Shurik. "This is what you intended all along, isn't it?"

"Not at all," the Qirsi said. "But what would you have had us do? Leave the bed as it was? Leave the lady's blood on the blankets and the bedding and the floor? We had the duke and duchess to consider. Our first duty was to them, and to the memory of their daughter." His expression changed, and Fotir suddenly had the impression that the man was enjoying himself. "Besides, it seems to me that Lord Tavis's blade was the single most important piece of evidence in the chamber. And if memory serves, First Minister, you shattered it that first morning."

Fotir took a step toward him. "You bastard!"

"That's enough, Fotir," the duke said. "What's done is done. We can still search the room. Perhaps the washers missed something."

He glared at Shurik for another moment before nodding and turning away. Xaver and Javan were already moving in slow circles around the perimeter of the chamber, examining the floor and the pieces of furniture that remained, the tapestries that hung on the side walls and the stones they covered.

Fotir crossed to the window. The wooden shutters were open, allowing the bright daylight to fill the room. It was hard to believe that Brienne had died here. He looked down at the inner ward far below, and at the closely fitting blocks of stone that made up the castle wall. The duke had suggested a few days before that the murderer might have entered the room through this window, but seeing now what that would have entailed, Fotir was even less inclined to believe it. Even assuming that someone could have made the climb, he felt certain that at least one of Kentigern's guards would have noticed.

"What do you think?" Javan asked, standing behind him. "Could someone have reached the chamber from below?"

"I think it unlikely, my lord," he said, not bothering to turn. "It looks like a difficult climb."

"Difficult, but not impossible."

"No. Not impossible."

"What about from another chamber on this level?"

Fotir hadn't considered this. Whoever it was would have had to come from the east; approaching the window from the west would have meant climbing past the duke's window as well as Fotir and Xaver's. This was the easternmost room on this, the south wall of the castle, and though there was a small ledge below the windows on this wall and on the east wall that abutted it, the rounded wall of the corner tower stood between. From what Fotir could see, climbing around the tower would have been difficult, but far from impossible and far less difficult than the climb from the ground below.

"Yes, my lord. It does look—"

It caught his eye like a ruby hanging from the throat of a noblewoman. It was small, no bigger than the tip of a finger, but it was unmistakable. On the far edge of the right-hand shutter, ending abruptly at the corner so that it looked like Ilias halfway through his waning, was a dried crescent of blood.

"It does look what?" Javan asked.

"My lord!" Fotir whispered, as if afraid that he might scare the stain away. "Come look at this!"

He stepped to the side, making room for the duke to join him at the window, but he kept pointing at the spot.

"Ean be praised!" Javan said, seeing it as well.

"You've found something?" Shurik asked, sounding doubtful.

"Indeed we have," the duke answered. He looked at Fotir, grinning for the first time in days. "Thank you."

The first minister joined them at the window, as did Xaver. Javan pulled the shutter back in toward the window and pointed at the stain.

"That's blood, First Minister," the duke said. "Somebody entered the room through this window, killed Brienne, made it seem that Tavis had done it, and then left, again through the window."

245

Shurik examined the spot for several moments, a slight frown on his narrow face. "I agree that this seems to be blood," he said at last, stepping back from the window and facing Javan. "But I fail to see how a single spot of this size supports such a wild claim."

"How else do you explain it?" Fotir demanded.

"Lord Tavis might have gone to the window after killing her."

Xaver shook his head. "You saw how much blood the murderer put on Tavis's hands. If he had gone to the window, there would be blood all over the frame."

"Perhaps there was, but the servants washed it away. Or, for that matter, maybe the servants got blood on their hands while they were washing the room and then put that spot there themselves."

"That's absurd!" said the duke.

"No more so than the notion of a wall-climbing assassin, my lord."

"You're just determined to blame this murder on my son! And so is your duke."

"And you, sir, are desperate to save him, even if it means fabricating these ridiculous tales."

"Watch yourself, Qirsi!" the duke said, leveling a rigid finger at the man. "Remember to whom you speak!"

"I wouldn't care if you were already king, my lord," Shurik said, meeting Javan's gaze. "Your son would still be in our prison and I would still be skeptical of all you've said. Justice in Kentigern is meted out fairly, without regard to station." He turned and started toward the door. "You found what you were looking for. Now I'd suggest that you return to your quarters."

"I demand that you inform your duke of what we've found!" Javan said, his voice booming in the small chamber.

The minister stopped just short of the doorway and faced the duke once more. "I have every intention of informing him, my lord," he said, his voice even and low. "I'll tell him as well what you think it means. And I'll offer my own opinion, which is that your little discovery does little to counter all the evidence pointing to Lord Tavis's guilt."

He turned again, and left the room, accompanied by one of the guards.

For some time, Fotir and his companions said nothing. Then the MarCullet boy returned to the window and stared at the crescent of blood.

"It has to mean something," he said. "Doesn't it?"

Fotir wanted to tell him it did, but he knew the true answer even before Javan spoke it aloud.

"It only means something," the duke said, "if Aindreas allows it to."

The screams of the other prisoner had become hoarse and ragged. They were softer as well, almost feeble, as if the man's strength was finally flagging. Since his first day in the dungeon, Tavis had tried to ignore the screaming. To some extent he was finally succeeding. He could sleep now, which was an improvement over the first several days, and there were times when the sound seemed to fade to the back of his mind, like the crash of the breakers on the cliffs below Curgh Castle.

Still, he always noticed when the sound stopped, because of the relief that silence brought, to be sure. But also because it meant invariably that someone was entering the prison.

So when the screaming stopped this time, trailing off uncharacteristically into a fit of coughing, he assumed that his father or Xaver had returned yet again. His father had already come to see him a second time this day, to tell him of the blood they had found on the window shutter outside his chamber. It was news that might have heartened him, had he dared to allow himself to hope. Perhaps another visit would again offer good tidings. Even after the prisoner's coughing ceased, however, the door at the top of the stairs did not open. Tavis waited, listening for the sound of the bolt being thrown or of voices on the far side of the door. After a time, he began to listen as well for some sound from the other man in the dungeon. But all in the prison remained still.

Had the prisoner lost consciousness? Had he died? It had never occurred to Tavis that he would, though of course it should have. The man was in the forgetting chamber. Ean knew how long he had gone without food or water. It was amazing that he had lasted this long. Yet Tavis could not bring himself to accept that the prisoner wouldn't resume his screaming in another moment.

He should have been relieved. How many hours had he spent praying for silence? How many times had he wanted to shout at the man to stop? At last he had peace. But at what cost? As unnerving as the screaming had been, the thought of being truly alone in the dungeon was worse. As ridiculous as it seemed, he had taken some comfort from the other prisoner's mere presence. Or maybe—was it possible?—he had taken comfort in the man's misery, in the knowledge that his own fate, though wretched, was better than that of the poor fool in the forgetting chamber.

Suddenly the dungeon felt darker, smaller, colder. The terror he had struggled for days to control began to rise again in his chest, clawing at his heart like some demon from the Underrealm. He thought about calling to the man, asking him if he was all right. But what if he answered? What if he didn't?

He closed his eyes, fighting desperately to resist the urge to start screaming himself, when at last he heard the opening of the prison door and footsteps on the stairs. Maybe this was why the man had fallen silent.

Opening his eyes again, Tavis climbed awkwardly to his feet and strained to look up at the stairs, expecting to see Xaver or his father. What he saw instead made his stomach heave.

Brienne's father had come, accompanied by two guards and the prelate of Kentigern's Cloister of Ean.

"I'm to be executed," Tavis whispered. "Ean have mercy."

"It pleases me to hear you invoke the god, my son," the prelate said, a smile on his thin, bony face. "Perhaps there is still hope for your soul."

"Have you come to hang me?" Tavis asked, his voice trembling like a child's. He looked briefly at the prelate, but then shifted his gaze to Aindreas.

The duke's expression was as hard as the prison walls, his eyes filled with loathing. Tavis had no doubt that the duke wanted him dead, and would have been happy to kill him with his bare hands.

But it was the prelate who answered his question. "No, my son. There will be no hanging today. But the time approaches and the Underrealm awaits. Have you made your peace with Ean?"

"I—I don't know."

"There is a cloister in Curgh Castle, is there not?"

"Of course, Father Prelate."

"And who is the prelate there?"

"His name is Nevyl. I can't remember his family name."

"Nevyl," the prelate repeated, his smile broadening. "Of course. Brother Ortishen."

Tavis nodded. Ortishen. That was it. The prelate was close to his mother, less so to his father, who still resisted the movement away from the older faith toward Ean worship. The duke journeyed out of the castle once every turn to visit with the prior of Curgh's Sanctuary of Elined. As Eibithar's future king, Javan often said, he had a responsibility to listen leaders of both faiths, as did Tavis. But the duchess disapproved, reminding him pointedly that other houses in Eibithar had embraced the cloisters and insisting that it was time Curgh did the same. For his part, Tavis preferred the ancient rituals and meditations of the sanctuary to the somber liturgies of the Ean worshipers. Still, his mother made certain that he spent at least a few moments of each day in the cloister.

"No doubt Nevyl has led you in the recitation of Ean's Teachings," the prelate went on.

"Yes, Father Prelate."

"So you know that Ean values truth above all else. 'Thy word shall be golden and thy deeds the reflection of thine heart.'"

Tavis recognized the phrase: Ean's Fourth Doctrine. Had his father been there, he would have pointed out that if Ean valued truth above all else, this would have been the first doctrine. Tavis, though, said nothing.

"Please, my son, you do not want to face Ean with deceit lying heavy on your heart. The Underrealm is a cruel place for those who hide the truth."

"Yes, Father Prelate, I'm sure it is." He knew where this was leading, what they wanted him to say. He faced Aindreas again, meeting the duke's glare as best he could. "You want me to confess to Brienne's murder."

"We want you to find peace," the prelate insisted. "You have taken a life, and must answer to the god for that. Do not face him as a liar as well as a murderer. Confess now, and perhaps your path into the Underrealm will be easier."

"I can't do that," Tavis said, still looking at the duke. "I didn't kill her."

"You lying pile of dung!" the duke said, striding forward and striking him with the back of his hand.

Tavis's ears rang with the blow and his cheek burned. He held his breath for a moment, fighting back the tears that had sprung to his eyes. He kept his face turned to the side, not daring to look at Aindreas again.

"Don't do this, my son," said the prelate, his voice as soothing as a balm. "Please. Your life has been destroyed by butchery and lies. Do not make the same mistakes as you go to face the god."

"I didn't kill her," he said again, knowing what the duke would do.

Aindreas's blow hammered his head against the stone wall. His knees buckled, but he managed somehow to keep his balance. He felt blood begin to flow from high on his cheek, where the duke had hit him, as well as from his temple, where his head had crashed into the wall. More than anything he wanted to be brave, to endure this in a way that would have made Brienne proud, but he could not hold back his tears.

"Confess, you craven bastard!" Aindreas hissed.

Tavis choked back a sob, but didn't answer.

"Confess!" he said again, mashing the boy's head against the wall. He brought his face close to Tavis's, his hands still pushing on the boy's head. Tavis smelled wine on his breath. "Confess, I say!"

The prelate cleared his throat. "My Lord Duke, I'm not certain that this—"

"Go!" Aindreas commanded, not even looking at the man. "Your work here is done."

There was a long silence. Tavis was aware of nothing save the duke's rasping breath warming his cheek.

"Very well," the prelate said at last. "Ean have mercy on your soul, my son."

It seemed to take the man forever to climb the stairs and leave the dungeon. All the while, Aindreas did not move, not even to release him. Tavis felt as though his skull would shatter like crystal under the duke's hand, and he wondered if that was Aindreas's intention.

But when the prison door finally opened and then closed, indicating that the prelate was gone, Aindreas backed away.

"I'm glad you refused him," the duke said. His face was red, and his eyes had a wild look to them. "I rather like the idea of you enduring the tortures of the Underrealm for all eternity. I was torn, for a time, because I want to hear a confession. The prelate has assured me, however, that a confession resulting from torture would not spare you after your death. That was why he insisted that I allow you the chance to give one freely." He shrugged. "Now that you've refused him, I'm free to do with you as I please."

"I swear to you, my lord, I did not do this."

Tavis would never have thought that a man of Aindreas's size could move so swiftly. But in a blur of light and steel and swirling cloth that he could barely follow, the duke drew his sword and slashed him across the shoulder.

The boy screamed in pain as blood began to soak into the tatters that were once his banquet clothes.

The duke held out his blade to that its point hovered like a bee just before Tavis's eyes.

"Every denial will draw blood," he said. "Every lie will bring pain."

"But it's the truth!"

Again the blade flashed, this time along his cheek. Tavis gasped. It felt as though his face were burning, as if the blood running down his jaw and neck were molten earth flowing from a fire crevice.

"Lie again and you'll lose an eye."

"When my father sees me—"

"Ah yes, your father." The duke shook his head. "I think it will be some time before your father or his companions will be allowed down here again. They probably won't see you until the day of your hanging."

Tavis closed his eyes, feeling the tears start to flow again.

"You thought that the blood they found today would win your release, didn't you?"

He said nothing, fearing that any response would bring the blade again.

But even his silence could not save him.

"Answer me!" the duke raged, pressing the point of his sword against the corner of Tavis's eye.

"Yes," he breathed. "That's what I thought."

Aindreas removed the blade, at least for the moment. "I thought as much. That seems to be what your father expected as well." He smiled thinly, shaking his head once more. "That blood means nothing to me, not compared to the blood on your dagger and on your hands." He stepped forward again, grabbing Tavis's shirt in his fist. "Look at this!" he said, his voice echoing off the walls. "Look at it! Her blood is still here on your clothes! And you want me to believe you're innocent, just because your friends found a drop of blood on a window shutter?"

Tavis was trembling. He looked to the side, then down at the floor. Anything to avoid what he saw in the duke's eyes.

"Do you?"

He nodded, and it probably saved his eye. The sword sliced into him again, but from the corner of his eye to the top of his ear. Even with the blood flowing into his eye, he could still see. His tears stung like a surgeon's spirits, but Tavis dared not make a sound. He merely clenched his teeth, waiting for the next cut and wondering what he had done to offend the gods that they should put him through this.

"You think me cruel," Aindreas said. He offered it as a statement, Tavis noted with relief. No question to answer. "You think that I'm inhuman because I take pleasure in causing you pain. If you had lived long enough to be a father, perhaps you would have understood."

I'm not dead, he wanted to say. *Don't speak of me as if I am.*

Instead he held his tongue.

The duke raised his sword again, but then frowned and lowered it. "If I'm not careful," he said, "you'll bleed to death. Best to find another method of persuasion. Unless you care to confess now."

Still Tavis said nothing. Aindreas came forward, grabbing his left hand and bending back his little finger.

"Answer! Will you confess?"

"No," Tavis said, as bravely as he could. "There is nothing to—" He broke off, hollering in agony as the duke snapped the bone.

Aindreas took hold of the next finger. "There are nine more. How many must I break before you'll tell me what I want to hear?"

"Would you have me lie?"

Pain like white fire flared in his mind. Whimpering like a babe, he sunk to the floor, though the duke still held his hand. He sensed Aindreas staring down at him, but he couldn't bring himself to look up. After a moment, the man dropped his hand and squatted down before him.

"Why do you deny it?" he asked, sounding almost kind. "You must know by now that it won't save your life, that it will only bring you more pain."

At that, Tavis did look at him, summoning courage he didn't know he possessed. "Yes, I do know it. And yet I persist. Doesn't that tell you something?"

Aindreas slapped him again, this time catching him in the temple where he had hit his head on the stone wall. Tavis held his breath, waiting for this new pain to recede.

That's my reward for courage.

"It tells me only that you are your father's son. Like him, you're stubborn and foolhardy." The duke looked at him for a few seconds more before standing and shaking his head. "I'll return tomorrow. We'll start with the thumbs, I think. I've been told that can be quite painful."

He started to walk away.

"Can I ask you something?" Tavis called to him.

"Of course."

"Without fear of being struck or maimed?"

Aindreas's face reddened again, and just for an instant Tavis thought the duke would kick him. After a brief hesitation, however, he nodded.

The boy closed his eyes for an instant. His hand was throbbing, as were his cuts and the bruises on his face. Perhaps it would have been easier to make up a confession. But he could not bring himself to surrender. In that respect he was his father's son.

"Well?" the duke said, sounding impatient.

"If I had killed her," Tavis said, looking up at him, "why would I have stayed there in the room with her. Why wouldn't I have fled from Kentigern?"

Aindreas shrugged. "You were drunk. You fell asleep. I don't think you planned to kill her. I think it was an act of blind passion, like your attack on Hagan's boy."

Tavis's eyes widened and he felt his face grow hot.

"Yes," the duke said. "I know about that. It seems drink has been your undoing."

"What happened with Xaver was different!" he said quickly. "I had just come from a bad Fating! I was distraught!"

"Of course," Aindreas said, sounding unconvinced. "And just what did this bad Fating show?"

Tavis faltered and looked away. How could he answer? "It doesn't matter."

"No," the duke said. "I don't suppose it does."

He turned again and climbed the stairs, followed closely by the two guards who remained. Tavis heard the door open and then he heard the duke say, "He's not to have any more visitors. Not even his father. If they protest, send them to me."

The door closed again and the voices began to recede. Tavis took a long breath and started to sob as he hadn't since he was a young boy. The pain in his hand seemed to hammer at him with every beat of his heart. He felt blood from his face and shoulder drying on his skin, the sword cuts burning like brands. The bruises on his face felt swollen and tender.

Yet it was not the pain that made him cry, at least not entirely.

He had been thoughtless on occasion. Certainly he had been foolish, perhaps even cruel. And he would never forgive himself for what he had done to Xaver. But in this instance he was innocent. He was almost certain of it. The spot of blood discovered by his father and Xaver had to mean something. What a harsh irony it was, that he should suffer so for the one dark act he had not committed.

He heard bells ringing in the city. Probably the prior's bells, though again he had lost all sense of time. But in the silence that followed the distant toll, he remembered the other prisoner, whose screams had tormented him for days. He strained his ears, listening for any sound, any sign of life. He knew, though, that he would hear none. The man was gone, dead in the forgetting chamber. Tavis had never felt so alone.

Chapter
Fifteen

✦

Southwestern fringe of Kentigern Wood, Eibithar

As a young man growing up in Aneira, Jedrek had spent much of his time hunting in the southern portion of the Great Forest, near where the Black Sand River meets the Rassor. His father, the most successful smith in Crieste, the second-largest city in the dukedom of Dantrielle, had considered hunting beneath Jedrek's station and had tried his best to convince the boy to learn smithing.

"Hunting is for idle princes and unskilled brutes," he often said. "Young men looking to make their way in the world need a craft."

Even as a youth, however, Jedrek knew where his talents lay, and he knew as well that his father was wrong. Hunting was a craft for those who treated it as such. Any fool, prince or brute, could travel the forest long enough to blunder across a bear or a wildcat and slaughter it. But to track and kill a single prey took forethought, cunning, and, above all, knowledge of the beast's habits and needs. By the time Jedrek was old enough for his Fating, he could track wolves over stone and wood elk through a streambed.

Not long after his Fating he learned that people could be hunted as well, and that the rewards were far greater. The skills required, though, were the same: patience, guile, and an understanding of one's prey.

In this case, Jedrek's prey was Qirsi, which made him dangerous in ways even the most accomplished Eandi swordsmen were not. But the fact that this man, Grinsa jal Arriet, was a white-hair also told Jedrek much of what he needed to know in order to track him

255

across Eibithar. Jedrek knew which inns he would seek out along the way and to whom he would turn for help. Other Qirsi were not likely to be very helpful if Jedrek went to them asking questions, but by the same token, those Eandi with whom Grinsa had dealings were far more likely to remember him. Lone Qirsi travelers were something of a rarity throughout the Forelands, particularly in the north.

It helped as well that Jedrek knew where the gleaner was going, just as it was easier to hunt a wildcat once he found its den. He had waited four days before going after him, just as the Qirsi woman had instructed. The trail was already cold between Galdasten and Curgh. He knew it, so he didn't even bother looking. He merely rode southward across the Moorlands, pushing himself and his mount as hard as he dared. Whatever the limits of the gleaner's magic, he was no match for Jedrek in strength or stamina. None of the Qirsi were. If Jedrek rode fast enough for long enough, he'd catch him.

When he neared Heneagh, as the sun set on his third day of pursuit, he began stopping in towns and asking questions. He was bone-weary, his legs and back aching. It had been some time since he had ridden a mount so hard. But when the Eandi smith in a farm village just north of Heneagh told him that he'd shod a horse for a tall Qirsi traveler two evenings before, all of Jedrek's pain seemed to vanish. The grey-haired man believed that the stranger had stayed in the village overnight—there was a tavern that catered to his kind on the far side of town, the smith said.

Jedrek couldn't have asked for more. He had made up two days on the gleaner already, and he could cover the rest of the distance in Kentigern Wood, where the Qirsi was less likely to notice his approach. He briefly considered going to the inn to check on the smith's story, but quickly thought better of it. It was a small town; chances were that the old man was right. Better to make an informed guess than to raise suspicions with too many questions. Thanking the smith with a five-qinde piece, he left the village and continued southward, crossing the Heneagh River by the light of the moons and riding to the northern boundary of the wood before stopping for the night.

Jedrek resumed his pursuit with the first light of dawn, feeling like an army commander who had guided his soldiers to the high ground for a coming battle. In the wood, he could track anything or anyone, and having grown up in Aneira's Great Forest, he could ride among the trees at a good pace. Even after nearly two days, the Qirsi's path was obvious. Hoof marks on the forest path, broken twigs and trampled leaves where the man's horse had rested and fed, and, late in the day, freshly blackened ground where the gleaner had cooked a meal and warmed himself as he slept. He even found a few white hairs in the dirt beside the remains of the fire. They were long and fine, obviously from a Qirsi. It seemed that the gleaner did not fear being tracked, or was merely too careless to know any better. Whatever the reason, his marks on the forest were unmistakable. By the time evening fell, they had begun to look very fresh as well.

The Qirsi was half a day ahead of him, no more. Jedrek could close the distance that remained tomorrow. By the time the moons were up tomorrow night, the gleaner would be dead.

The thought of it made his stomach tighten. He tried to convince himself that he always felt this way before a kill, but he knew better. Tossing the rest of the smoked meat he had been eating into the shadows cast by his small fire, Jedrek leaned back against the trunk of a large oak and pulled out his dagger, the one he had gotten in Thorald nearly two years before. He had used it quite often since then, but the Sanbiri steel glimmered like a mirror in the firelight, showing no sign of wear.

It was true that he had never killed a Qirsi, though he still was not certain why he had confided such a thing to the woman who had sent him after Grinsa. Even Cadel didn't know. Cadel always handled the jobs involving Qirsi because he was better with a blade than Jedrek, and because he kept all the difficult jobs for himself. It was part of their arrangement, and Jedrek had never challenged it. But Cadel would have been surprised to learn the truth. On the other hand, he might have understood. Tracking a Qirsi was one thing. Killing one of the white-haired sorcerers was something else again.

Jedrek didn't like to take a man in the back, without showing himself. That was a coward's way. But in this case, he thought, carefully testing the dagger's edge with his thumb, he'd have little choice.

"He's just a gleaner," she had said. "He shouldn't be any different from others you've killed."

Right. Except what if he knew Jedrek was coming for him? What if he had seen it, or dreamed it, or whatever they did? What then?

"He's still just a man," Jedrek said aloud. "Maybe he'll have a blade of his own, or even a sword. But he's still just a man, and a weak one at that."

Still, his doubts remained. Despite the woman's assurances, and those he offered to himself in the flickering light of the fire, he couldn't help but think that a Qirsi, no matter how limited his powers, presented unfathomable dangers.

Take him quickly, in the back. Better a coward than a corpse.

It was as good a thought as any to carry with him to sleep. He returned his blade to its sheath and laid it on the ground beside him before closing his eyes. But sleep didn't come easily, and when finally he drifted off, his dreams were haunted by strange images of the Qirsi and their magic.

He awoke before dawn, forced from sleep by his last dream. Daylight was just beginning to seep into the wood. A fine grey mist hung among the trees and a single jay called from far away, its cries echoing eerily through the still branches above him. Most of the images that had come to him in his slumber had left only vague, unsettling impressions. But this last one remained disturbingly clear. He had been here in the wood, the trees shrouded in darkness. The Qirsi woman had been with him, holding a flame in the palm of her hand as she had the night she came to his room. As he watched her, unable to move or even utter a sound, held, he realized, by magic, she came forward, smiling, the fire she held shining in her pale eyes. She raised her hand over her head, and in that moment, the shape of the flame changed, becoming a fiery dagger, which she plunged into his chest.

He stood, stretching out stiff limbs, and then stamped his feet. His clothes and hair were damp and the air felt too cold for Elined's Turn. He knew he should eat something, but the knot in his stomach remained and there was a sour taste in his mouth. Instead, he stooped to retrieve his dagger, tucked it into his belt, and climbed onto his mount.

For an instant he considered abandoning his pursuit. He was no gleaner, and his dreams could not foretell the future. But he feared there was an omen in the vision that had awakened him. It no longer mattered that he was in the wood, or that he had gained so quickly on the Qirsi. His passion for the hunt was gone. Just a day before he had compared himself to a battle commander on the verge of a great victory. Now he felt like a foot soldier marching toward his doom.

But Cadel needed him, though he knew nothing of the gleaner's approach. If the Qirsi managed to save Curgh's son, all would be ruined and their gold lost. This was why Jedrek had remained with the Revel: to make sure that Cadel wasn't followed. This was what Cadel expected of him, always: to protect his back, to guard against the unforeseen. With any luck at all, Cadel was already in Aneira, expecting Jedrek to join him at some point. The path to Aneira, it seemed, wound through Kentigern. Thrusting away his doubts, he kicked his horse into motion and resumed the hunt.

He picked up the Qirsi's trail almost immediately. Just before midday—earlier than he had expected—he came upon the blackened ground on which the man had made his fire the previous night. For the rest of the day, Jedrek had to force himself to slow down, not wishing to overtake the gleaner before he was ready. Still, the marks Grinsa left on the trail grew fresher, until Jedrek half expected the Qirsi to jump out in front of him at every turn. Late in the day, when he suddenly flushed a covey of quail from a thicket, he nearly cried out.

He halted then, swinging down off his mount to catch his breath and calm his pounding heart. He had a feeling that the gleaner was close, though he was not certain how much faith he could place in his instincts at that moment. In the end, he decided to trust himself. Better to be wrong in this, than to give himself away by stumbling into the Qirsi too soon.

When twilight began to darken the wood, Jedrek started forward again. He left the horse tied to a tree, choosing to follow the Qirsi's trail on foot. Thus far, Grinsa had stuck to the path except to rest and make camp, and Jedrek guessed that he would continue to do the same. Night fell, making the signs harder to read, but he followed the path, trusting that it would lead him to the Qirsi. After a time, Jedrek realized that his blade was in his hand, though he didn't remember taking it out. Cadel would have laughed at him, arming himself to fight wraiths in the wood, but the feel of the smooth wooden hilt in his palm comforted him, and he held it ready as he advanced through the darkness.

At last, as Panya rose above the trees, softly lighting the leaves overhead, Jedrek spotted the orange glow of the gleaner's fire. He froze in midstride for just a moment, his heart abruptly pounding in his chest until the sound of rushing blood filled his ears.

He hasn't seen you. Be calm and be silent, and he's yours. It was Cadel's voice he heard, and like the dagger in his hand, it eased his fears.

He crept forward, sticking to the path as long as he could before easing himself into the shadows of the wood. The Qirsi was on the far side of the fire and Jedrek had to move in a wide circle to get behind him without being heard. A light wind was blowing, stirring the trees and helping to mask the sound of his approach, but still he took his time, taking slow, deliberate steps, and doing all he could to avoid dried leaves and twigs.

By the time he was close enough to ready himself for the attack, the gleaner was settling down beside the fire. Jedrek paused in the shadows lurking just beyond the light of Grinsa's fire. The act of stalking the man had calmed him, but his right hand was sweating, and he had to shift his blade to the left for a moment to dry his fingers. This was no time for an uncertain grip.

Taking the dagger in his right hand again, he breathed in slowly and lowered himself into a crouch. *Do it quickly.* This time it was the woman's voice, and it reached him as more of a plea than a warning. He nodded, as if she could see him, and then lunged at the man, intending to plunge the blade into the gleaner's back as he landed on him.

It was not until his feet left the ground that he realized how badly he had miscalculated, and by then, of course, it was too late.

The Qirsi, lying on the ground beside the fire, rolled. Not away from him—that would have taken him into the flames—but toward him, so that Jedrek sailed over him, landing awkwardly on the hard ground and just missing the fire himself. It was as if the man had been expecting Jedrek's attack, as if he had known all along that Jedrek was stalking him.

Jedrek scrambled to his feet and spun toward the gleaner, his dagger ready again, but now the Qirsi was on his feet, holding a blade of his own.

The woman had described him as tall and broader than most Qirsi, but still Jedrek had pictured a typical white-hair—tall perhaps, but frail and narrow in the shoulders. Certainly he had not expected the formidable, powerfully built man who faced him, his yellow eyes flashing with firelight, his long white hair stirring in the wind.

"Who in Bian's name are you?" the gleaner demanded.

Jedrek said nothing, but dove at the man again, slashing at him with his dagger.

The Qirsi jumped back, dodging the attack. He waved his blade at Jedrek as he did, but without much effect. Jedrek grinned. The man might have been built like a fighter, but he had no skill with a weapon. Grinsa seemed to recognize this as well, for he began to back away slowly, circling the fire as Jedrek advanced on him.

"What is it you want from me?" he asked, his eyes flicking down toward Jedrek's blade.

Jedrek lunged at him again, but the Qirsi danced away.

"I think you know," Jedrek said.

The gleaner nodded and licked his lips, his eyes drawn repeatedly to the fire now, as if he was looking for a way to use it against Jedrek.

"Why?" the man asked. "You can at least tell me that."

"It's not my choice," Jedrek said. "I was sent after you."

"Sent?" he repeated, narrowing his eyes. "You're one of the singers, aren't you? From the Revel."

The gleaner had halted, and rather than answering, Jedrek leaped at him again, his blade raised. He knew that this time he was close enough, that Grinsa, his eyes widening, knew it as well. The Qirsi was a dead man.

But in that instant, just before he buried his dagger in the gleaner's heart, he heard a sound that reminded him oddly of his father's hammer ringing on hot steel. At the same time, the gleaming blade of his weapon splintered, as though it were mere glass. His attack carried him forward so that he hit the Qirsi's chest with the hilt of his dagger, but the man just staggered back a step. There was no blood on him.

Jedrek stared down at what remained of his weapon, unable to speak. After a moment he looked up at the gleaner, who was watching him with a grim expression, his own blade held before him again.

"How did you . . . ?" Jedrek trailed off, shaking his head. The answer was obvious. He probably should have run, but all he could do was stand there, his eyes drawn once more to the useless piece of polished wood that lay in his hand. "But she said you were just a gleaner."

Grinsa was about to order his attacker onto his knees when the full import of what the man had said hit him. He felt cold suddenly, as though the warm wind moving through the wood had turned frigid.

She?

"Who told you I was just a gleaner?"

The sound of his voice seemed to jar the man into motion. He whirled as if to flee into the woods. But Grinsa grabbed him from behind and they both tumbled to the ground. The man was strong—stronger than Grinsa—and he almost got free. But when Grinsa pressed the edge of his dagger against the man's neck, his struggles abruptly ceased.

Grinsa's horse, that was tied nearby, snorted anxiously and stamped his feet.

"Who told you?" the Qirsi asked again. He was shivering. How had it turned so damned cold?

"A woman in Galdasten," the man said. "A white-hair, like you."

He didn't want to ask. Qirsar knew he didn't. But what choice did he have?

"What was her name?"

"She didn't say."

Of course she didn't. "What did she look like?"

"She looked like a Qirsi. I can't tell one of you from another."

He was lying. She was beautiful. Even an Eandi brute like this one could see that. He tightened his hold on the man, pushing his blade against his skin until blood began to seep out from beneath the steel edge.

"What did she look like?"

"Young," the man said, his voice rising. "Pretty. Pale eyes, long hair. I swear, I don't know how to describe you people!"

It explained so much. Everything, really. He should have known. He could sense a man tracking him through the wood without even seeing him, yet he could not see through the deceptions of the woman sharing his bed.

He must have relaxed his hold on the man, because before he could ask why she wanted him dead, the dark-haired man grabbed hold of Grinsa's blade hand and at the same time dug an elbow into the Qirsi's side. Grinsa gasped and tried to hold the man down, but it was too late. He was on his feet again and bounding into the wood. Grinsa jumped up as well, but rather than giving chase, he formed a thought in his mind—an image really—and propelled it forward as if with his breath. The effort tore a second gasp from his chest and left him feeling light-headed for just an instant. But it worked.

A large branch from an oak snapped and crashed to the ground just in front of the Eandi man, forcing him to stop.

"The next one kills you!" Grinsa called, though he wasn't certain that he had the strength to do it again.

Fortunately, the man didn't make him try. He turned and faced Grinsa, looking like a frightened child.

"Come here," the Qirsi commanded.

Slowly, almost timidly, the man started back toward the fire.

Grinsa was lucky she had sent an Eandi. Another Qirsi would have better understood the limits of his power. The Eandi were too afraid of magic to learn its ways.

The man stepped back into the circle of light cast by the fire, eyeing Grinsa warily. There was a line of dark blood on his neck where the Qirsi's blade had cut him, and his hair and clothes were covered with dirt, but otherwise he was unmarked.

"Sit," Grinsa said, waving his dagger at the ground.

The man lowered himself to the ground, his gaze never straying from Grinsa's face.

"What's your name?"

He hesitated. "Honok."

It had to be an alias. The man was an assassin; he wasn't about to give his real name. But Grinsa merely nodded. It made little difference. He just needed something to call him.

"I'm going to ask you some questions, Honok. I'll know if you're lying, so you might as well answer me truthfully. You don't want to make me angry."

"Can't you just read my thoughts?" the man asked. "Why bother with questions at all?"

"I can divine your thoughts, yes. But it would be quite uncomfortable for you. I thought you might want to avoid that."

There was some truth in this. He did have the divining power, though it offered him little more than a indistinct sense of another's emotions, and it could have been unpleasant, even painful, for Honok. This wasn't why he chose not to use it, however. He was beginning to tire. He had shattered the man's dagger and brought down the tree limb in the span of just a few moments. There were limits to a Qirsi's magic, even his. The exertion of power necessary for a divining would probably leave him too weakened to do much more than just sleep.

Once again, though, Honok's ignorance proved to be Grinsa's ally. The man paled at the implied threat, and, after a moment, nodded.

"The woman who sent you—" He paused, gritting his teeth against a wave of nausea. "Did she say why she wanted me dead?"

"She didn't want you reaching Kentigern," Honok said.

"Why not?"

"She didn't want you helping the boy."

"The boy," Grinsa repeated.

"The duke of Curgh's son."

Grinsa wasn't surprised. Knowing what he did of Tavis's fate, and remembering all the questions she had asked about his gleaning, he could hardly expect anything else. But still his chest ached, as though the man's dagger had found its mark after all.

"Why did she send you?" he asked.

Honok looked away, saying nothing.

"You're an assassin?"

He nodded, still not looking at Grinsa.

The Qirsi stared at Honok for several moments, trying to recall the times he had seen him at the Revel. The more he looked, the more familiar the man's face appeared, until finally he began to nod.

"You have a partner, don't you?"

Honok looked at him sharply.

"That's why she went to you, because your partner is already in Kentigern. He's the one who went after Tavis in the first place."

"I work alone!" the man insisted. But Grinsa heard the lie in his voice.

Again the Qirsi nodded. He could see the other man in his mind. He could picture them singing together. "I remember him, too. Tall and thin. Built like me, wasn't he? But with black hair and a beard."

"No!" the man cried. Moving so fast that Grinsa was caught off guard, he jumped to his feet and hurled himself at the Qirsi. Somehow, he had a dagger in his hand—too late, Grinsa realized that he hadn't searched him for a second weapon—and he raised it over his head, once again aiming a blow at the Qirsi's heart.

Grinsa threw out a desperate hand, deflecting Honok's arm at the last instant. But the dagger blade sliced into his left shoulder as the two men fell to the ground again, Grinsa on his back and Honok on top of him. The dark-haired man yanked the blade out of Grinsa's shoulder and stabbed down with it again, this time trying to bury it in the Qirsi's throat.

Grinsa formed the thought and forced it from his mind so quickly, with such blind desperation, that he could barely control it. As it was, instead of hearing the clear ringing of shattering steel, he heard something duller, like the muffled snapping of wood. Honok screamed out in pain, his dagger falling harmlessly to the ground as he rolled off of Grinsa and began to writhe on the dirt, clutching his arm to his chest.

Grinsa's shoulder throbbed as though the blade were still in his flesh. He put a hand to the wound, exploring it gingerly as warm blood flowed freely over his fingers. The cut went all the way to the bone.

"Damn you!" he said, forcing himself to sit up.

Honok just glared at him, his own pain written plainly on his face.

In a way, the pain in his shoulder was the least of his problems. Honok knew he was a gleaner, and he had seen him shatter wood and steel, not to mention bone. Now Grinsa had to heal himself, and Honok as well, if he was going to keep him alive. How much could he afford to reveal? And what was he to do with Honok? He couldn't keep the man with him without putting his own life at risk. Nor could he take him to a town and have him imprisoned. If Honok and his partner were as skilled in their dark trade as he suspected, there were no prisons outside those of the major houses that could hold him. Releasing him, of course, was out of the question, not only because of who he was and what he might do to Tavis and others, but also because of what he knew. If word got back to Cresenne that Grinsa had other powers, it would raise her suspicions, and given what he knew of her now, that seemed the greatest risk of all.

All of which meant that Honok had to die.

Grinsa shivered. Over the course of his life, he had gone to great lengths to preserve his secret, but he had never killed for it.

He's an assassin, he told himself. *He would have killed you tonight if you hadn't stopped him. Who knows how many others he's murdered, or how many more he'll kill if you let him go?*

It was an excuse, nothing more. All of it might have been true, but if he did this, that wouldn't be the real reason. He was protecting himself, and no one else. He was trading the life of this man before him for his own.

Honok started to push himself up, and as he did, his gaze fell to the second dagger lying on the ground between them.

There was nothing else Grinsa could do. As Honok lunged for his lost dagger, Grinsa threw himself forward, grunting at the pain in his shoulder. It seemed to the Qirsi that they met in midair, like falcons battling over the Moorlands, and then crashed to the ground. Grinsa's good arm, dagger in hand, was crushed against his chest under Honok's weight. He was fortunate that the blade lay flat, or he might have taken his own life. As it was, he could not free the arm to stab at the assassin. The dark-haired man pounded his fist into Grinsa's side and then stretched out his arm for the blade that lay on the ground. It was enough to give Grinsa room to move. Arching his back as violently as he could, and exhaling sharply at the white hot pain in his shoulder, he threw the man off of him. Without hesitation, in one convulsive motion, he flung himself over and plunged his dagger into Honok's chest, collapsing on top of him as he did. The assassin screamed, his back arching as Grinsa's had a moment before. But then his entire body seemed to sag, and he lay utterly still.

For a long time, Grinsa couldn't bring himself to open his eyes, much less sit up. His shoulder ached, his fingers had started to grow numb, and his side was tender from where Honok had hit him, once with his elbow and once with his fist.

But it was fear that held him there, that kept his eyes closed so tight it hurt. He had killed.

You had to, he told himself. *To protect yourself, to save Tavis.*

"You had to." He said it aloud, as if hearing it could help.

Slowly, he opened his eyes and pushed himself up with his good arm. Honok's eyes and mouth were still open, his death frozen on his face for all to see. Grinsa pulled his blade free and wiped the blood on his sleeve so that it mingled with his own. He tried to stand, but his head spun until he thought he'd be sick and he had to sit back down.

His shoulder needed healing, but he wasn't sure he had the strength to tend to himself. He had already used his powers far too much this night. He rested a few moments before crawling to where his mount stood. Forcing himself to stand, he retrieved his waterskin and pulled some food from a sack hanging from his saddle. Then he returned to the fire and dropped down to the ground. He took a long drink and made himself eat, though he nearly gagged on the smoked meat and hard cheese.

Placing his good hand on his shoulder, he closed his eyes and reached with his mind for whatever power remained within him. At first he sensed nothing, and fear gripped his heart. But then he felt it, welling up slowly within him, like a warm spring bubbling forth from the earth. Through his chest it flowed and down his good arm to the hand resting on his wound. Under that healing touch, the icy numbness retreated, leaving a searing pain that made him wince and shudder. Still, he kept his hand there, until at last the fire in his shoulder began to subside. It seemed to take a long time—the gash was deep and the pain stubborn. But eventually his shoulder healed.

Grinsa opened his eyes, only to have the forest roll and spin around him like a whirlwind. Squeezing his eyes shut again, he lowered himself onto his back. He was asleep almost as soon as his head touched the ground.

When he awoke the next day the wood had already grown warm, though a thin mist still drifted among the trees. Sunlight brightened the leaves above him and the trees were alive with the scolding of finches and warblers. It had to be midmorning, perhaps later.

Sitting up carefully, he was relieved to find that his dizziness had passed. He looked at his shoulder and raised his arm, testing the wound. He still bore an angry scar, dark and shaped like a sickle—chances were it would remain with him for the rest of his life—but he could move his arm without too much pain.

Almost against his will, his eyes strayed to the body of the assassin, which lay nearby. The flies had found him, hordes of them with shiny green backs. They buzzed loudly, crowding to the dark wound on his chest and to his mouth and eyes. Grinsa knew that he should do something for the man. *You killed him.* But he hadn't the tools or the strength to bury him, and even if he could have built a pyre, he was only a day's ride from Kentigern and he feared that the smoke might be seen from the castle. He looked away.

"Qirsar forgive me," he breathed.

He climbed to his feet and walked to his mount, feeling just a bit unsteady. After eating a few bites of meat and taking a long drink that nearly emptied his waterskin, he threw his saddle onto the horse's back and strapped it into place. He started to swing himself onto the mount, but then stopped, looking back once more at Honok.

Muttering a curse under his breath, he returned to where the body lay. He exhaled heavily, then dragged the body deeper into the woods, dug a shallow grave with his hands, and covered the body with dirt and dried leaves. There was little he could offer in supplication to the gods on Honok's behalf, so in the end he merely said, "Be just with him, Bian. May there be a place for him in your realm."

He started back toward his horse, but seeing the assassin's second dagger lying in the dirt, he stopped again. After a moment's hesitation, he picked it up and slipped it into his belt. A man never knew when an extra blade might save his life.

He was closer to Kentigern than he had thought. Even with his late start, he emerged from the wood onto the broad plain that lay before the city and tor just after dusk. It had been only two turns since his last visit here with the Revel, but still he could not help but pause for a moment to admire the austere majesty of the castle and the city wall. It was by far the most imposing castle in Eibithar, perhaps in all the Forelands, and gazing at it now, Grinsa found himself wondering if he had been a fool to think his plan could work. Over the centuries, the walls of this castle, and the tor on which it stood, had stopped armies from Aneira and the most powerful houses in Eibithar. Even with the powers he possessed, and the secret he carried, who was he to attempt alone what all those men had failed to accomplish?

He flexed his shoulder again, wincing slightly at the dull pain that remained. The answer, he knew, lay in Honok's attack on him. And in Cresenne's betrayal.

He had managed to keep her out of his mind most of the day, but thinking of her now, he felt an unbearable tightness in his chest that threatened to still his breathing. He fought past it, forcing his mind back to Tavis and his reason for being there. The duke's son needed his help. The boy was on a path no one else could understand; one that Grinsa had foreseen nearly to its end. He was Tavis's only hope, and all he had to do was think of Cresenne and the lengths to which she had gone to stop him, to understand how important it was that the boy survive. As formidable as those walls were, he had to try. Besides, though few knew it, he had resources of his own that were, in their own way, just as formidable.

After a brief rest, he rode on, reaching the east entrance to the city a few moments before the bells rang signaling the locking of the city gates. Once inside the city, he dismounted and led his horse through the marketplace toward the castle, not wishing to appear to be in a great rush. He left his mount at the base of the tor, in a small common yard with several other horses and oxen. He didn't plan to be in the castle for long, but he couldn't risk leaving the beast in a more obvious spot.

With a quick glance over his shoulder to be sure he wasn't being watched Grinsa started up the castle road. He was tiring quickly. The day's ride, while not long, had worn on him, and he still felt weak from his battle with Honok. The magic he would need to get past the guards did not demand as great an effort as the healing or shaping he had done the night before, but it promised to be difficult just the same, particularly since Kentigern Castle had two sets of gates.

The lie had to be simple. Anything too intricate would demand that he expend more power than he could manage. So when the first guard confronted him at the wicket door of the castle's city gate and asked him why he had come, he offered the easiest answer that came to mind.

"Your duke sent for me," he said. "He seeks my counsel."

Simple as this was, even the dullest guard in the kingdom would have been skeptical under most circumstances. But as he spoke the words, Grinsa reached out with his power and touched the man's mind.

"All right," the guard said, stepping out of his way and motioning him through the wicket. "He'll be in bed by now, but someone in the castle can find a place for you to pass the night."

Grinsa smiled. "Thank you." He started through the stone archway leading into the castle.

"Hey now!" another man called, from the guardroom. "Who's he?"

With an inward curse, Grinsa halted and turned again.

"He's here to see the duke," the first man said.

"I'm sure he is. But how do we know the duke wants to see him?"

The guard faced Grinsa again. "You say he sent for you?"

"Yes," the Qirsi said, gently tapping the man's mind a second time. "In the message I just showed you."

"It's all right, Trent," the guard said, looking over his shoulder at the other man. "He showed me the duke's message."

269

Grinsa held his breath. He didn't want to risk using his power on a second man.

"Fine, then," the second guard called at last, turning and stepping back into the guardroom. "Let him go."

Once more Grinsa smiled, before hurrying through the gate and into the castle's first ward.

He used the same story, and the same magic, at the inner gate on the south side of the castle. Once more, he only needed to use his power on one guard, who then convinced the rest for him. Even so, he felt himself growing light-headed with the effort. At this point, however, he had no choice but to press on. He was surrounded by guards and the great stone walls of Kentigern Castle. And the hardest part of his task still lay before him.

Chapter
Sixteen

✦

Kentigern, Eibithar

H e should have been asleep. The gate bells had rung some time ago and a deathly stillness lay over the castle. But Fotir could only lie in his bed, staring out the chamber's small window at the stars. Judging from the way Xaver was tossing in his bed, it seemed that he couldn't sleep either. It wasn't as though they had much to do during the day to tire them out. Since Kentigern's duke had barred them from seeing Tavis, there was little any of them could do other than sit in their chambers or wander the grounds of the castle. And worry. They had plenty of time for that.

Javan, who had seemed immune to the passage of time in the years Fotir had known him, appeared to have aged ten years in the past few days. Suddenly his face was lined and his back stooped like that of an old man.

"He's dying," he had said today, staring out the window, as he seemed to do all the time now. "My boy is dying and there's nothing I can do for him."

Fotir wanted to reassure him, to offer some comfort, but his duke deserved more than empty words and false hope. So he kept silent, even as he seethed with frustration and outrage. In truth, he thought it likely that the boy was already dead. A few days before, he had overheard several of the guards speaking of Tavis's torture at the hands of Brienne's father and his dogged refusal to confess. He couldn't be certain that they weren't saying it all for his benefit, but their stories had the ring of truth to them. Tavis was just past his

Fating, and though he was strong and capable for his age, no boy could survive torture for long.

He didn't say any of this to Javan, of course, but he felt certain that the duke knew, as did the MarCullet boy. In the last day or two, it seemed that all three of them had abandoned their hope for the boy's release and begun a vigil for his death.

The knocking was faint at first, as if whoever had come feared waking them. It was only when the first minister heard soft footfalls in the corridor that he realized the first knocks had been at Tavis's door. When the sound commenced again, on their door, it was unmistakable.

Xaver and Fotir sat up in their beds and exchanged a look.

"Light the lamp," the minister said, his voice low.

The boy fumbled with the flint and steel for several moments before finally striking a flame. Fotir dressed and stepped to the door.

"Who's there?" he called quietly.

"An ally," came the reply. "And a friend to Lord Tavis."

The minister glanced back at Xaver, who raised an eyebrow and drew his sword. Fotir nodded his approval before opening the door.

A tall, powerfully built Qirsi man stood before him. He looked vaguely familiar, though Fotir could not place him.

"First Minister," the man said softly, offering a slight bow.

Fotir narrowed his eyes. "Do I know you?"

Before the man could answer, Xaver took a sharp breath. "The gleaner," he said. "From the Revel."

The minister began to nod slowly. "Of course. We met at the Silver Gull."

"Yes," the gleaner said, glancing from side to side. Clearly he wanted to enter the room, but Fotir wasn't ready to let him in just yet.

"What is it you want, gleaner?"

Their eyes met.

"I want to help," the man said, sounding earnest.

"You knew this was going to happen!" Xaver said. "You saw it in Tavis's Fating, and yet you let him come here!"

Fotir raised a hand, silencing the boy, but he kept his eyes on the man's face. "The Revel is in Galdasten now, isn't it?"

"Yes."

"And you came all this way just to help Lord Tavis?"

"Master MarCullet is right. I did see something of Lord Tavis's fate. Or more precisely, of his future."

"An interesting distinction," Fotir said. "Perhaps I wasn't as far off as you and your friends made it seem when I asked if you had misled him with the gleaning."

He heard voices approaching. The gleaner looked in their direction, then faced him again. Suddenly he looked frightened. But still Fotir did not allow him into the chamber.

"You asked me if what he saw was real," the gleaner said. "Obviously it was. I had reasons for not showing him his true fate. You must believe that I meant him no harm. I intended what he saw as a warning."

"Your warning nearly cost young Xaver here his life."

"I know that." He looked past Fotir to the boy. "I'm sorry for it."

The voices were quite close now. Guards, no doubt. They'd be turning the corner onto this corridor in a few more seconds.

"Why did you come here?" Fotir asked again.

"To help!" the man said, desperation creeping into his voice.

"So you've said. How?"

"By freeing Lord Tavis from the prison! But I can't do it alone!"

It was the last thing Fotir expected him to say. Indeed, the minister was so surprised that he nearly left the man standing in the corridor for too long.

Seeing the flicker of the guards' torches on the corridor walls, he quickly stepped aside, allowing the gleaner to hurry into the chamber before closing the door. They all remained silent as a moment later the guards walked past the doorway, their voices echoing loudly off the stone ceiling and walls.

"What's your name, gleaner?" Fotir asked, when the guards voices had faded.

"Grinsa jal Arriet."

"Where are you from?"

"I've lived in Eibithar all my life." He said it proudly, as an Eandi would, or as Fotir himself had on many occasions. "The duke is to be my king," he went on a moment later. "I wish him and his family no harm. The night we met at the Silver Gull, I offered to help you search for the boy. Now I'm offering my aid again."

"I remember your offer," Fotir said. "I also recall that you said you were a gleaner, with no deeper powers. What makes you think that you can free Tavis from the prison?"

The man hesitated, his eyes straying to Xaver. "I'd rather not say. You just have to believe me when I tell you that I can."

"Shouldn't we speak with the duke about this?" Xaver asked.

Grinsa shook his head. "Your duke shouldn't be party to this, Master MarCullet, any more than you should. Even involving the first minister is risky, but I need another Qirsi, one I can trust." A look of deepest sadness flitted across the man's features and then was gone. "If we fail," he continued, appearing to gather himself, "it would be far better that we fail alone. The duke of Kentigern can blame it on Qirsi conspirators, or some such thing. If you or your duke are involved, it becomes grounds for war."

The gleaner was right, though it made Fotir vaguely uncomfortable to admit it. He also found the mention of Qirsi conspirators disturbing, but he kept that to himself. "I have to agree, Xaver," he said. "We should say nothing to the duke, at least for now."

The boy took a step forward. "You'll need help, someone to stand watch while you help Tavis."

"No," Fotir told him. "The gleaner was right about that as well. You can't be involved. If this can be done, we'll do it. And if it can't, we'll have an easier time avoiding capture if it's just the two of us."

"You can't just expect me to stay here," the boy said.

Grinsa smiled at him. "I showed you a fine future at your Fating, Master MarCullet. The first minister and I don't want to do anything to endanger it."

Xaver frowned, but after a moment he gave a small nod.

"Try to sleep," Fotir said, stepping to the door. "And no matter what happens, don't say anything about this to anyone. If someone asks, you thought I was going to a tavern."

Again the boy nodded, this time with more conviction. "All right," he said. "May the gods be at your side."

The minister grinned, then led the gleaner into the corridor and to the nearest set of stairs. At the entrance to the stair tower, however, he stopped and faced Grinsa.

"Before we go any further, I want a better explanation of what we're about to do."

Grinsa blinked. "I've told you," he said. "We're going to free Lord—"

"Yes, I know. But how? The boy's not here—it's just the two of us. Now I want the truth, Qirsi to Qirsi."

Once more the man hesitated, although this time he did not look away. "I can't tell you everything. It's enough to say that I am more than I told you. I can heal and shape as well as glean."

"Why did you lie to me that night?"

"I wasn't certain that I could trust you," he said with a shrug.

"Trust is one thing, but why lie about your abilities, especially when you were offering your help?"

Grinsa took a breath, and again it seemed to Fotir that his expression was one of profound grief. "There are divisions among our people that run deeper than I ever thought possible. Even the simplest gestures of trust can be dangerous. You and I know nothing of each other except that we both wish to save Tavis's life, and even that we're each taking on faith. I joined the Revel as a gleaner and told no one of my other powers. I had my reasons for doing so, and if I had told you more than I told Trin and the rest, it might have gotten back to them."

It was the second time since their arrival in Kentigern that someone had spoken to him of the rift that existed among the Qirsi as if it was something new. In a sense, though, these divisions dated back to the Qirsi Wars and the betrayal of his people that ended them. His parents, particularly his father, had spoken of Carthach, the traitorous officer who helped the Forelanders defeat the Qirsi army during the ancient wars, as if he had been a demon sent by Bian from the Underrealm. The traitor Carthach. It might as well have been the man's name. Certainly Fotir had never heard him referred to any other way until he was well past his Determining. Traveling with the Revel because both his parents were gleaners, he constantly heard men like his father, and like Trin, their tongues loosened by wine, railing against Carthach and the Eandi. And like Trin, Fotir's father and his friends saved their harshest words for those Qirsi who served in the Eandi courts that the Revel visited.

It was funny in a way. At least it was until Fotir's Fating. His mother did the gleaning, rather than his father. Fotir was sixteen, and had long since begun to challenge his father's narrow view of the world. They barely spoke anymore. Which was fortunate, for had it been his father summoning the vision of his future from the Qiran, Fotir might never have seen his true fate. As it was, his mother cried out at what she showed him. An Eandi watching the gleaning might have thought that she saw an early death for her son, or some unspeakable disgrace. But no, it was just Fotir, grown into manhood, serving an Eibitharian duke.

Fotir left the Revel that night. He never saw his parents again, though he and his mother exchanged letters until her death several years later.

The unrest of which Shurik and now Grinsa had spoken might have been new, but the feelings behind it—the irrational resentment and prejudice—were as old as Carthach's memory, as old as the kingdoms of the Forelands. Fotir wanted no part of this fight. He never had.

"You're still not answering my question," Fotir said, unwilling to be swayed simply by talk of Qirsi resentments and conspiracies.

"No, I'm not. But I swear to you on the memory of my wife, whom I lost to the pestilence six years ago, that I wish you and the duke no harm. I came here to help Lord Tavis and will do so with or without you. We both know, however, that I have a far better chance of succeeding if you help me."

Fotir considered this in silence for some time. Whatever had driven Grinsa to come to Kentigern, he did appear to be their last hope for saving Tavis's life. If it could still be saved. The first minister exhaled loudly, allowing himself a small smile. "You can be persuasive, Gleaner. Did you know that?"

Grinsa grinned. "Actually, yes. Did I forget to mention to you that I have mind-bending magic? That's how I got into the castle in the first place."

They started down the stairs, stepping lightly and keeping watch for more guards, but Fotir could not keep his mind from returning to what Grinsa had just told him. Mind-bending was a powerful magic, one that worked best on the Eandi, who had no way of protecting themselves from Qirsi power. But more than that, with gleaning, shaping, and healing, the mind-bending magic gave the man four types of power, an uncommonly large number for even the most powerful Qirsi. The very idea of it raised a staggering possibility, one that Fotir had not considered for many years. Abruptly, he understood Grinsa's reluctance to tell him the truth.

At the bottom of the winding stairway, Grinsa led them toward another corridor rather than out into the ward.

"Don't we want to go this way?" Fotir asked.

"Not unless we want to be seen by the castle guards."

Still the minister hesitated, abruptly unsure of whether he'd been wise to follow this man.

"I know of a sally port," Grinsa explained. "You didn't really think that we'd just walk into the dungeon and free him?"

Fotir felt his color rise. "No."

"Trust me, First Minister. One of the advantages of traveling with the Revel is that I have the opportunity to explore the castles of all Eibithar's dukes. I'm quite familiar with Kentigern."

"And Curgh, too?" the minister asked as they started walking again.

Grinsa glanced at him and grinned. "Of course."

Reaching the sally port, the two Qirsi stepped out into the night air and circled around to the outside wall of the prison tower. There, near the ground, was a single small opening covered with an iron grate.

"This is it," Grinsa whispered. "There's a second grate at the base of the shaft leading up to here, so if you can break these bars, I'll get the ones below."

Fotir nodded. "All right." He knelt on the grass and prepared to use his shaping power on the iron, but Grinsa stopped him with a hand on his shoulder.

"Keep the breaks clean," the gleaner said. "If we have the time, we should repair the breaks before we leave."

"That will take a lot of magic."

"I know. Leave that to me."

Fotir shrugged, then set to work on the window grate. There were four bars going across and another three plumb. Fourteen breaks in all. He would have liked to do only a few of them, but as it was he had to break the bars as close to the stone as possible in order to give them enough room to fit through. It would have been easier as well to merely shatter the grate with one push of power, but Grinsa was right: if they didn't repair the grate, Tavis's escape might be discovered too soon.

As first minister to the duke of Curgh, Fotir was valued as much for his wisdom and his knowledge of Eibithar and the other king-doms of the Forelands as he was for his Qirsi abilities. Occasionally, a dream offered him some glimpse of the future that he shared with Javan, and one could claim that his ability to summon mists and winds might aid in the defense of Curgh Castle in the event of a siege. But the fact was, he had little opportunity to use his magic in his capacity as Javan's advisor.

It felt good to be tapping into his power, and when the first bar broke, the metal chiming like two swords coming together in battle, he could not help but smile. But his joy at using his abilities once more quickly gave way to the recognition of how his skills had diminished. He felt like a soldier who goes to war without having trained for many years. He could barely control his magic and he tired quickly. After struggling through only four or five clean breaks, he was sweating like a trench laborer. His hands had begun to tremble and his head was pounding. He was ashamed of his weakness and he tried to hide his fatigue from Grinsa, but the gleaner was watching him closely.

"You can rest if you need to."

Fotir shook his head. "We haven't the time. I'll be fine. It's just been a while since I've done anything like this."

"Perhaps you need help."

"No, I—" He stopped, suddenly unable to speak. For his weariness had vanished. Abruptly, power was flowing through him like moonlight through an open window. In part it was his own power— he felt its source within him, as one feels the heart pumping life through one's limbs. But this was Grinsa's power as well, bolstering his own, directing it, bringing to it the control that Fotir lacked. Somehow, the gleaner was sharing the burden of what Fotir was trying to do.

Somehow. Fotir knew how. There could be only one explanation.

"You're a Weaver!" he breathed.

"Later," Grinsa said quietly. "After we're finished."

The minister nodded and turned his mind back to the iron bars, though he was still awed by what the gleaner had done. *A Weaver.* By revealing the extent of his powers, Grinsa had literally placed his life in Fotir's hands. It was an act of unimaginable trust that left the minister humbled, and deeply troubled by his earlier mistrust and the things he had said to Grinsa outside the Silver Gull in Curgh.

"Does anyone else know?" he asked.

"Later," Grinsa said again. "I'll tell you what I can, I promise. But we must do this first."

They were through the last of the bars. Carefully, with as little noise as they could manage, they removed the grate. Grinsa started to lower himself through the window, but Fotir stopped him.

"Let me do the other grate as well."

"But I don't want you going into the dungeon," the gleaner said. "We should limit your involvement as much as we can."

The minister smiled. "It's a bit late for that. You'll need me to help you lift him out. And since I have no power to heal, you'll need to tend to the boy on your own. Let me do this much. After what you've given me, I feel I owe you that."

Grinsa hesitated, a look of uncertainty in his pale eyes. "All right," he said at last. "My thanks."

Fotir gave a quick smile, before lowering himself headfirst into the narrow shaft. It was a tight fit—it promised to be even tighter for the gleaner, who was broader in the shoulders than he—but he didn't have far to go to reach the second grate. The shaft widened slightly at the bottom and there were fewer bars here, only two in each direction. The air, however, was hot and fetid and he nearly gagged on it. The smells of human waste and rot and infection made his eyes water. He worked as quickly as he could, and with Grinsa's magic enhancing his own, he removed the grate in just a few moments.

He held on to the iron rather than letting it fall to the prison floor, and he called as loudly as he dared for Grinsa to pull him back out. He felt the man grab hold of his ankles and pull. His knees and elbows scraped painfully on the stone, but after a few seconds he was out, breathing the cool, clean night air again.

"Well done," the gleaner said. "Now the opening is far off the floor, so be ready for a long drop when we go back in."

"And you should prepare yourself for the stench."

Grinsa's brow furrowed. "Bad?"

"Awful."

"Like a rotting corpse?"

Fotir caught his breath. It hadn't even occurred to him. "A bit, yes," he said, "among other things."

A look of relief registered on the man's features. "Those other things are a good sign. Other prisoners will have died there. If it was Tavis's corpse, the smell would have overwhelmed everything else." He gestured toward the opening.

Fotir climbed in again, feet first this time. He took a long breath as he did, savoring this last taste of pure air. Then he lowered himself into the opening. His feet reached the bottom of the shaft and he tried to ease himself downward as slowly as possible. But with nothing against which he could brace his legs it became increasingly difficult to control his descent, until at last he could no longer keep himself from falling. His upper body slid quickly through the shaft and he crossed his forearms over his face so as not to hit his head on the top of the opening. There was little he could do, though, to keep his balance when he landed, and he sprawled onto the rank, damp floor.

"Xaver?" a voice croaked from the far wall.

The minister pushed himself up and peered through the darkness, but he couldn't see anything at all.

An instant later Grinsa dropped into the cell, stumbling a bit as he landed, but staying on his feet.

"Father? Is that you?"

"No, Lord Tavis," Fotir said, finally finding his voice. "It's not your father or Master MarCullet."

"Then who?" the boy said, his voice sounding thick and weak.

A flame jumped to life in the palm of Grinsa's hand, its light fighting through the black of the prison.

"Fotir!" the boy said. "And the gleaner?"

But the minister just gaped at the figure he saw before him, chained to the stone wall. He felt his stomach turn and he had to choke back the bile that rose in his throat.

"My lord!" he said, his voice cracking. "What have they done to you?"

Aindreas had come back to hurt him so often that Tavis had lost track of everything. He didn't know the day or which bells he was hearing on those occasions when he noticed them ringing. He was barely even aware of the rise and fall of the sun and moons. There was no dark or light anymore, no day or night. There was pain and there was sleep. Nothing else mattered.

The marks of the duke's sword were all over his chest and back, his limbs and head. Aindreas had even taken his sword to Tavis's groin, though he had yet to cut off his privates. That was coming, though; the duke had made a point of telling him so. It was, at this point, the only part of him the duke had spared. The prelate had been back once or twice as well, to urge Tavis yet again to confess and repent. During his last visit, Barret had expressed his concern about all the cuts on Tavis. Apparently a good number of them were oozing and raw. Aindreas had taken the prelate's concern to heart and had given up his sword for torches. Tavis had burns on his back, his legs, and his arms. Most of his fingers were broken as well.

But he had not confessed. His life, he had come to realize at some point, hanging on that wall, whimpering at his pain, and pleading with Bian to come for him before Brienne's father returned, had amounted to shockingly little. He had never distinguished himself in battle, he had never been king or even duke, he had never been in love. Xaver was the only true friend he could claim, and he had nearly ended that friendship with the act of a drunken fool. When he was gone, hanged for a murder he had not committed, he would leave no legacy, no achievement that his parents might point to with pride and say, "Our son did that."

But, he had decided, with a resolve that surprised him and would have shocked his father, that he would leave no false confession either. Even if he could not add to the glory of the House of Curgh, he would not sully it, at least no more than he already had. As legacies went, it was pitiably small. But it was all he had.

Sometimes the pain grew so unbearable that he was tempted to give in. Few believed him innocent anyway, and those who did, those who truly mattered, would understand why he had confessed. It was only pride that stopped him. Curgh pride. Some called it the curse of his house. Some claimed that it had been at the root of more than one of Eibithar's civil wars. But in those final days, as torch fire seared his flesh, it proved to be Tavis's salvation.

When he first heard the voices, he feared that Aindreas had returned. He opened his eyes slowly, expecting to see daylight or the damned torches. Instead he found absolute darkness, though the sounds continued to reach him. Voices, the occasional ring of metal. It might have been guards outside the prison door, but he had never heard them so clearly before. Or perhaps he was losing his sanity. Such things happened to prisoners, he knew, particularly to those who were tortured.

Abruptly the ringing of the metal grew louder, as if it was happening within the cell. Had they brought in another prisoner as he slept? Was this the sound of a second set of chains? Or was Aindreas, having broken his body, trying now to break his mind as well? He kept silent, listening as the metal rang again and again. It was coming from the window, he realized, feeling a surge of hope. Just as suddenly as it began, the ringing stopped and a voice cried out; he couldn't make out the words. He was trembling, his pulse racing. Something was happening, for good or ill, and he waited.

He heard someone scuffling on the stone—again the sound came from the window shaft—and then something, or someone, landed on the floor of the cell just in front of him.

"Xaver?" he said through cracked lips.

No answer. His fear returned.

Again something hit the floor. Terror seized his heart.

"Father? Is that you?"

A moment later a small flame illuminated the dungeon and he saw the two Qirsi men. Fotir he might have expected, but why would the gleaner from the Revel have come? He tried not to be frightened by the first minister's reaction to his appearance, but seeing the tears on Fotir's face was more than he could bear.

"Am I beyond healing?" he asked in an unsteady voice.

"No," the gleaner answered, whispering as his eyes flicked briefly toward the door at the top of the stairs. "But mending all your wounds will take time. We can only do so much right now." He glanced at Fotir. "His chains."

The minister nodded and stepped to the stone wall.

"You know me?" the man asked, as the first of the manacles snapped in two.

"I do, though I've forgotten your name. And I don't understand why you're here."

"My name is Grinsa, and I'm here to take you from this prison."

"Why? You showed me this place in the Qiran. Isn't this my fate?"

Another manacle broke and then a third. Fotir's breathing was growing labored.

"What I showed you was your future, but not your true fate."

"I don't understand."

"I know. I'll explain, but not now."

The last of the manacles fell to the floor and Fotir took a step back.

"You're free, my lord," he said. His face shone with sweat. "Can you walk?"

Tavis had been sitting with his back pressed against the rough stone and now the two men came forward and helped him to his feet. Once more he leaned back against the wall. He put out his right foot, intending to take a step, but he could not support his own weight. He crumpled to the floor, crying out at the pain, which seemed to pulse from every wound Aindreas had inflicted on him.

The gleaner spat a curse, looking up at the door once more. "He'll have to be healed before we try to move him." He pulled one of the torches from a sconce on the wall and held it to the flame that still burned in his hand. Then he placed the torch in a far corner of the dungeon, where its light would be less noticeable to the guards outside the door while still allowing them to see.

"Yes," Fotir said. "But where do we begin?"

"Anywhere," Tavis said. "Please. Just do something."

Returning to where Tavis lay, Grinsa knelt beside him and placed his hands on the boy's shoulder. "I'll cool the fevered wounds," he said. "Those are the ones making him weak. And I'll try to repair his hands. The rest can wait until we're someplace safer."

Even as the man spoke, Tavis felt the healing magic flowing, like water from a mountain stream, into the sword cut on his shoulder. Fotir knelt as well, supporting Tavis's head in his lap as the young lord closed his eyes.

Tavis must have dozed off, for when he awoke sometime later, the gleaner was healing one of the many wounds on his side. He was still in pain, but it was tolerable now—not at all like the agony he had known just a short time before.

The two Qirsi were in the midst of a conversation, and he said nothing, choosing instead to listen with his eyes still closed.

". . . You're the only one aside from my sister," the gleaner was saying in hushed tones. "And she and I have done all we can to conceal the fact that we're related."

"It amazes me that you've kept it secret for this long," Fotir said.

"At times it amazes me as well." A pause, and then, "I have to ask you, will my secret survive this night?"

"What do you mean?"

"You're a Qirsi in the service of Curgh's duke, a man who soon will be king. We both know how the Eandi of the Forelands feel about Weavers. Some in your position would see it as their duty to expose me."

Tavis had heard of Weavers, but he remembered little of what he had been told. He knew that Weavers had led the Qirsi invasion of the Forelands nearly nine hundred years ago, and that all the Weavers in the Qirsi army had been executed at the war's end. He knew as well what the gleaner meant about how Weavers were regarded in the Forelands to this day. They were feared, even hated. But he wasn't certain why.

"Let me ask you this," Fotir said, seeming to avoid Grinsa's question. "You spoke earlier of a Qirsi conspiracy. Did you mean it?"

"I merely said that Aindreas might suspect one if we were caught. I was trying to convince the MarCullet boy to stay out of harm's way."

"I understand that. But you've heard the talk, just as I have."

"Yes," Grinsa said, after a brief silence.

"Is it true?"

Again the gleaner hesitated. "I believe it is. An assassin followed me to Kentigern. I have good reason to think that he was sent by another Qirsi who didn't want me to help Lord Tavis."

"Where's this assassin now?" Fotir asked, sounding alarmed.

"He's dead. I killed him in Kentigern Wood, though only after he nearly killed me."

"Qirsar save us all!"

"Does Curgh's prelate know that you still invoke the Qirsi god?"

The first minister laughed. "I fear he suspects it." A moment later he went on, his voice grave once more. "What do you think these Qirsi want?"

"I'm not sure. It seems they wish to keep Tavis from the throne, perhaps his father as well. But I have no idea why. What does this have to do with what I asked you before?"

"That depends. Could you see yourself joining their cause?"

"No," the gleaner answered, his voice hardening. "They tried to have me killed."

"Is that the only reason?"

"Actually, it's not. Qirsi prejudice against the Eandi has cost me more than you can imagine. Now, I'll ask you again, what does this have to do with the fact that I'm a Weaver?"

"Probably very little. But it occurs to me that if there is such a conspiracy, and if I intend to oppose it, along with others who feel as I do, it might help our cause to have a Weaver on our side."

"If the conspiracy is real, First Minister, and if you pledge yourself to defeating it, I swear to you that you will."

For some time the two of them did not speak, although Tavis still felt Grinsa's power soothing his injuries.

"It must be strange for you," Fotir said at last. "You're probably the only Weaver in the Forelands. I can't imagine what that would be like, knowing that you're unique, that you're probably the most powerful Qirsi north of the mountains."

"Actually, I think it likely that you're wrong. I'm sure there are several of us."

Even with his eyes closed, Tavis could almost see Fotir shaking his head. "How is that possible?"

"You think I'm the only Qirsi who can keep a secret?" Grinsa asked. "Think about it. There had to be many Weavers in the Southlands before our people invaded the Forelands. The army was led by at least eight, and I doubt that all the Weavers came north, leaving the homeland unprotected. In the first century after the war, as our people settled in the kingdoms of the Forelands, a good number more were found and executed. Only later did Weavers become so rare. Do you really think the trait was bred out of us? Isn't it more likely that those who were born with the power learned to hide it?"

"I suppose you're right," Fotir said. "Which means there are others. I'm not certain that I find that comforting."

"You shouldn't."

Again they fell silent. After a few moments more, Grinsa removed his hands from Tavis's side and shifted position, taking one of the boy's mangled hands in his own.

"The hands are the last," the gleaner said. "I'll heal his other wounds once we're away from here."

"Should I wake him?"

"He's awake already. He has been for some time."

Tavis opened his eyes, feeling his face redden. "How could you tell?"

"Your breathing changed, as did your pulse. A healer can sense such things."

Fotir looked down at him. "How are you feeling, my lord?"

"Better. Thank you."

"I've taken the fever from your body," Grinsa told him, "but that's all. You may feel better, but you're still in no condition to travel far, and you still need several days of healing and rest."

He lowered Tavis's hand to the floor and took hold of the other one. To his great relief, Tavis found that he could move his fingers again, though they felt stiff and awkward.

"Where will we take him?"

The gleaner looked at Fotir and grinned. "*We* won't be taking him anywhere. Once we're out of this dungeon, you'll be returning to your duke. It's best you don't know where we've gone."

Fotir looked like he wanted to argue, but after a few seconds he merely nodded.

Turning to Tavis again, Grinsa took a breath. "You heard us talk about a lot of things, Lord Tavis."

"Yes."

"You understand that you can't repeat them to anyone."

"At this point, who'd listen to me?"

He tried to smile, but the gleaner shook his head. "This is no joke. Lives are at stake. Mine, the first minister's, those of people who matter to me a great deal. You must not tell anyone what was said here tonight."

The man's yellow eyes were locked on his, holding him as firmly as the manacles once had.

"You have my word," he finally said.

Still Grinsa's gaze did not waver.

The torch in the corner of the prison sputtered for an instant before starting to dim.

"We should go," Fotir said.

At last, the gleaner looked away. He let go of Tavis's other hand. It felt whole again as well.

"Yes, we should," Grinsa agreed. "Help me get him up."

They stood on either side of him, each taking hold of an arm, and carefully they pulled him to his feet.

Grinsa's healing had brought him relief from the worst of his pain, but when he tried to stand he grasped the severity of the wounds that remained. He had to bite his tongue to keep from crying out. They half carried him across the cell, leaning him against the opposite wall, beneath the window shaft. Every movement hurt, but smelling the sweet cool air descending from the shaft, Tavis didn't care. He'd have crawled through flames to get out of the prison.

"This is the only way out," Grinsa told him. "We're going to have to lift you into the shaft, and then one of us will pull you up, while the other pushes from beneath. It's going to hurt."

"I know," Tavis said. "I'd rather die trying than stay here."

The gleaner grinned. He turned to Fotir. "You go first, and I'll lift him into the shaft after you."

Laying a hand on the wall, Grinsa used his magic to carve a shallow notch out of stone, one that was small enough to escape notice, but deep enough to serve as a foothold. He made a second one a span or two above the first.

Fotir placed his fingers in the higher notch and the toe of his shoe into the lower one. In a matter of seconds he had climbed into in the shaft.

"Once you're in the shaft, my lord," he called, "grab hold of my feet."

"Ready?" the gleaner asked.

"Yes."

Grinsa lifted him off the ground as if he weighed nothing. Tavis had never guessed that a Qirsi could be so strong.

Reaching for the opening in the wall, Tavis tried to pull himself into the shaft, grunting at the effort and the agony in his arms and legs and back. Had Grinsa not been there, pushing him up, he would have failed. As it was, he barely managed to take hold of the first minister's ankles. Fotir started to climb and Grinsa continued to lift Tavis into the shaft.

Every second of it was excruciating. Each time his side or back or stomach scraped the stone, he felt as though Aindreas's blade were slicing into him again. The burns on his body screamed in his mind like wraiths. He feared that he would lose consciousness, he felt that he would have vomited had he not been starved for days. Closing his eyes, he did his best to push himself up with his feet, although this too brought him agony. But at least he was doing something to help the two Qirsi. He wasn't just some helpless babe having to be carried by others; he was Lord Tavis of Curgh. Clinging to that thought and to his name, as if they were the only things that could keep him afloat in his ocean of pain, he fought his way up the shaft.

The end came abruptly. One moment he was clawing his way up the narrow stone passage, and the next Fotir was pulling him out into the cool night and onto the soft grass of the castle ward. He lay there, with his face pressed into the earth, breathing in the glorious fragrance of the grass, as the throbbing of his wounds slowly subsided. In another moment, Grinsa was lying beside him, his chest heaving with every breath.

Fotir had vanished, and Tavis wondered if he had gone back to Xaver and his father. Only when the minister crawled out of the shaft a second time and started repairing the metal grate that had covered the window did Tavis realize what he had been doing.

"What now?" the minister asked.

Grinsa sat up. "Tavis and I need to get out of the castle."

"What about my father?" the boy asked, forcing himself to sit as well.

Grinsa shook his head. "You can't see him. If the duke of Kentigern has cause to believe that your father knew anything of your escape it could lead to war."

The Qirsi was right, of course. He was free, but to all in the land he was still a murderer. Ean knew how long he might have to run, how far he might have to go to keep his freedom. Suddenly, Tavis couldn't help but wonder if he'd ever see his father again.

"How will you leave the castle?" Fotir asked.

The gleaner climbed to his feet. "I'm not certain."

"Perhaps a hole in the castle wall?"

"That wall is as thick as you are tall," Grinsa said.

The minister grinned. "The tower walls are a good deal thinner."

The gleaner smiled in return, his eyes dancing with the light of the rising moons. "Do you have the strength?"

"Normally I wouldn't," Fotir answered. "But tonight I have a Weaver to help me."

Chapter
Seventeen

✦

H e heard the midnight bells echoing across the silent city like the tolling of funeral bells, and he raised the wine goblet to his lips to empty it yet again. He was alone, as he had been every night since Brienne's death. Shurik had retired for the evening a short while before, having sat with him dutifully for hours, waiting to be given leave to withdraw. Ioanna had been in bed for much of the day, rising only to stare at another meal until it grew cold, and then returning once more to the shuttered windows of their bedchamber.

We all deal with grief in our own way, Aindreas thought, pouring more wine. *She sleeps, I drink. And I torture.*

He had told himself from the beginning that he only wanted a confession. Brienne deserved that much. He couldn't allow the demon the solace of a quick death if he didn't first admit his crime. Usually he couldn't abide torture; certainly he rarely took such measures into his own hands. But under these circumstances he could hardly do less. Tavis had butchered his daughter, whom Aindreas had treasured more than his title, more than his house, more than all the riches in Eibithar. He had slaughtered her like an animal, and then left her lying there, half naked, in a pool of her own blood. What kind of a father would he have been had he not made her killer suffer as well?

All he wanted was the confession, he told himself. That's what he told the prelate as well, and Shurik, and anyone else who would have listened. But if the boy had confessed that first day, would he have stopped, and given him his execution? He wanted to say "yes" and believe it, but he knew better. So, he was sure, did Barret and Shurik. His demand for a confession was a pretense and nothing more. The boy's continued denials delighted him, for they justified every cut of his sword, every touch of the torch, every broken bone in the killing hands. Tavis truly was Javan's son, and his stubbornness was the source of Aindreas's only remaining joy, black though it was.

He did feel sorry for the duke himself. Knowing what it was to lose a child, he understood Javan's demands to see the boy and his threats of war when those demands were refused. Like his son, however, he could not be allowed to deny the undeniable. They might have been the boy's falsehoods, but by embracing them, the father became a liar as well.

Aindreas stood, draining his goblet again and placing it roughly on the table. He began to pace in long strides, flexing his hands like a battle-hungry soldier. Just thinking of Brienne and Tavis and Javan unsettled him, leaving him restless and eager for blood. It was late, and he should have been in bed, but sleep felt as distant as Glyndwr.

He was in the corridor on his way to the prison tower before he formed the thought. Everyone else was asleep; Ioanna, Shurik, even Barret. But the guards would be up, and he didn't really care if he woke the boy.

He found the two guards standing in the inner ward, just outside the entrance to the prison tower. They were supposed to be inside, guarding the door to the dungeon. Aindreas knew it, and judging from the fearful looks on both of their faces as he approached, they knew it as well. The duke could hardly blame them, though. Even with the door closed, enough of the prison's stench came through the small window in the door to make the entire tower reek. Had he been in their place, he would have been outside too.

"Open the door and get me two torches," he commanded, not bothering to say anything about where they were standing.

They both hurried to do his bidding, although one of them managed to remember a quick "Yes, my lord."

With the torches in hand, and the heavy prison door unlocked, Aindreas descended the steps. He felt a bit sleepy with the wine, but he was looking forward to this. He always did.

"Wake up, Tavis!" he called. "Time for us to have another—"

He froze, one foot suspended above a stair, not believing what he saw in the prison, or rather, what he didn't see. The last few times he had come to the dungeon he had been prepared for the fact that Tavis might be dead. He had not been gentle with his sword or the torches, and, for all the evil that lurked within him, Tavis was still just a boy. But Aindreas had never expected that Tavis could just vanish. It wasn't possible. No one had ever escaped the dungeon of Kentigern Castle. Yet there were his chains, hanging limply from the bloodstained wall.

The duke placed one of the torches he carried in a sconce by his head, then drew his sword and continued warily down the stairs.

"Guards!" he called. "Get down here! And bring more torches!"

Aindreas's heart hammered at his chest and his sword hand was shaking. Where were the damn guards!

"Hurry up!" he bellowed.

One of the men came running down the stairs, his sword already in hand.

"What is it, my lord?"

"Where's the other man?"

"Getting the torches, my lord."

The duke nodded and swallowed. Of course, that would take some time.

"Where's the boy?" he asked.

Even in the dim light he saw the man blanch, his eyes flying to the wall where Tavis had hung for days.

"I—I don't know, my lord!"

Aindreas gestured toward the far corner of the cell with his sword. "The forgetting chamber," he said in a whisper. "Check it."

The man nodded, then hesitated. Aindreas handed him the second torch.

The guard walked forward slowly, dropped to his knees, and, thrusting the torch into the narrow opening leading to the tiny cell, peered into the chamber. After a moment he straightened and, looking back at the duke, shook his head. He appeared to be clenching his teeth, as if to keep from being sick. After a few seconds he managed to speak again. "No sign of him, my lord. Just the brigand we put in there some time back. And he's . . ." He clamped his mouth shut again, shaking his head a second time.

"Has anyone been in this cell tonight?"

"No!" the guard said, his eyes widening. "I swear it!"

Aindreas glared at him. "Could someone have gotten in while you were outside?"

"I've had this the whole time," he said, holding up the iron key. "No one could have gotten in or out without my help."

"Apparently someone did." The duke walked over to the wall and bent down. The manacles lay on the floor, each of them broken in two.

The second man arrived, hurrying down the stairs with two torches in each hand. Seeing that the boy was gone, he halted and looked at his friend. "Where—?" He stopped himself, and glanced at Aindreas, appearing even more frightened than he had when the duke found them outside.

Aindreas grabbed one of the torches from him and began searching the dungeon. He didn't know what he was looking for, but it was all he could do to keep from running the men through with his blade.

Aside from the manacles, he saw nothing unusual on the floor. The iron grate still covered the window shaft, and while he wasn't certain he could trust these men even to look into the forgetting chamber without missing something, he wasn't about to stick his head in there. He could smell the brigand from where he was. He had to have gone up the stairs and through the door. There was no other way. Which meant that he had help. Not from these two. Neither of them was clever enough to be of any use in such a plot. They were much more valuable to his enemies for their incompetence than they would have been as allies.

Spitting a curse, he spun toward the men. "Raise the alarm!"

One of them started to leave, but Aindreas raised his sword to stop him. "On second thought," he said, starting up the stairs, "I'll do it myself. The two of you can stay down here."

"But my lord—!"

He didn't even break his stride. "Be thankful I don't kill you where you stand."

Reaching the top of the stairs, he slammed shut the prison door and ran into the ward shouting for his guards. With any luck at all Tavis had yet to leave the castle. If not, he might at least still be in the city. Not that it mattered. He'd track the boy to Uulrann if he had to. But he swore to every god who would listen that his daughter's murderer would not cheat the death he had earned.

Fotir managed to avoid Kentigern's guards as he made his way back to his chamber. He had thought that Xaver would be asleep again, but he should have known better.

"Is he free?" the boy asked, as soon as the minister opened the door.

Fotir raised a finger to his lips, quieting the boy. He closed the door gently before answering. "Yes," he whispered. "He's free."

"Is he all right?"

The Qirsi started to undress. "Get back in your bed and I'll tell you everything I can."

Xaver quickly returned to his bed and lay down.

"Lord Tavis needed a good deal of healing. He'd been tortured, just as we expected."

"But he's all right now."

"When I left him he was well enough to move. But he'll need several more days of healing, and even then some of his wounds may not heal fully. Many of the scars will stay with him for the rest of his life."

"I hope they all rot in the Underrealm!" the boy said. "Aindreas, his guards, all of them."

Fotir nodded, returning to his own bed. "I must admit, I feel the same."

There was a brief pause and then, "Where is Tavis now?"

"With Grinsa. They're out of the castle, but the gleaner didn't tell me where they were going. He thought it would be safer if I didn't know."

"Do you trust him?"

With my life, he wanted to say. *And with all of yours as well.* But how could he explain such a statement? Even if he tried, even if he told Xaver that Grinsa was a Weaver, and that his willingness to share his secret offered all the proof of his goodwill that Fotir needed, the boy wouldn't understand. Xaver was a loyal friend to his liege, courageous and intelligent beyond his years, but he was Eandi. Probably he wouldn't even know what it meant to be a Weaver, but if by some chance he did, he would see Grinsa as a threat, someone who should have been executed rather than entrusted with the life of the young lord. Fotir and the boy shared a common bond—their fealty to the House of Curgh—and the Qirsi saw qualities in Xaver that he had seen in himself years ago. But in this instance, all that tied them to each other could not bridge the chasm that separated Qirsi from Eandi.

"Yes," he told the boy, knowing that the question deserved a more thoughtful answer than he could give. "I trust him."

"When are we to join them?"

"I don't know."

Xaver propped himself up on one elbow. "You and Tavis made no plans?"

"Xaver, the duke of Kentigern still believes Tavis is a murderer. His escape doesn't change that. If anything, it makes your friend appear even more guilty than before. But given the condition he was in, we had little choice."

"What are you saying?"

"That Tavis will probably have to leave the kingdom. If he remains, he risks being hunted down and killed, or at least imprisoned again." Fotir hesitated. It had to be said, though he knew that it would pain the boy, and the duke and duchess even more. "We may never see Tavis again. We just have to take comfort in the knowledge that he'll be safe, even if we can't be with him."

Xaver stared at him for several moments, his expression unreadable in the darkness. Finally he lay back down, gazing up at the ceiling. They lay in their beds for a long time, neither of them speaking, until Fotir began to wonder if the MarCullet boy had fallen asleep.

"He was never an easy friend," the boy said abruptly, his voice so soft the minister could barely hear him. "He could be selfish, at times even cruel. But he was the only friend I ever had." He paused, but only briefly. "He didn't mean to hurt me. I know that now. I just wish I had told him that."

He doesn't deserve your regret. Even after all he's been through. He couldn't bring himself to speak the words, however. Not after risking his own life to save the boy. Not after devoting himself to the boy's father, who, though brave and wise, could also be humorless and cold. What was it about the men of Curgh that inspired such loyalty? Certainly it wasn't their charm or their warmth. "I'm sure he knows," Fotir said at last. "When we first reached the dungeon, and he still couldn't see who had come, yours was the first name he called out."

He was going to say more, but before he could, he heard someone shouting from the inner ward. An instant later the castle came alive with voices and tolling bells. Torchfire lit the walls of the fortress and cast flickering shadows within their chamber.

Fotir and Xaver leaped from their beds to the window and stared out at the men gathering in the ward. Aindreas stood at the center of the growing throng, barking commands to his men and gesturing frantically toward the towers and gates.

"They can't possibly know already," the minister said, his stomach clenching like a fist.

"Know what?" Xaver asked. "You mean Tavis? They've already learned that he's gone?"

"So it would seem."

"But how?"

"It doesn't matter. Come away from the window," he said, climbing back into his bed and gesturing for the boy to do the same.

Xaver backed away from the window and then turned toward the Qirsi, his eyes large and fearful, like those of a child.

"The duke can know nothing of what happened tonight," Fotir said, pointing to the boy's bed once more.

Xaver lay down again. "You mean our duke?"

"Yes. We'll tell him soon; he'll want to know that Lord Tavis is safe. But for now, don't speak of it, even if the three of us are alone. If Aindreas has any cause to believe that he knew, it could lead to war."

"But won't Aindreas suspect the duke?"

"Of course. But leave that to Javan. As long as he doesn't know anything of the escape, he'll be able to defend himself against Aindreas's accusations."

"All right."

Fotir heard footsteps in the hallway and the ring of steel as swords were drawn.

"Be brave, Xaver MarCullet," he said. "Remember who you are and all that your father has taught you."

Someone pounded heavily on their door.

"Open this door!" a voice called. "Or by authority of the duke of Kentigern we'll break it in!"

Fotir stepped to the door and pulled it open. Perhaps a dozen guards were crowded in the corridor, all of them with their swords drawn. Several held torches.

"The two of you will come with us," one of the men said.

Fotir nodded. "Of course. Can we dress first?"

The man nodded. Fotir and Xaver pulled on their clothes and stepped into the corridor. The guards had Javan as well. The duke looked sleepy and confused, his clothes thrown on hastily.

Before the guards could take them anywhere, however, Aindreas and Shurik came around the far corner, the Qirsi minister hurrying to keep up with his duke.

"Ah, good," Kentigern said, seeing Javan and the rest of them. "I was afraid the three of you would be gone as well."

Javan straightened, as if finally rousing himself from his slumber. "What is the meaning of this, Aindreas?"

Kentigern shook his head. "I should have known," he muttered. He turned to the captain of his guards. "Report."

"The duke was asleep, my lord. Or at least he seemed to be." He pointed to Fotir and Xaver. "These two were already awake."

"We're both light sleepers," Fotir explained evenly. "From all the noise outside we thought the castle was under attack."

The large duke sneered. "Of course you did."

"I demand an explanation!" Javan said, sounding, Fotir had to admit, like a peevish boy.

A guard who had entered Fotir and Xaver's chamber a few moments before emerged now and shook his head. A second man stepped out of Javan's room a few seconds later and did the same.

"Nothing, my lord," this one said.

"Very well, Javan," Aindreas said, looking at Curgh's duke once more. "If you insist on playing this game, I'll go along. Your son is gone from my dungeon. We don't know how he got out, or where he is now. But we're searching the castle and the city, and even now I have soldiers fanning out over the countryside. We will find him. So unless you wish to see him ridden down like an animal, or killed by my archers and dragged back to the castle behind a mount, you'd better tell me where he is."

The duke paled at the news—surely Aindreas saw it as well—and he put a trembling hand to his lips.

"Tavis escaped?" he said, his voice unsteady. "Ean be praised! When?"

Aindreas dismissed the question with an impatient gesture, turning to Fotir. But the Qirsi could see that he was unnerved by Javan's response.

"What about you?" Kentigern demanded. "What do you know about this?"

The minister shrugged, surprising himself with how calm he felt. "Nothing, my Lord Duke. As I told you—"

"Yes, yes. You thought we were under attack. No doubt you were hurrying to our aid when my men opened your door."

"Actually no," Fotir said. "We were about to check on our duke, just as one would expect of his loyal servants."

"My lord, my lord!" came a voice before Kentigern could answer. An instant later two more guards ran into the corridor, nearly crashing into several other guards. "My lord!" one of them said again.

Aindreas took an eager step toward them, pushing aside two of his men. "Yes, what is it? Have you found him?"

"No, my lord. Something else. A hole in the wall of the north city tower."

"A hole? In the stone?"

"Yes, my lord."

Aindreas whirled toward Fotir, grinning triumphantly. "I knew that there was Qirsi magic behind this! How else could his manacles have broken? How else could he have gotten out of the dungeon without being seen? How else could he have walked after all—?" He faltered, though only for an instant. "After all that time in chains."

Fotir almost forgot himself. He so wanted to reveal what Kentigern had done to Lord Tavis, here, in front of Javan and Xaver and the man's guards, that he nearly pounced on Aindreas's slip of the tongue. But by doing so he would have proven his own complicity in the boy's escape.

"I don't understand, my lord," he said instead. "Are you accusing me of helping Lord Tavis escape?"

"Well, who else would I accuse?" Aindreas gestured toward his first minister. "Shurik?"

Fotir allowed himself a smile. "And you believe that I used my magic to break a hole in your castle?"

"Would you have me believe that you used your hands?"

The Qirsi laughed. "One is as likely as the other, my lord. Even if I had the power to do such a thing, I would barely be able to speak for the effort, much less stand here as I'm doing."

Aindreas looked at him skeptically.

"You needn't believe me, my lord," Fotir said. "Ask your first minister."

The duke turned to Shurik, a question in his pale eyes.

Shurik cleared his throat awkwardly. "I'm afraid he's right, my lord. I don't possess the shaping power myself, but I know many who do. It's my understanding that, if the minister had done what you've accused him of doing, he would scarcely be able to stand for hours afterward."

"Well, perhaps you had help," Aindreas said.

Before Fotir could respond, Javan began to chuckle, shaking his head. "You're like an Aneiran constable, Aindreas, determined to blame the first person you find for each crime no matter what the facts tell you. Even the most plausible denials aren't good enough for you. You've made up your mind that Tavis is guilty, despite the blood we found on his window shutter. And now you're doing the same with Fotir, even after what your first minister just told you."

The duke's face shaded to purple, and Fotir feared that Javan had gone to far. It was bad enough likening a Kentigern to an Aneiran, but to do so under these circumstances, with Brienne dead and Tavis gone from the prison, bordered on cruel.

"Your son has escaped my prison," Aindreas said, biting off each word. "Whom else should I blame but one of your company?"

The duke of Curgh shrugged indifferently. "I don't know. I won't lie to you and tell you I'm sorry. I hope that my boy is already leagues away from this castle. I don't even care if he's in Aneira, so long as he's safe from you and your dungeon. But as your own guards have already told you, he's not in Fotir's room, nor is he in mine. So blaming one of us for his escape strikes me as rather foolish." He turned back toward his room. "I'm going back to sleep. I hope your search for Tavis proves as fruitless as your efforts to keep him locked away."

"Hold, Javan!" Kentigern said, his voice echoing in the narrow corridor.

The duke faced him again. "What is it now? You wish to search my chamber a second time? Perhaps you think I carved a hole in your castle wall with my sword, and you want to see if my blade is notched."

Aindreas bristled. "I see no humor in this," he said. "My daughter's killer has escaped and until he is found I plan to hold you and your company in his place." He glanced at his captain. "Take them. You're not to let them out of your sight. Do you understand?"

The man nodded. "You want them in the dungeon, my lord?"

The duke hesitated, his eyes flicking toward his first minister. Shurik held his gaze briefly, then shook his head.

"No, not to the dungeon," Aindreas answered, shaking his head as well. "Put them in the prison tower. See to their needs, keep them fed and reasonably comfortable. But they are not to leave the tower."

"You would make a prisoner of your future king?" Javan demanded.

"If I must."

"Though it mean civil war?"

"Wouldn't you do the same to save your son?"

Javan did not respond, but Aindreas must have seen the answer written on his features, for a moment later he gave a dark grin.

"Yes, of course you would. So how can you expect me to do any less as I seek justice for my daughter?"

Still Javan said nothing. What was there to say? The two dukes merely stared at each other, as if with swords drawn for a battle that would determine the fate of the entire kingdom. At last Aindreas looked away, though only so that he could nod to the captain of his guards.

An instant later the captain gave a sharp order to his men, and Javan, Xaver, and Fotir were led away to Kentigern's prison tower.

After nearly half a turn in the castle prison, Tavis was too stiff and weak to walk on his own. And after all he had done that night, bending the minds of the guards, helping Fotir break the iron bars, healing some of the young lord's wounds, Grinsa could hardly carry him. At another time, in almost any other place, the gleaner might have found the situation amusing. But scrambling down the side of Kentigern Tor in the shadow of Aindreas's great fortress, half supporting Lord Tavis, half carrying him, he saw nothing funny in it at all.

The boy hadn't said a word since they left the castle, though he had cried out in pain several times and was now sucking air through his teeth with almost every step.

"Do you need to rest?" Grinsa asked him. He didn't want to stop. They were only halfway down the tor. Grinsa couldn't even see his mount yet. But neither did he want to kill the boy.

"I'm fine," Tavis managed. "Don't stop."

The gleaner could tell that he was lying, that his fear of returning to the dungeon was simply more powerful than his pain. But Grinsa took the boy at his word, continuing to steer him down the mountain.

"I have a horse ahead," he said. "Not far from here."

"I'm no more fit to ride than I am to walk, gleaner. You'll have to sling me across his back like a corpse."

"If you can lie still enough, that may get us past a guard or two."

In spite of everything, the boy laughed. Perhaps there was more to him than the spoiled child Grinsa had seen at his Fating.

"Where will we go?" he asked a moment later.

Grinsa started to answer, then faltered. With all the boy had to fear just now, he didn't need this as well.

"A place where you'll be safe," he said at last. "I can't tell you more than that right now."

He expected an argument, but Tavis merely nodded, gasping once more as an awkward step jarred him. The moons were obscured by clouds at the moment and while their light might have helped the gleaner navigate the tumble of rocks and clumped grass, Grinsa was just as glad to see them darkened. Panya's bright glow was not their ally tonight.

The moons emerged again just as they reached the bottom of the tor and the ground started to level off. Panya's light touched the city once more, revealing Grinsa's mount standing in the field where the Qirsi had left him.

"This way," he said, leading the boy toward the horse.

Before they got to the animal, however, the gleaner heard a cry go up from the castle.

He whirled, nearly knocking Tavis to the ground.

"Already?"

"What is it?" Tavis asked.

"I fear they've already learned of your escape."

"Perhaps the gods aren't with us."

"Nonsense," he said, hurrying the boy to the horse and lifting him into the saddle.

Grinsa swung himself onto the beast as well, sitting just behind the young lord to keep him from falling. The shouting in the castle had grown louder. Fires were lit in the towers overlooking the city, to be answered a few seconds later by bright flames atop the city gates. If Grinsa had been planning to leave the city, all would have been lost. But he had another place in mind, one that was far closer, but just as safe.

He kicked the horse into motion, drawing another soft cry from Tavis. He needed more healing and a good deal of sleep.

Grinsa needed rest as well, but first he had to get them to the far side of the city.

The street that ran past the field connected the castle road to the city gate nearest the Tarbin, both of which were sure to be crawling with guards by now. The gleaner steered his mount across the lane and through a narrow yard between two small shops. They came to another field and, crossing that, reached another small lane. Grinsa pulled the animal to a halt and looked around briefly, getting his bearings.

"Are we there?" Tavis asked, sounding sleepy.

"Almost," the gleaner whispered.

They started forward again, turned onto the next street, and followed it in a wide arc to the gated walls of Bian's Sanctuary.

Stopping once more, Grinsa dismounted and stepped to the nearest gate.

A heavyset man emerged from the small guardhouse and regarded him coolly, glancing for a moment at Tavis, who still sat on the horse, before looking at the Qirsi again. The man was clean-shaven, with long silver hair that was tied back from his face. He wore a simple grey robe tied at his waist with a piece of rope. He didn't appear to be carrying a weapon; the clerics of the ancient gods rarely did.

"Good night to you, Brother," the Qirsi said. "This boy and I are weary from our travels and we seek rest in your sanctuary."

Guards were shouting all through the city now, and bells tolled from the castle as well as from the gates of the city wall. Grinsa tried to hold the man's gaze, but he couldn't help but glance over his shoulder as the shouting grew nearer.

"The prioress likes to know of all who seek refuge among us," the man said, his voice gravelly, his face betraying nothing. *Refuge, not rest.* He understood all too well. "Who shall I say has come?"

"Is Meriel still prioress here?"

The man's eyes widened, though only for an instant. "She is."

"Then tell her that Grinsa jal Arriet has come seeking her aid."

"And him?" the man asked, pointing at Tavis.

"He's a friend," Grinsa said, meeting the man's gaze as best he could. "He needs healing and rest."

The man gave a slight frown. But after a moment he nodded. "Very well. I'll return shortly."

"Thank you," the gleaner said as the man walked back toward

the center tower of the sanctuary. He looked back again. Torchlight flickered in the distance. "Be quick, Brother," he murmured.

Grinsa walked the horse slowly to the gate, marking the approach of the torchlight as he did.

"Where are we?" Tavis asked, warily eyeing the gate and buildings beyond.

"At a sanctuary," Grinsa told him. "I know the prioress here. I believe she'll be willing to help us."

"Are we still in Kentigern?"

"Yes," the Qirsi said, hoping the boy was too weary to put the pieces together.

Tavis nodded, but didn't say anything more, and Grinsa allowed himself a soft sigh of relief.

A few moments later, the heavyset man returned, unlocking the gate and waving them inside.

"The prioress will see you in the shrine," he said, locking the gate once more. "I'll take your mount to the stable."

"Thank you, Brother," Grinsa said, helping Tavis off the mount and leading him toward the shrine.

Like those in the sanctuaries of the other gods, the Shrine of Bian was simple, almost stark. Unadorned on the outside save for the narrow spire that rose above the other buildings in the sanctuary, the shrine contained several rows of dark wooden benches, and a stone altar that held a bowl and knife for blood offerings, both of which were also made of stone. Narrow tapered candles burned at either end of the altar, resting in plain wooden holders that were caked with wax. Behind the altar stood an enormous window of stained glass, a stunning contrast to the austerity of the rest of the shrine. In one corner of the window, raked by angry flames of orange and yellow and tormented by black demons, the damned writhed in anguish, their mouths opened in silent screams. On the opposite side, the honored walked in a garden filled with brilliant blooms of red, blue, violet, and gold. In the center, above all the dead, stood the Deceiver himself, cloaked in a shimmering multihued robe, his arms lifted before him, as if he were controlling both the flames and the bright silver light that shone on the garden. His ageless face wore a strange expression, one that seemed to change continually with the flickering of the candlelight. There was anger in it, even malice, but Grinsa thought he sensed kindness there as well.

He glanced at the boy once more, but Tavis was nearly asleep on his feet. He would learn soon enough where he was, but for tonight, at least, he was too consumed with his own weariness and pain to notice.

"Do you care to offer blood?" someone asked from behind them.

Grinsa turned toward the voice, knowing already whose it was.

"Gladly, Mother Prioress," he said, "if that is the price of our safety."

Meriel strode toward the altar on long legs. She was tall and straight-backed, though the years had left lines on her face and bold streaks of silver in her red hair.

"This is a sanctuary. There is no price for refuge here." Reaching the altar, she turned to face him. "I merely asked if you wish to offer blood to the god."

The Qirsi hesitated, then nodded. "I think I had better," he told her, his voice dropping to a whisper. "I sent a man to the Under-realm last night."

The expression on her handsome face did not change and her dark eyes continued to hold his. "Step forward then. The knife and bowl await."

Grinsa helped Tavis onto one of the wooden benches, then stepped to the altar. He held out his arm, turning it so that the underside was exposed. The prioress placed the bowl under it and raised the stone knife so that the milky white blade shone in the light of the candles.

"Hear me, Bian!" she said, her eyes closing and her voice ringing like the castle bells. "A man comes to you offering his life's blood for a life he has taken. Deem him worthy and accept this gift. Make room for the one who has died." She paused, looking at Grinsa. "Do you know the name of this man you killed?"

"I knew him as Honok. He was an assassin sent to kill me."

At that her eyes did widen, though only for an instant.

"And you offer blood for him?"

He shrugged. "I killed him."

After a moment she nodded. Closing her eyes again, she raised the knife a second time. "Make room for the one who has died," she repeated. "Judge him as you will. And remember Grinsa jal Arriet, who gives his blood. When his time comes, consider this gift."

She dragged the blade across Grinsa's arm, catching the dark blood as it welled from the wound. Though he had offered blood before, he could not help anticipating pain. The blade of the stone knife appeared jagged and uneven. But it was honed to such a fine edge that he barely felt the cut at all.

After a few moments the bleeding subsided and Meriel wrapped a cloth around his arm. He could have healed himself, of course. But he chose to let time mend this wound.

The prioress lifted the bowl and swirled it gently so that his blood covered the entire surface. Then she placed the bowl at the middle of the altar.

"Will your companion make an offering as well?" she asked, facing him once more.

From the way she asked the question, Grinsa could tell that she knew just who the boy was and what he was said to have done.

"There's no life on his hands," he said as forcefully as he could. "And he's already had more blood taken from him than he deserved."

"I'm the god's servant," Meriel said, "and my dukes all turned to the cloisters long ago. But I'm still a woman of Kentigern. I'll need more than the word of one man to trust that he's innocent. Even if that man is you."

"I understand, Mother Prioress. You'll give us refuge?"

"How could I not? Others in my family may have disapproved of you as a husband for Pheba, but I saw how she looked at you."

He felt the old grief rising within him, stronger than it had been in years. Perhaps it was being with Meriel again, or just the added pain of Cresenne's betrayal. "Her mother saw that as well," he said, unable to keep the bitterness from his voice. "It didn't seem to matter to her."

"My sister was small-minded and selfish. She cared more for what people said of her than she did for Pheba's happiness."

Grinsa nodded, not trusting himself to speak.

Footsteps echoed off the ceiling of the shrine and the Qirsi turned, seeing a robed cleric standing beside a door he hadn't noticed earlier.

"My pardon, Mother Prioress," the man said, "but there are soldiers at the gate." His eyes flicked toward Grinsa. "They are inquiring about our guests."

"Thank you, Osmyn," Meriel said. "I'll speak with them in a moment."

The man nodded once and withdrew.

"What will you tell them?"

"A lie," she said easily. Then she smiled. "I serve the Deceiver."

Grinsa merely stared at her, and after a moment her smile faded. "I'll tell them I haven't seen you or Lord Tavis."

It was the first time either of them had spoken the boy's name, and the Qirsi shivered slightly.

"When they don't find him elsewhere, they'll come back. Aindreas wants him dead."

"The sanctuaries cannot be violated, even by a duke bent on vengeance. Aindreas knows that."

"He tortured me, though it risked war with my father. Do you really believe he'll show any more regard for the sanctity of your shrine?"

Grinsa turned to look at Tavis, awake after all and very much aware of his surroundings. He was as pale as a Qirsi and he appeared to be trembling, as if the very act of sitting there was taxing him to his limits. But the look in his eyes was keen and alert.

"Fear of the Deceiver runs deep, Lord Tavis," the prioress said, showing no surprise at the boy's question. "It's one thing to challenge another duke, even one who would be king. It's another thing entirely to challenge a god. As you will learn soon enough."

The young lord frowned. "What do you mean?"

"This is Bian's Sanctuary, and the cycle of this moon ends two nights hence. Every turn, on Pitch Night, all who are in this place meet their dead. Lady Brienne will tell us if you are guilty or innocent. It's ironic, isn't it, that the truth of such things can best be learned in the shrine of the Deceiver."

Tavis had paled, but he did not look away.

"I'll go speak with the soldiers," Meriel said, a thin smile on her lips. She started to leave, then halted and returned to the altar. "Your offering has been accepted," she said, looking at Grinsa. "I hope that brings you some comfort."

She held up the stone bowl for both of them to see. It was as white as the knife, as white as it had been when first they entered the shrine. His blood had vanished entirely, as if it had been absorbed into the stone.

Chapter
Eighteen

✦

Glyndwr, Eibithar

ven before she reached the court hall, Keziah made up her mind to leave the banquet early. She had met the duke of Rouvin before and though he seemed a gracious man and a competent leader, he struck her as a typical Eandi lord: as bland as Wethy bread, too full of himself, and far less intelligent than he believed himself to be. The irony in this, one that Kearney was certain to point out to her, was that it had been her idea to invite him to Glyndwr Castle.

"It would be wise to maintain good relations with our Caerissan neighbors," she told Kearney at the time. "War may seem a remote possibility now, but by the time a threat appears, it's often too late to win allies."

Her duke had agreed, as a wise duke will when his Qirsi minister offers sound advice. It had helped, of course, that she had made the suggestion in his bed, as she straddled his back rubbing his shoulders. She had known at the time what it would mean—a formal dinner attended by the duchess, and a night passed alone in her bed—but she knew as well that Kearney needed to do this. Tensions along the Aneiran border remained high, and the lords of Caerisse were divided in their sympathies between Aneira and Eibithar. If the kingdom could not depend upon the support of Caerisse's northern lords in the event of a war, they had no hope of keeping their southern neighbor from allying itself with Aneira. With so much at stake, her personal concerns about the evening seemed selfish and small.

She had been alone before, and she had spent a good deal of time in the company of her lover's wife. One night more of one or the other would mean little to her.

Much as Keziah disliked Leilia, the duchess, she also felt sorry for her. The woman knew of Keziah's affair with the duke. By now she probably knew that he was in love with Keziah, and she with him. Yet there was little she could do about it. Yes, the love shared by the minister and her duke was forbidden by law—the sin of the moons—but had Leilia exposed them, she would have brought humiliation on herself as well. Besides, with other lovers would have come bastards, and a different kind of shame for the duchess. In noble houses of Eibithar, it was said, there were more bastards than there were heirs. But not in Glyndwr. Had Keziah become pregnant with the duke's child, it would not only have exposed their crime, it would also have endangered her life, for Qirsi women rarely survived the labor that brought forth the child of an Eandi man. As things stood, Leilia was still the mother of all Kearney's children, and Keziah and the duke were so discreet that few people, even within the castle, knew of their affair. Publicly, many noblewomen in the kingdom endured far worse than the duchess did. Her pain was private, a wound few could see. Keziah couldn't say which she thought worse. In truth, each seemed a cruel fate to bear. At times she felt ashamed for what her love did to the woman. But on nights like these, when Leilia could claim the duke as her own before all the dukedom, Keziah envied the duchess. She might even have hated her.

Stepping out of the cloister tower, the one nearest her quarters, Keziah crossed Glyndwr Castle's upper ward toward the court tower. Elined's turn was almost over, but here in the Glyndwr Highlands, the night air still carried a chill. She pulled her shawl tighter around her shoulders and quickened her pace. The gown she wore was cut lower in the back than it should have been for so early in the growing season, but Kearney loved it, and if he was going to pass the night in Leilia's arms he was going to do so thinking of Keziah in this dress. She reached the far side of the ward and entered the tower, nodding to the guards there as she did.

A great fire burned in the hearth of the court hall, warming the room. Many of the duke's guests had already arrived. His three children were seated at the main table at the far end of the room, and minor lords and lesser ministers sat at tables throughout the hall.

Keziah was to sit at the duke's table as well, as their guest would expect of the duke's first minister. But Leilia had made the seating arrangements, and the minister had no doubt that she would be as far from both the duke and duchess as possible. Last time the duchess had put her at the very end of the table, beside Gershon Trasker, Kearney's swordmaster, who hated the Qirsi almost as much as he did the Aneirans. The man said nothing to her all night, choosing instead to speak solely with Corinne, the duke's nine-year-old daughter.

Gershon was already there as well, but tonight he was seated next to his wife and the younger Kearney, the duke's eldest son and heir. She would, at least, be spared his company, she thought, removing her shawl as she approached the table.

Horns blew, the sound ringing through the hall and stopping her where she stood. A moment later Kearney entered the great room with the duchess on his arm. He was dressed as if for battle—appropriate for a banquet honoring one he sought as an ally. He wore a simple black shirt and matching breeches, and the silver, red, and black baldric worn by all dukes of Glyndwr. He was smiling broadly, his youthful, tanned face ruddy in the firelight and his hair, silver before its time, shining with the glow of the torches mounted on the walls. He was not particularly tall or broad-shouldered, but to Keziah he looked like a king.

The duchess, on the other hand, appeared older than her years, her face fat and pale, the smile on her lips forced and awkward. She scanned the hall nervously, her eyes finding Keziah immediately, and flicking away just as quickly. The minister wished she hadn't come at all. Better just to give the night to the duchess than to go through all of this.

The duke and duchess of Rouvin followed Kearney and Leilia into the hall, and Glyndwr's duke began to make introductions to the other lords and ministers. Seeing Keziah, his smile broadened and his eyes strayed briefly to her dress. With a quick, self-conscious look at his wife, Kearney beckoned to her. Taking a breath, Keziah joined them near the door.

"My Lord Duke," Kearney said, placing a hand lightly on Keziah's bare shoulder, "I'm certain you remember my first minister, Keziah ja Dafydd. First Minister, the duke and duchess of Rouvin."

"It's an honor to see you again, my Lord Duke," she said, making herself smile. "And a pleasure to meet you, my lady."

The duke of Rouvin smiled, taking her hand and saying something in a thickly accented voice that she did not understand.

Keziah nodded, continuing to smile. But she was aware of little other than Kearney's fingers on her skin. She felt the duchess watching them, though she dared not look Leilia's way, and long after he removed his hand and introduced his guest to someone else, the memory of his touch made her shoulder burn, as if she had stood in the sun for too long.

"You're at the end of the table," she heard a low voice say. "I put you next to Rouvin's Qirsi."

She looked toward the voice in time to see Leilia turning away from her, the same strained smile still on her face.

The end of the table again. With a Qirsi no less. Keziah wondered briefly if Leilia hoped to make a match. She grinned at the thought.

It was a fine meal, as were all Glyndwr's feasts. Servants brought platter after platter of spice-laden stews and roasted meats, tender mountain root and sweet greens, rounds of bread baked fresh that day, and pungent cheeses from the dairymen of the highlands. Dark ales and blood-red wines flowed at all the tables, and musicians played songs from both Eibithar and Caerisse. The duke of Rouvin's minister offered passable companionship, though Keziah was hardly in the mood for conversation. She ate little—Qirsi appetites were no match for those of the Eandi—and listened more to the music than to the man beside her. Mostly she tried not to look at the duke, even when she knew that he was looking at her. At last, when she could take it no more, she made her excuses to the Caerissan minister and left the hall, throwing her shawl around her shoulders and hurrying across the ward back to the warmth of her quarters.

The fire she had left burning in the small hearth of her room had all but burned out, leaving a bed of glowing orange embers and a few charred ends of wood that smoked and crackled. Keeping her shawl on, Keziah placed two logs on the coals and watched them catch fire.

Kearney would be disappointed that she had left the banquet so early. He might even be angry with her, though he could never remain so for very long. She had learned little from her conversation with the Caerissan duke's first minister, nor had she done much to further Kearney's pursuit of an alliance.

"Tomorrow," she said aloud. "I'll seek out the minister tomorrow." He deserved an apology, for her reticence as well for her early departure from the dinner. And her duke deserved a more determined effort on her part. "Tomorrow," she said once more.

The fire popped loudly.

Keziah removed her gown, carefully returning it to her wardrobe, before pulling on her sleeping shirt and climbing into bed. She had thought that she was tired, but once she lay down, she found that sleep did not come easily. She thought of Kearney and Leilia, of what it meant to be joined to someone for so many years, to bear his children.

Such thoughts do you no good, a voice said within her. *Sleep. Stop thinking.*

But still she lay there, watching the shadows cast by the fire dance on her walls.

When she finally did fall asleep she slipped almost immediately into a dream. She was standing on a barren stretch of the steppe on a cold, grey day. A steady wind blew across the tawny grasses and grey boulders, carrying the faint scent of the sea. Keziah recognized the place from her childhood. It wasn't far from the home in which she had grown up. She recognized the dream as well, for it had come to her many times before, and always it meant the same thing.

"Grinsa?" she called, turning slowly, scanning the plain. "Are you here?"

At first she saw no one and heard nothing save the keening wind and the rustling of the grass. But after some time a lone figure appeared in the distance and began to draw nearer. She could see it was a man, tall and broad, with long white hair that twisted like mist in the wind. His mouth was full and wide, his cheekbones high, like those of a Qirsi king, and his eyes were the same shade of yellow as hers. She recognized him instantly. She knew his walk, the way his hair moved as he approached her, and she knew and loved the smile that spread across his face as he came closer.

"You look well," her brother said. "Court life agrees with you."

She wanted to return the compliment, but she couldn't. Grinsa had dark circles under his eyes and his skin looked too white, even for a Qirsi.

"How is your duke treating you?" he asked.

Keziah felt her face color. "Very well, thank you. He heeds my counsel, he pays me more gold than I can spend—"

"That's not what I meant, and you know it."

Keziah smiled. "Yes, I do."

He appeared to be waiting for her to say more. But she just grinned at him, keeping her silence.

"Fine," he said at last. "Tell me nothing." He looked away, feigning indifference. "I'm not interested anyway."

"Well, you never tell me anything about your life. Why should I answer all your questions?"

Grinsa opened his arms wide. "Ask me anything. I'll tell you whatever you want to know."

"All right. You look terrible. What's the matter?"

He frowned. "You sound just like Mother."

"It looks to me as if you could use some mothering."

"Maybe," he said, looking away once more.

"Where are you?" Keziah asked.

"Kentigern, in the sanctuary."

"With Meriel? Is that why you look this way? Are you thinking of Pheba?"

"I think of Pheba every day," he told her, "but that's not . . ." He hesitated, shaking his head. "I'm used to that."

"Then what is it? Why have you come to me?"

Few Qirsi could have entered her dreams as Grinsa had done. Indeed, she knew of no others who were alive right now, though she was certain that there must be a few. A Weaver's magic allowed him or her to bind together the powers of many Qirsi and wield them as a single tool or weapon. Since the Qirsi controlled their powers with their minds, this meant that Weavers could also divine the thoughts of other Qirsi, and in some cases even enter their dreams, just as Grinsa had done tonight.

"I need your help," her brother said. "Has word reached Glyndwr yet of the murder in Kentigern Castle?"

"No."

He took a breath, as if preparing himself for an arduous task. Keziah had to remind herself that entering her dreams took a great effort on his part.

A moment later he began to tell her his tale. The words came slowly at first, as if he were uncertain of how to begin. He described the Fating he had done for Tavis of Curgh and his affair with the woman in Bohdan's Revel. As the story continued—his confrontation in the woods with the assassin, his rescue of Lord Tavis, and their escape from the castle to Bian's Sanctuary, all of which had happened in the last day—the words came faster and faster, until Keziah found it difficult to follow all that he was telling her. She grasped enough, however, to understand both his fatigue and the pain she read in his eyes.

One part of his story frightened her more than anything else, more than the idea that Brienne's murderer still roamed the land, more even than Grinsa's suspicions of a Qirsi conspiracy.

"This man who helped you, Curgh's first minister, he knows you're a Weaver?"

Grinsa nodded. "I had little choice but to tell him."

"Do you trust him?"

"Yes, I do. I wouldn't have before, but he risked his life for the boy, and he saw that I was willing to do the same."

"But still, he's a minister. His loyalties lie with the Eandi."

"That's a strange thing to hear coming from you."

"Nevertheless," she said. "I wish you had found another way."

"No one will ever know you're my sister, Kezi. You have nothing to fear."

She felt her features hardening. "I'm not worried about me," she said angrily. "How dare you even think it! This deception has always been your idea. I just don't want to see you burned like the ancient Weavers, and all the Weavers since."

Grinsa closed his eyes. "I'm sorry. I'm tired, and I'm not thinking clearly. Don't be angry."

She nodded, though she wouldn't meet his gaze. It had been his idea. They both knew it. But they both knew as well how necessary it had been. So great was the fear of Weavers among the Eandi that not only were all Weavers executed when they were discovered, but so were their parents, siblings, and children. It had been this way for nearly nine centuries, since the failure of the Qirsi invasion and the execution of the Weavers who commanded the army of the Southlanders. Grinsa and Keziah had no other siblings, and their parents had died many years before. But since realizing the extent of his power, as an apprentice, Grinsa had insisted that they hide their kinship. Only Nesta, the Qirsi master who had trained them both and had been the first to suggest that Grinsa might be a Weaver, had known the truth. And she had sworn herself to guarding their secret until the day she died.

Their deception was made somewhat easier by Qirsi custom, which dictated that all boys be named for their mothers and all girls for their fathers. Hence, she was Keziah ja Dafydd; he was Grinsa jal Arriet. It helped as well that he looked just like their father, while she favored their mother. Even those who saw them together would never guess that they were related.

"Please, Kezi," he said softly. "Forgive me. I'm so tired. I can't stay much longer, and I still need to ask your help."

Reluctantly she looked at him again, her eyes finding his. "What is it you need?"

"The duke of Curgh's minister told me that his lord threatened war if any harm came to his son, and that Kentigern countered with similar threats. Javan isn't king yet, but Aylyn has little time left. Everyone knows that. If he dies, making Javan king before all of this is settled, I fear that Aindreas will try to keep him from the throne. Eibithar will fall into civil war."

"It sounds as though the houses could go to war even if Aylyn lives."

He nodded. "Quite possibly."

"But what do you want of me?"

"I want you to prevail upon your duke to intervene."

"Kearney? What can he do?"

"He can ride to Kentigern and speak with both men. He can talk them out of going to war."

Keziah shook her head. She didn't like this idea at all. Kearney was likely to be killed if he tried to put himself between the armies of Curgh and Kentigern. "Why would Javan and Aindreas listen to the duke of Glyndwr? Kearney's house ranks below both of them. To the other major houses, Glyndwr is barely more than one of the minors."

Grinsa gave her a sour look. "We grew up in a minor house, Kezi. You know there's a great distance between Glyndwr and the minors, even Eardley."

She and Grinsa had grown up in the House of Eardley, the wealthiest and most influential of Eibithar's seven minor houses. Their father had been a minister to Eardley's duke. And Grinsa was right. Glyndwr had far more in common with the other major houses than it did with Eardley and the lesser houses. Just this night her duke had entertained a duke from Caerisse. None of the lesser dukes ever would; none of them brought enough to a potential alliance to attract such attention from the nobles of other kingdoms.

"You may be right," she said at last. "But I doubt that Curgh and

Kentigern would agree with you. To them Glyndwr is just a lonely fortress on the steppe. In the absence of a true threat from the eastern kingdoms, they'd just as soon ignore us."

"Perhaps," he said, conceding her point in turn. "But who else is there? Aylyn is too old to make the journey. The other dukes have always viewed Tobbar of Thorald as a regent and nothing more. And with Filib dead, he's not even that. The new lords of Galdasten are still four generations away from being recognized once more in the Order of Ascension. The minor houses haven't the strength to enforce the peace. Don't you see? Kearney is our only hope."

Of course she saw it. How could she not? *I don't want to lose him. Why can't we stay here, where we're safe, where the snows are the greatest threat and he only needs his sword for ceremonies?* She let out a long sigh. "How quickly do you need us there?"

Keziah couldn't help but smile at the relief she saw on her brother's face.

"Thank you, Kezi. I know I'm asking a lot, but this is the only way to stop a war. I'm sure of it. I wouldn't have asked this of you otherwise."

He was telling the truth. She had always been able to tell. But she heard something else in his words as well. He was asking even more of her than he was saying. Something was going to happen on this journey to Kentigern, something that would change her life and that of her duke. She suspected that Grinsa knew already what it was.

"How quickly?" she asked again, shivering slightly in the wind.

"Soon. Word of these events should reach Glyndwr in the next few days. You must convince him immediately. Things are happening very fast. Too fast really. Tavis's escape will only make matters worse."

She started to say something, then stopped herself.

"I had to save him," Grinsa said, reading her thoughts. "Another day in Kentigern's dungeon and he would have died."

"Was he worth saving? Can you justify risking civil war for this one life?"

She expected him to grow angry, but instead he merely shrugged, as if he had already asked himself the same question.

"I think so," he told her. "I know that our fates—his and mine— lie together, and I can only assume that he'll be needed in whatever conflict is coming." He took a breath. "I had a vision of Tavis's Fating before the Revel even reached Curgh. It showed the two of us journeying across the Forelands together, fighting battles side by side. It's little more than a guess, but I believe we were fighting against the conspiracy. I couldn't show him his real Fating without giving away too much about my powers. I had to change it." It seemed to Keziah that her brother was trying to convince himself of this, and that he failed. "I suppose you could say that I altered his Fating to save myself," he went on, shaking his head, "but I also did it to warn him of what was coming, to prepare him in some way. In the end, I think I just made things worse for him. I never imagined that he'd turn his blade on his liege man."

"None of us can foresee everything, Grinsa," she said softly. "Not even you."

"I know. I've wondered since Tavis's Fating if I read too much in that vision, if maybe his role in this conflict will be less than I thought." He met her gaze again. "Even if that's the case though, I'm still certain that his death would have brought war. By saving him, I might have kept Curgh and Kentigern from destroying each other, at least for a time."

Keziah nodded. Even as a child, Grinsa had been wise beyond his years. It almost seemed that the gods had prepared him to carry the burdens that came with being a Weaver. She could hardly question his judgment now, after all these years.

"As soon as word arrives, I'll talk to Kearney," she said. "I expect him to resist the idea. He's not usually one to involve himself in the affairs of other realms. But I'll try."

"Thank you."

Grinsa stepped forward and put his arms around her. She pressed her cheek against his chest, feeling warm and safe for just that moment. He smelled like home.

"Be well, Kezi. I hope to see you soon."

She didn't. As much as she missed her brother, she hoped that Kearney would refuse to ride to Kentigern. She kept this to herself, however. "I love you, Grinsa" was all she said.

An instant later she was awake. Her room was dark, save for the glowing remains of her fire. She rose from her bed and stepped to the window, staring out over the highlands and Lake Glyndwr. Panya hung above the lake, a thin white crescent reflected in the shimmering, windswept waters. Daylight was still hours away.

She wanted to go to Kearney then, without waiting for dawn, but she knew he was with the duchess. Not that she could tell him anything of her dream anyway. She couldn't even speak to him of the threat faced by the kingdom until news of Brienne's murder arrived from Kentigern. There was nothing for her to do but sleep. Still, she remained at the window, watching Panya climb higher into the sky, tasting the lake waters in the wind. After a time, Ilias appeared on the horizon, barely more than a sliver and the color of leaves on a highland oak during the harvest. The lovers.

Keziah turned away from the moons and returned to bed. Sleep wouldn't come easily, she knew. Too many thoughts raced through her mind. But better just then to try than to stand at her window thinking of Kearney. She had her days for that.

She slept later than she had intended, waking to the midmorning bells as sunlight streamed through her window. Still, she felt as though she could have slept for hours more. Her conversation with Grinsa had left her drained and troubled. Her slumber after the dream had been fitful.

She rose and splashed cold water on her face, before dressing and making her way to Kearney's ducal chambers. Reaching his door, she heard him laughing within. Apparently he wasn't alone. She passed a hand through the tangles in her white hair, wishing belatedly that she had taken the time to comb them out. Then she knocked.

"Enter!" he called.

She pushed the door open and found the duke at his writing table. Gershon, the swordmaster, stood next to him, the grin on his face vanishing as he saw her come into the room.

"First Minister!" the duke said, standing and stepping around the table to greet her. He took her hand in both of his. They felt warm, and she looked down at them, not willing to look into his eyes just yet.

"I trust you slept well," Kearney said.

"Quite, my lord. Thank you."

Gershon cleared his throat. "I should be going, my lord, I have men to train."

Kearney released her hands and grinned at the swordmaster. "Of course you do. Don't be too hard on them, Gershon."

The man grunted and started toward the door. He didn't look at Keziah again.

"I'll consider your counsel, swordmaster," the duke said as Gershon went past. "We'll speak of this again."

"Very good, my lord."

Kearney faced her again when Gershon was gone, and putting his arms around her, drew her into a deep kiss.

"I missed you," he said.

"Did you? I'd have thought the duchess would make you forget me entirely." She regretted the words as soon as they crossed her lips.

He released her, stepping back around the table to his chair.

Keziah closed her eyes briefly, cursing her stupidity. They had fought about Leilia countless times before, and always it came back to the same unalterable fact: she was his wife, the mother of his heirs, and nothing would ever change that. Bringing it up as she just had only served to make their time together awkward and sad.

He sorted through some of the documents lying before him, his eyes trained on the pieces of parchment. "You left early last night. Were you ill?"

I'm sorry. Don't be this way. "Just tired, my lord. I trust the banquet went well."

"Well enough. Farrar is a fine man. He may even carry some influence with the Caerissan king. But Gershon believes that he may bring less to a military partnership than we first thought."

"Of course he does," she said, unable to keep the ice from her voice. "Does Gershon base this on anything or is he just guessing?"

Kearney looked up. "First my duchess and now my swordmaster. Am I to ignore my other ministers as well? What about the prelate, or Morna's prioress down in the city? Should I ignore all of them, and listen only to you?"

Keziah felt her face shade to crimson. "No, my lord." She hesitated, struggling to hold his gaze.

"Go ahead," he told her. "Say what you will."

"We're not seeking the strongest lord in Caerisse. We're merely looking for allies in the event of a war with Aneira. The duke of Rouvin's influence with his king is far more important to us than his army. There are few dukes in Caerisse who are as strong as Eardley or Heneagh, much less Eibithar's major houses. I don't question Gershon's assessment of Farrar's army, but neither do I think it should be our first consideration in this matter."

The duke regarded her for several moments, saying nothing. Finally he began to nod. "You make a good point. Gershon is a fine swordmaster, but he sees the world through a warrior's eyes." He gave a slight frown. "Still, Keziah, that's no reason to hate him."

"I hate him because he has nothing but contempt for all Qirsi. It has nothing to do with his strange affection for swords and war horses."

He continued to stare at her, shaking his head now. After a time, a smile touched his lips. "You're a difficult woman."

"Thank you, my lord. I try to be."

He gave a gentle laugh.

"I'm sorry for what I said before about the duchess," she went on. "It wasn't fair of me."

"It's all right," he said, dismissing the apology with a gesture. But his green eyes flicked away from her gaze once more. It seemed she had hurt him more than he cared to admit.

Kearney picked up a piece of parchment from his table and motioned toward one of the chairs near where Keziah stood. "Please sit," he said. "There's other news we need to discuss."

She lowered herself into the chair, knowing what he would say before he opened his mouth to speak, and wondering if Grinsa had known that word would come this morning, or if it had just been coincidence. Suddenly she felt cold, though sunlight shone through the windows, warming the chamber.

"A messenger arrived this morning from Kentigern. It seems the duke's daughter, Lady Brienne, was found murdered in the bed of Lord Tavis of Curgh. Apparently Tavis was visiting Kentigern with his father, to arrange a marriage of all things." He paused, looking at her, waiting for some response. When she offered none, he went on. "Tavis has been imprisoned in Kentigern's dungeon ever since. Aindreas and Javan are both threatening war, and Aindreas has gone so far as say that he will oppose Javan's ascension to the throne when Aylyn dies."

He paused a second time, obviously expecting her to say something.

"Who sent the message?" It was all she could think to ask. Of course the message said nothing of Tavis's escape, but she needed to know if it cast any doubt at all on the boy's guilt.

The duke frowned, but he looked at the parchment once more. "One of Aindreas's ministers. I don't recognize the name. Why?"

Keziah shrugged. "What do they want from us?"

"A pledge of support should Javan try to take the throne before the matter is settled."

"Do they offer any proof that the boy did it?"

319

Kearney glanced at the message again. "There seems little doubt of that. I'll spare you the details, but it's enough to say that they as much as found him with the weapon in his hand."

She felt her mouth twitch, and she looked away. *What is it you ask of me, Grinsa?* "Shouldn't you hear from Curgh before you commit yourself to Aindreas's cause?"

"I suppose," he said, looking puzzled. "But under these circumstances I'm not sure what difference that would make."

"If the boy is innocent it could make all the difference in the world."

He tossed the message onto the table and stepped around it again so that he stood just in front of her chair. "This isn't like you, Kez. What's going on? Is this still about last night?"

"No," she said, crossing her arms over her chest. "But we can't just assume the boy is guilty and join Aindreas in opposing Javan. The Rules of Ascension date back nearly eight centuries. This is no trifle Aindreas is asking of you."

"I know that. But what if Tavis did kill her? Can we ignore Kentigern's plea and give the throne to a house of murderers?"

"Of course not. This is why we need to know more about what happened."

The duke gave a loud sigh and sat on the edge of his table. "I've never liked Javan. I've never trusted him."

"You like Aindreas that much more?"

A smile alighted on his face for an instant and was gone. "No. But my father and Aindreas's father were good friends. I suppose I feel that has to count for something."

"Something perhaps. But that's not much on which to base a decision of this magnitude."

Kearney nodded. "You're probably right." He looked at her again. "So you think I should do nothing for now."

Yes, she wanted to say. *Stay out of it. Let the fools tear each other apart.* But she had promised Grinsa.

"I'm not certain that you can," she answered, the words almost sticking in her throat. "It sounds as though Javan and Aindreas are on the verge of war. You may have to go to Kentigern, not as Aindreas's ally, but as a peacemaker."

His eyes widened. "Go to Kentigern?" he repeated. "Even Aindreas's minister didn't suggest that."

"Still, I think you should consider it."

"What would you have me do, Kez? Just ride to the tor unasked with a thousand soldiers at my back? They may be threatening war, but they're not at war yet. By leading my men to Kentigern, I might give them just the excuse they need."

"Or you might give them pause. If you wait until they're already at war, it may be too late. The entire kingdom could be drawn into their conflict, at a cost we can scarcely imagine. This may be the only chance you have to prevent civil war." She stopped, surprised by her own passion. Perhaps Grinsa's plea for help had affected her more than she realized.

Kearney stared at her for some time, offering no response. "You still surprise me sometimes, Kez. I don't know that I've ever heard you argue so forcefully for any action that involved Glyndwr's army."

"Does that mean you'll do it?" she asked, still half hoping he would say no.

"I don't know. It still seems rash to me. I know how I'd feel if one of the other dukes brought his army to Glyndwr unbidden."

She nodded. "I understand. No doubt you should speak with Gershon about this."

"*Gershon?*" the duke said, his features registering such shock at the suggestion that Keziah almost laughed out loud. "Now I know you're concerned about this. You actually want me to seek the swordmaster's advice?"

"You said yourself that Gershon sees the world through a warrior's eyes. In this case I think such a view would be useful."

"Gershon," Kearney said again, shaking his head. "Yes, I'll speak with Gershon."

"Good. I think he'll agree with me."

They sat in awkward silence for a few moments, Keziah gazing toward the window, though aware that he was watching her. At last she stood.

"I should go."

He caught her arm with a gentle hand. "Why?"

"You have to speak with Gershon, remember?" She couldn't help but smile.

Kearney stood, pulling her toward him. "He's training my men right now. He won't be finished until after the midday bells are rung."

Light from the windows lit his silver hair and made his green eyes sparkle like emeralds. He bore a small scar on his chin, white and crescent-shaped. It looked just as Panya had the night before. She traced it lightly with her finger, bringing a smile to his lips.

"Tell me how you got this."

She had heard the story a thousand times already. He had been eight when it happened, a boy in his father's court, and, on that particular day, mounted atop his father's steed. The horse had been far too big for him—his feet didn't even reach the stirrups—but when several older boys challenged him to a race he didn't hesitate to accept. He knew how to ride well enough, but the creature was too strong for him. When he tried to stop it, the horse reared and threw him, giving him the cut on his chin. By that time, though, he had won the race.

"You don't want to hear that story again."

They called him the silver wolf now, for his hair and the crest of his house, a wolf howling at the full moons. She thought it an odd name for a man with hands as gentle as his, but she knew that few saw him as she did. She knew as well that he could no more ignore a challenge now than he could as a boy. It was not in his nature. They would be riding to Kentigern. Not today perhaps, or even during this moon. But soon. And even with his arms around her, and his lips caressing hers once more, Keziah could not keep from shivering.

Chapter
Nineteen

✦

Kentigern, Eibithar

He awoke to the distant echo of thunder and the sweet, cool scent of rain. A soft grey light held the room and a bird called from just outside one of the windows, clear and urgent. For what seemed the first time in a turn, Tavis felt no pain. None at all.

For the past few days he had drifted in and out of sleep, usually waking to find Grinsa standing over him, healing his wounds, or soothing the fever that burned in his brow. Once he had opened his eyes to find the prioress sitting beside his bed, her stern expression unable to mask the concern in her dark eyes. This, though, was the first time Tavis could remember waking to an empty room since the dungeon. He should have been able to enjoy such solitude, but instead he felt a sense of dread rising in his chest, as if he expected Aindreas to enter the chamber in the next moment.

"Grinsa?" he called, throwing off his blanket. He stepped to the door, his legs stiff and weak. "Mother Prioress?"

He pulled the door open, expecting to find a corridor or a second room. Instead, he found himself looking out at an open courtyard of painted stone. A small fountain gurgled in its middle, surrounded by a modest bed of flowers. On the far side he saw other buildings like the one he was in, and beyond them, the back of the shrine. A gentle wind blew rain against his face and the thin white robe he was wearing.

"Grinsa?" he called again. "Is anyone here?"

No one answered, though the wind blew harder and another

rumble of thunder rolled among the buildings of the sanctuary. Reluctantly, Tavis closed the door and returned to his bed. He was tired still, and could easily have slept more, but he felt restless.

Standing again, he started to search the room for his clothes, only to remember an instant later that they had been matted with filth and blood, and cut to little more than ribbons by Brienne's father. No doubt they had been discarded or burned, and good riddance. But he saw no new ones to take their place. All that had been left for him was the simple white robe he was wearing, which was not at all appropriate for a duke's son, much less one who was in line to be king. It was intolerable really. There didn't appear to be any food either. Grinsa and the prioress had just left him alone in a room, unattended. What if Aindreas's men had come for him?

There was a knock at the door and before he could respond, one of the clerics poked his head in.

"Did I hear you calling, my lord?" the man asked.

"You certainly did. Where is Grinsa? Where is the prioress?"

The man smiled and stepped fully into the chamber, uninvited. Tavis thought of saying something, but he wanted answers, and there seemed no sense in driving the man away.

"Your friend, Grinsa, has left the sanctuary. I don't know where he's gone. He said he'd be back by tomorrow morning."

Tavis's throat felt dry. "Left the sanctuary?"

"For a time, yes. The prioress is in the shrine, performing her midday devotions. She should be available a bit later." He paused. "My name is Osmyn. We met two nights ago, though I doubt you remember. Can I help you with something?"

Grinsa had gone. Who knew if he would really return? Tavis truly was alone. "I need clothes," he said at last. "I have nothing but this robe."

The man nodded. "The vestments of a novice."

He narrowed his eyes. "A novice?"

"Yes. Grinsa and the prioress thought it best that you be dressed so. The duke's guards have been watching the sanctuary from afar. Wearing that robe, you're far less likely to draw their attention."

Tavis felt a sudden sharp chill, as though he were back in the prison again. "Very well," he said. "I'll wear this for now."

"Is there anything else, my lord?"

"Yes, food. I haven't eaten in days."

"Actually, my lord, I fed you some broth just yesterday. But I'll be happy to bring you some cheese and bread."

"That's hardly what I had in mind."

"I'm afraid it's all we have, my lord. Unless you care to wait until the evening meal. I believe we'll be having fowl and greens."

His stomach felt hollow as a gourd at the harvest. Cheese and bread would have to do.

"Fine," he said, turning away from the man. "Bring me what you have."

"Very good, my lord."

The cleric withdrew, closing the door gently, and leaving Tavis brooding by the window. They had him dressed like a novice, and eating even worse. He should have just left. Had he a mount, he would have. But with Aindreas's soldiers searching the city for him and his wounds only recently healed, he would have been just as well off walking back to Kentigern's dungeon and saving them the trouble of hunting him down. He had no choice but to wait for Grinsa. If and when the Qirsi returned, they'd leave this place together and set about restoring Tavis to his rightful place in the kingdom.

An image of his father's face entered his mind and Tavis shook his head, as if to rid himself of it. Did Javan even know where he was? Did he think Tavis had died? For that matter, was he even alive himself?

Another knock on the door announced Osmyn's return.

"Your food, my lord," the man said, hurrying into the room and setting a platter of cheese and dark bread on the small table beside the bed. "I'll bring some fresh water in a moment."

This was too much.

"Haven't you at least some wine?" Tavis asked, not even trying to mask his annoyance.

The man stopped and stared at him. "Of course we do, my lord. But we don't serve it on this day or through this night. You may have wine tomorrow."

It came to him in a rush: where he was, what this day had to be. Still, Tavis couldn't help but ask.

"What is today?"

"The last day of the waning, my lord. Tonight is Pitch Night."

Their eyes met for an instant; then Tavis looked away.

"I'll be back with your water presently, my lord," the man said in a low voice, reaching for the door again.

A moment later Tavis was alone once more, and he walked to his bed, his hunger abruptly gone. It was Elined's Turn, he knew, and he thought for a minute, trying to remember what the legends said about Pitch Night in the goddess's moon. Something about the plantings—it had to be that. If the seeds sown for the crop weren't up by tonight, the crop was doomed to fail. That was it. Not that it mattered. In this place, in the sanctuary of the Deceiver, all Pitch Nights were the same. Tonight, in the shrine, Tavis would meet his dead. He would meet Brienne.

He was certain that he hadn't killed her. He had tasted her lips and the soft skin of her neck. He had promised to guard her honor and had resolved to marry her. Murder had been the last thing on his mind that night. It had to have been someone else. That was what he had told her father and the prelate, and he had suffered greatly for it. Of course he was certain.

Except that the door had been locked, and he had awakened to find his dagger in her chest. His memories of that night remained clouded and confused. He remembered her falling asleep. He thought that he had as well, soon after. But he couldn't be sure. Not with all the wine he had drunk. Not after what he had done to Xaver.

Tonight, though. Tonight he would see Brienne again, for good or ill. And he would know. The thought brought no comfort. Just the opposite. He couldn't keep from trembling and he feared that his legs would not bear his weight.

Before he could make his way to the bed, however, the door opened again. Osmyn again, with his water.

But when he turned toward the sound, he didn't see the cleric, but rather Meriel in her black robe.

He started, taking a step back away from her, before remembering himself. "Mother Prioress," he said, fighting with only some success to keep his voice steady.

She gave him an appraising look. "I heard you were awake and demanding food. I trust you're feeling well."

"Well enough, thank you."

Meriel looked past him to the food on the table. "Our food isn't to your liking?"

"It's fine. My . . . I'm not as hungry as I thought I was."

"Perhaps you need more rest."

He nodded, looking away. "Perhaps."

"Grinsa said to tell you that he would return in the morning."

"The cleric told me. Do you know where he's gone?"

"No. I don't think where mattered very much. He didn't want to be here tonight. He doesn't wish to face his dead."

Tavis looked up at that, meeting the woman's gaze. Her eyes were almost black and she wore a thin smile on her lips.

"Maybe you'd like to leave as well," she said.

"You think I killed her."

"I barely know you. I can't say whether you killed her or not. I merely serve Bian. When your time comes, he will judge you."

"No," Tavis said, shaking his head. "There's more to it than that. I see the way you look at me. I hear the things you say. You've already made up your mind about me."

For the first time he saw her hesitate. "I believe you're capable of such a murder. And I sense that you fear this night. That's all."

He shuddered. Her opinion of him mirrored his own misgivings too closely. "Shouldn't I be afraid?" he asked, hoping she couldn't read his thoughts. "Grinsa has fled the sanctuary, yet you find no fault with him."

The prioress shrugged, the movement seeming odd for such a formidable woman. "I suppose I understand your fear. It's never easy to meet one's dead, no matter the circumstances. As for Grinsa, I've known him for many years, and I understand his grief. Many years ago he lost his wife, my niece, under . . . difficult circumstances. I believe he fears meeting her."

Tavis wasn't certain how to respond. "I'm sorry," he said, knowing how awkward he sounded.

She gave a queer smile, and looked at him for some time.

"You're a strange boy," she said. "You can be rude, as you were to Osmyn just now. Yet you can also be kind, though it makes you uncomfortable to be so. It think it is well that you'll never be king."

Tavis blinked, not quite believing what he had heard. "Of course I'll be king. After my father, I'm next in the Order of Ascension."

She shrugged a second time, though this time there was no uncertainty in the gesture. She was humoring him.

"I must be mistaken," she said. "Forgive me, my lord."

He heard irony in the way she addressed him, and he opened his mouth to demand an apology. But something stopped him. It might have been simply that she was a prioress of Bian and they were in her sanctuary. Or perhaps it was that somehow she already seemed to know him better than he knew himself. Whatever the reason, Tavis said nothing. He nodded, though he wasn't sure why.

"Osmyn will be in with your water in a moment," Meriel said, turning to go. "Be in the shrine at sundown. I'll await you there."

"Yes, Mother Prioress," he said, sounding like a dutiful child.

She started toward the door, then stopped. It was raining harder, though the thunder had moved off and sounded like a low whisper beneath the wind. "If you're innocent, as you say," she told him, "you have nothing to fear from Brienne's spirit. Seeing her may bring you grief, but she cannot harm you. If you're innocent."

Tavis nodded, then watched her go. *I am innocent,* he wanted to call after her. *I have nothing to fear.* But the words wouldn't come, and she wouldn't have believed him anyway. She could see how scared he was.

The rest of the day seemed to last an eternity. Tavis tried to sleep, but after two days of rest, he could only lie in bed staring at the rain and listening as thunderstorms drew near and receded like Amon's tides. Eventually he ate the bread and cheese the cleric had brought him, though only because he knew he should. He wondered if he'd ever be hungry again.

When the sunset bells finally tolled in the city, Tavis nearly leaped to his feet, hurrying out of his room into the steady rain and the gathering darkness. His heart was hammering against his chest and every part of him was trembling. For just an instant, he had to fight an urge to run, to leave the sanctuary and brave Aindreas's soldiers in the streets of Kentigern. If he was to prove Meriel wrong, however, and reclaim his place in the Order of Ascension, he had to do this first. But even more than that, he had to know for himself. He wanted to believe that someone else had killed her, but unless he faced Brienne, he would never be certain. In a way, the god was offering him a gift: a chance to find peace, one way or another. He would have been a fool to refuse it.

Tavis slowed as he reached the shrine, his apprehension growing. He had expected to find clerics standing before the doors to the temple, but there was no one. Entering the building slowly, he saw that it was empty as well, though candles lined the walls and covered the altar. He took an uncertain step toward the great portrait of Bian on the window, the soft slap of his bare foot on the floor echoing off the ceiling.

"I wondered if you would come," a voice said from the far side of the altar. "I thought you might be afraid."

"I am," he admitted, walking down the center aisle of the shrine. "But I wanted to prove to you that I didn't kill her."

"You needn't prove anything to me."

Tavis froze. This wasn't Meriel's voice. It was too high, too youthful. And even as he drew closer to the altar, it still sounded like it was coming to him from a distance.

"Come forward, my lord," the voice said. "You have nothing to fear from me."

In that moment, as the last faint remnants of daylight faded from the colored glass image of the Deceiver, Tavis saw her, his breath catching in his throat.

She stood before the altar, suffused with a pale white light, as if she held Panya in her hand. Her golden hair hung loose to her waist and her eyes glowed with the soft grey Tavis remembered from their night together. She wore the same sapphire dress, the one in which she had died, though there was no blood on it, no marks from the dagger.

"Brienne," he whispered, taking a faltering step toward her, then another. He felt tears on his face, and he wiped them away with a trembling hand. At the altar he halted and held out a hand to her.

"No," she said, backing away. "We cannot touch. It would mean your death."

"I don't know that I care." His voice sounded raw to his own ears, as though he had been crying for days. "You're even more beautiful than I remember."

She smiled shyly. It was so easy to forget that she was a wraith. "You look tired, my lord. You've suffered greatly since my death."

He wondered if she knew what Aindreas had done to him. It served nothing to tell her, he decided. "I've missed you," he said instead. "I so wanted you to be my queen."

"As did I, my lord."

"Are you . . . ?" He hesitated, unsure of how to ask the question. "Are you in the Underrealm now?"

She seemed to take a breath—did the dead do that? After a moment she nodded.

"What is it like?"

"He forbids us from speaking of it with the living. He says such things are only for the dead to know."

It took him a moment. Bian. She was speaking of the Deceiver.

"You've seen him?" he breathed.

She nodded again.

A sob escaped him. "I hope he's been kind to you."

"Please, my lord—"

"I'm so sorry, Brienne," he said, his tears falling freely once more.

The spirit offered a sad smile. "For what, my lord?"

"I feared . . . It was my dagger that killed you. And I've done things recently—terrible things, that I can't explain. So I was afraid that maybe . . ." He stopped, unable to say the words.

She shook her head. "No, my lord. You didn't do this to me."

"I didn't save you either. I was right beside you. I must have been. And I didn't protect you."

"Had you tried you would have been killed."

"I would have preferred that."

"No, Tavis. It would have been for nothing. He would have killed both of us."

Tavis stared at her. "He? You know who killed you?"

Brienne nodded, glowing tears appearing on her cheeks as well. "I was asleep when he came, but since my death I've seen it. All of it." She closed her eyes briefly. "Too many times."

"His name!" Tavis said. "Tell me his name!"

"I don't know it. It was one of the servants, the man who brought us the bottle of wine we carried from the banquet."

The young lord scoured his memory of that night, but he couldn't remember the man of whom she spoke. "What did he look like?"

"He was tall," she said. "And quite thin. He had long dark hair and a beard. His face was lean and his eyes pale blue. He had a pleasant face. He even smiled at me. As I said, he was a servant, but he wouldn't have looked out of place as a member of my father's court."

It seemed to Tavis that she could have been describing nearly anyone. But as she continued to speak, something appeared beside her. At first it looked like little more than a swirling cloud of white mist, an ocean fog turning in the wind. Gradually, though, the mist took shape and Tavis saw a man's face forming at its center.

"Is this him?" he asked, his voice dropping to a whisper once more.

The spirit glanced toward the image she had conjured. She nodded, her eyes widening, as if amazed by what she had done. "Yes. That's the man."

Tavis stood utterly still, staring at the face, afraid that any move he made would frighten the image away. After some time, it began to lose its form, becoming a mist once more and then fading entirely.

"I know him from somewhere," the boy said, as much to himself as to Brienne.

"Yes, from the banquet."

"No, that's not it." He closed his eyes, fighting past his grief and the haunting memory of Aindreas's dungeon, trying to recall where he had seen that face. The answer danced before him, just beyond his grasp. It was almost as though he were chasing his own shadow. Except that he felt himself getting closer with each moment.

"My lord?"

He raised a hand, silencing her. There was a song in his mind, one that sounded familiar, though elusive and faint. But it, too, was growing clearer.

"He was a singer!" Tavis said, abruptly opening his eyes. "I heard him sing during the Revel."

"This year's Revel?"

Tavis nodded. "I spent much of the Revel alone, wandering the streets of Curgh, watching the dancers and listening to the musicians. I only saw this man once, and briefly at that. But I remember him because he was so good." He paused, but only for a moment. "The *Paean*. He was singing *The Paean to the Moons*."

"So he followed you from Curgh?"

"He must have."

"But why did he kill me?"

Tavis gazed at her sadly. She was crying still, and he wanted more than anything to wipe the tears from her face.

"He killed you," the boy said as gently as he could, "so that I would be executed for your murder and our houses would go to war." There was an ache in his chest, as if Aindreas had laid one of his torches there, searing his heart. "You're dead because we were to be married."

"Are our houses at war?" she asked, sounding so young.

"Not yet. But I barely escaped your father's dungeon. Even now his guards hunt for me."

"Then you must find him, my lord. Don't allow my death to be the cause of a civil war. Please."

"I'll find him," Tavis said. "I swear it to you in the presence of Bian and any other god who will listen. I'll find him and I'll avenge you."

But Brienne shook her head. "Revenge is nothing. Prove your innocence and save the kingdom. The rest makes no difference to me."

He nodded again. "I will." In his heart, though, Tavis repeated the rest of his oath. The musician would die for what he had done. Even if it meant Tavis's life as well.

They had been in the prison tower for only two days, but already Fotir sensed that all of them were feeling the strain. The rooms were cramped, the air sour and still. The servants, all of them, had been given two chambers, and the forty guards who had accompanied Javan to Kentigern had been placed in five others. Fotir and Xaver were in one room together and the duke had the last chamber to himself.

To his credit, Javan asked Aindreas to put him in with Xaver and the first minister so that his soldiers might have another chamber. Kentigern refused, however. He never explained why, but the reason seemed obvious enough to Fotir. The soldiers' chambers were below them in the tower, where the men could neither see nor speak with their duke. Had Javan been allowed to give up his chamber for some of his men, they would surely have been in an adjacent room. Aindreas could not risk that. As it was, he appeared uncomfortable having Fotir so close to Javan, but his prison tower only had so many rooms, and the smallest ones could be found on the uppermost level.

During this second day of their captivity, Fotir had heard shouting coming from the tower's lower floors. Already the men of Curgh were fighting each other or their Kentigern jailers. And today it had rained. Had the sun shone, heating the tower and its chambers as it had the day before, matters would have been far worse. No doubt they would be soon, unless Aindreas let them go.

With dusk and the arrival of some food, all had grown quiet once more. The meal didn't consist of much—some dried meats, cheese, bread, and fruit. It was more than a prisoner in the dungeon would have gotten, and it was offered in ample amounts. But they had eaten the same foods in the morning and at midday, and twice the previous day. This would only add to the restiveness of Javan's men.

Xaver had spent much of the past two days staring out the narrow window of their chamber. He said even less than usual and ate little of his food, until prompted to do so by Fotir. The duke was silent as well, leaving the Qirsi to pace the small room and ponder this latest turn of events.

Aindreas had left them alone, and, aside from the guards who brought their meals, so had his ministers and men. Fotir had no wish to be interrogated, especially after seeing what the duke of Kentigern had done to Tavis. But a part of him wished that Aindreas or Shurik had come to ask them questions or threaten torture. At least then he could have been certain that Tavis and Grinsa were still safe. As it was he could only hope the very fact of their imprisonment meant that Aindreas's search for the boy had yielded nothing.

"Fotir!" Javan called from his chamber.

The Qirsi and Xaver exchanged a look. Even more than an interrogation at the hands of Kentigern's duke, the first minister dreaded questions about Tavis's escape from his own duke. He knew that he could deceive Aindreas, and Shurik if he had to. He felt less certain about the MarCullet boy's ability to lie, but he hoped that Aindreas would ignore him, seeing him as little more than a child. Javan, however, was a different matter. He loved his son in his own fashion, and Fotir knew that he would have given his life to save Tavis's. But if he knew of Tavis's escape, and the condition the young lord had been in when Fotir found him, not even his devotion to the boy would still his tongue.

And then there was the matter of the Weaver. Javan had become more tolerant of the Qirsi as he had grown older, thanks in part to the influence of the duchess. He seemed to appreciate the counsel offered by his underministers, and he paid them a generous wage. And Fotir felt certain that the duke had come to consider him a friend as well as a trusted advisor. But Weavers were another matter entirely, and even under these extraordinary circumstances he didn't know how Javan would respond to the news that a Weaver had saved his son's life.

"Yes, my lord," he said, stepping to the door of his room and looking through its small window.

Torches burned in the corridor between their rooms, casting dim shadows on the guard standing against the wall. Javan stood at his own door, looking haggard, his eyes fixed on Aindreas's man.

"My first minister and I need a moment alone to speak," the duke said.

The guard glanced at one of them, then the other. "I'm sorry, my lord," he said, sounding young and unsure of himself. "I was told to keep watch on all of you."

"Is my door locked?" Javan asked.

"Well, yes, my—"

"Is his?"

"Yes. But—"

"Then you have nothing to fear. Go down and talk to your friends for a while. By the time you return, we'll be done."

The man shook his head. "I have my orders, my lord."

"You know who I am?"

"Of course, my lord. You're the duke of Kentigern."

"And you know who I'll be a year from now?"

The guard swallowed, then nodded. "You'll be king, my lord."

"That's right. So what do you suppose you ought to do when your future king gives you an order?"

Fotir had to keep himself from laughing at what he saw on the man's face. For some time the guard stood there, chewing his lip, looking from one door to the other. Finally he checked the locks on both doors and with a last furtive glance toward Javan he walked to the stairs.

"I'll be right below you, my lord. If you try to escape, I'll know it."

"I understand," Javan said solemnly. "You have my word as your next king. We'll be here when you return."

The man nodded, as if satisfied. Then he started down the stairs.

Javan waited until his footsteps had died away before speaking. "He won't be gone for long," the duke said, meeting Fotir's gaze again. "So I'll make this quick. I'm guessing that you're not telling me all you know. I think I understand why. But I need to know if Tavis is safe."

Fotir took a breath. He would have preferred not to tell the duke anything at all. But Javan deserved this much.

"To the best of my knowledge, he is, my lord."

"Is he alone?"

"No."

"You trust those he's with?"

"Completely, my lord."

The duke nodded. "Do you know where he is?" Immediately, he held up a hand and shook his head. "Don't answer. I shouldn't know either way."

Abruptly Fotir knew how the guard had just felt and he regretted his amusement at the man's discomfort. Denying Javan anything could be difficult, even for his first minister. He sensed Xaver just behind him, listening to their conversation, and he could guess what the boy was thinking.

"I don't know where he is, my lord," he said at last, "nor do I know when any of us will see him again. But given the chance to choose his guardian from all the men and women of your kingdom, I couldn't have found anyone better."

It wasn't much to offer, probably less than Xaver thought appropriate. But it was far more than Fotir had intended to say.

Javan appeared to sense this as well. "Thank you, Fotir. I won't ask anything more."

"I think it best that way, my lord."

The duke nodded, looking away. "Of course."

Fotir heard voices from the stairwell, and a moment later footsteps as well.

"They may torture you," Javan said quickly, peering at him through the window once again. "Perhaps all of us. Ean knows what Aindreas is capable of doing."

I know, Fotir almost said, shuddering at the thought. *I've seen it.* "Yes, my lord. I'll die before I tell them anything."

"As will I, my lord," Xaver said from behind him.

Javan actually smiled. "My deepest thanks, to both of you. Your father would be proud of you, Xaver MarCullet."

The boy had no chance to respond. Fotir had expected the guard to return, though he had feared that it might be Aindreas. Instead, it was Shurik who stepped into the corridor, accompanied by two guards Fotir did not recognize. The Qirsi minister paused between the two chambers, looking first at Javan and then at Fotir.

"I hope you've enjoyed your private talk. I wouldn't expect to have many more. You may be interested to know that your guard has lost his wages for this turn as a result of his foolishness. None of his comrades is likely to make the same mistake."

"He was following the orders of his future king," Javan said. "He shouldn't be punished."

"He defied his duke. He's lucky to be alive." The minister faced Fotir, turning his back on Javan. "I'd like a word with you, First Minister." He nodded once to one of the guards, who stepped forward and unlocked the door.

"If you're going to torture one of us it should be me," the duke said, his voice rising.

Shurik looked back over his shoulder. "I assure you, my Lord Duke, if the duke of Kentigern decides that torture is necessary, he won't spare any of you." He turned to Fotir again. "As it happens," he went on, "I'll be speaking to your minister myself. And I have no intention of torturing him."

Even with the door to his room open, Fotir did not move. "Would you rather I remained here, my lord?" he asked, looking past the minister to his duke. Shurik might treat Javan with disdain, but Fotir never would.

"No, Fotir," the duke said. "Go with him. Perhaps some good will come of it."

"Very well, my lord." He looked back at Xaver and made himself smile. "I'll be back soon. Attend to the duke."

The boy nodded.

"No harm will come to the boy or your duke," Shurik said, gesturing for him to come forward. "You have my word."

Fotir looked one last time at Javan, who nodded his encouragement. Then he stepped into the corridor and followed Shurik down the stairs. He heard the door to his room being closed and locked and the guards joining them in the stairwell, but no one spoke until they reached the bottom of the tower.

"Remain here," Shurik told the guards. "I'll bring him back when I'm through with him."

"But, Minister, he's a prisoner. You yourself said that one of us—"

"I know what I told you, and now I'm telling you to leave us alone. Unless you care to take this matter up with the duke."

"No, Minister," the man said quickly, his eyes widening. "Of course not."

"Good." The Qirsi started walking away, motioning once more for Fotir to follow. "I thought we'd return to the Silver Bear," he said. "It seems as good a place as any to chat."

"Do all the duke's prisoners enjoy such treatment?"

Shurik gave him a grave look. "I think you of all people know that they don't."

It was all Fotir could do to keep his stride. They had been alone for just moments and already the minister had him backed into a corner. "I'm not sure what you mean," he said, knowing that the denial sounded forced and hollow.

Shurik merely glanced at him again, raising an eyebrow.

They walked the rest of the way to the tavern without speaking. Once inside, they made their way directly to the back room, where one of the serving girls brought them ale and two bowls of a flavorful, spicy stew.

"Pipeweed?" Shurik asked, breaking a lengthy silence.

"No, thank you." He would have liked some, but he could not help thinking of Javan and Xaver, and the tasteless meal they had been given in the tower. It was bad enough that he could enjoy the stew and ale. Pipeweed, particularly Uulranni weed, would have been too much.

"Don't tell me you're worrying about your duke even now," the minister said.

It was not a discussion Fotir wished to have, least of all with this man. "Why did you bring me here, Minister? What is it you want?"

"I want to avoid a war, if I can. I brought you here because I think you had a hand in Lord Tavis's escape, and because I hope that you and I can find a way to end this crisis quickly and peacefully."

"What makes you think I had something to do with Tavis's escape?"

Shurik grinned. "Come now, cousin. It's one thing to lie to the dukes. It's quite another to fool a Qirsi."

Fotir held the man's gaze, but offered no response.

"All right," the minister said. "If you insist on playing this game. I've been to look at the hole in the castle wall, the one through which Lord Tavis must have escaped. That hole was made by magic, First Minister."

"You're certain?"

"The edges of the hole were far too clean. No Eandi could have made such an opening."

"And you think I could have? You told your duke that I would have been too tired to stand had I even made the attempt."

"I tell my duke many things, First Minister. What I neglected to mention that night was that you could have done it if you had help from other Qirsi."

Fotir laughed. "You believe I was part of an army of shapers coming to Tavis's rescue?"

"It may be far-fetched, but it's possible."

"Then why didn't you say anything to the duke?"

"Come now, Fotir!" Shurik said, propelling himself out of his chair. He began to pace the room. "Did you listen to anything I said the night we spoke? I may serve the duke of Kentigern, but I'm Qirsi above all else. I'm sorry the duke lost his daughter, and I'm inclined to believe that Tavis killed her. All the evidence points to his guilt. But if you tell me right now, Qirsi to Qirsi, that he's innocent, I'll believe you."

Fotir stared at the man, trying to gauge what he saw in Shurik's pale yellow eyes. "He is innocent," he said. "I've been telling you so for days. Why would you believe me now?"

"Because the dukes aren't here. Because we can speak freely. We're Qirsi, Fotir. That bond goes far deeper than the petty rivalries that divide our houses. That's what I was trying to tell you the last time we were here. While you were fretting about loyalty to your duke and avoiding indiscretions, I was trying to find out what kind of a man you are. I couldn't tell then; I still can't. So I'm asking you now, straight to the point, does your blood flow Qirsi or Eandi?"

"You say that the issues dividing our houses matter less to you than the color of our eyes," Fotir said, evading the question for at least a moment. "Yet I told you in confidence of Tavis's attack on the MarCullet boy, and you wasted no time betraying that confidence to your duke."

Shurik stopped his pacing. "You're right, I did. As I told you a moment ago, I thought the boy was guilty of a foul crime. I did that more for Brienne than I did for the House of Kentigern."

Fotir wasn't certain that he believed this. Indeed, he couldn't say that he believed any of what the minister was telling him. The man had him badly confused, which might well have been Shurik's intention. For all he knew, Aindreas had arranged this meeting so that Fotir might reveal what Tavis had not, even under torture.

"Well?" the minister said. "Are you going to answer my question?"

"I'm not certain I can. You seem to believe that a man can't be

Qirsi and also a loyal subject of the kingdom. I disagree. As I tried to tell you the other night, my pride in being Qirsi does nothing to compromise my loyalty to Javan and the House of Curgh."

"So when you freed Tavis from the dungeon were you acting for our people or for your duke?"

It almost worked. He almost said, *Both*. He managed to stop himself, though not in time to keep Shurik from seeing the truth. He felt certain of that.

"You give me too much credit, cousin." He said it because he had to, because Shurik would be expecting some kind of denial. But Fotir felt once more that the minister had him trapped.

"There was one other possibility I considered," the minister said, resuming his pacing. "I suppose it's no more plausible than the idea of you leading 'an army of shapers,' as you put it. But it did occur to me that you might have been helped by a Weaver."

He felt the blood drain from his face, and this time Shurik smiled at his response.

"Don't worry, cousin. I've tried to make you understand: in a contest between my loyalty to Kentigern and my devotion to our people, the latter will always prevail." He returned to his chair and leaned his elbows on the table, bringing his face close to Fotir's. "Have you known the Weaver long, or did you meet him here?"

Fotir shook his head. "I don't know what you're talking about. There is no Weaver, and I had nothing to do with Tavis's escape." His voice was steady enough, but no one who heard him would have been fooled. In a way it didn't matter anymore. Shurik was well beyond believing his denials. But Fotir had to make it clear to him that he wouldn't admit anything.

The minister continued to stare at him a moment longer, his smile fading. Then he straightened. "What I told your duke was true, Fotir. When Aindreas turns to torture, which he's bound to do eventually, none of you will be spared. Not you, not Javan, not even the boy. You saw what he did to Tavis. And this time he'll be more careful. You'll have no hope of escape. Work with me, and I can save all of you. Defy me, and I promise you a long, painful death."

Fotir managed a dark smile. "So much for your devotion to our people."

"Damn you to the demons, Fotir! Don't you understand what's at stake here?"

"Apparently I don't. Perhaps you'd like to explain it to me."

For the first time that night, Fotir saw Shurik falter, as if he was the one who had said too much.

The minister stood once more. "It's time I returned you to the tower."

He picked up his tankard. "But I haven't finished my ale."

"That's too bad. Stand up."

Fotir did as was told and the minister gave him a firm shove toward the door.

The main room of the tavern was crowded and noisy. The sweet scent of pipe smoke filled the air and several men and women were laughing and singing out of key near the back of the room. Shurik kept a hand on the small of Fotir's back, pushing him through the throng. Before they reached the door, though, the barkeep called to the minister, forcing him to stop.

"Leaving so soon, Minister?" the man asked.

Fotir didn't hear Shurik's answer, for in that instant something caught his eye. The Weaver was there, sitting alone in the corner nearest the tavern's front door. His eyes were fixed on Fotir and he half rose, as if intending to approach them. Fotir glanced at Shurik to be sure the minister wasn't watching him. Then he gave the Weaver a slight shake of the head. Grinsa nodded, stood, and slipped out the door into the night.

"Come on," Shurik said again a moment later, pushing him once more.

Fotir walked slowly, hoping to give Grinsa time enough to slip away. But Shurik grabbed him by the arm and pulled him through the door and out into the street. The Weaver was nowhere to be seen.

"This is your last chance, Fotir," the minister said, as they started back toward the castle. "Tell me what you know, and I can still save you."

"There's nothing to tell you."

Shurik shook his head. "You're a fool."

He said nothing. He had already revealed far too much, and the appearance of the Weaver had left him badly shaken. No doubt the boy was safe; Grinsa wouldn't have left him alone otherwise. But Fotir had hoped they would be far from Kentigern by now. As long as they stayed here, within reach of Aindreas and his men, the kingdom remained at risk.

Chapter
Twenty

✦

Adriel's Moon waxing

H e wandered the streets of the city, walking among the empty markets, until he saw the first pale hint of day-break in the eastern sky and heard the dawn bells ringing from the city gates. Only then did Grinsa make his way back to the Sanctuary of Bian.

The Qirsi had tried to tell himself that it was the assassin he had wanted to avoid this Pitch Night, that after years of seeing Pheba on the last night of Bian's Turn in the cold of the snows, he didn't fear her spirit anymore. But he knew better. The assassin had earned his death. By offering blood for the man the night he entered the sanctuary, Grinsa had done more than anyone could have expected of him. Even now, though, after all this time, after loving Cresenne and feeling the anguish of her betrayal—especially after all that—the mere thought of seeing his dead wife pained him so that he felt a blade had pierced his heart.

He felt ashamed of his cowardice, not so much for Pheba as for Meriel. Living in the sanctuary, the prioress faced her dead every turn. Not just Pheba, but her parents, and the child she bore unjoined before she came to the sanctuary, who died in his infancy. If she could face them each turn, a voice within him demanded, why couldn't he face Pheba just this once? To which another voice replied simply, *Because it hurts too much.*

Returning in the growing light of day, Grinsa had thought to find the sanctuary still, save for the cleric posted at the gate. But upon stepping into the main courtyard, he saw someone standing at

341

the entrance to the shrine. It had to be Meriel, he realized, and he hurried toward her, wondering if something had happened to Tavis.

As he drew nearer, she held a finger to her lips, then slipped quietly into the shrine. Grinsa followed.

She had stopped just inside the door and was looking toward the far end of the temple. Following her gaze, he saw someone lying on the floor just before the altar.

"Is that Tavis?" he asked, taking a step forward.

She placed a hand on his arm, stopping him. "He's fine," she said. "He's just sleeping."

"How long has he been there?"

"Since before the midnight bells."

"Did Brienne come to him? Did you see her?"

The prioress looked at him. "I never see someone else's dead. None of us do. It's not the Deceiver's way. But she did come to him. I heard what he said to her."

"And?"

She faced the boy again. "I believe he is innocent. He shed tears for her and spoke to her of his love and his sorrow. He's no murderer."

Grinsa closed his eyes, knowing a moment of profound relief. Since leaving the Revel for Kentigern he had had his doubts about the boy. Usually he trusted his visions and the images he brought forth from the Qiran, but in this instance there had been so much else to consider.

"You weren't certain," Meriel said.

He opened his eyes and saw her grinning at him.

"The way you spoke to me the night you came here, I wouldn't have guessed."

Grinsa smiled as well. "I'm glad I was so convincing."

"His innocence does nothing to change the fact that he's rude, inconsiderate, and spoiled. You'll have a difficult time caring for him, if that's your intention."

The Qirsi nodded. "I know. But our lives are linked for some reason. I don't know why yet, but I think it must be important. I have no choice but to remain with him, at least for now."

"Then there's something more you should know," the prioress said. "From what I heard of their conversation, it seems that Brienne was able to show the boy an image of her killer."

"*What?* Is that possible?"

"I've never heard of such a thing, but then again I've never had one of the dead who was murdered so recently appear to someone in my shrine." She shrugged. "After all these years of serving the Deceiver nothing surprises me anymore."

"Extraordinary," Grinsa said softly. "Do you know what the killer looks like?"

"No, but the boy recognized him. It seems he was a singer in the Revel."

The Qirsi nodded, drawing a puzzled look from Meriel.

"You expected this?" she asked.

"I suppose in a way I did. The assassin I killed in Kentigern Wood also sang in the Revel. They must have been working together."

"So you might know this man as well."

"Possibly."

He stood staring at Tavis for several moments. After his silent encounter with Fotir in the tavern the night before, Grinsa had resolved to leave Kentigern as soon as possible. He had heard talk in the city—in the wake of the boy's escape, it was said, the duke of Curgh and his entourage had been imprisoned in the castle. Seeing Fotir with Aindreas's first minister, Grinsa had thought he had reason to doubt the stories. But then he saw how the minister from Kentigern pushed Javan's man through the tavern, and he knew that it must be true. No doubt the men of Kentigern were still searching for Tavis, and at this point, it was impossible to say what they'd do if they recaptured him. After leaving the Silver Bear he had even gone so far as to make arrangements with a Qirsi merchant he knew. The man was willing to offer passage to Tremain for both Grinsa and the boy. They could be out of the city before sundown.

Now, however, he had something new to consider.

He faced the prioress, fixing his eyes on hers. "Would you be willing to tell the duke of Kentigern what you've told me?"

"About the assassin?"

"Yes, that," he said. "But also your belief in Tavis's innocence, what you heard of his conversation with Brienne. All of it."

She held his gaze, pressing her lips into a thin line. "By telling him these things, I admit to harboring the man he believes murdered his daughter. There's no telling what he might do to me or the sanctuary."

343

"Two nights ago you said that the sanctuary can't be violated, that even Aindreas understood that."

"Yes, I did," she said. "And then the boy reminded me that Aindreas had already risked war with the future king over this matter. To be honest, I don't know anymore what the duke would do. But there are few things as dangerous as a man bent on vengeance."

"Tavis is innocent, Meriel. You know that now. Aindreas needs to be convinced of it as well. He's holding Javan in the castle, and he's hunting for Tavis as if the boy were an animal. With each day that passes Eibithar moves closer to civil war. And the more I think about it, the more I think that's just what Brienne's killer wants." He looked around the shrine before facing her again. "I don't want to see anything happen to this sanctuary, and I certainly don't want you to be harmed. But there's too much at stake here for you to keep silent."

She looked away, the muscles in her jaw tightening. "Even if I were to go to him, it might not do you any good. Like his father before him, Aindreas has little use for the sanctuaries. He belongs to the cloisters. In matters of faith, he listens to Barret, his prelate. And Barret will tell him I'm a demon worshiper and an enchantress."

She was right. As a member of the Revel he had seen how the courts of the kingdom looked upon the sanctuaries. Worship of the older gods was referred to as the Qirsi faith, and like so many things tied to his people, it was scorned. Meriel's word would carry no more weight with Aindreas than his own. Once more, Grinsa found himself thinking of Keziah's duke and hoping that she could prevail upon him to ride to Kentigern. Of all the dukes in Eibithar's major houses, he maintained the closest ties to the Old Faith. His best hope was to wait for Glyndwr's duke, and to do so as far from Aindreas as possible.

"You may be right," Grinsa told her. "This may not be the time to approach Aindreas with what you know. But when that time comes, can I count on your help?"

She managed a small smile. "Of course. Bian allowed the girl to show Tavis her killer. He must have had a purpose in doing so. Who am I to defy the god?"

He made no attempt to mask his relief. "Thank you."

They fell silent, watching the boy sleep.

"I'm sorry I wasn't here last night," Grinsa said at last.

"You needn't apologize to me," the prioress said. A moment later she added, "Or to Pheba, for that matter."

"Was it a difficult night?"

344

"I think it was for the boy."

He looked at her sidelong. "What about for you?"

She smiled wanly. "I've lived in this sanctuary for more than ten years, facing my dead at the end of every turn, and each night during Bian's Moon. I sometimes wonder if I'm more comfortable with them than I am with the living."

"Did you tell Pheba I was here?"

"I told her I had seen you, and that you looked well. I didn't tell her that you were in Kentigern now." She paused, leaning forward so that he had to look at her. "Even if I had, I don't think she would have found fault with you for leaving the sanctuary. She knows how you loved her, Grinsa. And she knows how you still grieve."

He nodded, not trusting himself to speak.

"You have enough to concern you right now. Don't trouble yourself about last night any more. It serves nothing."

He took a deep breath. She was right about this as well. "All right," he managed.

They fell back into silence, though Meriel didn't allow it to last very long. "So you're not ready yet to confront Aindreas. Does that mean you'll be staying with us for a time?"

Grinsa looked at Tavis once more. "No. I think it's time we left Kentigern."

"Are you certain? I believe the sanctuary is safe for now, and you're welcome to stay here as long as you like."

"Again, my thanks. But under the circumstances, the risks of keeping him here are too great. A friend of mine has offered to take us to Tremain. We'll be leaving late in the day."

"Tremain?" Meriel repeated. "I know the prioress there. A woman named Janae. Her sanctuary is devoted to Adriel, so this will be a difficult turn for her, but she might be willing to give you refuge if you mention my name."

The Qirsi smiled and shook his head. "How many times can a man say thank you? Maybe I need to offer blood again."

But Meriel shook her head. "I'd wait if I were you. If I remember correctly, Janae wields a thirsty knife."

His first thought, waking to find himself on a cold stone floor, was that he was back in Kentigern's dungeon. He sat bolt upright, wincing at the stiffness in his neck and shoulders.

"It's all right," came a voice from behind him. "You're in the sanctuary."

Tavis turned his head gingerly and found the gleaner sitting on the wooden bench nearest to him.

"You're back," he said. "I guess that means Pitch Night is over."

The Qirsi stiffened for just an instant. "It's morning, yes." He paused briefly, as if willing himself to relax. "The prioress tells me you had quite a night."

Tavis closed his eyes and rubbed a hand over his brow. "Yes, I did." He opened his eyes suddenly, grasping the full import of Grinsa's comment. "She saw Brienne, too? She knows what happened?"

"She knows you didn't kill her, and that you know who did."

"Ean be praised!" he whispered.

"Actually, you ought to thank Bian, don't you think?"

The boy grinned. "I'll thank any god you want me to." He climbed to his feet, moving slowly and flexing his muscles with care. "So when do we go back to the castle?"

"You mean Kentigern?" Grinsa asked with a frown.

"Yes. My father's still there, as is Xaver. They'll want to know. And we need to tell Aindreas as well."

"I'm afraid it's not that easy, Tavis. Aindreas has even less use for the Old Faith than your father does. All we can tell them right now is that the prioress and I believe you to be innocent. That won't carry much weight with Brienne's father."

"But Brienne said I was innocent. She showed me her murderer."

"So you claim."

"You said the prioress—"

"I said she knows that you didn't kill Brienne. But that's all." The gleaner exhaled heavily. "I don't understand the ways of the god as Meriel does. But from what she told me it seems she could only hear what you said to Brienne. She couldn't see or hear the spirit, nor did she see the image of Brienne's killer. What she heard from you was enough to convince her that someone else killed the girl. Beyond that, though, it does us little good. Aindreas won't believe her any more than he did you."

Tavis felt like someone had kicked him in the stomach. "So it was all for nothing," he said bitterly. "I'm no better off than I was before I saw her."

"That's not true. Meeting one's dead is never easy. If nothing else

you can take from last night the knowledge that you acted coura-
geously. But even more—"

"Pardon me, gleaner," Tavis broke in, unwilling to listen to such
things just now, "but I don't need lectures from you on the courage
needed to face the dead."

Grinsa stood abruptly, his cheeks reddening. "How dare you! I
have risked my life for you every day since leaving the Revel! And
now you presume to judge me for something you couldn't possibly
understand?" He turned on his heel and started toward the shrine's
door. "Find your own way back into the Order of Ascension!" the
man said, not bothering to look back. "I'm through with you!"

Tavis stood utterly still, baffled by the vehemence of the Qirsi's
reaction. Just as Grinsa reached the door, however, he called the
man's name.

"I'm sorry," he said. "I didn't . . . I shouldn't have said what I
did."

Grinsa just stood there, his hand on the door handle, his back
still to the boy.

"Please. I need you. I . . . I can't convince any of them alone."

"No," Grinsa said, turning to face him. "You can't. The sooner
you realize that, the sooner you'll stop acting like a spoiled child."

Tavis had to bite back a retort. He wasn't accustomed to being
spoken to in this way. But then again, he had been forced to endure
much that was new recently, and compared with most of it, this was
a trifle.

"You're right. This has been a difficult time for me. I'm not used
to depending on someone the way I have to depend on you right
now. I don't particularly like it."

The Qirsi pursed his lips for a moment, then nodded. "I can
understand that."

"You were telling me what I gained from facing Brienne," Tavis
said, trying to coax Grinsa back into the shrine. "I think I need to
hear that. It would do me some good."

"No more of your abuse?"

"I promise."

Grinsa stood at the door for another moment, as if he still
wished to leave. Finally he released the door handle and walked
slowly back toward the altar. "I was going to say that though your
encounter with Brienne may not have given you enough proof to
change Aindreas's mind, it did give you something. For one thing, I

know you're innocent now, as does the prioress." He hesitated, eyeing Tavis closely. "And now you're sure of it as well, which is more than you could say yesterday, isn't it?"

The young lord felt his mouth drop open. How could the gleaner have known?

"Am I right?" the man asked.

Tavis nodded.

"I thought so. Even if we can't go to Aindreas right now," the Qirsi went on, "we're better off than we were before. You need to be patient, my lord, difficult as that may seem."

"But if you and the prioress can't convince the duke, who will?"

"A good question," the Qirsi said, his concern written on his pale features.

But in that moment Tavis knew the answer to his own question. Perhaps seeing Brienne had given him what he needed after all.

"The murderer," he said, the word echoing loudly off the shrine's ceiling.

Grinsa looked at him with surprise. "What?"

"If we can find the murderer, Aindreas will have to believe us."

"Will he?" the gleaner asked, raising an eyebrow. "Do you plan to bring the man to him alive? Because a corpse will prove nothing. And even if he is alive, how do you plan to wring a confession from him?"

"But I know who killed her!" Tavis said, feeling hope slip away again. "I saw his face! I recognized him! That has to count for something."

"In the end I'm sure it will. But again, this may not be the time. Patience, Tavis. That's what will get you through this."

He shook his head. "No! Not with this. She showed me his face. She told me to find him. 'Prove your innocence and save the kingdom.' That's what she said."

"And that's what we'll do. But right now we don't even know where he is. He must have left Kentigern days ago."

"So we'll find him!"

"How, Tavis? As far as everyone else in the Forelands is concerned, he's a musician. No one knows to look for him. You, on the other hand, are a fugitive."

Tavis shook his head again, though not so violently this time. "He planned this very well, didn't he?"

"He didn't plan it alone. I know that offers little comfort, but it's true. You weren't undone by one man, but rather by a vast conspiracy. Defeating it will take time."

"How do you know this?"

"I don't for certain, but it makes sense. Far more sense than the idea of Brienne's murderer working alone. I believe the night we took you from the dungeon you heard me tell the first minister that I had killed a man in Kentigern Wood. I'm fairly certain that he was an associate of Brienne's murderer. And before I killed him, he told me he had been hired by a Qirsi woman I knew from the Revel."

Something he heard in Grinsa's voice as the Qirsi spoke of this woman made Tavis think that there was more to her than he was saying.

"Was she a Weaver, too?" he asked.

The man looked at him sharply, but his answer, when it came, was surprisingly subdued. "No, she wasn't a Weaver."

Tavis considered asking more, but quickly thought better of it.

"We can talk about this another time," the Qirsi said. "Right now I need to make some arrangements."

"What for?"

"Our departure. We're leaving Kentigern later today. I have to speak with the merchant who'll be helping us."

"What should I do?"

Grinsa shrugged. "Get something to eat. Rest. Whatever you choose. Just be ready to leave by the ringing of the prior's bells."

The boy nodded, then watched as the gleaner turned from him a second time and left the shrine. He had never had much use for the Qirsi. In that way, as in so many others, he was his father's son. But he found some comfort in the knowledge that Grinsa would be with him for a time, and he felt certain that he had never before met a Qirsi like this man.

Grinsa's friend, it turned out, was Qirsi as well, a cloth merchant headed for Tremain. His cart, which he steered to the sanctuary's rear entrance, was piled several fourspans high with large, folded sheets of broadcloth and buckram. Two large farm horses were harnessed to the wagon, one of them white, the other grey and black.

"You're to hide among the sheets," Grinsa explained, somewhat unnecessarily. "Hewson says you'll be better off under the broadcloth. The buckram is too stiff; the gate guards will be more likely to spot you."

"Seems to me they're going to anyway," Tavis said, eyeing the cart doubtfully.

"I've done this before, young master," the merchant said from atop his seat. He spoke with a thick Wethy accent, and with his pipe held tight between his teeth, Tavis could barely make out what he was saying. "Curl yourself up on your side and keep still, and I promise you'll have no trouble."

Several clerics helped them remove most of the broadcloth sheets, leaving just a thin layer over the wooden bed of the cart. The merchant then folded a number of sheets and placed them in such a way that they created a hollow in which Tavis was to lie. The boy began to nod, finally understanding how the deception was to work. From the sides and back, the pile of broadcloth would look perfectly normal. On the fourth side, the one hidden from view by the pile of buckram, there would be a narrow opening, through which Tavis would be able to breathe.

"Convinced now?" the merchant asked, regarding him with a sly smile.

Tavis had to laugh. "Yes."

"Good. Then climb on. I want to be moving before long."

The young lord turned to Meriel, who was already watching him.

"Many thanks, Mother Prioress. Whether I'm king someday or not, I will repay this debt."

"You owe me no debt, Lord Tavis. If anyone deserves your thanks it's Grinsa. And perhaps, Bian as well."

He glanced briefly at the Qirsi before nodding to Meriel. Then he climbed onto the cart and lay down on the broadcloth as the merchant had instructed. A moment later, the clerics began to pile the sheets on top of him again.

It took some time, and even with the folded sheets bearing some of the burden, he soon felt the weight of the cloth bearing down on him. He began to grow hot, and lying in the darkness, he had to keep himself from succumbing to panic. He found it difficult to breathe, though he could tell that some fresh air was reaching him.

It's better than the dungeon, he told himself again and again. He could hear nothing, and when the cart suddenly lurched forward, it set his heart racing.

"You could have warned me!" he shouted, knowing they couldn't hear him.

The cart bounced and rocked for what seemed a long time, until Tavis wondered if he'd be sick to his stomach. Just then, however, the cart stopped. An instant later, Tavis heard Grinsa calling his name.

"Yes," he shouted back. "Where are we?"

"We're a short distance from the east gate. I wanted to see if you were all right before we met up with Aindreas's men."

"The east gate? That's all?"

"Yes, why?"

"Demons and fire," he muttered. Maybe it wasn't that much better than the dungeon after all.

"Never mind. I'm fine. Just get on with it."

"Very well."

In a few seconds the cart started moving again, only to stop again several moments later, no doubt at the gate. Tavis lay perfectly still, breathing in silent shallow breaths and straining his ears to hear what the guards were saying to Grinsa and the merchant. For quite a while he didn't hear anything. But then he heard several voices, Grinsa's among them. They must have been standing right next to the pile of broadcloth. He began to shake so fiercely that he feared the whole pile had to be moving. Eventually though, the voices moved away. Still the cart did not move and Tavis lay there for what seemed an eternity, waiting and wondering what the guards were doing.

At last the cart began to roll forward once more and Tavis closed his eyes, more grateful than he could have imagined for the jouncing, rocking motion of the wagon.

After that he lost track of the time. He might even have fallen asleep. It was hard to tell in the unchanging darkness and warmth of his strange bed. At some point, though, he realized that the cart had stopped and that he heard voices again.

"Tavis!" Grinsa was calling.

The weight of the cloth seemed to be lessening.

"I'm all right!" he called. "Why have we stopped?"

Suddenly the entire pile was lifted off him. Grinsa and the merchant were standing on the cart, tilting up the broadcloth.

"Don't just lay there, boy!" Hewson said through gritted teeth. "Get out so we can put this blasted cloth down!"

Tavis rolled out from under the pile. His muscles were sore again—they always seemed to be these days. He wondered if Aindreas had injured him more permanently than Grinsa had let on.

Night had fallen and they were in Kentigern Wood. Aside from a small oil lamp one of the Qirsi had lit and placed on the ground, there was little light by which to see. Ilias hung low in the western sky, a thin sliver of red peeking through the trees and marking the start of the waxing. Panya would not be up tonight at all.

"Where are we?" Tavis asked, as the two Qirsi let the cloth drop back down onto the cart.

"We've come a league or so from Kentigern," Grinsa said. "We should be safe here for the night."

"Do I have to get back under there tomorrow?" He wasn't sure he wanted an answer, but he couldn't keep from asking.

Hewson shrugged. "It wouldn't hurt."

Grinsa must have seen Tavis's expression, because he began to laugh. "I think that depends on whether you're sitting in front of the cloth or lying beneath it."

Tavis gestured toward his clothes, which Meriel had given him. They were simple and stained, like those of a common laborer. "No one's going to recognize me in these," he said. "They'll just think I'm an apprentice."

The merchant chuckled. "I doubt that. You have the look of a court boy. It doesn't much matter what you're wearing."

The boy looked at Grinsa, pleading with his eyes.

"We can dirty his clothes and face a bit," the Weaver said. "That might help."

Hewson shook his head. "It's not likely to fool Kentigern's men if we run into them. You're just a gleaner, Grinsa. If we have to run, it'll be me calling up the mists."

Once again, Tavis cast a look at Grinsa, who glared at him, keeping him silent. Hewson might have been a friend, but apparently he knew nothing of Grinsa's other powers.

"I don't think we're likely to meet Aindreas's men out here," Grinsa said, facing the merchant again. "If we were on the road to Curgh perhaps, but they have no reason to look for Tavis on the road to Tremain."

Hewson waved his hand, as if losing interest in the conversation. "Fine. Do what you will. Just don't blame me when we end up with ropes around our necks."

He walked off, mumbling something about finding wood for a fire.

"He doesn't know?" Tavis asked.

Grinsa started pulling sacks of food from a small chest beneath the cart seat. "No, he doesn't."

"So how did you explain all this to him?"

The Qirsi stopped for a moment, eyeing Tavis as if looking for some sign that he was being difficult. "I told him that others got you out of the prison," he finally said, resuming his work, "and that I was called to the sanctuary to help you leave Kentigern and find refuge elsewhere."

"And he was satisfied with that?"

"Hewson doesn't ask many questions, nor do I ask many of him. A man so adept at deceiving gate soldiers isn't likely to want to discuss such matters."

Tavis weighed this for a moment. "Well, thank you," he said. "I'm glad to be away from Kentigern."

"As you should be. I expect the journey to Tremain will go smoothly. You'll have to hide again to enter the city, but that won't be for several days." He climbed down off the cart, carrying all the food he had found. "For now, Lord Tavis, you're a free man. Enjoy it while you can."

It was barely past time for dinner and still hours before the closing of the city gates, yet Kentigern Castle was already so quiet it might as well have been midnight. Soldiers spoke in hushed tones by the barbicans and guardhouses. Ioanna was still in bed, her ladies confined by propriety and custom to their chambers. The duke sat alone in his banquet hall, doing his best to empty the castle's cellars of Sanbiri red. And his ministers, including Shurik, took their meals in their private chambers, dismissed for the day by Aindreas.

The evenings had been this way since Brienne's death. Silent as a cloister, and somber as a funeral procession. Once, the castle had been a lively place, filled nearly every night with music and the smells of a feast. The duke drank his share of wine then as well, though usually in company and almost always with a grand meal. There was a reason he had grown so fat.

But those days were past. Shurik wondered if Kentigern would ever be like that again. Certainly he hoped it wouldn't. In their current state the castle's inhabitants would have a far more difficult time enduring the coming siege.

Finishing his meal, the first minister called to his servants to remove the dirty plates and tell the stable workers to ready his mount. They bowed, murmuring, "Yes, First Minister," until they were out in the corridor, then ran off to carry out his instructions. None of them asked him why he'd need a mount at this hour, or where he was going. They didn't even ask him if he wished to inform the duke of his plans. It was all so easy he had to laugh.

He walked down to the ward, where the stableboy brought him his horse, explaining that he had brushed the beast just that day. The boy fairly beamed when Shurik commented on how fine the animal looked. The guards at the inner and outer gates bowed to him, wishing him a pleasant ride and a good night. The soldiers at the road gate went even further, promising him that even if he returned after the ringing of the bells for gate closing, they would assuredly admit him to the city. He was Shurik jal Marcine, first minister to the duke of Kentigern. And they were Eandi fools. How could any of them have done different?

Upon leaving the city, he rode straight toward the Tarbin, so that it would seem to the guards at the gate that he was riding to the encampment of Kentigern soldiers who kept watch on the river. Only when he was out of sight of the city walls did he veer off to the south, toward the edge of Harrier Fen, where the Tarbin grew shallower and easier to ford. With Panya in darkness for another night, and Ilias little more than a narrow blade of red on the eastern horizon, he didn't fear being seen. He couldn't see much himself, but he trusted his mount to follow the river and deliver him safely to the meeting place.

As he rode, his mind returned once more to his conversation with Curgh's first minister the night before. He had been certain from the start that Tavis was freed from the dungeon by one or more Qirsi. It struck him as so obvious, he was shocked that even Aindreas hadn't seen it. Astonishingly, though, it seemed clear to him that there had been a Weaver involved. There could be no mistaking the terror he had seen in Fotir's eyes when he raised the possibility. Shurik knew what it was to work with a Weaver, to know that simply by associating with such a Qirsi one risked execution. He couldn't blame Fotir for paling at the mere mention of the word, or for maintaining his deception even after it had been exposed.

354

But he needed to know if Fotir's Weaver was also his Weaver.

It wouldn't have surprised him. The man who was paying him had shown, time and again, a willingness to pit one of his hirelings against another. Given his goals in this instance—civil war, the weakening of Eibithar's major houses, and war between Eibithar and Aneira—it certainly would have made sense to do so again.

Whether this was the case or not made little difference; either way Shurik would be expected to follow his orders. Nevertheless, he couldn't help but wonder if Tavis's escape was yet another element of the Weaver's plan, or an unforeseen reversal. Was it possible that he and Fotir were allies after all? Should he have been helping Aindreas recapture the boy or subverting the duke's efforts?

Something—a momentary flicker of light—caught his attention. He slowed his mount, scanning the far side of the river. An instant later he saw it again: a small flame, no larger than that of a candle, appeared briefly, and then was gone. Yaella.

Shurik steered his mount down the shallow riverbank and into the frigid waters of the Tarbin.

They'll say I'm another Carthach, he thought, as the river soaked his breeches and splashed his face and hair. *They'll look at me and see another Qirsi traitor.* It shouldn't have bothered him. Why should he care what Aindreas and the others said of him? Besides, nothing could have been further from the truth. Carthach betrayed his people to save his own life and line his pockets with gold. Shurik might have been betraying an Eandi duke, and getting paid for it, but he was doing this for the glory of the Qirsi people. Indeed, he liked to think that what he wrought tonight might help undo, after all these centuries, the terrible wrong committed by Carthach by the banks of the Rassor.

But still, the thought stayed with him as he emerged from the Tarbin on the Aneiran side and rode toward the place where Yaella and her duke waited. *The traitor walks a lonely path.* It was an old saying, dating back much farther than Carthach's treason. But Shurik couldn't help thinking that it carried more than a grain of truth.

A few moments later he reined his mount to a halt just in front of them. They were barely visible in the darkness, two dark forms framed against the stars and the pale red light of Ilias. Like Shurik, both of them were on horseback, Yaella on the smaller beast looking tiny beside the Eandi noble.

"Shurik jal Marcine," Yaella said, the words barely reaching him over the murmur of the river, "first minister of Kentigern, may I present Lord Rouel, duke of Mertesse."

"I'm honored to meet you, my Lord Duke," Shurik said, trying his best to sound like he meant it.

"Everything is ready?" the man asked, sounding impatient.

"Not yet, but it will be, provided I get my gold."

A pause, then, "Pay him."

A flame appeared, balanced like a juggler's blade on a stone that rested in Yaella's palm. With the other hand she held out a pouch that jingled invitingly.

"You can count it if you like," the duke said as Shurik took the pouch from Yaella, his fingers gently brushing hers.

Shurik tucked the pouch into a pocket hidden within his riding cloak. "That won't be necessary, my lord. I'm sure it's all there."

The duke frowned in the firelight. He was a large man, broad in the shoulders and chest, though not as fat as Aindreas. He had yellow hair and cold blue eyes that peered out from beneath a jutting brow.

"I was telling the duke as we rode here," Yaella said, "that given recent events in Kentigern, we might be well served to wait for the moons before beginning the siege."

Their eyes met and Shurik thought he saw the hint of a smile playing at the corners of her mouth.

"I'd have to agree," he said. "It's quite possible that the houses of Kentigern and Curgh will be at war by then, which should make taking the tor far easier."

"Is it true that the Curgh boy killed Aindreas's daughter?" the duke asked.

"Ah, so you've heard. Yes, I'm afraid it's true."

"I've always said the Eibitharians are brutes. This merely proves it."

Shurik grinned. "Strange that Brienne's death should affect you so, my lord."

The man glared at him. "My quarrel is with your king and your duke, not with innocent children."

"Of course, my lord."

A horse whinnied on the Aneiran bank behind Rouel and Yaella. Shurik started in his saddle, causing his mount to rear. It was all he could do to control the creature.

"Calm yourself, First Minister," Rouel said, not bothering to hide his amusement. "It's just my men. I don't venture this far from my castle unprotected."

Shurik took a deep breath and patted his mount's shoulder. He tried to smile, but knew that he failed. He suddenly felt vulnerable and he wished Yaella would let her flame die out.

"So then it's agreed?" Yaella asked. "We'll wait a bit longer?"

"Half a turn," the duke said. "But that's all. If the houses go to war before the Night of Two Moons, we'll use that to our advantage. But I won't wait past the third night of the waning. We need the moonlight to cross the river, and I don't want too much of the night to pass before we begin." He regarded Shurik briefly, a sour expression on his face. "You'll send word if the houses go to war before then?"

"If I may, my lord," Yaella said. "Perhaps we should just plan the attack for that night, the third of the waning. These meetings are dangerous for all of us. I'd rather not risk another."

"Is that acceptable?" the duke asked Shurik.

He sensed a purpose behind Yaella's suggestion, though he couldn't guess what it was. Half a turn was more than enough time for him to make his preparations, but he didn't know if the houses would be fighting so soon. "Yes, my lord," he answered. "I believe it is."

The duke nodded. "Good." He turned his mount and started back up the riverbank. "Come, Yaella," he called over his shoulder.

"Yes, my lord." But she remained as she was for just an instant, her eyes fixed on Shurik's.

"I can't be certain that Aindreas and Javan will be at war by then," he whispered to her.

She smiled, the look in her deep yellow eyes reminding him of nights they had spent together long ago. "I can," she said, and extinguished her flame.

Chapter
Twenty-one

✦

Glyndwr, Eibithar

Gershon finished reading what was scrawled on the parchment and placed it on the duke's table, watching as it curled up once more, like dried leaves in a fire.

"I see what you mean," he said, after a brief silence. "It's almost as if Aindreas wants a war."

"I can't say that I blame him," the duke said. "But that doesn't matter anymore. When he and Javan were merely threatening each other, I could afford to wait and watch. But now . . ." He shrugged. "I'm still reluctant to ride to Kentigern, but I don't know that I can just stay here and let them destroy the kingdom."

"And you say the idea of going to Kentigern came from the first minister?" Gershon asked again, still not quite believing what his duke was saying.

Kearney nodded, a small smile on his face, as if he didn't quite believe it either. "It surprised me as well. But she spoke rather forcefully on the matter, and she even suggested that I discuss it with you."

The swordmaster considered this, shaking his head. The Qirsi were full of surprises, and he wasn't ready to rule out the possibility that this was some sort of trick. It had always struck him as absurd that the sorcerer race, men and women who had first come to the Forelands as would-be conquerors, were now trusted as ministers in every court of every kingdom in the land. Hadn't any of the Eandi nobles learned their history? Didn't they know what Qirsi magic had done to the armies of the Forelands during the Qirsi Wars? Had they forgotten that the Qirsi themselves had been done in by a traitor? They were dangerous and deceitful, yet it sometimes seemed to the swordmaster that he was the only person who realized it.

Perhaps, as Kearney often said, he was too much of a warrior. He didn't fully trust the Caerissans either, though Caerisse and Eibithar had been allies for two centuries and hadn't fought a war in four hundred years. Once an enemy, always an enemy. It was an old soldier's credo, one Gershon's father had taught him many years ago. He knew that it could be taken too far—during its history, Eibithar had fought wars with just about every kingdom in the Forelands, and he couldn't expect the kingdom to stand alone, without allies. But neither would he expect any of Eibithar's dukes or thanes to turn to the people of Wethyrn or Caerisse for counsel. Yet none of them thought twice about turning to the white-hairs.

Gershon thought his duke the most intelligent and honorable man he had ever known. He understood the world as it truly was, unlike some, who seemed incapable of seeing beyond what they thought the world should be. As commander of Glyndwr's army, he appreciated the value of training and fine arms. As head of one of Eibithar's major houses, he knew when to talk and when to use his soldiers. As a friend, he expressed his opinions with candor, and expected the same in return, even knowing that he might not like all he heard.

A man—a soldier—could ask for no more from his duke. To Gershon's mind Kearney had but one flaw: his attachment to the first minister.

It was bad enough that he turned to her for advice at every turn. That he should love her as well seemed to the swordmaster uncharacteristically foolish. Gershon and Sulwen had befriended Kearney and his wife years ago, long before Kearney's father died, making the young man duke. The swordmaster knew that Leilia could be difficult, even cold at times. He knew as well that it was not at all uncommon for a noble to take a mistress, or even several. But a mistress was one thing; a Qirsi mistress who also served as first minister was quite another. Never mind that their love was forbidden, that they risked disgracing themselves and the House of Glyndwr every night they spent together. How was he to judge the soundness of the advice she offered if he listened to her as a lover rather than as a noble? The Qirsi had shown time and again that they could not be trusted, and yet Kearney had let the woman into not only his court but also his bed.

Gershon found it easy to hate her, and easier still to question her motives and the soundness of her counsel. All of which made those rare instances when he found himself agreeing with her deeply disturbing.

"You're very quiet, swordmaster."

Gershon looked up. Kearney was eyeing him closely, that same smile on his lips.

"I take it you think this is a bad idea."

The swordmaster cleared his throat. "Actually, I'm not certain what I think of it. It does sound like Kentigern and Curgh could be at each other's throats, and soon. I'd put our army up against either of theirs without a second thought, but I'm not anxious to get between them."

The duke looked puzzled. "So you do think we should stay out of it."

"I don't know that we can. She's right about that. If we have even the smallest chance of preventing a civil war, particularly one so close to the Aneiran border, we have an obligation to do so."

"We live in extraordinary times," the duke said, laughing and shaking his head.

"My lord?"

"First Keziah suggests that I speak with you, and then you tell me that you agree with her. I wouldn't be surprised if the king of Caerisse walked in here tomorrow and told me he'd signed a treaty with the Aneirans."

"Ean forbid," Gershon said with a frown.

There was a knock at the door, and the swordmaster felt his shoulders tightening.

"Are you certain you're up to this?" the duke asked.

"Of course, my lord. We're your most trusted advisors and you require counsel from both of us. That's what you'll have."

The duke nodded, then faced the door. "Enter," he called.

The door opened and the first minister walked in, her white hair and pallid skin making her look more like a wraith than a person.

Kearney rose from his chair and stepped around his table to greet her. "Good morning, First Minister."

"My lord," she said, giving a small bow, no doubt for Gershon's benefit. "You sent for me?"

"Yes." He indicated Gershon with an open hand. "We were just discussing your suggestion that I ride to Kentigern."

The minister faced him, her expression unreadable. "Good morning, swordmaster."

He nodded once, saying nothing.

"Did you decide anything, my lord?" she asked.

"Not yet, no. But you should know that I received another message this morning, this one indicating that Lord Tavis managed to escape from Kentigern's dungeon and that Aindreas has imprisoned Javan, his first minister, and a small company of his men in the castle. It seems he intends to hold them until the boy can be recaptured."

The woman rubbed her hands together anxiously. "Who sent the message, my lord?"

"That's the odd thing. It's not signed, and the messenger couldn't say."

"Perhaps it's meant as a deception, a trick to get you to ride to Kentigern."

"I thought you wanted him to go," Gershon said.

She hesitated, and the swordmaster could see that she was struggling with something. There was more here than the duke knew.

"I want nothing one way or another," she said at last. "If by going to Kentigern the duke can prevent a civil war, then by all means he should go. But only if the danger to him isn't too great." She gave a thin smile. "That's why I told him to speak with you, swordmaster. Who better to decide what's safe for him and what isn't?"

"Do you think this message is a trick of some sort?" Kearney asked, forcing them both to look at him again.

"It bothers me that isn't signed," Gershon said. "But with all we know of what came before, and all we know of Javan and Aindreas, I believe what it says."

The Qirsi woman crossed her arms over her chest. "So do I."

Again, watching her speak, Gershon had the sense that she was holding something back.

The duke, however, did not seem to notice. "I believe it as well," he said, "though I'm loath to admit it." He walked slowly to the hearth and gazed into it, though no fire burned there. "Left to themselves, Javan and Aindreas will destroy each other, leaving all of southwestern Eibithar exposed to Aneira." He faced them again. "That's where both of you think this will lead, isn't it? Unless I stop them."

"No one else will stop them, my lord," Gershon said, choosing his words with care. "The king is said to be infirm, Tobbar carries little weight with the other houses, and the same can be said of the new leaders in Galdasten."

He glanced at the first minister and found that she was watching him closely, as if seeing him for the first time. It made him uncomfortable to have her staring at him so.

"Did I say something wrong?" he asked sourly.

"No," she said. "Just the opposite. I was about to say much the same thing." She smiled. "I'm not accustomed to agreeing with you so often."

"Perhaps there's hope for Javan and Aindreas after all," Kearney said, grinning at them.

Gershon mustered a smile, but he remained uneasy.

"So," the duke went on a moment later, "I have no choice but to intervene."

"I don't believe that's what the swordmaster was saying, my lord. It may be that none of Eibithar's houses should intervene. You may even want to consult with them before you act. But if you feel that something should be done, you'll have to do it yourself. None of the others can."

She understood him well enough, though Gershon didn't like her speaking for him.

The duke looked at him, a question in his green eyes.

The swordmaster nodded. "She has it about right."

"I don't think we have time to consult with the other houses," Kearney said. "As it is we may not get to Kentigern soon enough to prevent a war." He returned to his table, pulled a piece of parchment from a drawer, and began to write. "How long will it take you to prepare the men?" he asked, not bothering to look up.

Gershon didn't hesitate. "We can be ready two mornings from now, my lord. How many men do you want to take?"

"As many as we can without leaving Glyndwr vulnerable."

Gershon thought for a few moments. He would leave three hundred archers and two hundred swordsmen to keep the city and castle safe. Fewer men might suffice, but he tended to be cautious in such matters. See first to defending yourself, for a victory in the field means nothing if home is lost. It was yet another of his father's sayings, and perhaps the most sensible of them all.

"I would take seven hundred, my lord. Two hundred bowmen and the rest swordsmen."

"That sounds fine." The duke looked up from his writing. "You'll see to their provisions?"

"Of course, my lord."

"So you've decided," the minister said.

"Yes. Given what I've been hearing from the two of you, I don't feel that I have any other choice."

"What is it you're writing?"

"A message to Aindreas informing him of my intention to ride to Kentigern and asking him not to do anything that might endanger the peace before I arrive."

"It's a bit late for that," Gershon said quietly.

Kearney glanced at him, smiling once more.

"You're certain this is wise, my lord?" the Qirsi asked.

"No," he said, still grinning.

The minister didn't respond, and Kearney's smile faded.

"I know it carries risks. But I believe it's the right thing to do."

She stood there for several seconds, looking as if she wanted to say more. Instead she turned and started toward the door. "Then I'll leave the planning to the two of you. I'm not very good with soldiers and supplies."

"Kez, wait." Kearney was on his feet again, stepping out from behind his table. "I must say, I'm as confused as Gershon was before. First you tell me I have to go to Kentigern, and then, when I make up my mind to do so, you act like I've just disappointed you terribly."

The Qirsi stopped at the door, but didn't face him again. "I don't mean to, my lord. I agree that you're doing the right thing. I . . . I'll pray to the gods for your safety."

"Our safety, Kez. You have to come with me."

She did turn then. "I'm no warrior."

Gershon had to keep himself from voicing his agreement. She wasn't a warrior, and she had no place in the company that would ride from the highlands to the tor.

"No, but you're my first minister. Gershon is a warrior and we may need him before all of this is over. But I have to stop a war, and I need to have someone with me who's as skilled in mediation as the swordmaster is in soldiering."

The look in her yellow eyes brightened. "Yes, my lord," she said. Neither of them had moved—half the room lay between them. Yet, looking from one of them to the other, seeing the way they gazed at each other, Gershon had to turn away. He could never approve of their love, but neither could he deny its power.

"I'll leave you, my lord," she said again, the words coming out as no more than a whisper.

"Very well. We'll speak again later in the day."

She bowed again before leaving.

For a moment Kearney continued to stare at the door, as if he could still see her standing there. Then he looked at the swordmaster, as if finally remembering that he was still there.

"Is there anything else, Gershon?"

Nothing that I can say, nothing that wouldn't end our friendship forever. "No, my lord. I'll prepare the men and speak with the quartermaster."

"Thank you." He glanced toward the door one last time, before returning to his table and the message for Aindreas.

The swordmaster left the duke's chamber, closing the door quietly behind him. The first minister was still in the corridor, making her way toward the court tower and the archway that opened onto the upper ward. Gershon hurried after her. His footsteps echoed off the low stone ceiling and he was certain that she could hear him. But the Qirsi didn't turn. If anything, she appeared to quicken her stride.

"First Minister," he called.

Still she kept walking.

"Would you stop!"

She halted, standing with her back to him for just an instant before turning. "What do you want?" Her cheeks were flushed, the blood beneath her pale skin as dark as bruises, and Gershon was struck by how young she looked.

"You're hiding something from us. I want to know what it is."

"I don't know what you're talking about."

He gestured over his shoulder toward Kearney's chamber. "I was watching you in there while you were talking to the duke. You weren't telling him everything. I can't tell if you want him to go on this journey or not, but whichever it is, there's more to your reasoning than you'd like us to know."

She chewed her lip, her eyes darting to his face, then dropping again. She looked so much like a child that Gershon couldn't help but wonder how old she was. Few of the Qirsi, he knew, lived to their fortieth year. And in that moment he thought she couldn't have been much more than half that old.

"Do you believe that I love him?"

He blinked, not certain that he had heard her correctly. "What?"

"I know that you hate me, that you hate my people. No doubt you fear our powers and see us as a threat to the kingdom. You think we can't be trusted. Probably you even think us strange-looking." She smiled, though the look in her eyes was sad. "I see from your expression that I'm right. But putting all that aside, do you believe that my love for the duke is real?"

"What does this have to do—?"

"Please just answer me."

It was more than he wanted to admit, but having confronted her, having demanded the truth, he could hardly give her less. "Yes. I think you love him."

She actually smiled. "Thank you. That couldn't have been an easy thing to say."

"Whether you love him or not has nothing to do with my question."

"It has everything to do with your question. Do you have any idea what it's like being his minister and his lover?"

He couldn't help but grin. "I can't say that I do."

The first minister laughed, though there were tears in her eyes. "That may be the first time you've ever made me laugh, swordmaster."

Gershon felt his cheeks coloring. "Your point?" he asked.

She wiped a tear from her face. "Every time I offer my counsel I'm torn between what I think the duke of Glyndwr should do, and what I want Kearney to do. He has to go to Kentigern. Both of us know that. But I'm afraid he's going to die there."

He was a warrior. He dealt with such fears quite often and had learned long ago to control them. But hearing these words from a Qirsi was another matter entirely. It almost seemed to Gershon that Bian had placed a deathly cold finger on his heart, chilling his blood. "Have you gleaned something? Is the duke in danger?"

"No, not that I know of. My fears aren't founded on anything I can name." She gave that same sad smile again. "This is just what I mean. I fear for him because I love him, and it makes being his minister . . . difficult."

Gershon wasn't sure whether to believe her. He had spent too long thinking of their love affair as a threat to the House of Glyndwr. None of this had ever entered his mind. "It seems to me there was more to it than that," he said at last. "The message that came this morning didn't seem to surprise you at all." It was little more than a guess, but apparently it was a good one.

"You're right," she said. "There is more. But I assure you, it won't compromise my loyalty to the duke, nor will it endanger our journey to Kentigern."

"You think I'll just accept that?"

"I'm afraid you have no choice."

"Of course I do! I can—"

She held up a finger, silencing him. "I didn't have to tell you anything, swordmaster. I could have lied, told you there was nothing more, and that would have been the end of it. But if we're to ride together off the steppe and keep Kearney alive, we have to begin to trust one another."

"This is your idea of trust?"

"Actually, yes. I trust that you won't tell Kearney what I've told you here today. And in return you trust that I will keep the best interests of the duke and his house foremost in my mind and heart, no matter what."

"Can you give me one reason why I should believe you?"

"I don't have to; you already know it."

Which brought them right back to where they had started. She loved the duke. She had wanted to avoid this confrontation—she had practically run from him. Yet Gershon abruptly felt that their entire conversation had gone just as she planned.

She turned from him, as if intending to leave.

"This thing you're not telling me," he said, stopping her again. "Is it dangerous for you?"

"Would it matter, swordmaster?"

"If you're in danger, I should know." He faltered, but only for an instant. "Perhaps I can help."

Her eyes widened slightly, as if, for the first time that day, he had surprised her.

"Once again," she said, "you have my thanks. I wish I could answer you, truly I do. But I don't know."

They gathered two mornings hence in the lower ward, Kearney in his riding clothes, mounted atop his great bay, looking as much the warrior as Gershon. The sky was the color of smoke, and a light drizzle darkened the pale stone of the castle. Row after row of the duke's soldiers stood in the grey light and mist, waiting for their orders. They filled the lower ward, spilling up the broad stairs at the south end into the upper ward as well. Gershon had said seven hundred the day before, but to Keziah it seemed that there were thousands of them.

All of them were Eandi, of course, and unlike even the most ancient armies of her own people, the armies of Eibithar's houses, great and small, included only men. She felt like a cleric from Morna's Sanctuary in the middle of one of Ean's cloisters. She did not belong.

As if to prove the point, Marwan, the prelate of Glyndwr Castle's cloister, was there as well, his bald head damp, tiny drops of silver rain clinging to his brown robe. He prayed to Ean for the safety of the duke and his men, without bothering to mention Keziah, without even looking at her.

Gershon wouldn't look at her either. She had hoped that with their conversation the day before they had at least started to move beyond the enmity that lay between them. It seemed, though, that her hope was misplaced.

Worse still, Kearney had made a point of telling her, late the previous day, what she already knew: they could not be together during the journey.

"There's no privacy in an army, Kez," he told her. "Everyone would know."

She didn't argue. She merely nodded and left him, so that he could dine with the duchess and spend the night with her.

Here she was, about to be escorted to Kentigern by over seven hundred men, and yet it promised to be the loneliest journey of her life. It should have been funny, but she couldn't bring herself to laugh.

The prelate finished his invocation and stepped back to stand beside Leilia, who had come to see her husband off. Like just about everyone else, the duchess refused to look at her, but Keziah knew that her presence in the company had to be gnawing at the woman like field vermin. It was small consolation really, but it was something.

Silence fell over the castle, as heavy as the mist. Gershon's grey horse whinnied, and a number of the men shifted uneasily on their feet, their eyes fixed on Kearney.

"We ride to Kentigern," the duke said, his voice ringing suddenly across the ward, "not to make war, but to stop it. We have no quarrel with the other houses, but we will not sit by, allowing them to destroy the kingdom. I wish to save Eibithar from the ravages of a civil war, and I need your strength and your skill to do so. You are to be the blade I wield in the name of peace. Men of Glyndwr, are you with me?"

The soldiers responded as one, raising their swords and bows over their heads and giving a thunderous roar that reverberated off the castle walls until Keziah thought the stone must surely give way.

"To Kentigern!" the duke cried.

"To Kentigern!" came the reply.

A moment later, Kearney started slowly toward the castle gate. A young man rode on each side of the duke, one bearing the silver and black banner of Glyndwr, and the other the purple and gold of Eibithar. Gershon and Keziah rode behind them, followed by the soldiers of Glyndwr, who were on foot. Emerging from the castle, they found hundreds of cheering people lining the broad lane that led from the castle's north gate to what was known as the highlands gate, at the west wall of the city. Children stared with wonder at the horses and the soldiers' weapons, and women waved to their husbands and brothers and sons.

"You'd think we were going to fight the Aneirans," Gershon said over the din.

At first Keziah said nothing, thinking that he had been speaking to Kearney. But a moment later she realized that the duke was riding ahead of them, and that the swordmaster had addressed the comment to her.

She nodded and made herself smile, not knowing what to say.

"These men have dreamed of this day all their lives," he said. "Marching with their duke is the greatest honor many of them will ever know." He gestured at the people along the rode. "Their families realize that as well."

"You make it sound like they want to go to war," she said, having to shout to make herself heard.

He frowned. "That's not what I meant at all. It has nothing to do with fighting or killing. They're serving their duke and their king.

They're journeying under the banners of Eibithar and Glyndwr. That's all the matters to them."

Again, she wasn't certain how to respond.

"You don't understand, do you?" He shook his head and faced forward again, as if dismissing her.

They soon reached the gate and rode out into the highlands, leaving the cheers behind them. Even on this day, with the sky dark and the fine rain falling, a wind blew across the high grasses and grey stone. They hadn't felt it in the city, but out here, among the tors and boulders, it stung their faces and eyes, keening like one of Bian's demons.

"I do understand," Keziah said at last, drawing Gershon's gaze once more. "I've devoted my life to serving the House of Glyndwr and I'm risking my life to save Eibithar. Don't tell me I don't understand, swordmaster. You don't know me well enough to judge such a thing."

She kicked at her horse, spurring him ahead of Gershon's. And for the rest of that day, she and the swordmaster rode separately, trying their best to ignore one another.

Despite the wind and the difficult terrain of the highlands, the company managed to cover nearly three leagues before stopping for the night beside a small tributary of the Sussyn River. They forded the river the following morning, continuing west until they met a second watercourse, which they forded as well. They made camp that night beside the third and last branch of the river, fording it the next day and riding on until they came within sight of the end of the steppe. Fording the streams was no small task, particularly for the quartermaster's men and the wagons they drove. But though these tributaries came together farther north, closer to the edge of the steppe, the river they formed was far too powerful and wide. Better to brave three smaller streams than chance crossing the Sussyn in all its might.

Even with the river crossings, Keziah found the journey tedious. Since their encounter the first day, Gershon had avoided her. Most of the men were either afraid of her or too wary of Qirsi sorcerers to come near her. It almost didn't matter which; the result was the same. No one spoke to her. Few of them even looked at her. Except Kearney, of course. The duke spent at least a part of each day by her side. Occasionally they spoke of what awaited them in Kentigern, but mostly they just rode in silence, savoring what little remained of the intimacy they had left in Glyndwr.

The nights were no better, though in truth she had little cause to complain. Several of the men took time each evening to erect a small tent that she had to herself, giving her comfort and warmth that no one else save Kearney enjoyed. Her evening meals consisted of more than just the hard cheese and dried meat rationed to the soldiers. She ate with Kearney and Gershon and so partook of whatever the quartermaster managed to find for the duke. The first night it was coneys, killed by several of the men as they marched. The second and third nights they ate ptarmigans roasted on spits and flavored with highland sage. The quartermaster had even brought a small amount of wine, which the duke insisted on sharing with the minister and swordmaster.

Even having to dine each night with Gershon, who brooded silently across from her at the small table in Kearney's tent, she should have been grateful. Compared with what the men of Glyndwr's army were enduring, she was not suffering at all.

But her fine meals and warm bed could not alter the fact that she was lonelier than she had been in years. She and Kearney were finally out of Glyndwr Castle together, leagues away from Leilia and her ladies, with their prying eyes and icy stares, and still they couldn't be together. They couldn't even touch without fear of drawing unwanted attention. And had they found a way to move beyond sight of the army, Gershon would have been there, glaring at them, his distaste for her written plainly on his blunt features.

So she rode, and when the others stopped, she did as well. But her days and nights passed without love, without companionship. After just three days she would gladly have given up warmth and good food for conversation or a shared smile. Instead, she finished her meal with the duke and swordmaster and quietly excused herself, walking back to her shelter as the last rays of daylight disappeared beneath the steppe and the moons hung overhead, midway through their waxing.

She didn't feel sleepy—she hadn't done enough during the course of the day to tire herself—but she lay down on the sleeping roll left for her by Kearney's soldiers and stared up at the roof of the cloth shelter, listening to the sounds of the camp. Voices and laughter drifted among the rocks and grasses of the steppe, mingling with the calls of larks and the whisper of the wind. Someone was singing in the distance, his voice high and sweet, like that of a boy. Keziah didn't recognize the song. Closer to her tent, horses nickered and stamped their feet.

Eventually, as darkness spread through the camp like mist, she felt her eyes closing and she gave in to sleep. An instant later, though, she opened them again, only to find herself standing in the middle of the steppe. The sun was up again, partially obscured by high thin clouds. Kearney and his men were gone.

I'm dreaming.

She heard a voice calling her name and she turned toward it. Grinsa was walking toward her.

"Why can't you let me sleep?" she asked as he drew near. "These conversations of ours leave me exhausted."

Her brother grinned. "No more than they do me."

He looked more rested than he had a few days before, though he still looked tired.

"You've left the castle," he said. "I can tell that much."

"Yes, with an army of seven hundred men."

"Well done, Kezi!" he said, his smile returning, even broader than before. "How far have you come?"

"We're still on the steppe, but we've crossed the Sussyn, and we should begin our descent tomorrow."

He seemed to consider this, as if measuring in his mind the distance they had covered.

"What's happened?" she asked. "Are they at war already?"

"Not as far as I know. I've left Kentigern with Lord Tavis. We're nearing Tremain. I need you to come here too, with Kearney of course."

"That shouldn't be difficult. It's a natural stopping point between here and Kentigern. I believe Kearney was planning to stop there anyway. He and Lathrop are on good terms."

Grinsa nodded. "Good."

"Aren't you worried about the two of us being together?"

"Of course I am," he said, frowning. "But I need to speak with your duke, and this is the only place I can do it where Tavis will be safe."

"Why do you need to speak with Kearney?"

He hesitated. "Are you certain you want to know?"

It seemed to Keziah that the wind on the steppe rose suddenly, chilling her. In truth, she didn't want to know. But whatever it was, Kearney would probably ask her counsel, and she wanted to be prepared.

"Tell me."

"I'm going to ask Kearney to give Tavis asylum in the House of Glyndwr."

She couldn't say that she was surprised. Had she been in her brother's position, she would have done the same. Just as Kearney was the only duke with any hope of stopping a civil war, he was also the best choice for this. Glyndwr's dukes had rarely held Eibithar's throne—the other major houses did not view the men of Glyndwr as ambitious, or as threats to their ambitions. Given how remote Glyndwr was from the others, Tavis was also likely to be safest there. It made perfect sense.

"All right," Keziah said. "Do you want me to plant the idea before we arrive, or would you rather it came from you the first time he heard it."

"That's it?" Grinsa asked, raising an eyebrow. "No argument? Just 'all right'?"

She shrugged. "He's really the only choice, isn't he?"

"Well, yes, but—"

"Then answer my question," she said, grinning slightly, "and let me sleep."

Grinsa laughed. "Fair enough. No, don't mention it to him. It might help smooth the way, but I'm afraid it will raise suspicions. This will strike them as a rather audacious proposal. They won't believe that we both thought of it on our own."

"Very well. I'll say nothing, then. But I'll do everything I can to make certain that we stop in Tremain."

"How soon do you think you'll be there?"

Keziah thought for a moment. "As I said, we're still on the steppe. We're at least twenty leagues away, and with the descent still ahead of us, I would imagine it will be at least seven days more."

"That gives us enough time to get there as well. I hope we'll be staying at the sanctuary, but you needn't worry about that. I'll find you."

She still felt cold, and she rubbed her arms.

"Are you all right, Kezi?"

Keziah nodded, making herself smile. "I'm fine. Just tired."

"Of course." Grinsa wrapped his long arms around her and kissed the top of her head. "I'll let you sleep. Journey safely, Kezi. I'll see you soon."

He released her and started to walk away.

"Grinsa, wait!" she called, without even thinking.

Her brother faced her again.

"Something's going to happen, isn't it?"

His brow furrowed. "I'm not sure I understand."

"The last time we spoke, I had the sense that you were keeping something from me. I think that you know what awaits us on this journey, but you're not telling me."

He just gazed at her, his expression revealing little, but his pale eyes looking sad. "You're right," he said at last. "I do know."

She shuddered, but she couldn't keep herself from asking. "Will you tell me now?"

"I can't, Kezi. It all has to happen as it's supposed to, with none of those involved knowing what will come. One person could change everything, and that could be extraordinarily dangerous."

"But you know."

He shrugged. "I'm the Weaver."

There had been a time, years before, when she had envied him his power. But as she came to appreciate the burden he carried, her jealousy faded, leaving her slightly awed that the boy she remembered from her youth could possess the wisdom and strength necessary to stand before her and speak those words with such calm. *I'm the Weaver.* No Eandi in the Forelands, not even one as intelligent as Kearney, could have possibly understood.

"This future you've seen," she said. "Is it terrible?" She was trembling and she felt a tear running cold down her cheek.

"Kezi, I can't—"

"Is it terrible?" she demanded.

Grinsa exhaled through his teeth. "I don't know if it's good or bad. I've seen glimpses, that's all. The only thing I know for certain is that we have to do this. There's too much at stake."

She didn't answer. She was cold and tired and too frightened to speak.

Grinsa gave a gentle smile and walked back to where she stood. Laying a hand gently on her brow, he kissed her cheek, and spoke a single word.

"Sleep."

She opened her eyes to the darkness of her tent. Night had chilled the air, and she was shivering. She longed to go to Kearney, just to feel him beside her. But instead she wrapped herself in a rough blanket and fell into a dreamless sleep.

Chapter
Twenty-two

✦

City of Kings, Eibithar

hey spoke in hushed tones, mindful of the king, who slept in his bed on the far end of the grand chamber. Servants came and went, bringing plates of food and cups of water that Aylyn did not touch, and removing them again some time later. An herbmaster lingered near the great bed, in case Aylyn needed an elixir to ease his pain or induce sleep, and priests of the castle's cloister prayed by the king's side. Occasionally, the healers came as well, but they had long since given up their vigil. Eibithar's king was dying, and all the magic in the world could not save him.

Natan still remembered seeing Aylyn for the first time, nearly seventeen years before. The king was already in his middle years by then, and more than sixteen years into his reign. His hair had begun to thin and grow grey, and he no longer looked like the lithe swordsman he was said to have been in his youth. But still, Natan had been impressed with the quiet strength he saw in the man, and the confidence and wisdom that lay behind his words.

Natan had been quite young at the time; he had never seen a king before, much less spoken with one. He hadn't even planned to come to the City of Kings, but his duke, Filib of Thorald, Aylyn's son, had insisted. The king's archminister had just died, and Aylyn was looking for a new Qirsi advisor.

"Much as I hate to lose you," the young duke had said, "I think you should go. My father needs you more than I do, and you should be in a court where your talents can be of most use."

It remained, to this day, the greatest act of kindness any Eandi had ever shown him.

Natan had been nervous about meeting the king, having far less confidence in his abilities than the duke had expressed. But despite the years that separated them, and Aylyn's unconcealed distrust of the Qirsi people, he and the king both realized almost immediately that they could work well together. In the years that followed, Natan had come to realize that Aylyn was not a great king. He was a competent military leader and a generous guardian of his kingdom and people, but that was all. Filib might have been great, had he lived. And Natan saw the seeds of greatness in his son, Aylyn's grandchild, who had visited Audun's Castle several times before his own tragic death two years before.

Even without achieving greatness, however, Aylyn had done all that Eibithar could ask of its king. He had tried to keep the peace, and failing that, had used his armies prudently, risking as few lives as possible. He had ruled the land for longer than any king in over two centuries, and throughout his reign Eibithar had remained one of the three preeminent powers in the Forelands, along with Braedon and Sanbira. A kingdom could ask little more of its sovereign. He deserved better than this ending, wasting away in his bed, without heirs, without a wife to offer comfort and shed tears. So though the healers no longer sat by his side, Natan had taken it upon himself to make certain that someone did. He and his fellow ministers had taken turns watching over the king, and would until the Deceiver came for him.

"Natan, are you all right?"

The Qirsi tore his gaze from the bed and found the other ministers watching him.

"I'm fine," he said. He looked at Wenda, who had spoken, and made himself smile. "What were you saying?"

She leaned forward and patted his leg gently.

Wenda had been in Audun's Castle serving Aylyn almost as long as he. He remembered seeing her for the first time as well. She had been rather plain-looking in her youth—the passage of the years and the gentle lines they had brought to her pale face had actually made her a more handsome woman—but Natan had fallen in love with her anyway. She was brilliant and she carried Bohdan's spirit in her heart. Even the king could not resist her humor. Wenda and Natan were both joined to other people; nothing ever came of his affection for her. But he liked to think that in some small way she had loved him as well.

Wenda became high minister shortly after Natan did, and four years ago, when Aylyn's archminister died, the king made it clear that he was considering both of them as possible replacements. In the end, the king chose Natan, largely because he had served the throne longer. If by some remote chance Natan died before Aylyn, no one doubted that Wenda would succeed him in the position.

"Paegar was asking if we could act as the king's surrogates," she said.

Natan glanced at the others. They were watching him, waiting for his reply. He was supposed to be presiding over this discussion. Actually Aylyn was. But with the king unable to join them, this responsibility fell to the archminister. And it was all he could do just to listen to what the others were saying.

He cleared his throat. "To what end?"

"To send the King's Guard to Kentigern," Paegar said. "To stop Aindreas and Javan from going to war." The man frowned, a look of concern in his yellow eyes. "Are you certain you're well, Archminister?"

"Yes, of course. Just a bit distracted, that's all." He smiled again, though these lapses concerned him. His father and mother had both died before their thirty-eighth birthdays and here he was nearing his fortieth. He should have been thanking Qirsar for his long life, but he couldn't help cursing the years for what they had done to him. Lately his mind wandered like that of a child, and he could barely keep himself awake during ministerial conclaves. Three nights before he had tried to summon a wind to his chambers, just to see if he could. The draft he conjured—it could hardly be called a wind—barely stirred the curtains by his window. Yet the effort left him breathless and damp with sweat.

"So what do you think, Archminister?" Paegar asked, the smile on his face not quite masking his impatience.

"I think it's a bad idea." Natan had to keep himself from grinning at the reaction of the other ministers. Even Wenda and Paegar looked surprised.

"You do?" Wenda asked.

"We're just ministers," Natan said. "It's one thing to collect tithe from the dukes in Aylyn's name, or even to extend trading privileges to merchants from other kingdoms. It's quite another to order the King's Guard to one of the dukedoms."

"But surely under these circumstances, we'd be justified," said Dyre. He was one of the younger Qirsi, the underministers, as they were called, though in truth any first minister in any dukedom in Eibithar would have gladly surrendered his or her place to be one of them.

"In whose eyes?" the archminister asked. "In our own? Perhaps. But to the captain of the guard and his men, we're sorcerers. They'd no more take orders from us than they would from the king of Caerisse."

"Not even to prevent a civil war?"

"We don't know this will end in war. We can't prove it to them. Unless you've gleaned something I don't know about."

Dyre's face reddened. After a moment he shook his head.

He reminded Natan so much of himself when he was young and new to the castle, when he had wanted nothing more than to wield his power in the name of the king. Natan had been fortunate to serve as a young man under a wise king, seasoned by years on the throne, who knew something of power and its limits. What would it have been like to come to the City of Kings as a young minister and find that the king one served was too infirm to lead? The archminister wondered if he had been too quick to dismiss the man's suggestion.

"I'd be willing to discuss the matter with the captain of the guard," he said after a brief silence. "He may be more open to the idea than I expect."

The young minister nodded. "Thank you, Archminister."

"Could we have one of the dukes act on the king's behalf?" another minister asked.

"I like that idea even less," Wenda said, before Natan could respond. "Enlisting the aid of a duke in the king's name could be very dangerous. For all we know, that could start the war we're trying to prevent."

"I have to agree," Paegar said. "If the archminister can't prevail upon the captain to take his men, there's little we can do."

A door opened near the king's bed and Obed, the prelate, stepped into the room. He glanced toward the Qirsi ministers, then quickly looked away, hurrying to his usual place beside the king to begin his whispered prayers. Ean worshipers had little use for the

Qirsi, and the prelate was no different. A moment later, though, the prelate stole a second look toward the Qirsi, and seeing that Natan was looking his way, Obed gave a small nod. The prelate had come to the City of Kings as a priest just a turn before Natan began his service to the king, and over the years the two men had come to understand one another. They weren't friends. Natan, who spent some time each day meditating in one of the city's four sanctuaries, had heard too many of Ean's servants railing against Qirsi heresies and the evils of the Old Faith to befriend any prelate. More often than not the two men offered Aylyn conflicting advice and sought to undermine each other's influence with the king. But while Natan had questioned Obed's judgment on many occasions, he never doubted the prelate's devotion to Aylyn, nor did he believe that Obed doubted his. Natan didn't have to imagine what the prelate was feeling at that moment, praying to his god, waiting for the king to die, for the Qirsi was feeling it as well.

He had lost track of the discussion again, but he couldn't bring himself to care. He was tired. All he wanted was to return to his chambers and rest.

"I hate to even ask this," Paegar said, eyeing Natan. "But have the healers given us any sense of how long the king . . . how much time he has?"

The rest turned to him. Wenda, the underministers. Glancing toward the bed once more, the archminister saw that even the prelate was watching him, awaiting his answer.

"I gather from all they've told me," Natan said, pitching his voice so Obed could hear him as well, "that they can only guess at such things. But he hasn't much time left. A few days. Perhaps half a turn. Perhaps less. It seems they almost lost him last night."

Paegar nodded, as if he had expected this. "And what happens if he dies, making Javan king, before this matter in Kentigern is settled?"

"I've thought of that as well," Wenda said. "If Aindreas truly intends to keep Javan from the throne, the king's death could bring war."

"All the more reason to send the guard," Dyre said, refusing to meet Natan's gaze.

The archminister shook his head. "All the more reason not to."

"What?"

"Think for a moment. If the king dies and the King's Guard is in Kentigern, they become Javan's men. Right now we have two dukes of roughly equal strength threatening to start a war, the end of which neither of them can foresee with any confidence. If Curgh suddenly adds the King's Guard to his army, it'll be a slaughter." Natan glanced around the circle of advisors. "Is that what we want?"

Dyre just shook his head, staring at Natan as if the archminister had shown him a new magic, a way to use his Qirsi powers that the younger man had never seen before. *There!* Natan wanted to say. *You see? Even as an old man, with one foot already in the Underrealm, I can think of things you've never even considered.*

Wenda cast a sly grin Natan's way. "I think we're done for the day," she said, looking at the others. "We'll gather again in the morning. In the meantime, pray for the king's comfort and for an easy journey to the Underrealm."

It was his place to adjourn them, but under the circumstances Natan did not mind at all. He had said his piece.

Most of the underministers stood and began slowly to file out of the king's chamber. Dyre lingered, however, seemingly intent on having the last word.

"You'll speak with the captain?" he asked.

Natan had to think for a moment before remembering that he had promised to do so. "Of course," he said. He already knew how the conversation would go, but he had given his word.

"Thank you." The man hesitated briefly, glancing first at Paegar and then at Wenda. After a moment he turned and left the room.

"The man's a fool," Natan muttered, watching him go.

Wenda smiled, placing a hand on his leg again. "He's just young, Natan. I remember when we were the same way."

"He's not just young," Paegar said. "He's also scared." He looked over at the prelate, before continuing in a lower voice. "So am I, to tell you the truth."

The archminister knew that he should have been as well. The kingdom had been through several civil wars over the course of its history; Eibithar's major houses had fought among themselves more frequently than the kingdom had fought the Aneirans. Natan did not doubt for a moment that Javan and Aindreas were capable of dragging the land into yet another war. But as with so many other things recently, this failed to arouse any feelings in him at all. He should have been frightened, or angry with the dukes' foolishness, or at least sad that the kingdom could still be threatened from within in this way. But he felt nothing.

"It would be best if Javan would simply abdicate," Paegar went on a moment later.

"And give the kingdom to Aindreas?" Wenda said. "He'd never do it."

It was one of the few flaws in Eibithar's Rules of Ascension. The rules had been created eight centuries before by the leaders of all twelve houses, and they remained, in Natan's mind, a most reliable and equitable method for choosing a leader. By allowing only the eldest son of a king to ascend to the throne, the dukes hoped to keep one house from becoming the sole ruling power in the kingdom. But by establishing an Order of Ascension, a hierarchy among the houses, they hoped as well to maintain some consistency of leadership. Occasionally, over the centuries, Thorald's supremacy had drawn the resentment of the other houses, leading to civil war, and in more than one instance, to experiments with other methods of selecting a king. Always, however, the houses turned back to the Rules of Ascension. Simply put, they worked.

But these were extraordinary times. The House of Galdasten was still recovering from its terrifying brush with the pestilence, which had killed the duke and his entire line. Under the rules, the new lords of Galdasten would have to wait four generations before they could lay claim to the crown once more. The House of Thorald, tragically robbed of both its duke and his brilliant son, did not have to wait as long as its rival to the south, but still it could place no heirs on the throne for another generation. With the land's most powerful families removed from the Order of Ascension, stability vanished, but not the rivalries that still existed among the other major houses and the outrage engendered by Brienne's death and Tavis's imprisonment. A duke of Thorald, and even Galdasten, might be convinced to give up the crown in circumstances such as these, knowing that under the Order of Ascension their houses, the preeminent houses in the land, would reclaim the throne in the foreseeable future. But for the men of Curgh and Kentigern, whose houses gained the throne but once or twice in a given century, abdication was out of the question. Javan could be expected to guard jealously Curgh's newfound status as the kingdom's highest-ranking house.

"Do you think Javan would renounce his son if Aindreas agreed not to take the throne himself? That way Javan would rule, but when he died the crown would fall to Aindreas's boy."

Wenda shook her head. "That would only work if Aindreas was willing to accept Javan as his sovereign, and Javan was willing to acknowledge Tavis's guilt. And if those things were possible, we wouldn't be worrying about civil war."

Paegar muttered a curse and propelled himself out of his chair. "So there's nothing at all we can do." He offered it as a statement, but he looked from Wenda to Natan, as if hoping one of them would contradict him.

"There's nothing we can do without a king," Natan said. "Under almost any other circumstance, I'd be in favor of sending messages to all the houses, telling them of Aylyn's state and asking them to allow his successor to take the throne. But we can't even do that right now."

The midday bells tolled from the city gates, their peals echoing among the great towers of Audun's Castle, and drifting into Aylyn's chambers like sweet spirits of the Underrealm. The priests kneeling at the king's bed climbed stiffly to their feet and stepped somberly from the room. Obed remained, however.

"I'll return later," Paegar said, his mouth set in a hard line. He glanced once at the king, then left, though through a different door from the one used by the Ean worshipers.

Wenda stood as well and smiled down at Natan. "I was thinking of walking to the marketplace. Join me?"

The archminister shook his head. "Perhaps another time. I'd like some time with Aylyn, and after that I need to rest."

"I understand." She took his hand, giving it a quick squeeze. A moment later she was gone as well.

Natan pushed himself out of his chair and crossed to the king's bed to stand next to Obed.

Noting that the prelate was in the middle of a prayer, the archminister kept his silence, looking down at Aylyn. The king was so pale, his hair so white and thin, that he could easily have been mistaken for a Qirsi. Even as an older man he had looked as an Eandi king ought to, handsome and tall, with icy blue eyes and strong, angular features. But now he just looked old and sickly, his hair disheveled and his cheeks so sunken that his skin seemed about to tear. His lips were cracked and dry, and his chest rose and fell unsteadily, with a high, rasping sound. Eibithar needed a miracle; it needed its king. But looking at him now, Natan knew that Aylyn would never open his eyes again. The most for which any of them could hope was that he would outlive the crisis on Kentigern Tor.

The prelate finished his prayer and rose, brushing off his robe. "He looks worse every day," he said.

"Yes."

"Your healers can do nothing more?"

They weren't his healers, of course. They were the king's. But they were Qirsi, and so his in Obed's eyes.

"He's an old man," Natan said. "If it were just the sickness they could heal him. But the king's body has given all it can."

Obed nodded. "I heard some of what you and your ministers were saying. Are you as concerned as the others?"

I should be, but I feel nothing. "The danger is real enough. It remains to be seen whether Javan and Aindreas will follow through on their threats or come to their senses."

"I've met both of them," the prelate said. "Neither has much sense."

Natan laughed, and after a moment Obed joined in. The archminister had known many prelates in his years and as far as he could tell, Obed was the only one of them with any humor. Their laughter faded quickly, and they stood, wordless, watching the king.

"It's time for my devotions," Obed said at last. "Be well, Archminister."

Natan nodded. "And you, Father Prelate. Pray for our king's long life."

He couldn't help feeling that they were being watched, that someone was marking their progress through the ward, wondering what they were doing together. He knew he was being foolish. No one would think twice about one of the king's Qirsi ministers speaking to one of his Qirsi healers, not when the king was so ill. Certainly none of the Eandi would notice. Most of the guards still didn't recognize him, and he had been living in Audun's Castle for nearly eleven years. To them he was just another Qirsi advisor. He could count on one hand the ones who knew enough to call him high minister as he walked by. He had nothing to fear from them. Nor did he have cause to worry about his fellow ministers. Only the day before he had seen the archminister speaking with a healer, just as he was doing now. He shouldn't have been nervous at all. Yet Paegar had to walk with his hands behind his back so the healer wouldn't see how they trembled.

"The king's master healer is very protective of his patient. He won't allow any of us to attend to the king unless he's there as well. As I said before, there's nothing I can do. With Natan insisting that you and your fellow ministers sit vigil with the king, you are the best choice to see to this matter."

Paegar nodded, but offered no other response. What they were asking of him went far beyond anything he had done for them before. Perhaps he should have expected it, given what he had heard of others doing, but somehow he thought that it would be different for him. Aylyn was old, and he was dying. The minister wanted to believe that they could wait half a turn for Bian to take him. But after all that he and the other ministers had discussed the past few days, it had become clear to him that they couldn't wait at all, not even a day.

He had hoped to have someone else do this. Since he ranked highest among the members of the Qirsi movement here in the City of Kings, it was within his power to assign the task to any of the others. So long as it was done.

"What about the herbmaster?" the minister asked, lifting a hand to greet one of the garden laborers who was working by the armory tower.

"The Eandi?" the healer asked, frowning at the idea.

"He takes our gold. He's administered sweetwort for us in the past. Not to kill, but nonetheless, there's no reason why he can't do this as well."

"Actually there is."

Paegar had to bite back a curse.

"When the king dies," the healer said, "no matter the cause, the master healer will examine the body. He'll know if Aylyn has swallowed anything. If the king were still eating his meals or even drinking water, it might work. But as things stand now, poison is out of the question."

"Then how?" the minister demanded, barely managing to speak the words.

"Suffocation," the man said, sounding unnervingly calm. "I'd suggest using a pillow."

He would have liked to strike him, or better yet, take a dagger to his heart. But that would have solved nothing. The Weaver expected Aylyn to die, and Paegar knew that the king's death had to appear natural. It was no more the healer's fault than it was the king's.

"All right," he said, his voice flat.

"Place a kerchief over his face first, and destroy it after. There should be nothing on the pillow to give us away. I'll be with the master healer tonight, so we'll find the body together. If there are any signs of what you've done, I'll do my best to conceal them."

He might as well have been speaking of the flowers in bloom along the path, so light was the man's tone. Paegar wondered if the healer would have been as composed had it been he himself who was to do the killing.

They reached the king's tower, whence they had started some time ago. The healer halted and faced him.

"I'm expected back in the master healer's chambers," he said. "Is there anything else, High Minister?"

Of course there was. He had never killed before. He had never thought he would. Others had died as a result of the movement. Paegar knew that. And so others in the movement had killed. But it hadn't occurred to him that he would have to as well. How was he to gather the courage to kill Eibithar's king? Did courage even play a role in such a murder?

"High Minister?"

"No," he said. "Nothing else."

"Fine then." The healer hesitated. At last he merely nodded and stepped into the tower.

Paegar closed his eyes and took a long breath. Suddenly he longed to leave the City of Kings, just for a while. Just until nightfall.

"High Minister!"

He opened his eyes, turning toward the voice. Dyre was hurrying toward him, his white hair twisting in the light wind, his yellow eyes looking almost white in the sunlight.

"May I have a word with you?"

No. Get away from me. "Of course, Minister. What can I do for you?"

"I saw you speaking with the healer," the younger man said, stopping in front of him. "Is everything all right?"

"My conversation with the healer is none of your concern." Paegar winced at what he heard in his own voice. He looked away briefly, trying to will his heart to slow down. "Forgive me," he said, facing the minister again. "These are ... difficult times."

"Of course, High Minister. That was why I was hoping we might talk." He gestured, indicating that they should walk.

In spite of everything, Paegar almost laughed aloud. If this continued, he'd spend the entire day walking in circles.

As they started along the path that followed the perimeter of the inner ward, Dyre spoke of his concerns about the archminister's reluctance to send the King's Guard to Kentigern. Paegar should have expected this in light of all that had been said during their discussion earlier in the day. But he was still thinking of how he had barked at Dyre when the man asked about his conversation with the healer. How was he supposed to fool Wenda and Natan, who had known him for so long, if he couldn't even keep himself calm around one of the underministers? If he wasn't careful, he would end up being hanged as a traitor before he even reached the king's chambers.

The young minister went on for some time, speaking his mind as if the two of them were great friends. Paegar couldn't follow all he was saying; in truth, he wasn't really trying. But he heard enough to know how to respond when Dyre finally turned to him again and said, "Can you speak with him, High Minister?"

"I can try, Dyre. But you must realize that none of us knows the king or the captain of the guard as well as Natan. He's been here the longest, and while I agree that he's been acting strangely in recent days, I do believe that he's right when he says that the captain will not act without a direct order from Aylyn."

"But does the captain know how ill the king is? Does he understand that Aylyn can't give orders anymore?"

"He's spoken with the healers. I'm certain he knows."

The man sighed and rubbed a hand across his lips. "The archminister promised me that he would speak with the captain," he said. "Would you at least see that he remembers?"

Paegar nodded, sensing an opportunity to end their conversation. "I give you my word. If Natan won't do it, I will."

"Thank you, High Minister," Dyre said, looking truly grateful.

"My pleasure."

He stopped walking, glancing for a moment up at the sun. "If there's nothing else—"

"No, nothing at all," the man said quickly. "I've already kept you too long." He took a step back, smiling now. "Again, my thanks. I feel better having spoken with you."

"I'm glad to hear it."

Paegar turned and walked away, hoping that Dyre wouldn't call him back, and that no one else would stop him. He needed time alone, to prepare himself for what he had to do. He couldn't leave the city, he knew. Not with the king dying. Instead he made his way back to his quarters, entering the prison tower and walking through the cool stone corridors of the castle. It would have been quicker to cross the ward once more, but in the middle of such a warm, sunny day, he was far less likely to be accosted within the hallways.

Entering his small chamber, Paegar locked the door and stepped to the small window. A warm breeze touched his face, carrying the faint smell of roasting meat from the castle kitchens. He hadn't eaten since breakfast, and his stomach rumbled loudly. The prior's bells had yet to ring; the sun would be up for hours more. Certainly he had time enough to eat. But despite his hunger, the thought of eating nearly made him retch.

He remained by the window, staring out at the castle's outer ward and the great towers of its middle wall. The sun turned its slow arc across the bright sky, casting deep shadows across the north barbican and the deep green grass that grew in front of it. After some time, guards at the city gates rang the prior's bells. Still Paegar did not move. A flock of doves flew above the walls and towers, turning together in tight circles like trained horsemen. A bank of dark clouds appeared in the western sky, blocking out the sunlight. The air turned colder and the minister thought he heard thunder roll in the distance.

A short time later it began to storm, the gusting wind driving rain into his chamber. Reluctantly the minister closed the wooden shutters on his window and lit a candle by his bed. He thought about lying down and trying to sleep, but, fearing that he would sleep too long, immediately thought better of it. After sitting in the candlelight for just a minute or two, he extinguished the flame. He had been in his room long enough. Better to return now to the king's chambers, and remain there for as much of the night as was necessary, than to appear there suddenly just a short while before Aylyn was to die.

Wenda and Natan were with the king when he got there, as

were the ever-present priests. Paegar had hoped—vainly, he knew—that Aylyn might die before nightfall, but the king looked just as he had that morning.

The minister stepped to the foot of the bed, bowing once to his sovereign, before he joined the older ministers at Aylyn's side.

"He actually stirred at the sound of the thunder," Natan said softly, his eyes never straying from the king's face. "We hoped that perhaps he would awaken. But he hasn't moved or made a sound since."

Paegar shuddered at the notion that the man could move at all. He was supposed to be one step from death. The minister felt his hands start to tremble again and he balled them into fists.

"Is everything all right, Paegar?" Wenda asked.

"I had hoped the king might show some improvement."

Natan shook his head. "He's past that."

Wenda stepped closer to Paegar. "I'd like to get some sleep now," she whispered. "That way I can stay with the king through the night. Can you remain with the archminister until I return? I fear for his health."

"Actually," Paegar said, also lowering his voice, "I slept during the day so that I could relieve you both for the night."

She smiled, looking a bit surprised. "How kind of you."

"What's that?" Natan asked.

"Paegar is going to stay with the king tonight so that you and I can rest."

"I don't want to rest."

Wenda frowned. "Natan, don't make me call the herbmaster for a sleep draught."

The archminister glared at her for several moments, then shrugged and looked away. "All right," he muttered. He quickly looked up again. "Not yet, though. I'm not leaving yet."

Wenda took his hand. "No," she said gently. "Not yet."

The priests left a short time later, with the ringing of the twilight bells. They would pass the night in the cloister, returning the next morning at dawn. At least that was what they did most nights. Tonight would be different.

Wenda and the archminister lingered far longer than Paegar had wished they would. And just as they finally resolved to leave, the healers arrived to check on the king. Natan insisted on staying for this, of course, and it was another hour or more before Wenda could lead him away.

At last, however, Paegar found himself alone in the chamber with the king. There was no light save for the low fire that burned in the great hearth, and a single candle that flickered by Aylyn's bed. The castle had grown quiet. Most were in bed by now. But still he waited. The minister told himself that he had all the night, that if he killed the king too early he would invite suspicion. But he knew that wasn't why he waited.

There were several pillows on the bed other than the two on which the king's head rested. He had only to take one in his hands. His stomach felt hollow and sour, and his throat was so dry he couldn't swallow.

The king had never been especially kind to him—certainly not as he was to Natan and Wenda. But neither had he ever been cruel or even discourteous. He had done nothing to deserve this death. Paegar could never claim that he had. The men and women of the movement had offered him gold and spoken to him of a glorious future for his people. And after so many years of living in this castle and serving this Eandi king, of offering counsel that was ignored as often as it was accepted, that had been enough. That was why Aylyn was about to die. That was the only reason.

He stepped forward and picked up one of the pillows. He was breathing hard and his hands felt sweaty. Only at the last minute, just before he covered the king's face, did he remember what the healer had said about a kerchief. Pulling one from the pocket of his robe, he placed it carefully over Aylyn's mouth and nose. The king didn't move.

Paegar closed his eyes and lowered the pillow onto the old man's face, pushing it down harder and harder until he was nearly lying on the bed himself. Still Aylyn offered no resistance and for a long time the high minister remained there, wondering if the old man was dead yet.

Finally he stood and removed the pillow and kerchief. The king looked just as he had before. Paegar bent over and laid his cheek on the king's chest. He heard no heartbeat and sensed no movement. Straightening, the Qirsi carried the kerchief to the hearth and threw it on the fire. It blazed briefly before shriveling into a small blackened mass, which he stirred with a poker until it vanished.

His hands were still shaking, but that didn't matter anymore. They'd expect that, just as they would expect the tears that ran down his cheeks.

"Guards!" he shouted, returning to the king's side. "Wake the castle! The king is dead!"

Chapter
Twenty-three

✦

Tremain, Eibithar

"Ask a noble the difference between a minor house and a major house," an old Eibitharian saying went, "and his answer will tell you to which he belongs."

Like so many of the old adages this one carried more than a grain of truth. The only differences the dukes of Eibithar's minor houses saw between themselves and the leaders of the major houses were a few hundred men in their armies, a few thousand qinde in their treasuries, and the chance to become king under the Rules of Ascension. To the dukes of the major houses, even Kearney, whose house ranked lowest among the five, the distinctions were far greater. With each house's army including fewer than two thousand soldiers, a difference of a few hundred could be significant. But more than that, the men of Thorald, Galdasten, Curgh, Kentigern, and Glyndwr were the land's finest and best trained. Kentigern and Glyndwr were expected to protect Eibithar's borders; Thorald, Galdasten, and Curgh her shores. Their armies had to be the best. And since the dukes of the five were in line for the throne, their courts had to be worthy of receiving nobles from all the kingdoms of the Forelands. Their castles were larger and more elegant, their cities were more prosperous. "No one who has lived in a major house could ever mistake a minor for one of the five," it was often said. "And no one who leaves a minor house for one of the five will ever return home."

Keziah, who had spent her childhood in the House of Eardley, the most prosperous of the minors, and her adult years in Glyndwr, was inclined to agree with the nobles of the five. The castles of the major houses were finer in every way. Eardley's army was only slightly smaller than Glyndwr's, but Eardley's men were no match for those commanded by Kearney. It was true that the houses had been ranked centuries ago, according to their strengths at the end of the clan wars. It might even have been true that in some ways the hierarchy no longer reflected reality. Many believed that Sussyn, the lowest in rank of all Eibithar's houses, was actually stronger and more prosperous than both Domnall and Labruinn. Most agreed that there was little difference among the armies of Galdasten, Curgh, and Kentigern.

But there could be no disputing the fact that only five dukedoms deserved to be called major houses. Far from being a relic of a forgotten time, the distinction between the majors and minors continued to provide a legitimate basis for determining who among Eibithar's nobles should be king.

Keziah was reminded of this upon their arrival at Tremain Castle eight days after her last conversation with Grinsa. Among the kingdom's seven minor houses, Tremain was ranked fourth. The castle, perched just at the edge of the Heneagh River and within sight of the eastern fringe of Kentigern Wood, rose high above the surrounding city, its round towers bearing banners of tawny, black, and gold. Keziah could see the famous Tremain orchards on the eastern side of the castle, just beyond the low grey wall that surrounded the city. There could be no denying that it was one of Eibithar's more beautiful fortresses, but it was no larger or more imposing than the castles of thanes and earls living in the Glyndwr Highlands. Compared with Glyndwr Castle itself, Tremain looked small and vulnerable.

Riding with Kearney and Gershon just a few hours past midday, Keziah crossed the Tremain Bridge and approached the city's north gate. There, Lathrop, duke of Tremain, met the company with a full complement of guards. Kearney had sent a small party of soldiers ahead to Tremain two days earlier, to ask Lathrop's leave for the Glyndwr army to rest in his dukedom.

Of course the duke had given his permission. As Keziah had told Grinsa, Kearney was on good terms with the duke and they visited yearly, to hunt for elk in the highlands or boar in the nearby wood. Indeed, not only had he agreed to let Glyndwr's men set up camp in the shadow of the city walls, he had made Kearney, Gershon, and Keziah guests of the castle.

Lathrop had been a friend of Kearney's father before the old duke died. His hair and beard were the color of steel, and there were deep lines around his pale blue eyes. He had grown heavy in recent years and he walked with a pronounced limp. But he was still quick to smile and he greeted Kearney and Gershon with great enthusiasm, embracing them as brothers after the riders from Glyndwr dismounted.

Lathrop had been accompanied to the city gate by his young wife, Tabya, who, to Kearney's obvious surprise, was large with child.

"A duke needs heirs," Lathrop said in a deep voice, chuckling at the reddening of Kearney's face. "My first wife, Bian keep her safe, gave me only daughters."

The duchess appeared unconcerned with all the attention being given to her belly. She merely stood beside her duke, playing absently with her red curls and smiling as he spoke. She couldn't have been more than three or four years past her Fating.

The duke of Tremain's first minister was there as well, an older Qirsi woman named Evetta, whom Keziah greeted warmly. Keziah would have been happy to pass the evening speaking with the minister and drinking the rich pear spirits made here in Tremain's cellars. But already she was scanning the faces of those who peered out through the city gate, searching for Grinsa. The spires of the Sanctuary of Adriel rose into the sky just beyond the city wall. She could hear the clerics chanting where she stood. Her brother was nearby. She could feel him.

"First Minister?" she heard Kearney say.

She made herself face the two dukes, her cheeks burning. "Yes, my lord."

He nodded toward Lathrop. "The duke was just asking you how you enjoyed traveling the land in the company of such an army."

"My Lord Duke, forgive me," she said, bowing deeply to the grey-haired man. "I'm weary from our journey and I had forgotten how beautiful your city and castle are." She smiled, her eyes flicking toward Gershon, who was frowning at her. "Riding with the duke and his guard is always an honor, but I'll be grateful for a comfortable bed and a meal prepared in your fine kitchens."

Lathrop smiled. "You're most kind, First Minister. Be welcome. I know that my first minister has been looking forward to seeing you."

"And I her," Keziah said, though she felt her stomach tightening. Leaving the castle to find Grinsa would not be easy.

A few moments later, Gershon rode back to Glyndwr's men to give the orders to set up camp. At the same time, Lathrop, the duchess, and Tremain's first minister led Kearney and Keziah through the city toward the castle. Evetta walked beside her, speaking of recent events in Tremain. There had been a flood early in the planting season—word of it hadn't reached Glyndwr—and dozens had died of the pestilence in one of the more remote baronies, though the disease had come no closer than that. Keziah did her best to listen to what the minister was saying, but she could not keep herself from looking for Grinsa. He should have been easy to spot, tall as he was. Fewer Qirsi lived in the cities of the minor houses than in Glyndwr, Thorald, and the other majors. There weren't as many opportunities for them in the smaller castles. But she didn't see him, though they walked right past the sanctuary and through the city marketplace. Keziah wondered if he had come to Tremain after all, or if something had happened to change his plans.

"He would have told you," she told herself. "He would have come to you again."

"What?"

She looked at Evetta, feeling herself grow pale. "Did I say that aloud?"

"You said something. I couldn't tell what it was."

"I'm sorry, Evetta. I'm afraid I won't be very good company. I've a lot on my mind."

The woman pushed a strand of white hair back from her brow. "Of course you do. If I was riding to Kentigern these days, I would as well."

"Thank you for understanding. I probably just need some sleep."

Evetta gave a strange smile. "Perhaps. Or maybe you need some time alone in our sanctuary. That can be quite restful, I hear."

Keziah froze in midstride for just an instant. Before she could say anything, the minister pulled a small folded piece of parchment from her robe and placed it in her hand, the movement so fluid and subtle that no one would have noticed had they not been looking for it.

"This came for you in the morning," Evetta said in a low voice.

"One of the clerics brought it to me. He made it sound as though this was a matter of some urgency. I didn't open it, of course, but I assume you'll need to get to the sanctuary as soon as possible. I can help you get out of the castle and accompany you as far as the marketplace. I'd take you farther, but I expect you'd prefer to go the rest of the way alone."

"Thank you," Keziah whispered, keeping her gaze fixed on the road before her, but unfolding the parchment as quickly as she dared. She glanced down at it for just an instant, but that was long enough to see that it was from Grinsa, and that the entire message consisted of just two words: prior's bells.

"Is everything all right?" Evetta asked.

"Yes, fine." She looked up at the sun, trying to gauge the time. "How long has it been since the midday bells?"

"Several hours. The prior's bells should be rung in another hour or so. Is that when you're to be there?"

Keziah faltered. She had always liked Evetta, but enjoying the woman's company was one thing; trusting her under these circumstances was quite another. Grinsa had relied on her to deliver his note, but he had kept his message so brief as to reveal almost nothing.

The minister saw Keziah's hesitation, her features hardening. "I see," she said, facing forward again.

"Forgive me, Evetta. The letter took me by surprise."

"Did it?" the woman asked, still not looking at her. "It seems to me you've been looking for someone since the moment you passed through the city gate."

Keziah felt herself growing cold. Had she been that obvious?

"It's your choice, First Minister," Evetta went on before she could say anything. "I've offered my help. It's yours if you decide you need it."

"I do," Keziah said, making up her mind in that moment. "You're right. I need to be at the sanctuary with the prior's bells. I'm meeting—"

"No." The woman shook her head. "Don't tell me. I'm not certain that I want any part of this."

You don't, Keziah wanted to say. *No more than I do.* Instead she nodded, saying only, "I'll be grateful for whatever aid you can offer."

They came to the castle a short while later and entered the larger of the structure's two wards. There Lathrop presented his daughters and Tremain's swordmaster, a dour man who barely even looked at either of the first ministers. Keziah was sure that he and Gershon would be fine friends.

They were shown to their quarters—hers was on the same corridor as Kearney's, but several doors away from it. It was a small room, but comfortable, with an ample bed, a washbowl, and a pitcher filled with water so warm that steam still rose from it. The lone window afforded a fine view of the river and, in the distance, the abrupt cliffs of the steppe.

Lathrop had said that there was to be a banquet that night in honor of Kearney and the rest of Tremain's guests, but it was not to begin until dusk. Whether he had known this or not, Grinsa had planned their meeting perfectly.

Keziah was not alone in her chamber for more than a few moments when there came a knock on the door. Pulling it open, she found Evetta standing in the corridor, looking as withdrawn as she had before. Keziah felt a fool for not trusting her. She feared that she had lost a friend.

"If you want to be at the sanctuary when the bells ring, we should go now."

Keziah nodded. More than anything she wanted to wash herself with that water while it was still hot.

"You do still want to go," the woman said, eyeing her curiously.

Keziah shook her head. "No. But I have no choice."

That drew a smile from Evetta.

She stepped out of the chamber and pulled the door closed behind her. "I'm sorry for not confiding in you before," she said, as they started toward the nearest tower and the stairs down to the ward. "It's not a matter of not trusting you. Much of this isn't mine to tell. Nearly all of it, really. I was afraid to say too much; I still am."

"I understand," Evetta said, smiling again. "In our position, it's sometimes hard to separate ourselves from the affairs of our dukes."

Keziah didn't bother to correct her; best for now to let her think that she was acting on Kearney's behalf. They descended the winding steps of the tower and hurried through the castle wards to the streets of Tremain. They were crowded still, though not as they had been earlier in the day, when Tremain's people had turned out to greet Kearney and his company. Sunlight slanted sharply across the low buildings, casting odd shadows on the narrow stone lanes. The bells tolled as the two ministers neared the cluster of merchant stalls in city marketplace, the sound filling the streets and halting conversations momentarily.

"Follow this lane back toward the north gate," Evetta said, stopping at the north end of the marketplace. "You'll see the sanctuary just beside it. You passed it when you entered the city."

Keziah nodded. "I remember. Thank you, Evetta. I'll see you at the banquet."

She could see the spires already, and she walked quickly toward them, her pulse quickening. In spite of everything else, she was eager to see her brother again. It had been more than half a year since the Revel's last visit to Glyndwr, and even then, she and Grinsa had not dared spend too much time together for fear of drawing attention to themselves.

The sanctuary gate was open and she made her way through the courtyard to the grand shrine with its narrow, soaring towers. This was Adriel's Turn, and later that night, after darkness fell, the shrine would be filled with young lovers seeking the blessings of the goddess and offering their devotions in anticipation of the Night of Two Moons, three nights hence. That night, perhaps the most anticipated night of the year among the men and women of the Forelands, they would consummate their affairs and, according to legend, assure themselves of everlasting love. But with the golden light of late day shining through the brilliant stained-glass windows behind the altar and along both sides of the building, the shrine was nearly empty.

Keziah made her way toward the altar slowly, wondering suddenly if this was where she was to meet Grinsa, or if he was in another part of the sanctuary.

"May I help you?" someone asked from behind her.

She turned so quickly that she nearly lost her balance. A woman stood before her, a cleric, judging from the color of her robe.

"You seem lost," the woman said, smiling kindly.

"No, I'm not. I'm just . . . I'm looking for someone."

The cleric glanced around the shrine. A young couple sat close together on one of the wooden benches near the back of the building, and an older woman was kneeling before the altar, crying quietly. Otherwise there was no one in sight.

"Perhaps this person intended to meet you here tonight. It's a bit early yet."

Keziah smiled, though she felt herself blush. She was about to explain that she wasn't meeting a lover, when it occurred to her that this would only make the woman curious. Maybe it was best to play along. "No," she said. "We were to meet now, at the ringing of the prior's bells. I'm sure of it."

"Well, maybe we should look else—"

"It's all right, Sister," came another voice.

Keziah turned again, and saw a woman in a robe of deepest red standing behind the altar. The prioress.

"She's here to see me."

The cleric's eyes widened slightly, but she recovered quickly, nodding once and withdrawing.

"Do you care to offer blood?" the prioress asked, gesturing for Keziah to approach the altar.

"Of course," she said, wondering if she truly had a choice.

She walked toward the altar, which was made of dark wood with a wide swirling grain and exquisitely intricate carvings of the various gods and goddesses. An ornate sconce stood at the center of the altar, holding four long, tapered candles of red and white. Beside it rested a stone bowl and a long-handled knife, also made of stone.

Keziah stepped past the crying woman and around to the far side of the altar where the prioress waited for her. She held out her arm and, as an afterthought, looked away.

"My name is Janae," the woman said, as she lifted the bowl and dragged the blade across the minister's arm. "I assume you're Keziah."

"Yes." She barely noticed the cut at all, though she did feel warm blood flowing down her arm and dripping to the bowl.

"You don't like to see blood, Keziah?"

"Not my own, not if I don't have to."

The prioress laughed.

"I'll take you to them in a moment," the woman said after a brief silence.

Them. Grinsa was with Tavis. Keziah had been so intent on finding her brother that she had forgotten the young lord entirely. She was nearly as reluctant to meet him as she was impatient to see Grinsa. It was because of him that they had left Glyndwr, disrupting her life and putting Kearney's at risk.

"There," Janae said, dabbing at the cut with a soft cloth. "We should bind your arm before we go to them. Unless you care to heal yourself."

She shook her head. "I don't have that power."

The prioress nodded, pulling a long cloth from within her robe and wrapping it around the wound with sure hands.

"You've a deft touch, Mother Prioress."

"I should. I've lifted that blade many times."

A moment later, the bandage was in place.

"Come with me," Janae said, starting toward a small door near the altar.

Keziah followed. In a moment they were in a second courtyard, smaller than the one between the gate and the shrine. It opened onto several small buildings, each of them appearing to be a dwelling for clerics. The prioress led her to the last of these, pushing open the door and indicating with a hand that Keziah should enter.

The minister hesitated, but only briefly. Grinsa was reclining on a small bed by the far wall, looking tired, though no more so than he had the last time he entered her dreams. He rose when he saw her, smiling broadly and walking to her to take her in his long, strong arms.

He looked and felt and smelled just as he had in the visions. But the dreams, real as they were, could not replace actually being with him.

He kissed the top of her head. "It's good to see you, Kezi."

She nodded, but she wasn't ready to speak just yet. She merely dried her tears on his shirt and stepped back, returning his smile.

His eyes strayed toward the window, and she followed the direction of his gaze. A young man sat in a chair, watching them, his expression unreadable. He had straight hair the color of wheat, and dark blue eyes. His features were fine and youthful, without being womanly, as those of young Eandi nobles sometimes were. Had he been smiling, and had it not been for all the dark angry scars on his face—one at his temple, another near his right eye, and one more across his other cheek—she might have thought him handsome. Even with his wounds, even wearing the fine white robe of a sanctuary novice, the young lord was hardly what she had expected. He didn't look like a murderer or a spoiled court boy. He looked, she had to admit, strong and thoughtful, as a young king should.

"Keziah ja Dafydd, first minister of Glyndwr," Grinsa said, still looking at the boy, "allow me to present Lord Tavis of Curgh."

Keziah bowed, searching for something appropriate to say. "My

Lord Tavis. I'm . . . honored to meet you. I wish I could have done so under different circumstances."

The young lord offered only the slightest of nods in response, his dark eyes going from Keziah to Grinsa and back to Keziah again. "So the two of you are sister and brother," he finally said, his expression still revealing little. "I never would have guessed from looking at you."

She glanced at her brother, unnerved by Tavis's comment.

"It's all right," Grinsa said softly. "Keziah is Lord Glyndwr's most trusted advisor," he told the lord. "I thought the two of you should meet before we went to the duke to ask for asylum."

Tavis seemed to consider this. "Glyndwr never struck me as a particularly bold man," he said to her at last. "Do you think he'll agree?"

She had to fight an impulse to just walk out. Tavis was about to ask Kearney to grant him a great kindness, one that carried grave dangers for the entire dukedom, and not only had the boy insulted her duke, he hadn't even shown the courtesy of referring to him as Lord Glyndwr. Despite his regal looks, she found it very easy to dislike this young lord. Already she couldn't imagine counseling Kearney to grant the boy's request. "I don't know, my lord," she said. "Do you intend to be as rude with him as you're being with me?"

"Keziah!"

She ignored her brother, keeping her eyes on Tavis.

"I wasn't aware that I was being rude," Tavis said. "You'll have to forgive me for not getting up to kiss your hand. After the half turn I spent being tortured in Kentigern's dungeon and the two days I had to ride in a merchant's cart, buried under a mountain of broadcloth, I still have trouble moving my legs without it causing me a good deal of pain. But I suppose you're right. I should be polite. Perhaps you'd like me to be cheery as well. And why not? I'm so looking forward to passing the rest of my days in the highlands. Better that than the dreary future I would have endured as duke of Curgh and king of Eibithar."

"That's enough," Grinsa said. He cast a disapproving look at Keziah. "Both of you."

The room felt terribly small. She wanted to be far away from Tavis. She didn't even wish to be near her brother just then. Part of her was so angry with the boy, she would have liked to strike him. Another part of her was so ashamed of herself she couldn't bring herself to look at either of them. She couldn't imagine what Tavis had been through over the course of the past turn. What bothered her, though, was that she hadn't even tried. She should have been able to muster some compassion for the boy. His scars screamed out for it. Yet his manner made such feelings nearly impossible, and she hated him for it.

An uneasy silence settled over the chamber, heavy as an early snow. Keziah needed to return to the castle to prepare for the banquet. They hadn't much time and there were matters they needed to discuss, but she couldn't bring herself to speak.

"Is Kearney planning on leaving in the morning?" Grinsa finally asked.

Keziah nodded, keeping her eyes fixed on the stone floor.

"So you'll have to convince him tonight to speak with me."

"I'll try."

"It's not enough to try, Kezi."

She looked up and found him staring at her, a pained expression in his yellow eyes.

"We've been through all this before," he said, pleading with her. "You know what's at stake. Don't make me convince you again, Kezi. We haven't the time."

She ran a hand through her white hair, glancing briefly at Tavis. He was still watching her, wearing that same placid expression. If he was angry with her or afraid that she wouldn't help them, he showed no sign of it. *What are you thinking?* she wanted to scream at him. *Do you feel anything anymore?*

She faced her brother again. "Kearney won't want to stay," she said. "He was reluctant to stop here in the first place. We could have covered another league today had we kept going, and had it not been for Gershon arguing that the men needed to rest, we would have."

"What if you told him that I had just come from Kentigern and that I had information about Brienne's murder?"

"That might persuade him to speak with you," she said. "If I told him that Lord Tavis was with you, that would certainly do it."

Grinsa shook his head. "No. In his eyes, and those of Lord Tremain, Tavis is guilty and a fugitive. I don't want Tavis being arrested the moment he sets foot in the castle."

"Kearney wouldn't do that! If he agrees to meet with both of you, that's what he'll do, without breaking faith!"

"I'm not worried about Kearney," Grinsa said. She could tell that he was struggling to keep his voice calm. "But Lathrop will be there as well—courtesy dictates that Kearney invite him to such a meeting. And as a minor lord he can't risk angering Aindreas by harboring the man all the kingdom believes killed Lady Brienne."

He was right, of course. Again. There was nothing worse, Keziah decided in that moment, than being caught between Kearney and her brother when both of them had set their minds to something.

"All right," she said. "When do you want to speak with him?"

"Midmorning. We'll be at the castle gate when the bells ring."

She nodded. "I'll ask Evetta to leave word with the guards that you're to be allowed in. How will you disguise Lord Tavis?"

"He'll still be wearing the novice's robe. And I'll be dressed as a cleric. Have the guards looking for visitors from the sanctuary."

She nodded a second time and peered out the window. The sky was darkening.

"I should go," she said. "I'm expected at the banquet."

Grinsa's smile looked forced. "Of course."

She wanted to put her arms around him again, but at that moment she didn't feel that she could. How could the distance between them seem so great in a room so small?

"My lord," Keziah said, offering a small bow to the boy.

"I've heard your duke is fair-minded, First Minister. I'm sure he'll grant our request."

The minister thought it a strange comment. But she had the distinct impression that the boy was trying to show his gratitude. "Until tomorrow, my lord."

She started toward the door, but Grinsa caught her hand. "Kezi," he said, making her look at him. "When this is over we'll have some time together, just the two of us. I promise."

It was an apology of sorts, an acknowledgment of how much he had asked of her already, and how much more was to come.

She tried to smile—he deserved that much. But in the end she failed. "I'd like that," she said. "But when will this ever be over?"

They followed a roundabout path to the castle gate. There weren't many Qirsi serving as clerics in the sanctuaries of the Forelands, but there were enough to make the brown robe Grinsa had borrowed convincing. Even in his white robe, however, Tavis did not look like a novice, especially with the scars he bore on his face. Better to avoid the crowds in the marketplace, Grinsa decided. It was going to be hard enough getting past the castle guards.

Tavis said little as they walked through the lanes of the city, and Grinsa was grateful for his silence. The boy had a way of finding just the right words to infuriate him. The evening before, just after Keziah left the sanctuary, her expression so sad that Grinsa wished they had never come to Tremain, Tavis had turned to him and asked, "So how long has she been sharing her duke's bed?"

Never mind that the young lord was disturbingly perceptive. He should never have asked the question at all. Tavis knew that such a love was forbidden by law. Everyone did. He had to know as well that merely to speak of it was to risk disgracing both Keziah and the duke.

Grinsa didn't even answer the question. He merely walked out of the dwelling, not returning until well after the evening meal. They hadn't spoken of the matter since, but Grinsa feared that before this day was through, the boy would say something even more damaging.

"No one is to know that Keziah is my sister," he said, looking at Tavis sidelong as they walked.

"I know. You've told me three times now."

"They can't know that I'm a Weaver, either."

The boy let out a short, mirthless laugh. "I know that, too."

"If someone asks, you were healed by other Qirsi in the sanctuary at Kentigern."

"Anything else?" Tavis asked, his voice flat.

"Actually, yes. It would be helpful if you managed to treat Lord Glyndwr with some courtesy. If he grants you asylum he'll be putting his house at risk. Aindreas might take it as an act of war and attack him."

"And Curgh will come to his defense. Kentigern can't possibly defeat both his house and mine."

Grinsa stopped, grabbing the boy's arm to pull him to a halt as well. Tavis wrenched his arm out of the Qirsi's grip and stood there, glaring at the gleaner.

"You're missing the point, you fool!" Grinsa said. "We're trying to stop a war, not start one on terms more favorable to the House of

Curgh. As long as you're living under the formal protection of Glyndwr, you can't take the throne. I'm hoping that will satisfy Aindreas enough to keep him from starting a war with your father."

"I understand," the boy said through clenched teeth. "But before you said that Glyndwr is risking war with Kentigern, and I was just saying that my father won't allow any harm come to Glyndwr if Kearney agrees to grant me asylum."

Grinsa looked away; after a moment he nodded. He had to remind himself that Tavis was barely past his Fating and had endured more in the last turn than most young nobles did in a lifetime.

"Come on," he said, starting to walk again. "The bells will be ringing soon."

They reached the gate a few moments later and the guards waved them through. As they hurried into the ward, however, crossing the gardens toward the duke's chambers, one of the guards called after them.

"What happened to the lad's face?"

"Thieves," Grinsa called over his shoulder, not bothering to stop and hoping the guards wouldn't ask why thieves would trouble themselves with a novice who carried no gold or valuables.

Keziah was waiting for them at the far end of the castle's second, smaller ward. There was another Qirsi with her, an older woman with short white hair whom Grinsa recognized as Tremain's first minister, the woman to whom he had instructed the cleric to deliver his message.

He could tell from looking at his sister that she was unsure of how to handle the introductions, so he introduced himself to the first minister.

"I take it you're not really a cleric," Evetta said.

Grinsa grinned and shook his head. "No."

The minister narrowed her eyes. "You look familiar. Have we met before?"

"Not formally. For the last few years I've traveled with the Revel. You've probably seen me at the banquets."

"Yes, of course," she said, nodding and smiling. "That's it." She turned to Tavis. "And who is your companion?"

Grinsa and Keziah exchanged glances, and after a moment she nodded.

"This is Lord Tavis of Curgh," Grinsa said.

Evetta's eyes flew to his face as if searching for some sign that he was joking. An instant later she looked at the boy again, with fear in her eyes, and loathing as well.

"Why have you brought him here?" she demanded. "Are you trying to drag Tremain into a civil war?"

"I'm trying to prevent a civil war," Grinsa said. "We've come here to ask Kearney to give the boy asylum. If he agrees, we'll be leaving with the Glyndwr army. If he refuses, we'll try one of the other major houses. Either way, we'll be out of Tremain before nightfall. You have my word."

"What makes you believe that Kearney would agree to such a thing?"

"Foolishness. Blind hope. Desperation. Take your pick. Most likely it's a combination of the three."

"Grinsa and I discussed this matter yesterday," Keziah said. "I think there's a good chance the duke will grant the boy's request. Certainly I intend to advise him to do so."

Evetta continued to stare at the young lord. "His wounds are mending nicely," she said at last, much to Grinsa's surprise. "The healing was done well." She looked at the gleaner. "Your work?"

He shook his head. "No. It was done by friends of mine in the sanctuary at Kentigern."

The woman nodded, facing Tavis once more. "The whole kingdom wants to know if you killed her, boy."

"Are they ready to believe that I didn't?" the boy asked.

"Is it the truth?"

"Yes," Grinsa said, before Tavis could answer. "He's innocent. I'm certain of it, as is the prioress of Bian's Sanctuary in Kentigern, who heard him speak with Brienne's spirit this past Pitch Night."

Evetta appeared to consider this. "Even serving my duke, I remain devoted to the Old Faith. The word of a prioress carries some weight with me. Still, I want to hear it from the boy."

Grinsa saw Tavis bristle and the Qirsi held his breath, fearing that the young lord would lash out at her as he had at Keziah the day before.

"I didn't kill her," he said after a brief silence. "I can't seem to convince anyone of this, but I had already started to love her. I wanted her to be my queen."

"You seem to have convinced Grinsa," the woman told him. "And Keziah as well. That's a good start."

"What about you?" Keziah asked. "Are you convinced?"

The minister gave a thin smile. "Not yet. But I'll let you take him to my duke, and I won't call the guards."

It was as much as Grinsa could have asked. "My thanks," he said, as the minister led them into the castle.

It was a short walk through the dark corridors to Lathrop's chamber. Evetta knocked on the door, and hearing her duke call for her to enter, she pushed it open and ushered them inside.

Lathrop was seated at his table, appearing too large for his chair. Kearney sat nearby, his legs crossed casually, his silver hair and easy grace giving him an air of elegance that Grinsa had seen in few others, even among the nobles of Eibithar. A third man stood beside Kearney's chair. He was bald with blunt, crooked features and a hard look in his eyes. A sword hung on his belt, and it seemed to Grinsa that his hand strayed to the hilt as they entered the room. He had never seen this man before, not even at the Revel banquets in Glyndwr, but Grinsa knew from all that Keziah had told him that this must be Gershon Trasker, Kearney's swordmaster. He knew as well that this would be a far more difficult conversation with the swordmaster present.

Keziah looked at Evetta, as if waiting for her to make the introductions. But Tremain's first minister shook her head.

"You requested this meeting," Evetta said. "It's yours to oversee."

"Who are these men, Keziah?" Kearney asked, getting to his feet.

"This is Grinsa jal Arriet, my lord. He's a gleaner with the Revel."

The duke was eyeing Tavis closely. He glanced at Grinsa for an instant and nodded. "I recognize you from the banquets," he said. "I also recognize the boy, though I'm not certain from where or when." He stepped closer to the young lord, examining his scars.

Tavis stood utterly still, suffering the man's stares, his eyes lowered.

"Where did you get these wounds, boy?" the duke asked.

Tavis looked at Grinsa.

"It's all right," the Qirsi said. "It's why we're here."

The boy raised his eyes, meeting the duke's gaze. "I got them in Kentigern's dungeon, my lord, from the duke himself."

Grinsa saw recognition flash like lightning in the duke's green eyes. "Tavis," he whispered. He took a step back, then whirled toward Keziah. "Demons and fire! You brought him here? What were you thinking?"

"I brought him here, my lord," Grinsa said. "Keziah merely arranged for us to meet. And she did so as a favor to me."

"To what purpose?" the duke demanded.

"Am I to understand that this is Lord Tavis of Curgh?" Lathrop asked, standing as well and stepping out from behind his table.

The boy had sense enough to bow to him. "My Lord Duke," he said. "I know that my presence here places your castle at risk. I wouldn't have come if I had anywhere else to turn."

"To turn for what?" Lathrop asked. "What is it you want?"

"We've come to ask Lord Glyndwr to grant Tavis asylum," Grinsa said, "pledging his protection to the boy until we can prove his innocence."

The duke of Tremain gaped at him, a look of utter disbelief on his face. Grinsa, though, was more concerned with Kearney, who kept silent at first, his expression betraying nothing. After several moments he turned to Keziah.

"You knew of this?"

"I met with Grinsa yesterday, my lord, at the sanctuary. We spoke of this then."

It was cleverly done. Keziah had made it clear to Grinsa that she didn't wish to lie to her duke any more than was necessary. He believed that eventually she would have no choice in the matter, but for now it seemed the truth was enough to mislead him and preserve their secret.

"And how is it that you know this man?" Kearney asked, sounding just for that instant more like her lover than her duke.

Keziah heard this as well, for a smile flitted across her features. "Grinsa and I grew up together, my lord. I've known him and trusted him all my life."

The duke frowned, but he seemed to accept this. "How has this come to concern you, gleaner?" he asked Grinsa. "The Revel is no closer to Kentigern than it is to Tremain."

"No, my lord, it's not. But I gleaned for the boy when we were in Curgh and I saw what awaited him in Kentigern."

"Is it common for gleaners to involve themselves this way in the lives of those they meet under the tent?"

"No. But neither is it common for a gleaner to foresee such plain injustice. What kind of a man would I be had I done nothing?"

The duke regarded him coolly. If he heard the goad in Grinsa's words he ignored it.

"You believe him innocent."

"I do. He was in Bian's Sanctuary this past Pitch Night, my lord. The prioress there heard him speaking with the Lady Brienne's spirit. They spoke as lovers, my lord. She didn't accuse him, and he showed no fear of her."

"Sorcery and a sorcerer's faith," the swordmaster muttered, shaking his head.

Kearney raised an eyebrow. "You wish to say something, Gershon?"

"You read the message from Kentigern, my lord." He gestured toward Tavis. "You know how they found him and the girl. Just because this Qirsi says he's innocent—"

"The prioress isn't Qirsi," Grinsa said.

Gershon glared at him a moment, then turned back to the duke. "Just because this Qirsi says he's innocent, doesn't make it so."

"Do you think the prioress would lie?" Kearney asked.

"She might. That's not the point. I'm sure this Qirsi would lie about what she said."

Grinsa saw Keziah open her mouth, her pale eyes blazing, and he shook his head. She clamped her mouth shut again and turned away.

"The gleaner isn't lying."

They all turned toward Tavis, who had spoken.

"I didn't murder Brienne, and I did speak with her in the sanctuary. Yes, it was my dagger that they found in her chest. And yes, they found me covered with her blood, in a room that had been locked from within. But I swear on her memory that I didn't kill her."

"And why should we believe you, Lord Tavis?" Kearney asked, his tone surprisingly gentle.

"You can see the scars on my face, my lord. The marks on my back and chest are far worse. Aindreas spared nothing with his torture. All because he wanted me to confess, and I wouldn't." His mouth twitched, as if he was trying to smile. "Call it Curgh pride if you want. Kentigern did. Certainly it would have been far easier for me to confess and be done with it. But I didn't kill her, and I would rather die than lay claim to another man's crime. Aindreas thought to brand me a murderer with these scars, when in truth, they're the most visible proof of my innocence."

For some time, none of them spoke. Kearney stepped to the window and stared out at the morning. The sky had turned grey and the air smelled like rain.

"Why seek asylum for the boy?" the duke asked. "You've gotten him out of Kentigern. Why not just flee the kingdom? He'd be just as safe that way."

"True," Grinsa said. "But as long as he's running, Aindreas will pursue him, and he and Javan will continue to threaten war."

Kearney turned and grinned. "You'd rather have him threatening me than Javan?"

Grinsa smiled in return. He could see why Keziah was drawn to this man. "As long as Tavis is under the shield of another house, he has no claim to the throne. I'm hoping that Aindreas will be satisfied by that."

"From what I've heard," Lathrop said, "he doesn't even want Javan to be king."

Grinsa nodded. "I've heard that as well. But none of the other houses will join him in opposing Javan, not if Tavis is removed from the line of ascension. There's also another matter to consider. If you grant him asylum, when we find the man who killed Brienne, Tavis can reclaim his legacy. If he flees the land, no one will ever accept him as duke or king. This is an innocent man, my lord. Someone has murdered Brienne in order to deny him his rightful claim to the throne. They can't be allowed to succeed."

Kearney seemed to weigh this briefly before turning to his swordmaster. "Gershon?"

The man shrugged. "I'm not convinced this will keep them from going to war."

"Perhaps not alone," Grinsa said. "But combined with your presence in Kentigern, it might."

"And where will the boy be while we're in Kentigern," Gershon asked.

"With you, of course."

"What?" the swordmaster said. "That's madness."

"Actually, it's not," Kearney said before Grinsa could answer. "In flight, Lord Tavis appears guilty. But by returning to Kentigern, even under my protection, he demonstrates his faith in his own innocence."

"Does that mean you'll grant his request?" Grinsa asked.

Before the duke could answer, the city bells began to toll, the sound drifting among the castle towers and walls like the singing of sanctuary clerics on the Night of Two Moons.

Kearney gave Lathrop a puzzled look.

"I don't understand it," Tremain's duke said, moving to stand beside him at the window. "The midday bells shouldn't ring for hours yet."

The tolling continued and soon they could hear people shouting as well, the voices growing nearer by the moment. Grinsa felt his stomach turning to stone, and he strained his ears trying to make out what Tremain's people were saying.

"What could it be?" Evetta asked. "Is there war? Has the pestilence come?"

No one answered. They were all listening, some with their eyes closed. Tavis appeared to be trembling, as though he thought that Kentigern's men had come for him.

It was Gershon who first heard, his face turning white as Keziah's hair. "Ean save us all," he breathed, looking at Kearney.

"What is it, Gershon?"

The man was crying, the tears running a crooked course down his face. "My lord," he said, his voice trembling. "The king is dead."

Chapter
Twenty-four

✦

Curgh, Eibithar

ven before Shonah crossed through the inner gate to the city ward, she could hear Hagan barking commands at Javan's men, his voice echoing off the castle walls. The swordmaster had been working the men far harder than usual for the past half turn. The duchess didn't have to watch the training sessions to know that much. She had heard the guards talking in the corridors outside her chambers. She had seen how weary Hagan himself looked, and she was certain that if the swordmaster was that tired, his men had to be suffering far more.

She had thought at first that Hagan was driving them so relentlessly out of frustration. Since word first came from Kentigern of all that had happened there, she had been terribly cross with her ladies and servants. She understood how difficult it was to keep from lashing out in fear and anger. It wasn't Hagan's boy who had been accused of murder, but he did have a son on the tor, just as she did. And if there was one man in the dukedom whose love for Javan could be said to run as deep as her own, it was Hagan. Who could blame the swordmaster for allowing his rage at Aindreas to affect him so?

Only in the last few days, however, since the arrival in Curgh of a messenger bearing word of Tavis's escape and Javan's captivity, had it occurred to her how foolish she had been. Hagan, she understood abruptly, was working the men so hard because he expected to lead them to war.

They hadn't spoken of it. In truth, they hadn't spoken at all since the arrival of the last message. Even before Daria's death eight years ago, Hagan had seemed uncomfortable around women, the duchess in particular. In the years following his wife's death he avoided her entirely. Perhaps she reminded him of Daria—many said that they looked alike. Or perhaps the pain of losing her had been such that he couldn't bear to be near any woman. Whatever the reason, they never saw each other except at banquets and, occasionally, when their paths crossed in the castle corridors.

Which was why on this day, at last, she had resolved to seek him out. With the duke and her son gone, she commanded the castle. The time had come for her to speak with the captain of the duke's guard.

Passing through the gate, she followed the stone path toward the south end of the city ward, where the men were training. They were paired off to practice their swordwork, not with wooden blades, she noted, but with steel, the ringing of their weapons filling the ward like Revel music. They even had on their mail and armor. Shonah shivered, despite the sun and the warm air blowing in off Amon's Ocean.

"Watch your footwork, you dullards!" Hagan shouted, as he walked among them. "Balance is everything!"

As Shonah reached the men and continued past some of them toward Hagan, several of them stopped fighting to stare at her, as if she were one of Ean's prelates entering a brothel.

His ire drawn immediately to their silence, Hagan whirled toward them. "Sluggards! Who told you to—?" He stopped, following the line of their stares and seeing the duchess. "My lady!" he said, his expression quite similar to those of the soldiers.

"Good day, swordmaster." She regarded the men briefly. "I take it the training goes well."

"It does." He narrowed his eyes. "Is there something I can do for you, my lady?"

"I'd like a word, yes," she said.

"Of course." He glanced at his men, all of whom had stopped to listen and look at the duchess. "Train, you dolts!" he shouted. "This doesn't concern you."

Shonah and the swordmaster walked off a short distance, stopping in the shadows of the south gate.

Hagan faced her, his light curls ruffled by the breeze. "What can I do for you, my lady?"

414

"You've heard nothing more?" she asked.

His mouth twitched. "No. You?"

In spite of everything, Aindreas appeared to be placing no limits on the number of messages Javan wrote, or Xaver, for that matter. Missives arrived from them both every few days. But though she knew Javan's hand, she could not tell if the content of the letters was his as well. They were vague at best. Each one assured her that he was well, that he was not being mistreated by Aindreas or his men. But he never mentioned Tavis by name, and he offered no guidance as to what she should have been doing to help him. She couldn't tell if he was trying to protect her, or if he was being told what he could and could not write. It seemed from Hagan's expression that he had similar doubts.

The duchess shook her head. "I don't know how much longer we can wait to do something. But I do know that Javan wouldn't have waited even this long."

His expression didn't change, but after a moment he nodded. "I agree. I . . . I haven't wanted to push you." He gestured toward the soldiers. "In the duke's absence, these men are yours to command. I've tried to see to it that they're ready for whatever you decide to do with them."

"And what do you think that should be?"

He looked away. "It's not my place to say, my lady."

"Nonsense! If Javan were here, asking you the same question, you wouldn't hesitate to give your counsel. I'm not asking any more of you than he would."

"Actually, my lady, you are," he said, still not meeting her gaze. "The duke has the first minister to rely on as well as me. But the Qirsi isn't here. And the duke also can draw on his own knowledge of military matters. You can't. You're asking me to make the decision for you, and I won't do that."

She had to admit that there was some truth to what Hagan was saying. She would be relying in great part on what he told her. But the rest of it was rubbish, and it was time he learned something about her.

"Hear me well, swordmaster," she said, her tone forcing him to look her way. "I may be a woman, and I may never have ridden to battle, but that does not mean that I will cede command of these men to you!"

"My lady!" he said, looking aghast. "That's not wh—"

"You may offer me what counsel you will, but I will decide what is to be done about Kentigern and his accusations against my son. And even if that means ordering you into a war of which you disapprove, I will expect you to follow my orders. If you feel you can't do that, tell me now and I will have you relieved of your command until my husband returns."

Hagan stared at her for several moments, saying nothing. Then he began to nod, the hint of a smile alighting on his lips.

"Your point is taken, my lady. My apologies."

She did her best to keep her expression grave. "None is necessary, Hagan. Now, please, answer my question. What do you think we ought to do?"

He looked back at his men, as if appraising the progress of their training. "In all honesty, my lady, I'm not certain. It was one thing for Kentigern to accuse Lord Tavis as he did and put the boy in his dungeon. But it's quite another to imprison the duke this way. It's almost as if he wants a war."

She didn't want to ask—she dreaded not his answer, which would be polite and vague, but the manner in which he offered it— but she had been grappling with the question alone for too long. "Do you think Tavis killed the girl?"

His eyes flicked to her face for just an instant. "I'm no judge of such a thing, my lady."

Just as she expected, but she had asked and there was no turning from it now. "But you saw what he did to your son."

"Yes, I did." He glanced at her again. "I'm sorry, my lady."

"It's all right. It's nothing I haven't thought on my own. You may not believe it, Hagan, but the boy's no murderer. His attack on Xaver was unforgivable; I wouldn't blame you if you hated him for it. Had Xaver done the same to Tavis I'd feel the same."

"If Xaver had done the same to Tavis," the man said quietly, "he'd have been hanged by now."

She stared at him, feeling her color rise. There was no arguing the matter. The swordmaster was right.

"For what it's worth, my lady, Xaver argues as you do. The one time he mentioned Lord Tavis in a letter, he made it clear that he thinks the lord innocent. And if he still believes that, who am I to doubt it?"

She smiled for just an instant. "Thank you, Hagan." She stared at the guards, as the swordmaster had done a moment before. "Are the men ready if we . . . if I decide to send them to war?"

This time he didn't hesitate at all. "They're ready, my lady. Kentigern's men can't stand against them. But with the duke held in the castle, I'd be reluctant to send them into battle. There's no telling what Kentigern might do if the fighting goes badly for him."

Shonah exhaled, knowing a moment of profound relief. She had thought of this as well, but had been afraid that Hagan might see her as weak for worrying about it.

"So that leaves us just where we were," she said.

He looked past her to the soldiers. "I suppose it does. So we'll wait?"

The man kept his tone even, but she read his disapproval in his dark eyes and the tightening of his jaw. Which was fine. She felt the same way.

"I'm tired of waiting," she said, drawing his gaze. "It may not be wise to start a war just yet, but perhaps a show of our resolve would help matters along."

"My lady?"

"Prepare the men, Hagan. If we hear nothing in the next three days, we'll ride to Kentigern. That should give the quartermaster time enough to prepare provisions for the journey."

"More than enough time, my lady."

Shonah nodded. "I know. But we'll give Aindreas a few days more to relent. Perhaps Javan would be bolder, but I must do this as I know how."

"You might be wise to speak with the duke's other advisors, my lady, to be sure you're doing the right thing. The first minister may not be here, but the second minister is, as are the underministers."

She knew that she should. She knew as well how difficult it must have been for Hagan to suggest such a thing. He agreed with what she had decided to do, and there was a chance the ministers would not. But while Shonah had come to respect Fotir, even to like him, she did not feel the same way about the other Qirsi who advised Javan. She thought them arrogant and she could tell that they had little regard for her. She had no desire to ask them for their counsel. The duchess smiled to herself. It seemed that the Curgh pride for which her husband and his ancestors were so famous had found its way into her blood as well.

"I'll inform them of my intentions," she said. "I see no need to trouble them beyond that."

Hagan raised an eyebrow, that small smile returning. "Are you certain, my lady?"

The duchess nodded, as if she had convinced herself. "Yes I am. Please see to it that the quartermaster is given all he needs, Hagan," she said, turning to walk away.

"I will, my lady."

She started back toward her chambers, frightened by the decision she had made, but comforted by the knowledge that they were doing something at last. She had only taken a few steps, however, when the swordmaster called to her.

"My lady!"

She stopped and faced him again.

"I think the duke would be pleased."

Shonah couldn't keep the smile from springing to her lips. She was certain that Hagan was right.

"Please keep me informed as you make your preparations," she said, turning once more.

"Of course, my lady."

Over the course of the next day it seemed to Shonah that the entire castle came to life, as if all the people who lived and worked there had been waiting for her to give them some purpose to which they could apply themselves. Perhaps she should have sensed this before—she felt certain that Javan would have—but she had been too absorbed with her own fears. Now, though, she felt their will, their mettle. The duke had spoken to her of the way a group of laborers with no common bond could come together if set to a task, or an army of men could find strength and courage in each other simply by readying themselves for war. But until now, she had not understood.

Late the following day, just after the ringing of the prior's bells, Hagan informed her that the quartermaster and his workers had readied the provisions.

"All the carts are loaded, my lady," the swordmaster said, as they walked slowly through the city ward, looking over the quartermaster's work. "We can begin our journey whenever you choose."

Hagan's men were training again, just beyond the last of the carts. It seemed to Shonah that there was a crispness to their movements that had been lacking just the day before. Even they were not immune to the excitement that had gripped the castle.

"Please commend the quartermaster for me," the duchess said, "and convey my thanks."

"I will, my lady."

They walked a short distance in silence. Then Hagan took a breath, as if readying himself to say something. Shonah knew what he would say before the words crossed his lips. They had both gotten messages that day, his from Xaver, hers from the duke. As always, the swordmaster was reluctant to ask her what the duke had said, as if Javan would be writing her love letters from Aindreas's prison tower.

"It's all right, Hagan," she said, suppressing a smile. "You can ask."

"Thank you, my lady. Did the duke write anything new?"

"No, I'm afraid he didn't." It had been a short letter, as most of them were. He and Fotir were fine. He hadn't seen the rest of his men, but he had no reason to believe they were being mistreated. He did mention Tavis by name, if only to say that there was no word on his whereabouts, but aside from that the letter contained nothing of note. "Did Xaver?"

The man shook his head, looking, despite his great height and powerful build, like a small boy. "Nothing at all."

She took his arm. "Patience, swordmaster. Aindreas hasn't done anything to harm them, and he'd have nothing to gain from doing so now."

He nodded, but kept his silence.

They had walked among the quartermaster's wagons and then completed a great circle around them. Returning to where they had started, Hagan stopped and the duchess released his arm.

"If there's nothing else, my lady, I should get back to training the men."

"You don't fool me, Hagan MarCullet. You want to yell at someone, and you're afraid to yell at me."

He grinned. "Yes, my lady."

She smiled as well. "Very well, Hagan. Go to your soldiers. But don't be too cruel to them. They've a long journey coming."

The swordmaster opened his mouth to reply. But before he could speak, a bell began to toll from the far end of town.

Shonah frowned. The prior's bells had already been rung; the next bells weren't to be struck until dusk.

"What do you think—?"

Hagan shook his head and raised a hand, silencing her. An instant later more bells began to ring.

"The first was the Moorlands gate," he said, his voice low, his head cocked so as to hear better. "The stone gate and far gate just joined in."

The duchess could hear voices now. At the far end of the city a great many people were crying out. Hagan's men had stopped their fighting with the first bells, and were now approaching Shonah and the swordmaster, their weapons ready.

Shonah's heart was pounding and she felt as if all the blood had left her body, leaving her cold and breathless.

"What is it, Hagan?" she whispered. "Are we under attack?"

The shouts were coming closer and bells were tolling at all the city gates.

"We're not being attacked," the swordmaster said, a single tear rolling down his face. "Listen to the cries and you'll understand."

It had happened only once before in his memory. Ailell of Thorald died when he was just a babe, too young to understand. But Hagan still remembered the death of the first Aylyn as clearly as he recalled the birth of his son and the death of his wife. He had been eight at the time, a mere boy in the court of his father, who was a thane in the Curgh countryside. His father's castle now belonged to Hagan's brother. As the secondborn, Hagan was given MarCullet Manor and the earldom that went with it. Daria's tomb was on the manor's grounds, and he rode to it several times each year, often with Xaver.

Living most of the time in Curgh Castle, they both considered the manor little more than a large country home. Even MarCullet Castle seemed insignificant and run-down. Certainly it was no fortress. And though a part of Hagan's heart belonged to the place, he was just as glad to live apart from it.

But thirty-three years before, when the elder Aylyn died, the castle had seemed to him the grandest place in the world. His father's servants and guards treated him as a prince, and he had spent his days pretending to be that and more. Until a man arrived on horseback, travel-stained and so weary he could barely stand, bearing the news of the king's death. He stayed but a few moments, long enough to water his horse and eat a small meal himself, before continuing on to Curgh Castle. But in that short time—a matter of just minutes—Hagan MarCullet realized that beyond the walls of MarCullet Castle lay a far greater world, one of which he wanted desperately to be part.

In most respects, Aylyn the First's death did little to change the course of life in his home. But Hagan never again saw the place as he had before the messenger arrived. Suddenly it seemed too small, too quiet, too far from anything of importance. Later in his life he came to understand how fortunate he was that his father didn't expect him to fulfill the duties of his earldom, for he would have gone mad had he been required to remain in the manor for all his life. As it was, the years leading to his Fating passed as slowly as a prison term. As he grew older, he also learned that the effect the king's death had on his youth was not at all unusual. Almost everyone he knew who was old enough to remember that day, did so with extraordinary clarity. And a great number of them still pointed to that day as a portentous one in their lives.

No doubt there were children in Curgh on this day who would remember hearing of Aylyn the Second's death until the end of their days.

Even before the messenger stepped into the castle to deliver his news to the duchess, cries of "The king is dead!" and "Bian spare our king!" reached the ward. Shonah's tears flowed freely from her bright green eyes and her face had turned pale. She looked in that moment so much like Daria that Hagan found it difficult to breathe.

The soldiers had gathered around them, waiting for the messenger to arrive. But already the news of the king's passing had left many of them too stunned to do more than just stand there, their arms hanging limp by their sides, the points of their swords resting on the ground. Hagan had rules about such things. Letting one's weapon touch the ground usually meant a run through the towers. But not today. Most of these men had never known another king of Eibithar. Probably they couldn't even imagine one. This was the worst possible time to send them to war. Yet Aylyn's death made war all but inevitable.

There was a brief commotion from the barbican. No doubt a crowd had followed the messenger all the way from the Moorlands gate only to be stopped now by the castle guards. An instant later the messenger stepped through the gate and entered the castle's city ward. Hagan couldn't help but stare at the man. It had been thirty-three years. The messenger who had told his father of Aylyn the First's death was an old man now. But this man looked just like him.

He could barely stand. Most likely he had covered the thirty-five leagues that lay between the City of Kings and Curgh with only a few brief rests. He might have gotten a new horse in one of the towns on the Moorlands. Messengers from Audun's Castle often did, knowing that anyone in his right mind would trade for a royal mount. But chances were the man hadn't slept in more than a day. His clothes were stained with mud and his face was streaked with dirt and sweat. Behind him came one of the guards, leading the man's mount to the castle's stable. The beast walked slowly with its head held low. It had been pushed to its limits as well.

The messenger stopped in front of the duchess and managed a deep bow.

"My lady," he said in a raw voice. "I come to you bearing heavy tidings. Our Lord Sovereign, King Aylyn the Second, has died."

"When?"

"Two nights ago, my lady. His ministers sent us to the twelve houses the following dawn."

Shonah's eyes met Hagan's. "They won't know in Kentigern for another day."

He had been thinking the same thing. "Were you told to speak with the duke?" he asked the messenger.

"No, my lord. They told me to find the lady."

Hagan nodded. Apparently the king's ministers knew of what had happened in Kentigern. That was something at least, though not much.

"Is there more to their message?" Shonah asked.

"No, my lady. Just that the king is dead."

She and Hagan exchanged a look. The ministers knew enough to send the messenger to Shonah, but they had nothing more to offer. It seemed that whatever was to happen in Kentigern would unfold without the intervention of the King's Guard.

"Very well," the duchess said at last. She actually managed a smile for the man. "You must be hungry and tired."

"Yes, my lady."

She gestured for a pair of the soldiers to come forward. "The two of you will take this man to the duke's hall. Be sure that he is well fed, and then find him a room in which to sleep."

The soldiers bowed to her and led the man away.

"Dismiss your men, swordmaster," Shonah said, facing Hagan again. "We have much to discuss. I'll be in the duke's chambers with his ministers. Join us there."

She was walking back toward the duke's ward before Hagan could respond. It was so much like something Javan might have done that he had to grin.

"You heard her," he called to the guards. "You're dismissed. But don't go far. I expect we'll be leaving for Kentigern within the next day."

Leaving his men, Hagan hurried to find the quartermaster. After a brief word with him, he continued to Javan's chambers, where he found the duchess already discussing the death of the king with the duke's Qirsi.

"Hagan, good," Shonah said as he entered the room. She was standing behind Javan's table looking discomfited, her color high.

The second minister appeared displeased as well, though as much by Hagan's arrival as by anything that had come before.

"Is there a problem, my lady?" the swordmaster asked, taking his customary seat by the duke's table.

"We're disturbed by this talk of leading the army to Kentigern," the second minister said before she could answer. "It's reckless. The duke would not approve."

Hagan had never been fond of the Qirsi. They were as arrogant as they were strange-looking. Perhaps he was too much a man of the sword, but he could not bring himself to trust their magic. There was something unnatural about it; such powers belonged with the gods, not with men and women of this earth. He had come to accept that the duke relied upon Fotir, but why Javan had ever seen fit to trust Danior jal Dania, the second minister, was beyond him. Given the choice between bold action and caution, he invariably chose the latter. Hagan had never heard him speak in favor of any use of the duke's army. It was almost as if the man wished swords and bows didn't exist.

"You believe you know better than the duchess or me what Javan would want?"

"The duchess, quite understandably, is concerned for her husband and her son. I don't believe she can consider this matter with a clear mind. And since you also have a son in Kentigern, I'm forced to question whether you can either."

Hagan glared at him. "How dare you!"

"I intend no offense, swordmaster, but you must admit that you have more on your mind just now than the well-being of the House of Curgh."

"Demons and fire, man! Shouldn't we all? The duke is in line to take the throne. From this day on, every hour that we tarry is an hour that Eibithar stands without a sovereign against the Aneirans and the emperor of Braedor. We must act now, not for this house, but for the entire kingdom!"

Danior snorted. It took Hagan a moment to realize that he was laughing. "Spoken like a true warrior, swordmaster. We must go to war to keep our enemies from starting a war."

"Better a warrior than a coward, you Qirsi bastard!"

"That's enough!" Shonah said, standing and stepping to the window. Hagan had seen the duke do much the same thing a thousand times. "You were starting to say something else, before Hagan arrived," she went on, glancing back at Danior. "What was it?"

"It was about the message, my lady. You said that the king's ministers sent no word other than tidings of Aylyn's death."

"Yes."

"Well, that should tell you something. If they thought that Curgh should march on Kentigern, they would have advised you to do so. They may even have offered to send the King's Guard."

"Don't be a fool," Hagan said. "They couldn't do anything of the sort. They don't advise the duke, nor can they expect to when he becomes king. He'll take his own ministers to Audun's Castle." *Hopefully he'll have sense enough to leave you here.* "They'd no sooner offer counsel to him than they would to Aindreas. And as to the King's Guard, when Aylyn died he left them powerless to do anything with his army. The guard isn't theirs to order about."

"I believe you're wrong on that point," Danior said. "Until the new king is formally enthroned, Aylyn's reign continues. His ministers can act on his behalf."

Hagan frowned. "So the king dies, and suddenly all power in the land falls to his Qirsi? I don't believe that for a moment."

"Believe what you will, swordmaster. The fact remains that the king's ministers could have sent word in support of the steps you're advising the duchess to take. But they didn't, and that should tell us something."

For several moments, no one spoke and the chamber was silent save for the soft calls of a dove perched on the castle wall somewhere near the window. The underministers had said nothing at all, which was probably wise. No matter what counsel they offered, they were bound to offend someone. And every person in the chamber had the power to keep them from ever becoming more than underministers.

"Aylyn is dead," the duchess said at last, "and so Javan should be king." She still looked frightened, as she had in the ward. But there was a look of resolve in her eyes as well. "I can't be certain what the duke would tell me to do under these circumstances. But I do know this: he would never abdicate, at least not without a fight." She faced the minister. "I hope you will forgive me, Danior, but I have to do this. Yes, I fear for my husband and my boy, but that's not why I'm doing this. It's Javan's way. It's the Curgh way. Surely you must see that."

"I do see it, my lady, though I'm not certain that the Curgh way, as you put it, is the wisest course. You realize, of course, that by marching on Kentigern you risk your husband's life." The Qirsi cast a look Hagan's way. "And your son's as well."

She nodded once. "I know that. I plan to make Aindreas understand that if he kills the duke, Curgh's army will destroy all of Kentigern." She turned to Hagan. "Can we leave at once?"

"No, my lady. I had a word with the quartermaster before I came here. We may be forced to lay siege to Kentigern's castle. In which case we'll need more men to build engines. The quartermaster will need a few hours more to add provisions to those he's already gathered. I'm afraid we'll have to wait until daybreak to leave."

"So you knew that I would take the army to Kentigern?"

He felt the second minister's eyes on him, but he refused to look at the man. "I had faith that you would choose the wisest path."

"I see," she said, sounding grateful. "Very well, we'll leave in the morning."

"I must say, my lady, that while I feel you've made the right decision, I don't believe you should be part of this journey. The dangers to you—"

She held up a hand, stopping him. "This is my war, Hagan, if it's to be a war. Would you tell Javan to remain here while his army marched to battle?"

He grinned. "Every time, my lady. But he wouldn't listen either."

"My lady," the minister said, "I must tell you one last time, I think you're making a grave mistake."

"I understand that, Danior. You and your ministers are free to go. I appreciate your counsel. It may not seem that way to you, but it's true nevertheless. I'll expect you to ride with us. You have the power of mists, don't you?"

"Yes, my lady."

"Good. We may need that before this is over." She faced Hagan again, as if dismissing the Qirsi.

Danior looked over at the other ministers, appearing unsure of what to do. After a moment they all stood and filed out of the chamber. The second minister hesitated at the door, as if intending to say more. But instead he merely shook his head and left.

"That was well done, my lady," Hagan said, standing as well.

"Thank you. I suppose you think that I've learned well from my husband."

"You wouldn't be the first to do so, my lady."

"Must a woman be taught such things by her man? Did it never occur to you that I might have come to our joining already possessing an aptitude for statecraft?"

He had to smile. It was something Daria would have said. "Of course it did. I don't think Javan could have loved you so much if you hadn't."

She smiled as well, though sadly. "Perhaps not."

They stood for some time, neither of them speaking, until finally the swordmaster cleared his throat and glanced toward the door.

"I should inform the men of what's been decided here. As it is, they'll be awake much of the night preparing and saying their goodbyes."

Shonah nodded, and he started toward the door.

"Hagan."

The swordmaster stopped, waiting.

"Are we about to start a civil war? Is that where all of this is leading?"

"This may bring us to war," he said, his voice hardening. "But we didn't start anything. Nor did Aindreas. Whoever killed Lady Brienne bears the blame for all of this. But Kentigern has imprisoned our duke, and now he holds our king. What kind of people would we be if we remained here doing nothing?"

Chapter
Twenty-five

✦

Kentigern, Eibithar, Adriel's Moon waning

rey light from the windows seeped across the chamber like a river fog, illuminating the parchment on Aindreas's table, but casting no shadows. Raindrops tapped softly on the castle roof and darkened the wooden shutters. The duke's midday meal sat before him, untouched and still warm. The flask of Sanbiri red was nearly empty.

Ioanna would have told him that it was too early to be drinking. She would have said that a man who was about to lead an army to war needed to be sober, that he needed to think clearly and be able to make decisions in an instant. Had she known this was his second flask, she would have been deeply disappointed. She might even have been ashamed. Had she known. Had she cared about anything anymore.

The Curgh boy had not only taken his daughter, but also his wife. Ean knew Aindreas hadn't been the best of husbands. He had taken pleasure in more than his share of serving girls over the years and had done a damned poor job of keeping it from Ioanna. But he had never taken a mistress, or loved any woman other than his duchess. He still remembered how beautiful she looked the night he met her at her father's castle, her golden hair falling to her waist, her dark eyes sparkling with candlelight. She had been like a gem, so exquisite he was almost afraid to approach her. Brienne had looked the same way the night she died. Brilliant as a jewel, more dear to him than all the riches in his treasury. The boy had taken everything from him. Or so it seemed. He had to remind himself at times that

429

he still had Affery and Ennis, that they were suffering even more than he, for they had lost a sister to murder and their parents to grief. He should have been with them. In spite of the war that loomed before him, he should have been comforting them, assuring them that they were still loved. But he could no more give up his wine than Ioanna could give up her bed and the solitude in which she had taken refuge since Brienne's death.

Instead, he pushed aside the plates of food, drained his glass, and poured the rest of the wine. Then he picked up the scrolls that lay before him. The first had come a few days ago, the same day that the messenger arrived from Audun's Castle bearing news of the king's death. Aindreas would never have believed that any letter could compete with such tidings for his attention. Yet this one had. It was from Kearney, the duke of Glyndwr, and it announced his intention to ride to Kentigern as some sort of peacemaker.

Kearney was a decent man. His father and Aindreas's had been friends and allies, and for that reason alone Aindreas had a certain affection for the man. But perhaps owing to the remoteness of his dukedom and the low station of his house, Kearney remained younger than his years. He clung to ideals that had no place in the real world and he was prone to making grand, foolish gestures, as his letter made all too clear. His army, though reputed to be well trained, was small. Even if he left just a token force to guard his castle, he couldn't have been bringing more than seven or eight hundred men. How could a force of that size hope to keep the armies of Kentigern and Curgh from going to war? Aindreas had every reason to ignore the message. Glyndwr was powerless to stop this war and he had no business trying.

Still, the letter remained on his table, and though Aindreas had not allowed it to stay his hand, neither had he been able to put Kearney's plea for restraint out of his mind. Maybe it was because the letter and word of Aylyn's passing had come on the same day, as if the gods themselves were warning him away from this war. Perhaps Aindreas had been moved by the sheer folly of what the man was doing. Surely Kearney and his renowned swordmaster knew that they were no match for the two armies. But they hadn't allowed this to deter them.

Aindreas couldn't say for certain why he kept the letter, or why he found himself reading it again and again. There was little to it really. He and Leilia were deeply saddened by the news of Brienne's death, he would be leading a contingent of soldiers to Kentigern immediately, and he hoped that Aindreas would do nothing to bring the kingdom any closer to civil war. That was all. Even the language was rather plain. Save for the ending.

> Brienne's death is a tragedy for the entire land. They will
> sing of her beauty and strength long after you and I are
> gone. Let us not allow those songs to become dirges for
> the young men of Kentigern and Curgh. Let us not allow
> her memory to be darkened by the shadow of civil war.

Aindreas had intended to go to the prison tower the night Aylyn died, to tell Javan once more that he would never allow him to take the throne, that notwithstanding the Order of Ascension, he would spend the rest of his life making certain that no man of Curgh ever wore Audun's crown. After reading Kearney's message, however, he went to the cloister instead, and spent the evening chanting for the king. He hadn't been to the prison tower since. No doubt Javan had heard the bells tolling and the people crying in the castle wards and city lanes. Curgh knew that Aylyn was dead and that the throne should be his. That was enough to satisfy Aindreas; at least it had been until this morning.

He should have expected this second message, the one that had arrived just a few hours before. The only thing surprising about it was that it hadn't come sooner. But still it had caught him unaware. Aindreas was furious with himself. He had allowed Kearney's maudlin sentiments to cloud his judgment and distract him from what he should have been doing, readying his men and his castle for battle.

According to this paper, which was written the day before he received word of the king's death and signed by one of his agents in the north, Javan's army had left Curgh Castle four days ago, led by Hagan MarCullet and the duchess. Aindreas had always been fond of Shonah; he didn't relish the idea of facing her in battle. But she had left him little choice. He had only five or six days to prepare, and he could hardly afford to waste any time worrying about her. Hagan would have his men battle-ready—no doubt he had been working them like plow horses since he first heard that Tavis had killed Brienne. Aindreas could only hope that Villyd, his own swordmaster, had been doing the same. He muttered a curse, knowing that he should have seen to it himself days ago.

There was a knock at his door. Shurik, at last.

"Enter!" he called.

The Qirsi walked in, looking like a living corpse in the silver light. "You called for me, my lord?"

"Just after the midmorning bells," the duke said acidly. "Where have you been?"

"My apologies, my lord. I was observing the swordmaster as he trained the men. And after that I went to check on our guests from Curgh. I got here just as your meal arrived and I assumed you'd want to dine alone."

Aindreas waved a hand, dismissing the man's excuses. "Fine, fine. You're here now."

"Yes, my lord."

"How's Villyd doing with the men?"

"Sir Temsten has them performing quite well, my lord. I know little of swordplay, but they look most impressive to me."

"Good. It seems we'll be sending them to war before too long."

"My lord?"

Aindreas handed him the parchment. The Qirsi took a moment to read it, an eyebrow going up as he did. Then he placed it on the table once more.

"Do you think Curgh's men will fight for their duchess as they would for their duke?"

"Hagan will see to it that they do," Aindreas said. "And they won't be fighting for their duke or their duchess. They'll be fighting for their king. Curgh's army is not to be taken lightly."

"Of course not, my lord."

Aindreas glanced at his wineglass. He dearly wanted to empty it and have the cellarmaster bring him another flask. But he thought it wise to wait until the first minister had gone.

"I want you to go back to Villyd. Tell him that he and his men are to see to the castle's defenses. Then go to the quartermaster and tell him to make preparations for a siege. I want this castle ready to withstand Curgh's assault in four days. That should leave us a bit of time before Hagan and his men arrive."

"You'll pardon me, my lord, but I don't think that would be our wisest course."

Aindreas stared at the man, wondering if he had heard him correctly. "What? Why not?"

"It's been nearly a full year since the harvest, my lord. The season's crops will be bountiful, but they're not ready yet and our stores are low. The castle is ill prepared to withstand a siege."

"Don't be ridiculous! This is Kentigern Castle you're speaking of! This house has withstood sieges from the most powerful armies of the Forelands. It's not going to fall to Curgh!"

"I would hope not, my lord. But the fact remains that our stores of food are rather low and unless you're ready to turn away the people of the city, or at least let Javan and his men starve in the prison tower, we have too many people to feed."

"So you're saying the castle would fall?" Aindreas asked, still not willing to believe what the man was telling him.

"I'm saying it might."

"Impossible," the duke said. But he had to admit that it had been several turns since he had checked on the stores. He rubbed his brow, thirsting for that wine more than ever. "How long could we hold out?"

The Qirsi shrugged. "I don't know for certain, my lord. I can find out for you."

It wasn't likely to matter much. Aindreas had never endured a siege as duke, but he had read accounts of them written by his ancestors and he knew that even the threat of starvation could break the spirit of a defending army.

"What would you have me do?" he asked, his stomach feeling empty and hard.

"The castle might not be fit to hold off a siege," the Qirsi said, a grin spreading across his face. "But the army is more than ready to go to war. Take the battle to Curgh, my lord. The duchess and her swordmaster are expecting you to wait for them atop the tor. But if you can beat them to the northern fringe of the wood, you can force them to fight with the Heneagh River at their backs."

This was the last thing Aindreas had expected him to say. It was a bold idea, one that hadn't even occurred to him. Perhaps it was time the duke put his wine flasks away and took up his sword again. He squeezed his eyes shut, trying to clear his head. The north edge of Kentigern Wood was just under twelve leagues from the castle. If they left that day and used the light of the moons to march by night, they could be there within three days. Then again, if this weather held, their progress would come slower, and they would have a harder time marching at night.

"How quickly can the quartermaster be ready?" Aindreas asked.

"I'll have to ask him, my lord. But the men won't be going far and we'll need only a half turn's supplies. Besides, he's been preparing already. It's no secret that you've been threatening Lord Curgh with war. It should take him less than a day to prepare."

"What if we don't reach the edge of the wood before they're across the river? What if we have to fight them in the forest?"

"We know the wood better than they do, my lord. I believe the swordmaster has trained the men to fight among its trees and hollows. There isn't a wood of any size within twenty leagues of Curgh. Javan's men may be ready to wage a war on the Moorlands, but in the wood the advantage is ours. And don't forget, Kentigern's army will be led by its duke. The men of Curgh will be led by a woman."

Aindreas nodded, but said nothing. He turned in his chair to look out the window. The rain was falling harder now, though the sky near the horizon appeared somewhat brighter than it had a short time before. He felt the minister watching him, yellow eyes fixed on the back of his head, but all he could do was sit there, wishing for a sip of wine and wondering what his father would have done. This castle, and the tor on which it sat, had always been the foundation of his house's strength. It seemed folly to leave it now. But with the stores low and Curgh's army commanded by its duchess, Shurik's counsel made a great deal of sense.

"Perhaps I've overstepped," the Qirsi said, seeming to misinterpret Aindreas's silence. "Forgive me, my lord. In all likelihood the castle can endure a siege. We may have to limit meals at the end, but chances are we will prevail. As you say, this is Kentigern Castle. Marching to the river carries risks. We'd be foolish to try something so daring."

The duke glanced back at him for a moment before turning his gaze to the rain once more. He had never considered himself a cautious man. Javan was cautious. Aylyn had been cautious. But not he. Living so close to the Tarbin, the men of Kentigern had to be fearless and venturesome. The Aneirans regarded caution as a sign of weakness. None of the other Eibitharian dukes understood that, because none of them lived each day under the threat of war. The other houses saw him as reckless, just as they had his father before him.

Aindreas didn't recognize himself. Curgh's army was being led to Kentigern by a woman, and he was content to sit in his castle and await a siege? That might have been how they did things in Wethyrn or Caerisse, but not in Eibithar, and certainly not on the tor. Aindreas was ashamed that it had taken the words of a Qirsi to remind him of this.

"Are you well, my lord?"

"I'm fine," the duke said, facing the minister again. "Go to Villyd and the quartermaster. Tell them we march with the prior's bells. If the quartermaster isn't ready by then, so be it. He and his men will have their carts. They'll catch up with us when we stop to make camp."

"But the prior's bells, my lord. That's but a few hours from now. If we wait for dawn, we should still have time to reach the river before the Curgh army."

"Possibly. But if we leave today we'll be certain of it." He stood, grinning at the Qirsi. "You've roused me from my torpor, Shurik. This is no time to grow timid."

The man gave a small smile. "No, my lord."

"Go on then. See to it that the preparations go smoothly. Villyd doesn't like to be rushed, even when he needs to be. So make certain he understands that I'll be ready to go when the bells are rung. And have my horse brought to the duke's tower. Let the men see that I intend to ride with them."

"Very good, my lord," the Qirsi said, turning to go.

"Shurik."

The minister stopped and looked at him again, waiting.

"You understand that you'll be coming as well."

"Of course, my lord. I wouldn't have it any other way."

The Qirsi bowed to him and left the chamber. Aindreas pushed himself back from his table and stood, hesitating for a moment as he looked down at the dark wine in his glass. He shook his head once and walked to the center of the room. There, he pulled his sword from its jeweled scabbard and examined the blade. Even in the dull light of this grey day, it shone like Panya on a clear, cold night, drawing another smile from the duke. It had been too long since he last raised his weapon in battle. This was what he needed, more than

DAVID B. COE

wine, more than finding Tavis. Kearney had sent his plea for restraint to the wrong castle. Curgh was marching against him, and though he had put off his vengeance longer than anyone could have expected, that time had now passed. They wanted war, and he was glad to give it, finally. He would strike a blow against all of Curgh, not from his chamber, but from his saddle, not as the defender against a siege, but as a warrior. It was perhaps the wisest counsel Shurik had ever given him.

Xaver's clothes reeked of sweat and felt stiff and filthy against his skin. His hair was matted and his head itched. Occasionally the guards brought them warm water with which to bathe, but their bedding hadn't been changed since the morning they were brought to the prison tower, and the lone window in their small room did not allow in enough air to carry away the sour smells of their captivity.

It had gotten so bad that the previous night, Fotir had conjured a wind to stir the stale air in their chamber. Then he had sent a second wind across the narrow corridor to the duke's room, drawing the ire of the two guards, who commanded him to stop. The minister ignored them at first, allowing the air to flow through the narrow grate at the top of the door, but when they threatened to withhold meals from all of them, including Javan, he let the wind die out.

They had been prisoners for nearly half a turn, though it seemed far longer to Xaver. They had heard no news of Tavis in that time, leading Xaver to hope that perhaps his friend had managed to escape the city. Certainly, if Aindreas had captured the young lord again, he would have come to gloat. But it had been days since they had seen either the duke of Kentigern or his first minister.

They knew the king was dead, having heard the bells ringing and the cries going up throughout the castle. A short time later a guard came to deliver the news to them, a small courtesy that stood in stark contrast to the treatment they had received before and since. Javan offered no response to the news of Aylyn's death, other than to say that he had been a fine king. He kept his silence the rest of the day, not even bothering to come to his door to receive his evening meal. Usually when a king died, Fotir explained later that night, speaking in a whisper, the dukes of Eibithar's major houses traveled to the City of Kings for his funeral and the investiture of the new

436

king. Clearly, though, Javan would not be going, and, he guessed, neither would Aindreas.

"The other dukes are about to find that they have no king," the Qirsi said, candlelight flickering in his bright yellow eyes.

"And what will they do?"

"It's hard to say. I find it hard to imagine any of them wanting to get between Curgh and Kentigern. If they act together, they might, but that's even harder to imagine."

Xaver shook his head. "You mean they'd let us go to war?"

"I'm not certain they're capable of doing anything else."

The next two days passed much as had the ones before Aylyn's death. Guards came and went, sometimes bringing meals or fresh water. But neither Aindreas nor Shurik came to the tower, and no one acknowledged what seemed so obvious to Xaver: that Javan was now king, and that Aindreas, by continuing to imprison him, was guilty of treason.

The third day dawned grey and rainy, a welcome respite from the heat and sunshine of the previous several days. Otherwise, that morning was no different from those that had come before. But an hour or two after the midday bells, Xaver heard voices calling from the stairway and, soon after, footsteps on the stone stairs.

The two guards abruptly straightened, standing stiffly with their arms at their sides. A moment later, Aindreas stepped into the corridor. He wore gloves and riding boots and a cape of silver and blue that bore the Kentigern crest. His sword hung on his belt, and he carried a second, two-handed weapon in a baldric strapped to his back.

Despite his warrior's dress, however, the duke looked terrible. His eyes were red and sunken, his face unnaturally flushed. Xaver wouldn't have thought it possible for a man of Aindreas's size, but the duke looked gaunt and sickly.

Xaver made room at the door for Fotir so that both of them could peer out through the grate. Javan stood at his door, staring at Aindreas as well, his mouth set in a thin line.

"Have you come to fight me, Aindreas?" the duke asked. "Or have you started a war with the Aneirans?"

Kentigern grinned in a way that made Xaver shudder.

"Neither, Javan. Though I am going to war. You were right about that much." He stood there a moment, looking first at Javan and then at Xaver and the first minister. "Well?" he said at last. "Aren't you going to ask who we're to fight?"

Xaver didn't have to ask. In that instant, none of them did.

"Who?" Javan finally said, his voice flat.

"Your army, of course. Word came this morning. They marched from Curgh four days ago."

Four days ago. Most likely the same day the people of Curgh learned of Aylyn's death. Xaver should have expected this, even before Aindreas came to them. His father would never allow Kentigern to deny Javan the throne. In many ways, Hagan had just as much pride as the men of Curgh. Add to that the MarCullet temper, and it was a wonder this hadn't happened sooner.

"You shouldn't be here, Aindreas," the duke said. "You should be at the sanctuary, praying to Bian for kindness and mercy. If you're going up against Hagan you'll need it."

Kentigern stepped so close to Xaver's door that the boy could see the dark tiny veins of red in the man's eyes. "Is that what you think, boy?" he said. "Is Daddy going to come and rescue you?"

"Leave him alone, Aindreas! He's done nothing to you."

The duke laughed, his breath stinking of wine. He turned and walked slowly to the duke of Curgh's door. "Actually, Javan, Hagan isn't commanding your army. He is with them," he added, glancing over his shoulder, as if he was saying this for Xaver's benefit. "But the army of Curgh is commanded by the duchess."

Javan's face blanched. "Impossible. Hagan wouldn't allow it."

Xaver knew better. His father would have been powerless to prevent it.

"Nevertheless, I'm told that she rides at the front of your army, just as a commander should. From what I hear, she's even carrying a sword, which, if I'm not mistaken, gives me the right to kill her."

"You bastard! You wouldn't dare!"

"We both know what your son took from me. Why shouldn't I take someone just as dear from you and him?"

"Bian damn you to the fires!"

"Come now, Javan," Aindreas said with a grin. "This isn't my fault. She chose to come. What kind of a soldier would I be if I didn't meet her blade with my own?" He paused, a sly look on his face. "Of course, if you really want to save her, there is something you can do."

The boy saw his duke waver, as though he knew he shouldn't ask, but couldn't keep himself from doing so.

"What can I do?"

"Give me Tavis," Aindreas said quickly, moving as close to

Javan's door as he had been to Xaver's a moment before. "Tell me where I can find the boy and I'll let you and your men go. This war will be over before it ever begins and Shonah will be safe."

Javan stared at him, shaking his head. "You want me to trade one of them for the other? You're mad! I'd never do such a thing, and Shonah would never forgive me if I did."

"Then I'll take her from you," Aindreas said, ice in his voice, "just as Brienne was taken from me."

"You'll die trying."

"I don't think so. I have considered, however, whether it might break the spirit of Curgh's soldiers to see their duke's head mounted on a pike and carried along with Kentigern's colors before my army."

Javan's face stretched into a grin. "Let's find out, shall we? I think you'll find that it will do the opposite. They'll fight like Bian's demons, for you'll not only have killed their duke, but also their king."

"You're no one's king!" Aindreas said, his hand flying to the hilt of his sword.

"Aren't I? Didn't I hear bells ringing in the streets of your city three days ago? Didn't I hear your people crying for Aylyn?"

"That doesn't make you king!"

"The Rules of Ascension say otherwise."

"The Rules of Ascension be damned! They mean nothing without the consent of Eibithar's dukes! And as long as I draw breath, I will not honor Curgh's claim to the throne! You will never be king, Javan! I swear it to you before all the gods! I swear it to you on Brienne's memory!"

"Tavis will be proven innocent," Javan said. "And when he is, every house in the land will recognize me as their king. If you refuse to do the same, you will be branded a traitor and executed, and your house will be removed from the Order of Ascension for a hundred years. Think of it, Aindreas. You know the law. As things stand now, your boy might someday be king. Continue with this folly, however, and he will inherit nothing from you but a shamed house."

"Don't you dare to speak to me of shame! You continue to defend your son, though all the land knows him to be a drunkard, a murderer, and a coward! You shame the entire kingdom! And you doom your wife to a bloody death!"

He turned on his heel and started toward the stairs.

"Aindreas!" Javan called. "Don't do this! You can still stop this war!"

The duke paused at the top of the stairwell, but only for an instant. He didn't even turn.

"Aindreas!" Javan cried again, as the large duke disappeared down the steps. "Aindreas!" Curgh's duke closed his eyes and rested his forehead against the bars of his door. "Ean forgive me," he whispered. "I've killed her."

"No, my lord," Fotir said. "The duchess leads the army by her own choice and, I'm certain, over the objections of Lord MarCullet. Your men will give their lives to guard her, just as she has chosen to risk hers to win your freedom. Take pride in her, my lord. She is an extraordinary woman. I expect the duke of Kentigern will find that she is a more formidable foe than he anticipates."

"Perhaps," the duke said. "She is extraordinary. But she's no warrior. Leading the army to war is one thing, leading them into battle is quite another."

"My father knows that, my lord," Xaver said. "He won't allow her to ride into the fighting."

The duke managed a smile. "You're still young, Master Mar-Cullet, and so have yet to learn that women like the duchess, and your own mother for that matter, rarely ask permission to do anything. If my wife decides to lead the charge, there will be nothing your father can do about it. I just hope she has sense enough to stay back when the battles begin."

"I find it strange that the duke is riding to battle at all," Fotir said. "Why would he leave the castle when Kentigern is renowned for its ability to withstand any siege?"

"He must believe there's an advantage to be gained by meeting the Curgh army," Xaver said. "Perhaps he means to use the wood."

The Qirsi nodded. "Or the Heneagh. If the Curgh army left only four days ago, he still has time to beat them to the river."

Javan took a long breath. "That may be it," he said. "It's also possible that he's so desperate to leave this castle that he's making poor decisions."

Fotir frowned. "My Lord?"

"He's been searching for Tavis for half a turn, with no success. As much as he talks of killing me and denying me the crown, he can't hurt me. It would appear that he was trying to win the throne for himself. He'd risk war with all the other houses. This is his best chance to strike a blow against the House of Curgh. He may be so eager for war that his judgment is clouded."

"Good," Xaver said. "That should work to our advantage."

The duke shook his head. "Desperate men make for dangerous opponents, Master MarCullet. I'd have thought your father had taught you that."

He had, of course, though only in the context of single combat. It hadn't occurred to Xaver to apply the lesson to a conflict with the commander of an entire army. He could only hope that his father wouldn't make the same mistake.

Even before his meeting with Kentigern's duke, Shurik had ordered Villyd and the quartermaster to prepare for the march to the Heneagh River, so certain had he been that Aindreas would follow his counsel. On his best days, the duke could be steered one way or another with little effort. When he was drunk, it became laughably easy. If anything, the minister had been too successful. He had hoped to leave with first light the following morning, not this same day. He had a task to complete before they marched from the castle, and it promised to be far more difficult in daylight than it would have been at night. But having convinced the duke that they should try to beat Curgh's army to the Heneagh, he couldn't very well argue for a delay until dawn.

The minister made his way back to the castle's inner ward to check on the quartermaster's progress. Two of the carts needed repairs, but the castle's wheelwright was already working on them. They weren't likely to cause any delays. On the other hand, the kitchenmaster had been stingy with some of the food, particularly the cheese and dried meats. The quartermaster had been forced to send some of his workers to the marketplace to buy some supplies, slowing his preparations considerably. Apparently food stores in the castle were dwindling, though they weren't yet as low as Shurik had made it seem when he spoke with Aindreas.

Leaving the quartermaster, the Qirsi walked to where Villyd was shouting orders to Kentigern's soldiers.

Seeing the minister approach, Kentigern's swordmaster raised a hand as if to beckon him over, his brow furrowed with concern.

Villyd was a compact man. He was actually a bit taller than Shurik, but because of the swordmaster's broad chest and shoulders and his muscular limbs, he looked shorter than he really was. He had a round face and small blue eyes, and he always appeared to be squinting. Despite his appearance, he was a skilled swordsman who had earned the complete respect and loyalty of his men. For a man of war, he was also surprisingly tolerant of the Qirsi who served in Kentigern Castle. Shurik actually liked him.

"First Minister," he said as the minister stopped in front of him. "Did the duke tell you how many men he wished to keep here in the castle?"

Perhaps he could have lied, telling the man to take more soldiers to the Heneagh than was necessary. But such a lie carried great risks; it was too obvious, too easily traced.

"No, swordmaster. He didn't tell me anything. I believe he was leaving this to your discretion."

Villyd nodded. "He often does. In that case, I intend to leave seven hundred men here and take the rest. That's a thousand men. I can't imagine Hagan will have any more."

Shurik frowned. Seven hundred men to defend the castle and city. He wondered if Yaella and the duke of Mertesse would be expecting that many.

"You think I should take more?" the swordmaster asked, looking concerned. "I hate to leave the castle undermanned. The Aneirans will know we've gone. They might use this opportunity to attack."

"I suppose they might," Shurik said. "I'm sure a thousand men will be enough. And if the Curgh army manages to break through our lines, there'll be plenty of men here to hold them off."

"So you do think I should take more."

"I'm just a minister, swordmaster. I know very little of such things."

"But you know the duke. You know what he wants."

Shurik grinned. "He wants to win this war, swordmaster. He wants to avenge the murder of Lady Brienne. All of us do."

Villyd nodded. "Yes. Yes, of course." He stood there for a moment, appearing to consider the minister's words. "Perhaps we can spare another two hundred men," he said at last.

"Whatever you think best," Shurik said, suppressing a smile.

"Five hundred should be enough to defend Kentigern," he went on, as though still trying to convince himself. "And with twelve hundred men marching against the Curgh army, we shouldn't be away from the castle for very long."

"That strikes me as sound reasoning, swordmaster." Shurik glanced up at the sun. He hadn't much time before the prior's bells. "Now, if you'll excuse me, I have other matters to which to attend before we leave."

"What? Oh, of course, First Minister. Please forgive me."

Shurik was already walking away. "Think nothing of it, swordmaster."

"And thank you," the man called.

The Qirsi raised a hand, but didn't bother to look back. The man would have kept him talking all day long.

He made his way out of the inner ward through the south gate, then entered the nearest tower of the outer wall and followed the tight, dark corridors to the castle's western gate, the Tarbin gate as it was called. Unlike the city gate, which was kept open during the day except in times of war, the Tarbin gate almost always remained closed, even the wicket gate. The gate faced Aneira. Indeed, since no structure in all of Eibithar stood closer to the Aneiran border than Kentigern Castle, one could argue that the Tarbin gate was the kingdom's first defense against an Aneiran invasion.

Standing at the entrance to the gate, Shurik could not help but admire its sheer power. Each of the four portcullises was as thick as a man's thigh, and constructed of oak from Kentigern Wood and iron from the city's forges. Beyond the portcullises stood an equally dense door, also made of oak and locked with massive iron bolts. And beyond that lay a drawbridge, raised, of course, which could be lowered to provide passage across the deep pit separating the barbican from the road leading up the tor from the river. There were arrow loops on both sides of the gate, with chambers behind them for the duke's archers, and murder holes in the ceiling, from which soldiers could attack intruders. But so strong were the defenses at this entrance that the only guards stationed here stood outside, manning the wall between the towers on either side of the gate and the smaller spires at the outer edge of the Tarbin barbican. Within the gate, Shurik was completely alone.

For years he had been telling people that he possessed three magics: gleaning power, the power of fire, and the language of beasts. He told Fotir as much the first night they spoke in the Silver Bear. Like so much else he told his duke and others, however, this was only partially true. He did have all those powers. But unlike most Qirsi, he had a fourth as well. He was a shaper. He decided long ago to keep this a secret. Many Qirsi became first ministers possessing only three magics; he didn't need to reveal the full extent of his power to gain a position of influence. And he had learned long ago that it could be helpful to know more about his adversaries than they knew about him.

For obvious reasons he didn't use his shaping power very often, and he knew that he would tire quickly using it this day. But he didn't have to destroy the door or the portcullises, he merely had to weaken them.

He started with the iron hinges of the door, closing his eyes and pushing the power out from his mind as if it were a bad memory. Almost immediately he felt a dull, throbbing pain building behind his eyes. He was going to be in sorry shape before this was over. He wondered if he'd be able to ride with the duke. He could hear the metal creaking under the strain of what he was doing to it, and he made certain to stop before the hinges failed entirely.

He only weakened two of the door's four hinges, leaving the others for Mertesse and his men. There was nothing he could do about the drawbridge, either, but the Aneirans would find a way around that. The Qirsi was most concerned with the portcullises, and, once he was done with the door, he directed his magic at them, attacking the wooden crossbeams on all four of the immense lattices. He worked as quickly as he could, wiping the sweat from his face, and fighting the nausea that seemed to grow with each pulse in his aching head. He felt the magic flowing through him, as he had in times past. But he was older now—he hadn't exerted himself like this in years—and he could almost feel the life pouring out of his body. For a moment he feared that he would fail before the castle's defenses.

Again, he didn't weaken all of the beams. It would have been too apparent if every one of them failed at the same time. But he worked on enough of them, stretching and thinning the wood in certain places so that it would be far easier for the rams of the Aneiran army to break the portcullises down.

When he finished, he staggered to the nearest wall and fell back against it, struggling to catch his breath. His hair and clothes were damp with sweat and there was a pounding in his head that made the ground seem to pitch and roll like a ship at sea.

He had known that it would be this way, though perhaps not quite this severe, and he knew what he would tell the duke. He could even guess how Aindreas and his men would respond, and while he was not looking forward to their taunts, that seemed a very small price to pay. Pushing away from the wall, he stepped unsteadily back into the narrow corridors and returned to the inner ward the same way he had come from it, taking care once more that he wasn't seen until he was a good distance from the gate.

Stepping into the ward, Shurik immediately spotted the duke sitting atop his great mount, his blue and silver cape soaked with the rain that continued to fall. The minister's smaller horse stood nearby, and Shurik hurried to it.

"We were looking for you, First Minister," Aindreas called to him as he approached.

"I was . . . walking, my lord."

"You don't look well. Are you ill?"

Shurik glanced toward the soldiers, making himself appear embarrassed. "It's . . . it's been some time since I rode to war, my lord," he said, lowering his voice.

Aindreas stared at him a moment before starting to laugh. The Qirsi also heard a few snickers from the men who stood nearby.

"You have battle sickness, First Minister," the duke said, still laughing. "All of us have had it at one time or another. It's nothing to be ashamed of. I've seen many a fine swordsman reduced to little more than a quivering babe by the prospect of an actual war." He gestured toward Shurik's mount. "You'll feel better once you start riding."

"Yes, my lord," the minister said, swinging himself onto the horse. His head spun as he did, but the pain had started to ebb.

A moment later Aindreas shouted an order to the men and kicked at the flanks of his stallion. The soldiers of Kentigern gave an earsplitting cheer and started to march out of the ward. There would be people lining the streets of the city, Shurik knew, cheering as well, sending their heroes off to war, none of them knowing that war would be coming to them long before these men saw battle.

As they rode slowly ahead of the soldiers, the duke looked at him, shaking his head and laughing again. "Battle sickness," he said. "I wouldn't have expected that from you, Shurik."

Laugh all you want, you fat fool. Because of me, the famed walls of Kentigern are finally about to fall. "I didn't expect it either, my lord," the Qirsi said. "But as you say, I should be feeling better soon."

Chapter
Twenty-six

❖

Mertesse, Aneira

I t seemed to Yaella that she had been asleep only a few moments when the dream began. She recognized it immediately, her stomach turning sour, and her hands starting to tremble. Even in her sleep, even as she began to feel her way across the familiar terrain of this vision, she wondered how the Weaver could know when she slept and when she was awake.

She walked carefully, stepping among the strewn boulders and clumps of tall grasses toward the high mound where she knew he expected her to go. During earlier dreams, Yaella had tried to figure out where she was, though without any success. Land of this sort could be found throughout the Forelands, in the southern plains of Aneira, the moorlands of western Eibithar, the northern steppe country of Caerisse, or the highlands of Glyndwr and Wethyrn. Had she been able to see beyond the nearest rocks and grasses, she might have been able to determine at least which kingdom she was in. But in these dreams the sky was always dark and starless. Even the moons did not shine here. It was as if the Weaver had mastered Elined and Morna, Qirsar and Amon, shaping the earth and sky to match his desires. In this realm, he was greater than the gods.

Yaella felt herself beginning an ascent and knew she had come to the Weaver's mound. Her heart began to pound in her chest, and not simply owing to the effort of climbing this rise. She had been first minister to the duke of Mertesse for nearly nine years. Twice she had met Aneira's king. In her first year of service to Rouel, she had ridden with him into battle against the men of Kentigern. And for more than three years, she had been a part of the Qirsi movement to win control of the Forelands, living a lie every day, her life constantly in danger. Yet nothing else filled her with the cold, bone-deep dread that came with these dreams. No one but the Weaver could make her shiver simply with the sound of his voice.

She continued up the rise, her legs growing heavy and her breathing labored, until at last the ground began to flatten out, telling her that she had reached the summit. She stopped to wait, staring into the darkness in what she knew would be a vain attempt to catch a glimpse of the Weaver's face.

The light blazed so suddenly that Yaella had to raise a hand to shield her eyes. It was as bright as the sun and as white as Panya's glow, and it appeared to flow from the earth itself, like steam rising from the heat springs of Wethyrn's Grey Hills. An instant later she saw the Weaver walking toward her, as if emerging from the brilliant light. Framed as he was against the radiance, a cape draped over him, he appeared as little more than a living shadow, faceless and formless. She could tell that he was tall and that he walked with long, confident strides. But that was all. Even his hair, which had to be as white as hers, looked black and wild, like the mane of some beast from the underrealm.

He stopped before her, and she bowed to him as she would to a Qirsi king.

"Are they at war yet?" he asked, his voice cutting through the stillness like a noble's blade.

"No, Weaver. But soon." She sounded small and frightened to her own ears, like a child answering an angry parent.

"Why this delay? Aylyn is dead. The Curgh army marches on Kentigern."

"Yes, but—"

"Has Kentigern led his men from the castle yet?"

"It's been more than a day since they left, Weaver. My duke's scouts saw them marching from the city just after the prior's bells on the third day of the waning."

"That was later than we agreed."

Yaella faltered. She wanted to protect Shurik, but not in a way that would bring the full weight of the Weaver's wrath down on her.

"Well?"

"I'm certain there's a reason, Weaver. Aindreas can be a difficult man, and under these circumstances—"

It suddenly felt as though the Weaver had placed a hand over her mouth to keep her from speaking, though neither of them had moved. She felt fear rise in her chest like a moon tide, and she had to remind herself to breathe through her nose.

"Never speak to me of circumstances or difficulties or excuses of any sort. We are part of a great movement, one that will wipe the Eandi nobles from the Forelands and bring a Qirsi king to power. Our people have dreamed of such a day since they first set foot on this land. Nine centuries ago, one man's betrayal condemned us all to thralldom and persecution. To this day, our people are forced to serve and entertain men of limited capacity, just as are you. To this day, Weavers live in constant fear of execution. All because of the traitor Carthach.

"We are closer to our dream right now than we have been at any time since the ancient wars. Yet, even today, the failure of just one man or woman can destroy our cause again. Circumstances are nothing. Difficulties don't concern me. Each of us has a task to perform. Each of us carries in his or her hands the fate of our movement. That should be enough to ensure the success of all. And in case it's not, you and your friend are being paid a great deal of gold to do what I tell you to do, when I tell you to do it. Do as I ask, and you'll have power and riches for the rest of your days. Fail me again, and this hand you feel covering your mouth will be at your throat. Do you understand?"

Yaella nodded, still unable to speak.

"Good," he said. "I expect you to make certain that Shurik understands as well."

As abruptly as it had come, the hand was gone from her face. Yaella took a long breath, closing her eyes for just an instant. "Yes, Weaver," she said. "I'll tell him."

"When will Mertesse march on Kentigern?"

"We can attack tomorrow night, Weaver. My duke is ready now." She hesitated, fearful of angering him again.

"You may speak. Say what you will."

"I think we would be wise to wait another day, until we're certain that Kentigern is too far away to save his castle. A siege can take time. I know that you want this war to begin immediately, but if we strike too soon—"

"I agree. Have your duke wait another day."

She nodded. Rouel was almost as impatient for this war as the Weaver, but Yaella felt certain that she could persuade him to wait.

"Is there anything else?"

Again she faltered, though only briefly. "I feel I must tell you that Kentigern Castle has resisted sieges for hundreds of years. Shurik has promised to weaken its defenses, and I'm sure he has. But still, the fortress is strong."

"I don't care if the castle falls. I want there to be war between Aneira and Eibithar. The rest is unimportant. If the siege succeeds, war becomes that much more likely, but even if it ultimately fails, it won't matter, so long as it leads to war."

"Yes, Weaver."

"We'll speak again soon," the Weaver said.

Yaella wanted to ask him what he intended to do once the war had begun. She understood so little of his plan. Indeed, she barely grasped how his movement worked. She knew that the Weaver had his chancellors, Qirsi who spoke on his behalf, but it seemed that he ceded little of his authority to others working for him. She didn't even know how he managed to pay her. All the gold she had earned had been left in her quarters, appearing as if by magic. Someone must have put it there, a castle servant perhaps, turned by the Weaver to his cause. But Yaella had never seen this person; she had no idea who it might be.

She did know that the Weaver expected his underlings to bring new Qirsi to the movement, and that he paid them handsomely for doing so. Shurik once told her that he had received two hundred qinde for convincing her to join the conspiracy. That, however, was the extent of her knowledge. She longed to know more, but she had learned long ago that questions angered the Weaver, and that the same magic he had used to silence her could be used to cause pain.

With the Weaver's last words still echoing in her mind, she awoke, gasping for breath as one might rising to the water's surface from the depths of a cold lake. Somehow she was sitting up in her bed, the golden sunlight of early morning making the walls of her chamber glow. She felt as though she hadn't slept at all and she silently cursed the Weaver, wondering as she did if he could sense even this.

She swung herself out of bed and padded across the cold stone floor to her washbowl. The water had grown cold, but she rinsed her face anyway, shivering slightly as she reached for a cloth to dry herself.

No doubt the duke was already up, ordering his men about and overseeing the final preparations for the siege. He had a quartermaster, of course, as well as a master armsman. But he was the type of man who trusted no one to do what he believed he could do himself. Despite her assurances to the Weaver that she could convince Rouel to wait another day, Yaella was dreading this encounter.

She dressed and made her way down to the north ward, where she knew she would find the duke. He was already dressed for battle, his black and gold cape stirring behind him as he strode among the wagons and men. Usually the commander of an Aneiran army would not have thought to carry so much to war, but with the enemy so close—Castle Mertesse stood just over a league from the south bank of the Tarbin, and Kentigern was even closer to the north bank—Rouel had decided that it made more sense to bring the materials they would need for the siege. Yaella had to admit that it made a great deal of sense. Rather than wasting valuable time gathering wood for the siege engines and the hurling arms, they would be able to begin their assault on the castle almost immediately. With much of Kentigern's army gone, and the castle's west gate weakened by Shurik's magic, speed promised to be their greatest advantage. Anything that could further hasten their attack could only increase their chances for success.

Enormous carts holding long beams of hewn oak and ironwood lined the side of the ward, waiting for the teams of horses that were to pull them across the river and up the tor. In addition to the soldiers, Rouel intended to bring more than one hundred laborers and a dozen master carpenters. Because of this, the quartermaster and his men had been forced to load their carts with even more provisions than usual.

In all, this promised to be one of the largest undertakings attempted by Mertesse's army since the Harvest War, nearly a century and half before. It was small wonder Rouel seemed so eager for it to begin.

Yaella fell in step just a stride or two behind the duke and joined him in looking over the carts and the men. They appeared nearly ready to go. Certainly nothing she saw would provide her with any justification for asking Rouel to delay their departure.

451

After a time, she realized that the duke hadn't yet noticed her and she cleared her throat.

"Good day, my lord."

He stopped and looked back at her. "First Minister! Good morning." He tipped his head to the side. "Have you been here long?"

"Just a few moments, my lord."

He nodded and resumed his walking, gesturing for her to do the same. "What do you think?" he asked.

"It seems to me that your preparations are going quite well."

"I agree. For centuries the men of Kentigern have boasted that their castle is unassailable. But I believe this siege will be their undoing."

Yaella didn't bother to point out that were it not for Shurik's magic, they wouldn't even be attempting this assault. There was no sense in angering the duke, particularly now.

"There's something I wish to discuss with you, my lord."

"You there!" Rouel shouted, stopping abruptly to watch two men who were practicing their swordplay. "Do that against one of Kentigern's men and he'll run you through! You have to raise your shield arm more," he said, demonstrating the movement as he spoke. "Try it again." He stood and watched them for several moments before nodding. "That's better. Keep working on that." He began to walk again, a frown wrinkling his brow. "I shouldn't have to correct them on such elementary movements."

They walked in silence for a few seconds before the duke looked at her again. "I'm sorry, First Minister. You were saying something."

"Yes, my lord." It was best just to say it and have it done. "I feel that we would be better off delaying our attack for another day."

He stopped again, facing her. "Demons and fire, woman! Why would we do that?"

"To ensure our success, my lord."

"Absurd!" He started forward again, shaking his head. "We march today! We've already waited longer than I had wished. I won't put it off yet again!"

"If we attack tonight, my lord, the siege will fail. I'm certain of it."

"How can you know that? Has your friend failed? Is that it?"

"Shurik has nothing to do with this, my lord. He marched with his duke two days ago, which means that he's already seen to the weakening of Kentigern's west gate. He's done all he can on our behalf."

"Then why delay at all? When we spoke with him, we agreed to begin the assault on the third night of the waning. I made it clear that we would need the moonlight. That night has come and gone, and still we tarry!"

"Yes, my lord. But at the time we assumed that Kentigern would leave the castle before he did."

"So your friend did fail."

The duke was walking so quickly that she could barely keep up with him. He seemed to have no destination in mind and at last the minister held out a hand, forcing him to halt.

"Please, my lord. Listen to me. Kentigern has lost his daughter. He's waging a war of vengeance against Curgh. It was too much to hope that the timing of his departure from the castle would be precisely what we wanted. This delay is no one's fault."

"Of course it is! We paid the man a great deal of gold so that this siege would succeed, and now we find that he didn't get his duke out of the castle soon enough."

Yaella nearly laughed aloud. If anyone had suggested to Rouel that she could get him to do anything at a time of her choosing he would have been incensed. But, she knew, the Eandi were like this. They needed someone to blame when things didn't go as they wished. It was part of what made serving them so trying.

She would have liked to let the matter drop, but she couldn't allow Rouel to blame Shurik for this. She and Kentigern's first minister had known each other for nearly twenty years, since beginning their apprenticeships with the same Qirsi master in Caerisse shortly after her Determining. Together they had learned to wield their magic; she was one of only a handful of people in all the Forelands who knew the full extent of his powers. He had even been her first lover and she his. She still remembered their first night together so clearly that she could make herself feel his lips on her skin. It had been the night of their Fatings, and though she had been with other men since, she always found herself returning to the comfort of Shurik's arms, even to this day, despite the danger to both their lives. Now that Shurik had betrayed his duke, there was a chance that he would need to seek asylum in Aneira. If Rouel blamed the minister for this delay, he would never agree to offer Shurik his protection.

"If you're going to blame anyone, blame me," she said. "You

wanted to meet with Shurik again. I was the one who suggested that we decide then to begin the assault on the third night. I should have allowed for more time."

He didn't respond at first, but she could tell from his expression that he preferred to find fault with Shurik. More than that, though, he looked deeply disappointed, like a small boy who has been told to wait for a sweet. He didn't want to delay the siege, but he was too dependent on her counsel to dismiss the idea.

"Why do you think we should wait?" he finally asked, his voice low and his eyes fixed on the ground in front of him.

"Kentigern has been gone less than two full days, my lord. As soon as we begin the assault, as soon as Kentigern's guards see us on the river plain, they'll send a messenger after their duke. He'll be on horseback, and he'll be able to reach Aindreas in no more than a day. Kentigern's army will be back before we can clear the castle of those men who remain. But if we wait, if we give Aindreas another day to march eastward, the messenger will have farther to ride, and the army will have farther to march. By the time they return, we'll have the castle. Then the tor and the castle's defenses become our allies."

He recognized the logic of her argument. She could see it in the way he rubbed his jutting brow and clenched the muscles of his jaw.

"Our plan is sound, my lord. The damage Shurik has done to the gatehouse is not going to be discovered in the next day. This is the greatest opportunity any duke of your house has ever had to take Kentigern and hold it. We mustn't allow impatience to undo all our planning. One day simply isn't that important."

They resumed their walking, the duke brooding in silence. But at last he gave a slight nod, the movement of his head almost imperceptible.

"Very well," he said. "Tell the others. I actually believe the quartermaster will be glad to hear it. And this way I can go back to those men and show them how to fight without getting themselves killed."

Yaella smiled, her relief genuine. "Yes, my lord. We will succeed. I'm certain of it."

The duke nodded again before walking off. It would take him some time to get over his disappointment. It always did. But at least he had agreed. Perhaps if word of their siege's success reached the Weaver soon enough, she wouldn't have to dream of him again for some time.

The minister went to the master armsman and quartermaster to inform them of Rouel's decision. Wyn Stridbar, the armsman, offered little by way of response, but as the duke had anticipated, the quartermaster looked profoundly relieved. After speaking with them, Yaella returned to her chamber. Perhaps because she was a woman, or perhaps due to Rouel's tendency to oversee everything himself, the duke asked little of her as the castle prepared for this war. For the rest of that day and the morning of the next, she was able to keep to herself, only returning to the ward after the ringing of the midday bells on the fourth day of the waning.

Men were securing teams of horses to the carts bearing wood for the siege engines and tying down the last of the quartermaster's provisions. Soldiers spoke quietly as they polished their swords or tested the tension of their bows. Few were practicing. It seemed the time for that had passed.

As he had been the day before, Rouel was dressed for war, and seeing that Yaella had put on her riding clothes as well, and strapped a sword to her belt, he approached her, smiling broadly.

"You look like a soldier, First Minister."

She made herself smile in return. "Hardly, my lord."

"I took the liberty of having your horse groomed and saddled. I hope you don't mind."

"Not at all, my lord. My thanks."

He cleared his throat, glancing over his shoulder toward the master armsman before facing her again. "I've been thinking that it might be wise to leave a bit earlier in the day than we had first planned," he said. "We want to be certain that we're on the river plain just at nightfall, and this way we guard against unforeseen troubles along the way. The forest will keep the Eibitharians from marking our approach."

Mertesse Forest was a narrow strip of woodland that lay between the castle and the river. Compared with Aneira's Great Forest, which lay to the south, it was little more than a viscount's garden. It didn't even rival Kentigern Wood, which most Aneirans dismissed as an inconsequential grove. But it would provide cover for their advance.

The duke stood before her, looking once more like a child awaiting the judgment of a parent.

"I think it a fine idea, my lord," she said, pretending not to notice how pleased he seemed by her reply. "It may allow our scouts to determine how many guards remain in Kentigern and how they're stationed."

"I agree," the duke said, his blue eyes widening eagerly. "I'll let the captains know."

He hurried away and Yaella started toward her mount, nodding to the men as she passed among them. Most of the time soldiers had little use for Qirsi ministers. On a given day, she could walk every corridor in Castle Mertesse and draw little more than stares from the guards she encountered. From what Shurik had told her, Yaella gathered that he was treated much the same way in Kentigern.

But on this day the men of Mertesse greeted her as if she were one of their own. For this night, they knew, she would wield her magic on their behalf. The mists she called forth would conceal them from Kentigern's archers and the fires she conjured would burn the gates and doors that guarded their enemy's castle. Even if she never drew the sword she carried, she was, at least for a time, as much a warrior as each of them. In spite of everything, she had to admit to herself that she liked being treated this way.

She walked an easier road than Shurik and so many of the others. She had known it for some time, but only today did it occur to her how fortunate she had been. Her betrayal was subtle. She could continue to serve her duke to the best of her abilities and still be true to the Qirsi cause. If all went well, Rouel would not learn of her deception until long after she was gone from Mertesse. Shurik, on the other hand, was likely to be branded a traitor for the rest of his days no matter what happened. His was a cruel fate, and realizing this made her that much more determined to secure his safety when he was forced to flee Kentigern.

Reaching her horse, she stroked his mane and kissed him on the nose. Her saddle needed a few slight adjustments, but the stableboys had done a fine job combing him and readying him for the journey. She pulled on her riding gloves and checked her sword again. It would be hours still before the siege began, but Yaella felt her anticipation growing. She never expected to respond to the prospect of battle this way, and she tried to tell herself that she was merely eager for her role in the Qirsi movement to begin in earnest. But a part of her knew better. The truth was, she found war exciting. The army of Mertesse needed her magic, but Yaella almost hoped that she would be forced to fight with her blade. She had practiced swordplay almost all her life, and though she was not nearly as powerful as Rouel's soldiers or the men of Kentigern, she was quick and skilled with a sword.

It was mere fantasy. Rouel would never let her fight, not only because she was a woman, but also because he valued her magic too highly. Still, as she waited for the duke and his men to complete their preparations, Yaella drew her sword and checked the blade, wiping away a small spot of dirt and some finger marks so that the steel gleamed.

The army marched from the castle a short time later, with Rouel riding before it escorted by two men bearing the black-and-gold banners of Mertesse. Yaella rode just behind the duke, as did Wyn. The city's streets were choked with people who cheered for their duke and his army so loudly that the minister feared the sound would reach Kentigern, alerting the Eibitharians to their advance. It took some time for the entire procession of soldiers, laborers, provision carts, and supplies for the siege engines to leave the walled city.

Once they were in Mertesse Forest, however, they quickened their pace. Their route carried them eastward toward the edge of Harrier Fen, rather than directly north toward Kentigern. The Tarbin grew shallower as one traveled east, and the larger encampments of Kentigern's men kept to the west, nearer the castle. They reached the edge of the wood well before dusk, but Rouel wisely chose to keep his men in the shelter of the trees until nightfall. They could hear the river from where they were, its slow waters looking dark and angry beneath the grey clouds that had hung over the land throughout the day. The white mass of Kentigern Tor loomed over the river plain, appearing far closer than Yaella had imagined it would from the forest. Atop the tor stood Kentigern Castle, its grey stone a perfect match for the color of the sky.

As daylight finally gave way to darkness and torches appeared on the castle walls, the duke led his army from the shadows of the forest onto the river plain. They moved quickly and with astonishingly little noise given the size of the army. Yaella could smell the fen from where they were, but the ground was still firm, a far cry from the rank ooze of the slough itself.

The men forded the river far faster than the minister would have thought possible, but the carts proved to be another matter. Loaded down as they were, a number of them became mired in the river's silted bottom. Soldiers scrambled back into the river to throw their weight against the carts, but the crossing proved difficult. And before all of the wagons had emerged from the water, several of the horses began to whinny sharply in their distress.

Rouel, who had been watching the crossing from the north bank of the river, spat a curse at the sound and whirled in his saddle to look up at the castle. At first nothing happened, but then they began to hear shouts coming from farther up the river. Bright ward flames leaped to life on the castle's towers and more guards appeared on the walls, many of them bearing torches.

"Get those carts onto the riverbank!" the duke bellowed, his horse rearing in the sudden turmoil. He turned again, looking at the soldiers who still stood on the riverbank near him. "You men, light some torches. Then unload the carts that have gotten across and get the laborers working. I want the snails built first, then the ram, and then the hurling arms. Lord Stridbar will direct you."

The duke and his master armsman exchanged a brief look before Wyn swung off his horse, calling out instructions to his men. They were taking a risk, though not a great one. Kentigern had men stationed nearby, but their numbers were small. The encampment by the river was intended to keep Aneiran raiding parties from attacking houses and villages outside the walls of Kentigern. It wasn't nearly large enough to repel a full invasion. No doubt those men were already on their way back to the castle, where they would make their stand with the other soldiers who had not gone with Aindreas to meet the force from Curgh. Even now the castle was being readied for the siege, something Rouel had hoped to avoid by waiting for darkness to cross the river. But at least here, the duke and his army remained beyond the range of Kentigern's archers.

Still, just hearing the men of Eibithar call to their castle, and seeing those cries met by the bright yellow fires that sent dark smoke into the night sky, made Yaella tremble upon her mount. She was aware once more of the sword she wore on her belt, but she realized in that moment how foolish she had been to fancy herself a soldier. All she wanted was to raise her mists without delay and hide herself within them.

She stayed by the duke's side waiting with him until all the carts had been pulled from the waters of the Tarbin. Then they dismounted to help Wyn oversee the construction of the siege engines. The snail, as it was called, was a low shelter mounted on wheels that the attackers would use to approach the castle. It was covered with two layers of wood thick enough to block arrows and even crossbow bolts. The wood was then covered with wet animal skins, to protect against fire. It moved slowly, particularly up a hill as steep as that which led to the castle gate—hence the name—but it would offer protection to the men as they filled in the road pit with soil and stones.

The ram would follow close behind it, also covered with a roof of wood and damp skins. If Shurik had succeeded in weakening the gate, it would take only a few blows to breach the gates and portcullises, but even with the damage he had done, they would need the ram.

The hurling arms might not be necessary. Once the Mertesse army gained access to the castle, they would not need them anymore. But the men of Kentigern would expect the attackers to build the engines—all armies did when they began a siege. By not having them built, Rouel risked drawing the defenders' attention to the weakening of their defenses.

The construction of the snail and ram took some time, though not nearly as long as it would have had the army not brought wood from Mertesse. As soon as both engines were ready, Rouel and Yaella led at least half the Mertesse army along the riverbank to the base of the tor. The rest of the men stayed with the master armsman to complete the hurling arms. The minister and her duke met no resistance along the way, nor did they see any awaiting them on the road winding up the rocky slope to the castle gate. No doubt Aindreas's men were all within the walls of Kentigern, awaiting the commencement of the siege.

Yaella turned her eyes to the sky, looking for arrows from Aindreas's archers.

"You'll never see them until it's too late," Rouel said, following the direction of her gaze.

"Perhaps they'll use fire on them."

The duke shook his head. "Not yet. Not until we approach the gate. Until then, their arrows will be far more deadly if we can't see them."

Yaella nodded, though she couldn't keep herself from looking up once more.

Nearly a hundred men fit inside the snail and several dozen more walked beneath the roof on the ram. But the rest would have to climb the tor unprotected. "Spread out along the road, men!" the duke called to them. "If you walk in a cluster you'll give their archers a target."

He faced Yaella again. "We need your mists now, First Minister, over the length of the road for as long as you can manage."

"Yes, my lord."

Before she could summon her magic, a cry went up from the castle.

"Shields!" Rouel cried out, raising his own shield over his head.

Yaella grabbed at hers, which was still strapped to her saddle. In pulling it loose, however, she allowed it to slip out of her hand to the ground. An instant later she heard the harsh whistle of falling arrows. Unable to do anything else, tasting her death in the breath she took and held, the minister threw her arms over her head and neck, huddling down close to her horse's mane. The arrows dropped all around her, burying themselves in shields and the ground, or bouncing off rocks, their barbs sparking with the impact. Men screamed out in pain, as did at least one horse, its shriek echoing like the cry of a demon off the side of the tor. But the minister was spared.

"Your mists, First Minister! Now!"

Yaella closed her eyes, and reached down into herself with her mind, as a singer might just before beginning "The Elegy for Shanae." Except rather than reaching for that brilliant high note, she was reaching for her power, drawing it from her blood, from her heart, from the very essence of who she was. She had heard Qirsi argue for hours over the root source of their magic, some saying it was part of their corporeal being, and that was why the use of power left them so tired and shortened their lives. Others, like her father, believed that magic existed within their minds, like memory and thought, and the cost it exacted, while no less real, came from the spirit rather than the body. At times like these, Yaella found it impossible to distinguish between the two. She felt as though she lived solely to bring forth this magic, as if her body and her spirit were nothing more than conduits for the power that dwelled within her. It was glorious. She felt like a flame, like light. This, she had decided long ago, was what it meant to be Qirsi. The Eandi looked at her people and saw white hair and yellow eyes, pallid skin and frail bodies. But she knew that there was so much more. The ability to glimpse the future, or to create fire in the palm of her hand. The ability to draw mist from the earth.

Opening her eyes, the minister saw the first pale strands of vapor rising from the ground and drifting over the men of Mertesse. Within moments they had been enveloped by a great billowing cloud that continued to build. She summoned a light wind that carried the mist to all of Rouel's soldiers and up the road toward the fortress, until the entire face of the tor was shrouded in a dense fog. Kentigern's archers could still loose their arrows and bolts in the direction of the road, but they could no longer see their targets. Even the torches carried by Rouel's men could not penetrate her mist. At the same time, though, she was able to leave some clear air between the bottom of her cloud and the ground. The duke and his men could see each other and the road reasonably well.

"You and your men can approach the castle, my lord," Yaella said, her voice tight with the strain of what she was doing.

"How long can you hold the mist in place?" Rouel asked.

"I don't know. Summoning the mist is the most difficult part. Maintaining it takes far less magic."

"But it takes some."

"Yes. I'll do the best I can, my lord. But for the sake of all of us, work quickly."

The duke nodded, then turned his horse and called for the men to follow him up the road.

Arrows continued to rain down around them, hissing angrily, like Kebb's serpents. Kentigern's men couldn't see Rouel's army any longer, but they knew the twists and turns of the road, and the mist muffled the sound of their arrows' descent, giving the soldiers of Mertesse less warning of their approach. Still, fewer men were struck by these new volleys than had been by the first, and the army advanced steadily up the tor.

Yaella's head had started to pound and she was shivering in the damp cold of her mist. Had she been on foot, her legs would have failed her by now. But she clung to her horse as if he were a spar of wood floating in a dark sea, her eyes closed and her mind fixed on nothing save her magic.

So intent was she that the duke had to call out her name to keep her from riding her mount into the men walking in front of her. Opening her eyes, she saw that the snail had reached the great pit at the top of the road and that the men beneath its shell were filling in the hole with stones large and small. Arrows and bolts struck at the snail almost continuously now, many of them flaming. The wood had started to burn, the smoke mingling with her mist and the bright glow of the fires to suffuse the very night with a baleful orange hue.

Pots of lime and burning tar dropped down upon them, scoring the siege engines and splattering on many of the men, who howled in pain like burning wraiths from the Underrealm. The smoke and the smell of the fire pots stung Yaella's nostrils and her eyes until tears ran down her face. She was seized by a fit of coughing that almost made her black out and left her throat raw and sore. Soldiers were dying all around her, yet somehow she was spared, as was Rouel, who rode from one side of the snail to the other, shouting commands and exhorting his men to work faster.

Soon they had filled in the pit, and moving the snail away from the gate, they brought forward the ram. Yaella stopped drawing forth her mists long enough to set fire to the raised drawbridge with her magic. And as it burned, the men within the ram began to hammer at it with a heavy rhythm that seemed to shake the entire tor. More fire pots fell, more men screamed and died. Even with the mist around them, they were easy targets for Kentigern's archers. There was no mystery anymore. The invaders were at the gates, and Aindreas's bowmen loosed their darts as rapidly as they could.

Yet, amid the din and confusion of the siege, the minister heard the low rattle of another engine coming up the road.

Apparently Rouel heard it as well.

"Drop your mists, First Minister!" he called to her. "Wyn is here with the hurling arms!"

Immediately, Yaella let the mists begin to fade, even going so far as to summon a wind that scattered the remnants of her cloud like the dry seeds of a harvest flower. Wyn's men had already drawn back the arms on all three engines and fitted large stones in the great round hands. As soon as the top of the castle came into view, the master armsman barked a command and the first arm flew forward, propelling a missile toward the nearest of the towers. Kentigern's archers dove out of the way, though the stone passed harmlessly above them.

The second rock flew too low, smashing against the castle wall, but doing little damage. The third, however, found its mark, striking the top of the south gate tower and sending men of the castle flying in all directions.

After that, Yaella saw little of the fighting. With her mists gone, no one was safe, and since Qirsi were often the first targets in battles of this sort, Rouel insisted that she seek shelter in the snail with the wounded. After hurriedly sending her mount back down the road, she slipped into the engine, regretting it almost instantly. The space was cramped and overly warm, and it smelled of sweat and blood and fear. Already there were too many wounded to fit comfortably. They seemed to be lying on top of one another, groaning in their anguish. Two Qirsi healers crawled over each other, trying to ease the men's pain as quickly as they could.

"First Minister!" the older of the two men said as she entered the snail. "Are you hurt?"

Yaella swallowed and shook her head. "The duke sent me here. He didn't want me getting killed."

"Can you heal?" the man asked.

"No. I have mists, fire, and gleaning."

The healers looked at each other, both of them frowning. In that moment Yaella would have given up all three of her magics just to be able to help them.

"Will you at least help us tie bandages?"

"Of course," the minister said quickly.

For a time that defied measure, the minister's entire existence seemed to reduce itself to the act of tearing and tying strips of cloth around wounds that made her gag. Some of the men had burns that covered faces and hands. Others had arrows lodged so deeply in their flesh that the healers could do nothing more than break off the shafts and try to stanch the bleeding. Yaella refused to look at the faces of the soldiers to whom she attended. She merely moved from wound to wound, marking the progress of the siege by what she heard over the moans and sobbing around her.

After some time, a triumphant shout went up from Mertesse's soldiers, and she guessed that the raised drawbridge had finally been broken. Soon after, she heard another cry, and then a third. The portcullises were falling. Shurik, it seemed, had earned his gold.

More shouting still, the ring of swords being drawn, and finally the more desperate cries of battle and the frenzied clatter of steel striking steel. Men were fighting not far from the snail. She heard Rouel's voice over all the others, crying out, "For Mertesse!"

Still Yaella tore cloth and bound wounds, her clothes covered with blood. Gradually the sounds of the battle receded into the castle. One of the trailing soldiers stuck his head into the shelter, a fierce smile on his young face.

"We're in!" he said. "Kentigern's gates have fallen!"

She looked at him briefly and nodded, before turning her attention back to the man lying in front of her.

But a few moments later, a second man came. He had a jagged gash on the side of his head which had left a trail of dark, dried blood all the way down to his chin and onto his shirt of mail.

"You need healing," Yaella said, as he peered in at them.

"I'm fine, First Minister. The duke wants you in the castle."

Had Kentigern fallen already? She followed the man out into the night.

There were bodies all around the snail, most of them with arrow shafts jutting from them like cooking spits. The ground was still blackened and smoking in spots from the lime and tar, and the grey walls of the castle were pocked where they had been struck by missiles from the hurling arms. Kentigern's drawbridge, charred by her fire, had been splintered and broken in two, each half still hanging from the castle gate by thick iron chains. The portcullises lay twisted and fractured just beyond, as if a whirlwind had passed through the gatehouse.

Yaella could still hear men shouting from within the castle. Dark smoke billowed into the night sky, reflecting the light of torches and ward fires and the flames of battle. She heard the clang of steel above her. Soldiers were fighting on the castle walls; the siege wasn't over yet.

She found Rouel just inside the gate, his face begrimed with soot and dirt and sweat. He had a cut on his shoulder and another on his thigh, but otherwise he appeared unhurt.

"You sent for me, my lord?" Yaella asked, stopping in front of him.

"How are the wounded?"

She shrugged, swallowing. "Some are better than others, my lord."

"Are there many of them?"

"Yes."

The duke took a breath, glancing over his shoulder at the sound of voices from the far side of the ward.

"How goes the fighting, my lord?"

He faced her again, nodding and baring his teeth in what she took for a grin. "Kentigern's men are putting up a battle. They know the lay of the castle better than we, so it may take some time before we prevail. But we're in, thanks to you and your friend. They'll be hard-pressed to push us back out."

"Yes, my lord."

"I sent for you because the smoke from these fires is drifting to the north and east, right toward Aindreas and his men."

She glanced up into the darkness. He was right.

"Can you make a wind that will drive it back toward Mertesse, or out to sea? Anywhere else will do."

She nearly laughed aloud. Had she not been bone-weary, had she not poured so much of herself into the mist that concealed their advance, she still would have been incapable of summoning such a wind. She was a lone Qirsi, she wasn't Morna.

"No, my lord. My power doesn't go that deep. I'm sorry."

He frowned, raising his eyes to the sky. "Aindreas will see that smoke, and he'll know what's happened."

"Yes, my lord."

"We were wise to wait an extra day."

"Yes." But abruptly her mind was elsewhere. The prevailing wind in Kentigern, as in Mertesse, blew inland from Amon's Ocean. The smoke should have been drifting toward the fen and the Caeris-san Steppe, not toward Heneagh. It almost seemed that someone or something wanted Aindreas to know. Perhaps this was Morna's doing. Or the Weaver's. For his powers did go this deep, and no one wanted war between Eibithar and Aneira more than he.

Chapter
Twenty-seven

✦

North edge of Kentigern Wood, Eibithar

lmost from the moment Aindreas led his men from Kentigern, nothing went as he had hoped. Just after the ringing of the midday bells on that first day, as Villyd finished readying the men to march, the skies appeared to brighten, despite the rain that still fell on the castle. The duke convinced himself that the weather would break before they left, or at least by dusk. It didn't. If anything, the rain began to fall harder just as he led the army from the castle gates down into the city.

He had decreed that all Kentigern's people should be out in the streets to see the army off, and, of course, no one in Kentigern dared to defy him. But they had to wait some time for the army to emerge from the castle and wind down the steep road from the castle, all the time standing in that cold, driving rain. By the time Aindreas and his soldiers reached the first of them, Kentigern's people were soaked, and their cheers sounded hollow and forced. Nor was Aindreas the only one to notice this. Rather than drawing strength from the throng that filled the lanes, the army appeared to grow grim, almost angry, as if they resented being forced to march to war under such conditions.

Once they were out of the city, on the broad road leading toward Kentigern Wood, Aindreas began to push them harder. What else could he do? They had to reach the Heneagh before Hagan and the men from Curgh. But on the wide plain that lay between the city and wood, he could see that the sky looked grey and dark in every direction. The road had been turned to little more than a strip of reddish brown mud that was so thick in places as to be almost impassible. He allowed his soldiers to break formation and take to the high grasses rather than have them tramp through that muck.

The wagon horses, however, had no choice but to stay on the road. Their carts sinking deep into the mud, the horse teams strained to pull them forward, snorting loudly, their great muscles quivering. Two of the carts threw wheels and had to be fixed in the waning light of day. None of the provisions spilled when the wagons failed, but that was the only good fortune they enjoyed that day. It was almost dark before they even entered the shelter of the wood.

If Aindreas entertained any hope at all of being able to rest that first night, it died on the road. They had so far to go, and they had covered so little ground. There was no moonlight, of course. They had to march by the glow of their torches, but march they did. The rain still fell, but the trees blocked most of it. Still, even if they weren't getting any wetter, the air was too heavy for them to dry off. Aindreas tried to tell himself that his men were better off than he was. At least while walking, they would keep warm. He was cold and miserable atop his mount, so much so that he finally dismounted and began to lead the beast on foot. A moment later he heard Shurik do the same.

The duke glanced back at his minister and gave a small smile, which the Qirsi returned, though it vanished almost immediately. Looking beyond Shurik, Aindreas frowned at what he saw on the faces of his men. He didn't expect them to look happy. He was no fool. But they didn't even look angry or resentful. Their expressions were utterly devoid of expression, as if they cared nothing for their cause, or their duke. None of them spoke. The only sounds in the wood were the trudging of a thousand pairs of feet, the occasional nicker of a horse, and the incessant drip of rain on the leaves above them.

"Do you know any war songs, Shurik?"

The minister looked at the duke as if he had just asked the man to fly. "No, my lord. None."

"We need a war song. These men look like they're marching home from a rout, rather than to a great battle."

He searched his memory; his father sang them all the time when Aindreas was young. In truth, the duke hated them. But that was beside the point.

We walk with the goddess to glory and song,
Our steel it is gleaming, our quivers are filled;
Our loves lie behind us, the journey is long,
But there's battles to win, and there's legends to build.

It was called "Orlagh's March," for the goddess of war. It was one of his father's favorites, and one of the few war songs Aindreas had ever really liked. The duke glanced back once more. A number of his men had looked up from the ground to stare at him, several of them smiling. When he began to sing again, his wasn't the only voice to rise above the rain.

Through forest and hillside, o'er rivers and field,
By the warm sun of day or the lovers' bright glow;
We've faith in the goddess, she lends us her shield,
And the steel of her blade, strikes bold at our foe;

We fight for our kingdom, not silver or gold,
And we'll give up our lives to save land and king;
We fear not Bian and his realm dark and cold,
For Orlagh walks with us, of her glory we sing.

By the time they reached the last verse, the wood rang with their voices. And when the song was done, his soldiers cheered so loudly he was certain they could be heard in Braedon. In spite of all that had gone wrong that day, Aindreas couldn't help but smile.

"That was well done, my lord," Shurik said quietly, walking beside him now.

"It was nothing," he said. "I shouldn't have had to do it at all. It's the damn rain."

"Yes, my lord." The man paused, but only for an instant. "Will we be stopping soon, my lord?"

Aindreas looked at the Qirsi. He looked wan and tired, as if he had been taxed well beyond endurance. It was hard to believe that such awesome magic could exist in bodies so pale and slight and weak.

"No," he said. "Not soon. We lost a good deal of time between the city and the wood. If you're weary, I suggest you ride the rest of the night. Let your mount do the work."

The minister made a halfhearted attempt at a smile. "Yes, my lord. Perhaps I will."

Shurik might have been suffering, but the rest of the men seemed to have been revived by their singing. The rest of the night passed quickly. The rain didn't stop, and they walked for hours more, but at least the men were talking and laughing again, as warriors should.

They rested only a short while in the last hours before dawn, long enough for a small meal and perhaps a quick nap on the damp ground. When the wood began to brighten with the first grey strands of daylight, they resumed their march.

It wasn't until late in the morning that the rain finally slackened. Still, the cloud cover did not break, and as the day dragged on, Aindreas realized they would have to do without the moons again that night. If they were to march past sunset they would need light, and he didn't want to use all their oil for torches. The first minister looked somewhat better this day than he had the night before, but as they continued on through the wood, taking only the briefest of rests, he appeared to wilt in his saddle. Aindreas was reluctant to ask him to expend any more power than was necessary. Once more, however, the weather left the duke with few options.

He slowed his mount to ride beside the Qirsi. "When night falls, First Minister, I'll need you to illuminate the wood for us. We can't afford to burn torches for another night."

Shurik looked at him. "Of course, my lord. I'll do what I can."

The duke heard nothing unusual in the man's tone. But for the merest instant before Shurik spoke, Aindreas thought he saw a look of utter contempt and malice flash across the man's pale features. A trick of the light, no doubt, an illusion born of the grey shadows of the wood. He was weary himself, as they all were. Yet Aindreas couldn't help but stare at the man, as though waiting for the expression to return.

"Is there anything else, my lord?"

"No," the duke said, shaking his head. "We'll be grateful for whatever light you can provide. When you tire, we'll stop for the night."

"Very good, my lord."

Aindreas clicked his tongue at his mount, riding ahead of the Qirsi again, and telling himself that he had imagined it.

When night finally crept through the wood, Shurik raised his dagger and drew forth a bright golden flame that balanced on the blade and shone like a beacon among the trees. The men walking at the back of Kentigern's column still had to light torches, but only half the number that the army had used the previous night.

It wasn't long before the first minister's face shone with sweat and the hand holding the flame began to tremble. After a time he switched hands, the way a servant in the kitchens might move a plate of food from one palm to the other. But his weariness grew more apparent by the moment.

Once more the duke steered his horse to the minister's side.

"Do you need to stop, First Minister?"

"Not yet, my lord. But soon."

Aindreas heard the strain in the man's voice and he didn't expect the minister to last more than another few minutes. In the end, though, they managed to cover over half a league more before Shurik finally let his flame die out.

The duke would have liked to keep going, but he knew that his men needed rest. He did, too. If he pushed himself or his army much further, they would be in no condition to fight even if they did beat Curgh's men to the river. They still hadn't covered as many leagues as he had hoped they would by the second night. But they had managed to make up some of the time they had lost the day before.

The following morning dawned grey and cool. The rain didn't return, but the clouds showed no sign of breaking up. Standing in a small clearing in the wood, staring up at a patch of leaden sky, Aindreas let loose with a string of curses. After all he'd been through, why wouldn't the gods be with him in this war? He deserved better than this.

He had the army moving again within an hour of dawn. Even with the time they'd lost, he felt certain that they could reach the north edge of Kentigern Wood before they slept again, and he told Villyd to have the soldiers maintain as fast a pace as the swordmaster thought they could endure. The first minister looked better than he had since before they left the castle. A night's rest had done him some good. Perhaps the Qirsi could provide light again that night, if they needed it.

As it turned out, they didn't, but for all the wrong reasons. As the duke had hoped, they managed to reach the end of the wood just as the last silver light of day was starting to fail. But from within the shelter of the trees, they could see the Curgh army making camp on the open plain that lay before them. They had already crossed the river and had put enough distance between themselves and its banks to have the advantage in any fight on the plain. The army of Kentigern would be too close to the wood when the battle began to have any chance of flanking them. Aindreas could try to lure Javan's men into the wood, where the fight would be on more equal terms, but Hagan wasn't likely to cooperate. He'd bide his time, waiting for Aindreas to make the first assault.

Their best hope lay in the woods. Shurik had said a few days before that in a battle among the trees, Kentigern's army would have the advantage. Seeing the Curgh army before him, at least a thousand men strong, their helms and swords glittering in the dying light, Aindreas wasn't so certain. But at least they would be on equal footing, which was more than he could say about the plain as the armies stood now.

He briefly considered pulling his army back a league or so into the wood and lying in wait for the men of Curgh. Hagan's scouts hadn't seen them yet, and if they could surprise the Curgh army in the forest they certainly would have the upper hand.

An instant later, however, that possibility vanished as well. Two scouts burst from the wood, one a short distance to the west of Kentigern's men, the other an equal distance to the east. Both men were on horseback, riding their mounts at a full gallop. They shouted as they rode, and even from this distance, Aindreas could see men of Curgh turning to look toward the wood.

"Archers!" Villyd shouted almost immediately.

Several bowmen ran forward, their arrows already nocked.

"Hold!" Aindreas called to them.

The swordmaster looked at him. "But, my lord—"

"It's too late. Let them go." He would have liked to kill the two scouts with his own hands. But Javan's men were already fighting for their duke—actually their king, as they saw it. There was nothing to be gained by giving them two deaths to avenge as well. At that moment, he would have given his sword for a flask of wine.

"They know we're here," Aindreas said, looking first at Villyd, then at Shurik. "What now?"

The swordmaster cleared his throat. "They hold better ground than we do, my lord."

"Demons and fire, man! I can see that! I'm asking you what we should do about it."

"Talk to them," Shurik said, his voice low. "Find out how confident they are. They hold the plain, but they don't have their duke. We do. We also have MarCullet's son. They may not want to fight us, in which case the advantage is still ours."

The duke nodded. A parley made a good deal of sense right now. "See to it," he said.

The Qirsi took one of the blue-and-silver banners carried by Aindreas's soldiers and rode with it out onto the plain, his white hair flying loose behind him. He rode a good distance toward the Curgh army before reining his horse to a halt, dismounting, and driving the banner's pole into the ground. Then he climbed back onto his mount and rode back toward the wood. Behind him the banner of Kentigern stirred in the light wind.

Shurik returned to the duke's side and together they watched for Curgh's reply. It took several moments, but at last a lone rider rode out from the opposing camp carrying the gold and brown flag of Curgh. The rider was Eandi, with light brown hair—it might very well have been Hagan himself. He stopped a short distance from the Kentigern banner and placed the Curgh flag in the ground as well, so that the two danced together in the breeze.

The lynx and the bear. Not long ago, barely more than a single turn, the two houses had been on the verge of an alliance. Now they were readying for a parley of war.

"Shurik, Villyd. I want the two of you with me. And four bowmen." He would have felt safer with more, but four was customary.

"Yes, my lord," the swordmaster said. "Do you wish to ride forward now?"

Aindreas shook his head. "Wait until they come out."

"They'll be waiting for you, my lord," Shurik said quietly. "You requested the parley."

They're marching on my castle! he wanted to say. *Doesn't that count for anything?* Instead, he just nodded. "All right. Then let's get this over with."

Daylight was slipping away quickly, though it was brighter on the plain than it had been among the trees. To his credit, Hagan didn't keep him waiting long. Before Aindreas and his company had reached the Kentigern banner, Curgh's swordmaster was already riding forward to meet them, accompanied by the duchess, a thin, balding Qirsi whom Aindreas had never seen before, and four archers.

"Your army looks small, Hagan," Aindreas said as the sword-master reined his horse. "You had hoped to topple my castle with so few men?"

Hagan bristled, but said nothing.

Rather it was the duchess who spoke. "You'll address yourself to me, Aindreas. In Javan's absence, this is my army and my banner."

She wore a coat of mail and carried a sword in a simple leather scabbard that hung from her belt. Her golden hair was pulled back from her face, and her cheeks were flushed. She looked small atop her white mount, but she sat confidently. If she feared the coming battle, she hid it well. Aindreas didn't think that he had ever seen her looking more lovely.

"As you wish, my dear," the duke said. "That should make this far more pleasant. It's not often that a duke gets to parley with such an enchanting foe."

"Tread lightly, Kentigern!" Hagan said. "That's the queen you're addressing."

Shonah lifted a hand. "It's all right, Hagan." Her eyes were fixed on Aindreas's face, as green as emeralds in the twilight. "You asked for this meeting," she said. "What is it you want?"

"I may have offered the first flag, but it's you and your men who march on my castle. I'd ask you the same."

The duchess didn't hesitate for a moment. "Very well. I want my husband, his first minister, the MarCullet boy, and the rest of their company released from your prison immediately. If you refuse, we'll wipe out your army and take your castle."

It was well said. Aindreas was forced to wonder if he and Shurik had taken her too lightly. Of course, he kept these thoughts to himself, laughing and shaking his head.

"It's an empty threat, Shonah. A more experienced warrior would know that. Kentigern hasn't fallen in centuries, and it's not about to fall to you."

"No? How many of your men remain there, Aindreas? Perhaps five hundred? My force is at least as large as yours, and we hold the plain. If we defeat you here, who's to stop us when we reach your castle?"

No doubt Hagan's spies had told her all she needed to know about Aindreas's strength, both here and in Kentigern. Still, the duke found it disquieting to hear her speaking with such certainty on these matters.

"This is foolish, Shonah," he said, fighting to keep his temper. "Your entire premise is wrong. Javan and his men are not prisoners in my castle. They're my guests. Do you honestly think they'd choose to leave before your son was found and his fate decided?"

Hagan leveled a finger at him as if it were a blade. "You're a liar!"

"Now it's you who should tread lightly, swordmaster. I am duke of Kentigern, and I expect to be treated as such."

"You're a traitor, who has imprisoned his king!"

"That's enough!" Shonah said, glaring at both of them.

Hagan looked away, though he fingered the hilt of his sword. Aindreas continued to stare at the man, but he was aware of Shonah watching him.

"You say my husband is a guest," she said, her voice even. "His letters say something else. He's in the prison tower, as are the others in his company. He cannot leave, he cannot speak with his men. Are all your guests treated so?"

"Not all, my lady. Only those whose heirs murder my children." He swung his gaze to her, not caring anymore who held the plain or whose army had more men. He would crush them all, the duchess as well as the swordmaster. "If he was a prisoner, he'd be in my dungeon, as your son was until he managed to escape. I should have hanged them all the day Brienne died. That was my great mistake, and it's one I intend to correct as soon as I finish destroying you and your army."

He didn't wait for a reply. He didn't even glance at Shurik or Villyd. He merely wheeled his horse away and started back toward the wood, spurring the beast to a run. He sensed that the Qirsi and his swordmaster were just behind him, but his mind was already on the coming battle. The position of Shonah's army posed problems, but they could be overcome. Tavis had escaped him, and he had spared Javan, though he suddenly couldn't say why. But with dawn he would finally have his revenge.

The duchess was silent as they rode slowly back to the encampment. Hagan watched her closely, trying to gauge her thoughts, but she was as skilled as the duke at keeping her features from revealing anything of her feelings.

"That went as well as one could expect, my lady," the second minister said, riding on her other side. "Lord Kentigern wasn't interested in preventing this war. I think it far more likely that he was trying to determine whether you were committed to attacking him."

Hagan didn't like the minister, but he couldn't help but agree with him in this instance.

"Danior is right, my lady. There was nothing you could say that would have resolved this matter without bloodshed."

"What?" Shonah said at last, looking from one of them to the other. Then she waved her hand impatiently, as if their words had finally reached her. "Oh, I know all that. Stop treating me like a dullard. Aindreas wanted to see if I was afraid of war. That's why he offered the flag." She shook her head, her expression softening. "But I find him sad. He's so desperate to avenge his daughter that he barely knows what he's doing."

Hagan and the minister exchanged a look. "My lady," the swordmaster said, "he's imprisoned the duke. He just said that he means to kill him. This is not a man deserving of pity."

"Of course he is, Hagan. You think me soft because I'm a woman. But right now you're the fool. Both of you are," she added, glancing at the Qirsi. "I have no intention of sparing him or his army. If Aindreas is bent on war, then I'll give him war, and more than he can handle. But don't mistake, he does deserve our pity and more. He's lost a child, and you, swordmaster—who have lost a wife and now fear losing a son—you of all people, should understand his grief. More than that though, you should know that to defeat an enemy, you must first understand him."

She was indeed a formidable woman, worthy of being Eibithar's queen. In that moment Hagan wondered if Aindreas truly understood what he faced in the coming battle.

"What is there to understand?" Danior asked. "That he's a madman?"

Hagan shook his head, though his eyes remained fixed on the duchess. "That he fights out of grief and rage. That he's not interested in conquering the House of Curgh, but rather in hurting it. At this moment I would guess that he'd gladly trade the lives of all his men just to kill the duchess with his own blade."

Shonah gave a thin smile. "I suppose I should be flattered."

Hagan laughed, struck once more by how much she shared with her husband.

"Well, if that's what he has in mind, my lady," the minister said, sounding alarmed, "you'll have to keep to the rear of the army. Our first concern must be your safety."

"Again, he's right," Hagan said.

"No, he's not, swordmaster, and you should know this as well. A man who fights out of rage makes mistakes. As long as he can see me and direct his hatred at me, he'll be guided by his passions rather than by reason."

"A man who fights from rage may make mistakes, but he's also far more dangerous than any other foe. He's erratic. He follows none of the accepted rules of warfare. We can't risk your life in the hope that Aindreas will stumble."

"That's not your decision to make, swordmaster!" the duchess said.

Hagan looked away. "No, my lady."

Reaching the camp, the duchess swung herself down from her horse and tossed the reins to one of her servants.

"Tell the men to prepare for battle," she said, looking up at Hagan. "I want the army ready at first light. And double the watch, particularly on our flanks. I don't want Aindreas thinking he can surprise us."

"Yes, my lady."

She started away, then stopped herself, heaving a big sigh and facing him once more. "Forgive me, Hagan. I have every confidence in you and your men. But this is my first battle."

"There would be no shame in letting me lead the charge, my lady. The army is yours, but so is the dukedom, some would say the entire kingdom. We can't lose you."

"And you won't. But if I don't lead us into this battle, Aindreas will think he's won already and that will only embolden him."

"Will you at least allow me to assign some men to guard you?"

She shook her head. "We need every man fighting Kentigern. Besides," she added, smiling now, "I don't plan to stray from your side. That should be all the protection I need."

The swordmaster felt his color rising. "Very well," he said, quickly, steering his horse away. At times she reminded him too much of Daria.

"Swordmaster."

He glanced back, frowning for just an instant at the sight of Danior riding after him.

"Yes, Second Minister."

"Do you still think you'll need my mists?"

Hagan shrugged. "I can't say right now. We'll have to see what the morning brings."

"I see," the Qirsi said.

"Is something troubling you?"

Before the minister could answer, one of the men called to Hagan. Several of his soldiers were standing, their eyes fixed on Kentigern Wood.

Following the direction of their gazes, Hagan saw a long line of torches spreading in either direction along the fringe of the wood.

"What are they doing?" Danior asked.

What, indeed? The torchlight didn't appear to be drawing nearer to their position, but Aindreas's army was definitely on the move.

"Swordmaster!" he heard the duchess call.

"Yes, my lady," he answered, his eyes still on Kentigern's men. "I see them."

A few moments later the duchess was beside him again, watching the torches as well. "Are they already on the attack?"

"I don't think so."

"Then what?"

He shook his head, and for some time they merely stood there, watching. Hagan sensed that his entire army had ceased doing anything else, that all of them were staring to the south much as he, Shonah, and the second minister were doing.

After a while, a pattern emerged. It seemed only some of them were on the move. Aindreas had split his army into thirds, positioning one cluster of men to the west and another to the east, while keeping the rest where they had been.

"Damn him," the swordmaster said quietly.

Shonah frowned. "What is it?"

"It's as if he knew the minister had the power of mists. By dividing his army this way, he makes it dangerous for us to shroud the battlefield. We won't be able to keep watch on all three groups of men."

"Can we split our army as well?"

"We can, but we don't know how their numbers are divided. All we can see are the torches. He may be trying to trick us into doing just that. Damn," he said again. "Say what you will about the man, but he is clever."

"So what do we do?" Danior asked.

Hagan thought for several moments, rubbing a hand across his face as his eyes continued to scan the plain. "Nothing for now," he finally said. "We'll keep watching them and see what the morning brings. If he had an ally in this, another army to throw at us, I'd worry about our flanks. But I'd guess that he still has only as many men as we, in which case we should be able to guard the east and west without weakening our center too much."

"Very well," the duchess said. She remained there for several minutes more, her gaze still fixed on the distant torchlight. "Wake me if anything changes," she said at last.

"Yes, my lady."

She walked away, leaving Hagan and the second minister.

Danior cleared his throat. "If there's nothing else, swordmaster, I think I'll get some sleep as well."

"Actually, there is, Minister." Hagan faced the Qirsi. He still didn't like him, he wasn't even certain that he trusted him completely. But he had nowhere else to turn under the circumstances. "I've promised the duchess that I would remain by her side when the fighting begins, and I intend to. But I want you to be there, too. If something happens to me, or if I'm too occupied by the battle to guard her and you judge her to be in danger, I want you to raise a mist and get her away."

The minister regarded him with unconcealed surprise, his yellow eyes gleaming with the light of Curgh torches, his thin face looking almost hawklike.

"Is there something wrong?"

The man shook his head. "No, nothing. I just never imagined you would trust me with any task at all, much less guarding the lady's life."

Hagan hesitated, uncertain of what to say. "I'm sure the duchess will be safe with you."

"Thank you, swordmaster. I'll do my best to justify your faith in me."

Hagan watched the Qirsi ride toward the back of the camp before turning his attention once more to Kentigern's army and assigning the watches for the night. He didn't expect to get much sleep, but neither did he trust himself to keep watch on Aindreas and his men until dawn. And this gave him something to do. The swordmaster would never have admitted this to the duchess, particularly now, but he had never led an army to war before. He had been training the men of Curgh for more than ten years, and he had led small parties into the Moorlands and the coastal hills to capture bands of brigands. But Curgh's army hadn't been in a full battle in over a century.

His reputation as a warrior, which had spread throughout much of the Forelands, was founded almost entirely on the success he had enjoyed in sword tournaments at castles in Eibithar, Wethyrn, and Caerisse. He had studied military tactics nearly all his life. He knew what to do with an army. But unlike Aindreas and his swordmaster, Villyd Temsten, who had at least fought skirmishes with the Aneirans, Hagan had almost no experience with true warfare.

He tried to tell himself that it wouldn't matter, that Aindreas and Villyd hadn't been to war in years and the soldiers of both armies were new to combat. He knew better, though. At that moment he would have given up half his men to have Javan there with him. Not that the duke had been in battle any more than he, but Hagan would have felt far more comfortable relying on Javan's instincts than his own.

After taking his own watch, and then riding among the men with one eye still on Kentigern Wood, Hagan finally lay down on his damp bedroll and tried to sleep. He had seen no further movement by Aindreas's army, nor did he expect any more. Reluctant as he was to give himself over to sleep, he knew that he should, that he and his men would be better off in the morning's battle if he did.

He had expected to lie awake for much of the night, but almost immediately fell into a deep slumber, only awaking when the first pale glimmerings of day had started to touch the eastern horizon. Many of his men were already up, as was the duchess, who rode among the soldiers, greeting them with a confident smile and soft words of encouragement.

She's better suited to this than I, Hagan thought, feeling a surge of fear. *I should have been doing that.*

He rose, and looked toward the wood. There was already a good deal of movement in Aindreas's three camps, and the swordmaster cursed himself for sleeping so long.

"Swordmaster!"

"Yes, my lady," he said, tearing his gaze from the torches of Kentigern's army.

The duchess looked tired, as though she hadn't slept, and in spite of the smile she had offered the men, she looked pale and afraid in the faint light of the coming dawn.

"Have you thought of a way to position the men that will counter what Aindreas has done with his army?"

He nodded. This much, at least, he had done. "We should divide our bowmen as they've divided their army, positioning enough of the archers on each of our flanks to keep Aindreas's men from getting around behind us. We'll lead with our third group of archers. I want to try to thin their numbers somewhat before the close fighting begins. Aindreas has come this far to meet us, so I doubt he'll wait for us to attack first. He can't allow us to get past them or his castle is lost. We, on the other hand, can afford to take a more defensive posture. As long as our lines hold, we should be fine."

She gave a wan smile. "I'll have to trust you, Hagan. I understand so little of this."

The swordmaster nodded, saying nothing, but wondering if he really deserved the faith she had placed in him.

The duchess watched him expectantly for several moments. "Should we ready the men?" she finally asked.

"Yes, of course. Forgive me, my lady. I'm . . . I'm still shaking the sleep from my head."

"Are you sure you're all right?"

"I'm fine." His horse stood nearby, and he walked to the beast now, swinging himself into his saddle and riding with the duchess back to where the men awaited them. As quickly as they could, Hagan and his lieutenants arranged the men in a broad curving formation, the archers set as he had described to the duchess, and the pikemen and swordsmen arrayed around them.

The sky remained grey and the air misty. They couldn't see the sun as it rose behind them, but there could be no mistaking the brightening of the plain, or the strains of "Orlagh's March" drifting toward them from Aindreas's army.

Aindreas's men had arranged themselves in tight formations, the center one led by the duke himself, high upon his great horse. Villyd and Kentigern's Qirsi led the other two. The singing of Aindreas's men had grown louder, but still they hadn't started toward the center of the plain. Hagan wasn't certain why.

He glanced back at his men, only to find that nearly every one of them was watching him. Most of them looked so terribly young, barely older than Xaver, that the swordmaster felt his chest tighten at the sight of them. How many would survive this battle? They knew how to fight; he had trained them well. But seeing the fear in their eyes, he suddenly doubted that would be enough.

It took him a moment to realize that they were waiting for him to speak. Abruptly feeling self-conscious, he looked toward the duchess and Danior and found that they were eyeing him as well. This was the last thing he needed just then. He had never been good with words. Inspiring an army was the province of a duke, and though he had been born a noble, he had spent his life as a warrior.

He cleared his throat. "We fight for Curgh," he said.

The men gave a cheer, though not one that was likely to strike fear into the hearts of Aindreas's army.

"We fight as well for our duke, who is to be king."

Again, they shouted their agreement.

"But most of all," he said, facing Shonah, and drawing his sword. "We fight for our queen." He raised the flat edge of his blade to his forehead and bowed to her.

This time the Curgh army gave a full-throated cry that reverberated across the plain like thunder.

Kentigern's army shouted as well, as if answering Curgh's challenge, and an instant later, a single arrow arced into the sky from the center of Aindreas's army. The last echoes of both armies' war cries faded away and it seemed to Hagan that all eyes were on that barb as it paused high above the open ground before beginning its swift descent to the earth. And when it struck, burying itself in the ground between the two camps, both armies surged forward, the roar of hoarse voices and the ring of drawn steel shattering the brief silence.

Chapter
Twenty-eight

✦

It was what she imagined it would be like to be caught in a whirlwind. Amid the fearsome din of screaming men and clashing steel, the dizzying tumult of flailing limbs and slashing weapons, Shonah could barely remember where she was and which men were hers. There was something terrifyingly arbitrary about the violence that surrounded her. This wasn't war, at least not as she had thought it would be. This was a maelstrom of blood and pain and death. There was no control here, no tactics were at work. Men were maiming and killing each other, bleeding until the grasses of the plain were darkened and slick. Call it frenzy. Call it madness. But to make more of it than that would have been a lie.

The duchess held her sword in her hand and there was blood on the blade. Riding beside Hagan as the battle began, she had fought alongside the men of Curgh just as Javan might have, hacking at the foot soldiers of Kentigern who grabbed at her and tried to pull her from her mount. She was so close to Aindreas that she could see the spittle flying from his mouth as he shouted commands to his men. Atop his enormous horse, the duke fought like one of Bian's demons, whirling his horse from side to side with astonishing agility and leveling blow after bloody blow at Javan's men.

Shonah had told Hagan the night before that she hoped her presence on the battlefield would force Aindreas into a mistake. Instead, it appeared to embolden Kentigern and his men. They surged in her direction, as if they believed her death alone would bring them victory. After only a few minutes—though it seemed far longer than that—Hagan's defense began to sag under the weight of their assault and the swordmaster screamed for her to go.

She tried to turn away, to ride back toward the rear of their lines, still swinging her sword at the men who reached for her. But she saw no path of retreat. Arrows hissed by her head and still more men pressed toward her.

I'm going to die here, she thought, fear seizing her heart like a taloned hand.

But in that instant a voice cut through the bedlam, so calm that it startled her.

"This way, my lady."

She turned and saw Danior at her side, a reassuring smile on his pale lips. He gestured toward a small gap in the fighting, and as he did, the duchess suddenly found herself surrounded by a rising mist, as cool as rain, and as impenetrable as mail. She could still see the minister, but little else. Even the cries and the clatter of weapons were muffled by the Qirsi's cloud.

"Follow me," he said. "And stay close."

The duchess hesitated, straining to see Hagan through the swirling mist. She didn't want to leave him, though she knew that she was of no help in this fight, that indeed she was endangering everything.

"My lady, please."

"Yes, I know."

Still she lingered. In her mind's eye, Shonah could see the swordmaster fighting, his sword dancing, wraithlike, a blur of glittering steel and bright blood. He hadn't Aindreas's bulk and brawn, but he was quicker than the duke, and, she believed, smarter as well. Long ago, Javan had told her that when it came to battle, he would always trade strength for speed and wits.

"Duchess, we must go!"

This time she kicked at her horse's sides, following the Qirsi back toward safety. There was a tangle of men in their path, all of them locked in combat, and the minister wound his way through them as quickly as possible, like a man trying not to be noticed. Seeing Shonah ride past, a few of Aindreas's soldiers tried to extract themselves from their battles to strike at her, but the men of Curgh wouldn't allow it. When one man did manage to take hold of her leg and try to pull her from her mount, Shonah hacked at him with her sword. He howled in pain and she sped forward, out of his reach.

Once she and the minister were finally beyond the last of Curgh's men, Danior's mist began to dissolve and fade, allowing the duchess to see the battle once more. The war cries still reached her, as did the howls of the wounded and dying. But she could see little of the fighting and so had no sense of how the battle was going.

"Are we winning?" she asked the minister, not taking her eyes from the knot of men before her.

"I don't know, my lady. Kentigern appeared to be pushing back our center, but I believe our flanks are holding."

It was more than she could tell. She should have been up there still. This was her army. She had said so again and again since leaving Curgh, to Aindreas as well as Hagan. Yet here she was hiding at the rear of the army, waiting for a victory or a defeat in which she would have no part. She would have given anything in that moment to have Javan beside her.

He'd be beside Hagan, as you should be.

"I should go back."

"You'll be killed, my lady. And dozens of men will die trying to protect you."

She bit off a curse that would have shocked her husband, galled by the truth she heard in the minister's words.

"My apologies, my lady," he said quietly.

Shonah shook her head, closing her eyes briefly. "You have no reason to apologize, Danior. You're merely telling me what I know to be true." She glanced at him, making herself smile. "You saved my life, and you have my thanks."

"The duke would have expected no less of me, my lady. He expects—" The Qirsi stopped, his eyes widening and his narrow face turning even whiter than usual. "Demons and fire," he whispered.

Turning in her saddle to see what had come, Shonah felt her stomach heave. A long column of soldiers was approaching the battle plain from the east, following the course of the river. They bore a banner of black, silver, red, and white. The wolf and the moons. Glyndwr.

Javan had never had any quarrel with Kearney, but neither had they ever been friends. Kearney's father, on the other hand, had been closely allied with the House of Kentigern.

"It'll be a slaughter," Shonah said. "Hagan hasn't a chance."

"Shall I raise—?"

She didn't wait for the Qirsi to finish his question. Spurring her mount to a full run, the duchess rode toward the Glyndwr army, her sword raised, her golden hair falling free so that it trailed behind her. She might not have been a warrior, but she knew how to ride, and she knew that she could get to Kearney long before he joined the battle. She had no idea what she'd say or do once she reached the duke, but that seemed far less important than just getting to him. She could hear Danior calling to her, trying to convince her to turn back, but she didn't even look at him.

It was only when she drew near the Glyndwr army that she realized there was more to Kearney's appearance than she had ever imagined possible. He had two Qirsi with him rather than one, and another man who looked oddly familiar.

She reined her mount to an abrupt halt, her hands suddenly trembling so fiercely that she dropped her sword. It was Tavis. Kearney had Tavis.

The duke rode toward her, as did the two Qirsi, her son, and one more man who she guessed was Kearney's swordmaster.

Tavis reached her first, dropping himself off his mount almost before the creature had halted. Shonah dismounted as well and ran to him, wrapping her arms around him and burying her face against his shoulder, her body racked by sobs. At length, she pulled back, looking at him through her tears. He had scars all over his face, as though he had already been through a battle. He flinched slightly as she looked at him, his dark eyes flicking away, his own tears dampening his cheeks. She couldn't begin to imagine how he had suffered. Just the thought made her chest ache.

"Are you . . . are you well?" she asked, forcing him to meet her gaze.

"As well as I'm likely to be."

She opened her mouth, shut it again, unsure of how to ask what she wanted to know most. But it seemed words weren't necessary.

"I didn't kill her, Mother. I give you my word as a Curgh."

She embraced him again. "I believe you." She truly did, though only now, feeling relief warm her heart like sunlight, did she realize how deeply she had doubted him.

"Why are you here?" she asked a moment later, releasing him once more. "Why are you with Glyndwr?"

Tavis shook his head. "I couldn't possibly explain all of it right now. It's enough to say that the duke has granted me asylum."

"Asylum?" She looked up at Kearney, who had stopped his mount a few strides from where they stood. "You give him asylum and then you bring him here?"

"Mother—"

She held up a hand, silencing the boy. "What is this, Kearney? Are you playing games with my son's life?"

"Hardly, my lady," the duke said. He was a handsome man, his youthful face belying the silver of his hair, even now with his expression so grave. "Lord Tavis is here at his own insistence and that of his companion."

"His companion?"

"That would be me, my lady," one of the Qirsi said.

She had barely taken note of him before, but now, eyeing him closely, she saw that he was unlike any other man or woman of the sorcerer race she had ever seen. He sat tall on his mount, with broad, powerful shoulders that gave him the look of a soldier rather than a minister. Like all the others of his kind he had yellow eyes and pale skin, but rather than giving him an appearance of ill health as these features so often did, they made him look formidable, almost frightening. He wore his hair long and loose, and it danced around his face now in the freshening wind.

"And who are you?" Shonah asked.

"My name is Grinsa jal Arriet. I'm a gleaner with the Revel."

"And how have you come—?" She stopped, staring at him. "A gleaner? Are you the one who attended his Fating?"

"Yes, my lady."

His eyes had wandered beyond her, and for a moment the duchess thought he was avoiding her gaze.

"What role have you played in all that's happened to my son?"

"I'd be happy to answer that, my lady. Later. But right now, men are dying before my very eyes. I think it's time we stopped this war."

Reminded of the fighting, Shonah turned to face the battlefield. She wasn't thinking clearly. Tavis, the war, Javan. It was all too much for her. Of course they had to do something. It shouldn't have taken this strange Qirsi to remind her of that.

The men of Kentigern and Curgh showed no sign of having seen the Glyndwr army. They were far too intent on slaughtering each other.

Shonah retrieved her sword and climbed back onto her horse. Tavis remounted as well.

Kearney steered his horse next to hers and stared toward the battle. "How do we stop them?"

"Your army?" she suggested.

"No," the Qirsi said. "That will only add to the carnage."

Shonah regarded the man through narrowed eyes. There was something about him that commanded her consideration. She couldn't help thinking that he was more than he claimed to be. Certainly he didn't speak with the voice of a mere Revel gleaner.

"Then what?" Kearney demanded.

"A wind." This time it was the other Qirsi who spoke. She was as attractive as Grinsa was impressive. She wore her hair tied back in twin braids and she wore mail and a sword that looked slightly foolish on one as slight and delicate as she. Then again, she was no smaller in stature than Shonah herself. *Is this how I appear to the men?* the duchess asked herself.

"My first minister," Kearney said, glancing quickly at Shonah. "Explain yourself, Keziah. What would we do with a wind?"

"Draw their attention, at least for a moment. That may be all we need."

Glyndwr nodded. "Do it."

The woman glanced for just an instant at the gleaner, before closing her eyes and taking a long breath. At first there was nothing, indeed an unnatural stillness fell over the plain, so that it seemed to Shonah that the only sounds in the world were the clashing of blades and the cries of dying men. In the next moment, however, the air around her began to stir, as if Morna herself had waved her hand over the three armies. It built quickly, until it was a gale racing over the grasses. Shonah's hair whipped around her face, and she felt her horse pushing back against the wind just to stand upright.

Within a few seconds it had reached the two armies, hammering at them so forcefully that they couldn't help but pause in their fighting to look in the direction from which the tempest had come. Seeing the banner of Glyndwr, many of Kentigern's men let out a cheer. But Aindreas and Hagan sat unmoving on their mounts, glaring at one another, as if each was trying to gauge what the other intended to do next.

"It worked, Keziah," Kearney said, hollering to be heard over the roar of her gale. "You can stop."

Almost immediately the wind began to slacken. The woman opened her eyes, glancing once more toward the gleaner and favoring him with a small smile.

Aindreas shouted an order to his men, and though Shonah couldn't hear what he said, his tone was such that she half expected the armies to resume their fighting. Instead, men on both sides lowered their swords.

Kentigern started toward them, to be joined a moment later by his first minister. Hagan followed close behind. All of them had sheathed their swords, but when the duke spotted Tavis, he drew his again and kicked at his horse's flanks.

Glyndwr rode forward to meet him, drawing his blade as well.

"Yield, Kearney!" Aindreas said as he approached. "I've no quarrel with you. It's the boy I want."

"Stop where you are, Aindreas. Lord Tavis is under my protection now."

Kentigern halted abruptly, his face contorting with rage and disbelief. *"What?"*

"I've given him asylum. Until all this is resolved, any harm you do to him will bring vengeance from the House of Glyndwr."

Aindreas stared at him, his face reddening. Finally, he lifted his sword and raised himself in his saddle. "So be it."

"Gershon!" Kearney said sharply.

Suddenly there were six archers standing beside the duke of Glyndwr, all of them with arrows nocked and their bows drawn back. Kearney's swordmaster had done little more than move his hand.

"The House of Kentigern has lost too much already, Aindreas. Don't make me take its duke as well."

"Bian throw you to the fires!" the large duke said. "Why would you protect him? After what he did to my daughter—"

"He claims to be innocent."

"And there are whores is Kentigern who claim to be virgins!"

"You tortured him, and still he wouldn't confess. Doesn't that tell you something?"

Shonah looked at her son again, feeling herself wince at the sight of what had been done to the boy's face. To his credit, her son was not shying from Aindreas's glare. He sat straight-backed on his mount, his cheeks pale, but his gaze steady. She had once thought of his features as handsome in a boyish way, but the scars Aindreas had given him changed all that. He still didn't look old; his skin was smooth and he hadn't anything resembling a beard. But he would never look young again.

"All it tells me," Aindreas said, "is that you're a far greater fool than I ever imagined you could be."

Kearney's swordmaster opened his mouth, but the silver-haired duke silenced him with a quick shake of his head.

"Perhaps you're right, and I am a fool. But I won't allow you to destroy this kingdom."

"Do you think you can stand against my army, Kearney? If I choose to take the boy from you, do you honestly believe that you can stop me?"

"He can with Curgh's men fighting beside him," Shonah said, drawing a withering look from Aindreas. "If you move against Glyndwr, our two houses will crush you."

"Lord Kentigern," Tavis began.

But Aindreas held out his sword, its point aimed straight at the young lord's heart. "Not a word, boy," he said, shaking his head. "Not a word, or I swear I'll cut you down where you sit. Let them kill me if they wish. Better to die with your blood on my blade, than to live knowing that you're free."

"Aindreas—"

"How can you do this, Kearney? What of the alliance forged by our fathers? Does that mean nothing to you?"

"On the contrary. It means a great deal to me. But the boy—"

"The boy is a murderer! Damn you, man! Don't you understand that? He killed my girl. I saw her blood on his hands and his clothes. I saw his dagger in her—" His voice broke, his body heaving with sobs. He squeezed his eyes shut, tears streaming down his cheeks into his red beard. Shonah could see him gritting his teeth, as if the struggle to regain his composure pained him.

No one said a word. Kearney and the gleaner kept their eyes trained on the ground in front of them. Even Tavis had the good sense to look away. Shonah looked past the duke to Hagan, who shook his head slightly. She understood. More than anything, she wanted to hate this man. He had tortured her son, imprisoned her husband, and brought her to a war she didn't want. But she had lost a babe herself, and she remembered the grief with a clarity that made her eyes sting. True the child had been a turn short of being born, but that hardly diminished the pain she had felt. She couldn't begin to guess how Aindreas and Ioanna had suffered since Brienne's death. *If it turns out that the boy is guilty*, she told herself, *I'll have him hanged myself.*

"I should have killed him when I had the chance," Aindreas finally said, his voice ragged.

"Then you would have killed an innocent man," the gleaner said.

Aindreas regarded him warily, his eyes red. "Who are you?"

"A friend of Lord Tavis's, and of yours as well, though I doubt you'll believe that."

The duke's eyes widened with recognition. "You're the one who freed him, aren't you? You're the bastard who took him from my prison!"

"I helped him get out of Kentigern, yes."

A dangerous smile spread across Aindreas's face. "You I can kill."

"Enough, Aindreas!" Kearney said. "If I have to I'll grant him asylum, too. But this talk of vengeance has to end."

Kentigern shook his head in disbelief. "Now you're protecting a Qirsi? This is a conspiracy, isn't it? I've heard rumors of such a thing. But I never thought that you'd be party to it, Kearney."

"The rumors you've heard are true," Grinsa said. "There is a movement growing among some Qirsi in the Forelands whose aim is to wrest control of Braedon and the six kingdoms from the Eandi. And I believe your daughter was a victim of this movement. But the duke of Glyndwr is no more a conspirator than he is a sorcerer, and the same can be said for Lord Tavis. Indeed, I believe that he's a victim of the movement as well."

"The boy? Absurd!"

"Is it? What better way to weaken the Eandi courts of Eibithar than to plunge the land into civil war. And what better way to do that than to take the land's two most powerful houses and turn them into bitter enemies?"

"So you believe that a Qirsi killed Brienne?" Shonah asked. "And then made it seem that Tavis had done it?"

"I believe that Qirsi gold paid the assassin who murdered her. I can't be certain of anything beyond that."

Tavis started to say something, but the gleaner stopped him with a hard glare and a shake of his head. Shonah would have liked to know what her son was thinking, but she trusted this Qirsi and if he wanted the boy to keep silent, she wouldn't pursue the matter. If there truly was a conspiracy—and at the mere mention of the possibility, an icy fear had settled deep in her bones—there was no telling who among them could be party to it.

"What do you think of all this?" Aindreas asked, his eyes fixed on his first minister.

The man gave a small shrug. "We've all heard the rumors. There's nothing new in that. But I've seen no evidence of this movement in Kentigern, and I can't believe that a band of Qirsi could defeat our defenses so thoroughly as to murder the Lady Brienne and implicate the boy."

The duke nodded. "I'm inclined to agree."

"I'm sure you are," said the one named Keziah. "And two turns ago you would have said the same if asked whether a man could escape your dungeon."

Aindreas's face reddened.

"Both our houses have suffered, Aindreas," Shonah said, keeping her tone so gentle that she might have been speaking to a frightened child, "though I'd never deny that Kentigern has lost far more than we have. But if there's even a chance that this conspiracy exists, don't we owe it to the land to learn more before we try to destroy each other?"

"You all just expect me to let the boy go, to forget what I saw the morning after she died?" Aindreas shook his head. "You're all mad."

"There's little else you can do, Aindreas," Kearney said. "Unless you're willing to risk war with both my house and Javan's."

"The dukes of Kentigern will never forget this, Glyndwr. Long after I'm gone, my people will curse your name, just as they do Curgh, all because of what you do here today."

"That saddens me, Aindreas. I gave the boy my word that I would protect him. I certainly intended no offense to you or your people."

"You chose Curgh over Kentigern!"

"I chose peace over war, and would do so again without hesitation! But know this." He paused, looking at Shonah as well. "If I learn that Tavis is guilty in this matter, I'll return him to the prison in Kentigern myself. Glyndwr does not knowingly harbor murderers."

The duchess glanced at Tavis, who met her gaze and gave a single nod.

"I understand, my Lord Duke," she said. "I thank you for the consideration you've given my son and I accept those terms."

Kearney inclined his head slightly, acknowledging what she had said. Then he turned to Aindreas. "Lord Kentigern?"

"As you say, Kearney," the duke muttered, refusing to look at any of them, "my only choice is to make war on both your houses." After a few seconds he raised his eyes, glowering at Tavis. "If you want that demon in your castle, you can have him. If you've any sense at all, you'll lock him away until he rots."

"Does that mean we can end this war?" Shonah demanded. "Will you let my husband go?"

Aindreas hesitated, the hand gripping his sword tightening until his knuckles were the color of Qirsi hair. "Yes," he finally said. "I'll let him go. But I will not allow his ascension to the throne."

Hagan drew his sword. "Then there's a war to be fought after all."

The duke turned his horse to face the swordmaster. "So be it, MarCullet. But I will not allow a house of liars and butchers to rule this land."

"And I won't allow one man's blind need for vengeance undermine the Rules of Ascension!"

"This war is over!" Kearney said, spurring his mount forward until he was between the two men. "If I have to I'll place my army between the two of you. But I will not allow you to destroy this kingdom." He pointed at the gleaner. "Didn't you hear what he said? Don't you understand that this weakens us?"

Before either of them could answer, a cry went up from the battle plain. Shonah spun around, expecting to see the armies fighting again. Instead, however, she saw several men running in their direction, some from Curgh and some from Kentigern. Ahead of them rode Villyd, Aindreas's swordmaster. All of them were pointing to the south toward Kentigern Wood.

Looking that way herself, Shonah saw immediately what had alarmed them. The low heavy clouds that had darkened the past several days had lifted with the morning. The clouds that remained continued to cover the sky, blocking the sun. But the threat of rain had passed, and one could see clear to the horizon where there were no trees blocking the view. To the south, however, the sky remained murky, and the light mist that had hung over the wood the night before had been replaced by a sooty grey haze. Somewhere beyond the wood, something was burning.

"I can smell it."

The duchess didn't realize she had spoken aloud until Hagan looked at her and nodded.

"It might just be the wood," Kearney said.

"Or it might be my castle," Aindreas said, staring grimly at the sky. He looked at Hagan again. "Is this your doing?"

"I swear to you in the sight of all the gods, it's not. All the Curgh army is either here or back at the castle."

Aindreas turned to Glyndwr. "Kearney?"

"I have no reason to attack the tor, Aindreas. I think you know that."

By this time Villyd had reached them, breathless and wide-eyed. "It's the Aneirans, my lord. Mertesse, probably. I'd wager all the qinde I have to my name."

"Their spies must have seen you leave," Hagan said.

Aindreas nodded. "So it seems."

"We mustn't rush to conclusions, my lord," said Kentigern's first minister. "As Lord Glyndwr said, it could just be the wood, or a fire on the grasses east of the tor."

"After three days of rain?" Hagan asked. "I find that hard to believe."

The sky was darkening with each moment that passed, the smell of smoke growing increasingly pungent.

"He's right, Shurik," Aindreas said. "That's no grass fire. I have to get my men back to the castle."

"Would you allow me to ride with you, my Lord Duke?" Kearney asked. "We've a long way to ride and the Aneirans may have the castle when we get there. Another army might give you the advantage you need."

Kentigern took a breath, then nodded. "My thanks."

"We'd ride with you as well, my lord," Shonah said, "if you'll have us. I know that when this day dawned we were adversaries, but we're all subjects of this kingdom, and we'd be honored to stand beside you against the Aneirans." *And my husband is a prisoner in your tower.*

The duke's mouth twitched, as if he found the very idea of riding with the men of Curgh distasteful. But after a moment he nodded again. He turned toward Tavis, his expression hardening.

"I suppose you'll be riding with us as well."

The boy's eyes flew to Shonah's face, then to Grinsa's. Neither of them moved or said anything.

"Yes, my lord," Tavis said at last. "I offer my sword and my life to the defense of Kentigern."

"Fine." Aindreas turned away, but quickly faced the young lord a second time. "Just stay away from me, boy. If you come within reach of my blade, I swear I'll kill you on the spot, Glyndwr's asylum be damned."

He swung his mount away and started back toward his men, not bothering to wait for a reply. Shurik and Villyd followed, saying nothing.

The duchess and the rest sat in uneasy silence and watched them go.

"I didn't kill her," Tavis said again. He was looking at Shonah, but she could tell that his words had been intended for all of them.

"I believe you, Tavis. I told you that already."

He nodded, staring after Aindreas. "I know you did. But sometimes I think that I'll be protesting my innocence until the day I die."

"You've convinced the duke here," Hagan said, nodding toward Kearney. "And this gleaner as well. That's good enough for me."

For the first time since being reunited with him, Shonah saw her son smile. "Thank you, Hagan," he said. "You and Xaver have proven to be far better friends to me than I deserve."

"It's about time you realized it, boy," the swordmaster said, his words softened a bit by a broad grin. He faced the duchess. "I'll ready the men to march."

"What about the dead?" the duchess asked, wiping the smile from his face. "Are we just going to leave them?"

"You offered Kentigern our aid, my lady. If we're to be of any use to him, we have to march now."

She nodded, knowing that he was right. "Very well. Prepare the men." To herself she added, *May Orlagh forgive us.*

Shonah turned to Tavis once more, favoring him with a smile. "Ride with me?"

"That wouldn't be wise, my lady," Grinsa said, before Tavis could answer. "He's under Lord Glyndwr's protection and so should ride under the duke's banner. It would be presumptuous of him to ride at the head of the Curgh army. It might also be very dangerous."

She felt the color drain from her face. She so wanted for all of this to be over. But even now, with the armies of Curgh and Kentigern preparing to fight side by side, there was no peace for any of them.

"It's all right, Mother," Tavis said, though she read the hurt in his dark eyes. "I'll be fine riding with Lord Glyndwr and the gleaner."

She made herself smile. "Of course you will."

They remained there a moment longer, gazing at one another. Shonah wanted to put her arms around him again and hold him close as she had when he was young. She sensed that perhaps he wanted the same. But that time seemed impossibly far away.

"You're welcome to ride with us, my lady," Kearney said. "If you have no objection to riding under Glyndwr's banner."

"My thanks, Lord Glyndwr. I have no objection at all. I believe it would be appropriate for me to lead Curgh's army from the battle plain. But once we're under way, I'd be most honored to join you."

Kearney smiled. "The honor will be ours, my lady."

Shonah tipped her head in thanks. She glanced at her son one last time, searching for something to say. In the end, though, she merely turned away and followed Hagan and his men.

Smoke continued to darken the southern sky, and the fine haze that had drifted through the wood now covered the plain as well. Aindreas's army had gathered near the edge of Kentigern Wood, while Hagan had assembled Curgh's men on the near side of the bloodied field. Beyond them lay the dead, their bodies strewn on the grasses like the discarded playthings of some spoiled child. Already a pair of buzzards circled above them. Several crows had landed a short distance away and were hopping in ever-closing circles around the bodies, as if summoning the courage to begin their feast.

These men deserved better, and yet the fires burning beyond the wood demanded that they be left there. Javan might have been fighting for his life at that very moment. Or he might already have been dead. They couldn't afford to linger here, not for a moment.

"Be kind to them, Bian," she whispered, turning her back to the battle plain. "Kinder than we've been."

Chapter
Twenty-nine

✦

Kentigern, Eibithar

X aver was asleep when the first cry of warning went up from the westernmost towers of Kentigern's outer wall. At first he thought that he was dreaming once again of the night they found Brienne's body in Tavis's bed, when the voices of Kentigern's guards and their pounding on the young lord's door roused him from his slumber. As the shouting continued, though, he forced his eyes open to find his chamber being brightened by ward fires burning atop the castle's towers. For an instant he feared that Aindreas had returned already, and that he had found Tavis.

"The castle's under attack."

He turned toward Fotir, thinking the minister had spoken. But the Qirsi was looking toward the door.

"Did you say something, my lord?" Fotir called.

"Yes," the duke answered.

Fotir rose from his bed and stepped to the door, as did Xaver.

Javan was already up, peering into the corridor through the small barred window near the top of his door, his eyes gleaming with torchlight. "I said that the castle is under attack."

"You don't know that," one of the guards said, sounding frightened and terribly young.

"Listen to the cries of your comrades, man! Look at the ward fires! What else could it be?"

"The duke went to stop Curgh's advance! He wouldn't have failed, and even if he had, your army couldn't be here already."

Javan closed his eyes briefly, as if fighting an urge to rail at the man. "It's not Curgh attacking, it's the Aneirans, probably Mertesse."

"Impossible!" But the guard didn't sound as if he believed his own denials.

"Maybe I should check," the man's companion said in a low voice.

The guard eyed Javan warily, but after a moment he nodded.

"If you're right, my lord," Fotir said, "and Mertesse finds you here, he'll execute you. As far as the Aneirans know, you're Eibithar's king."

The duke gave a slight shrug. "That may be so. But this is Kentigern Castle, First Minister. Even with Aindreas away and much of his army with him, the siege is likely to fail."

"So what should we do?" Xaver asked.

"We can't do much of anything, Master MarCullet. That is, unless our friend here would like to free us from these cells."

The guard frowned, and looked away, drawing a smirk from the duke.

The second man returned a few minutes later, breathless and flushed. "He was right," he said, nodding in the direction of Javan's door. "It is the Aneirans. They're by the river still, building their engines. But it seems they're planning a siege."

"What are we supposed to do?"

The man gestured at the two rooms. "Stay here and guard them, at least for now."

For what seemed an eternity, they all just waited, listening for any sound that would tell them what was happening beyond the castle walls. After a time, Xaver returned to the window and looked down on the castle's outer ward. Kentigern's soldiers were running in every direction, no doubt trying to prepare the fortress for the coming assault. But Xaver had little sense of what they were doing. He saw no sign at all of the Aneirans. Eventually, he crossed to the doorway again.

"The danger lies mostly in Aindreas's absence," Javan said abruptly, as if continuing a conversation that had been going on for some time. "It doesn't take many men to defend a castle like this one. In fact too many soldiers can cause a good deal of confusion during a siege. But without a seasoned commander, soldiers tend to make mistakes. If the castle falls, that will be the reason." He glanced at the guards. "Who's in command right now?"

The two men exchanged a look, appearing uncertain as to whether or not they should answer.

"The night captain," one of them finally said.

Javan shook his head. "No, I mean who's in charge of the castle's defenses. Not who's overseeing tonight's watch."

"The night captain," the man repeated. "He not only commands the night watch, he's second captain of the guard." The man glanced at his friend again, swallowing nervously. "He's a good soldier and skilled swordsman."

The duke started to respond, but in that instant, another cry went up from the west. A few moments later the shout came again, and then it repeated a third time.

"The master bowman," Javan said. "Mertesse must be approaching the west gate."

Xaver rubbed his hands together, hoping the first minister wouldn't see how they shook. Despite the duke's faith in the strength of Kentigern Castle, he didn't like being locked helpless in the prison tower during a siege.

"You're sure we're supposed to stay here?" one of the guards asked.

The other nodded, but kept his silence.

The rhythmic cries of the master bowman continued, to be joined a short time after by additional shouting. Xaver peered across the corridor, trying to see from the duke's expression if he was alarmed by what they were hearing. Javan seemed intent on the noises of the fight, but he didn't look concerned.

At least not until the castle suddenly shuddered with a blow that seemed to come from the earth itself. The next moment brought a second crash and then another and another.

Javan's brow furrowed. "That's a ram. They're probably trying to bring down the drawbridge."

A moment later a different kind of crash rattled the castle, not as heavy as the ram, but sharper. Several more followed, and with them came screams of anguish.

"Hurling arms?" Fotir asked.

Javan nodded. "Perhaps. Mertesse is sparing no effort."

Again they lapsed into silence, waiting for the next stones to strike the walls, the next blows to hammer at the drawbridge. Dark, bitter smoke floated into the chamber, carrying with it the ragged desperate wails of the wounded. Men were dying beyond the castle walls, and Xaver wondered how long it would be before the fighting breached the gates.

They knew immediately when the bridge failed. The castle shook one last time and an enormous cheer rose from the Aneiran army. Xaver took a long ragged breath, clamping his mouth shut against a wave of nausea.

"Courage, Master MarCullet," said the duke. "The bridge is but the first barrier they have to defeat, and by far the weakest. The Tarbin gate of Kentigern Castle has several portcullises and a door that could stop Orlagh herself."

"Yes, my lord," he said weakly. "Forgive me. This is my first siege."

"You've no need to apologize. I've seen far more seasoned men than you lose their nerve under similar circumstances." He eyed the guards for a moment. "In fact, I don't think you're the only one worrying. These two—"

The castle shook again, even more violently than before.

Javan shook his head, frowning. "That didn't sound good."

Another jolt, and more cheers from the Aneirans.

"Impossible!" the duke breathed. "Something's not right. That door should have held for hours, if not longer."

A few moments later, three more blows made the castle heave and quake. And once more the men of Mertesse roared their approval.

"This makes no sense," Javan said.

The guards had grown pale, and with this last shout from the Aneirans, one of them left, saying that he would find out what was happening.

The assault on the gates went on, the castle seeming to groan under the pounding of the ram, and Mertesse's army letting out more cheers.

The guard returned a short while later, his face a mask of utter despair.

"The gates are failing!" he said. "All of them!"

"How can that be?" Javan asked, sounding truly frightened.

"Magic."

They all looked at Fotir.

"Mertesse may have a shaper with him," the minister went on. "A Qirsi wouldn't have to destroy the gates. Just weakening them would be enough."

The duke shook his head again. "But surely Aindreas's bowmen know enough to kill any Qirsi who tries to approach the gates. A shaper wouldn't have time to do all this."

"Then maybe it was done before," the Qirsi said. "But that's the only explanation that makes any sense. No ordinary ram could do this."

"If you're right," Javan said, "it won't be long before the outer gate is breached and the Aneirans lay siege to the inner walls."

As if in answer, the castle trembled again and yet another cry echoed through the ward.

"You have to free me and all the men of Curgh you hold in this tower," Javan told the guards. "With the gates failing, you're going to need every able-bodied man you can find."

One of the men shook his head, though he didn't look very sure of himself. "You're prisoners of the duke. We can't free you without him saying so."

"I assure you, your duke would want you to do everything in your power to guard his castle. That's what I'd want from my men. You know who I am. You know that I'm to be king. Who do you think will do a better job leading the defense of this castle: your night captain or me?"

The guards just stared at him. They were ill suited to make a decision of this magnitude and both of them seemed to realize it. Again the castle rocked, like a ship buffeted by storm winds.

"Wouldn't another Qirsi help you against the Aneirans? Wouldn't forty-three more swords?"

"You want us to give a sword to the boy?"

Javan pointed at Xaver. "That boy happens to be the son of Hagan MarCullet, of whom I'm certain you've heard a great deal. He may be young, but I'd wager a hundred qinde that he could best half the men in your army."

In spite of everything, the heavy fear that had settled in his stomach and the racing of his pulse, Xaver couldn't help but smile at the duke's praise. For all he knew, Javan was just trying to get the guards to release them, but it was rare indeed to have one's duke— one's king?—say such things.

Once more the walls rose and fell, as if from a land tremor. And this time, the shouts that followed took on a chilling urgency. Voices filled the outer ward below their tower. Hurrying back to the window, Xaver saw soldiers streaming into the castle, most of them wearing the black and gold of Mertesse.

"The last of the gates has failed, my lord!" he called over his shoulder. "The Aneirans are in the castle."

"Do you hear that?" the duke said. "We can't wait any longer! Release us now, before it's too late!"

Still the men said nothing. Xaver lingered at the window a moment longer, watching the men of Mertesse swarm through the ward, his heart in his throat. Over the last turn, he had come to hate the duke of Kentigern and his castle. But seeing the famed walls of Kentigern fail now, he felt as a child might learning for the first time that his father was mortal and flawed. If this castle could fall, no fortress in all of Eibithar was safe.

"If you don't release us," Xaver heard Fotir say, "I'll destroy the locks on these doors. I'm a shaper myself, and that's well within my power."

The boy turned at that and returned to the door.

The guards were staring at the Qirsi as if he were some fearsome wraith from the Underrealm.

"I think you're lying," one of them said, in a voice that held little conviction. "If you can do that, why haven't you before now?"

"Because I told him not to," Javan answered. "Nothing good would have come of it. Even if he defeated the locks and shattered your swords, there were always more guards waiting at the bottom of the stairs. Eventually he would have tired, and then, chances are, all of us would have been killed."

"But—"

"Enough!" the duke said. "Mertesse is in your castle! The siege has moved to the inner walls and you've less than half your army here to defend against it. Now free us, or stand aside while we free ourselves!"

The guards glanced at one another again, each appearing to wish that the other would make the decision.

"Well?" demanded the duke.

"All right," one of them said at last, fumbling for his keys.

Javan nodded as the guard approached his door. "Good man. Your duke would approve. I'm certain of it."

Xaver felt far less certain of this, but he wasn't about to say so to his duke or the soldiers.

After trying one or two keys, the man opened the duke's door, eyeing Javan with just a touch of fear, as if he expected the duke to attack him immediately.

"We'll need our weapons as well," Javan said, stepping into the corridor.

The guard opened the door to Fotir and Xaver's chamber before facing the duke again. "I don't know where they are, my lord," he said.

"Then any weapons will do."

The guard hesitated.

"Demons and fire, man! What's the sense of releasing us if you're not going to let us fight?"

"There are pikes and swords in the arms chamber at the base of the tower," the man said, sounding defeated.

Javan nodded. "Lead the way, friend. Whatever you may think of me, I am of Eibithar before Curgh. And I'll die defending your castle if I have to, as will the men you hold in the chambers below us."

The man actually smiled. "Yes, my lord."

The two guards led them down the stairs and in a few moments had freed all of Curgh's men. They made their way to the arms chamber, where they found the weapons brought to Kentigern by Javan's army. Javan's sword wasn't there, nor were Xaver's or Fotir's. Most likely Aindreas had taken them to his quarters. But that was of little importance just then. There were enough blades, shields, and mail coats for all of them, and after arming themselves, they stepped out of the tower into the inner ward. Soldiers of Kentigern were hurrying through the north gate from the outer ward and walls, pursued by the Aneirans who fought to break through to the interior of the castle.

"Find me your night captain," Javan told the guard, surveying the scene before him. He turned to Fotir. "Take the men and help defend that gate. If we can't keep them out now, we have no chance."

"Yes, my lord."

"Master MarCullet," the duke said, facing him. "You stay with me. I'll need someone to run messages to Fotir and the captain, and I'll need your sword, if the walls don't hold."

He nodded and swallowed. "Of course, my lord."

The guard returned a few moments later with an older man who had to be the night captain. His head was clean-shaven, like that of a prelate in a court cloister, but the similarities ended there. He was tall and barrel-chested, and he wore a thick mustache and beard. He bled from a gash on his brow and there were raw burns on both his arms, but otherwise he appeared unhurt.

"My lord," he said, stopping in front of Javan, a scowl on his crooked features. "I see these men freed you. That wouldn't have been my choice."

"I don't imagine, Captain. But it was the right thing to do. I've added more than forty men to your army, and I've given you a Qirsi who has mists and winds as well as shaping power. You'd be a fool to keep us in that tower."

The captain conceded the point with a single nod. "I take it you intend to take command of our defense of the castle."

"I was hoping we could share that responsibility. I'd guess that I have more experience commanding armies. But I lack your knowledge of Kentigern or her men."

"Very well," the captain said after a brief pause. "We started the night with about six hundred, including those at the river, in the castle, and in the city."

Javan raised an eyebrow. "That's all?"

"The duke was intent on defeating your army," the man said with a shrug. "Fewer than half were here when the Aneirans crossed the river, though our men by the river made it back to the castle in time to meet the siege. Still, I've only four hundred men here in the castle and while I'd like more, I'm reluctant to weaken the city's defenses just now."

"I agree. How many sorcerers do you have?"

"Six. Two shapers and three with mists and winds. The other is a gleaner and all but one of them are also healers."

"What happened to the outer gates?"

The captain shook his head, his mouth twitching. "I don't know. They just failed. I can't explain it."

"My first minister suggested that they were weakened by magic."

"There were no Qirsi near the gates during the assault," the man said, his voice rising. "I wouldn't have allowed that."

"Then I'd say you have a traitor in your castle. Unless you want me to believe that the fame of Kentigern is based more on myth than truth."

The captain's face reddened. "What would you have me do now, my lord?"

Javan looked at the man a moment longer, the hint of a grin on his lips. "Secure that north gate," he said. "And then get your bowmen on the inner walls. Mertesse has the upper hand right now, but as long as we can keep him from breaching the inner keep, we should be all right. That is, unless the inner gates have been weakened as well."

"The bowmen are climbing the towers already, and the battle at the gate was going our way."

"Good. Go back to your men." Javan laid a hand on Xaver's shoulder. "This is Xaver MarCullet. He'll carry messages between us. Use my men however you see fit. Tell my first minister that he's to follow your orders as if they come from me."

"Yes, my lord." He started to turn away. Then, seemingly as an afterthought, he offered a small bow.

"Oh, Captain, I forgot to ask. Is the duke's family safe?"

The man hesitated, his eyes narrowing as if he wasn't certain he could trust the duke with an answer.

"Yes," he said at last. "As soon as I heard the Aneirans had crossed the river, I had the duchess and her children taken to the sanctuary."

"That was wise," Javan said.

The man nodded and walked away.

"The guards were right," the duke murmured, watching him go. "He is a good soldier." He glanced at Xaver. "Come along, Master MarCullet. We should be on the walls."

Since Brienne's death, Javan had appeared to age before Xaver's eyes, his facing growing gaunt and pinched, his back more stooped by the day. But as the duke hurried up the winding stairs of the nearest tower, a sword in his hand, Xaver following close behind, the years seemed to fall away from him once more. The boy couldn't help thinking that Javan was enjoying this.

For his part, Xaver had never been more afraid. He had no desire to walk the walls with the duke, in plain sight of the Aneiran archers massing in the outer ward. Yes, he was good with a blade. His father had taught him a great deal. But he had never fought for blood, and he certainly had never killed, or defended himself against a foe who truly wished him dead.

"You're very quiet, Master MarCullet."

"Yes, my lord."

"You're scared."

"I'm sorry, my lord."

"It's all right. Only a fool knows no fear. The measure of a warrior is how he overcomes his fear. Always remember that."

"Yes, my lord."

"Besides, I intend to keep you so busy that you won't have time to be afraid."

They stepped out of the stairwell and onto the castle wall, and Javan spat a curse. Already men in black and gold had reached the top of the wall and were battling Kentigern's soldiers. More were climbing onto the ramparts by the moment. Scanning the rest of the inner wall, Xaver could see that Mertesse's men were everywhere. The defenders tried to use forked sticks and even their pikes to push the hooked ladders away from the wall. But for every ladder they defeated, two more took its place. Archers loosed their arrows at the climbers, but they were too numerous to be driven back. It wouldn't be long before the Aneirans controlled the wall.

Javan started forward, his sword held ready. Xaver did the same, though his legs felt so uncertain that he barely trusted them to keep him standing.

"No, Master MarCullet," the duke said, casting a quick look over his shoulder as one of Mertesse's men advanced on him. "I need your legs more than I need your blade. Go to the captain. Tell him we need Fotir and the other shapers up here immediately. If we can't break those ladders, we're lost."

"But, my lord—"

"Go, boy! Now, before it's too late!"

Reluctantly, Xaver turned away from the duke and hurried back down the stairs, faltering only for a moment when he heard the ring of clashing swords just behind him. He was back in the ward within just a few moments, and, sprinting across the trampled grasses to the north gate, he soon found the captain.

"Yes, boy, what is it?" he said, his gaze flicking in Xaver's direction for but a moment before returning to the fighting just in front of them. "Tell the Qirsi to use their fire!" he hollered, before Xaver could answer. "We have to drive them back and get those portcullises down!" He looked at Xaver again. "Speak, boy! I haven't time for shy children."

"There are Aneirans on the wall, sir. They've got ladders and the men can't hold them off for much longer. The duke wants his first minister and the other shapers up there to break the ladders. He thinks it's the only way to stop them."

"Demons and fire," he man muttered. "I can give you one and the minister. My other shaper also has fire. I need her here."

Xaver was speaking for the duke, but he was doing so in Kentigern. He couldn't argue with the man.

"Very good, sir."

"Tell your duke the Qirsi will be there shortly. I'll see to it myself."

"Thank you, sir."

Xaver ran back to the tower and started up the stairs, taking the steps two at a time. The mail slowed him some and made it seem a far warmer night than it really was, but he still had his wind. His father would have been pleased, the boy thought, a smile briefly touching his lips. Running the towers of Curgh had prepared him well for this night.

Stepping out onto the wall's walkway, Xaver felt his heart turn cold. There were even more men in black and gold than there had been a short time before. Kentigern's men still fought, but they were outnumbered and falling back. Javan was still near the opening to the stairs, fighting off two Aneirans. Xaver's father had spoken to him often of the duke's brilliance with a blade, but until this night, Xaver had never seen his duke fight. The Aneirans he battled were far larger and brawnier than Javan. Indeed, the duke looked like a frail old man beside them. But it seemed to Xaver in that moment that the duke had been born to fight. He used his shield as if it were part of his arm, blocking every slash and thrust of the soldiers' swords with apparent ease. All the while, the duke's own steel whirled and flashed as if it were alive, flicking out like a serpent's tongue to strike at the soldiers. Both of the larger men were bleeding from small cuts on their faces, arms, and shoulders. None of the wounds was enough to drop them, but together they had to take a toll.

Sweat ran down Javan's face like early rains off the steppe, and his teeth were bared in a fierce grin. One man already lay dead behind the two Aneirans, his blood on the duke's sword. Javan had to be tiring, but he showed no sign of weariness. Instead it was the soldiers who appeared to be laboring, every blow they aimed at the duke seeming more desperate than the last. Even faced with two men, both of them younger and stronger, the duke was controlling this battle.

Which was why Xaver was still standing by the top of the stairs merely watching when the Aneiran swung himself onto the wall from an unseen ladder, landing just beside him. He was just about as tall as Xaver, but far broader in the chest and shoulders. He had a youthful, clean-shaven face, and Xaver had time to note that he couldn't have been a year or two past his Fating.

For just an instant, the two of them stared at each other, the Aneiran seeming as surprised to find the boy standing there as Xaver had been by the man's appearance. Then the soldier hacked at him with his blade and Xaver abruptly found himself battling for his life, his sword absorbing blow after arm-numbing blow. He heard someone grunt and fall to the walkway nearby, but he couldn't even look away to see if it was Javan or one of the men the duke had been fighting.

He did see a second Aneiran climbing onto the wall from the same ladder his own foe had used, but he could do nothing about it. The soldier had driven him back against the rampart and was still hewing at him with his blade. Thus far Xaver had managed to block every blow, but the muscles in his shoulder were screaming, and his blade was notched.

The man raised his shield with his other hand and swung it at Xaver's head. The boy blocked it with his own shield, his knees buckling under the weight of the blow. But even as he struggled to recover in time to block the man's sword yet again, Xaver heard a voice in his head. His father's voice.

The first thing an inexperienced warrior forgets in the heat of battle, is that he has two hands. Every time you defend with your sword, you miss a chance to strike at your opponent.

Of course.

When the Aneiran brought down his blade again, Xaver raised his shield to meet the blow. At the same time, he swung his own sword at the man's side. The soldier lowered his shield in time, but already Xaver was starting his next attack, this one at the Aneiran's shoulder. Again, his foe managed to block it. But the man stepped back, as if realizing for the first time that he was truly in a fight. Xaver gave him no time to rest, leaping forward with his sword raised once more. He was still tired. His blade arm ached. But his fear had vanished. In his mind he was in the city ward of Curgh Castle with his father shouting instructions to him.

Don't get careless! You should always be most careful when you're certain the advantage is yours. A man who feels he's losing is liable to try anything.

The man parried Xaver's blow, then raised his blade as if to strike at the boy's head. Xaver raised his shield, only to find that the soldier had dropped to one knee and was slashing at his legs. It was all he could do to wrench himself out of the way, tumbling hard onto his back so that all the air was forced from his lungs. Still on his knee, the soldier sought to finish him with a chopping blow. Again Xaver raised his shield in time, slashing at the man's arm with his blade at the same time.

The soldier cried out in pain and stood again, backing away. Xaver scrambled to his feet. He was breathing hard, and he wiped the sweat from his brow with the back of his sword hand. The Aneiran was bleeding from his wrist, just below the edge of his mail sleeve. Their eyes met, and in that moment it seemed to Xaver that the world stood still. This soldier had a name, a life, people who loved him. Xaver could imagine the Aneiran with his mother and father, doing chores outside a small home in the Mertesse countryside. Perhaps he was married already. Perhaps he had children.

Always remember that you carry more into battle than just a sword and a shield. Any part of the body can be a weapon. Your elbows and shoulders, your legs and feet, even your head. Most soldiers forget this. They think only of their steel. The man who uses all his weapons has a distinct advantage.

They sprang forward at the same time, swords raised, shields ready. Xaver was staggered by the collision with the larger man. He managed to keep his balance, but once again he found himself forced against the wall. The soldier wasted no time, jumping at him once more. Xaver raised his sword again, but as the Aneiran moved his shield to ward himself, the boy lashed out with his foot, catching the man in the thigh with the toe of his boot.

It wasn't enough to knock the man over, but it did throw him off balance long enough for Xaver to hammer his sword into the man's side. The soldier's mail kept the blow from drawing blood, but he fell onto his stomach. And without hesitating, without even thinking, Xaver pounced on him, driving the point of his blade into the man's back. The soldier's body arched for an instant, as if he were a Revel tumbler in the midst of his performance, and he took a long shuddering breath. Then he collapsed onto the stone, limp and lifeless.

Xaver didn't move. He just remained there on his knees, watching the blood flow from the wound into the grey metal circles of the soldier's chain armor. He had stabbed a man in the back. It wasn't a proper kill.

Someone shouted his name in warning and he turned in time to see another Aneiran coming at him, weapon raised, rage in his dark eyes. Xaver didn't even raise his shield. There was a sharp musical sound, like a bell ringing, and the man's sword broke in two. The Aneiran stared at what was left of his steel, looking shocked. He spun around and in that moment Fotir stabbed him with his sword. The man grunted and dropped to his knees, sliding off the Qirsi's bloody steel and lying down almost gently on the stone. The Aneiran had been unarmed. That wasn't a proper kill either.

The first minister strode to where he was kneeling and tried to hoist him onto his feet. "Stand up, Xaver, before you get yourself killed!"

"These weren't proper kills," the boy said, shaking his head.

"What are you talking about?"

"I stabbed him in the back." Xaver looked at the Qirsi. "And you killed an unarmed man." He shook his head again. "That's not the way you're supposed to do it."

"Xaver . . ." Fotir exhaled, closing his eyes for a moment. Then he lifted the boy to his feet. "This isn't a tournament, Xaver. This is war. You kill however you can, and you do whatever is necessary to stay alive."

"But it wasn't right." He felt a tear rolling down his cheek, then another. An instant later he was sobbing, his arms hanging limp by his sides.

Fotir wore a pained expression and it seemed for just a second that he wanted to put his arms around the boy. But a noise from behind him made him spin, his sword flashing again at yet another Aneiran climbing onto the wall. The soldier blocked Fotir's sword with his shield and raised his blade to strike. Before he could, however, the minister shattered his sword as well. He pulled back his blade arm as if intending to kill the soldier, but at the last moment appeared to change his mind. He swept his sword low, catching the

Aneiran on the side of the knee. The man fell to the ground, clutching his leg, and Fotir slammed the hilt of his sword into the base of the soldier's skull, knocking him senseless.

Fotir stepped to the wall and stared over the edge. Xaver didn't see him move, but after a moment he heard a sound like the rending of wood, and then screams that faded before ending abruptly.

He faced Xaver again. "I need you now, Master MarCullet." He gestured toward another Qirsi, who was standing near the top of the stairs, his face as white as Panya. "The underminister and I have to get to the rest of the ladders before any more of Mertesse's men gain the wall. We'll need another sword."

Xaver was still wiping tears from his face, but he nodded. He returned to the man he had killed and, gripping the hilt of his sword, pulled the steel from the soldier's back. He desperately wanted to wipe the man's blood from his blade, but he didn't know what to use.

When he turned again, Javan was there, a dark bruise on his brow and blood oozing from a wound on his shoulder. He and Fotir were speaking in low tones. As Xaver approached them, the duke looked at him gravely.

"The first minister has told me of your battle, Master MarCullet, and of your misgivings. As your duke, I feel I must commend you for both."

He felt his color rising and he couldn't decide whether he was angry with the Qirsi or grateful to him. For the moment he merely said, "Thank you, my lord," hoping that would be the end of it. Fortunately, the battle demanded no less.

With Javan leading them, followed by the two Qirsi and then Xaver, they made their way along the wall, fighting past the Aneiran soldiers they encountered so that the two sorcerers could destroy the siege ladders that hung on the castle like vines. Gradually, men of Kentigern joined them, swelling their numbers to some twenty or more men, and they swept along the walkway like a tide, driving the Aneirans back and slowing the flow of attackers onto the wall.

Xaver remained in the middle of their small group and though he struck at a few Aneirans with his blade, he hit only steel. The other men around him were older and more seasoned. Most of them were also quite a bit larger than he. But the blood on Xaver's blade, which had brought him such pain a short time before, now glimmered in the torchlight like a medal, marking him as one of them.

Within a short time, they had secured the entire west wall and much of the south. But near the towers of the south gate, the army of Mertesse rallied. Xaver could see them still climbing onto the wall on the far side of the castle, fanning out in both directions. He could see as well small groups of Aindreas's men trying to hold the Aneirans back, but with more of the enemy joining the fight each moment, they were clearly doomed.

Xaver knew that Javan saw this as well. He lashed his sword at the men of Mertesse like Binthar himself, calling for Fotir and the other Qirsi to shatter their swords. But the ministers were tiring and the sheer numbers of the Aneirans began to turn the battle. Soon Javan and the others were falling back again, giving ground grudgingly, but giving it nevertheless.

One of Kentigern's men called out, pointing at something beyond the wall and below. Stepping to the rampart, Xaver felt his blood turn cold. The Aneirans had steered their ram into the outer ward and were pushing it slowly toward the south gate. Much of the fighting thus far had been at the north gate, and Xaver feared that Kentigern's captain might still have his attention fixed there. It seemed Javan had the same thought.

"Master MarCullet!" he called over his shoulder, still fighting one of the men in black and gold. "Go back down to the captain! Tell him what we've seen! Hurry!"

Xaver turned to go, but then stopped abruptly. The Aneirans had retaken much of the west wall. But more than that, it seemed they had already found a way to repair or replace the ladders broken by the Qirsi, for they were swarming onto the walkway again. Xaver thought he could just make it to the nearest tower and its stairs before the men of Mertesse reached them. That way at least he could warn the captain. But he feared that if he left the duke and Fotir now he might never see them again. They were trapped on the castle wall.

Chapter
Thirty

✦

ven having been to war once before, Yaella remained ignorant in the ways of battle. She had been young the first time she rode into battle with Rouel and, mercifully, the fighting had ended quickly with the men of Mertesse being driven back across the Tarbin. It hadn't truly been a war so much as a skirmish, and an inconsequential one at that. So perhaps she shouldn't have been surprised to find that her expectations were so wrong in so many ways. But as she watched this battle unfold, she felt as though the lessons of a lifetime were being discredited one by one. War, she had been led to believe, was a disciplined endeavor. Men followed orders. Battle plans unfolded as intended. Large armies defeated smaller ones, and unexpected betrayal led inexorably to defeat. She never imagined that the fortunes of war could change so swiftly or so often, or that the ebb and flow of battle would be as fickle as storm winds in the Scabbard Inlet.

When the last portcullis in Kentigern's west gate finally fell, and Rouel's men rushed through, their weapons held high and a war cry on their lips, she was certain that the castle would be theirs before long. The duke seemed just as confident, going so far as to leave the ram by the outer walls while he and his men attempted to take the inner keep. It didn't take long, however, for the resistance put up by Kentigern's men to start to take its toll. Rouel's hooked ladders allowed some of his men to reach the top of the inner walls, but many more were struck by arrows and crossbow bolts, and several were maimed and killed when Kentigern's shapers destroyed the ladders.

Soon the duke was forced to turn once more to his ram, and this time, because Shurik had done nothing to weaken the inner gates, the castle's defenses proved far more stubborn. Gradually, the fighting atop the walls started to turn Mertesse's way, not because the duke's soldiers were any better trained or his captains more adept, but rather because there were simply more Aneirans than there were defenders.

Seeing the great number of men in black and gold on the ramparts, Yaella felt her initial confidence return. But once more, the Eibitharians managed to deny them a quick victory. They battled fiercely, and when it became clear that they couldn't stand against Rouel's men, they still found a way to confound them. Ceding the walls to the Mertesse army, the soldiers of Kentigern retreated to the towers, which were far easier to hold. Denied access to the stairways, the Aneirans became easy targets for Aindreas's archers, who loosed their darts from the turrets. After several hours of this, the men on the walls began to climb back down to the relative safety of the outer ward. A few tried to stay on the walls and lift their ladders up to the walkways so that they could then use them to descend into the inner ward, but neither Yaella nor her duke believed that they had any chance of succeeding.

As they watched the fighting go on, Rouel and the minister received word from one of the captains that Javan of Curgh and his formidable Qirsi, Fotir jal Salene, were now commanding the defenders. Far from facing an army with no leader, the duke abruptly found himself at war with a man who was generally believed to be bolder and more cunning than Aindreas.

Night gave way to a morning that dawned grey and cool, and still the fighting went on. Fires burned throughout the outer ward, some of them set by the army of Mertesse, others by the fire pots dropped by Kentigern's men. Black smoke poured into the sky, and somehow the winds continued to carry it northward toward the wood and Heneagh.

The pounding of Rouel's ram echoed through the castle like waves crashing against the Aneiran shore. The great door of the inner gate had finally fallen shortly before the sky began to lighten, but the first of the portcullises still held firm.

Men cried out from the top of the inner wall, and though Yaella could still see black and gold heralds from where she stood, she could tell that their numbers were dwindling. Mertesse's advantages—the size of Rouel's army and the suddenness of their attack—seemed to be fading with each hour that passed.

She sensed Rouel's frustration mounting, and though she was starting to believe that this was just what the Weaver had intended, she couldn't help but feel sorry for her duke. He had hungered for this war for as long as she had served him, and had truly believed that he could take Kentigern, despite the castle's deserved renown. No one who wasn't of the royal family ever ruled Aneira, but that didn't keep dukes from the other houses from vying with each other for influence. Mertesse was already one of the most important family names in the kingdom, and Rouel hoped that in the wake of this siege it would be second only to the royal house.

He spent much of his time near the inner gate, overseeing the assault on the two remaining portcullises. But even when the first of these gave way late in the morning, it didn't seem to cheer him. His men started to celebrate, but he silenced them immediately.

"Stop your cheering!" he yelled, drawing their stares from beneath the ram's roof. "We should have been through here hours ago. So keep your silence and get back to work."

They eyed him a moment longer but then did as they had been told. Yaella could see, though, that the battle had begun to wear on all of them, including the duke. It had been nearly a full day since they left Mertesse, and longer still since any of them had slept. And as the morning had progressed, the fighting had taken a new, darker turn for the Aneirans. Kentigern's men knew the fortress as well as Rouel's men knew their own. There was no surprise in that, of course. But the duke and his soldiers were learning that there was even more to Kentigern Castle than they had thought. Using hidden sally ports and unseen passages, Aindreas's men were attacking from all sides, striking at the army of Mertesse with sudden brief volleys of arrows and bolts before vanishing again. In the time it took them to defeat that first portcullis, the Aneirans lost scores of men.

From the murder holes above the gate, defenders dropped lime on the ram until its roof was nearly gone. At the same time, archers standing within the walls of the gate loosed more arrows at the ram and the men inside. Rouel's soldiers tried to fight back, but the arrow loops were small, and most of their arrows bounced off the thick stone walls and fell harmlessly to the ground.

Yaella couldn't even set fire to the second portcullis, as she had to the first and to the heavy oak door before that, because Kentigern's bowmen wouldn't allow her to get close enough. She tried to raise a concealing mist, but within the narrow confines of the gate, her magic did little good. There were too many archers hiding within the chambered walls; even loosing their arrows blindly into the mist, they kept her from approaching the last portcullis. And failing that, there was little else she could do to aid her duke. She was more a burden than a help, just another life to be guarded by men who should have been protecting themselves. Rouel's other Qirsi weren't doing much more. The men of Mertesse were falling so fast that the duke ordered his Qirsi healers to tend only to those whose injuries were slight, so the injured men could return quickly to the fighting. The rest of the wounded were left to die.

Just when Yaella had decided that war was far better suited to the Eandi than to the people of her own race, the sorcerers fighting to defend the castle proved her wrong. Peering into the archway of the gate to see how the men within Mertesse's ram were fairing, she saw a group of bowmen standing on the far side of the portcullis, all of them with arrows nocked. The men within the ram shouted a warning and began to scramble for safety. But the soldiers of Kentigern did not draw back their bows. Instead, another man stepped into view. A Qirsi. He was tall and bearded and he wore his white hair tied back. Seeing him, Yaella could not look away from his eyes, which were as yellow as the eyes of a cat.

An instant later the man vanished within a swirl of dense mist, no doubt of his own making.

Hearing the commotion from his men, Rouel had hurried to the minister's side, and now he called for his own bowmen to strike at the Eibitharians. Before they could, however, the Qirsi raised a fearsome wind that whipped through the gateway with a high keening sound, like the cry of some dying wild creature. Still the mist poured forth, carried by the gale. Yaella could see nothing of the sorcerer or even of Rouel's ram. But she did hear a ringing sound over the wind, like of two swords meeting, and for an instant she feared that Kentigern's men would step from the mist and cut down all of them. Then another noise reached her, like the rending of wood, and she knew what had happened. She knew as well who it was she had seen before the mist swallowed him.

In another moment, the wind began to diminish, dying away as if it were a retreating storm and carrying with it the last strands of white mist.

The Qirsi was gone, of course, as were the soldiers of Kentigern. Yaella saw nothing to indicate that any of the bowmen had let fly even a single arrow. None of Rouel's men had been wounded or killed. But seeing the wreckage of his ram, the duke's body sagged as if his entire army had been wiped away by Kentigern's assault. The steel chains by which the thick tree trunk hung from the ram's roof beam had been snapped, and what remained of the roof itself had shattered like glass.

"It was Fotir," Yaella murmured. She hadn't intended to speak aloud, and when Rouel looked at her, his expression sour, she felt the blood rush to her cheeks.

"You know this?" he asked.

Of course she did. Who else among the Qirsi of Kentigern and Curgh could have raised such a tempest and still had power enough to destroy the ram? Besides, she had heard others speak of the man's eyes, and she knew what she had seen.

"Yes, my lord."

"And why does it matter who it was?"

She faltered, lowering her gaze and shaking her head. "It doesn't, my lord. My apologies."

Rouel shook his head as well, spitting a curse. "We can't even have the men retrieve the wood. They'd be slaughtered by Aindreas's archers before they had the chance to carry anything out."

"Perhaps with the snail, my lord. They'd be protected, and we wouldn't have to build a new ram from the wheels up."

His face brightened. "Yes, the snail! A fine idea, First Minister! Thank you."

He turned and called to one of his runners, ordering the man to have the snail brought to the inner gate. Then he faced Yaella again, opening his mouth to say more.

It happened so swiftly that the minister didn't truly understand until it was too late. One moment the duke stood before her, smiling once more, and the next he was falling backward like a felled tree, a crossbow bolt buried nearly to its quills in his brow.

For several moments, Yaella could do nothing more than stare at him, watching blood flow from the wound and over his face. Soldiers called frantically for a healer, but Rouel was far beyond a healer's touch. He was with Bian already.

She felt her chest tightening and realized with great surprise that she was crying, although she couldn't imagine why. She had betrayed him long ago, ever since the day she pledged herself to the service of the Weaver. It didn't matter that her betrayal had yet to take her from his side, or even force her to deceive him in any meaningful way. She hadn't truly served him for years.

But seeing him dead was another thing entirely. She and Shurik had convinced him to wage this war, at the Weaver's behest it was true, but that hardly mattered. She had killed him; she might as well have been the one holding the crossbow. Still, even that didn't explain her tears. If she was to blame for the duke's death, wasn't she responsible as well for the life of every dead soldier in the castle and the Tarbin road? Was it possible that she actually cared for Rouel, that she would mourn him as she would a friend?

"First Minister?"

She looked up into the face of a soldier, a boy really. He couldn't have been more than a few years past his Fating.

"What should we do?" he asked.

"What do you mean?"

"Do we continue with the siege?"

"I'm not—" She clamped her mouth shut and swallowed, fighting back a wave of nausea. She had no desire to lead an army, nor was she capable of doing so with any hope of success. But she was still first minister of Mertesse and the highest remaining authority of the house in Kentigern. "Get me the master armsman," she said, her voice fluttering like the wings of a moth. "Tell him what's happened and that I request his aid in commanding the army."

"Yes, First Minister."

The boy ran off, and another soldier stepped forward, as if awaiting her next command.

One of the healers knelt beside the duke's body—she hadn't even seen him come. He looked up at her and shook his head, his expression bleak.

Yaella turned away, searching around her for anything else at which to stare. Her gaze came to rest at last on the ruined ram at the far end of the gate.

"The duke called for the snail," she said, facing the soldier again.

"Yes, First Minister. I believe they're bringing it now."

"Go make certain. And tell them to hurry."

The man nodded once and ran toward the outer gate.

Rouel hadn't truly been her duke for years. But he had paid her and trusted her. More than anything, he had wanted to conquer this castle, and in this one instance, his ambitions and those of the Weaver were the same. She could be true to both of them.

"You intend to continue this war?" the healer asked her, still on his knees.

"I do. It's what the duke would have wanted."

"We've already lost hundreds of men. And now the duke as well. What if this castle can't be taken?"

"It can," she said, believing it true.

The master armsman would know what to do. Together they could do this, in spite of her doubts. Abruptly she wanted nothing more than to avenge Rouel's death. Perhaps it was the one way she had left to make up for her betrayal. Whatever the reason, she had no intention of retreating now.

The healer stood, making no effort to mask his disapproval. *You're Qirsi,* his expression seemed to say. *You should know better.* "What shall I do with the duke?"

She looked down at Rouel's body one last time, fighting an urge to avert her gaze. "Have two of the men carry him to the outer gate. We'll give him a proper funeral when the castle is ours. In the meantime," she went on, not bothering to face the Qirsi again, "return to your healing. We need all the soldiers you can manage to save."

Rumors of Rouel of Mertesse's death spread through the castle like the black smoke that poured from a dozen fires in the outer ward. Fotir and his duke first heard the whisperings around midday, but they did not learn for certain that it was true until just before dark. By then it was clear that the death of the Aneiran duke had done nothing to dissuade his army. If anything, it made them fight harder. This had become more than a siege; it was a war of vengeance.

Another one, Fotir thought, rubbing a hand across his face.

He had hoped that by destroying Mertesse's ram, he would force the Aneirans to abandon their assault on the south gate. But as with Rouel's death, it seemed only to spur them to redouble their efforts. Within just a few hours the attackers had retrieved the remains of the engine using their snail, and by the following morning they had repaired it enough to begin pounding at the portcullis once more. Javan sent Fotir and the bowmen back to the gate so that the minister could try to disable it again, but this time the Aneiran archers were ready for them. The Qirsi couldn't get close enough to use his magic, and eventually he and his men were forced to retreat to the towers. The last portcullis gave way a short time later.

With nothing keeping them from the inner ward, the men of Mertesse swarmed into the keep and turned their weapons on the inner towers, where Kentigern's defenders and the small number of Curgh soldiers who had survived the fighting thus far now found themselves trapped. As long as they still held the ward, Javan and his men had been able to move freely from tower to tower. But with Mertesse controlling the walls and winning the ward, that now changed. Each group of men was forced to defend itself, with no hope of relief or aid. Kentigern's captain still managed to get messages to Javan—his knowledge of the castle was truly impressive. But Mertesse still had the larger force, and with the fall of the south gate that advantage began to grow again.

Once the siege gave way to close combat, Fotir and the other Qirsi became simple soldiers, like everyone else. He and the other shapers could still shatter blades and, if they were lucky, arrows as well. But there were no more ladders and siege engines to destroy, and their mists and winds were of little use.

The first minister stayed near his duke and the MarCullet boy. Javan still fought like a man half his age, his sword bloody now but still whistling as it slashed at Aneiran soldiers. Xaver had recovered from his first kill and was fighting well, though he hadn't the strength of the older swordsmen. But all of them were terribly weary. They had been fighting for nearly two days without rest. As another night approached and the tower grew dark, Fotir wondered if any of them would be alive come morning.

Fortunately, Mertesse's army must have been just as tired. As darkness fell, the fighting slackened, allowing Javan to rest his men in turns while still keeping watch for new attacks. Small groups of Aneirans harassed the defenders throughout the night, as if to make clear that this lull in the battle in no way signaled an end to the siege, but the fighting did not begin again in earnest until daybreak.

Fotir had just awakened when the new assault began, and though he was grateful for a few hours sleep, he was far from rested. All of the men still looked tired, even the duke. It didn't help that they had eaten little since the gate fell the morning before, or that their store of water was running low.

As the shouts of the Aneirans drew nearer and they began to pound at the door to the tower, Kentigern's bowmen took their places at the arrow loops located at intervals along the winding stairway. Unlike the gates, the tower doors were tall enough only for a man to pass through. The ram, which had been so effective against the portcullises, would have hit too high on the tower wall to be effective against the doorways. Instead, the Aneirans had to hammer at these doors with their hands, shoulders, and feet, and though the doors were not as strong as the gates, they were sturdy enough to hold for a time.

"Loose your arrows at will," Javan called to the bowmen. "As soon as they're close enough you can begin."

"We've less than a hundred arrows left among us, my lord," one of the archers called down to him.

"Demons and fire!" the duke said under his breath. "What about the crossbows?" he asked, closing his eyes, as if he expected to be pained by their answer.

"We have about the same number of bolts, my lord."

The first minister felt as if a demon's hand were squeezing his heart. The bolts would last longer than the arrows, simply because they couldn't be loosed nearly as quickly. But two hundred arrows and quarrels wouldn't hold off the Aneirans for long.

The duke turned to the MarCullet boy. "Look in the weapons chamber. See if there are any more there."

"Yes, my lord."

Javan faced Fotir as the boy hurried off. "He's not likely to find more than a few dozen shafts. Do you have any ideas?"

"We still have a bit of lime and a few fire pots in one of the chambers near the top of the tower. But after that's gone, we'll have to rely on our blades."

"If it comes to steel, we're lost. There are just too many of them."

"We don't have to hold out forever, my lord," one of the Curgh men said. "Just until the duke of Kentigern returns."

The minister saw Javan's jaw tighten and he thought he could guess what the duke was thinking.

"The smoke has been blowing north," the Qirsi said, lowering his voice. "Aindreas may have turned back before the armies ever met."

"Or he may have waited until Shonah and Hagan were dead."

He couldn't think of anything to say that might ease the fear he saw in Javan's dark eyes. When Xaver called to the duke a moment later, Fotir was more than happy to look away.

"We found no more bolts, my lord," the boy said as he stepped into view, his arms laden with arrows. "But there were at least two hundred arrows. This is only some of them."

Javan smiled, though Fotir could see that it was forced. "Well done, Master MarCullet. Leave those here and get the rest. I'll have them distributed among the bowmen."

"Yes, my lord."

It was something at least, though not much. Far less than an hour if the arrows were distributed among all of the bowmen in this tower, even if they were used sparingly.

"Take some men to help you with the fire pots," the duke said, looking at the Qirsi again. "But keep yourself out of view. I don't want a stray arrow to find you. We may have need of your magic before long."

Fotir nodded and started toward the stairs, gesturing for several of Curgh's swordsmen to follow him.

The pounding at the door continued, and one particularly heavy blow brought the sound of splintering wood and a cry of triumph from the Aneirans.

"Quickly, First Minister!" the duke shouted as Fotir and his men bounded up the stairs. "They'll be in before long!"

Reaching the chamber, which was located directly above the doorway, Fotir let out a curse of his own. Most of the fire pots and containers of lime were gone. Three of Aindreas's bowmen stood in the room, each stepping to the window in turn to take aim at the Aneirans as the other two nocked new arrows.

"What happened to the rest of the pots?" the Qirsi demanded.

"They needed them atop the tower, Minister, to guard the door leading to the walls."

Of course. He could hardly be angry with them. If the men of Mertesse defeated either door, the tower would be lost.

"Should we hold the rest of them?"

"No. The duke wants them dropped on the men at the ward door."

"The duke?" another of the men repeated. "Aindreas has returned?"

"Forgive me," Fotir said, suddenly feeling uncomfortable. "I meant my duke."

The man frowned and turned away.

The Qirsi glanced back at the men who had followed him to the chamber and nodded once. Two of them stepped to where the pots sat on the floor and readied them. The other two walked with Fotir to the window.

Arrows, some of them still burning, jutted out of the wood shutters like quills from a hedgehog. Staring out at the ward, though taking care not to present too clear a target, Fotir saw men in black and gold massing at towers all around the castle. A few of the doors had already given way and the entrances were choked with soldiers locked in bloody combat. Two of the towers were ablaze, black smoke pouring from their arrow loops and twisting in the light wind as it rose into the sky. The castle would belong to the Aneirans by dusk if the course of the battle didn't change soon. And Fotir had no idea how Javan and Kentigern's captain could possibly turn the fighting their way.

"We're ready, First Minister," said one of the Curgh men. "Should we start with the fire pots or the lime?"

It doesn't matter. "Start with the lime. Maybe we can make them wary of approaching the door."

The man nodded, and he and his companion lifted the pot of lime carefully, carried it to the window, and began pouring it on the soldiers below. Almost immediately screams floated up to the chamber.

"Stop pouring," Fotir commanded. "Don't use it all at once."

An arrow soared into the room, narrowly missing the men and clattering off the stone wall before falling to the floor. Another followed and then several more, until they had no choice but to pull the shutters closed.

"They'll be back at the door in no time," one of Kentigern's men said, as if chastising him.

Fotir knew he was right, but he couldn't help glaring at the man.

"Light one of the fire pots," the Qirsi said.

A Curgh soldier lit the pot using a flint and steel. Fotir took it from him and crouched by the window. Taking a breath, he pushed open one of the shutters and dropped the pot before ducking down again. Almost immediately four more arrows flew into the chamber, two of them flaming. The soldier from Kentigern grabbed the burning arrow and used it to light the remaining four pots.

"Might as well use them now," he said. "They won't do us any good once Mertesse has the tower."

The minister opened his mouth to argue, then closed it again. After a moment he gave a single nod.

More arrows whistled through the window, many of them marked with Kentigern's colors. Now that the Aneirans controlled the wards, they were free to scavenge for arms. Still, Fotir and the soldiers didn't bother closing the shutters again. As long as they stayed low and to the sides they were safe, and this way the Aneirans didn't know when to expect the pots.

Within a few minutes they had dropped all of them and poured out what remained of the lime. The men of Mertesse continued to send arrows and bolts into the chamber, but Fotir and the other soldiers had forced them to break off their assault on the ward door, at least for a while.

"What now, First Minister?" one of Javan's men asked.

The Qirsi glanced at the bowmen "How goes the fight at the top of the stairs?"

The one who lit the pots shook his head. "The door's held so far, but the archers on the tower haven't enough shafts to keep the Aneirans away."

"We found more arrows in the weapons chamber. They'll have more soon."

"Enough?"

Fotir narrowed his eyes, wondering if the man was baiting him again. After a moment though, he shook his head. "No. Not enough."

The man looked around the room, as if searching for something else to throw at the Aneirans. "If the duke had been here, we could have beaten them. They would never have even tried this."

The minister stiffened. "Javan has done all he could to—"

"I'm not blaming your duke. He's done as well as anyone could expect with so few men. I do hold the boy responsible, though. It's his fault we're at war with Curgh. If my duke had been here, and the rest of his army with him, there would be no siege, and I'd be sleeping late today."

Fotir started to tell the man that Tavis was innocent, that he was certain someone else had killed Lady Brienne. But this was no time for that fight, and the man never would have believed him anyway. Still, he felt that by holding his tongue, he was betraying both the duke and the boy.

"Our houses shouldn't be at war," he said at last. "I'll grant you that much."

The man started to respond, but shouting from the stairway stopped him. All of them sprang to the door, and just as they reached it, the tower shook with a loud crash that seemed to come from overhead.

"The door to the walkway!" the Kentigern guard said. He threw down his bow and pulled his sword from the scabbard on his belt. "Seems we were wasting our time with those fire pots."

The minister didn't agree with the man on this either. Better to have only one door fail than both of them. But again, that was an argument for another day. Drawing his blade, seeing the men of Kentigern do the same, Fotir rushed out the door and started up the stairs, taking them two at a time.

They met the Aneirans just short of the top of the stairway, and before the men in black and gold could even raise their weapons, Fotir shattered their blades and ran them through. In his mind he heard Xaver MarCullet saying, *That isn't a proper kill,* and he hesitated for just an instant. But as the next wave of Aneirans came at them, he summoned his magic again. Was it proper to drop lime and burning tar from a high window? Was it proper to loose arrows from murder holes and arrow loops? He had never considered himself a warrior; few of his people had since the time of Carthach. But he served an Eandi duke and had pledged himself to fight and die for the man. He felt his sword pierce the mail shirt of another Aneiran soldier. He smelled blood and sweat and smoke. *This is war,* he had told the MarCullet boy. But he couldn't help but be surprised by his own lust for battle. It almost seemed to the Qirsi that all the anger and frustration of the past turn was pouring out of him now, guiding his sword, giving added potency to his magic. He wasn't tired anymore. On the contrary, every blade he splintered, every life he took, left him wanting more. It didn't matter that his wrath was directed not at Kentigern and his men, but at the soldiers of Mertesse. He was fighting back, finally.

For what seemed a long time, Fotir's power and the sword skills of the men beside him were enough to hold the Aneirans back.

Sword fragments were strewn on the steps, and dead soldiers, most of them wearing black and gold, lay on top of one another, their blood flowing down the stairway like melting snow from a mountaintop. But there were so many soldiers from Mertesse, and even in his battle rage Fotir's lack of rest and food began to wear on him. Eventually the Aneirans began to force the defenders back down the steps. The minister tried to direct his power at their blades, but he was tiring and every blade he broke made it that much harder for him to fight off the next man.

The stairs narrowed as they descended, making their footing more treacherous and the fighting more difficult. The muscles in Fotir's sword arm and shoulder and back burned like embers in a fire. He had cuts on his other shoulder and on his jaw just below his ear. For some time now he had been calling to Javan for help, hoping that the duke would send more men up the stairs to fight back the Aneirans. But thus far no men had come to his aid. He hadn't even heard a reply.

A few moments later, he realized why. From beneath them, echoing in the stairwell, came the clash of swords and the shouts of yet another sword battle. The ward door had given way as well. Javan and his men were being driven up the stairs just as Fotir and the others were being forced down.

"Are you all right, my lord?" Fotir called down, even as he continued to fight.

"I'm alive."

"And Master MarCullet?"

"He's with me. Many of the others wound up in the ward. I fear they haven't a chance."

And what chance do we have?

They battled on, the sound of Javan's struggle growing louder and closer by the moment. It wouldn't be long before the first minister and his duke were fighting back to back.

Fotir heard more cries from outside the tower and he felt despair seeping into his heart. All the towers were falling just as theirs was. Kentigern was lost.

"Do you hear that?" It was Xaver's voice, and something in his tone gave the Qirsi pause, making him listen again, more closely.

This time he did hear it. These weren't death cries from the soldiers of Kentigern or cheers from the Aneirans. They were simply the voices of men from every corner of the castle. And all of them were saying the same two words again and again.

"The duke!" they called. "The duke! The duke!"

With the consent of the duke of Glyndwr and Tavis's mother, Aindreas had driven the three armies back toward Kentigern Tor at a punishing pace. They hadn't slept more than an hour or two since leaving the battle plain, and they had taken their meals without stopping. Tavis was so weary that he could barely carry on a conversation, much less lift a weapon and fight a war. And he had been on horseback the entire way. He couldn't imagine how the foot soldiers continued to march.

Yet, when they finally emerged from Kentigern Wood and saw the castle belching smoke like some creature from a child's nightmare, it seemed to the young lord that the burden of the march fell away, leaving him almost eager for battle.

He had dreaded seeing Kentigern again—the image of its dungeon had haunted his sleep since his escape. But the siege changed everything. This might have been Aindreas's home, but it was also Eibithar's first defense against the Aneirans. In spite of all that had happened and all that the duke had done to him, he meant what he said a few days before, beside the waters of the Heneagh. He would give his life to guard this castle.

His mother had ridden with him and the army of Glyndwr for more than two days, but seeing the castle now, she reined her mount to a halt and faced Tavis, who did the same.

"I should return to Curgh's army," she said. "My place is with them."

As is mine.

She glanced at Kearney, and it appeared that she intended to say something. After a moment, though, she merely offered a sad smile and turned her horse to go.

"May the gods keep you safe, Mother," Tavis said. "We'll meet again in the castle."

"Be careful," she said, looking back at him, her eyes wide. "Orlagh guide your sword."

She rode on without looking back a second time, and Tavis watched her go.

"Come, Lord Tavis," Kearney said at last. "Hagan will keep your mother safe."

The boy nodded and started forward again, following the duke and his dour swordmaster to battle.

As they crossed the open land between the wood and the tor, Aindreas broke away from his army and rode to Hagan and Tavis's mother. The three of them spoke for a few moments before the duke turned from them and steered his mount toward Kearney and Tavis.

"I've told MarCullet and the duchess to ride around the tor to the Tarbin gate," he called as he drew near. "Your army should stay with mine. We'll ride through the city and enter the castle from the east."

"Very well," Kearney said. "You command us today, Lord Kentigern. My men and I are yours to use as you see fit."

Aindreas frowned, as if he had hoped for a fight. "My thanks," he said, his tone gruff. His eyes flicked to Tavis, but he said nothing to the boy. After a brief, awkward silence, he wheeled his mount away and returned to his men, leaving Tavis to wonder if he wanted Glyndwr's army with his own so that he could find a way to avenge Brienne during the battle.

"No one would blame you if didn't join this fight, Tavis."

The boy looked to the side to find Grinsa eyeing him closely, and for just an instant he wondered if the gleaner had been reading his thoughts. Could the Qirsi do that? Could a Weaver?

"Given what Kentigern did to you . . ." the man went on.

"I pledged my sword to the defense of his castle," Tavis said, his tone harsher than he had intended. "A Curgh doesn't break his word."

The Qirsi shrugged. "All right."

"Have you ever been to war, Lord Tavis?" the duke asked.

He felt his cheeks grow hot. "No, my lord. I haven't."

"Then may I suggest that you stay close to Gershon and me? I haven't fought many battles, certainly none of this magnitude. But I have been in my share of fights."

Tavis had to keep himself from refusing outright. He was, he realized, too much his father's son. True, he was a man of Curgh, but that didn't mean he had to let his pride get him killed.

"I'd be grateful, my lord." He made himself smile. "And I believe my mother would appreciate it as well."

Kearney grinned. "For her then." The duke turned to his first minister, the gleaner's sister. "I want you nearby as well, Kez."

"Don't worry, my lord. I won't let anything happen to you."

For the first time in days they all laughed, even the swordmaster, who seemed to have little use for either the minister or her brother.

They reached the city gates a short time later, and as Hagan and Tavis's mother led the men of Curgh around the city walls toward the Tarbin, the armies of Kentigern and Glyndwr marched through the gates and along the city lanes toward the castle. There were few guards in the city—no doubt most of them had gone to defend the castle. But as the armies entered the city, people spilled out of their homes and shops to cheer Aindreas and his men, as well as Kearney and the soldiers of Glyndwr.

Tavis sat motionless on his mount, his eyes fixed on the road before him, fearing that at any moment, the crowd would topple him from his mount and exact their revenge for Lady Brienne's death. But if any of the men or women on the streets recognized him, they didn't let it show.

"No matter what fate awaits you, Tavis," Grinsa said to him quietly, "today you're a hero. All of us are. Enjoy it."

The boy looked at him sidelong, drawing a smile from the gleaner. Tavis nodded once, then faced forward again, his hand straying to the hilt of his sword.

As they approached the base of the tor, arrows began to rain down on the road, whistling like slashing blades. The two armies were still beyond the reach of the Aneirans' bows, but the warning was clear. The ascent to the castle would be deadly.

Aindreas rode toward them again, this time accompanied by his first minister.

"I had hoped that I would never have to retake my castle," the duke said, as he pulled his mount to a halt. "Just for this reason."

"My minister can cloak us in a mist, Lord Kentigern," Kearney said. "If you think that would help."

"I do."

"The fires are still burning," Grinsa said. "I don't think the Aneirans hold the castle yet. Perhaps the defenders that remain can keep Mertesse's archers busy a while longer."

Aindreas twisted his mouth, looking like he didn't wish to say anything to the gleaner. Once more, his gaze shifted to Tavis, though only for an instant. "Perhaps," he finally said. He faced Keziah again. "Weave your mists, First Minister. A wind might help us as well."

The woman bowed her head. "I'll do what I can, my lord."

Kentigern rode off again, though his minister lingered a moment, his eye fixed on Grinsa. "My duke has asked a great deal of her," he said, nodding toward Keziah. "Perhaps you can help her?"

"I don't have the magic of mists," the gleaner said.

The minister gave a thin smile. "Of course not. A pity." He clicked his tongue at his mount and rode after Aindreas.

"What was that about?" Kearney asked.

"It was nothing, my lord," Grinsa answered with a shake of his head. "Some court Qirsi have little regard for those of us who work in the Revel."

The duke raised an eyebrow and nodded, as if satisfied by this. But judging from the brief look that Grinsa shared with his sister, it seemed clear to Tavis that there was more to it than that.

Keziah took a long breath and closed her eyes, as a strange stillness settled over the two armies. A moment later strands of grey mist began to rise from the road, swallowing the soldiers and horses like a highland fog. At the same time, a wind rose, blowing from the north across the road. Tavis had thought that the Qirsi would have the gale blow back toward the castle, to knock down the arrows loosed by the men of Mertesse. But he saw now that this made more sense. With the mist covering the armies of Glyndwr and Kentigern, the Aneirans would have enough trouble aiming their darts. A crosswind would make it nearly impossible.

Shrouded in the sorcerer's cloud, the armies started up the road, their swords drawn and their shields held high. Occasionally arrows struck the shields, and a few men fell, but for the most part Keziah's wind and mist protected them.

To Tavis, who didn't know the road, their ascent seemed endless. He felt his fear mounting by the moment and he had to wipe the sweat from his sword hand several times. The fog was so thick that the young lord didn't realize they had reached the castle until the great stone gate loomed just before him.

Aindreas bellowed to his men; Kearney called out, "For Glyndwr!" And the men marching behind them surged forward, to be met by a mass of men in black and gold. Abruptly Tavis found himself being swept forward by a turbulent sea of men and horses.

Somewhere behind him, Kearney called to his minister to drop her mists. Almost immediately the air began to clear, the gale to subside. But Tavis still felt as though he were in a storm, the rush of the wind giving way to the wails of the dying, the impenetrable grey of the mist replaced by the whirling confusion of battle. Not knowing what else to do, he kicked at the flanks of his horse and swung his sword from side to side, desperate to free himself from the grip of the battle.

Before he knew it, he was through the castle gate and in the first ward. Grinsa was calling to him, as was the duke of Glyndwr, but they were both far behind him. Tavis was surrounded by Aneiran soldiers. Men clawed at his legs and arms, trying to pull him from the horse, and he slashed at their arms with his blade. He pulled hard on his reins, trying to turn his mount and ride back to the gleaner. The animal reared, nearly throwing him. But the Aneirans backed away for an instant, giving him just enough room to spur the beast toward the gate. A moment later the soldiers closed on him again, and he hacked at them like a madman, ignoring the smell of blood and the screams from those he wounded.

The gleaner and the duke were only a few fourspans away, and men from both Glyndwr and Kentigern had gained the ward, pushing back the army of Mertesse. Somehow, Tavis had managed not to get himself killed. Or so he thought.

In that second his horse reared again, letting out a screech that echoed off the stone walls, making every man pause in the midst of the combat. Even as he felt himself start to fall Tavis saw the arrow that had pierced the beast's neck, and he threw himself to the side to keep the horse from falling on him.

He landed hard on his shoulder, tumbling over once and winding up on his back, dazed and breathless. Instantly, before he could even try to stand, a soldier was above him, chopping at him with a sword. Tavis didn't know he had managed to hold on to his own blade until he raised it to block the blow. Rolling to the side, he scrambled to his feet just as the Aneiran sprang at him again, his sword arcing toward Tavis's head. The young lord parried this strike as well, though the force of it sent a stinging pain up his arm and knocked him off balance. Rubbing his arm and backing away, Tavis saw that the soldier was grinning as he advanced on him, as if he knew that Tavis couldn't hurt him.

He swung his weapon again and though Tavis managed to deflect the blow, he couldn't block it entirely. The man's blade pounded into his side, driving the boy to the ground and making him gasp at the pain. His mail shirt kept the soldier's sword from drawing blood, but his ribs ached and Tavis wondered if any were broken. He tried to crawl away, but he could barely move at all.

The Aneiran walked toward him, raising his blade for the killing strike. Tavis felt tears on his face and he choked back a sob. Had he survived Aindreas's torture only to die here fighting for the man's castle? Certainly there was nothing he could do to stop the soldier. He raised his sword, hoping at least to make a fight of it. But just as the man reached him, something hit the Aneiran's leg, causing him to pitch forward. The soldier threw out his arms, grasping for anything that would stop his fall, but there was nothing. He toppled onto the young lord, his neck impaling itself on Tavis's blade. Hot blood flowed over the boy like bathwater. He opened his mouth to cry out, only to have the man's life pour down his throat.

All around him men were fighting and dying. Any Aneiran who saw him there, who thought him worth the effort, could have killed him with a single thrust. But all Tavis could do was push the man off of him, roll over onto his stomach, and retch like a sick child.

Chapter
Thirty-one

✦

Shurik fought for his life, his horse dancing like the mount of a Revel performer, and his sword rising and falling until he thought his arm would never be of any use to him again. In some small corner of his mind, one his fear couldn't reach, he saw the humor in it all. After this day Aindreas would praise him for his bravery and the fervor with which he had fought for Kentigern, when all he wanted to do was survive.

Eandi warriors were trained to attack Qirsi ministers in a fight of this sort. Nothing could tip the balance of a battle more quickly than a shaper or a sorcerer with mists and winds. Even a smaller army could prevail in such a fight if it had the aid of a powerful Qirsi. Since there was no way to determine just from looking at a man or woman of his race what kind of magic they possessed, the Eandi saw all white-hairs as equally dangerous. He could hardly blame the men of Mertesse for massing around him. They didn't know that he didn't have mists and winds or that he couldn't afford to reveal that he was a shaper. They saw his hair, his yellow eyes, and they attacked.

Don't you know who I am? he wanted to scream at them. *Don't you know what I did for you and your duke?*

But all he could do was fight. He did manage to use his fire magic on a few of them, setting their shirts and hair ablaze, and that forced the rest to reconsider their attack for a time. Before long, however, they gathered their nerve and he found himself besieged once more.

Even as he struggled to stay atop his horse, Shurik was able to sense the course of the battle, and he knew that Mertesse's army was on the verge of being vanquished. The men of Curgh, led by Hagan MarCullet and Javan's extraordinary duchess, had already forced their way past the Aneirans at the Tarbin gate and were slowly establishing control over the western half of the castle. Aindreas's army, fighting alongside the men of Glyndwr, were close to doing the same on the eastern side. Those Aneirans who remained in the inner keep had nowhere to go. They couldn't retreat—their path to the river now belonged to Curgh—and they were being slaughtered by the Eibitharians. They could surrender, or they could fight to the last man. Either way, Shurik didn't believe they would last the night.

Which meant that the Eandi soldiers he was fighting were the least of his problems. The Weaver wanted this war to continue far beyond a few days. Or so Shurik guessed. The Weaver had revealed almost nothing of his plans in their conversations, and had told Yaella little more. But from all that Shurik could divine, he thought the Weaver wanted the Aneirans to take Kentigern, thus sparking a prolonged war with the other houses of Eibithar. With the kingdom already weakened by the blood feud between Javan and Aindreas and the inability of the major houses to select a king, the Eibitharians would be forced to turn to their allies to the south and east, Caerisse and Wethyrn. The Aneirans, in turn, would look to Braedon for help. Within a few turns, nearly every kingdom of the Forelands would be party to this war. Such a conflict couldn't help but weaken the Eandi courts, giving the Weaver the opportunity he needed to lead a Qirsi uprising.

The last thing the Weaver wanted, Shurik felt quite certain, was a quick, unsuccessful end to the siege, particularly if Mertesse's failure fostered an alliance among the houses of Glyndwr, Curgh, and Kentigern. Shurik had done his part. He had been weary for two days after using so much magic to weaken the Tarbin gate, and still it wasn't enough. He would have to ask Yaella how the Aneirans had managed to fail despite his aid.

With the thought, he suddenly knew a moment of utter dread. What if she had been killed? What if she was still in the castle and was about to be captured? Aindreas might spare the foot soldiers, but he was certain to execute Rouel, his advisors, and his captains if he was given the chance. More than anything Shurik wanted to search the castle for her, to be sure that she was all right and to find a way to get her out of Kentigern. But even if he could have fought his way through the knot of soldiers in front of him, Aindreas wouldn't have allowed him to leave his side. Hacking once more at the nearest Aneiran, the minister stood in his stirrups, scanning the ward for any sign of her.

At first he saw only soldiers, some in the black and gold of Mertesse, others wearing the colors of Glyndwr, Kentigern, and Curgh. When he finally spotted the white hair of a Qirsi, he nearly cried out. An instant later, though, he saw that this wasn't Yaella, but rather Javan's first minister, and the duke of Curgh was fighting beside him. They were just outside the prison tower. The MarCullet boy was there as well, as were a few of Javan's men, probably the surviving members of the company that had come to Kentigern the previous turn.

"What is it, Shurik?" Aindreas called. "What do you see?"

The minister glanced at his duke before pointing toward Javan and Fotir.

Aindreas's face turned crimson, his lips pressed into a thin dark line. After a few seconds, however, he shook his head, as if arguing with himself.

"They would have needed his sword," he said at last. "And those of his men. I can't blame them."

"Of course, my lord."

But Shurik couldn't help but think that the Weaver wouldn't like this at all.

Scanning the ward again, Shurik saw that Hagan and the duchess had fought their way to the inner gates. If Yaella hadn't escaped, she was dead already. A cheer went up from the far side of the castle, and looking in that direction Shurik understood. One of the Aneirans had raised the banner of Mertesse, except that it had been turned on its head, so that the great golden oak was standing on its crown. The Aneirans were offering their surrender.

The combat went on for several minutes more. Men in the throes of battle weren't likely to notice a flag on the other side of the ward. Eventually, though, the fighting subsided and Aindreas rode forward to speak with the man bearing the banner. Shurik and Villyd Temsten rode with him, as did Kearney, his first minister, and his swordmaster. Grinsa was there as well, and Lord Tavis, who shared the Qirsi's mount, his face and shirt covered with drying blood. Hagan and the duchess joined them, and a moment later

Javan, Fotir, and the MarCullet boy reached them. Hagan and Shonah dismounted at the same time, the swordmaster fiercely embracing his son and the duchess rushing into her husband's arms. An instant later, Tavis joined them and both mother and father put their arms around him.

Aindreas watched all this with barely concealed distaste before facing the Aneiran.

The man had long black hair that he wore tied back from his face. His eyes were almost black and they appeared too big for his face. He was built like a fighter, wiry and muscular, though he wasn't particularly large.

"Who are you?" the duke demanded. "Where is your duke?"

"My name is Wyn Stridbar," the man said, his voice even. "I'm master armsman of Mertesse."

"And your duke, Sir Stridbar?"

"My lord duke is dead."

"Why should I believe you? For all I know he's escaping as we speak, leaving you to die in his place."

"Rouel of Mertesse would never have done such a thing. He had more courage than all the so-called nobles of Eibithar taken as one."

The man was brave, though some might have called it foolishness. A murmur of protest rose from the soldiers of Eibithar, and Shurik noticed that at least a few of the bowmen pulled arrows from their quivers. Aindreas silenced them with a raised hand.

"It's all right," the duke said. "Every man here would say the same of his duke. It's as it should be." He eyed the Aneiran again. "So you were the only one of Rouel's advisors to survive?"

"No. I sent our first minister back to Mertesse with the duke's body and as many of the men as we could save."

"You're willing to die for them?"

Stridbar grinned. "Would your swordmaster do any less?"

The duke gestured toward the Aneiran soldiers who remained in the ward, surrounded by the armies of Eibithar. "And what of these men? Are they ready to die as well?"

The man paled. "Only a butcher would execute vanquished soldiers. You have their commander. Let them go."

Aindreas nodded. "Perhaps I will. But first you need to answer some questions for me."

Stridbar glared at the duke, saying nothing. After a moment, though, he nodded.

"Kentigern is the mightiest fortress in the Forelands. Yet your army almost managed to take it in a matter of days. How is that possible?"

Shurik felt his stomach heave.

"Maybe your castle isn't as mighty as you think," the man said, a thin smile on his lips. "Or perhaps the army of Mertesse is more powerful than you anticipated."

Aindreas shook his head. "I don't think so. I think you had help."

"Something was done to the west gate," Javan said, drawing Aindreas's gaze.

"How do you know?"

"It's the only explanation that makes any sense. It wasn't a matter of days, Aindreas. The Aneirans got through that gate in a matter of moments. It had to have been weakened somehow."

Aindreas stared at Javan a moment longer before facing the Aneiran again. "Well?"

"I don't know what he's talking about. We defeated your gate with a ram, just as any army of the Forelands would."

Shurik started to relax. The man had made up his mind to die for Yaella and the soldiers of Mertesse. Aindreas couldn't frighten him into revealing anything. Or so he thought.

"Bowmen!" the duke called, his gaze still fixed on Stridbar. "Ready your arrows and bring me an Aneiran soldier."

The armsman's eyes widened, making him look like a frightened boy. "What are you going to do?"

Aindreas shrugged. "I'm going to execute your men one at a time until you tell me what I want to know. What else can I do?"

Maybe he doesn't know, Shurik thought. *Yaella and the duke might have kept this to themselves.*

The man's eyes flicked in his direction. It was only for the merest instant, but it was long enough to shatter this last hope like glass.

"Executing foot soldiers is not worthy of you, my lord," Shurik said quietly. "It's the act of an Aneiran, not a duke of Eibithar."

"I'm forced to agree, Lord Kentigern," Glyndwr said from atop his mount. "I dislike torture, but in this case I think that would be the better course."

Aindreas glared at the minister as if his words alone had been a betrayal. But in the end he nodded. "Fine," he said, his voice like ice. "Take him to the dungeon."

"What of my men?" Stridbar asked.

Truly a leader to the end. He was to be admired. But more than that, perhaps now he could be trusted. Shurik could only hope that by saving the man's soldiers, he had won his silence, at least long enough to make his way out of the castle to Mertesse.

"We'll take their weapons and then send them back to Mertesse," Aindreas said. He straightened in his saddle. "You have my word."

The Aneiran took a breath and nodded. Aindreas lifted a finger, no more, and two men walked to where the man stood, grabbed hold of his arms, and led him toward the prison tower.

"Villyd," the duke said, turning to his swordmaster. "Have the Aneirans stripped of their weapons and shields. Then have two of your captains and a hundred men escort them to the river. They aren't to be harmed unless they turn on you." He paused, his eyes sweeping the ward, a sour expression on his face. "The rest of your men should begin cleaning up this mess and fixing those gates."

"Yes, my lord."

"My men will be glad to help in any way they can," Javan said, looking up at Aindreas.

Kearney nodded. "As will mine."

Aindreas's jaw tightened. Clearly he wanted no help of any sort from Javan, but his castle was in ruins. Merely removing the bodies would take the better part of a day. "My thanks," he said, his voice thick.

A moment later Aindreas's swordmaster began shouting commands at his soldiers, as did the dukes of Curgh and Glyndwr. Soon men were moving off in all directions to gather bodies and begin repairs to the castle.

"You said something was done to the gate," Aindreas said, facing Javan once more. "What do you mean?"

"I don't know anything for certain," said Curgh's duke. "But my first minister suggested that it might have been weakened by magic. I agree."

"What kind of magic?" Aindreas asked, shifting his gaze to Fotir.

"Shaping, most likely. Do you have any shapers in the castle?"

The duke glanced at Shurik. "Do we?"

"Yes," Shurik said, pleased to hear that his voice remained steady. "Two of the underministers are shapers."

"Is that all?"

Shurik turned at the sound of the voice to find Grinsa eyeing him closely. He felt a shudder go through his body. It almost seemed that the man could tell he was hiding something.

Ever since his second conversation with Fotir in the Silver Bear, Shurik had believed that the minister was the one who freed Tavis from the prison, and that he had been helped in this by a Weaver. And since meeting Grinsa for the first time, he had wondered if this gleaner was the one. A Weaver could discern the powers of another Qirsi simply by looking at him, so it was possible that this man knew he was a shaper as well. But even as they stared at one another, like two warriors gauging each other's strengths before a fight, Shurik realized that neither of them could say anything about the other. The gleaner couldn't reveal that Shurik was a shaper without giving away the true extent of his powers, and Shurik couldn't accuse the man of being a Weaver without betraying his own secret. The gleaner seemed to sense this as well, for after several seconds he looked away, saying nothing.

"I'm fairly certain that is all," the minister said, facing Aindreas again. "Of course, there's nothing to prevent a Qirsi from lying about his or her powers. Any Qirsi in the castle could be a shaper."

"Including you." Fotir.

Shurik forced a smile. "Yes, First Minister, including me. And you."

"I've never concealed the fact that I am a shaper. But I was in your prison tower when the gates fell."

"This is foolishness," Aindreas said, sounding impatient. "I want to speak with those two underministers, if they're still alive. Find them for me, Shurik."

"Of course, my lord."

He turned his horse away and started toward the nearer of the two inner gates, taking care not to appear to be in a hurry. There were things in his chamber that he wanted: a pouch filled with gold, several bound volumes, some articles of clothing, an ornate dagger that his father had given him years ago. But none of them mattered anymore. If the gleaner didn't give him away, the Aneiran armsman would. Either way, his life would be forfeit before long. This might be his only chance to get away. None of the soldiers would think to stop him, and for once he had nothing to fear from the Aneirans guarding the far bank of the river, most of whom had probably gone back to Mertesse with Yaella and what remained of Rouel's army.

It seemed an abrupt end to his years in Kentigern, he mused, passing through the north gate. He always knew this day would come, but still it felt strange to make his decision so quickly. But what choice did he have? He had done what he could to help the Weaver's cause. Perhaps it wasn't enough, and perhaps the Weaver would kill him for that. But he had no wish to die by Aindreas's hand. The Eandi fool didn't deserve that satisfaction.

It was Shurik. Grinsa had no doubt. His eyes met Fotir's, and he could see immediately that the minister felt the same way. He couldn't say anything about it here, of course, not in front of the Eandi, not without raising their suspicions about his own powers. But there was nothing stopping him from following Aindreas's minister and questioning him somewhere more private.

Before he could make his excuses and ride after the man, however, the conversation among the dukes took a dark turn, forcing him to remain with them at least a few moments longer.

Aindreas had dismounted and was standing in front of Javan. Both of them bore cuts and welts, though the Curgh duke looked to be the far more battered of the two.

"It seems my prisons can't manage to hold any of you," Aindreas said, his hand resting on the hilt of his sword. "Why is that?"

Javan shrugged, though his blue eyes never strayed from Kentigern's face. "I don't know. I've heard it said that the gods won't allow any prison to hold an innocent man. It seems as good an explanation as any."

"You want me to accept a Qirsi plot to free your boy as a test of his innocence? Never!"

"Did you see Tavis fight today, Lord Kentigern?" Grinsa asked.

Both men looked his way.

"No," the duke said. "Why?"

"Because if you had, you would have seen a young man—a child really—struggling to master his fear. And you would have seen that he was sickened by the act of killing a man, though that man had been intent on killing him. The boy's no murderer; he's not even a soldier yet. He hasn't the stomach for it, or the courage." The Qirsi glanced at Javan. "Forgive me, my lord, but I speak the truth."

Tavis was looking down at his feet, the dried blood of the

Aneiran he had killed still staining his face and neck. Grinsa had no desire to humiliate him, but better to be thought a coward than a butcher. That at least was the choice the gleaner would have made. He couldn't tell just then if Tavis agreed.

"You offer that as proof?" Aindreas asked. "It means nothing! Of course he was scared today! He wasn't murdering a defenseless girl this time." He glared at Tavis, flexing his sword hand. "I should have killed you that first day, boy. I never should have offered you the chance to confess."

Tavis raised his eyes to look at him. "Is that what you were doing? In Curgh we call it torture."

Aindreas drew his sword, growling like a wild beast. Javan raised his weapon to defend the boy, as did Fotir and Hagan MarCullet.

"Hold!" Kearney said from atop his mount. "Lord Tavis is still under my protection, Aindreas. Harm him and it means war with Glyndwr."

"And Curgh," Javan added.

"You have no place in this matter, Javan," Kearney told him. "Your son has requested asylum from the House of Glyndwr. If you wish to protect him, I'll withdraw my offer of protection. But since he can't escape Kentigern's justice in his own court, I'd suggest you leave this to me."

The duke of Curgh's face reddened and he opened his mouth. But the duchess laid a hand on his arm, stopping him.

"You're right, of course, Lord Glyndwr," she said. "Please accept our apologies."

Kearney nodded to her, before facing Aindreas again.

After several moments, Kentigern sheathed his sword, looking off to the side. "Fine, Kearney. You win. But you'd best get him out of my castle, before one of my men decides to take matters into his own hands."

"That, too, would be an act of war," Kearney said, refusing to back down.

"Which is why you'd do well to get him away from here. You threaten war, Kearney, but we both know that Glyndwr's army is no match for mine."

Glyndwr's swordmaster gave a harsh laugh. "I'm not so sure of that."

"Quiet, Gershon," Kearney said. He faced the duke again, taking a long breath. "Our threats serve no purpose, Aindreas. This land—this castle—has seen enough war for one day. We need to honor our dead and rebuild Kentigern. Having just fought as allies to drive the Aneirans from our kingdom, can't we all agree to do those things?"

Aindreas and Javan glanced at each other, their eyes meeting for a moment. Both of them appeared to consider Kearney's plea, and Grinsa believed he saw their expressions soften.

The gleaner wanted to believe that they could work together, at least for a time. Not only because the kingdom's future depended upon it, but because he was anxious to leave them. A voice in his mind was screaming for him to go after Shurik. If the minister had betrayed Kentigern to the Aneirans, he wouldn't be coming back from the errand on which Aindreas had sent him. The risks to the man were too great.

With every day that passed, with every new revelation, Grinsa grew more convinced that talk of a Qirsi conspiracy in the Forelands was more than just the idle prattle of frightened Eandi nobles. He had no real evidence; he was guessing, groping for answers to questions he only barely understood. But Cresenne—just thinking of her made his heart ache—Cresenne had sent an assassin to keep him from reaching Kentigern. Brienne had been killed and Tavis made to look guilty. And now Shurik had betrayed his duke and his castle to the Aneirans. These things had to be connected. He was sure of it.

He was just as certain that he would never find Cresenne again. Even if they found the assassin who murdered Brienne, the gleaner doubted that he would know any more about this conspiracy than the man Cresenne had sent for him. Shurik, though, was a different matter. He was first minister to one of Kentigern's major houses. If he was involved, he would know a good deal. More than anything, Grinsa wanted to find the minister and question him, even if he had to beat the answers out of him.

But the three dukes standing before him had more to do than just honor their dead and mend the castle gates. The shadow of civil war still hung over the land, and at that moment he seemed to be the only one who realized it.

"With all respect, Lord Glyndwr," he said, glancing over his shoulder toward the north gate for just a moment, as if he could will Shurik to remain in Kentigern a bit longer, "I'm afraid that you and the other dukes have greater responsibilities than seeing to your fallen soldiers."

Kearney narrowed his eyes. "What do you mean?"

"Your king is dead, and the land awaits his successor."

"Javan of Curgh is his successor," said Hagan MarCullet. "The Rules of Ascension are clear."

"Damn the Rules of Ascension!" Aindreas leveled a rigid finger at Curgh's duke. "I've told you before, Javan, you'll not rule so long as I live! The boy is beyond my reach, but this isn't. I will never consent to a Curgh king."

"Even at the risk of war?" Kearney asked.

The duke nodded. "Even so."

Glyndwr turned to the duke of Curgh. "Javan?"

"What?" the man said. "He's threatening war, not me."

"But you can avert this war by renouncing your claim to the throne."

Javan stared at Kearney as if he thought the duke mad. "And give the crown to him? Never!"

"It seems, Lord Glyndwr," Grinsa broke in, "that there's only one solution. You must take the throne."

"What?" It was Keziah, of all people, who in that instant spoke for all of them. "You can't be serious."

"There is no other choice," the gleaner said. "Thorald and Galdasten are powerless in this matter. Not only do they lack legitimate heirs, they don't even have the authority to go against the Rules of Ascension. If we take this to a council of the major houses, Curgh will prevail, regardless of how Glyndwr votes. If there's a solution to be found, the three dukes you see before you must find it. Kentigern will not accede to a Curgh king, nor Curgh to one from Kentigern. That leaves Lord Glyndwr."

Grinsa could see that he was hurting her, that she saw her life and her love crumbling before her eyes. It was one thing for a duke to take a Qirsi as his mistress. It was quite another for Eibithar's king to do so. *I'm sorry,* he wanted to say. *It's the only way.* But all he could do was gaze into his sister's pale eyes and hope that she understood.

"I have no wish to be king," Kearney said. "I never have."

From any other man it would have sounded hollow and false. But Grinsa believed him.

The gleaner nodded and offered a small smile. "Which is why you're such a fine choice, my lord."

He looked at Javan, then Aindreas. "My lords?"

"Kentigern's threats should not keep Lord Curgh from the throne!" Hagan said, shaking his head. "The Rules of Ascension—"

Javan stopped him with a hand on his shoulder. "It's all right, Hagan." He pressed his lips together, looking first at Grinsa and then at Kearney. At last, his eyes came to rest on the duke of Kentigern. "I'll consider this, Aindreas, if you will as well. We both lost good men today, and our houses have suffered a good deal more in the last turn. I don't want another war."

Aindreas gave a reluctant nod. "I'll think on it."

"Lord Glyndwr?" Grinsa asked.

Kearney was gazing at Keziah, as if he too realized what his ascension would mean for them. "If the other choice is civil war," the duke said, "I can hardly refuse." Grinsa sensed that he wasn't answering the question. Rather, he was reasoning with Keziah, trying to make her understand. But the others couldn't have known this, except perhaps Tavis, who was watching them both, his expression unreadable.

"We should see to the dead," Javan said after a lengthy silence. "It'll be dark before long."

The others nodded and started to walk off, but Grinsa caught Fotir's eye.

"A word?" he said.

The minister looked to his duke, who nodded before walking toward one of the towers, hand in hand with the duchess. Tavis watched them go, before joining Kearney, his expression like that of a lost babe.

"I want to find Shurik," the gleaner said, lowering his voice so that only Fotir could hear him.

"Now?"

"I don't think we'll have another chance. If I were in his position, I'd be looking for the quickest route to the Tarbin."

"Then let's go," the minister said.

Grinsa held out a hand. Fotir gripped it and swung himself onto the gleaner's horse. They rode quickly through the north gate into the outer ward, then turned west toward the Tarbin gate. Grinsa saw no sign of Shurik. The minister had been on horseback, too. There was a chance he was already in Aneira, though Grinsa thought he would have ridden slowly, to keep from drawing attention to himself.

The two Qirsi crossed through the outer gate, past the twisted iron and wood of the ruined portcullises, and followed the winding road down toward the river. At the bottom of the tor, they turned south again, following the curving bank of the Tarbin toward the shallows. Only then did they spot Shurik. He was a good distance ahead of them and had already turned off the road and ridden down the bank to the water's edge. There was no way they could reach him in time to keep him from crossing.

"Damn him!" Grinsa said, spurring his mount to a full gallop though he knew the effort would be in vain.

"Isn't there some magic we could use?" Fotir asked.

"Not at this distance, not unless you think a wind would stop him."

"It might."

"Can you raise it while we ride?"

Fotir said nothing. An instant later, however, a wind began to rise, slowly at first, but building swiftly until the river waters grew turbulent and white, like the Western Sea during a storm. Shurik's horse struggled against the gale and the rough waters, but the traitor continued to cross. Had the water been deeper it might have stopped him; as it was, Grinsa and Fotir were going to have as much trouble reaching him as Shurik was having fording the river.

"Can you add your magic to mine?" Fotir asked, his voice strained.

"Not without revealing to Shurik that one of us is a Weaver."

By the time they came to the shallows, Shurik had managed to reach the far bank. The minister was watching them, the smile on his lips seeming to say that he knew he was beyond their reach. Fotir allowed his wind to die away, and Shurik's grin broadened. After a moment he raised his sword, as if saluting them. Then he turned his horse from the river, and disappeared into Mertesse Forest.

"We might be able to catch him before he makes it to Castle Mertesse," Fotir said.

"And what if we meet up with the rest of the Mertesse army?"

"You're a Weaver!"

Grinsa looked back at him. "Are you serious?"

"I'm not suggesting we fight them. But certainly we could raise a mist to get away if we had to."

"No," the gleaner said, shaking his head. "Shurik won today. There's nothing more we can do."

He faced the river again, gazing at the line of trees beyond its waters. A part of him wanted to go after the man. He deserved to be punished, not only for his betrayal, but also for the role he had played in Tavis's suffering. More than that, though, even without bolstering Fotir's wind with his own magic, Grinsa had begun to wonder if the man knew somehow that he was a Weaver. He couldn't stop thinking about the minister's strange comment on the road leading to the castle, and the way Shurik looked at him during their brief silent exchange in the keep. In all likelihood, he was merely imagining things. As a Weaver, Grinsa lived in constant fear of having his true powers revealed, and in the past he had allowed such concerns to get the better of him. But in this case, the danger felt especially real. Shurik had already shown himself to be a cunning enemy. Armed with this knowledge, he would be a threat to Grinsa's life, and perhaps to Keziah's.

"I'll find him eventually," Grinsa said, his voice low. "I won't even have to work very hard. I have a feeling that Shurik will be looking for me as well."

Chapter
Thirty-two

✦

Xaver and his father were still in Kentigern's inner ward when Fotir and the gleaner returned to the castle. Xaver's father was overseeing the gathering of the Curgh dead, not something he would usually have been anxious to let Xaver watch. But Hagan had not strayed more than a step or two from Xaver's side since their reunion a short while before. It almost seemed to the boy that his father feared letting him out of his sight, lest they be separated again. In truth, Xaver was just as reluctant to leave Hagan.

He had already told his father much about their time in Kentigern, particularly about the last few days as they battled the Aneirans, and the swordmaster was eager to thank Fotir for all the minister had done to keep Xaver safe.

Before they could reach the Qirsi, however, the minister and Grinsa rode to where Aindreas stood. The two sorcerers dismounted and began talking to the duke and gesturing toward the gates.

"Impossible!" Xaver heard the duke say. Aindreas started to walk away from the Qirsi, shaking his head and saying, "I won't listen to this."

Grinsa followed him, speaking once more, though in a voice too low for Xaver to hear.

After a moment Aindreas whirled on the man, raising a finger as if in warning.

By this time Kearney had joined them, and a few seconds later Javan and the duchess did the same.

"Come, lad," Hagan said, hurrying to the duke of Curgh's side with Xaver close behind him.

"Is this some Curgh trick, Javan?" Aindreas demanded, his face crimson.

The duke stared at him, his expression blank. "Is what a trick?"

"This gleaner and your first minister are telling me that my first minister is a traitor, that he's the one who weakened my gates."

"Is it true?" Javan asked, facing Fotir.

"I believe so, my lord."

Aindreas shook his head again. "It can't be true. Shurik isn't even a shaper."

"That's what he told you, Lord Kentigern," Grinsa said. "But he might have been lying."

"Or he might have been telling the truth," Fotir added, "and working with a second traitor who is a shaper. Either way, the man has betrayed you. And now he's crossed the river to Aneira."

"What?" Javan said. "You saw him go?"

"Yes, my lord. Grinsa—" He hesitated, glancing briefly at the other Qirsi. "We both have had our suspicions about him and when we saw him leave the keep, we followed. He managed to get across the river before we could stop him."

"There must be another explanation," Aindreas said, beginning to pace. "I've known Shurik for nearly ten years. He'd never do this to me."

"Have you noticed him behaving strangely?" Kearney asked.

"He's Qirsi! Of course he behaved strangely!"

"More so than usual? Perhaps just before you left the castle to march against Curgh?"

Aindreas stopped in midstride, his eyes flying to the face of his swordmaster. "Demons and fire!" he whispered. "The day we left. When he claimed he'd been walking and that he was feeling ill. 'Battle sickness,' I called it. He was sweating and he looked like he hadn't slept in days."

Fotir glanced at the gleaner. "That's how I'd look if I'd just come from weakening all those portcullises."

The duke squeezed his eyes shut, as if his head were hurting. "Bian throw him to the fires." He opened his eyes again, looking warily at Grinsa and the minister. "I swear I'll never trust one of you people again."

"We're not all traitors," Fotir said.

"Perhaps not, but it does seem to run in your blood."

Fotir glared at the duke, but he kept his silence.

"There's nothing more we can do," Grinsa said. "He's well into Mertesse Forest by now."

Javan nodded. "Then we should return to what we were doing. I'd like to have some daylight by which to make camp, and we still have work to do here."

The three dukes began to walk off in different directions once more, like warriors at a tournament returning to their corners of the field. Hagan turned to join Javan, but Xaver hesitated, watching Tavis follow Kearney. The young lord had washed the dried blood from his face, but he still moved stiffly, no doubt from the injury he had suffered earlier that day. He stared at the ground as he walked. No one said anything to him or walked with him. It almost seemed that he was of another world, that the others in the castle couldn't see him.

The two of them hadn't spoken since the last time Xaver saw his friend in Aindreas's dungeon. Earlier in the day, when they were all standing in the center of the ward, Tavis barely even looked at him. Xaver wanted to go to him. A part of him felt that it was his duty to do so. In spite of all that had happened, he was still Tavis's liege man. Yet something held him back. The distance between them felt greater now than it ever had before. He couldn't begin to comprehend all that his friend had been through since Brienne's death, nor could he guess at what the young lord was feeling now. The expression Tavis bore in his dark blue eyes made him look far older than his sixteen years, and the scars he carried had changed his face, making it severe where once it had been youthful and handsome. Had Xaver seen him on a farm lane, far from the walls of Kentigern or Curgh, he might not have recognized him. In a sense, with Tavis now under Glyndwr's protection, they weren't even of the same house anymore.

"You coming, Xaver?" his father called to him.

Xaver continued to watch his friend, unsure of what to do. Finally he turned to his father and shook his head. "I'll be along soon," he said.

Hagan's eyes flicked toward Tavis for an instant, as if he had read Xaver's thoughts. He nodded his consent.

Taking a breath, Xaver ran after Tavis, calling to him as he drew near.

The young lord stopped, but at first he didn't turn. It almost seemed that he was trying to decide whether to speak with Xaver or flee.

Xaver halted a few steps from him. "If you want me to leave you alone, I will."

He saw Tavis take a breath. "No," the boy said, facing him at last. "I almost looked for you earlier. I've wanted to talk to you. I just . . ." He shrugged, then winced slightly, rubbing his side.

"You all right?"

"You mean this?" he asked, patting his side. "I'm fine." He dropped his gaze. "I got lucky, Stinger. He would have killed me if he hadn't fallen."

Xaver shuddered, remembering his own first kill from the night the siege began. "You know what my father says. 'I'd rather be a poor swordsman with luck than a good one without it.' "

Tavis smiled, though even then he looked sad. "A poor swordsman with luck," he repeated. "That definitely was me today."

"You should have seen me a few night ago," Xaver said. "I was fighting like we used to when we were ten. If my father had been there he would have had me running the towers. Right then, in the middle of the siege."

The smile lingered on Tavis's face a few seconds longer, before fading like the last light of day. "How's your arm?"

It took a moment. "It's fine. I'd almost forgotten about it."

"I find that hard to believe."

Xaver racked his brain for something to say, but nothing came to him.

"I saw Brienne," the young lord said, making Xaver shudder a second time. "I was in the Sanctuary of Bian on Pitch Night and she came to me." He swallowed, and Xaver thought he saw a tear in the corner of Tavis's eye. "She said I didn't kill her, Xaver. She even showed me an image of the man who did."

"I'm not surprised. I've believed you were innocent for a long time."

"I wasn't certain until I saw her. I wanted to be, but I kept thinking about what I did to you."

Xaver didn't want to talk about this at all. He had been telling the truth a moment before. He had managed to forget about it. But speaking of it was rekindling his anger and making his chest ache again. It almost seemed that his forearm was beginning to throb once more.

"So what will you do now?" he asked. "Are you going to live in Glyndwr until her murderer is found?"

"That would mean living there forever. I have to go after him, Xaver. I have to find him."

"You're not serious."

"No one else will. No one in Kentigern believes he exists, and I wouldn't ask anyone in Curgh to do it for me. Besides, I'm the only person who knows what he looks like."

"He's an assassin, Tavis. Even assuming that you can find him, he'll kill you the first chance he gets. And if he doesn't, one of Kentigern's assassins might. Kearney can't protect you if you leave Glyndwr."

"What's my choice, Xaver? Living the rest of my life among people who think I'm a murderer, in exile from my family and the court of my ancestors?" He shook his head. "I'd rather be dead. At least this way I'll be doing something." He smiled, perhaps the first true smile Xaver had seen from him since they left their home to come to Kentigern. "I'm a Curgh, Stinger. Could you imagine my father living his life under another man's protection? Could you imagine him living in the highlands, forty leagues from Curgh?"

Xaver had to grin as well. The fact was, he couldn't imagine either Javan or Tavis doing anything but what his friend had in mind.

"You should at least take someone with you," he said. "You can't expect to do all this alone."

"I don't. I think Grinsa will be with me."

"The gleaner?"

"Yes. I don't understand all that he's told me, but it seems that our lives are linked in some way. He's had visions of this. He says it's why he freed me from Aindreas's dungeon."

"So you trust him."

"I suppose I do. He saved my life, at considerable risk to his own. I don't have many people I can trust. There's my parents, you and your father, Fotir, and the gleaner. None of the rest of you can come with me, and I don't want to go after the assassin alone."

"For what it's worth," Xaver said, "Fotir trusts him, too. He told your father that he couldn't have chosen a better guardian for you."

"I think that may be true."

It seemed to Xaver that there was more to this than what Tavis was telling him, and he thought about pursuing the matter. Perhaps two turns ago he would have. But something in the young lord's manner stopped him. For the first time, Xaver felt far younger than his friend. Perhaps it was the scars on his face, or the scars Xaver couldn't see. Whatever the reason, he couldn't help thinking that Tavis had earned the right to keep some things to himself.

"I haven't told anyone else what I intend to do," Tavis said. "Not even Grinsa, though I think he knows what I have in mind."

Xaver nodded. "I understand. I won't mention it until you've had a chance to speak with your mother and father."

His friend smiled again, though the look in his eyes remained grave. "No, Stinger. You don't understand. I'm not going to tell my parents, at least not for now. My father would think me a fool, and my mother would worry about me day and night."

"Actually, I think you're wrong about them. You said it yourself: your father would never sit idly in another man's castle while the assassin who had ruined his life walked the Forelands, a free man. And though your mother might worry, she'd also understand. She doesn't want you to be known as a murderer for the rest of your life any more than you do."

Tavis gazed off to the side, as if considering this. "You may be right," he said after some time. "Perhaps I will tell them eventually. But not yet, not until I've spoken with Grinsa."

"And Kearney. You have to tell him."

The young lord nodded. "I know."

They lapsed into silence, both of them gazing around the ward, as if unwilling to look at each other. After several moments of this, Xaver made up his mind to leave his friend, at least for the day. Before he could say his goodbyes, however, the young lord surprised him.

"I'm going to miss you, Xaver. I already have. I know I never told you this back when we . . . before we left Curgh, but you've been a good friend. Better than I had any right to expect."

He shook his head. "Tavis—"

"Let me finish. You've been far more than a liege man to me, though there have been too many times when I've treated you like a common servant." He paused, taking a long breath. "But I think the time has come for me to release you from your oath."

"We've already talked about this."

"Yes, I know. But everything is different now. I'm not in line to be king anymore, or even duke. I'm no longer a lord of Curgh. A man in my position doesn't need a liege man. And a man in your position shouldn't be tied to a disgraced noble."

Xaver knew he was right. He could hardly serve as Tavis's liege man with the young lord living in Glyndwr or traveling the Forelands in search of Brienne's killer. But while much had changed since the last time Tavis offered to release him from his oath, Xaver's feelings about this had not. If anything, he felt less inclined to accept the offer this time than he had after the incident at Curgh. In spite of the humiliation and suffering Tavis had endured since then, or perhaps because of them, the young lord seemed more worthy of his service now than ever before. Standing with him in the middle of Kentigern Castle, Xaver saw little of the spoiled child who only two turns before drank himself into a stupor and came at him with a dagger. He did see a darkness in Tavis that frightened him, but he also saw a maturity that he had long hoped for, but had never truly expected. At last, this was the man he wanted to serve.

"I've told you before, Tavis, I don't want to be released from my oath."

"Don't be a fool, Stinger. You can't serve me anymore. Let me release you, and you'll finally be done with all this."

"Are you going to find the man who murdered Brienne?"

His friend faltered for a moment, then nodded.

"And once you do, you'll be returning to Curgh, won't you?"

"I might."

"So you'll need a liege man then."

"That could be years from now, Xaver."

"Then grant me leave to serve the House of Curgh in your absence, in whatever way your father and I deem appropriate. And when you return, I'll still be there to fulfill my oath."

The young lord weighed this briefly. "I guess I could do that."

"It would be easier. We wouldn't have to involve our fathers at all."

Tavis smiled. "A good point."

It almost seemed that the duke had been waiting for that moment to approach them, for suddenly he was there, his expression grim. Xaver would have liked to leave, having been witness to more than his share of difficult conversations between these two. But there was nowhere for him to go.

"Kearney and I are on our way out of the city," the duke said to his son. "We've done all we can for today, and we have a lot to talk about."

Tavis nodded, suddenly looking uncomfortable. "What should I do?"

"Come with us, of course." Javan glanced at Xaver. "You, too, Master MarCullet. This concerns you and your father as well."

"Yes, my lord. Are we done here, Lord Tavis?"

His friend grinned. "So it would seem."

The three of them started toward the nearest gate, to be joined a few moments later by Shonah, Xaver's father, Grinsa, and the duke of Glyndwr and his advisors. Together they left the castle, descended the winding road to the city, and passed through the north gate into the Kentigern countryside. The armies of Glyndwr and Curgh had already started to make camp, and the smells of roasting meat drifted with the light wind, making Xaver's stomach growl. He could hardly remember the last time he had eaten a decent meal.

"I had started to wonder if I would ever leave that city," Javan said, drawing a smile from the duchess.

Xaver looked back over his shoulder at the castle, remembering how it looked when he first laid eyes upon it more than a turn ago. The fortress didn't look as formidable as it had that day. The tor seemed lower, the walls more vulnerable. Still, he felt a chill go through his body. He wasn't awed by the place anymore, but it would haunt his dreams for the rest of his days. A part of him hoped that he would never have to pass through its gates again.

The two dukes led their parties to Kearney's tent in the midst of the Glyndwr army. There was no discussion of why, but it seemed clear to Xaver that they did so for Tavis's benefit. As long as he was with the Curgh army, he was considered to be under his father's protection and not Kearney's. As they walked among the soldiers of Glyndwr, however, Xaver wondered if his friend was any safer with Kearney than with Javan. Glyndwr's men stared at the young lord with such venom and loathing that it made Xaver's stomach churn. They had made up their minds about him. Tavis was right: he was better off chasing Brienne's assassin through the Forelands than trying to make a life for himself in the highlands.

The men were cooking venison and fowl provided by Aindreas's kitchenmaster. No doubt Kentigern had been loath to extend any offer of hospitality to either duke, and certainly Javan would have refused him if he had. But after Glyndwr and Curgh helped save the castle, Aindreas had little choice but to give them something. Under the circumstances, providing meat, bread, and ale for the two armies was the least he could do.

For a time, Tavis, Xaver, and the rest ate wordlessly, savoring their meal. Xaver was simply too hungry to speak and he guessed that Fotir and the duke felt much the same way. But he also knew that all of them were reluctant to begin this discussion.

"Has either of you given more thought to what I said earlier today?" Grinsa finally asked, eyeing Javan and then Kearney. It was strange that this Qirsi should have felt so comfortable taking charge of their conversations, as he had that day in the castle and again just now. He was a Revel gleaner, nothing more. Yet dukes, ministers, and warriors appeared more than willing to defer to him in these matters, and Xaver could see why. Unlike so many of the Qirsi Xaver had seen over the years, this man had the build of a warrior and carried himself with the confidence of a king. His voice was deep and powerful. Unlike most of the sorcerer race, who seemed to be diminished by the magic they wielded, Grinsa's presence was enhanced by it. With his bone white hair and pale yellow eyes, he might have been the most formidable man Xaver had ever met.

"I certainly have," Xaver's father said, chewing a piece of bread. "It seems to me that the Rules of Ascension demand that a king be chosen by all the houses of Eibithar. Sure the king comes from one of the majors, but the dukes of all twelve houses have a say in this. One house shouldn't have the power to overturn the will of the rest, particularly when it would also mean ignoring the Order of Ascension."

Grinsa nodded, his eyes fixed on the flames of the cooking fire. "Usually I'd agree with you. But these are extraordinary times. If the houses follow the traditional order, and give the crown to Javan, it could mean civil war."

"And what happens the next time we have to choose a king? What's to stop another duke from threatening war because he doesn't like the man in line for the throne?"

"He has a point," Fotir said quietly. "The rules depend upon the consent of all the houses. If we allow one house to withhold consent this time, and thus alter the Order of Ascension, we weaken the entire foundation of the kingdom."

"Wouldn't a war weaken it more?"

"Maybe not," Hagan said. "If the other houses stand together against Aindreas, it may end up strengthening us. In the past, challenges to the rules have led to civil wars, but only because the challenges have come from more than one of the majors. Aindreas is alone this time."

"How do you know?" Grinsa asked. "Word of Brienne's death is still spreading through the land. And Tavis is still being blamed. Hearing of her murder and the evidence against Lord Curgh's son, other dukes may join Aindreas's cause."

"Aren't they just as likely to view Glyndwr's ascension with suspicion?" Kearney's first minister asked. "Particularly when they learn that the duke has granted asylum to Lord Tavis?"

"Not if Aindreas agrees to it. In that case, both Curgh and Kentigern will have been passed over in favor of Glyndwr."

The Qirsi woman looked down at her hands, which she was rubbing together as if the night were cold. "And what if something happens to him? Thorald won't have a viable heir for another generation, Galdasten for three. This could all come up again before long."

"Nothing is going to happen to me."

They all turned to Kearney, who had kept his silence until then.

"I find it a bit curious that those of us who have the most at stake in this are the ones saying the least."

Javan grinned. "I noticed that, too."

"Few people in the kingdom would believe it," Kearney said, "but I meant it when I said today that I don't want to be king. It would mean leaving my home and my people." He lowered his gaze. "It would mean giving up much in my life that I treasure. That said," he went on, looking at the duke of Curgh once more, "my sacrifice would be nothing next to yours. This is not my decision to make." He paused, looking briefly at Tavis. "I should also tell you, though, that if you decide to take the throne, I can't stand with you in any conflict with Kentigern. Were I to do so, I would be placing everyone in my court at risk, including your son. Especially your son. I've pledged myself to his protection and won't do anything to undermine that pledge."

"Well, that's convenient!" Hagan said, wearing a harsh grin. "You say that you don't want to be king, but then you turn around and say that if the duke doesn't cede the crown to you, you'll do nothing to stop Kentigern from plunging the land into war."

Glyndwr's swordmaster bristled. "He said nothing of the sort!"

Xaver's father started to stand, but Javan gripped his shoulder, stopping him. "That's enough, Hagan," he said in a low voice. "Kearney's right. His promise of asylum to Tavis takes precedence over everything else. You don't really think I'd want it any other way, do you?"

Hagan shook his head, though he still glared at Gershon Trasker.

"I won't lie to any of you," Javan continued. "I do want to be king. I've wanted it all my life. It's been over sixty years since Skeris the Fourth died. And before he took the throne it had been nearly a century since a man of Curgh wore Eibithar's crown. Who knows when our house will have another opportunity like this one? I regret the tragedies that have placed the House of Curgh in this position, but I'd be a fool not to take advantage of them. At least I would be under different circumstances." He looked at the duchess, taking her hand and raising it to his lips. "More than anything, I wanted you to be my queen. I hope you can forgive me for this."

Shonah gave a small breathless laugh, her pale green eyes sparkling like gems in the firelight. "There's nothing to forgive, my love. You're doing the right thing, not that I expected anything less."

"Are you sure of this, my lord?" Hagan asked. "As you say, you've wanted to be king all your life."

"Yes, I know. But my ambitions are of little consequence next to the well-being of this kingdom." He stood, facing Kearney, who climbed to his feet as well. "Lord Kearney of Glyndwr, I, Javan of Curgh, swear this oath to you now, that I will renounce my claim to the throne in favor of your ascension, provided Aindreas of Kentigern does the same."

"Lord Javan of Curgh," the duke answered, "I, Kearney of Glyndwr, hear your oath, and swear to you that I will accept the call to ascend when it is issued by the twelve houses of Eibithar." He bowed, then met Javan's gaze once more. "I will never forget what you do here tonight, Javan, nor will I allow the rest of Eibithar to forget. You would have been a noble and worthy king. I only hope that I prove myself deserving of the honor you do me here."

"I believe you will," Javan said. "And I'll gladly pledge my sword and my house to your service."

Watching the two men embrace, Xaver felt his heart expand with pride at what his duke had done. He thought this must have been what it was like to watch Audun take the throne as Eibithar's first king. He glanced at his father, who still gazed at Javan.

"He would have been a fine king," the swordmaster whispered. "A rival to old Skeris himself."

The two dukes bade each other good night a short while later, the company from Curgh, including Xaver, standing and stretching their legs before starting back toward the Curgh encampment.

Tavis walked with them part of the way, to the edge of Glyndwr's camp, before embracing his mother and father.

"I'm sorry, Father," Xaver heard the young lord say as Javan gripped his shoulders. "I've cost us the crown."

"The man who killed Brienne did that, Tavis," Javan said, looking sad. "And I fear the cost to you has been far greater than it ever will be for me."

"But I—"

"Don't think of it anymore. You, your mother, and I have survived two battles now. The gods are smiling on us. I'm duke of the finest house in Eibithar. How much more can a man want?"

The boy nodded, embraced his father again, and pulled away, starting back toward Kearney's tent.

"It's only going to get harder for him," Shonah said, watching her son walk away.

Javan put his arm around her. "Yes, but he's a Curgh."

She shook her head. "He's a boy."

Keziah stared off to the west, toward the Curgh encampment. She had long since lost sight of Javan and his duchess, but she couldn't bear to look at Kearney or her brother just then.

It had all happened so quickly that it left her dizzy. Her duke— her lover—was to be king. He hadn't even asked her counsel. Perhaps he knew how much she wanted him to refuse the crown. Perhaps he knew as well that had he asked, she would have told him to do just what he was doing, and that speaking the words would have hurt her more than anything.

She felt Grinsa's eyes upon her, and she willed herself not to face him. She could see his expression in her mind. The concern in his furrowed brow, the sorrow in his pale eyes. He would plead for her forgiveness when both of them knew there was nothing to forgive. There was no doubt in Keziah's mind that by suggesting this compromise, Grinsa had saved the land from civil war. But she couldn't bring herself to say this aloud, at least not yet.

So it was that she still faced toward the west when Tavis returned to them, looking pale as the white moon, save for the angry scars Aindreas had given him. However much Kearney's ascension pained her, she knew, it was nothing compared with what this boy was going through. His mere presence made her ashamed of her self-pity, as it had so many times in the past several days.

But it was not the boy himself that caught her eye as he approached. It was the looks of loathing from Kearney's men, which followed him like the shadows cast by the two moons. Earlier in the day, she had heard whispered conversations between Kentigern's men and the soldiers of Glyndwr. Word of Tavis's alleged crime had spread swiftly through Kearney's army. The minister had even heard some of Glyndwr's men questioning the duke's decision to grant the boy asylum. For now, Tavis had only to cope with glares and whispers, but it wouldn't take much for this to become something far more serious.

"Given the opportunity," Grinsa said quietly, "I think they'd kill him right now."

Keziah turned to look at him, but her brother was speaking to Kearney.

"I gave the boy asylum, and my soldiers know that I'd view the merest threat on his life as an act of treason."

"That may be true, my lord," Gershon said. "But we can't afford to weaken ourselves in any way, particularly now."

"I understand what you're saying, Gershon. I've thought of this myself."

The swordmaster nodded. "Very well, my lord."

Tavis stepped into the circle of firelight, and the three of them fell silent.

"I'm sorry," the boy said, his face reddening. "I didn't mean to interrupt."

"You didn't, Lord Tavis," Kearney said. He gestured for the boy to sit. "Please join us. We have matters to discuss."

Tavis lowered himself to the ground, eyeing the duke and appearing unsure of himself.

"Your father did a very brave and honorable thing tonight. There aren't many men in all the Forelands who would have made the same choice."

"Yes, my lord."

"When I granted you asylum, I did so as duke of Glyndwr, and though my ascension to the throne in no way abrogates my pledge of protection, it does change our arrangement in certain ways."

"My lord?"

"I can still offer you the refuge of my house, but I can't see to your protection personally. I'll be in the City of Kings, and I don't think it would be appropriate for you to be living in Audun's Castle."

The ghost of a smile touched the boy's lips and was gone. "Of course, my lord. I understand."

Kearney smiled as well, looking relieved. "I'm glad to hear that. Gershon will be leading a group of my men back to the highlands in the next day or two so that he can escort my wife and children to the City of Kings. You can ride with him if you like."

"Actually, my lord, I have something else in mind."

Kearney blinked. "Excuse me?"

"I'm grateful for your offer of protection, and I know that I would be very comfortable in Glyndwr Castle. But my life has been taken from me, my lord, much as Brienne's was taken from her. Yes, I'm still alive, but I've lost my title, my claim to the Curgh dukedom, and even my right to live with my family and friends. I want to find the man who did this to me, who did this to us. I want to find Brienne's killer. That's the only way I can prove my innocence, not just to you and Aindreas, but to all the people of Eibithar."

"We've talked about this, Tavis," Grinsa said.

"Not to my satisfaction, we haven't. You've told me that our lives are linked in some way, you said that you've seen this. But that doesn't make you my master."

"I never—"

"I have to do this, gleaner. With all respect to the duke, there's no life for me in Glyndwr. I'll be alone and miserable."

"I can't protect you beyond the walls of my city," Kearney told him.

The boy smiled, though there was a brittleness to it, as if he could start to cry at any moment. "I've seen the way your men look at me, my lord. I'm not convinced that you can keep me safe within your walls."

The duke stared at him, but said nothing. Perhaps he was starting to question this as well.

Tavis turned to Grinsa again. "I'll do this alone if I have to, but

I'd be grateful for your company. If the conspiracy you fear is real, finding the assassin might help you learn more about the people who lead it."

"Have you spoken to your father of this?" Kearney asked, his voice low.

"Not yet, my lord. I'm no longer my father's charge. I thought I should speak to you and Grinsa first."

Kearney nodded, saying nothing for a moment. Then he faced Grinsa. "I have no power to stop Tavis from doing this. He's under my protection, but he's not my ward. Nor do I have any sway with you, gleaner. But I think we both know that he'll be safer if you're with him. You asked me to take the throne, now I'm asking you to take care of him."

Keziah could see her brother waver. He was struggling with something, though she could only guess at what it might be.

"This all began with the boy's gleaning," he finally said. "I knew then that it wouldn't be over for some time." He turned to Tavis and even managed a smile. "Yes, I'll go with you. The conspiracy of which I've spoken is real, and I don't think anyone in the Forelands has more cause than you to want to see it defeated."

Again the boy smiled, and this time it appeared genuine. "Thank you." He glanced at Kearney. "And thank you as well, my lord. I hope you don't think me ungrateful."

"Not at all, Lord Tavis. In truth, I didn't envy you the life that awaited you in Glyndwr. You're taking a great risk, but it's one I would take if I walked your path."

Tavis nodded and took a breath. "It's been a long day," he said. "I think I should get some sleep." He glanced at Keziah and Gershon before nodding once more to the duke and Grinsa. Then he walked off to find his sleeping roll.

Kearney and Gershon exchanged a look.

"I'll make sure he's all right," the swordmaster said, standing and starting in the same direction. "I could use the rest, too."

Grinsa rose a moment later, his gaze falling on Keziah. There were so many things she wanted to ask him, so much she still didn't understand. But with Kearney right there, and Glyndwr's men all around them, she knew she would have to wait a while longer.

"Will you and Tavis be leaving right away?" she asked, dreading his answer.

"With the duke's permission, I'd like to accompany you to the

City of Kings. I want to see this through to Lord Glyndwr's investiture, and I'd like to give Tavis a bit more time with his mother and father."

"You're welcome to remain with us through the ceremony," the duke said. "Beyond that, I don't think it would be wise. I don't want to begin my reign by driving a wedge between Aindreas and the throne."

"Of course, my lord," her brother said, bowing. "Thank you." Grinsa turned to Keziah once more. "It seems you'll have to put up with me a while longer." He bowed to her also, a grin playing at the corners of his mouth.

She smiled. As children, they had bowed to each other whenever they said goodbye, mocking the somber formality of the court in which their father served. Kearney couldn't have known this, of course. He would have thought it perfectly natural for a Revel gleaner to bow to the first minister of a major house.

"I've put up with you for many years," she said. "Another turn or two shouldn't be too difficult. Good night, Grinsa."

Smiling broadly and bowing once more to the duke, he left them. For the first time in days, Keziah found herself alone with Kearney.

"You're angry with me," he said, his eyes searching hers.

"What right do I have to be angry? You're saving the kingdom."

"But I didn't ask for your advice on the matter. I didn't even discuss it with you."

She shrugged, looking away. "You know what counsel I would have given."

"Yes, I do."

For some time neither of them spoke. She could hear men laughing in the distance; some were even singing. Keziah had to remind herself that they had won a war this day. She stole a look at the duke. He was gazing into the flames, his eyes wide, as if he could see within the fire all that he had taken on by agreeing to be king, the burdens and the power.

"I have to bring her here," he said abruptly. "You understand that."

The minister felt her throat constrict. "Of course. She's to be your queen."

"It's more than that, Kez. I'm to be king, a living emblem of the land and its laws. To defy those laws—even for you, even for us—would be to weaken all of Eibithar."

She would have liked to tell him that a king deserved to be happy, that he deserved to love. She wanted to ask if he really believed other kings in the Forelands gave up their mistresses when they took the throne. But Kearney wasn't like other men. She, who loved him more than she had ever dreamed possible, knew that better than anyone.

After some time he looked up, his eyes meeting hers. "Will you stay on as my archminister?"

"You'll have your choice of any Qirsi in the kingdom, my lord, including many of those who have served Aylyn. You shouldn't offer to make me archminister until you've spoken to others."

"Who else would I want, Kez?"

She wanted to look away again, but his eyes held her. "I don't know if I can do this," she whispered. "How can I continue to serve you if I can't love you?"

"I don't know. But I need you, Kez. No one understands me better than you do, and there's no one I trust as much." He paused, a pained look in his eyes. "Will you at least think about it?"

She nodded. "All right." After another brief silence she rose, forcing a smile. "It's late, my lord. We can speak of this more in the morning."

Kearney stood quickly. "Kez, wait." He hesitated, suddenly looking like a shy boy, despite his silver hair and the cuts and bruises on his face. "I was hoping you might stay with me tonight. This isn't a night for either of us to be alone."

The minister gazed at him, her heart hammering so hard within her chest that she thought she could hear it. Her throat was dry, and there were tears on her face. More than anything, she wanted to take his hand and lead him back to his tent. But after all that had been said this night, how could she?

"I can't lie with you, my lord," she told him, her voice barely carrying over the sounds of the camp. "If I'm to spend the rest of my life thinking of you as my liege rather than as my love, I have to begin now, tonight."

"But, Kez—"

She shook her head, tears flying off her face. "Please," she said, turning away from him. "Don't say anything."

The minister started to walk away, though she didn't know where to go. Kearney was everywhere—his soldiers, his tent, his banners. There was no escaping him here.

She almost wished that he would call to her, knowing that she couldn't refuse him a second time. But the duke let her leave, and Keziah wondered how she would ever find the strength to stop loving him.

Chapter
Thirty-three

✦

Mertesse, Aneira

Yaella rode back to the castle with Rouel's body, which
they carried on one of the carts that had borne wood for
siege engines. She never strayed from the wagon, even
when the mud of the Tarbin sucked at its wheels and her
mount grew restive in the swirling waters. But neither did she look
upon the duke. She had seen enough blood and death during the
previous three days; she couldn't bear to look upon more.

Instead, she tried to choose what words she would use to tell the
duchess that her husband had been killed. She could still hear faint
cries coming from behind her, and she shuddered, wondering if she
had been wrong to leave Wyn and the other soldiers behind. The
master armsman had encouraged her to go. Indeed, he had made it
sound like an order, though she was the duke's highest-ranking
advisor. The oath she had taken to serve Rouel and the House of
Mertesse demanded that she stay. But her allegiance to the Weaver
said otherwise, and so she fled, though it was a decision she would
regret for the rest of her life.

The minister, and the soldiers who accompanied her, reached
the walls of Mertesse City shortly before nightfall. Word of their
approach had spread through the city and castle, drawing people
from their homes. Many of them cried out at the sight of their duke,
and before the cart came to the castle gates, bells were ringing in
guard towers along the city walls and in the spire of the Sanctuary of
Elined.

The procession moved slowly, as if Rouel's funeral had already

565

begun. The streets grew more crowded, and the people more subdued, until it seemed that Yaella and the duke's corpse were passing
through the sanctuary itself. They entered the castle through the city
gate, crossed the north ward, and came at last to the duke's ward,
where the duchess awaited them. She was sobbing already, and
when she saw the duke, the killing bolt still embedded in his skull,
she let out a wail that reverberated off the walls of the keep, mingling with the sound of the bells.

Her son was beside her, and she buried her face against his chest,
her body convulsing with the power of her grief.

Rowan, the boy—the new duke—held his mother in his arms,
staring down at his father, dry-eyed and impassive. His hair was red,
like his mother's, but in every other way he was his father's son. He
was only two years past his Fating, but already he was nearly as
broad in the chest and shoulders as Rouel. He had the duke's broad
mouth and prominent brow, as well as his icy blue eyes.

"Where's Wyn?" he asked, his eyes flicking to Yaella before
returning to his father's shattered face.

"We left him in Kentigern, my lord. He and a large number of
soldiers were still fighting Eibitharians." She swallowed. "He told
me to bring the duke home and he sent some of the men to guard us."

"The siege was going that well?"

"No, my lord. It was going that poorly."

He looked up at her again. "How is that possible?"

"Lord Kentigern returned, my lord, with his army. And the
armies of Curgh and Glyndwr marched with him. We had taken
much of the castle by then, but we couldn't hold it against so great a
force."

"So Wyn is lost as well."

"I fear he is, my lord."

"And how many men?"

"We haven't made a count yet. I returned with well over a hundred men, maybe as many as two hundred, and Kentigern may spare
the foot soldiers who survive the last of the fighting. I'll let you know
as soon as I can."

He nodded. "Yes, do that. I'll want to speak with you further
about this."

"Of course, my lord."

Rowan started to lead his mother away, his eyes lingering a
moment more on his father. "See to it that the body is handled prop-

erly, First Minister," he said. "We'll discuss plans for my father's funeral later."

She just stared after him, not knowing what to say. A first minister didn't do such things; at least, she never had. But she couldn't bring herself to say this, and by the time she managed to mutter, "Yes, my lord," he was too far away to hear her.

The soldiers who had led the cart back to Mertesse were watching her, as if awaiting instructions.

"Take the duke to his chambers," she said, still refusing to look at Rouel's corpse. "And summon his surgeons. They'll know what to do."

"Yes, First Minister."

She dismounted, tossing the reins to another soldier, and made her way back to her chambers. More than anything, she wanted to strip off the oppressive mail coat and her filthy riding clothes, and bathe herself with a fresh bowl of steaming water. The stench of blood, smoke, and horse sweat clung to her like sodden cloth. But all she could bring herself to do was roll onto her bed and close her eyes. Every muscle ached and her head spun for want of sleep.

Just as the minister felt herself drifting toward slumber, however, she heard a knock at her door. She lay still, hoping whoever it was would go away, but when the knock came again, she opened her eyes.

"Demons and fire!" she spat under her breath. "What is it?"

"There's a man at the outer gate, Minister." A man's voice, one of the guards, no doubt. "He's asking for you."

She swung herself off the bed and stepped to the door, pausing with her fingers on the door handle until her sight cleared and the dizzying motion of the chamber stopped. Then she pulled the door open.

"What man?" she asked the soldier who stood before her.

"I don't know his name. He's Qirsi, and he claims to be the first minister of Kentigern."

She was past him almost before he finished.

"He is Kentigern's first minister," she said over her shoulder. "Or at least he used to be. You haven't harmed him, have you?"

"No, First Minister. We're holding him at the gate, and we took his sword, but we've done nothing more."

"Good."

She hadn't expected Shurik so soon. Tomorrow perhaps, or the day after. But not this night. His arrival here probably meant that the battle had already ended. She was fortunate to have left when she did.

He was grinning when Yaella found him, though she could see the strain of the last few days in his pale eyes. He was surrounded by Rouel's guards, and he looked like a child beside them.

"It's all right," Yaella told the soldiers, dismissing them with a wave of her hand. "Return his sword to him, see that his horse is taken to the stables, and leave us."

The men did as they were told and in a moment the two Qirsi were alone.

"It's over?" Yaella asked, as they walked back toward the inner ward.

"Your master armsman had just surrendered when I left."

"So Wyn was still alive."

"For the time being, yes. But Aindreas had him taken to his dungeon. My duke is intent on learning how his precious gates were defeated so quickly."

"Is that why you left?"

Shurik shrugged, the familiar ironic smile springing to his lips. But Yaella could see that he was troubled. "I left because I sensed that one of the Qirsi riding with Kearney of Glyndwr knew what I had done."

"But that's impossible."

He glanced at her. "Not entirely."

It took her a moment. "You think he's a Weaver?" she asked, her voice dropping to a whisper.

"I think it's possible. I'm just not certain if he's our Weaver or not."

"Why would our Weaver be helping Glyndwr? Why would he scare you into fleeing?"

"Why does he do any of this? I believe this Weaver helped the Curgh boy escape Aindreas's prison, which carried us one step closer to a war between Kentigern and Curgh. Yet then he brought the houses of Eibithar together and ended Mertesse's siege." He shook his head. "I don't know what to believe anymore. Which seems more likely to you: that there are two Weavers walking the Forelands, or that our Weaver is influencing both sides of this conflict?"

Yaella weighed this for some time. Neither choice made much

sense to her, but both seemed at least vaguely possible. "So what can we do?"

"I can't answer that, either. I wouldn't want to risk asking the Weaver about any of this, but if there is another of his kind, he should know about it."

"Well, I'll leave that to you," she said.

He grinned again. "Coward."

They passed through the inner gate and followed a narrow path toward the tower nearest her quarters. Usually she would have taken Shurik to the duke immediately. The minister was here seeking refuge in the House of Mertesse, and though Rouel had already agreed to grant him asylum, there were formalities to be observed. With Rouel dead, however, and Rowan grieving and so new to his power, she thought it best to wait.

She explained this to Shurik as they entered the torchlit corridors and made their way to the nearest stairway, their footsteps echoing loudly off the stone ceiling.

"But where am I to sleep?" he asked.

"You're welcome in my chambers." Seeing his grin, she shook her head. "Sleep, Shurik. That's all." Then she smiled as well. "For tonight at least."

The following morning she took Shurik to the duke's chambers, only to be turned away by guards who told her that Rowan was still attending to his mother, and wouldn't be ready to speak with her until later that day. These soldiers also informed her that just over two hundred men had returned from Kentigern late the previous night, all of them unarmed and most of them uninjured. All told, the army of Mertesse had lost more than seven hundred soldiers, far more than half the number of men who had marched on Kentigern a few days before. Such news wasn't going to make her conversation with the new duke any easier.

Yaella spent much of the day overseeing arrangements for Rouel's funeral. Without being able to speak with Rowan or the duchess, she was forced to make a number of decisions on her own, but in the end she realized that neither of them was likely to find fault with much of what she did. The duke would be honored in a manner befitting his life and his station. What more could they ask?

She had dreaded this task when Rowan gave it to her, but she found that it made the day pass quickly and, oddly, it took her mind off the grief she still felt for Rouel. Shurik remained with her for much of the day, although he returned to her chambers just after the ringing of the prior's bells. She met him there a short while later and escorted him once more to the chambers of the duke. This time the guards let them pass.

Rowan was standing at his father's writing table, reading by candlelight. All the windows in the castle had been shuttered, and would remain so for a full turn. Yaella cringed at the thought of it. The chamber felt small and there was already a staleness to the air. She wasn't certain she could live this way for a turn.

"Who is this?" Rowan asked, eyeing Shurik with unconcealed distaste.

Yaella cleared her throat. "This is Shurik jal Marcine, my lord. Until yesterday the first minister of Kentigern. First Minister, I present Rowan, duke of Mertesse."

Shurik bowed. "An honor, my Lord Duke. I'm deeply sorry for the loss of your father. He was a wise and courageous man."

Rowan stared at the minister for a moment, saying nothing. Then he swung his gaze back to Yaella. "Why have you brought him here? I have no wish to speak to this man today."

"Shurik helped your father plan the siege of Kentigern, my lord. And in return, your father promised him asylum."

"My father employed a Qirsi traitor?" the duke asked, narrowing his eyes.

A look of purest hatred twisted across Shurik's features and was gone, appearing and vanishing in the time it might take an arrow to fly from a soldier's bow to his enemy's heart. Rowan gave no sign that he noticed.

"Your father understood that his assault on Kentigern stood little chance of succeeding without my aid," the minister said, somehow managing a thin smile. "Even your fine army could not defeat the castle's gates without my magic."

"Yet even with your magic, the siege has failed and my father is dead." The duke cast a dark frown at Yaella. "I'm told that we lost more than half the men my father took across the river. Is that true?"

What sense was there in denying it? "It is, my lord. I believe the number is near seven hundred men."

Rowan shook his head, looking so much like Rouel that he could have been one of Bian's wraiths rather than a fatherless boy. "It seems, sir, that your magic did my father and his men little good."

"With all respect, my lord, my magic nearly allowed them to take the castle. Your father's siege only failed because Lord Kentigern returned too soon and brought with him the armies of Curgh and Glyndwr. This was regrettable, to be certain, but it was beyond my control."

The young duke looked down at his table, his mouth twitching. "I take it you've already been paid handsomely."

"I have, my lord."

"And though I still know little of such things, I would also guess that you're still owed more gold."

Shurik glanced at Yaella for just an instant. "That was our arrangement, my lord. Under the circumstances, the siege having failed and the duke having been lost, I expect no more gold. But there is no longer a life for me in Kentigern, or anywhere in Eibithar for that matter. I do humbly ask your protection."

"Yes, very well," Rowan said, a sour expression on his youthful face. "I grant you asylum. And if my father promised gold, you'll have that as well. The word of a Mertesse is as true as the sun." It was an old saying, as old as the house itself, from all that Yaella could tell.

"You're most gracious, my lord," Shurik said. "Just as your father was."

Rowan eyed him for a moment. "How much do we owe you?"

Shurik looked at Yaella once more.

"He was promised three hundred qinde, my lord," she said, "and he's still owed half."

The duke's eyes widened slightly, but then he nodded. "See to it, First Minister. And then make certain that he remains as far away from me as possible."

Yaella faltered, glancing quickly at Shurik. "Of course, my lord."

"My lord is too kind," Shurik said, bowing once more. Yaella heard sarcasm in his voice, but again the duke didn't appear to notice.

Rowan said nothing, his eyes fixed once more on the papers in front of him.

The two Qirsi exchanged another look.

"We'll leave you now, my lord," Yaella said. "You must be terribly weary."

"Why did you do it?" Rowan asked.

Yaella frowned. "My lord?"

But when the duke looked up, his gaze fell upon Shurik's face. "Why did you help my father? Was it just the gold?"

Abruptly Yaella's heart was pounding like a smith's sledge. She stared at Shurik, scouring her own mind for some answer that would satisfy Rowan without revealing too much. Her friend, though, gave no indication that he was shaken by the question.

"I served Aindreas of Kentigern for nearly ten years," he said. "And never once did I feel that my duke appreciated my counsel or my powers. But more than that, I never felt that I was in the court of a great man. Do you have any idea, my lord, what it's like to devote your life to serving a man you don't respect?"

Yaella knew how much truth there was in Shurik's answer, not only because he had expressed similar sentiments to her, but also because she had pledged herself to the Weaver's cause for much the same reason.

"Yes," the Qirsi went on after a moment's pause, "I wanted your father's gold. But just once I wanted as well to find myself in the service of a man I could honor."

She felt certain that he was speaking of the Weaver, but Rowan couldn't know this.

"I see," the duke said, his voice low. "I appreciate your candor."

"Your question demanded nothing less, my lord."

Rowan nodded, suddenly looking tired and pale. "Leave me now. I wish to be alone."

"Yes, my lord," Yaella said.

The two Qirsi bowed to him one last time and left the chamber, keeping their silence until they were far from the duke's guards in the dark corridors leading back to Yaella's chamber.

"You handled that well," she finally said. "Better than I would have."

"I simply told him what he wanted to hear, and in a way that was so vague that I didn't even have to lie." Shurik grinned. "But you give yourself too little credit. You would have done the same had you been in my position."

Yaella shook her head, unable just then to share in his mirth. "It will be much more difficult to explain all this to the Weaver. He expected a successful siege and a prolonged war between Aneira and Eibithar. We've given him neither."

"I don't know what he expected. As I told you before, I think it possible that he had much to do with our failure." He stopped her beneath one of the torches, taking both her hands. "We did what we could. We did what the Weaver told us to do. How can he ask more of us than that?"

Someone stepped into the corridor at its far end, the footfall startling her.

The two Qirsi began walking again, although Shurik continued to hold one of her hands in his own. They passed a guard, who nodded to them, his gaze straying to their entwined hands.

"He saw," she whispered, after she could no longer hear the man's footsteps.

"So what?" Shurik said. "I'm tired of keeping up appearances for these Eandi fools. Besides, I live here now. Chances are I'll be one of the duke's underministers before long. Isn't it natural that I should seek the affections of his lovely first minister?"

She did smile at that.

A few moments later, they reached her door, pausing for a moment in the corridor.

"Will I be using my sleeping roll again tonight?" he asked, smiling and stepping closer to her.

Yaella felt her cheeks color and nearly laughed aloud at herself. Was she a girl again, about to share her bed with this man for the first time? She put her arms around his neck and kissed him lightly on the lips.

"The duke did say to make certain you were comfortable."

"A fine man, this new duke."

Yaella kissed him again, deeply this time, before opening her door and drawing him into her chamber.

Lying in the darkness with Yaella naked beside him, her breathing slow and deep, her hand resting lightly on his chest, Shurik struggled to slow the beating of his heart. His brave words in the corridor notwithstanding, he feared the Weaver, as any Qirsi in his right mind would. Shurik considered himself a formidable man. Few Qirsi could lay claim to wielding even three forms of magic, much less the four that he possessed. He had served in the court of one of Eibithar's most powerful dukes and had, for the past several years, succeeded in concealing his betrayal. He might not have been the finest warrior in Aindreas's army, but swordsmanship was an Eandi talent. In the most important respects, those that mattered to his own people, he was a man to be respected.

Yet, next to the Weaver, he was nothing. The man could read the thoughts and harness the powers of other Qirsi as if they were his own. He could enter the dreams of those who served him, and could compel their obedience without saying a word or lifting a hand. Shurik had dreamed of such power for years; he had never imagined that another would use it to bend his will.

If he could have divined the purpose behind the Weaver's instructions it might have helped to ease his mind, but even in this way, the man was beyond him. Would the Weaver be angry that the siege had failed, or had he been responsible for its failure? Either way, Shurik felt certain that the man was waiting for him, ready to invade his sleep and carry him to the mysterious rise where they always spoke. So the minister lay awake, fighting his weariness, groping in the darkness for the words he would use to explain all that had gone wrong in the last few days. He longed to get up and step to the window so that he might look upon the moons and feel the cool touch of night on his face. But with Rouel dead and the castle mourning, even that was denied him. He felt himself drifting toward sleep, and though he tried to resist, it was as futile as swimming against a storm tide. It almost seemed that the Weaver had found a way to control his body as well as his mind.

At last he closed his eyes, thinking to do so only for a moment. But when he opened them again he was on the plain, standing in tall grasses amid the hulking shadows of boulders. The sky above him was black as night, but starless and moonless. Without even thinking, he started to walk toward the rise where the Weaver awaited him.

It was a steep climb that always left him winded and sweating, but this night it seemed especially arduous, as if the Weaver was already punishing him. Shurik felt as though he were ascending the highest peaks of the Basak Range rather than the grassy mound he had encountered here before. His legs ached and the slope grew so severe that he had to scramble on his hands and feet for the last part of the climb. When at last he reached the top, he could barely stand and his breath came in ragged gasps that tore at his chest.

He stood there for a long time, bent at the waist, his head spinning until he thought that he might be sick. The wind had ceased, as if the land itself were waiting for him to recover. At last he straightened, and only then did the light blaze, stabbing like a blade into his eyes. He looked away, raising a hand against the light. When he faced forward again, the Weaver was there, walking toward him, his wild hair and flowing cape framed by the radiance like a cloud that has blotted out the sun.

The Weaver stopped a few paces from where Shurik stood. He looked taller than Shurik remembered, more powerful, more frightening, his face obscured by the shadows.

"The siege is over." The Weaver offered it as a statement, his voice as hard as the stone boulders strewn across the darkened landscape.

"Yes, Weaver."

"And there is no war."

"No."

"How is it that you've managed to fail so miserably?"

How many times would he have to explain this? "Kentigern returned too soon, and he brought the armies of Curgh and Glyndwr with him."

"I had heard of this as well. Not only did you fail to give me the war I desired, but you have allowed the major houses of Eibithar to unite. Only days ago, Curgh and Kentigern were on the verge of civil war. Now they've fought side by side against their kingdom's most hated enemy. There's no telling how many turns it will take to drive them apart again."

"There was little I could do to—"

Shurik's head snapped back, his cheek stinging as if he had been struck. But the Weaver hadn't moved at all.

"You're Kentigern's first minister!" he said, his voice low and menacing. "You were there as all this was happening! And you want me to believe that you couldn't prevent any of it?"

"There were other forces at work, Weaver."

"Yes, of course there were."

Shurik heard sarcasm in the Weaver's tone and he had to bite back a response.

"The boy is free again?" the man asked a moment later. "Under Glyndwr's protection?"

"Yes."

"In other words, the only thing that worked out as you had hoped was your request for asylum in Mertesse. How fortunate for you. Under such circumstances, a man in my position might feel that his generosity had been exploited, that his gold had gone for nothing at all."

"The boy's presence in Glyndwr may prove to be of some use to us," Shurik said quickly, expecting the Weaver to hurt him again at any moment. "My former duke may have been helped by Curgh and Glyndwr, but he remains convinced that Tavis killed his daughter. Given time, I believe the rift between Javan and Aindreas will widen again. With the boy in Glyndwr, it shouldn't be difficult to draw Kearney into the fray."

"Interesting. You may be right. But in the meantime, whose time is being wasted? Whose gold is being spent to turn Kentigern against Glyndwr?"

Before Shurik could answer he was staggered by another blow, this one to the temple.

"*Mine!*" the Weaver roared, his voice rolling like thunder over the grasses and boulders. "Never forget that! Every time you fail, I pay the cost. I'm a patient man. I've waited many years to achieve as much as I have. But my patience is wearing thin and my tolerance for mistakes is waning. From now on, when you fail me, you'll be punished. And not just you, but all the Qirsi in my service, including the one sleeping beside you. You can tell her that in the morning, when you wake."

"Yes, Weaver."

Shurik thought the man would let him go then, but he was wrong.

"You said a moment ago that there were other forces at work. What did you mean?"

The minister hesitated. This was not a matter he wished to discuss just now, with the Weaver already enraged.

"You do remember saying it."

"Yes, Weaver. But I meant only that Tavis's escape had drawn Glyndwr into the conflict and that the duchess of Curgh had been surprisingly generous in her offer to help Aindreas defend his castle."

"I don't believe you. There's more to it than that. I sense your fear, your reluctance to tell me all that you're thinking."

"Anything else is conjecture on my part. Nothing more."

"Then amuse me with your theories. But tell me quickly. I grow tired of these games. I can just as easily compel you to speak as ask you. And I don't think you want that."

Shurik's throat was tight. In that moment he wasn't even certain that he could speak. He felt a strange pressure on his eyes that swiftly turned to agony. Again the Weaver had not lifted a hand or taken a single step toward him. But it seemed to the minister that the Weaver's thumbs were pushing his eyes into his head, until he thought that he would never see again.

"All right!" he cried. "I'll tell you! Please, just stop!"

Abruptly the pressure was gone.

"Of course," the Weaver said, his tone mild. "I don't want to hurt you. I just want to know what you meant."

The minister took a long, shuddering breath, wishing that he had held his tongue rather than making excuses for the failed siege.

"Well?" the Weaver demanded, his voice hardening once more.

"As I told you before," Shurik began, "I didn't foresee the involvement of Glyndwr, or for that matter, the boy's escape from Aindreas's dungeon. As far as I can tell, one man was responsible for both. He's Qirsi, I don't know his full name, though I heard others call him Grinsa. I've also heard him referred to as the gleaner, leading me to believe that he was with the Revel."

"So all this fuss is about a resourceful Qirsi?"

"No, Weaver. I believe he's far more than that. When Tavis escaped the castle, those who helped him managed to shape a hole in the stone wall of a castle tower. And when I denied having shaping power myself, I had the distinct impression that he knew I was lying."

"What are you suggesting?" the Weaver asked. But Shurik knew from the sound of the man's voice that he already understood. For the first time since he had pledged himself to this cause, Shurik heard fear in the man's voice. If Grinsa was a Weaver, he certainly wasn't this Weaver.

"There may be another Weaver in the Forelands," Shurik said, trying to keep his voice even. If he was right, his Weaver needed him more than ever. Who else knew where Grinsa was or what he looked like? Who else understood the courts of Eibithar well enough to predict with any certainty where he might go next? "I don't think there's any other explanation."

"Of course there are other Weavers in the Forelands, you fool. Do you honestly believe I thought myself the only one? The danger lies not in his existence, but rather in the interest he's taken in the boy and your activities. Most Weavers choose to stay away from the intrigue of the courts for just this reason, the fear of discovery. That's probably why he was hiding in the Revel. But something must have happened to lure him out of the gleaning tent. Something that—"

He fell silent, standing before Shurik as still as the boulders that surrounded them.

"Weaver?" the minister said at last.

"You're to remain in Mertesse," the Weaver said at last. "You and your friend. In time, there will be more for both of you to do, but for now, I want you to stay there. Earn the trust of the new duke. Learn something of the Aneiran courts. Do you understand?"

"Yes, of course. But what about this other Weaver?"

"Never speak of him again. Not to anyone."

"But I know who he is. I've seen him. I can help you find him and keep watch on him."

"You're an exile and so you're of no use to me at all."

"What if—?"

A hand grabbed hold of his throat, unseen, but as powerful as a demon's claw.

"Enough!" the Weaver said. "You will stay in Mertesse. Question my commands again, and I'll hurt you in ways that will leave you wishing you'd remained in Kentigern to face your duke's torture. Defy me and I'll kill you."

His lungs burned for air. It felt as though the Weaver was crushing his throat. He tried to plead for the man's pity, but he couldn't make any sound at all.

And then he was awake in Yaella's chamber, with daylight seeping through the shuttered windows. She was sitting beside him, wrapped in a robe, her eyes wide with terror and tears on her face.

"I couldn't wake you," she whispered, her voice quavering. "I tried and tried, but it was as if you couldn't hear me."

He lay very still, saying nothing, his eyes closed, his chest rising and falling with each precious breath.

"Were you with the Weaver?"

Shurik nodded.

"Was he angry?"

"Yes," he said, his voice weak and raw. "But more than that, I think he's scared."

Chapter
Thirty-four

✦

City of Kings, Eibithar, Shyssir's Moon waxing

E|ibithar's nobles came to the City of Kings from all corners of the kingdom to attend Kearney's investiture. Of course the dukes of the twelve houses were there, including Kearney's eldest son and namesake who would become duke with his father's ascension. But lesser nobles came as well, from the most powerful thane in Thorald, to the most obscure of Sussyn's barons, and nearly all in between. It had been over thirty years since the last ascension. Given Kearney's youth and the longevity for which Glyndwr's dukes were renowned, there was no telling when there might be another.

Nobles came from Wethyrn, Caerisse, and northern Sanbira as well. There were even rumors that Braedon's emperor intended to send a representative, though no one had arrived from the empire as of yet. Many of these nobles brought their families, and the families brought gold. So Grinsa was not surprised to see the broad avenues of the city choked with peddlers and merchant carts. "Whither court gold, so go the traders." It was an old saying, but one that still rang true.

But neither the noble families of the Foreland's courts nor the merchants with all their wares held any interest for the gleaner. He cared only for Bohdan's Revel, which had arrived late the previous night, sometime after he and Tavis returned to their chamber in the great castle. The Revel had been in Eardley, of course, as it always was during Morna's Turn, and would usually have traveled west anyway as far as Labruinn. It was one of the longest journeys of each year for the festival, made even longer this year by the celebration at Audun's Castle. The musicians, dancers, and gleaners would have had to journey an additional twenty leagues and cross Binthar's Wash and the Thorald River, both of which were swelled by the rains of the growing season. No doubt they had been weary when they arrived, hungry for a warm meal and eager for sleep. But this was the Revel. When Grinsa and the young lord awoke, the gleaning tent was already raised, its flags visible from their window.

The gleaner was reluctant to leave Tavis's side, particularly with the city so crowded. Aindreas had promised to support Kearney's ascension and, though clearly unmoved by Tavis's claims of innocence, he had made no more threats against the boy. But Kentigern's soldiers and lesser lords were everywhere. Kearney had vowed to hold Aindreas responsible for any harm that came to Tavis, but as a practical matter, there was only so much he could do if one of Kentigern's underlings made an attempt on the boy's life.

As soon as he caught sight of the gleaning tent, however, feeling his heart jump like a Revel tumbler and his stomach turn to stone, he knew that he would have to leave the boy alone, at least for a time.

"What is it?" Tavis asked, eyeing him closely. "Are you ill?"

In spite of everything, Grinsa managed a smile. "No, not ill. I have to do something this morning." *I have to kill the woman I love.*

"That tent," Tavis said, following the direction of the Qirsi's gaze. "It's the Revel, isn't it?"

"Yes."

"You're going to see that woman. The one I asked you about in the Sanctuary."

Grinsa clenched his jaw, still staring out at the gleaning tent. He had no wish to discuss this with anyone. "Can you amuse yourself in the castle until I return?" he asked. "I shouldn't be long."

"Of course. I may go out to see the musicians, but I'll be back by midday if you wish."

He didn't like the idea of the boy leaving the safety of the castle, but he couldn't make him a prisoner. "That will be fine," he said after a moment's pause. "Just watch yourself."

Tavis grinned. "I'm no dolt, Grinsa. I'll find Xaver or my father. I won't be alone."

The gleaner left their chamber a few minutes later, following the most direct route out of the castle and into the streets of the city. He walked quickly, fighting the urge to run.

Eager as he was to confront Cresenne, he knew that he was taking a great risk. He wasn't so foolish as to think that he had stopped loving her, even after all that had happened. A part of him wanted only to hold her again, to taste her lips and smell her hair. He had to remind himself that she had betrayed him, that she had sent a man to kill him.

There was already a long line of children outside the gleaning tent, but Grinsa strode past them, flinging open the tent flap and stepping into the shadows. Trin was there, seated before the stone. A young girl sat across from him, and she turned to look at Grinsa, her face almost as pale as that of the fat Qirsi.

"Grinsa!" Trin said brightly, smiling up at him. "What a pleasure this is! I'm afraid, though, that you've come at a bad time. We were just about to begin this young lady's Determining. Perhaps we can meet later—"

"Leave," Grinsa said to the girl, fighting to keep his anger from spilling over.

"But she's just come in."

He glared at the man, silencing him. "She can come back later." He glanced at the child again. "Go back to the front of the line. When the gleanings resume, you'll go first."

She nodded and ran out of the tent, leaving the two Qirsi alone.

"I'm surprised at you, Grinsa. I've never known you to be rude to—"

Grinsa stepped to where the man sat, pushing over the table, grabbing Trin by his shirt, and lifting him out of his chair.

"Where is she?" the gleaner demanded.

"Who?"

Grinsa raised a hand, as if to strike him.

"You mean Cresenne?"

He let his hand fly, slapping the Qirsi with an open palm. "Of course I mean Cresenne, you fat fool! Now tell me where she is!"

"She's gone! I swear it!"

"What do you mean, she's gone? Gone where?"

"I mean she's left the Revel."

He felt his body sag. After a moment he lowered Trin back into the chair, though he didn't let go of the man's collar. "Did she say where?"

"Back to the Wethy Crown to see her family. She said a sister of hers had fallen ill."

It was probably another lie, one among many. For all Grinsa knew, she had never lived a day in Wethyrn, or Braedon for that matter.

"I was sorry that things didn't work out between you," Trin said, speaking slowly, as if he expected every word to anger Grinsa again. "I thought you'd be together for a long time."

"Stop it." Grinsa tightened his hold on him. "I want to know what your role was in all of this."

"My what? I don't know what you're talking about."

"You practically pushed us into each other's arms. Why? Was that part of your plan? Did you choose me from the beginning, or was it only after Tavis's Fating?"

"This is nonsense, Grinsa! I have no idea—"

He slapped Trin again, harder this time. In a few seconds a red imprint of his hand appeared on the man's cheek.

"Stop lying to me, Trin! I know about the conspiracy! I know that you're both involved!"

"I know of the conspiracy as well," Trin said. "But I'm not a part of it. And until this moment, I didn't know that Cresenne was."

Something in the man's voice stopped Grinsa, forcing him to listen, despite his rage and his grief and the ache in his chest.

"I promise you, Grinsa, I had nothing to do with this. I'm sorry that Cresenne was involved. Truly I am."

Grinsa shook his head. He felt as though he were in a sorcerer's mist. "But you hate the Eandi so. You spoke of Carthach as if he was a demon."

"I do hate them. And Carthach was a demon." The fat man smiled. "I'm not saying that I don't sympathize with their cause. Perhaps if I was a younger man, and a braver one, I would be aiding them." He gestured toward himself, the smile lingering on his lips, though the expression in his pale yellow eyes grew sad. "Look at me, Grinsa. I'm old. Not to the Eandi, perhaps. Maybe not even to our own kind. But at my age and with my girth, I hardly have the strength to do my fair share of the gleanings. I'd guess that I have five years left to live, a few more than that if I'm lucky. I'm not interested in changing the world. And even if I were, why would the leaders of such a conspiracy be interested in a fat old Qirsi like me?"

Grinsa stared at him a few moments more. Then he released him and straightened, looking off to the side.

"I'm sorry, Trin."

"You loved her very much."

He nodded.

"She said that you left the Revel after she told you she didn't love you. She said you couldn't stand being near her if you couldn't have her."

It was a strange lie. If he hadn't known better he might have thought that she really did love him, that she had said this as a matter of pride, to mask the pain she felt when he left.

"Did you believe her?" he asked.

"I had no reason not to. Is it true?"

Enough people knew he was traveling with Tavis so that it wasn't a secret anymore.

"No. I went to Kentigern to try to win Lord Tavis's release from the duke's prison. I saw in his Fating what awaited him there and I felt that I had to do something."

Trin raised an eyebrow. "It seems you succeeded."

"After I left, Cresenne sent a man to stop me. He was a singer in the Revel, and an assassin. Do you know the man I mean?"

Trin gaped at him. His expression might have been funny had they been talking about almost anything else. "No," the Qirsi finally said. "I remember hearing that a musician left the Revel shortly after you did, but I didn't know who he was, and, to be honest, I gave the matter little thought." He shook his head. "She sent him to kill you?"

"Yes."

"And how did you escape him?"

"I didn't. I killed him."

"I see," Trin said in a small voice, what little color he had draining from his face. "Am I to assume then that you're in league with those fighting against this conspiracy?"

Grinsa hesitated, wondering how to answer. Did he tell the man the truth, that there was no true opposition to the Qirsi movement? Did he admit that he could only count on support from Keziah and Fotir? Or was he too quick to accept the weakness of his position in this coming struggle? Wasn't Tavis an ally as well? And wouldn't his support and Fotir's bring Javan to their cause? If he could count on Keziah wasn't there a chance that he could look to Eibithar's new king for help?

"Yes," he said at last. "I guess I am. Does that make us enemies, Trin?"

The Qirsi shook his head. "No. I'm no friend of the Eandi, and, as I said, I understand the sentiments behind this conspiracy. But I have a nice life here in the Revel. I'd rather not see it upset by a war between the courts and the white-hairs. As much as I'd like to see Qirsi nobles in the Forelands, I'm not interested in changing things that much."

Grinsa stared at the man, unsure as to whether he was hearing him correctly. "What are you saying?"

"That I might be willing to help you. In small ways, mind you. I'm not about to risk my life, and I'd rather that no one on the other side learned of my activities. But if you need information, or if there's a message you want carried from one of Eibithar's houses to another, I might be able to help you."

"For a price?" the gleaner asked with a grin.

Trin smiled, an innocent look on his broad face. "Would you trust a man who did such things for free?"

Grinsa laughed. "A fair question." He regarded the man a moment longer, then nodded. "Very well. Thank you, Trin. If the need arises, I may call on you."

"So will you be gleaning for us while we're here?" Trin asked, changing the subject so easily they might as well have been discussing the recent rains. "Qirsar knows we could use the help."

"I don't think so," the gleaner said. "But I'll try to come by again before I leave the city."

The Qirsi nodded. "I'd like that."

Grinsa righted the table he had overturned and put the Qiran back on its stand, before turning to leave.

"How did you manage to save the boy?" Trin asked, just as he was reaching for the tent flap.

Grinsa stopped and faced him again. "I think it best if I don't answer. The more you know, the more the danger to both of us."

Trin nodded. "You're probably right. But tell me this: did the boy kill Lady Brienne?"

"No."

"You sound certain."

"I am."

"Well, we've just come from Eardley, as you know. And before then we were in Thorald. Most of the people in those cities believe Lord Tavis is a murderer. We left Thorald before word of Glyndwr's ascension reached the city, but in Eardley they thought Kearney a wise choice. Nevertheless, that hasn't stopped them from taking sides in the conflict between Aindreas and Javan. Even with a new king, the events in Kentigern could still tear this kingdom apart."

Grinsa had heard much the same thing about Eibithar's other cities. The houses were starting to line up behind the two dukes. Most, including Galdasten, one of the major houses, were allying themselves with Aindreas, because so many of the dukes still thought that Tavis was guilty. But a few had thrown their support to Javan, among them Heneagh and Labruinn, which had strong ties to Curgh. Thorald and Glyndwr had yet to commit to either side, and with Kearney as king, Glyndwr was likely to keep itself out of the fray. As long as Thorald did the same, the chance of civil war remained remote. But if the kingdom's most powerful house eventually allied itself with either Curgh or Kentigern, even a king as well-meaning as Kearney might not be able to maintain the peace.

"Thank you, Trin," Grinsa said quietly. "I appreciate the information."

"You're welcome. Be careful, Grinsa. If Cresenne was willing to send an assassin for you, others will also."

He nodded, making himself smile. Then he left the tent and made his way back toward the castle. He found Tavis in the moat ward of the palace, walking among the peddlers who had spread their wares on the grass there. Xaver MarCullet was with him, and the duke and duchess of Curgh were nearby. Assured that the boy was safe, Grinsa returned to the inner ward in search of his sister. They had spent some time together since the night Kearney agreed to take the throne, but Keziah remained distant. With the king's investiture set for the next day, and Tavis and Grinsa intending to leave the City of Kings soon after, Grinsa wasn't certain when he might have another chance to speak with her alone.

He found her in the castle's enormous hall, where the ceremonies would take place. She was overseeing the hanging of the pennons of each of Eibithar's houses. They were to hang in normal order of ascension except for Glyndwr's, which would be placed first for as long as Kearney and his line ruled. Already, seats for the visiting nobles were in place, row after row stretching the length and breadth of the hall. There must have been a thousand of them. Tapestries hung on the inner walls, one from each house, glorifying the achievements of each family's greatest hero. At the front end of the hall sat Audun's throne, moved here for the ascension from its usual place in the king's presence chamber. It was made of oak, carved with intricate images of the gods and goddesses, and though ancient, the wood still shone as it must have eight centuries before. A second, smaller throne stood next to it, also made of carved oak and obviously intended for Kearney's queen. Grinsa couldn't help but wonder how its presence here was affecting his sister.

"They're still too low," Keziah called to one of the men hanging from the ceiling of the hall. "They're better than they were, but I'd like them a bit higher."

The man shouted something in return that Grinsa couldn't hear, and Keziah nodded.

"The hall looks magnificent," the gleaner said.

She turned, her face brightening at the sight of him. "It certainly looks better than it did last night. With any luck, we'll actually be ready by tomorrow."

"I had hoped we could talk, but if you're too busy . . ." He shrugged, leaving the thought unfinished.

"It seems I'm always too busy. This is as good a time as any."

She glanced around the hall briefly, as if to convince herself that she could afford to leave for a moment or two. Then she led him to the nearest door and out into the bright sun of the ward.

They followed one of the stone paths leading through the castle gardens, and just like every other time they had been alone since leaving Kentigern, they fell immediately into an awkward silence.

"I feel like I need to apologize," Grinsa said at last, stealing a look at his sister, who had her eyes on the path before her. "I don't know what for, but I sense that you expect it of me."

"Did you know this would happen?" she asked. "Did you know that Kearney would become king?"

"I had some idea, yes. It was the obvious solution, Kezi. We all should have seen it from the start."

"Well, I didn't," she said, her voice rising.

"You didn't want to. Neither did Kearney. And certainly Javan and Aindreas didn't. That's why I had to say something."

"This is what you saw, isn't it? This is the future I asked you about when you came to me on the steppe."

"Yes. You asked me if it was terrible and I told you that I couldn't say whether it was good or bad. Do you remember?"

"Of course."

"So now that you know, how would you answer that question?"

"What?"

"Is it terrible to see the man you love crowned as our king? The way you've been for the last turn, you seem almost like you've been in mourning. Is it really worth all that? Do you honestly think this compares with what Tavis has been through, or the duke and duchess of Kentigern?"

They both stopped walking. Keziah's face had reddened and she was glaring at him as if she wanted to rail at him. But after a few moments she shook her head and lowered her gaze.

"I love him, Grinsa. And I've lost him. It may not be a tragedy to anyone else, but it hurts."

"I know. I'm sorry for it. If there had been another way, I would have found it. I hope you believe that."

She looked up, a small smile on her lips. "I do."

They resumed their walking, following a winding course among the flowers and small trees.

"I take it you and Tavis will be leaving soon?" she asked after some time.

"The morning after Kearney's investiture. It wouldn't be wise for us to stay much beyond that."

"And where will you go?"

"South. Shurik escaped to Aneira and I assume that Brienne's assassin did the same. I don't want to chance crossing the Tarbin, so I guess we'll go up onto the steppe, cross into Caerisse, and enter Aneira from the east."

Keziah pressed her lips together and shook her head. "I don't like the sound of that at all. It's bad enough that you're chasing an assassin, but to do so in Aneira." She shook her head a second time.

"To be honest, I don't like it any more than you do. I'd rather be going after Shurik. I think he probably knows more about the people leading the movement than would an assassin. I'm still hoping I can convince Tavis that Shurik is the safer quarry. But either way, we have to go to Aneira."

"Are you certain there isn't another you'd rather find in Aneira?"

This time it was Grinsa's turn to color. He had told his sister very little about Cresenne, but no one knew him better than she and some things couldn't be hidden.

"How did you know? I thought she was with the Revel until this morning."

"I knew that you would go looking for her today. And you would have said something if you had found her. The rest was a guess."

"She's in Aneira as well," he said. "I'm sure of it. But I don't know what I'd do if I found her. I think I'm better off going after Shurik and the assassin. Cresenne is . . . dangerous."

Keziah took his hand, and they walked a while longer, speaking of the ceremony to come and the troubles that awaited the new king.

But as they circled back to the hall, she stopped and made him face her.

She opened her mouth to speak, then closed it again, as if unsure of what to say. "I love you, Grinsa," she said at last. "Promise you'll come back to me."

"I promise. And in the meantime," he added, smiling, "I know how to find you."

She gave him a sour look. "I'm going to be archminister to the king. I need my sleep."

He laughed and took her in his arms, holding her close for a moment before bending to kiss her brow.

"Be well, Keziah," he said. "May the gods keep you safe and bring you peace."

"And you," she whispered. She pulled away and walked quickly back into the hall. But as she stepped through the doorway, Grinsa saw her wipe away a tear.

The investiture of King Kearney the First of Glyndwr began the next day with the ringing of the midmorning bells. A long procession, led by the King's Guard, and including soldiers from every house in Eibithar, marched through the streets of the City of Kings before entering Audun's Castle through the south gate. Behind the soldiers came the lesser nobles, beginning with the barons, then the earls, and finally the thanes. They were followed by those nobles visiting from other kingdoms.

The dukes of the twelve houses came next, arranged by order of ascension, except for Kearney's son, who took the place of honor at the end of the column. Because Tavis was under Glyndwr's protection, he walked with clerics and underministers from Kearney's house, just behind the new king's sons and daughter. Still, he wore the brown and gold of Curgh, though he knew it would make him conspicuous in the procession. It didn't take him long to wish that he hadn't.

The people lining the city's streets, who cheered for the soldiers and the other nobles, fell silent as he walked by, or shouted at him, calling him a butcher and worse. One man stepped into his path and spit on the road in front of him, before letting him pass. Several people applauded. Had it not been for Grinsa walking a few strides behind him in the column, the young lord might have feared for his life. As it was, he was aware of every pair of eyes upon him, every whisper that marked his progress through the avenue.

When finally he walked through the outer gate of the castle and stepped onto the moat bridge, leaving the streets and hostile stares behind him, he knew a moment of profound relief. The feeling lasted only a moment, however. The soldiers who had led the procession had now positioned themselves on either side of the outer ward, so that they might honor the nobles who walked around the inner keep toward the east gate. They stood silently, their swords raised in salute. But the expressions on their faces as they watched Tavis walk by held as much hatred as those of the commoners outside the castle walls.

Even after walking past the last of the soldiers, his gaze lowered, his cheeks burning like Qirsi fire, Tavis found that his ordeal was still not over. For after entering the inner ward and walking past the statue of Binthar that stood at its center, the men and women of Eibithar's courts filed into the great hall and took their seats, the lesser nobles sitting closest to the rear doors. A crier stood next to the hall entrance, announcing each noble as he or she entered. Awaiting his turn, his dread deepening by the moment, Tavis briefly considered stepping out of the column and retreating to his chamber in the castle. He knew what it would be like, how they would look at him, what they would say to each other as he passed them, row by row. He could almost hear the hushed voices already.

"They all know you're here," someone whispered behind him.

He looked back and found Grinsa standing close, the gleaner's yellow eyes fixed on his own.

"How is it you know what I'm thinking?"

"If you leave now," the Qirsi said, ignoring the question, "they'll all know why. In their minds it will offer further proof of your guilt."

Tavis swallowed, then nodded once.

"This is another test for you, Lord Tavis. One among many that you'll face in the years to come. If you truly want your life back, you must fight for it. Starting today with this simple march to your place in the front of the hall."

Grinsa was right, of course. But contemplating what he had to do, Tavis wasn't certain he did want his life back. Perhaps it was better to live in the comfort and safety of court exile than to face this.

"Lord Tavis of Curgh!" the crier said, his voice echoing through the hall.

Everyone turned to look at him. Everyone. Even the dukes were watching him, standing on either side of the two thrones at the far end of the hall, an impossibly long walk from where he stood. Aindreas was there, beside Tavis's father, murder in his pale grey eyes.

"Walk, Tavis," the Qirsi whispered. "Hold your head high. You're innocent, and you're still a noble in this land."

He started forward, his legs feeling weak, his color high. And the stares followed him. As he had so many times before, Tavis wished for the courage to scream at them all, to tell them that he hadn't killed her. Yet it was all he could do simply to walk and to keep from crying. He kept his eyes on Audun's throne, refusing to look at anyone. He knew that Xaver and Hagan were somewhere in the hall, sitting with the other earls of the Curgh countryside, and he knew as well that another few strides would carry him past his mother and Fotir. But he didn't dare search for any of them. Brienne's mother, Ioanna, was somewhere in the hall as well, as were her other two children. Tavis just walked, the hall seeming to stretch on and on, like one of those bleak uncurving lanes in the Moorlands.

He reached the front row at last, slipping into the first empty seat, which happened to be next to Kearney's daughter, Corinne. She said nothing to him, and gave him a look that conveyed more than a bit of fear. This, though, he could accept. She was a child. Had he been in her position, he would have been afraid as well.

A few seconds later, Grinsa took the chair beside him, a small smile on his pale features.

"Congratulations," he said in the same low voice. "You've fought and won your first battle."

"I hardly feel that I've won anything."

"Victory comes in many forms, Lord Tavis. Before this is over, you'll come to appreciate all of them."

The young lord frowned, wondering what the gleaner meant,

but Grinsa said nothing more. Before Tavis could ask him to explain, everyone in the hall rose. The king had arrived.

The boy stood as well, turning to look at the hall entrance. A prelate was walking down the center aisle. He was dressed in white, instead of the usual brown, and he carried a heavy volume—the Book of Ean, no doubt—along with a tall golden staff. Behind him came several priests, all wearing brown robes. Two carried censers, from which came the fragrant smoke of the incense burned in the cloisters. All of them chanted to the god.

Finally, walking behind the clerics, their expressions suitably grave, came Kearney and Leilia. Tavis had never seen the queen before, though he had heard stories of her beauty. Her hair was black and her eyes so dark that they might have been as well. She was dressed in a long blue gown, the train carried by two small girls dressed similarly. Jewels sparkled on her neck, her ears, her fingers. She even wore a glittering tiara, as if unwilling to be outdone by the crown to be placed that day on her husband's brow. Yet rather than looking elegant, she merely looked sad. Tavis could see how she might have been beautiful as a younger woman. But she was heavy now, her face too fleshy for such delicate features, her figure too round for the close-fitting dress. She looked far older than her husband, though his hair was silver and hers had no grey at all.

Kearney wore a soldier's clothes. His boots had been polished to a high shine and the hilt of his sword gleamed like gold. But there was something comforting about his simple attire. Here is a man, it seemed to say, who will rule without arrogance, just as he came to the throne without ambition. He wore the purple and gold of Eibithar, as a king should. But he also bore a second sword held in the silver, red, and black baldric worn for centuries by dukes of Glyndwr. The colors didn't work, yet this only added to the impression of unaffected modesty. He was nothing at all like his queen, and Tavis was certain that everyone in the hall knew it.

Kearney and Leilia stopped before the throne. The prelate had halted there as well, turning to face the king and opening the volume. He began to read aloud and those in the hall fell silent. In the cloister such readings seemed endless to Tavis, and this one was no different. His eyes wandered the hall cautiously and he was glad to see that all were gazing at the new king. For now, at least, he had been forgotten.

After a time his own gaze was drawn back to the ceremony as well, though rather than looking at Kearney, he found himself watching his own father. There was no bitterness on Javan's face, no envy. But Tavis knew it had to be there, burning like a smith's forge in the duke's chest.

His father had told him it wasn't his fault, and though Tavis still felt responsible, he truly believed that Javan did not blame him. But watching his father watch another man's ascension, the boy vowed once more to find Brienne's killer. It might not place his father on the throne, or even restore his own place in the House of Curgh. But at least it would prove to all who stood today in this castle that he had not forced Javan's abdication.

Eventually, the prelate finished his reading. He closed the Book of Ean and handed it to one of the priests. Then he stepped around the throne to a small table Tavis hadn't noticed before. On it sat a simple wooden box. The prelate opened it and carefully lifted from it a circlet of gold. It was completely unadorned, save for a gleaming violet jewel mounted in the center of its browpiece. The prelate walked back to Kearney, raising the crown over the king's head.

"Repeat what I say," the cleric commanded. "I, Kearney the First of Glyndwr . . ."

"I, Kearney the First of Glyndwr . . ."

". . . Pledge life and sword to the service of Eibithar, as the kingdom's sovereign and champion . . ."

". . . Pledge life and sword to the service of Eibithar, as the kingdom's sovereign and champion . . ."

". . . To lead her people and enforce her laws as provided by the Rules of Ascension . . ."

". . . To lead her people and enforce her laws as provided by the Rules of Ascension . . ."

". . . With the consent and for the glory of Ean."

". . . With the consent and for the glory of Ean and all the gods."

The prelate frowned, but after a moment's hesitation he placed the crown on Kearney's head. The king turned to face his subjects, who all dropped to one knee in obeisance.

"Please rise," Kearney said, smiling at last.

They did, and as one they shouted, "Ean guard our king!," again and again.

Servants appeared in the back of the hall, bearing great trays of food and flask after flask of wine. Musicians from the Revel began to play in the ward and Tavis caught sight of dancers leaping and spinning in the gardens.

"This will last all day and through the night," Grinsa said. "Do you wish to stay?"

Tavis looked at him, searching for some sign that he was joking. But the Qirsi wore a mild expression and there was little mirth in his yellow eyes.

"Of course," Tavis said. "Don't you?"

Grinsa shrugged, but said nothing.

Kearney walked slowly toward the back of the hall, Leilia on his arm, both of them nodding and waving to the nobles who watched their every move.

After making certain that Aindreas had walked to another part of the hall, Tavis joined his father, and together they found Shonah, Fotir, Xaver, and Hagan, before making their way toward the tables of food. Grinsa, the boy noticed, was soon at his sister's side.

For a time, Tavis was so glad to be among those who loved him that he paid little attention to anything or anyone else. But as the day wore on, he began to notice the stares again. He might as well have been wearing Aneiran colors, or worse, Brienne's blood. Slowly he came to understand Grinsa's question.

When the Qirsi found him again, he was almost relieved.

"Enjoying yourself?" the gleaner asked, sipping some wine, his eyes wandering the hall.

"No. Just as you knew I wouldn't."

Grinsa turned to face him.

"I take no satisfaction in being right about this, Tavis. I hope you know that. They're not ready to accept you, and you're not yet able to be comfortable without their acceptance."

"I guess. I'm ready to leave when you are."

The Qirsi shrugged. "I'm ready now."

"What about your—? What about the archminister?"

"We've said our goodbyes."

Tavis nodded. He wasn't sure he was ready for this, but he had endured enough shame for one day. "Let me find my parents."

Leaving his mother and father proved easier than he had expected. His mother cried, but he expected that. His father tried one last time to convince him to go to Glyndwr, but Tavis had made his decision. Seeing that his son could not be dissuaded, Javan gave him a pouch of gold pieces.

"I don't know how long this will last," the duke said. "But it should keep you fed and housed for a few turns at least."

The young lord was most surprised by how hard it was to say goodbye to Xaver. There were tears in his friend's eyes as they embraced, and Tavis would have teased him had he not been crying also.

"May the gods watch over you, Tavis," Xaver whispered, still holding him tightly. "Whatever else you seek, I hope you find peace."

Tavis stepped back, making himself smile, even as he blinked back his tears. "Gods keep you safe." He should have said more, but nothing seemed sufficient. He could only hope that Xaver understood.

Fotir grasped his shoulder and wished him well, as did Hagan. And abruptly there was nothing holding him there any longer. Or almost nothing.

He and Grinsa had already started toward the rear doors when he thought of it.

"Wait for a moment," Tavis said, laying a hand on the Qirsi's arm.

Grinsa gave him a puzzled look, but Tavis didn't stop to explain. Instead, he walked to the king, who was speaking with the dukes of Sussyn and Thorald.

"My pardon, Your Majesty," Tavis said, bowing to Kearney. "With your leave, I feel it's time I began my journey. Before I go, I wanted to offer you my most humble thanks for your kindness and your generosity."

The king regarded him for a moment and then placed a hand on his shoulder. The conversations around them had ceased and Tavis was aware of others watching them. At that moment, though, he didn't care.

"You have leave to go, Lord Tavis," Kearney said. "And you do so with my friendship. I hope that you find what you seek, and I look forward to your return."

It was more than Tavis could have asked, and perhaps more than a king new to his power should have offered. The boy bowed again and walked away. Grinsa joined him as they reached the doorway and stepped out into the sunlight.

"That took courage," the Qirsi said. "And it might have been the wisest thing I've ever seen you do."

Tavis looked at him and grinned. "You could at least try to say that without sounding so surprised."

They returned to their chamber, gathered what few things they would need, and packed them in a traveler's sack. Then they left the castle and made their way to the south gate of the city, the steppe gate as it was called. When they were outside the city walls, the sharp cliffs of the Caerissan Steppe loomed before them. In the distance, to the south and west, Tavis could see Blood Falls, where the Sussyn flowed off the highlands. If they followed the river to its source, they would be only a few leagues from the Caerissan border.

"Are you sure about this?" the Qirsi asked one last time. "It's not too late to go to Glyndwr."

"I've already told you: there's nothing for me in Glyndwr."

"And you won't consider going after Shurik either? At least we know where he is."

"Shurik didn't kill Brienne, and finding him won't help me prove my innocence."

Grinsa opened his mouth, then stopped himself. The boy could see that he wasn't pleased. He had promised Kearney that he would stay with Tavis and keep him from harm, but clearly he regretted making that pledge.

"I want to find him, Grinsa," Tavis said, a plea in his voice. "I know you want to go after Shurik. But if we can find the assassin we may be able to learn who paid him. Wouldn't that be helpful?"

The gleaner stared up at the falls, looking sadder than Tavis had ever seen him. "I think I know who paid him," he said quietly. "But we'll try to find him anyway. In time, he may lead us to Shurik."

Chapter
Thirty-five

✦

Noltierre, Aneira

He preferred the southern cities. He always had, he realized, sipping an ale in the garden court of the inn at which he was staying. Part of it was that they reminded him of his home in Caerisse. Not that Castle Nistaad could compare to the fortress here in Noltierre, but there were similarities. Even had there not been, though, Cadel simply preferred the architecture of the south. The castles of Eibithar and Wethyrn, as well as those in northern Aneira and Caerisse, had been designed for war and little else. They were ponderous and ugly, as if those who built them had hoped that brute force might compensate for what they lacked in elegance and subtlety.

Noltierre, on the other hand, managed to combine formidable strength with uncommon grace and beauty. The castle and its walled city sat nestled in the hills overlooking the east bank of the Black Sand River, within sight of the southern fringe of Aneira's Great Forest. Its walls, carved from the same stone that had given the river its name, were black as pitch and easily as tall as those guarding the cities of Kentigern and Thorald. The towers were slender, almost delicate in their appearance, reaching high above the city and affording the bowmen who stood among the carved turrets a commanding view of the river, the hills, and the roads leading to the city gates. Even the shops that lined the narrow, curving lanes had been built with care and refinement. Doorways and windows were arched rather than square. The façades of the most common structures were sculpted, a luxury usually reserved in the north for only the highest courts. The shared garden plots were bordered with flowers, and even the lowliest merchants displayed their wares with taste.

Cadel had been here for nearly a turn, and already he was trying to find ways to remain a while longer even after Jedrek joined him. Aneira's Festival, while no match for the one in Sanbira or for Eibithar's Revel, offered one possibility, though eventually it would take them back north to Mertesse and some of the other, less attractive cities. There were a few singing companies that remained in Noltierre throughout the year, but he and Jedrek sang too well for any of them. They would become too famous too quickly, something no assassin ever wanted.

Over the past few days, for the first time in his life, he had actually considered giving up completely the life he had led for so long. He could just remain in Noltierre and do nothing. They wouldn't even have to sing. He and Jedrek had more gold than they could spend in a lifetime. Cadel grinned at the thought. He was sure that he had enough. Jedrek, however, was capable of spending a great deal.

The assassin shook his head at his own foolishness. Even if there were a way to stay, their Qirsi employers wouldn't allow them to remain in any one place for very long. Certainly they wouldn't let them stop working. They knew who Cadel was, where he came from, what he had done as a boy and as a man. They could make him do almost anything. For now, they continued to be generous, paying more than Cadel had ever dreamed anyone would. But he found the jobs increasingly distasteful. This last one had been the worst yet. He could still see the girl's face, the smile she gave him in Kentigern's great hall when he handed the wine to Tavis. She had haunted his dreams ever since, something that had never happened before in all his years as a hired killer.

He forced his mind past the image, draining his ale and signaling the serving girl for another. It would be another half turn before Jedrek arrived, perhaps a bit more. He could at least enjoy Noltierre until then.

Cadel couldn't say what made him notice her from so great a distance. There were Qirsi in all the cities of southern Aneira, just as there were all through the Forelands. Sitting in the courtyard, he had seen literally dozens of white-hairs walk by, without stopping to look at any of them.

It might have been that she looked so familiar, or perhaps the fact that she was staring at him. It might have been that she was the most beautiful Qirsi woman he had ever met, and that he remembered thinking the same thing on the rocky shore near Curgh. Whatever the reason, he could do nothing but gaze back at her as she approached him, her white hair falling loose about her shoulders, her pale yellow eyes looking almost white in the sunlight.

He felt his body growing tense, the way it did before a kill. Another job already. This had to stop.

She halted beside his table, glancing casually around the courtyard.

"May I join you?" she asked.

She looked younger than he remembered, and despite the lightness of her tone she wore a grim expression.

"I suppose," he answered, trying to convey as little warmth as possible.

She sat, waving a hand at the server.

"I've been looking for you for several days. I had heard you were in Noltierre, but—"

"What is it you want?" he demanded, fighting to keep his voice low. "I'm not ready to work again so soon. It's too dangerous. You may be paying us well, but that doesn't give you the right to put our lives at risk."

He stopped himself as the serving girl arrived with another ale.

"I didn't come to give you more work," she said, once the girl was gone.

"Then why?"

She faltered, looking away. "I need to speak with your friend."

"My friend?"

"Jedrek. There's something I have to ask him."

"He isn't here yet. I don't expect him before the waning begins."

Her face blanched. "He should have been here long ago."

"No. We agreed—"

"His plans changed. After you left the Revel, the gleaner who showed the Curgh boy his Fating followed you. I went to Jedrek and told him to go after this man, to keep him from reaching Kentigern. He was to join you here once he . . ." She swallowed. "Once he was finished."

"What right do you have to give orders to my man?"

"You told me yourself that he was supposed to watch out for

you, to take care of the unexpected especially when it placed your life in danger. You even told me his name so that I could go to him if I thought it necessary. In this instance, I felt that it was."

She was right. This was just the type of thing Jedrek was supposed to do. *I need you to guard my back.* He had said this to Jed more times than he could remember. Was it possible that Jedrek had gotten himself killed doing his job?

"Why would the gleaner go to Kentigern?" he asked, as much of himself as of her. "And how would he have managed to fight off Jedrek?"

Again she hesitated, staring at her ale. "I think the gleaner felt responsible for the boy in some way. I think that he saw what was going to happen in Kentigern and he wanted to stop it. As for your friend," she said, looking up at Cadel again, "he told me that he had never killed a Qirsi before. Maybe his fear of our magic got the better of him."

Jedrek had never killed a Qirsi? Cadel thought back on the jobs they had done together. As far as he could remember, he had taken care of all the white-hairs they had been hired to kill.

"But still," he said, unwilling to accept any of this. "This was a gleaner." Surely Jedrek couldn't be dead.

"He might have been more," the woman said, her voice dropping so low that Cadel wasn't certain he had heard her correctly.

"What do you mean? More in what way?"

She shook her head. "I'm not sure. It's not important."

"It is important!" he said, far too loudly. People at other tables stared at them for a moment before resuming their conversations. "It is important," he repeated, quietly this time. He grabbed hold of her arm, gripping it like the hilt of a blade. "My closest friend, the man I've worked with for sixteen years, may be dead. Now I want to know what you meant."

"You're hurting me!" she said through clenched teeth, wrenching her arm from his grasp. She rubbed her forearm, glaring at him. He could see red marks where his fingers had bruised her skin. "It's possible that he had other powers," she said at last. "Mists and winds, perhaps others. I honestly don't know. But if your friend was expecting to face a man with only gleaning magic, he might have been surprised."

Jedrek. Dead. "How long ago?" he asked.

"Two and a half turns."

Long enough. He should have been in Noltierre long before this. "I'm sorry," she said.

It was this last job, the Kentigern job, Jedrek had called it. Nothing good had come of it. It didn't matter how much they had paid him, not if the gold had Jed's blood on it. Suddenly he wanted nothing to do with this woman, or any of her kind. They knew too much about him, so at some point he'd have to kill for them again. But until then, he'd stay as far away from sorcerers as possible. Except one.

"What's the gleaner's name?"

Her eyes widened slightly. "Why?"

Because Jedrek had been his friend, practically his brother, and this was the only way Cadel knew to honor him.

"Because," he told her, "if he knew enough to follow me to Kentigern, he's a threat to all of us. And because you were eager enough for his death to send Jedrek after him. I owe it to Jedrek to finish his work."

She seemed reluctant to answer, but after a moment she said, in what was barely more than a whisper, "Grinsa jal Arriet."

He nodded, pushing himself out of his chair and reaching into his pocket. He threw a gold piece onto the table.

"That should pay for a few more ales," he said, starting to walk away. "Enjoy them. And enjoy Noltierre. That's what I was doing before you found me."

Cresenne couldn't take her eyes off the gold coin. For all she knew, it was one she had given the assassin in Curgh three turns before.

Twice now she had sent men to kill Grinsa. Or to be killed by him.

"He's just a gleaner," she had told Jedrek. And today she had said, "He might have been more." But how much more? She had wondered ever since the Weaver came to her in a dream during Adriel's Turn, demanding to know all she could tell him about Grinsa. The Revel was in Thorald at the time and Cresenne, hearing nothing more from Jedrek, assumed that Grinsa was dead.

As soon as the dream began that night, she had known that this encounter with the Weaver would be different from the others. Rather than having to walk across the dark, windswept landscape, she entered the dream atop the rise. She didn't even have to wait for the Weaver to show himself. She found him waiting for her beneath that strange black sky. Immediately he began to question her about the gleaner. What was his name? How long had he been in the Revel? Where had he lived before joining the festival? Had she ever learned what he saw in Lord Tavis's Fating? Where was he now? When she told him about sending Jedrek to keep him from reaching Kentigern, his tone grew less urgent, but still the questions continued.

"Did he ever show signs of possessing more than just gleaning magic?" he asked her.

Because of who and what he was, she had resisted the urge to lie, knowing it would only bring her pain. "Yes," she said. "He admitted that he had mists and winds, though he claimed his power was limited."

"Anything else?"

"No." Then, without thinking, she asked, "Why does this matter? I told you, he's dead."

He was silent for so long that Cresenne feared she had offended him.

But he didn't hurt her. "You still love him." A statement. A Weaver would know.

"Yes."

"Yet you sent a man to kill him."

"Yes."

"This was before you knew, before you fully understood what you were doing?"

The question shocked her, made her shiver, even in her dream. Again she had to remind herself that he was a Weaver, that no secret lay beyond his reach.

"Yes," she said. "It was before. It would have been harder had I known."

"Of course it would have," he said. "Still, I'm pleased. Qirsar was with me the night I chose you to be my chancellor. If others in this movement are like you, we cannot fail."

When he finally left her, and she awoke to a room still dark with night, Cresenne was so shaken by the dream that it was all she could do to keep from being ill. But as her fear subsided and she was able to look back over their conversation, she began to wonder why the Weaver would be so interested in Grinsa. It was her first inkling that the gleaner might still be alive. But more than that, it forced her to consider that his powers might go beyond gleaning, beyond even the small mist he had conjured for her in the bed they shared.

As the days passed she had tried to put the matter out of her mind. It was dangerous to show too much interest in the affairs of the Weaver. Everyone in the movement knew that. Besides, Grinsa was dead.

Still, the questions stayed with her. What if he wasn't dead? What if the Weaver asked so many questions because he saw in Grinsa a potential rival? It made no sense, really. Who would a Weaver view as a rival except another Weaver? Which, she had realized at the time, brought her to the heart of the matter. Leaving the Revel to come south had been dangerous. The Weaver had not ordered her into Aneira, and he might be displeased. But she had to know if Grinsa was alive. Even the Weaver would understand that.

Her meeting with Cadel only served to make her more certain of what she already knew. For now it seemed that Grinsa had survived his encounter with Jedrek. Once more, still eyeing the assassin's gold, Cresenne found herself thinking about that night at the inn in Curgh, when his tiny mist spun in her hand. She had never seen anyone do such a thing. Grinsa claimed that he could only conjure a small mist, but she felt certain that few Qirsi possessed the power necessary to create and control such a perfect little cloud.

All along, there had been more to him than she could put into words, more than she had ever dreamed she would find in a mere Revel gleaner. How else had he managed to make her love him so? He was a Weaver. It explained so much.

It also changed everything. Grinsa was far more than an inconvenience, a problem to be addressed and forgotten. He was a threat to the entire movement.

Or was he? For the first time, sitting in that sunny courtyard in Noltierre, Cresenne considered an enticing possibility. For so long she had assumed that only the Weaver she knew, the one who had darkened the sky in her dreams, could bring Qirsi rule to the Forelands. But what if there was another way? What if Grinsa, who had loved her and might love her still, and whose child she carried, could be convinced to embrace this cause? True, he opposed them now. But this new life growing inside her might be enough to turn him. Though there was no way to be certain, it was possible that their son or daughter would be a Weaver as well. If the child grew up under

Eandi rule, he or she would live a life of fear and forced deception, just as had Grinsa, and so many Weavers before him.

But if the movement were to succeed, bringing Qirsi rule to the Forelands, all that would be altered. Weavers would be revered rather than persecuted. Instead of concealing their power, they would rejoice in it. Instead of pretending to be mere gleaners, they would aspire to be kings and queens.

What kind of father—what kind of Qirsi—would not want to create such a world for his child?

The problem was the assassin. Grinsa had defeated Jedrek, but Cadel was a far more dangerous man. One could tell simply from looking at him. If she could have lied to him this day, rather than revealing Grinsa's name, she would have. But to do so would have been to risk her own life and that of her child. She had no choice but to send the assassin after him, again. *It would have been harder had I known*, she had told the Weaver. It was.

She had to trust that Grinsa could protect himself. She had to believe that the gods would watch over her baby's father.

Above all, she had to hope that the Weaver wouldn't find Grinsa before she did.

About the Author

✦

David B. Coe grew up just outside of New York City, the youngest of four children. He attended Brown University as an undergraduate and later received a Ph.D. in history from Stanford. He briefly considered a career as an academic, but wisely thought better of it.

David has published three other novels and is the 1999 recipient of the William L. Crawford Memorial Fantasy Award. He lives in Tennessee with his wife, Nancy J. Berner, their daughters, Alex and Erin, and of course, Buddy, the wonder dog. *Rules of Ascension* is the first volume of *Winds of the Forelands*. David is currently working on volume two, *Seeds of Betrayal*.